## INTO NARSINDAL
### The Fourth Chronicle of Hawklan

Roger Taylor was born in Heywood, Lancashire and qualified as a civil and structural engineer. He lives with his wife and two daughters in Wirral, Merseyside, and is a pistol shooter and student of traditional aikido.

# Into Narsindal

## The Fourth Chronicle of Hawklan

Roger Taylor

**HEADLINE**

ISBN 0 7472 3353 5

Printed and bound in Great Britain by
Collins, Glasgow

HEADLINE BOOK PUBLISHING PLC
Headline House
79 Great Titchfield Street
London W1P 7FN

To Jo Fletcher, Keith Jones and Mike Tibbs

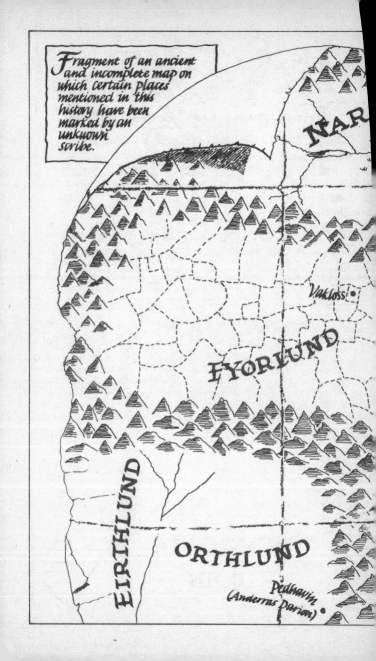

Fragment of an ancient and incomplete map on which certain places mentioned in this history have been marked by an unknown scribe.

NAR

Vakloss •

FYORLUND

EIRTHLUND

ORTHLUND

Pedhavin
(Anderras Darion) •

*'The time of Hawklan is so far in the past that it could be the distant future.'*

# Prologue

Hawklan's face was desolate.

'I remember the enemy falling back and standing silently watching us. I remember the sky, black with smoke, and flickering with fighting birds. There was a raucous command from somewhere, and the enemy lowered their long pikes – they were not going to close with us again. Then the figure next to me shouted defiance at them, hurled its shield into their midst and reached up to tear away its helm.' Hawklan paused and his eyes glistened as he relived the moment. 'Long blonde hair tumbled out like a sudden ray of sunlight in that terrible gloom.' He shook his head. 'I hadn't realised who it was. A great roar went up from the circling army. I called out her name . . .' He opened his mouth to call again. Both Gulda and Andawyr watched, lips parted, as if willing him this release, but no sound came from any of them.

'Without taking her eyes from the approaching enemy, she reached back and her hand touched my face briefly. "I am here," its touch said. "I am with you to the end." I threw away my own helm and shield and took my Sword two-handed as she had. Then the figure at my back cried out in recognition. He too I had not recognised in the press. Thus by some strange chance, we three childhood friends formed the last remnant of our great army.'

He paused again and clenched his fist, as if around his Sword hilt. 'A group of the enemy threw down their pikes and rushed forward to take . . . the girl. She killed three of them with terrible skull-splitting blows, but . . .

'So I slew her. I slew my friend. With a single stroke. I saw her head tumbling red and gold down the slope and into the darkness under those countless trampling feet.' He shook his head. 'Better that than that she be taken alive . . .

'The rest of her attackers fled back to their pikes and the enemy began its final slow advance. Back to back we held. Pushed aside and broke their long spears. Killed several. Then my last friend and ally fell and I . . .' He faltered.

'He said "I'm sorry," even as he fell . . .
'That last burden was my end and I too sank to my knees . . .'

# Chapter 1

Startled, Jaldaric spun round as the rider appeared suddenly out of the trees and galloped to his side. His right hand began moving reflexively towards his sword, but a cautionary hiss from Tel Mindor stopped it. Abruptly, a second rider appeared on the other side of the road and moved to flank Arinndier.

Tel Mindor looked behind. Three more riders were following. Despite himself, his concern showed briefly on his face. Not because the five men seemed to offer any immediate menace, though they *were* armed, but because he had not seen them, and that indicated both wilful concealment and no small skill on their part. However, his Goraidin nature did not allow the concern to persist. Instead he began to feel a little easier; the actual appearance of the men confirmed the unease he had felt growing for some time.

'Hello,' said the first new arrival to Jaldaric, his face unexpectedly friendly. 'I'm sorry I startled you. We've been following you since you came out of the mountains, but your friend here,' – he nodded towards Tel Mindor – 'was on the point of spotting us, so I thought it would save problems if we approached you directly.'

His manner was pleasant enough but, still unsettled by the man's abrupt arrival, Jaldaric's reply was harsher than he had intended.

'Following?' he said. 'Do the Orthlundyn always follow visitors to their country?'

'No, no,' the man replied with a smile. 'You're the first.' His smile turned into a laugh. 'In fact you're the *only* people who've come out of Fyorlund since we started border duty. It was good practice for us.' He extended his hand. 'My name's Fyndal, and this is my brother Isvyndal.'

Jaldaric's natural courtesy made him take the hand, though part of him remembered Aelang, and was alert for a sudden attack. 'This is the Lord Arinndier, the Rede Berryn and his aide Tel Mindor,' he said, indicating his three companions. 'I'm Jaldaric, son of the Lord Eldric.'

This time it was Fyndal who started. 'Jaldaric,' he echoed,

his eyes widening. Then, as if uncertain how to phrase the question; 'Jaldaric who came with Dan-Tor and kidnapped Tirilen?'

Jaldaric's face coloured at the reminder of his previous visit to Orthlund. 'Yes,' he said awkwardly, looking down at his hands briefly. 'To my shame.'

'And was taken by Mandrocs?' Fyndal continued. Jaldaric looked puzzled, but nodded.

Fyndal reined his horse to a halt, as if he needed a moment's stillness to assimilate this information. His brother too seemed to be affected.

The three riders behind them also stopped.

Then Fyndal clicked his horse forward again. 'Why have you returned?' he asked, his manner still uncertain.

'You not only follow, you interrogate,' Jaldaric began, but Arinndier leaned forward and interrupted him.

'We're representatives of the Geadrol,' he said. 'We've important news for all the Orthlundyn, and Isloman told us that we should seek out his brother Loman and the Memsa Gulda at Anderras Darion.'

Again Fyndal showed surprise. 'You've spoken to Isloman?' he said. 'Where is he? Was Hawklan with him?'

He gestured to the following riders, who spurred forward to join the group. Jaldaric and the others exchanged glances. 'Who taught you the High Guards' hand language, Fyndal?' Jaldaric asked.

'Loman,' Fyndal answered. 'He taught it to all of us.'

'Us?' queried Arinndier.

'The Helyadin,' Fyndal replied.

All Fyndal's answers were uttered straightforwardly and in the manner of someone stating the obvious. Arinndier opened his mouth to ask for an explanation, but Fyndal repeated his enquiry.

'When did you see Hawklan and Isloman?' he said, concern beginning to show through his affability. 'Where are they? Are they safe?'

Arinndier shook his head. 'We don't know where they are,' he said, then pausing thoughtfully he added, 'They left Fyorlund some time ago with two of our men to return to Anderras Darion. I had hoped they'd be in Orthlund by now.'

Fyndal frowned unhappily and made to speak again, but this time Arinndier took the initiative.

'What we do know about Isloman and Hawklan we'll tell to

Loman and Memsa Gulda when we meet, Fyndal,' he said. 'That and a great many other things. Then it's up to them what they choose to tell you. You understand, I'm sure. In the meantime, perhaps you could tell us who *you* are. And what the Helyadin are, and why you follow and question visitors to Orthlund. And why this man Loman should see fit to teach you *our* High Guards' hand language.'

'We're just . . . soldiers,' Fyndal answered, with a slight hesitation. 'We're on border patrol, making sure that nothing . . . unpleasant . . . comes into our land unchallenged again. Loman taught us the hand language because he said it was a good one' – he gave a subdued laugh – 'and it was the only one he knew. He's taught us a lot of other things as well.'

'Soldiers eh? So the Orthlundyn *have* been preparing for war.' It was Rede Berryn and his tone was ironic. 'How typical of Dan-Tor to tell the truth and make it sound like a lie.' Then he looked at the young Orthlundyn again. 'Who are you preparing for war against, Helyadin?' he said.

Fyndal looked at the old man. 'Sumeral, Rede,' he said simply. 'Sumeral. And all who stand by his side.'

The Rede met his gaze and idly rubbed a scar on his forehead. Since Hawklan and Isloman had left his village with their Mathidrin escort he had heard only rumours and gossip about what was happening in Vakloss and the rest of the country. Such instructions as he had received told him nothing, and such enquiries as he made were ignored. The local Mathidrin company was suddenly greatly strengthened and the patrolling of the Orthlund border increased dramatically. Then a ban that they imposed – and enforced – on virtually all travelling ended any hope he had of obtaining accurate information from such friends as he had in the capital.

Throughout these happenings Berryn had followed the ancient survival technique of the trained soldier and kept himself inconspicuous while clinging to what he knew to be right and true. In his darker moments, he tried to console himself with the thought that this madness *must* pass; the spirit of the Fyordyn surely could not be so easily crushed.

And the memory of his brief encounter with Hawklan and Isloman persisted in returning like some kind of reproach. Hawklan, the strange healer from wherever it was down there, looking every inch the warrior, yet playing the coward before the crowd until his horse laid Uskal out. And Isloman, revealed suddenly as one of the Orthlundyn Goraidin. The two of them, alone, seeking out Dan-Tor to demand an accounting for an incident that could not possibly have happened. Armed Mandrocs marching through Fyorlund to commit atrocities in Orthlund?

Yet the two men had patently been telling the truth.

The paradox had cost him sleepless nights. He, who could sleep in his saddle in the middle of a forced march.

Then it was over. First, a flurry of increasingly improbable rumours: Dan-Tor attacked! The King slain? Rebellion? Then, a dreadful silent lull and, as abruptly as they had come, the Mathidrin had left; the whole complement riding off secretly one night without a word of explanation. The villagers had scarcely had time to assimilate this change when Jaldaric and Arinndier had ridden in with a good old-fashioned High Guard escort, and announced the defeat and flight of Dan-Tor and the Mathidrin.

But they had brought worse news. Ludicrous news. Dan-Tor was Oklar, the Uhriel. Sumeral had come again and raised Derras Ustramel in Narsindal. No, Berryn had thought, rebelliously. Lord or no, Arinndier, you're wrong. Dan-Tor was a bad old devil, but I can't accept that kind of nonsense.

And he had resolved to bring himself nearer the heart of this turmoil. *Someone* had to start talking sense.

Thus when Arinndier had dismissed his escort, fearing that such a patrol might be none too popular in Orthlund, Rede Berryn had offered the services of himself and Tel-Mindor as guides.

'We know the border area well, Lord,' he had said. 'Tel-Mindor doesn't look like much, but he's worth the three of us put together. And no one's going to be upset by a limping old duffer like me.'

On the journey, however, Arinndier had talked quite freely of all the events that had happened since the Geadrol had been suspended, and Berryn had found the threads binding him to his old commonsense reality were stretched to breaking point. Now, in his simple statement, the young Orthlundyn had severed them utterly.

Oddly, the Rede felt more at ease, as many past events took on a new perspective.

Battle nerves, he thought suddenly. Just battle nerves. All that furious turmoil before you finally turn round and face the truth. The realisation made him smile.

'You find the idea amusing,' Fyndal said, misinterpreting

6

the smile and uncertain whether to be indignant or reproachful.

The Rede looked at him intently. Young men preparing for
war again, and doubtless old men encouraging them. Well he'd
be damned if he'd play that game!

'No,' he said, his voice stern but sad. 'I've ridden the Watch
and done my time in Narsindal.' He tapped the scar on his
head. 'I'm only sorry I stopped watching too soon. Sorry for
my sake, sorry for your sake.'

Something in the man's voice made Arinndier look at him.
'Don't reproach yourself, Rede,' he said. 'You weren't alone.
And at least we can see more clearly now. We've no time for
self-indulgence. You ensured that Hawklan reached Vakloss.
Without that, all could well have been lost.' He turned back to
Fyndal. 'We need to bring our news to Loman and the Memsa
as soon as possible,' he said. 'Have you made your judgement
about us yet, soldier?'

'Yes,' Fyndal replied, taken unawares by his kindly bluntness. 'Some time ago.' Then his youth showed on his face.
'Can you tell us nothing about Hawklan?' he asked, almost
plaintively.

Arinndier shook his head regretfully and repeated his
previous reply. 'At Anderras Darion, soldier,' he replied. 'And
only then as determined by Loman and Memsa Gulda.'

For a moment, Fyndal seemed inclined to pursue the
matter, but then with a resigned nod of his head, he let it go.
'I'll ensure that you're not delayed then,' he said. 'I'll have the
post riders send news of your arrival ahead. That will save you
a great deal of time, though I fear you may find Loman and
Memsa away with the army in the mountains still.'

'You have an army mobilised?' Arinndier asked, trying to
keep the surprise out of his voice.

Fyndal nodded.

Arinndier pulled his cloak around himself as a sudden gust
of the cold raw wind that had been blowing in their faces all
day buffeted them.

'There's winter in the wind,' he said. 'I don't envy anyone
doing a mountain exercise in it.'

'It's no exercise, Lord,' Fyndal said, his face suddenly grim.
'They're out trying to deal with an unexpected foe.'

Arinndier raised his eyebrows and opened his mouth to
speak, but a brief knowing smile from Fyndal stopped him.

'I'll find out at Anderras Darion?' he asked.

7

Fyndal's smile broadened, though it did not outshine the concern in his face. 'Indeed, Lord,' he said.

Arinndier accepted the gentle rebuke at his own secrecy with good grace. 'You won't be accompanying us yourselves?'

Fyndal shook his head. 'No,' he replied. 'We have to finish our tour of duty here first.'

'I doubt you'll see any more travellers from Fyorlund,' Arinndier said. 'If you feel you'll be needed with your army.'

Fyndal bowed his head in acknowledgment. 'Thank you, Lord,' he said. 'But had we been needed, we'd have been sent for. Our orders were to watch, and watch we must.'

Berryn nodded in approval.

Then Fyndal glanced at his brother and the three others, and they were gone, disappearing silently back into the noisy trees.

'Just stay on this road,' he said, turning back to the Fyordyn. 'It'll carry you straight to Anderras Darion. And don't hesitate to ask for food or shelter at any of the villages. They'll be expecting you by the time you arrive.' Then, with a brief farewell, he too was gone.

As the sound of hoofbeats dwindled, Tel Mindor rode alongside Arinndier. 'I didn't see them following us, Lord,' he admitted. 'Whoever they were, they weren't ordinary soldiers. And it almost defies belief to think that anyone could have been trained so well in just a few months.'

Arinndier nodded. 'I agree with you,' he said. 'I think that whatever problems the Orthlundyn are having in the mountains, they're still keeping a *very* strict watch on their border with us, and, frankly, I don't blame them. As for the training –' He shrugged. 'The past months have reminded me of the service they gave against the Morlider, and it was considerable. The Orthlundyn are a strange people. I've heard them referred to as a remnant people at times. Not a phrase I'd care to use myself, but there aren't many of them, for sure, and it does beg the question: remnant of what?'

As the day progressed, the quartet trotted steadily south through the cold damp wind.

At the top of a long hill, Arinndier grimaced. 'It's neither mellow like autumn, nor sharp like winter,' he said, reining his horse to a halt. 'Let's walk awhile, give the horses a rest.' Then he looked around at the countryside they had just ridden through. After a moment, he nodded reflectively to himself.

Despite the unwelcoming wind and the dull hues of the dying vegetation, the place had its own strange peace.

A sudden intake of breath cut across his reverie.

Turning, he saw that it was Jaldaric, and even as he looked at him, he saw the young man's face, already pale with cold, blanching further until it was almost white.

'What is it, Jal?' he asked anxiously.

Jaldaric opened his mouth to speak, but at first no sound came. 'It was here,' he managed eventually, gazing around. 'I didn't recognise it until I turned round and looked back down the hill. It was here. The Mandrocs.'

Arinndier's eyes narrowed at Jaldaric's patent distress.

Tel Mindor caught Arinndier's eye and drew his gaze to the bushes and shrubs that lined the road. They still bore signs of the damage where the Mandrocs had crashed through in pursuit of the High Guards.

'Would you like to be alone?' Arinndier asked.

Jaldaric shook his head. 'No,' he said. 'I stand here alone every night as it is. Watching . . . Aelang . . . struggling with his cloak and then smiling.' He put his hand to his face involuntarily as if to block Aelang's swift and savage blow. It was a well-rehearsed movement. As Arinndier watched him he noted with regret the grimness in his face and abruptly he was reminded of Eldric's ferocious father.

Tel Mindor stepped forward and took Jaldaric's arm. 'Say farewell to your friends now, Jal,' he said gently. 'Leave them here. There are no good places to die violently, but there are worse than here.'

Jaldaric clenched his teeth. 'I *will* stay a moment,' he said. 'You carry on. I'll join you shortly.'

The three men were silent for some time as they walked away from the young man. Each knew that there was little they could do to ease Jaldaric's burden, and while grief is a rending emotion, watching it in someone else is precious little easier.

Eventually Jaldaric rejoined them, his face set and emotionless. No one spoke and, mounting up, the party set off again.

As Fyndal had promised, the villagers they encountered had been told of their coming and they found themselves being offered an abundance of food and drink. Having brought adequate supplies with them, they tried to decline this generosity, only to find that Fyndal had laid gentle traps for them.

'Yes, we know you're in a hurry with your news, but you can

9

eat this while you ride,' was the comment that invariably ended their hesitant refusals.

Jaldaric in particular was visibly moved by the warmth of the greeting he received.

After passing through Little Hapter, Arinndier carefully stowed a large pie in his saddlebag and looked at the others a little shamefacedly. 'I couldn't refuse the woman, could I?' he asked. 'They must think we've had a famine at home, not a war. Are there many more villages between here and Anderras Darion, Jal?'

'I'm afraid there are,' Jaldaric replied, now much more relaxed, and smiling broadly.

'We should've brought another pack-horse,' Tel Mindor said, chuckling.

Jaldaric nodded. 'They *do* take some pride in their hospitality,' he said. 'But if you want the benefit of my local knowledge: whatever you do, don't start admiring their carving, or we'll never reach Anderras Darion.'

Their first encounters with the Orthlundyn, however, whilst burdening their packs had eased their unspoken concerns greatly. The people apparently held no ill-will towards the Fyordyn who had inadvertently brought such trouble to their land. Even the chill wind seemed to lose some of its edge.

After they had passed through Perato, Berryn remarked on the absence of young people from the villages.

'They must all be with this army of theirs in the mountains. It must be a civilian militia,' he said. No one disputed this conclusion and the Rede nodded to himself. 'I know there aren't many Orthlundyn,' he went on, 'but if those villages are typical, then they've got a *big* army, and if they're all in the mountains, then they're having to deal with a *big* problem.'

Arinndier looked at him. It was a valid deduction, but still it made no sense. Who could threaten the Orthlundyn from the east? The chilling thought occurred to him that while Fyordyn had been looking towards Vakloss, some army had swept down the Pass of Elewart to overwhelm Riddin and was now moving against Orthlund prior to attacking Fyorlund's southern border.

*And we sent Sylvriss there!*

The panic-stricken thought nearly made him voice his fear, but it was followed immediately by the memory of the faces of the villagers they had met. These were not the faces of a people facing imminent destruction at the hands of an army powerful enough to have overcome the Riddin Muster.

None the less, the Rede's comments had given him a problem that would not be set lightly aside, and at the next village he asked directly what the army was doing.

The villagers made reassuring noises. 'Don't you worry yourself about that, young man,' came the reply, from a man whom Arinndier judged to be somewhat younger than himself. 'It's just a little trouble with the Alphraan. I'm sure Loman and Memsa Gulda will sort it out soon. Not many things argue with Memsa Gulda for long.'

This last remark brought some general laughter from the group that had gathered around the new arrivals, but Arinndier sensed an undertow of concern that was more serious than the levity indicated.

'Who in the world are the Alphraan?' he asked his companions as they continued on their way. The name was vaguely familiar but he had been loath to show his ignorance to the villagers.

Jaldaric was frowning. 'The only Alphraan I've ever heard of are in . . . children's tales,' he said awkwardly. 'Little people . . . who live underground and . . . sing.' Rede Berryn and Tel Mindor both nodded.

Arinndier looked at them sternly, then his own memory produced the same image from somewhere in his childhood. He cleared his throat. 'Perhaps the word means something different down here,' he said.

Tel Mindor laughed softly. 'Perhaps Fyndal's sent more than one message to the villagers,' he said significantly.

The following day the wind had eased, but it was still cold, and the winter chill in the air was unequivocal. And as if to emphasise this, many of the already snow-capped mountains to the east were whiter than they had been on the previous day.

Looking at them, the thought of Sylvriss, Hawklan and Isloman came inexorably to Arinndier's mind. They *should* be through the mountains by now . . .

But the route taken by Sylvriss's party was little used, and that taken by Isloman's was virtually unexplored. And as far as could be seen from Eldric's stronghold, snow had come to the higher, inner mountains unexpectedly early. Of course there was nothing he could do, but it took some effort to lay the thoughts aside.

'What's that?' Tel Mindor's voice interrupted Arinndier's broodings.

The Goraidin was holding his hand up for silence and

11

craning forward intently. Unconsciously, the others imitated him.

Faintly, the sound of distant singing reached them. It came and went, carried on the slight breeze that was blowing.

'I hope it's not some kind of celebration for us,' Arinndier said, patting his stomach.

The remark brought back to Jaldaric his tormented evening at Pedhavin when the villagers had held an impromptu feast for them before he had had to return silently on his treacherous errand to snatch away Tirilen. Several times during that evening he had forgotten utterly why he was there in the whirl of the music and the dancing. Then his purpose would return to chill him to the heart like a mountain wind striking through a sun-baked and sweltering walker breasting a ridge.

Since his welcome by the Orthlundyn however, this sad, dark thread running through his memory had faded a little, and the happiness he had felt had become more dominant.

He smiled. 'Don't worry, Lord,' he said. 'If it's a celebration, they'll soon dance the food off us.'

When they reached the next village however, despite the fact that there was quite a large crowd of villagers on the small central green, there was no special celebration awaiting them. In fact, though they were again offered food and drink, the attention that was paid to them was markedly less than that they had received hitherto. The main topic of interest was the distant singing.

For distant it still was. As the Fyordyn had neared the village, the singing had grown a little louder and clearer, but its source was obviously not near at hand.

'What is it?' Arinndier asked, but the villagers did not know and with polite head shaking declined to be drawn into conjecture by these outlanders.

Pausing by the village leaving-stone, Arinndier turned to the others. 'Something strange is happening,' he said. 'Whether it's bad or good I don't know, but I think we should move a little faster.' No one disagreed.

Over the next few hours, the singing grew louder and louder and, despite their concern, the four men could not be other than swept up in its elaborate pulsing rhythms and joyous melodies.

'Somebody, somewhere, is celebrating without a doubt,' Berryn said. 'That is amazing singing.'

But Arinndier frowned slightly. 'Amazing indeed,' he said.

'But who could sing so long and so well, and with such power that it carries so far and so clearly?'

As the question left his lips, the four riders, line abreast, clattered over the top of a small rise. Arinndier gasped at the sight before them, and signalled to the group to halt. For a time they were motionless and the singing rose around them to fill the air so that it seemed to be coming from every conceivable direction.

# *Chapter 2*

Andawyr dived into his small tent, sealed the entrance and, rubbing his hands together ferociously, swore roundly, in a manner most unbecoming in the chosen leader of the ancient Order of the Cadwanol.

It was bitterly cold in the tent and his breath steamed out in great clouds, but at least he was now out of that merciless wind.

Gathering his cloak tight about him, he crouched down and fumbled in his pack. After some muttering he produced a small bag and immediately began to struggle with its tightly laced mouth. It took him some minutes of finger blowing and further profanity, together with judicious use of his incisors, to release the leather thong, but eventually he succeeded and with some relief emptied the contents onto a small tray.

He looked at the radiant stones dubiously. He'd never been any good at striking these damned things. And they didn't look very good either. He'd bought them very cheaply from that shifty-eyed blighter at the Gretmearc. Rubbing his still frozen hands together again, he decided now that that might have been a mistake – a very false economy.

The wind buffeted the tent to remind him where he was, and he shrugged his self-recriminations aside; good or bad, there'd be something in these things and he must get them lit quickly. Delving into his pack again, he retrieved the striker and, his tongue protruding slightly, scraped it along one of the stones. Somewhat to his surprise a glowing white line appeared and spread out across the surface of the stone. Less to his surprise, it faded almost immediately into a dull red. He eyed the stone malevolently and struck again, but the result was the same. Turning his attention to the striker he adjusted it and tried again, but still the stone refused to ignite satisfactorily.

Several minutes later he had made little further progress, though he was a good deal warmer by then, and his face was redder by far than most of the stones he had managed to strike into some semblance of life.

He threw the striker down irritably. There was a soft, deep chuckle.

14

'I can do without any of your comments, thank you, Dar,' Andawyr said testily. 'It's all right for you, snug in your own place. I'm freezing to death here.'

'I never said a word,' came the injured reply, radiating insincerity. 'I told you that you should have brought a proper travelling tent, but –'

'Don't say that again,' Andawyr said warningly. 'It's hard enough on foot through these mountains without struggling with a pack-horse.' He held out his hands over the dull red stones. 'And these things are useless as well,' he added.

'*You* bought them,' came Dar-volci's unsympathetic voice.

'These were matured stones when I bought them,' Andawyr protested unconvincingly. 'I'll lay odds that that beggar at the Gretmearc switched them when he bagged them.' He turned one of the unstruck stones over with an expert frown on his face. 'I'll report him to the Market Senate next time I'm there.'

'Matured,' Dar-volci was scornful. 'You couldn't tell a matured stone from a potato. They were baked. I told you that, but you wouldn't listen.'

Andawyr grunted sulkily, and muttered something about the Market Senate again.

'The Senate would throw them at your silly head,' Dar-volci said. 'You're so naïve. Why don't you listen to someone who knows, once in a while?'

'They were a bargain,' Andawyr said indignantly.

Dar-volci made a disparaging noise. 'Well, warm yourself on your cheery profit then,' he scoffed. 'You and your bargains. They see you coming, great leader. You shouldn't try to horse-trade; you don't have the eye for it. You should know that by now. Do you remember that *bargain* cooking pot you bought – *very* cheap –'

'Dar!' Andawyr's eyes narrowed menacingly, but Dar-volci continued, warming to his theme.

'– Genuine Harntor smithing . . . where the Riddinvolk get their precious horseshoes from.' His deep laugh filled the tent. ' –backside melted out of it the first time you used it. What a stink! Then there was that –'

'That's enough,' Andawyr snapped. 'Go to sleep.'

Dar-volci chuckled maliciously. 'Good night, then, old fellow,' he said. 'Sleep snug.'

Andawyr ignored the taunt and turned his attention back to the sulky radiant stones, struggling fitfully to shed their red warmth. Unnecessarily, he glanced from side to side, as if someone might be watching, then, muttering to himself, 'Well, just a smidgeon,' he brought his thumb and first two fingers together, and with a flick of his wrist, nodded them at the stones.

There was a faint hiss, and a white light spread over the reluctant stones.

'I heard that,' Dar-volci said, knowingly.

'Shut up,' Andawyr said peevishly.

The heat from stones filled the tent almost immediately, and Andawyr removed his cloak and loosened some of the outer layers of the clothes he had hastily donned at the sudden onset of the snow storm.

He had always been reluctant to use the Old Power for simple creature comforts, sensing that in some way it would weaken, even demean his humanity. And since his ordeal in Narsindal and his flight along the Pass of Elewart, this reluctance was even stronger. Still, the others *did* twit him gently about his excessive concern . . . and this *was* an emergency, he reassured himself faintly.

The wind rattled the tent again as if in confirmation of this convenient rationalisation.

After a little while, he reached out and dimmed the bright glow of the stones. Then he lay down and, staring up at the roof of the tent, listened to the howling wind.

What would tomorrow bring? When he had set off for Orthlund he had expected a cold, perhaps dismal, journey through the mountains, and had equipped himself accordingly. But this . . . ? This was winter. Granted he was at the highest point of his journey, but such a storm was still unexpected, and he hadn't the supplies to sit for the days it might take to blow itself out; the journey had already taken him longer than he had anticipated. He would have to move on tomorrow, and would probably have to use the Old Power both to guide himself and to survive.

He frowned as he realised just how deep was his reluctance to use this skill that he had struggled so long to master. He recalled a comment his old teacher had made many years earlier.

'I sometimes wonder whether we use *it*, or it uses *us*,' he had said. 'It's so beyond our real understanding.'

It had been a passing comment, lightly made, but it had stuck like a barbed dart in his young acolyte's mind, subsequently making him work as hard at being able to sustain himself without the Power as he was skilled in using it. When later he had become head of the Order, this attitude had inevitably percolated down to permeate all its members.

'We're teachers,' he would say. 'We can't teach people anything if we can't live as they live, strive as they strive.'

But he knew that his real motivation was deeper than that, and not accessible to such simple logic.

The Old Power was the power of the Great Searing, from which and by which all things were formed, and from whose terrible heat had walked Ethriss and the Guardians, followed silently by Sumeral with lesser banes at His heels.

Faced with the terrible dilemma that Sumeral's teaching of war had presented him, Ethriss had given the Cadwanol the knowledge of how to use the Old Power so that they might aid both the Guardians and the mortal armies of the Great Alliance of Kings and Peoples, against the Uhriel and His vast and terrible hordes.

However, as his teacher had said, to understand its use was not necessarily to understand its true nature.

Andawyr turned on his side and gazed at the stones, glowing even now with this very power. 'How can we understand the true nature of such a thing?' he muttered softly.

Even Ethriss himself may not have understood it. According to the most ancient documents in the vast archives of the Cadwanol, when questioned by his first pupils, all he had said, with a smile, was, 'It *is*.'

'It *is*,' Andawyr echoed softly into the still air of his tent.

He was right, he knew. While skill in the use of the Old Power must be studied and practised and improved, it should be used by humans only where all human skills had failed and great harm threatened. Its use was not part of the gift that Ethriss had given to humanity.

'I created you to go beyond it,' he had also said; an enigmatic phrase that had taxed minds ever since.

It was a knowledge that he had reluctantly thrust into the hands of men for use as a weapon only when their very existence and that of all things wrought by himself and the Guardians were threatened. Its inherent dangers were demonstrated all too clearly by Sumeral's use of it to corrupt the three rulers who were to become His Uhriel.

'Some part of all of us is Uhriel.' Andawyr's eyes widened. That phrase too, was one his teacher had used, but it was one he had not recalled for a long time.

He closed his eyes and tried to let the topic go. The debate was an old one amongst the Cadwanwr, and none disagreed in principle with Andawyr's thinking, though the consensus was that the revered Head of the Order was a little over-zealous in his reluctance to use the Power for minor matters.

Andawyr smiled to himself as he felt the warmth of the stones on his face. He had seen the unsuccessfully hidden looks of patient tolerance, not to say irritation, as he had scratched vainly at stones in the past, or struggled with some heavy burden – and made others struggle with him – instead of lifting it the *easy* way!

Yet they too were right. It *was* a mistake to be too zealous in avoiding the use of the Old Power. Why should he have even hesitated here in this biting cold, where failure to ignite the stones might have proved, if not fatal, certainly very dangerous for him?

Balance, he thought. That's all it is. Balance. Too much either way is wrong. But where *was* the balance? Only one thing was certain: the route to it lay along no easy path. Always judgement had to be used, and always judgement was flawed in some degree.

His thoughts began to wander as the day's walking and the last hours' increasingly anxious toiling began to take their toll.

'G'night, Dar,' he muttered faintly, but there was no reply.

Twice he jerked awake suddenly as the dark horror of his journey out of Narsindal came briefly and vividly into his deepening sleep. This happened almost every night, though much less so now than when he had first returned. He bore it with a snarl; I survived the deed, I refuse to fear its shadow, was the sword and buckler he reached for whenever he found himself hesitating to close his eyes.

The third time, however, it was no fearful memory that awoke him. It was the entrance to his tent being torn open and a body crashing in, accompanied by whirling flurries of snow and the icy blast of the storm.

Instantly bolt upright, his heart racing, Andawyr raised his hand to defend himself against this apparition. No hesitation to use the Old Power when it mattered, he noted briefly. However, a mere glance showed that the intruder not only held no weapon, but was exhausted. No threat here, he realised.

'Unless it's to freeze me to death,' he muttered out loud. Hastily he seized the body and, with a great effort, dragged it into the tent, nearly upsetting the radiant stones in the process.

18

As he sealed the entrance again, a hand clutched at him. He turned with a start, ready again to defend himself.

'My horse,' said the new arrival, his voice very weak. 'My horse.'

Andawyr looked at the snow covered figure and the few small flakes still whirling in the light of the glowing stones.

'Please,' said the figure, weakly but urgently.

Andawyr gave a resigned sigh. 'Riddinvolk I presume,' he said and, without waiting for an answer, he gathered his cloak about himself tightly and, with an ill grace, stepped out into the howling darkness.

Fortunately the horse was nearby, standing at the edge of the circle of light cast by the tent's beacon torch. Andawyr suddenly felt his irritation and concern pushed aside by a feeling of humility at the sight of the animal standing patiently in the snow-streaked light, head bowed against the storm. Few travelled these mountains at any time, and none would normally be travelling at this time of year, yet, on an impulse he had lit his beacon torch; and now it had drawn this lone traveller and his mount here and undoubtedly saved his life.

He struck his hand torch and walked over to the horse, staggering a little as the powerful wind drove into him. 'Come on, Muster horse,' he said, taking the animal's bridle. 'It's a little more sheltered over here. Your duties are over for the night. I'll look after your charge.'

The horse looked at him soulfully for a moment, then yielded to the gentle pressure.

Returning to the tent, Andawyr found the new arrival's concern unchanged. 'My horse?' he said, his voice still weak.

'I've thrown a couple of your blankets over him and put him in the lee of some rocks,' Andawyr said. 'It's not ideal, but he should be all right. I've given him a fodder bag as well.'

The man relaxed visibly and Andawyr shook his head. 'You people and your horses,' he said. 'You're incredible. Now let's have a look at *you*.'

The man offered no resistance to Andawyr's examination.

'You're lucky,' Andawyr said when he had finished. 'There's no frost damage to your hands and face, and judging from your boots I presume you can still feel all your toes?'

The man nodded. 'I should have stopped sooner,' he said, still weak. 'I misjudged the storm.'

'You're not alone,' Andawyr said. 'Luckily you're only chilled and exhausted, but it's a good job you saw my light.

You wouldn't have made it through the night.' He moved the tray of radiant stones as far away from the man as he could, then with a flick of his fingers he made them a little brighter. 'Keep away from the stones,' he said. 'Just lie still and rest. You'll soon warm up in here, it's a well-sealed tent: airy and snug.'

The man nodded again, sleepily. 'Thank you,' he mouthed softly. He made an attempt to say something else but it turned into an incomprehensible mumble as he succumbed to his fatigue.

Andawyr looked at him closely. He was a heavily built man, in late middle age, he judged, and from the quality of his clothes, wealthy; definitely not a man one might expect to find roaming the mountains alone at this, or for that matter, any other time of the year.

Nodding to himself thoughtfully, he lay down again. There would be plenty of time tomorrow to find out who the man was and why he was there.

Another flick of his fingers dimmed the radiant stones to their original redness. No point using the Old Power too much. He smiled as he caught the almost reflexive thought. The tent would retain the heat, and the stones, baked or not, would take back any excess and mature a little.

'I'll keep out of sight until we're sure of this one,' came Darvolci's deep voice softly. Andawyr muttered his approval, then allowed himself a brief smugness as he closed his eyes; it had been a good day.

The next morning he was wakened by a gentle shaking. He sat up jerkily, scratching himself and yawning. His guest was holding a bowl of food out to him.

'I took the liberty of making some breakfast for you,' he said. His voice was quite deep, and rich with the sing-song Riddin lilt. 'It's from my own supplies,' he added hastily.

Andawyr squeezed the remains of his broken nose. 'Thank you very much,' he said. 'That was kind of you. I'm afraid it's a meal I'm apt to neglect.'

'No, no,' the stranger said. 'It's I who must thank you for looking after my horse and taking me in.'

Andawyr smiled behind his bowl and paused. Typical Riddinvolk, he thought. Horse first, rider second. Without asking, he knew that the man would have been out to check on the animal before attending to his own needs.

The man misunderstood Andawyr's hesitation. 'Is the food

20

not warm enough?' he asked, his voice concerned. 'I had a little difficulty with your stones; they're not very good. They look as if they've been baked to me.'

Andawyr shot the stones an evil glance then returned to his guest. 'Yes,' he said. 'The stones could be better, bad bargain I'm afraid. But the food's fine.'

'My name's Agreth,' the man said sitting down heavily and extending his hand. 'Don't do the travelling I used to,' he added, then flicking a thumb upwards. 'This lot wouldn't have caught me out once. Judgement's going, I'm afraid,' he added.

'I'm not so sure,' Andawyr said. 'It's unseasonal to say the least, and it came on very suddenly.' His face became intent. 'Agreth?' he said, testing the name until its familiarity brought it into place. 'You're one of Ffyrst Urthryn's advisers aren't you?' He was about to name Agreth's House and Decmill by way of a brief cadenza, but he remembered in time that the Riddinvolk enthusiasm for lineage and family was not something to be lightly released, and he held his tongue.

Agreth smiled. 'Indeed I am,' he said. 'Though when he finds out I nearly froze to death like some apprentice stable lad, he might be looking elsewhere for advice.'

Andawyr laughed and, laying his bowl down, wiped his mouth with the back of his hand. 'And what's one of the Ffyrst's advisers doing alone in the middle of the mountains, half-way to Orthlund, if I might ask?' he asked jovially. 'Morlider come back again?'

He noted the flicker of reaction in Agreth, though it barely reached the man's eyes before he had it under control. 'No, no,' the man replied, with a hint of surprised amusement. 'Just some private business in Orthlund.'

Andawyr nodded, and waited for the counter-attack.

'And may I know the name of my rescuer?' Agreth asked.

Andawyr teased him a little. 'Ah,' he said smiling broadly. 'That's the name of your horse. I'm only your host. But my name's Andawyr.'

This revelation produced a reaction that he had not expected. Agreth frowned briefly then, as recognition came into them, his eyes widened and, reaching forward he seized Andawyr's wrists.

'From the Caves of Cadwanen,' he said almost breathlessly. 'Oslang's leader. On your way, as I am, to Anderras Darion, to spread your news and to see what's happened to this man Hawklan.'

21

Despite himself, Andawyr's mouth fell open.

'Yes,' he managed to stammer. 'But –'

Agreth raised a hand. 'Excuse me,' he said, and unsealing the entrance he thrust his head outside. Drawing back, he said, 'The wind's dropped, but it's still snowing. Let's get moving while we can still see. With luck the travelling should get easier as we move down.'

Andawyr opened his mouth to speak again, but Agreth was taking charge. 'I know Oslang's tale, and therefore yours,' he said, cutting ruthlessly through all discussion as he quickly fastened his cloak about him. 'Let me tell you mine as we travel.'

Andawyr looked through the open entrance. Agreth's advice was sound. Visibility was reasonable, but the sky was leaden and the snow was falling heavily. Nothing was to be gained except danger by staying here to relate histories.

'Very well, Line Leader,' he said with a smile. 'We'll walk and talk awhile.'

It took the two men only minutes to dismantle and stow the tent and soon they were strapping their packs onto Agreth's horse.

As he secured the load, Agreth looked around, his face anxious.

'What's the matter?' Andawyr asked.

'I've never travelled these mountains before,' Agreth replied. 'I have a map, but it's hard to read and I've been relying on the path to a large extent. Now . . .' He shrugged and gestured at the snow-covered landscape.

Andawyr looked at him and then followed his gaze, trying to view this cold, beautiful terrain with the eyes of a man brought up on the broad, rolling plains of Riddin. The Riddinvolk loved the mountains that bordered their land – but only to look at.

'Give me your map,' he said simply.

Agreth fumbled underneath his cloak and eventually produced the document. Andawyr pulled the Riddinwr towards him and, with their two bodies sheltering the map from the falling snow, carefully unfolded the map.

'It's a long time since I travelled this route,' he said. 'But I can remember it quite well. However, there's no point in you just following me. If I get hurt or if we get separated, you'll have to lead, so, with respect, adviser to the Ffyrst, I'll spend a portion of our journey showing you how to read this.' He tapped the map gently.

Agreth seemed doubtful, and anxious to be on his way, but Andawyr was insistent.

'This is not bad,' he said after a moment. 'There's some very good detail. See, we're here.' Agreth screwed his eyes up in earnest concentration. Andawyr's finger jabbed at the map and then out into the greyness. 'That is that small peak over there, and that is the larger one next to it.'

For a few minutes, for the benefit of his reluctant pupil, Andawyr identified on the map such of their surroundings as could be seen, then the two men set off slowly and cautiously through the deepening snow.

As they walked, Agreth told Andawyr of Sylvriss's unexpected arrival in Riddin, and of her strange tale of the corruption and decay of Fyorlund. He concluded with the interrogation of Drago, and the news that the Morlider were preparing to attack Riddin, united now by a leader that was presumed to be the Uhriel, Creost.

Andawyr stopped walking and looked round at the mountains, grey and ominous in the dull wintry light. Not a sound was to be heard except the soft hiss of the falling snow.

Oklar ruling a divided Fyorlund, Creost uniting and guiding the Morlider, Rgoric murdered, Vakloss torn apart, Hawklan struck down and perhaps even now lost in these snow-shrouded hills. He put his hand to his head.

'Are you all right?' Agreth asked anxiously.

No, Andawyr cried out to himself in self-disgust. No. How can I be all right? Me; leader of the Cadwanol; Ethriss's chosen watchers and seekers after knowledge, who slept when all the demons of the ages were waking and running amok! I just want to lie down in this cold grey silence and become part of it and be free from all this horror forever.

'Yes,' he said out loud, letting the now familiar reproaches rage unhindered and unspoken. 'It's just that so many things seem to be moving against us.' He looked up at the snowflakes spearing down into his face, grey and black against the dull sky. 'Even the weather's moving against us,' he said as his distress slowly began to fade away. It would return many times yet, he knew.

Agreth looked on, uncertain what to say.

Andawyr gave a dismissive grunt. 'Still, all we can do is walk forward, isn't it?' he said, stepping out again. 'And we find help in the strangest places, don't we?' He looked at his companion. 'In the midst of this lonely and ancient place, you find a cosy billet for the night, and I find someone to carry my pack.'

He laughed suddenly, and held out his arms wide. 'I used to love this weather when I was a boy,' he said. 'Sledging, snowballing. How can *this* be against me?' Impulsively he walked over to a nearby rock and scooped the snow on top of it into a single heap. Then he began compacting and shaping it.

Watching him, Agreth's uncertainty returned. This was the man that Oslang called his leader? What *was* he doing?

Finally, Andawyr bent down, made a snowball, placed it carefully on top of his handiwork and stood back to admire the result – a tiny snowman.

'There,' he said, beaming. 'Isn't that splendid?' He saluted the small figure. 'Enjoy the view little fellow. Enjoy the peace and quiet. No one will disturb you when we've gone. Have a happy winter. Light be with you.'

Brushing the caked snow from his arms, he turned to Agreth who was struggling to keep his doubts from his face. Andawyr laughed. 'Don't worry,' he said. 'I'm still here. But the day I can't appreciate being eight years old, will be a sad one for me.'

Then he was off again, as briskly as the snow would allow. 'Come on, ' he shouted, turning back. 'We've a long way to go yet.'

Agreth patted his horse hesitantly, as if for reassurance, then set off after him.

Later in the day, the snow stopped falling, and the sky lightened a little, bringing more distant peaks into view, which Andawyr identified for Agreth on his map. They walked on slowly and carefully; sometimes talking, sometimes in silence, sometimes just concentrating where they were putting their feet as they negotiated steep and treacherous slopes.

As they walked, however, they moved gradually down-wards, away from the colder heights, and the snow became less deep. Eventually, reaching the valley floor, Agreth announced that they could ride for a spell, and Andawyr found himself astride the horse in front of the Muster rider.

'Feel like an eight-year-old again?' Agreth asked, laughing.

Andawyr looked down nervously at the snow-covered ground passing underneath his dangling feet. It was much further below than he had imagined when he had been looking up at the horse. 'It'll take me a little time,' he said dubiously.

Agreth laughed again.

Being able to ride from time to time enabled them to make good progress, and late in the afternoon Andawyr professed himself well pleased. Towards nightfall, however, the snow started to fall again, and the wind rose suddenly, obliging the two men to make their camp in some haste. As they pitched Andawyr's tent, the landscape around them slowly began to disappear in a whirling haze.

At last, Andawyr ushered Agreth into the tent and then struck the beacon torch with some relish. As he joined him inside he found that the Muster rider was examining one of the radiant stones.

'These *have* been baked, without a doubt,' he said in a tone of irritated regret, throwing the stone back with the others. 'You should have a word with whoever does your buying.'

'I will,' Andawyr replied, a little more tersely than he had intended, then without hesitation he ignited the stones as he had the previous night.

Agreth started at the sudden flare of light, his face suddenly fearful.

'I'm sorry,' Andawyr said. 'I didn't mean to startle you. There's nothing to be afraid of. It's just –'

'I know what it is,' Agreth interrupted. 'It's the same power that Oslang knocked Drago down with. The same power that Oklar used on Vakloss.' He looked distressed. 'You saved my life and I feel no harm in you – nor does my horse, and he's a far better judge than I am – but I *am* afraid of *that*.' He pointed to the stones. 'It's terrifying.'

Andawyr stared into the warm comfort of the stones. The sudden tension inside the tent was almost palpable. Only the truth could ease it, he knew. 'Yes, you're right,' he said after a long silence. 'It *is* terrifying. But not here, not in this tent. Here it's warmth and light. You don't need to be told that the essence of a weapon lies in the intention of the user, do you?'

He looked up at Agreth, his face stern. 'We've hard times ahead of us, Muster rider,' he said. 'We must learn to see things the way they are; with our fear acknowledged, but bound by our judgement. Fear this power as you would any other weapon; when it's used against you by your enemies, not when it brings you aid and comfort in the darkness.'

Agreth was unconvinced. 'My head accepts what you say, but here –' He patted his stomach and shook his head. His face contorted unhappily as he searched for an explanation. 'I don't understand what it is,' he said finally. 'And how can I defend myself against such a power when it *is* used as a weapon?'

Andawyr looked into his eyes, and then returned his gaze to the stones. Again, only the truth was safe. 'You can't, Agreth,' he said quietly after another long silence. 'You can't. Only I and my brothers can protect you.'

Agreth stared at the prosaic little man with the squashed nose; the little man who made snowmen and was nervous on a horse.

'Are you enough?' Agreth said after a brief hesitation.

Andawyr shrugged. 'Who can say?' he replied. 'But that's a two-edged question. Are *you* enough in the Muster to protect *us* against the swords and arrows of Sumeral's mortal army, when we're extended to our full protecting you against His Power and that of His Uhriel?'

Agreth looked at him intently, then he too shrugged.

Andawyr leaned forward. 'We'll all have our separate parts to play,' he said. 'And we'll all be dependent on one another as well. We must learn each others' strengths and weaknesses – what we each can and can't do – and we must learn to trust where full understanding is not always possible. What else do we have?'

Agreth nodded slowly, and the tension seemed to ease. 'I suppose you're right,' he said. 'Oslang said more or less the same.'

Despite himself, Andawyr chuckled. 'I should imagine he did,' he said. 'A Goraidin's knife at your throat could breed great eloquence. I'm sure. Poor Oslang.'

Agreth stared thoughtfully at the radiant stones. 'It'll take some getting used to,' he said. 'But you *are* right. Without your power, we'd be having a very uncomfortable night tonight, perhaps even be at risk of dying. And what would be the consequences of *that*? I'd probably be no great loss; but the leader of the Cadwanol . . . ?' He let the question hang. 'So just keeping us warm here is using this terrible power of yours – whatever it is, or whoever's it is – to oppose Him already.' He lay down and gazed up at the roof of the tent. 'These flickering stones are the lights of the vanguard of the army that will come forth to meet the Great Corrupter,' he said with mock rhetoric.

Andawyr laughed at his mannerism. 'Very metaphorical, Muster rider,' he said. 'Very metaphorical. I see you've a flair for the broad sweep.'

'I've painted a few house ends in my time,' Agreth said drily.

Andawyr laughed again then he too lay down. The tent was warm now and he dimmed the glow of the stones. 'Better if the enemy doesn't see us coming too soon,' he said, still chuckling. Agreth grunted amiably.

Soon the two were sleeping soundly, oblivious to the moaning wind that twisted and swirled the snow around their small shelter, streaking black-shadowed and white across the bold unwavering light thrown by the beacon torch.

A figure stepped cautiously to the edge of the light, and two more, swords drawn, moved silently to either side of its entrance.

Something nudged Andawyr gently into silent wakefulness. It was Dar-volci. 'Visitors, Andy,' he said. 'Very quiet, too.'

'Stay out of sight, and watch,' Andawyr whispered.

Then, giving Dar-volci the lie, a voice cried out above the wind.

'Ho, the camp.'

# *Chapter 3*

'Look,' said Loman, pointing up at the four figures on the
skyline. 'That'll be them. Fyndal's post rider said they'd be
here soon.'

Hawklan followed Loman's gaze and smiled. He reached up
and touched Gavor's black beak. 'Go and show them the way
home,' he said. 'They'll be frightened to death by all this.
We'll join you as soon as we can.'

The raven chuckled, then reached out his great wings and
flapped up into the air.

Hawklan's comment was accurate; the scene around them
was indeed intimidating. A great host of people was strung out
in a long winding line that disappeared into the woods fringing
the nearby hills to the east. Some were riding, some were
walking, and some were riding on the equally long line of
wagons that was threading its way through the centre of the
crowd.

Even as Hawklan was speaking, the head of the procession
was spreading out like a great delta, and as the crowd reached
the road it divided into two separate streams, one moving
southwards, the other northwards.

Gavor circled high and wide, and glided silently down onto
the watching group from behind.

He landed abruptly on Jaldaric's shoulder, startling him
violently.

'So glad you've come, dear boy,' he said with huge menace.
'We've gathered a few interested souls to hear your . . .
*accounting*.'

He drew out the last word malevolently and then laughed
raucously.

'Isn't it marvellous to be back home, dear boy?' he
continued, jumping up and down excitedly on his reluctant
perch. 'I'm not,' Jaldaric offered as he gathered his scattered
wits, but Gavor ploughed on, oblivious. 'It was very pleasant
in the mountains, but one gets *so* weary of camp cooking and
frozen extremities. I can't wait to get back to a little decent
food, some warmth and, of course, my friends. And it's so nice
to see you all again. Come along, hurry up, hurry up,

everyone's waiting for you. You can tell me what's been happening as we go.'

Berryn and Tel Mindor looked on wide-eyed at this apparition, then with a little 'Hup,' Gavor hopped up on to Jaldaric's head and, tapping his wooden leg in time to the rhythms pulsing around them, focused beadily on the two Fyordyn.

'Ah,' he exclaimed, as if reading their names from some terrible register of his own, 'you will be Tel Mindor and Rede Berryn.' Both opened their mouths to speak, but Gavor rattled on jovially. 'How *are* you? Welcome to Orthlund. Isn't the music fine? Rather a lot of it, I'm afraid, but they're celebrating, you see. How's Uskal, these days? In pain I trust? Never mind, tell me later, I always prefer the good news to be last.'

'What's happening, Gavor? And where's Hawklan?' Arinndier managed to find a momentary opening in this barrage.

Gavor's response was to click loudly. Jaldaric's horse started forward under the command, and Arinndier could not stop himself from smiling at the young High Guard's continuing discomfiture. Then he moved after him, motioning the others to follow.

As they neared the approaching throng they saw that the predominant emotion was happiness. Some of the people were dancing impromptu steps to the music, others were clapping, some were singing, and overall there was a great deal of laughing and talking. The four men found themselves recipients of many friendly gestures and comments.

None the less, Rede Berryn could not forbear saying to Arinndier, very softly, 'This is Orthlund's army, Lord? It's more like a Festival Tournament crowd.'

'Steady on, Rede,' Gavor interposed. 'You're not the only one who can hear a smart-alec whisper from eight ranks back.'

Berryn looked at the bird suspiciously and tried to recall when he had last used the phrase.

Before the Rede came to any conclusion, however, Arinndier had taken hold of his arm excitedly.

'Look,' he said. 'It's Hawklan. He's well again.' He raised his arm in a frantic salute, and called out Hawklan's name, but his voice was lost completely in the all-pervading clamour.

The distant figure was looking at them, however, and raised his own hand in reply, before turning and trotting his horse back along the line to attend to some matter.

Arinndier made to urge his horse forward, but the press of the crowd prohibited anything other than a very leisurely walk and with a slight frown he let the reins fall idly on the horse's neck.

'Hawklan's well, then, Gavor?' he said.

Gavor nodded. 'He's well, Lord,' he replied. 'We're all well, and all anxious to be back home.'

'Your army's in good voice, Gavor, but seems to have precious few weapons.' Jaldaric said, his face puzzled.

'That's the Alphraan making all the noise,' Gavor replied, slightly less enthusiastically than previously. 'The rest of us are just trying to make ourselves heard.' He looked towards the mountains. 'One can have too much of a good thing, can't one?' he added, very loudly.

Jaldaric's bewilderment merely increased. 'But why no weapons?' he persisted, clinging to the same question in the hope that one strand of clarity might lead to others. 'We heard your army was in the mountains facing an unexpected foe. What's happened? These people don't look as if they've been defeated and disarmed.'

Gavor fidgetted restively. 'It's unbelievably complicated, young Jal,' he said patronisingly. 'As, I've no doubt, is your own tale. I can't begin to explain everything in the middle of all this. Let's get to Anderras Darion, take the weight off our feathers and have a talk at our leisure.' He paused and nodded to himself, well satisfied at this suggestion. 'I seem to remember that you Fyordyn are very good at talking,' he added with a laugh, and then he launched himself forward and soared up into the air to avoid any further questions.

Arinndier too laughed and, patting Jaldaric's arm, said, 'That's the best we're going to get. Let's take the bird's advice and get to Hawklan's castle. It's good enough news now just to see him up and riding again.'

Gradually, the four Fyordyn eased their way through the crowd until eventually they were clear of it and cantering along the empty road. Gavor circled high above them, occasionally swooping upwards steeply and then, with an uproarious laugh, tumbling back down precipitately like a tangled black bundle.

As they moved further from the following army, the pervasive music faded and eventually it could hardly be heard above the clatter of hooves on the intricately paved road.

The daylight was fading rapidly when they eventually came into Pedhavin but, high above the village, light streamed out through the Great Gate of Anderras Darion which stood wide and welcoming. It had been visible to the four riders long before they had seen the village, and had drawn them forward like a bright guiding star.

As the Fyordyn passed the leaving stone and the small sorry heap of Dan-Tor's decaying wares, Gavor flew past them noisily. 'Up the hill, up the hill,' he shouted. 'Door's open, and Gulda will be back by now. I'll join you later.' Then he was gone, into the deepening darkness. As the four men peered after him, the sound of a rather hoarse nightingale drifted down to them, followed by a fit of coughing.

The village itself was alive with torches and bustling activity, with people running hither and thither through its rambling maze of streets in happy confusion. Most of those that the Fyordyn encountered acknowledged them, and once again Jaldaric found himself moved as apparent strangers came up to him and took his hand sympathetically.

Arinndier gazed around, and then shook his head.

'This is a bewildering little place,' he said. 'Everything's covered in carvings and they all seem to be moving.'

'Amazing,' said Rede Berryn, gazing around in awe. 'I knew the Orthlundyn were carvers, but this . . .'

He fell silent as his eye caught a small plaque on which was carved what seemed to be a field of wheat. Under the touch of the torchlight, shadows rippled across it as though it were being stirred by a warm summer breeze. Berryn sat motionless, spellbound, while the others waited for him patiently.

'Up the hill, up the hill.' A friendly voice broke into their calm as a passer-by, thinking that the four outlanders were lost, pointed in the direction they should take.

Arinndier thanked him, and the group moved off again.

'What do you think of their communications, Goraidin?' Arinndier asked Tel Mindor with some amusement.

The Goraidin raised his eyebrows. 'Widespread,' he replied enigmatically.

The Goraidin's manner made Arinndier's amusement billow out into a great laugh which rang around the small square they were crossing. 'Very true,' he said, after a moment. 'But they've not told *us* anything, you'll note.'

Tel Mindor nodded his head in acknowledgement.

Then they were out of the village and heading up the steep winding road towards the castle. The activity was still continuing however, a small but steady stream of torch-bearing villagers moving slowly up and down the slope like a trail of tardy glow-worms.

As they neared the top of the slope, two figures came into sight. One was tall and straight and wearing a green robe decorated with a single black feather. The other was short and squat and leaning on a stick. Even though the light from the courtyard fell on her, she seemed to be as black as a silhouette.

Reaching the Gate, all four men dismounted to find themselves submitting to Gulda's inspection. Tirilen smiled slightly at the sight, though her eyes narrowed a little when she looked at Jaldaric and saw the subtle changes that the ordeals of the past months had wrought on his round, innocent face.

Gulda saw it too even though she had never seen him before.

'You'll be Jaldaric, young man,' she told him. 'I hear you've had troubles of late.' Jaldaric met her piercing gaze, but seemed uncertain how to reply. After a moment, she nodded. 'You'll live, Jaldaric, son of Eldric. You'll live,' she said, a gentleness in her voice and manner belying the seemingly harsh words.

Then, Jaldaric released, she raised her stick horizontally and pointed to each of the others in turn as she pronounced her conclusions. '*Your* names have come before you as well,' she said. 'Rede Berryn; an old High Guard if ever I saw one. You've ridden the Watch, haven't you?' She did not wait for an answer, but moved on. 'Tel Mindor.' She looked at him intently. 'Special,' she concluded after a moment. 'Goraidin, probably. Fine men.' Then: 'And last, as is the protocol of the Geadrol, I believe: Lord Arinndier.' She inclined her head slightly to Arinndier, who bowed his in reply. 'Don't be too distressed, Lord,' she went on. 'You're not the first to have been quietly led astray by Sumeral and his agents.'

'You must be Memsa Gulda,' Arinndier said as courteously as he could.

But Gulda, her inspection complete, was gracious. 'I am indeed,' she said. 'And this is Tirilen, a healer, and daughter to Loman, Hawklan's castellan. Welcome to Anderras Darion, all of you. We're honoured to have you here and you come at a propitious time . . .' Unexpectedly, she chuckled. 'We've just routed an ally.'

Then, without offering any explanation for this remark, she turned and stumped off through the Gate, beckoning the men to follow.

'You'll want to tend your own horses, I presume,' she said as they strode out to keep up with her. 'I'll show you to the stables, then' – she signalled to a young apprentice who had been hovering like a tiny planet some way from this weighty group – 'this young man will show you to your rooms. You'll be able to bathe and change out of your travelling clothes. Then we can eat and talk.' She nodded to herself. 'Considerable talkers, you Fyordyn, as I remember. I'll look forward to it. I've no doubt we've a great deal of news for one another.'

'That would be most welcome, Memsa,' Arinndier said. 'But we need nothing to eat at the moment. The villagers on the way have been more than generous.'

Gulda nodded again. 'That's as may be, young man,' she said. 'But *I'm* ravenous. It's been a long walk today and I've had nothing but camp fodder for the past few days.' And without further comment she walked off into the Castle.

Some while later the Fyordyn were ushered into a large room. A blaze of glowing radiant stones formed a focus for the warmth that filled it and a bright but mellow torchlight brought alive the carvings of rural scenes which decorated the walls. The ceiling was a great skycape in which huge heavily laden clouds seemed to make a slow, endlessly changing progress.

The four men were soon lounging luxuriously in the long-stored sunlight being released by the torches and the fire. For the most part, they were silent; even Jaldaric, who had seen the Castle before, was awed by the craftsmanship and beauty that he found surrounding him once again.

Of the four, Rede Berryn was the most vocal, moving from carving to carving like an excited child examining his Winter Festival gifts.

'This place is amazing,' he said finally, flopping down noisily on to a long, accommodating settle, and carefully straightening his stiff leg. 'Look at those torches. And those radiant stones. They splutter and crackle like burning logs. This room, this whole building, must catch and return every spark of their warmth for them to have matured like that. Marvellous, I haven't seen anything like them in years, if ever. And these carvings defy description. I must get my old wood chisels out when I get home. I'd almost forgotten about them, there's been so much sourness in the air these last few years, but at the first opportunity . . .' He left the sentence unfinished, but beamed a great smile and waved his clenched fist as a token of his resolution.

Arinndier and Tel Mindor smiled in return, though Jaldaric seemed a little uncertain about how to handle this sudden onset of childlike enthusiasm.

As they rested, each felt the calm of the room beginning to unravel the tangles of dire concerns that had grown over the past months to cloud their hearts and minds. Gradually they all became both silent and still, until eventually the only sounds in the room were the occasional murmur of the radiant stones, and the muffled echoes of the activities outside as the Castle prepared to receive again its key-bearer and the many others for whom it was now home. But neither these nor the various people who came in from time to time to enquire solicitously about their comfort, offered any disturbance to the calm of the four men.

Slowly but perceptibly the noises from outside changed in character, becoming more intense and purposeful, like a distant wind gathering energy.

Then, abruptly, Hawklan was there.

The large doors of the room flew open and a clatter of laughter and noise cascaded over the four Fyordyn, swirling the warmth around them, and lifting them out of their reveries. They all stood up expectantly.

For a moment Hawklan stood motionless, framed in the doorway and gazing around the room. It seemed to Arinndier that the dancing music that had flooded through the land earlier that day, was still washing around the feet of this strange, powerful man. Then the lean face split into a broad smile and Hawklan strode forward to greet his guests affectionately. Behind him came Loman and Isloman, followed in turn by Tirke and Dacu and several others, including Athyr and Yrain. Following them all, like a dour and watchful shepherdess herding her sheep, came Gulda.

There was a great flurry of introductions and greetings including an alarming bear-hug of forgiveness and welcome for Jaldaric from Loman. Then the questions that both parties had been quietly fretting over for the past hours began to burst out, and very soon there was uproar, with everyone talking at once.

Arinndier looked plaintively at Hawklan, who smiled and brought his hands together in a resounding clap. 'Friends,' he said loudly into the surprised silence. 'We all have too much to tell for us to learn anything like this.' He affected a great sternness. 'We must therefore comport ourselves in the

Fyordyn manner, so I shall put our meeting in the hands of the Lord Arinndier. No one may now speak without his permission.'

There was a little spatter of ironic applause, but the clamour did not return and as the company settled itself about the room, some on chairs and settles, some on the floor by the flickering fire, Arinndier rather self-consciously began relating the events that had occurred in Fyorlund since Rgoric had suspended the Geadrol.

As if listening themselves, the torches dimmed a little, and the yellow glow of the radiant stones became tinged with red and orange.

Despite Arinndier's succinctness, it proved to be a long telling, and the bringing of food and drink for the latest arrivals, proved a timely interruption.

At the end there was a murmur of general satisfaction at the news of the defeat and flight of Dan-Tor, but it was Tirke who yielded to temptation.

'He's *really* gone?' he exclaimed, unable to restrain himself. 'We're free of him? That's –' He clenched his fists and looked upwards for inspiration. 'Incredible . . . marvellous,' he produced, rather inadequately. 'I'm only sorry I missed the battle.'

Arinndier gave him a stern look for this breach of etiquette. 'Don't be, *Fyordyn*,' he said grimly, putting his rebuke into the last word. 'There was no joy in it, and there'll be others that you won't miss, I fear. That's why we're here. We're not truly free of him. He's alive and unhurt and ensconced in Narsindalvak with a large part of his Mathidrin intact. I doubt he intends to stay there long, and I doubt it's in our interests to leave him there unhindered too long, though what we should do remains to be seen.'

Hawklan lifted his hand to speak. Arinndier nodded.

'We must talk further about these blazing wagons that Dan-Tor used,' Hawklan said thoughtfully. 'And the materials that were in the warehouse that Yatsu fired.'

'Indeed we must,' Arinndier said. 'They were terrifying. With a little more thought, he would have destroyed us.' With a frown, he set the thought aside. 'Still, there are many things we need to discuss in due time, but tell us of *your* journey now, Hawklan, and your illness and your apparently miraculous recovery.'

Hawklan shrugged apologetically.

'What happened to me after I struck Oklar and until I was awakened, I haven't the words to tell. I'm sorry,' he said, holding out his hands towards Dacu.

It was thus the Goraidin who told the tale of their journey from Eldric's stronghold and of their strange encounter with the Alphraan and the mysterious awakening of Hawklan. His spare, unadorned, Fyordyn telling forbade interruption, but a deep, almost fearful, silence fell over his audience as he described Hawklan's brief but terrible battle with the monstrous remnant of Sumeral's First Coming.

Then he was concluding his tale. Telling how, after leaving the Alphraan's strange caverns, they had found the gulley that had led them safely across the shoulder of the mountain, and how their journey thereafter, though slow, had become gradually easier as they moved south and out of the premature snowfalls.

'We have the route well mapped now,' he said casually to Arinndier. 'But it'll need a lot of work – roads, bridges and so on – to make it suitable for use by a force of any size.'

He finished his telling with the mysterious and sudden disappearance of the Alphraan in the last part of the journey; if, as he wondered, disappearance were the correct word for the sudden absence of beings they had never actually seen.

'They used to join in our conversations, just as if they were with us,' he said. 'Then –' he snapped his fingers – 'they were gone. Silent. It was very strange. We'd grown used to this disembodied voice talking to us, but there was nothing until we walked into your . . . army and that . . . whatever it was . . . that great clamour.'

'It was an ousting of the old and inflexible, by the new.' Unbidden, Gulda interrupted the proceedings, though she threw an apologetic glance at Arinndier. 'Or perhaps, more correctly, it was the ousting of the old by the very ancient.' She shrugged. 'It doesn't matter anyway. They're a people . . . a race . . . almost beyond our understanding. We'll probably never know what happened. In fact I doubt they'd even be able to explain it to us. Suffice it that in some way they're now whole again, and our friends, or at least our allies. Something that hasn't happened since the beginning of the First Coming.'

'Hence the singing, the – celebrations – we heard, several hours ride away?' Arinndier said.

Gulda nodded, and Arinndier motioned her to continue. 'Geadrol protocol demands that the first shall be last, Memsa,' he said wryly, twitting her gently for her own remark earlier.

Gulda looked at him sideways, and the Orthlundyn waited expectantly. But no barb was launched at the Fyordyn lord. Instead, it was launched at them as, very graciously, Gulda said, 'Thank you, Lord. It's a refreshing change to be amongst people who know how to discourse in an orderly and rational manner.'

Her own telling however, was almost breathtakingly brief: the Orthlundyn had been made ready for war; the Alphraan had interfered, first by causing accidents and then by stealing the labyrinth that guarded the Armoury. They had been contacted and confronted . . .

'The rest you know,' she concluded. 'And the details we can discuss later.'

She ended abruptly and there was a long silence in the room.

'They sealed the labyrinth?' Hawklan asked eventually, almost in disbelief.

Gulda nodded. 'It's open again now,' she said almost off-handedly. 'First thing I checked when I got back. To be honest I'm surprised they're not here, but . . .' She shrugged, reluctant to speculate on the behaviour of these strange people. 'The whole thing was very worrying, but it's been a useful exercise and we've learnt –' She pulled a rueful face. '– re-learnt, a great deal about our command structures and the logistics involved in moving so many people about.'

'And your verdict?' Hawklan asked.

Gulda paused thoughtfully. Loman found his eyes narrowing in anticipation of some caustic reply, but Gulda just nodded and said, 'Not bad. There's plenty of room for improvement, but I think they've got the wit to see that for themselves now. Not bad at all.'

'Good,' Hawklan acknowledged, smiling slightly at the confusion of relief and surprise that Loman was struggling to keep off his face.

Arinndier looked round at the others. Several wanted to speak, but many were also showing distinct signs of weariness.

He glanced quickly at Hawklan, who nodded.

'We've heard enough for tonight, I think,' he said firmly, pulling himself upright in his chair. 'Even though we've raised more questions than we've heard answers. I think it's going to take us some considerable time to acquaint one another thoroughly with what's been happening and I see no benefit in going without sleep while we're doing it.'

Gulda nodded approvingly, and soon the group was breaking up noisily. Hawklan took Arinndier's arm as he rose to leave. 'First light tomorrow, Arin, we'll send messengers to Riddin to find out what's happened to your Queen,' he said.

Arinndier bowed. 'Thank you,' he replied. 'She's probably all right. She had a good escort and she's not without resource as you know, but these early snows . . .' He shrugged helplessly.

Hawklan walked with him to the door. 'Your people did well, but I grieve for your losses,' he said.

Arinndier nodded. 'Your arrow bound him, Hawklan, and gave us the chance. Without that –'

'It's of no relevance now,' Hawklan said, raising a hand. 'Loman's arrow. Ethriss's bow, my –' he smiled self-deprecatingly – 'marksmanship. Many things made the whole, not least the courage and discipline of your men, and it was the whole that tilted the balance and gave us all a little more time. What's important now is that we use it to the full.' He motioned to Tirilen, standing nearby. 'We've a great deal to talk about yet. I'm glad you're here. Tirilen will show you and the others back to your rooms. We'll talk further tomorrow.'

As he closed the door behind them softly, Hawklan paused. Then he turned and with a gesture further dimmed the torches.

Only Gulda remained in the room. She was sitting by the radiant stones which were now glowing red and, in the reduced light, casting her shadow onto the walls and ceiling like a great, dominating presence. In her characteristic pose, resting her chin on her hands folded over the top of her stick, she seemed the stillest thing in the room.

Hawklan sat down opposite her quietly. Gulda looked up at him and, for an instant, in the light of the dimmed torches and the glowing fire, he saw again a fleeting vision of a powerful woman of great and proud beauty. But as quickly as it had come the image was gone and she was an old woman again.

'You knew that Dan-Tor was Oklar, and didn't tell me,' Hawklan said, his voice even.

'I thought –' Gulda began.

'You *knew*,' Hawklan said, before she could continue.

Gulda lowered her eyes.

'You reproach me,' she said into the firelight.

'Should I not?' Hawklan replied.

Gulda was silent for a long time, then, 'You had Ethriss's

sword and bow, arrows as good as could be made in this time, a fine horse, a stalwart friend –'

'Yes, you let Isloman go too,' Hawklan interrupted. 'Two men against an elemental force.'

Gulda looked up, her face scornful. 'Don't whine, Hawklan,' she said. Her anger carried through into her voice all the more powerfully because it was commanding in tone and quite free of the rasping irritation that normally laced her more severe rebukes. 'Oklar is no elemental force, he's a mortal man as you are. A *flawed* mortal man, corrupted by being given too great a power, as perhaps you might have been had you stood too close to Sumeral with your whingeing begging bowl of desires.'

Hawklan's eyes narrowed in response to Gulda's biting anger. 'Don't quibble, *Memsa*,' he said, almost savagely. 'You understand my meaning well enough. You knew who he was and you let me – us – go without any warning.'

Gulda turned her face towards the glowing stones again. 'And you'd have me explain?' she said. There was a strange helplessness in her voice.

Hawklan stared at her, his anger fading. 'Yes,' he said, 'I'd have you explain that and many other things as well. Who you are. How you come here. How you know so many things about this Castle, about wars and armies. The list is long.'

Gulda nodded slowly but did not speak for some time. When she did, her voice was quiet.

'I am what I am, Hawklan,' she said simply. 'And I am here because of what I was.' She looked at him. 'As are you. As are we all. And how I came to know what I know, *you* don't need to know.'

'Gulda!' Hawklan made no effort to the keep the exasperation out of his voice.

She held his gaze. 'Had I told you that Dan-Tor, that dancing twisting tinker who came to torment your little village with his corrupt wares, was Oklar the Uhriel, Sumeral's first and greatest servant, with power to lift up whole mountain ranges or hurl them beneath the ocean, would you have believed me? And would you have done anything other than go and see for yourself in your doubts? And Isloman with you?'

Hawklan did not reply.

Gulda continued, 'And *had* you believed me, would you still have done anything other?'

Hawklan lowered his eyes. 'Damn you,' he said after a long silence.

'We had choice and no choice, Hawklan,' Gulda said softly. 'Both of us were free to walk away, but both of us were bound to our paths. It was ever thus for people such as you and I, people with the wit to see. And it ever will be.'

A faint reproach still flickered in Hawklan's voice. 'Perhaps had we known, we might not have confronted him so recklessly,' he said.

Gulda turned back to the softly whispering stones. Idly she prodded them with her stick, making a small flurry of cached sunlight spark upwards. Unexpectedly, she chuckled.

'What would you have done to meet such a foe, assassin?' she said mockingly. 'Crept into his room at night to smother him or stab him? Bribed the Palace servants to poison his food?'

Hawklan frowned uncertainly.

'No,' Gulda went on. 'You'd still have had to see first. Then having seen and decided, I suspect you'd have shot an arrow into his malevolent heart, wouldn't you?'

Despite himself, Hawklan smiled at this cruelly perceptive analysis.

'I was no different, Hawklan.' Abruptly Gulda was explaining. 'I could see no other way than to wait and see what would be. I could not face him myself . . . not yet. I was a spectator whether I wished it or not. All I could do was arm you with weapons of some worth, and have faith in the resources I saw within you.'

'And had we died?'

'You didn't,' Gulda's reply was immediate.

'But . . . ?'

'You didn't,' she repeated.

'We might have!' Hawklan insisted through her denial.

'You might indeed,' Gulda replied passionately. 'But you still know *I* could have done nothing about it. I *knew* that you had to see him for what he truly was, and both my heart and my head told me that even if I could have given you a measure of the man – which I couldn't, as you know now, he's beyond description – it would have hindered you more than helped you. Clouded your vision with fear. Marred the true strength that only your . . . innocence . . . could take you to.'

Gulda turned again to her contemplation of the radiant stones. Hawklan leaned back into the comfort of his chair and looked at her stern profile, red in the firelight.

'You were so certain of the outcome?' he said after a while.

Gulda smiled ruefully. 'Certain?' she said. 'Certainty's a rare luxury, Hawklan. The butterfly beats its wings and stirs the dust, which moves the grain, which moves the pebble, which –'

'Moves the stone, the rock, the boulder, etc., etc., and down comes the mountain.' Hawklan finished the child's lay impatiently, though as he did so, the memory returned to him of colourful wings stretching luxuriously on the toe of his boot as he had sat shocked and bewildered in the spring sunshine after he and Isloman had fled from Jaldaric's doomed patrol. He recalled that the butterfly too had fled at the approach of a shadow.

Gulda's voice returned him to the present again. 'I went as far as my reason and my intuition could go, Hawklan,' she was saying. 'After that all I had was faith and hope.'

'Faith and hope in what?' Hawklan asked.

Gulda shook her head and, after a moment, began to smile broadly. 'Just faith and hope that my reason and my intuition were right.' Her smile abruptly turned into a ringing laugh that rose to fill the room.

'Have you finished my trial, judge,' she said, turning to Hawklan, still laughing. 'Me, who gave you Ethriss's bow and made Loman forge those splendid arrows for it? Me, who you would have brushed aside if I'd fallen weeping at your knees imploring you not to go. Me who, above all, told you to *be careful*.'

She drew out her last words and, despite himself, Hawklan fell victim to her mirth.

Yet even as he began to smile, the thought came to him that he had done right to make Gulda release her doubts and fears; she would be less impaired now. It was a cold and sudden thought, and it repelled him, for all its truth. I had the same need, for the same reason, he thought in hasty mitigation of this unwonted harshness.

Gulda's laughter gradually subsided and she took out a kerchief and began to wipe her eyes. 'Who knows what butterfly blew us all here, Hawklan?' she said, still chuckling. 'And who knows where it'll blow us next. Let's take some joy in the fact that what happened, happened as it did and that Oklar's hand is stayed for the moment. And that you and Isloman and all the others are alive, and unhurt, and wiser, and *here*.'

41

Abruptly she jerked her chair nearer to Hawklan and, reaching forward, seized his wrists affectionately. Once again Hawklan was surprised by her grip. It did not crush or hurt, but he knew that it was more powerful even than Loman's or Isloman's.

'Now *I* must interrogate *you*,' she said, releasing him, but still staring at him intently. 'What has Oklar's touch taught you, key-bearer?'

Hawklan turned away from her gaze. 'His touch on Fyorlund and its people taught me that there's no end to his corruption; it's unfettered, without restraint of any kind,' he said. 'It taught me that I must seek him out again, and his Master, and . . . destroy . . . them both, and the others, wherever they be.'

'Has Hawklan the warrior slain Hawklan the healer then?' Gulda asked.

Hawklan looked at her, uncertain of her tone.

'There's no warrior in this room, unless it's you, swords-woman,' he said after a moment.

Gulda looked at him enigmatically and, sitting back in her chair, placed her stick across her knees.

Confused by his own strange remark, Hawklan glanced awkwardly round the darkened room, his huge shadow seeming to turn and listen to him.

'I doubt there's any difference between warrior and healer here anyway,' he said diffidently. 'Oklar is a disease beyond help; his Master, more so. Excision is probably the only treatment.'

'You already knew that,' Gulda retorted, leaning forward. 'Any half-baked stitcher of gashes could have told you that. Now answer the question you know I was asking. What has Oklar's touch taught you?'

'I don't know,' Hawklan replied after a brief silence.

Gulda's eyes narrowed. 'Go back to the source, Hawklan,' she said purposefully, leaning back in her chair again.

Hawklan looked into the fire and welcomed its warmth on his face. The terrible confrontation at the Palace Gate came to him again as it did every day, as did all his doubts and questions.

'I was frozen with terror after my arrow hit him,' he began. 'I felt his malevolence overwhelming me before I could even reach for a second one. Then Andawyr's voice came from somewhere, very weak and distant. "The sword," he said.

"Ethriss's sword." ' Hawklan's eyes widened as the scene unfolded before him inexorably, their green eerie in the red firelight. 'But I didn't know how to use it against such a foe – no part of me knew how to use it – no dormant Guardian rose up from within to protect me when his power struck me – nothing. I did what I could. I tried to heal. I felt the sword severing his dreadful destruction but still it came on, pushing me deeper into . . . darkness.'

He stopped and looked at Gulda. 'Perhaps if I'd not used the sword . . . not cleaved his power . . . those two great swathes of destruction wouldn't have been cut across Vakloss. Perhaps all those people would have been spared.'

Gulda shrugged, though in helplessness, not callousness. 'They would have been spared had you kept to your bed that day,' she said relentlessly. 'But a thousand times their number would have died the sooner if you hadn't defied him.'

'It's a bitter consolation,' Hawklan said.

'There's none other,' Gulda replied gently. 'Finish your tale.'

His doubt not eased, Hawklan hesitated, then his face darkened. 'As I fell, I felt His presence . . . icy . . . terrible.'

Gulda leaned forward, her face urgent and intent. '*He* came there?' Her voice was the merest whisper. 'He reached out from Narsindal?'

Abruptly her face was alive with pain and uncertainty. Hawklan reached out and took her hands. She was trembling and her pulse was racing as if with passion. For a moment she did not respond, then with a casual gesture she freed herself from his grip and motioned him back to his chair.

'How did you know it was Him?' she said stonily.

'How could I not,' Hawklan replied. 'And He spoke.' Gulda sank back into the shade of her chair. 'He called me . . . the Keeper of Ethriss's Lair.'

Hawklan wrapped his arms about himself and shuddered. As if in response, the radiant stones flared up brightly, throwing up a brilliant cascade of sparks and sending a myriad subtle shadows dancing through all the ancient carvings.

For a long time, the two sat silent, and the fire subsided, clucking and spluttering to itself unheeded.

'Only the pain and terror of His Uhriel could have lured His spirit from Narsindal,' Gulda said eventually, her voice low as if fearful that her very words could bring Him forth again. 'Only that could have enabled it to happen. I think Loman's arrow was truer than even I thought. And perhaps you too wielded the sword better than you knew. Perhaps you did not divide Oklar's power, but cut the heart out of it and returned it whence it came, as Ethriss himself might have done.'

Hawklan looked at her. 'I am not Ethriss,' he said.

'Perhaps,' Gulda said, 'perhaps not. You're certainly Hawklan the healer, as you ever were, though more knowledgeable as I fancy you'll tell me in a moment. But you're something else as well.' Hawklan scowled, but Gulda waved his denial aside. 'Sumeral's Will reached out to His Uhriel, but He didn't destroy you, as He could have done, protected though you were by Ethriss's sword. He let you be.'

Hawklan shook his head and wrapped his arms about himself again. 'I felt Him,' he said.

Gulda shook her head. 'No,' she said. 'He didn't touch you. His voice alone would have shrivelled you. You caught the edge of His merest whisper. He let you be, and He bound His Uhriel to ensure that he too would not assail you further.'

'*He* bound His own?' Hawklan repeated surprised.

'None other could,' Gulda replied.

'But . . . that would have left Oklar defenceless,' Hawklan said.

'We have no inkling of Sumeral's intent,' Gulda said. 'And the binding would be subtle. Oklar would not be defenceless, have no fear.'

'It cost him Fyorlund,' said Hawklan emphatically.

'We *have* no inkling,' Gulda repeated deliberately, to end the conjecture. 'Tell me of the darkness.'

Unexpectedly, Hawklan smiled. 'Have *you* any words to describe sleep?' he asked. Gulda did not reply. 'I remember nothing,' he went on. 'Nothing until a dancing spark of life reached out and touched me.'

'Sylvriss's baby?' Gulda asked.

Hawklan nodded. 'From then on, it was like a strange dream. I was awake, but not awake. There but not there. Resting yet striving. Listening, learning, understanding, but not fraught, anxious, concerned – not even at the pain I knew my condition was causing to Isloman and the others. It wasn't good, but . . .' His voice trailed off. 'I'm sorry,' he said. 'I can't explain. I don't know how long I would have stayed like that. Nothing seemed to change until . . . the silence.'

'Yes,' Gulda said. 'Dacu spoke to me of that almost within minutes of our meeting. It seemed to have had a profound effect on him.'

'It had a profound effect on us all,' Hawklan said. 'It wasn't just a silence, it was a great deep . . . stillness . . . but not the stillness of emptiness. Whatever it was, there was a powerful will at work. Benign I'm sure, but powerful. It reached out and . . . brought me together . . . woke me, if you like; and it stunned the Alphraan utterly.'

A thought came to him suddenly. 'It was searching for something,' he said. 'Or someone.'

Gulda nodded. 'Other forces are moving with us, Hawklan,' she said. 'We need our every ally, we must find the source of this will. I'll speak to the Alphraan about it. Perhaps they understand it better now.'

Hawklan smiled. 'They might,' he said. 'But even if they do, there's every chance they won't be able to explain to you in our "crude" language.'

'None the less . . .' Gulda said, leaving her intention quite clear and refusing to be deflected by Hawklan's levity.

Then she leaned forward and, folding her hands over the top of her stick, rested her chin on them again. 'And your own new knowledge, healer?' she asked, reverting to her original question.

'New and not new, Gulda,' Hawklan replied flatly. 'No great blinding revelations. It was like a wind slowly blowing sand away and exposing a familiar rock. What I know now, I also know was there all the time.'

He paused. Gulda waited silently.

'I've knowledge of the governing of a great people, of the leading of a great army, of a life of learning and effort to make my body and mind what they are now.' He smiled ruefully. 'No magical gift from some ancient Guardian made me what I am. Just effort and fine teachers. But –' he entwined his fingers and brought his hands together tightly as if trying to wring the truth out of something – ' . . . no names, no faces, no . . . small memories to tell me who or what I truly am . . . or was.'

He paused again, his face pained.

'Also I have the memory of a terrible battle – or part of it,' he said. 'The last part. The air full of awful noises, the sky flickering black, the ground uncertain under our feet, and hordes upon hordes of . . . them . . . coming eternally against us, regardless of their own losses . . .'

He shook his head as if to dismiss the thought forever.

'What else?' Gulda prompted.

Hawklan did not answer immediately. Instead he looked down at his still-clenched hands. 'I led them there, Gulda,' he said reluctantly. 'In my arrogance, I led my army, my whole people, to annihilation.'

'You *know* this?' Gulda asked.

Hawklan leaned back and looked up at the ornate ceiling, red in the firelight like towering storm clouds at sunset.

'We were the last,' he said softly. 'The rest of the army had been . . . destroyed. Destroyed by sheer numbers . . . savagery . . .' He looked back at Gulda. 'Perhaps treachery. I don't know,' he added uncertainly. 'We stood alone, back to back, a shrinking circle . . .'

He paused again. 'And I know nothing other than that. That and my terrible grief and despair.'

'Nothing?'

Hawklan fell silent again for a moment, then said, 'Something . . . touched my shoulder . . . I think.' His face was puzzled.

'It's a vivid memory?' Gulda asked.

Hawklan nodded. 'It's the clearest memory I have. It comes to me every day. Without the pain of the despair and grief – that's only a faint, distant echo now. But the images are intense.' His hands separated. 'What does it all mean, Gulda?'

The old woman shook her head. 'I don't know,' she said simply. 'You're beyond my reach and beyond my vision, and always have been. All we know is that Sumeral fears you sufficiently both to spare you when He could have destroyed you, and to bind His Uhriel to ensure he would not use the Old Power against you again. But why He should fear you?' She shrugged. 'You're as profound an enigma as ever, Hawklan.'

'Could it be that He wishes me spared for some more devious reason than just fear?' Hawklan suggested hesitantly.

'It's a risk,' Gulda said. 'Always has been. But there's nothing we can do about that. We must play the parts we see, and keep our wits about us for ambushes.' Then she leaned forward and looked intently at Hawklan again. When she spoke, her voice was almost a whisper. 'You're someone who might be turned to His way, Hawklan. Someone even who could become one of His Uhriel. Perhaps that's what He had in mind for you.'

Hawklan shrank back in his chair, his eyes wide. 'No,' he said hoarsely, his voice both fearful and savage. 'Never.'

'All the Uhriel were great men once,' Gulda said grimly.

'They weren't made the way they are at a flick of His hand. They were led to Him step by patient step, until they found they could not retreat.'

Still shaken, Hawklan caught an unexpected note in her voice. 'You sound almost sorry for them,' he said hesitantly.

Gulda was silent for a moment, then, with a slow shake of her head, she said, 'We all choose our way.'

Before Hawklan could speak again, she waved a dismissive hand. Whatever doubts she might have, they were not to be pursued further here.

'What are you going to do now?' she asked, relaxing.

'Stay here for a few days to rest,' Hawklan replied after an uncertain pause. 'And talk, and think, and walk around the castle, and just sit. I've travelled so far since I left for the Gretmearc, I need a little stillness for a time.'

Gulda nodded. 'And when you've finished this comprehensive list of chores, what then?' she asked.

Hawklan chuckled and retaliated immediately. 'You're relentless, Gulda,' he said. 'But when I've satisfied myself about everything you've all done so far, I intend to accept your original advice – and Andawyr's.' His face became anxious. 'That strange little man saved my life at the Gretmearc and has woven himself into it in some unfathomable fashion. He sought my help twice and I couldn't – wouldn't – give it. Then in my darkest moment he reached out, just as Sumeral reached out, and aided me.' He looked up at the red clouds overhead. 'We will need this Old Power to face Sumeral, just as surely as we will need men. None here can use it, but Andawyr could. I must seek out the Cadwanol.'

# *Chapter 4*

Hawklan stood on the battlements of Anderras Darion and looked out over the Orthlund countryside.

It was subdued and dull, and the horizon merged uncertainly with the grey sky in a vague mistiness. Coupled with the cold, raw weather, it was the very opposite of the rich, vigorous landscape he had left in the spring. Yet there was still a calmness about it: a calmness that said that all was as it should be; that this was the preparation for the long winter resting that would see the land renewed again in its due time. And even as he looked at it, Hawklan realised that this was where some part of him had been aching to be ever since he had left; this was where he belonged, for all his strange knowledge of other places and for all the strange compulsions that had drawn him to the Gretmearc and then to and fro across Fyorlund; this was his home.

He wrapped his warm cloak about himself and slowly drew in a long, cold breath. Then, equally slowly, he released it again, relaxing as he did so into the deep truth of his surroundings, into the Great Harmony of Orthlund.

Isloman, standing next to him, watched the slight movement silently. He laid his hand on the finely crafted stone of the wall.

'If we don't destroy Him, He will strike to our very heart,' he said.

The remark bore no relation to anything they had been discussing, but it chimed with Hawklan's mood, and he nodded in acknowledgement.

Why? he asked himself briefly. Why could not he and the Orthlundyn and the Fyordyn be left in peace? Why should Sumeral so seek to dominate them? What was to be gained by it? What creation could Sumeral offer that would match the harmonies of these lands and these peoples? And what others would He assail should these obstacles to His Will be swept aside?

Ethriss had given the joy of being. What would Sumeral give? Not being? A great barren stillness in which He alone *was*?

Hawklan did not pursue the questions. They had come

before and he had failed to find answers to them. Perhaps, he thought, such questions could not be answered, any more than could 'Why the mountains? Why the sea?' They *were*. Sumeral was. They should be accepted. That was sufficient answer for the needs of the times.

Hawklan smiled gently to himself. Whether a question could be answered or not was irrelevant. While there were minds to enquire, there would always be more questions and always further striving for answers; those same needs of the times would always set aside too idle a speculation.

It came to him suddenly that, whatever His motivation, Sumeral would not merely dominate the peoples He conquered, He would destroy them, and their lands, and everything else that the Guardians had created.

It was a chilling revelation, but Hawklan knew that it was true beyond all doubting. What he had learned from his studies at Anderras Darion had told him of a foe who had left a trail of every form of treachery, deceit and savagery; treaties broken, people enslaved, lands ravaged. Yet these were only the words of men; men long dead and beyond questioning; men who too could lie and deceive; men who could make honest mistakes as time stretched between the deeds and the writing of them. The inner knowledge that welded these words into the truth which now stood before him stark and clear, he had gained from the horror around Lord Evison's castle, from the downing of Isloman near the mines, from the countless tiny cries of all the living things around Vakloss that had reached out to him as he neared his goal, but, above all, from the naked fury of Oklar and the icy whispered touch of his Master.

Hawklan knew that he could not have such knowledge and turn away from it. He must become a greater healer yet, and a greater warrior, and each must accept the other without rancour or confusion.

A movement caught his eye.

'Who's that?' he said, pointing to a small group of riders far below.

Isloman peered forward intently. 'I've no idea,' he said. 'I think it's that group that Loman packed off into the mountains on an exercise when the rest of us were leaving the main camp.'

Hawklan recalled the incident. 'Tybek and Jenna were the two in charge,' he said.

'There's no point trailing back to the Castle and then trailing out again, is there?' Loman had replied to Tybek's injured

49

protest. 'We're far enough behind with our training as it is, thanks to our new friends. Take your winter gear. Cut a broad circuit round those peaks and come down onto the Riddin path. I'll send Jenna out in an hour or so with a hunting group. It'll be excellent practice for you both.'

Subsequently Loman had become concerned when snow-storms were seen on the distant peaks.

'Don't worry about them until they're overdue,' Gulda had said, less than sympathetically. 'They're as good as you could have made them. An experience like that will make or mar them.'

'And if they're marred?' Loman had queried angrily.

'Then they'd have been no good as Helyadin, would they?' Gulda replied sharply. 'Better fail now than when others' lives depend on them.'

Hawklan smiled as he remembered Loman's frustrated scowl.

'They've got someone with them.' Isloman broke into his reverie. 'And it looks as if there are two riding the one horse.' He screwed his eyes up. 'Yes, there are,' he added. 'And it's a fine horse too.'

Hawklan leaned forward on the parapet wall and watched the approaching group patiently. After a few minutes he began to make out the details that Isloman had described. That horse had to be a Muster horse, and that tiny passenger . . . ?

He was familiar . . .

He started, as a bedraggled Gavor bounced down onto the wall beside him, flapping excitedly and staggering a little.

'Come on, dear boy,' the raven said, jumping up and down and at the same time trying to preen himself. 'Shift yourself.'

Hawklan looked at him. 'Ah, good of you to join us again, Gavor,' he said. 'I presume all your friends were at home, by the look of you. Are you sure you can remember how to fly?'

'Very droll, dear boy,' Gavor replied, with great dignity, still struggling with his more recalcitrant feathers. 'Like you, I have a wide circle of affectionate friends and acquaintances who've been most anxious about me in my absence. It would have been churlish in the extreme not to accept their hospitality.'

'Yes, I didn't think you'd been refusing anything, judging from the way you landed,' Hawklan said, and both he and Isloman laughed.

Still dignified, Gavor walked to the edge of the wall and

peered over cautiously. 'Well, *I'm* going to join our friend Andawyr,' he said. 'Do feel free to join us if you can spare a moment from your gossiping.' And with an alarmed 'Whoops!' he launched himself unsteadily into the cold wind.

Andawyr watched as the black dot tumbled precipitately through the air then suddenly swooped up and round in a great majestic arc. As it neared, his face broke into a smile. 'Gavor?' he enquired of Tybek who was riding alongside him.

Tybek nodded, but before he could speak, Gavor had landed gently on Andawyr's outstretched hand. Agreth started at this unexpected arrival, and his horse reared a little, causing Andawyr to seize its mane hastily and Gavor to extend his wings to preserve his balance.

'Steady, horse,' Gavor said sternly.

Agreth's look of surprise turned to mild indignation at this usurpation of his authority.

Gavor turned and looked at him. 'So sorry, dear boy,' he said. 'Quite forgot who was in charge. Do carry on.'

Agreth had heard about Gavor from Sylvriss and the Fyordyn but, expecting an amusing pet, he was quite unprepared for the piercing black-eyed gaze and the forceful presence.

'Ah,' Gavor said, raising his wooden leg by way of a salute. 'I *thought* it was a Muster nag, quite handsome in a horsy kind of way.' Then, staring at Agreth, he asked abruptly, 'Is the Queen safe and well?'

'Yes,' Agreth replied hesitantly. 'She's with her father down at Dremark.'

'Good, good, good,' Gavor said rapidly. 'I was concerned about her when the weather changed. Fine woman.'

Andawyr's smile broadened. 'It's good to see you,' he said. 'Your friends here tell me Hawklan's returned safe and well, too. I was very alarmed for him when Agreth told me what had happened to you at Vakloss.'

Gavor affected casualness. 'Yes, nasty piece of work that Dan-Tor,' he said. 'Gave us a most unpleasant reception, but we got over it.' Then he extended his neck and peered at Andawyr. 'That said, *you* look as if you've been through the mill a little, dear boy,' he went on, his voice concerned. 'That ghastly little bird from the Gretmearc give you a bad time?'

'That and one or two other things,' Andawyr replied. 'But I got over it too. I'll tell you later. Tell me what happened to

51

waken Hawklan on your journey from Fyorlund.'

Gavor ruffled his feathers. 'Oh, it's far too much to talk about on horseback,' he said. 'And I've had a frightfully busy time since I got back. Such demands. I've not had a moment to myself. Let's get out of the cold and get some food inside us then we can have a good old natter.' He lowered his voice. 'That's always assuming the Fyordyn's haven't organised all the talking by now; you know the way they are.'

Andawyr laughed then, responding to a touch on his arm from Tybek, he looked up the road ahead. The tall black-clad figure of Hawklan was striding down to meet the group. He was accompanied by a powerfully built individual of similar height.

Gavor extended his wings and floated up into the air. Andawyr twisted round to Agreth. 'Set me down, please,' he said quickly.

Agreth dismounted and held out his arms to receive the Cadwanwr, who jumped down like an excited child and began walking briskly up the hill.

As he reached Hawklan, Andawyr seized his extended hand tightly in both of his own, his face a confusion of emotions and questions.

'You're really here this time,' he said. He patted Hawklan's arm as if he were testing a horse for purchase. 'Yes, you really are.' Then he stepped back and looked the bargain up and down. 'You've changed,' he said. 'You're different in some way.'

Hawklan nodded. 'A great many ways, I'm afraid,' he said. 'We all are. And you and I have got a great many things to talk about.' The two men stood for a moment just looking at one another, then Hawklan glanced at Isloman standing next to him, and at Tybek and the others waiting a discreet distance away.

'This is Isloman, Andawyr,' he said. 'He stood with me against Oklar and saved my life. Introduce us to your Muster escort, if you would.' Gavor dropped gently on to his shoulder.

Agreth watched as Andawyr led the two men towards him. From the descriptions Sylvriss had given him he recognised both immediately. These then were the two who had faced Oklar. Isloman was visibly powerful, but what was there in this other one that had had such an effect on Sylvriss and the Goraidin? No sooner had the thought occurred to him than he felt uneasy – afraid even – and his horse too inched back uncertainly, for although Hawklan was smiling and his manner offered nothing but welcome, there was a force in his presence that was almost tangible, Agreth had felt a similar power in Urthryn on occasions, but this was more powerful by far.

'This is Agreth,' Andawyr said. 'He's one of Ffyrst Urthryn's closest advisers. We met by chance in the mountains and he's made my journey over the mountains a great deal easier in every way.' He looked significant. 'He also has a great deal of news for us. Agreth, this is Hawklan, the man you've been seeking, and his friend Isloman.'

Agreth bowed and Hawklan held out his hand. 'Welcome to Anderras Darion,' he said. 'When you've rested and eaten we'll hear all your news and you ours, but if it's breaking no confidences we're both of us anxious to know . . .' He paused.

'Queen Sylvriss is well,' Agreth volunteered in anticipation of the question.

Hawklan smiled. 'Good,' he said. 'And the baby?'

Agreth shruggd. 'I'm more used to horses when it comes to pregnancy, but to the best of my knowledge, the foal – the baby,' he corrected hastily, 'is also well.'

'Good,' Hawklan said again. 'I'm greatly in debt to that young . . . person.'

Agreth looked puzzled by the remark, but Hawklan excused himself and turned his attention to Tybek and the others.

Both Tybek and Jenna watched Hawklan intently. In common with most Orthlundyn, they knew of him as the healer from Pedhavin, and of his mysterious arrival some twenty years earlier to occupy the long-sealed Anderras Darion. However, apart from a brief introduction amid the whirling noisy confusion of the Alphraan's sudden change of heart and the clamorous welcomes of Loman and the others, neither had really met the man that Loman referred to as their leader.

Both were sufficiently master of their new skills however, to realise that here they would judge and be judged.

'Any problems on the way back?' Hawklan asked simply, looking from one to the other. 'The cold get to any of you? Exhaustion, frostnip?'

'No,' Tybek replied, shaking his head. 'The sudden snowfall gave us a fright, but we had everything we needed. It was interesting – and very useful for the trainees. They did well. We kept the pursuit going until we ran into –' He nodded towards Andawyr and Agreth.

53

'I'm afraid we gave *them* a bit of a fright,' Jenna said softly, leaning forward a little. 'Waking them up in the middle of the night, swords drawn, but we just didn't know what to expect when we saw the tent. Who in the world travels the mountains at this time of year?' She lowered her voice further. 'We told them we were on an exercise, but we told them nothing about the Alphraan.' She went on: 'I think they took our caution in good part once we'd identified ourselves.'

Hawklan nodded and, looking back at Andawyr, smiled, 'I'm sure they did,' he said. 'I should imagine the Riddinwr's had greater frights than you in the past, and I *know* Andawyr has. Get yourselves fed and rested and we'll talk afterwards.'

As the party trooped up the last portion of the road to the Great Gate, Agreth watched Hawklan moving among the trainees who had been with the two Helyadin. He talked and listened and there was a great deal of laughter. In the few minutes it took them to reach the Gate, Agreth knew that Hawklan had won the loyalty of the entire group, himself included. It no longer surprised him that Sylvriss had been so affected by the man even though Hawklan had been unconscious.

Just before they came to the Gate, Gulda emerged, her long nose sniffing the cold air like a stalking hound. Immediately she went to Agreth's horse.

'Ah, a Muster horse,' she said, smiling and patting the animal affectionately, then, turning to Agreth: 'And a Muster rider too. You're welcome to Anderras Darion . . .' She paused and glanced at Hawklan for the arrival's name.

'Agreth,' Hawklan said. 'Adviser to Ffyrst Urthryn.'

Gulda nodded an acknowledgement. 'You're welcome to Anderras Darion, Agreth of the Decmilloith of Riddin, friend of Urthryn and son of the Riddinvolk,' she said. Agreth started slightly. Gulda's welcome was the formal Riddin greeting to a friendly stranger. It was a pleasant surprise; these Orthlundyn generally seemed to be so careless in their forms of address. How they knew who was who in their ordinary lives he couldn't imagine.

He smiled and bowed but before he could speak, Gulda had turned her attention to Andawyr.

She looked at the little man narrowly. 'A Cadwanwr, I see, from your garb and your manner,' she said. 'And from your appearance –' she flicked the end of her nose, apparently casually – 'you must be Andawyr, the saviour of our healer

54

here and self-styled Leader of the Cadwanol.'

Andawyr returned her gaze unflinchingly. 'My brothers call me their leader, Memsa Gulda,' he replied, equally casually squeezing his own nose. 'And I do my best to guide them when my advice is sought, but most of the time I follow, really.'

Gulda nodded slightly then walked over to him and looked at him even more intensely than before.

'How is your vision, Cadwanwr?' she said.

To Hawklan, it seemed that in some way, two great forces were confronting one another, although Andawyr looked relaxed and comfortable in the cold, grey, wintry light.

For an instant, however, the Cadwanwr's eyes flashed as if they had seen something strange and bewildering, and he frowned.

'Uncertain,' he replied after a moment.

Gulda nodded again. 'You too are welcome to Anderras Darion, Andawyr, Leader of the Cadwanol. Many threads are starting to pull together. Perhaps time and debate may show us a pattern, eh?' And with a grunt she turned and stumped back into the courtyard.

As the others made to follow her, a sleek brown form scuttled between the legs of the waiting group, and made straight for Andawyr. Reaching him, it began jumping up, chattering excitedly.

Andawyr bent down and it scrambled sinuously up into his arms.

'Where did you get to?' he asked it.

Gavor suddenly recognised it, and with a most unravenlike squawk, hopped nimbly up on to Hawklan's head.

'It's that rat thing of Dar-volci's,' he said, rather hoarsely. 'You remember – from the Gretmearc . . .' He bent forward. 'With the teeth,' he whispered urgently.

The animal, however, seemed to hear the remark and turned to eye Gavor purposefully. Andawyr smiled and laid an affectionate hand on its head.

'Hawklan, Gavor, this is –'

'Still carrying that crow-thing about, eh, Hawklan?' The animal said. Its deep voice was unmistakable.

'– Dar-volci,' Andawyr finished. 'An old and dear friend from the Caves. A *felci*, Gavor,' he added, giving the raven a knowing look.

Gavor cleared his throat. 'Ah,' he began uncertainly. 'A slip of the tongue, dear . . . boy. A slip of the tongue. You startled me. I can see now that you're not . . .' He cleared his throat again and changed tack. 'I've been looking forward to a chance to thank you for your good offices at the Gretmearc.'

'And I,' Hawklan added, sparing Gavor any further embarrassment.

Dar-volci seemed mollified. 'That was my pleasure entirely,' he said, wriggling round in Andawyr's arms and baring his enormous teeth in a terrifying smile that made Gavor tap his wooden leg nervously on Hawklan's head.

Then the felci was whispering frantically in Andawyr's ear and pointing towards the mountains.

Andawyr made a few brief interjections in an attempt to slow down the rate of this telling, but to no avail. Finally, Dar-volci nuzzled into Andawyr's bushy beard, sneezed, and then slithered from his arms to run off down the road at an enormous speed, leaving the Cadwanwr mouthing a vague, 'But –' while everyone else looked on in amazement.

A bubble of excited enquiry welled up out of the group, but Andawyr ignored it and turned to Hawklan.

'Dar-volci says that there are Alphraan in the mountains and that you've spoken to them and persuaded them to help us,' he said.

Hawklan nodded. 'Indeed,' he said. 'But circumstances and deeds persuaded them as much as anything that was said. Have they alarmed your friend?'

Andawyr shook his head. 'Quite the contrary,' he said. 'But he'll probably be gone for some time.' He turned to Gulda, who had returned to investigate the reason for the delay. 'Many threads . . . Memsa,' he said.

Hawklan's remark that there might be a great deal of talking later proved to be apt, as did Gavor's that the Fyordyn might have taken charge of it, though it had to be admitted that the buttressing presence of Gulda generally prevented their having to exercise their authority in the many discussions that took place during the following days as each of the new arrivals told or retold their tales and answered questions about them.

For all her stern presence however, Gulda seemed easier in her manner than she had at any time since her arrival at the Castle. Some days later, sitting with Hawklan and Andawyr in one of the halls, she said, 'Courage and good fortune have given us a little time in which to think and learn, and to be glad that all our friends are returned unhurt . . . if not unchanged, though one cannot but grieve for the Fyordyn in their pain.

We can be glad too that our enemy stands clearly exposed now for all to see. We must all rest and accept the healing benison of Ethriss's great castle. It will restore us now, and sustain us in the future.'

Hawklan was less sure. 'Oklar is safe and armed in Narsindalvak, Creost seemingly threatens Riddin,' he said. 'We can't afford the luxury of dawdling.'

Gulda laid a hand on his arm. 'Oklar is bound by his Master. The Fyordyn have been greatly hurt, but they'll set their house in order and won't let the Watch falter again. The Riddinvolk will watch the sea for the Morlider's islands. If I'm any judge, the Morlider will find swords, spears and arrows a-plenty waiting for them before they even touch the shore.'

Hawklan remembered the terrible power that had seethed around him as he stood small and impotent clinging to Ethriss's sword in the face of Oklar's fury.

'And Creost?' he said.

Gulda looked at Andawyr. 'The Riddinvolk have Oslang and the Cadwanol by their side,' she said. 'Much of Creost's strength will be spent in uniting the Morlider and in guiding their islands. Should he falter in the first, the Morlider will quarrel within a week and should he falter in the second, then the older, deeper writ of Enartion will run, and return the islands to their true courses.'

Andawyr nodded in agreement. 'Memsa is right, Hawklan,' he said. 'The enemy stands exposed and for various reasons is, like ourselves, far from full strength. The Fyordyn and the Riddinvolk will act as our eyes and limbs to watch and hold Him at bay if need arises. *We* here must be the head and heart. We must talk and think and plan. Learn and learn. Try to see to the heart of His intentions and reasons, to see the strategy that must lie behind all these happenings.'

Hawklan shook his head. 'That needs little learning,' he said. 'His intention is the destruction of us and all the works of the Guardians, and the reasons for that will be beyond us always. As to His strategy and tactics –' He smiled ironically. 'They'll shift and change as need arises, as will ours . . . though His will be hallmarked by their treachery, His indifference to the fate of His allies, and by His endless patience, while ours . . .'

He fell silent as his thoughts stumbled over his own words.

Endless patience.

He felt his eyes drawn upwards to the round window high

above, with its scene of a warrior parting from his wife and child. How old was that scene even when the artist caught it and trapped it there for future unknown generations?

Endless patience.

As he looked, he recalled vividly the memory of the sunny spring day when Tirilen's clattering footsteps had called him forth from his twenty years of peace. Part of him ached to return to that earlier time, but he set its longings aside gently. He was a warrior and a healer and he must carry his peace with him in his every action, or it was not a true peace. He had been brought into this world mysteriously and been given the stewardship of this great Castle presumably to face this foe, and whichever way he turned, he would be drawn back to that path inexorably.

Yatsu's words floated in the wake of this acceptance, uttered in the moonlit calm of Eldric's mountain stronghold. 'You carry more weight on the playing board than I do, you're nearer the player.'

Nearer the player?

Gulda touched his arm again to bring him back to the present. 'While ours?' she prompted.

Hawklan rested his head on his hand. His forehead furrowed. 'We must be *aware* of His treachery and cunning, but I think it would be a mistake to try and emulate it,' he said slowly, speaking the thoughts as they occurred to him. 'He is our master there, beyond a doubt, and to oppose Him thus would be to fight only with the weapons He offers us. I think that simplicity and directness will serve us better by far.'

Gulda and Andawyr exchanged glances.

'But surely we must ponder His deeds, try to fathom His intentions?' Andawyr queried.

Hawklan shook his head slightly. 'According to Arinndier, Eldric set up the cry "Death to Oklar" in the battle, and aimed his cavalry in close formation directly at him; directly at the source of Fyorlund's ills,' he said, his face grim. '*Nothing* was to stand in the way of this goal. And Oklar had to flee the field. Eldric's was the shrewd instinct of a true and hardened warrior. We should think about Sumeral's scheming, and make due allowance as appropriate. But not to the extent of faltering in our own straight sword thrust to His heart. Our single simple killing stroke which must be delivered regardless of all else.'

There was a coldness in his voice that seemed to chill the

hall. He looked again at the window picture above him. A man torn away from the simple pleasure of his daily life, from the warmth and closeness of his wife and the innocent but absolute trust of his child, to face who knew what horror that was none of his making. And his final parting was both marred and made strangely whole by his child's honest but fearful response to his grim armour. Whether such ties of affection would prove a strength to sustain and bolster him in battle, or a weakness to drag him to hesitant defeat, would be his own choice.

'When we look at His strengths,' he went on, still pensive, 'we must see in what way they are also His weaknesses.'

Andawyr looked puzzled. 'How can a strength be a weakness, Hawklan? He has no weaknesses such as you and I might perceive. He's profoundly armoured in every way.'

Hawklan nodded. 'Yes, but every strength shows where a weakness lies,' he said. Then his thoughts became clearer. 'Why does He come to destroy us as a man? As a man leading great armies of men? Why doesn't He come as earth, sea, air, which seemingly His power could shape to smash us all; or as some other terrible life-blessed creature of His own making such as still lingered in the Alphraan's heartplace? Why does He come in human form?' He leaned forward, his brow furrowed.

'That's all it is,' Andawyr said dismissively. 'A mere form. A shell to house His true Self –'

Gulda laid a hand on his arm to stop him.

'No,' Hawklan said firmly. 'He comes thus for a reason. If it were just a shell, He'd find a better one. Perhaps it's in the nature of the Old Power itself that only like can truly destroy like.' He paused thoughtfully, then shrugged. 'However, whatever the reason, He's chosen it and He must accept with it the flaws of that form: vanity, anger, jealousy, physical vulnerability.'

Andawyr shook his head. 'Everything that's known about Him says otherwise, Hawklan,' he said, almost impatiently. 'He shows only a cold, unending patience, and an indifference to everyone and everything around Him that goes beyond words such as ruthlessness.'

'Human traits, Andawyr,' Hawklan said quietly. 'There's an Uhriel in each of us.'

Andawyr's eyes widened as if he had been struck at this echo of the words he himself had only recently recalled.

'And where does your knowledge of Sumeral come from to

deny His humanity, Andawyr?' Hawklan went on forcefully.

'From . . . from the recorded words . . . of those who knew
Him . . .' Andawyr stammered at this unexpected assault. 'I
don't deny His humanity . . . I . . .' He paused, shaking his
head. 'I never thought about it, I suppose. Ethriss took our
form – or gave us his. It never occurred to me . . .' His voice
trailed off.

Hawklan ignored the little man's confusion. 'And what of
the knowledge of the hidden time? The time before He was
known. The time when He walked among men *as a man*, just
as Dan-Tor did in Fyorlund these past years. When even
Ethriss didn't know of Him.'

'Little or nothing is known of those times, Hawklan,'
Andawyr said, recovering some of his composure. 'Except
legend and story. We separate the two clearly in our
scholarship.'

Hawklan nodded. 'The legends and stories of Sumeral the
wicked adviser to Kings and Princes. The wizard granting
boons to men in return for terrible payments.' He raised a
conclusive finger. 'In His humanity is His greatest weakness,'
he said. 'As a human, He faltered and He fell to human
missiles as He assaulted the Iron Ring. He wouldn't come
again in such a vulnerable form if He were not constrained to it
by some need beyond our sight, or because of some overween-
ing trait of vanity or arrogance.'

Gulda raised an eyebrow. Hawklan caught the movement
and its implication.

'If it was through vanity or arrogance that He made the
choice, then it's a trait that lies in His *true* self, not in the form
he chose,' he said carefully. Abruptly he smiled. 'Perhaps the
traits we call human are Ethriss's own; inherent in the nature
of things.'

'Perhaps Sumeral is the essence of Ethriss's weakness and
frailty splintered from him in the Great Searing,' Gulda said
darkly.

Hawklan looked at her enigmatically, then his smile
broadened out into a bright laugh which warmed his listeners
as previously his manner had chilled them. 'I think we're
getting well beyond ourselves,' he said. 'It just shows how we
need the Fyordyn to keep our debates from rambling.'

Gulda smiled, but Andawyr still seemed discomposed.

'There's no harm in rambling,' he said, a little tetchily.
'Providing you know you're doing it. Many things are to be

found by walking a different way down a familiar path. But let's see if you were looking where you were walking, Hawklan. Where has your rambling led you?'

The brief irritation had been replaced by a stern seriousness which dampened Hawklan's levity. He looked intently at the bright-eyed little man who had faced his greatest trial at the Gretmearc while he, the warrior, the healer, whose life Andawyr had just saved, had stood by helpless.

He leaned back in his chair and was silent for a while.

'Whatever Sumeral truly is, Andawyr, *we* face a man,' he said eventually, his voice thoughtful. 'You and your brothers with those special skills that the chances of history have granted to you. We with our swords and spears. All of us with whatever wit and courage we can find. But still He is, or chooses to be, a man, not a god, and He can and will be defeated as such.'

'That's rhetoric,' Andawyr replied. 'I'll grant that it's important for firing the will of the people, but what does it give us in the way of specific tactics?'

Hawklan was at a loss. 'He can do nothing that we cannot do,' he said uncertainly. 'His power against us is levied through humans: his Uhriel, the Mathidrin, the Morlider and doubtless many others. All weak and fallible as we are.'

'Be specific,' Andawyr pressed.

'I can't,' Hawklan admitted. 'But the simple realisation of Sumeral's humanity is important. I feel it.'

Andawyr nodded reflectively. 'You may be right,' he said, abruptly ending his interrogation.

'He is,' Gulda said firmly. 'Sleep on it, both of you.' Then she stood up. 'You must excuse me,' she said. 'I've things to attend to.' And with a brief nod, she was gone.

Hawklan watched her black, stooped form departing. For an instant he seemed to feel an overwhelming sense of her great pain and loneliness.

'Who is she, Andawyr?' he said after the door had closed softly.

Andawyr turned away from his gaze. 'I don't know,' he said simply. 'I feel many things when I'm with her – pain, fear, excitement . . .' He shook his head. 'Many things. But she's more hidden from me than even you are.'

# Chapter 5

Over the next few weeks, Hawklan felt the whole Castle responding to the arrival of Andawyr and the others. And indeed, it seemed to him that every step *he* took through its countless corridors and hallways rang out like a small peal of welcome. He remarked on it to Loman. The smith smiled.

'It's been like that ever since you left and we started studying and training in earnest,' he said. 'New people coming and going all the time. Debating, thinking, planning. The Castle seems to thrive on it in some way. As if it were waking after a long sleep. You can feel it all around like the opening of thousands of flowers.'

Hawklan gave his castellan a look of great gravity at this poetic image, but Loman ignored the gentle taunt and ploughed on.

'I find new things every day, in the carvings, the pictures, everywhere, even whole new rooms. Things that perhaps I've been looking at but not seeing for years.' He paused. 'In truth I don't know whether it's the Castle or me, but it's wonderful.'

Hawklan agreed. 'It's probably both,' he said, smiling.

Isloman too noted a difference, and not just in the Castle. 'Have you seen some of the carvings that are being done?' he asked, eyes wide in appreciation. 'And with everyone having less time for it as well. I'll have to look to my chisels if I'm not to be replaced as First Carver.'

'You don't seem too concerned,' Hawklan said.

Isloman gave him a large wink. 'It won't happen,' he said, banging his fist on his chest and laughing. 'I've learned a trick or two from those wood carvers up north.'

Yes, Hawklan thought. And you faced and survived Oklar's storm fully conscious. That will add qualities to your work beyond measure.

He himself, however, felt oddly unsettled. This was his home; and yet not so. These were his people; this his time; and yet not so. A restlessness niggled deep inside him like a burrowing worm.

He succeeded for the most part in disguising this unease, but Gulda saw through him and brought him down with brutal ease.

'Sit!' she said, entering his room unannounced and finding him peering out through the window, frowning.

Hawklan's legs responded before his mind caught up with them.

Gulda swung a chair round and sat down facing him, hands folded over the top of her stick and her chin resting on them as usual.

'Where's your pain?' she said.

Hawklan looked bewildered. 'I don't understand,' he replied.

Gulda glanced towards the window. 'What were you frowning for then?'

Hawklan shrugged uncertainly. 'Nothing in particular.'

Gulda's eyes widened. 'You're unhurt, you're in this most wonderful of places, and surrounded by splendid friends, yet you frown at nothing in particular,' she said. 'Heal yourself, healer.'

It occurred to Hawklan for a moment to protest, but the thought wilted under Gulda's penetrating gaze.

'How?' he asked simply.

'Face again what you've faced in your journeyings,' Gulda replied. 'Face again what you must face in the future.'

Hawklan frowned again. 'I've no problems with what happened on my journeyings, as you call them. Unpleasant though some of it was. But how can I face what I was before or what I'll become? The one I'm striving to remember, the other I'm striving to see.'

Gulda fixed him with a steely gaze. 'Leave them,' she said with stark finality. 'Your past will return to you when you need it, and none can see the future – not even Sumeral. Have you forgotten the butterfly's wings so soon? Your future will happen regardless, and your frowns now will merely become unhappy memories where there should have been happy ones.'

There was a humour in her voice but Hawklan felt the cold inexorability of her words exposing the folly of his fruitless concerns. It happened with such suddenness that for a moment he felt almost winded.

'You're right,' he said, with a brief grimace of self-reproach. 'I'm sorry. They sneaked up on me.'

Gulda laughed. It was like sunshine melting the frost. 'They do,' she said. 'And they will again. But be more careful in future. Neither the warrior nor the healer can risk being ambushed like that too often.'

Hawklan nodded, then stood up and walked back to the window. Gulda joined him.

Below them was a cascade of windowed walls and a patchwork of rooftops, glistening silver-grey in the drizzling rain. Beyond was the curving sweep of the wall of the Castle, and beyond that was a vague, rain-shrouded impression of the rolling Orthlund countryside. A few hunched figures walked to and fro along the wall. Hawklan smiled; for all its damp bleakness, the scene had a peace of its own which had eluded him but minutes earlier. No, he corrected himself gently. The peace had not eluded him, he had simply allowed his darker nature to turn his heart away from it.

Graudally the days shortened, and Anderras Darion began to sparkle with its winter lights, shining out through the dark nights as brightly as it gleamed in bright summer days.

And within it was the constant shimmer of activity as its occupants worked and talked and planned for the day when Sumeral's cold hand must inevitably draw them forth.

Yet for all the grim prospect that lay ahead, the Castle's inner light forbade entry to its dark shadow; as also did Hawklan, now keenly alert for signs of the clinging ties of fear and doubt that might appear like silent cobwebs to mar that very future by shrouding the present.

Many other threads of endeavour were woven through the weeks. A messenger was sent to Fyorlund with the news of the safe arrival of Arinndier and the arrival and recovery of Hawklan. A messenger too was sent to Riddin, but he was obliged to return as the snows took possession of the higher peaks and valleys.

Andawyr and Gulda wandered the Castle together, pored over tomes in the library together, and talked and talked.

The Fyordyn joined with Loman and the other Morlider veterans in the training of the Orthlundyn army, Dacu and Tel Mindor taking a considerable interest in the Helyadin. All however, sat at the feet of Agreth to learn about cavalry warfare.

Jaldaric and Tirke were offered the opportunity to train with Athyr in the Helyadin.

Rede Berryn eventually took his stiff leg to Hawklan.

Dacu and Tel Mindor were impressed by the Helyadin. 'I'd never have thought it possible to achieve so much in so short a time,' Dacu said. 'You're to be commended, Loman. Your people are remarkable and you yourself must have learned a great deal during your service under Commander Dirfrin.'

Loman grimaced. 'Not from choice,' he said. 'It was learn or die. One doesn't forget such teaching. And Gulda knows a great deal, though how she came by such knowledge I'm not even going to think about asking.'

The two Goraidin agreed with that sentiment and concentrated on adding their own expertise to that which Loman and Gulda had already taught. They had already bruised themselves badly against Gulda by casually protesting about the physical dangers to the women in training alongside the men, especially in the severe training required of the Helyadin. Hearing their unexpected complaint and being in no position to advise against its utterance, Hawklan and Loman had both developed a sudden deep interest in nearby carvings as Gulda had stopped writing, paused, and then slowly looked up from her desk.

'The Muster women seem to manage,' she began. 'As did those who fought by Ethriss's side.'

Although her voice was soft, it was withering in its disdain, and her blue eyes defied description. When she had finished, Dacu and Tel Mindor retreated from the field in disarray to the barely disguised amusement of Hawklan and Loman. Dacu was heard to mutter, 'Poor Sumeral.'

Apart from minor frictions however, the Fyordyn and the Orthlundyn worked well together and to their considerable mutual benefit. The Goraidin in particular responded to the intuitive flair of the Orthlundyn while they in their turn came to appreciate the Fyordyn's painstaking thoroughness.

Both Tirke and Jaldaric welcomed the opportunity to join the Helyadin under Athyr's command. Tirke accepted with enthusiasm, having been much impressed by Dacu on their journey through the mountains and presuming that he in turn could impress Athyr with some of his new-found knowledge. Jaldaric, however, accepted grimly, carrying within him desperate memories of his capture first by Hawklan and then by Aelang, but worst of all, the memory of the impotent witness he had borne to the massacre at Ledvrin.

These initial intentions however, began to change rapidly as the two young men faced the Helyadin's simple but effective aptitude test. It involved a leap from the edge of a sheer rock face onto a nearby flat-topped spur. The gap was not too wide, but the top of the spur was small, and the drop beneath breathtaking. Roped for safety, but nevertheless terrified, both managed to pass the test, and both grew a little in wisdom.

Rede Berryn, a robust bachelor, was slightly embarrassed by the presence of Tirilen, but he watched intently as Hawklan carefully examined his knee. It was stiff as a result of a riding accident many years previously and various healers had shaken their heads over it from time to time. He could not avoid a small sense of disappointment however when Hawklan too shook his.

'Never mind,' he said philosophically. 'I'm glad you've had a look at it. If you can't do anything for it, then I doubt anyone can.'

But Hawklan had not finished. 'I can't loosen the joint for you, Rede,' he said. 'Like you, that's well set by now. But Tirilen will show you how to massage it and how to exercise these muscles here' – he prodded dispassionately – 'and here, so that they'll carry more of your weight. It'll be a little uncomfortable at first, but it should ease the pain considerably.'

'Oh, that won't be necessary –' began the Rede with spurious heartiness, but a gentle hand on the chest prevented his attempt at a hasty departure.

Tirilen smiled at the old man's discomfiture. 'Come now, Rede,' she said, rolling up her sleeves. 'I've seen uglier things than *your* leg.'

Berryn cleared his throat and coloured a little. As Tirilen approached he caught Hawklan's sleeve and pulled him forward. 'Perhaps . . you . . . . or maybe . . . the Memsa . . .' he whispered tentatively.

Hawklan sucked in his breath and shook his head, frowning 'Different school of medicine, Gulda,' he whispered back earnestly. 'Different entirely. Takes no prisoners and dispatches her wounded,' And with a broad wink he was gone.

'Come in,' Andawyr said.

The door to his room opened slowly and Hawklan peered in.

'I'm here,' Andawyr said, striking a small torch into life. 'I was just relaxing.'

The torch gently illuminated the chaos of books and scrolls

66

that filled the small room Andawyr had chosen for his study, but he himself was not to be seen. Hawklan gazed around uncertainly for a moment until, abruptly, a bushy-haired head appeared above a stack of books. A beckoning hand followed it.

'I'm sorry, I didn't mean to disturb you, Andawyr,' Hawklan said, entering and treading warily around the books and scrolls that littered the floor.

Andawyr shook his head decidedly and beckoned again. Hawklan advanced further, eventually finding the Cadwanwr sitting cosily in the lee of a broken cliff-face of books and other documents illuminated warmly by the small torch and a fire of radiant stones.

Andawyr motioned him to sit down, and with great care lifted a mound of papers from one chair to another. As he released them, they slithered gracefully to the floor.

With a small click of irritation, he bent down and gathered them together loosely then, after looking vainly for a blank space on a nearby table, he dropped them unceremoniously on top of another pile of papers. Hawklan watched the small drama with great interest, and could not forbear smiling.

'You're a profoundly untidy man, Andawyr, Leader of the Cadwanol,' he said.

Andawyr shrugged a small concession. 'But not here,' he pleaded, tapping his head.

Hawklan eyed the shadowy crags and peaks of the impromptu mountain range of documents that Andawyr had built, and looked conspicuously doubtful.

His doubts however, rolled serenely off Andawyr's beaming face. 'You're a fine and generous host, Hawklan,' the little man said. 'And you keep a fine inn here, with rare bedside reading.'

Hawklan nodded graciously. 'Didn't there used to be windows in here once?' he asked.

Andawyr looked vaguely over his shoulder. 'I'll put all these back when I've finished,' he said earnestly, like an ingenuous child.

Hawklan waved a dismissive hand. 'I know,' he said reassuringly. '*Gulda* looks after the library.'

Andawyr surrendered to this threat of vastly superior force with a chuckle, then he settled back in his chair.

'What did you want to talk about?' he asked.

Hawklan shook his head. 'Nothing special,' he replied. 'I

thought I'd let you know that a messenger just arrived from Fyorlund to say that Arinndier has been empowered unconditionally by the Geadrol to speak for them in whatever military arrangements we're making.'

Andawyr looked surprised. 'Remarkable,' he said. 'I presume that this is the Lord Eldric stamping his will on the Geadrol, Ffyrst or no.'

'Stamping reality on them more likely,' Hawklan replied. 'He and Darek and Hreldar.'

'Does the message say anything about Oklar, or about what they're going to do with their errant Lords?' Andawyr went on.

'The High Guards are patrolling the northern borders, but the Mathidrin have entrenched themselves along the approaches to Narsindalvak, so presumably Oklar is free to come and go about Narsindal as he wishes.' Hawklan looked regretful and there was a slight note of irritation in his voice.

'We're lucky he's not coming and going about Fyorlund, Hawklan, and don't you forget it,' Andawyr replied with some reproach, then, more anxiously: 'And the Lords and everyone else who supported Dan-Tor?'

Hawklan smiled appreciatively. 'I always knew Eldric was a considerable leader,' he said. 'But he's proving to be quite a healer as well. As far as I can gather, there's a great deal of accounting and breast beating going on, as you might expect. Individuals who were involved in acts of violence, other than in the battle itself, are being tried openly before the courts. But those who helped Dan-Tor in other ways are being given the choice of join us or join him – no punishment either way.'

Andawyr looked relieved.

'I agree,' said Hawklan speaking to the Cadwanwr's unspoken approval. 'Any acts of vengeance would have been very detrimental, however they were disguised in law. We need a united Fyorlund, not one riven with embittered factions, all piling up scores to settle.' His voice was hard.

Andawyr threw him a mocking salute. 'Shrewdly said, Commander,' he said.

Hawklan could do no other than laugh self-deprecatingly at the gesture. He leaned back in his chair.

'Tell me about Dar-volci,' he said unexpectedly.

Andawyr looked at him steadily for a moment, then said, 'Dar's an old friend and a typical felci pack leader,' he said. 'What do you want to know?'

Hawklan gestured vaguely. 'Nothing special,' he said. 'I'm just idly curious. I've never seen anything like him before, that's all. Why was he so excited by the Alphraan?'

Andawyr shrugged. 'Dar's Dar,' he said, with a gesture which indicated that that was a complete explanation. 'He comes and goes as he pleases – as I said, a typical felci pack leader.'

Hawklan shifted a little uneasily. 'There's something odd about him,' he said.

'Odd?' Andawyr said, watching Hawklan's face intently.

'I don't know,' Hawklan said uncertainly. 'Nothing specific; just . . . unusual, strange.'

'They're unusual creatures for sure. They burrow through rock,' volunteered Andawyr. 'Hence the teeth. And they've got claws to match. And minds both as sharp and as strong as their teeth and claws, as I've no doubt you'll find out when he condescends to come back.'

Hawklan shook his head. 'I'm sorry to be vague,' he said. 'It's not important. It's just that there seems to be something *profoundly* different about him . . . something very deep. Alien almost.'

Andawyr smiled gently. 'According to their own legends – which are very colourful, I might add – they were here before our time; even before Ethriss's time.' Then, intoning deeply in imitation of Dar-volci: 'Creatures of the deep rock, brought unwilling to this new world when the deeplands were desecrated by the plundering mines of Sumeral . . .' His mimicry broke down into a happy laugh.

Hawklan's unease faded in this sudden sunshine and he smiled in response to the little man's merriment. 'I gather *you* don't feel anything strange about them?' he said.

Andawyr's laugh carried over. 'I feel great affection for them,' he said, reaching up to wipe his eye. 'But you didn't come here to talk about Dar-volci, did you?'

Hawklan shifted in his chair awkwardly again. 'No,' he said after a pause. 'I suppose not.'

Andawyr opened his hands as a signal for him to continue.

Hawklan hesitated, uncertain again. 'We've all been working, studying, re-organising. You've spent a great deal of time with Gulda and . . .' He gestured around at the stacks of documents. 'I feel we're nearing the time when we have to decide what we must do next. I thought we ought to start talking about it.'

Andawyr bowed his head slightly in acknowledgement and then turned to stare pensively into the fire.

'Gulda tells me you remember things,' he said abruptly.

Hawklan started a little. 'She'll have told you what things, then, I presume,' he replied, though not unkindly.

Andawyr nodded. 'Yes,' he said. ' More awareness of your skills. Hazy memories of your life' – he looked up at Hawklan – 'but no details of who, what, when; no faces, no names . . . nothing to tell you who you were, or are.' He leaned forward. 'Would you like me to search your mind as I did at the Gretmearc? We're both wiser than we were.'

Hawklan looked at him narrowly. 'You still think I'm Ethriss, don't you?' he said.

Andawyr pulled a wry face. 'I don't know,' he said hesitantly. 'You've been given his Castle and his sword. And you wielded the sword to some effect against Oklar.' Hawklan shook his head in denial, but Andawyr went on. 'It occurs to me that perhaps you wielded the sword too well. That in protecting yourself and your friends you did not receive the power that would almost certainly have awakened your true self . . .'

Hawklan's face was suddenly angry. 'It was a happy chance then,' he said. 'I might be incomplete, but *this* is my true self.' He struck his chest forcefully. 'If this . . . great Guardian requires the sacrifice of a city for his rebirth, then better he stays asleep.'

Andawyr flinched away from Hawklan's powerful denunciation but only briefly. 'That confrontation was of *your* choosing,' he said, struggling with his own anger, which had risen in response to Hawklan's. 'And don't forget that the sword which you feel you used so inadequately may have *halved* the destruction of Vakloss, and that Sumeral Himself reached out from His fastness and bound His own servant rather than see you assailed further.'

'Damn you,' Hawklan said softly, his green eyes black and ominous in the red glow of the fire.

Andawyr met his grim gaze squarely. 'Ethriss was cruel only in the clarity of his vision of the truth,' he continued. 'He bound nothing lightly; either by chains or deceitful words. He let things be free. He gave us the freedom that he himself cherished, to do with as we will. *Sumeral* is the one who binds; the manipulator, the deceiver, the twister of minds and realities.' His finger jabbed out. 'You yourself uttered what

70

were virtually Ethriss's own words when you said that to fight Sumeral with treachery and cunning would be to choose to fight Him only with the weapons He offers us; when you said that we should fight him with our greatest strengths: with simplicity and directness.'

He stopped speaking and slowly sat back in his chair.

Hawklan looked away from him and rested his head on his hand.

'I'll oppose Sumeral to the end, Andawyr,' he said after a long silence. 'I see no alternative. But understand, I faced Oklar's power and felt no vestige of godhood in me. You must look elsewhere. Whatever I was, I was not Ethriss. I was as I am; mortal and frail. *That* I know.'

Silence seeped down from the waiting books to surround the two men like a mountain mist.

'And ponder this,' Hawklan said quietly. 'Why did Sumeral reach out to save me? Is it not possible that He, the deceiver, the manipulator, might seem to protect me, perhaps even conspicuously bind one of His Uhriel, with the intention of leading astray those who were searching for His most feared enemy?'

Andawyr stared at him, unmoving.

'Damn you,' he said viciously.

Hawklan lowered his eyes and, after a moment, gave a single ironic grunt. 'Now I've given us no choice,' he said. 'With my own inept manipulating. Now we'll *have* to find out who I am if Ethriss is ever to be found.'

Andawyr pursed his lips and nodded.

'Sit back and relax,' he said, standing up. 'Just remember that whatever you see and hear, you'll be here all the time. You'll hear me; feel my presence. Nothing can harm you except yourself.'

Hawklan closed his eyes. Andawyr reached out and placed the palms of his hands on Hawklan's temples.

Hawklan felt their gentle warmth, and then, as he had at the Gretmearc, he found himself floating free in a strange world of shimmering, fragmented sounds and images.

'Open your eyes,' came Andawyr's voice.

Hawklan did as he was bidden, but no barren empty plane appeared this time. Instead, he was still floating, drifting amidst elusive, disjointed images, and vaguely significant whisperings.

A woman on his arm, laughing . . . ?

71

An aching memory of a swirl of auburn hair and the soft irresistible curve of a cheekbone. Hawklan reached out to touch it again . . .

Warm and comforting sunlight, and the scent of fresh grass and yellow flowers . . .

Children, running, playing, more laughter . . .

Fond, stern voices commanding and teaching . . .

Music and beauty in a shining singing castle . . .

Darkness at the edges . . . nearing.

Darkness on the horizon. Smoke . . . Burning . . .

Fear . . .

Then *he* was there. Simple, but radiant and powerful. Yet pained and guilt-ridden. His presence standing against the darkness. But he could not stand alone . . .

Choices . . .

'Men must fight men.' A chilling knell . . .

The fearful stirring clarion call of battle trumpets . . .

Turmoil . . . Flickering flames and choking smoke . . . Destruction, terror . . .

'You're here, Hawklan,' came Andawyr's voice gently. 'Still safe, in Anderras Darion.'

Hatred . . .

But still hope shone, like a silver twisting thread glittering through the gloom . . .

'Stand your ground,' was the command and the intention.

Then, like black vomit, memories that could not be faced. Failure. Defeat. Broken ranks. Rout. The finest destroyed under the endless waves of . . .

'You're here, Hawklan,' Andawyr's presence was beginning to waver.

And then there came the memory that Hawklan knew too well. His body and heart wracked beyond all pain and weariness. Endless, endless hacking and killing, and all to no avail; a mere sideshow as His army swept past unhindered. On and on they came . . . unending . . . chanting, screaming . . . eyes and swords glinting red in the blazing fires . . . the sky black with acrid smoke and the great birds, also fighting their last . . .

And the ground under his feet, uneven, treacherous – a ghastly mound of the broken bodies of his men.

And this was his doing! This was the fruit of his arrogance and folly.

A distant cry of horror and guilt began to form inside him.

'Hawklan, you are here,' said Andawyr's voice, anxious and more distant. 'You are safe. Nothing can harm you.'

But the cry grew, long and agonised.

He felt his last friend die at his back, gasping out, 'I'm sorry,' even as he fell.

Hawklan's terrible cry grew until it seemed to fill the sky, mingling and overtopping the final triumphant roar of his enemy, as blades and malevolence closed around him . . .

'Hawklan!' Andawyr's voice was faint and desperate. 'Hawklan. You are here –'

But Hawklan could not hear it. He was plunging headlong into the dreadful, bloody darkness.

Then, abruptly, a hand was laid on his shoulder.

Eyes wide in horror, mouth gaping, he lurched foward, but the hand sustained him, and others reached out to support him.

He sank into their strength.

Slowly, the darkness of the battlefield faded to become the gentle light of the small torch and the radiant stones that lit Andawyr's room, and his scream dwindled to become his own gasping breath.

Andawyr's arms were wrapped about him as if he were a hurt child, and the little man's face was both pale and covered with perspiration. It was suffused with a mixture of concern and distress.

A hand still rested on his shoulder, still sustaining him until he was truly back in Anderras Darion.

He turned his head and looked up. The hand was Gulda's. She seemed to tower over him though her face was full of compassion, and tears shone in her eyes. Gavor sat on her shoulder, head bent forward, eyes intense.

'You are with us,' Gulda said, part statement, part question.

Hawklan nodded and Gulda slowly released his shoulder.

Andawyr too gradually let him go, helping him back into his chair. Then he sat down heavily on his own and, producing a large kerchief, began to mop his face in undisguised relief.

'Thank you, Memsa,' he said. 'I didn't expect such . . . power.' He looked uncertain.

Gavor hopped onto Hawklan's shoulder and closed his one claw about it reassuringly, though he did not speak. Hawklan reached up and touched his beak.

Gulda liberated a chair from its burden of documents, and sat down between the two men. 'You'd have got him back,' she replied to Andawyr simply. 'I shouldn't have interfered, but . . . I couldn't bear his pain, I had to . . .' Uncharacteristically, she left the sentence unfinished.

Andawyr looked at her and then laid his hand on hers. 'Thank you,' he said again.

Hawklan watched vacantly, as the memory of the turmoil that had so nearly overwhelmed him washed to and fro like an frustrated ebb tide.

'What . . . ?' he began, but Gulda held out her hand gently to quieten him.

'Rest a little while longer,' she said. 'We can talk in a moment, when the Castle's seeped back into your bones completely.' She smiled.

You were very beautiful once, Hawklan thought, though even as the thought formed itself, it became you *are* beautiful, and his head began to swim as his eyes tried to focus on the confusion of images that was Gulda's face.

She reached out and put her hand on his forehead. Its coolness cleared his vision. 'I'm sorry,' she said. 'Rest.'

The four sat in silence for some time and gradually the intensity of the eerie happening began to dwindle. As a sense of normality returned, Hawklan's breathing quietened and Andawyr finished wiping his face, though even in the red glow of the fire he was still pale.

'Not as . . . easy . . . as last time,' Hawklan said eventually, his voice unsteady and hoarse.

Andawyr shook his head. 'All things happen in their time, Hawklan,' he said. 'I hadn't the knowledge to take you further then though I didn't realise it.' He smiled a little, reflectively. 'I thought at the time that your early life had been sealed away by some other hand. Now, I think perhaps it might have been a deeper, wiser part of either you or I who created that strange barrier we found, for our own protection.' His smile became a chuckle. 'It's very difficult to be simple and straightforward when we have such a capacity for deceiving ourselves.'

Hawklan tried to smile, but his face did not respond. 'And what else have you learned?' he said. 'Those memories were mine, I know, but I'm no wiser.' He spread his arms out, hands palm upwards in a gesture of helplessnes. 'And where was Ethriss in all that whirling confusion except as someone other than myself? He it was I followed and failed.'

Andawyr and Gulda exchanged glances.

'And how are you here?' Hawklan asked, turning to Gulda.

74

She looked at him. 'I was drawn by your joy and happiness and then by your pain,' she said, then, lowering her eyes. 'I'm not sure I should have interfered. Perhaps what we need to know lies in the darkness that came after you fell on that field.'

Hawklan's eyes opened wide in horror and he wrapped his arms about himself. 'After my . . . death?' he said very softly. 'No, I'll not go back again.'

Gulda nodded. 'Neither of us would take you,' she said.

'You did not die,' Andawyr said.

Gulda looked at him sharply.

Andawyr shook his head. 'There's an inexorability about death that would have drawn us in like a great maelstrom. *No* power could have pulled us from it. Even Hawklan's own memory of his . . . end . . . was nearly irresistible. It was folly on my part to venture so close. I should have known from what you told me that that memory dominated all others.'

Gavor flapped his wings restlessly, throwing great shadows over the walls and ceiling and the waiting mountain range of books.

Andawyr looked at Hawklan, his expression enigmatic.

When he spoke, his voice was flat and toneless. 'You are not Ethriss, Hawklan,' he said. 'And I fear our position is more grave than I had thought.'

Hawklan felt suddenly like a small guilt-ridden child. 'Who am I then?' he asked.

Andawyr turned to Gulda. 'Tell him about the Orthlundyn, Memsa,' he said.

# *Chapter 6*

Gulda looked uncertainly at Andawyr.

The little man nodded and gestured her to begin.

A brief look of pain passed over Gulda's face and, fiddling nervously with her stick, she glanced awkwardly about the room as if looking for something that might tell her where to start her tale.

'The war of the First Coming was unbelievably long, Hawklan,' she began at last. 'And it was fought on many levels and between many different peoples in many different ways. Some, mostly the battles of men, we know a great deal about. Some, involving other than men, like the Alphraan and the Mandrassni, we know a little of. Others, like the terrible cloud wars of the Drienvolk, the vengeance of the great ocean mammals, we know mainly by repute – by legend. Ethriss rarely spoke of them. "All must be won," he would say. "But men must fight men, and Sumeral has come as a man among men, thus man's burden will be the greatest, for they must fight Him in His mortal frame."'

'I know this,' Hawklan said impatiently. 'You may recall that I spent long enough in the library here before I left and' – he raised his hand to his temple uncertainly – 'I knew anyway.' He grimaced. 'Old and new memories,' he said. 'I can't separate them any more.'

'It's of no consequence,' Andawyr said. 'Knowledge is knowledge.' He motioned Gulda to continue.

'I mention those other aspects of the war to remind you that while man did indeed carry the greatest burden, it was but a portion of the whole, and not one hundredth part of it rested on the shoulders of one single man. Each . . . leader, commander . . . carried what he could to the best of his ability. Few failed Ethriss and he did not reproach those who did.'

Gulda looked at Hawklan anxiously.

'Andawyr and I have talked about you a great deal over these past weeks,' she said. 'And I tell you what we believe now, not simply to assuage your curiosity, but because you must know the truth to be free of the burden of guilt which you seem to be carrying.'

'And while I am so burdened, my judgement is marred and my value lessened,' Hawklan said coldly.

Gulda nodded. 'Yes,' she said. 'That's true as you above all know. But we also care for you.'

Hawklan bowed his head, momentarily ashamed of his harshness. 'I feel no guilt,' he said, uncertainly. 'Not when I remember the . . . end.' He hesitated. 'Only when . . . I'm there. I . . .'

'Just listen,' Andawyr said powerfully, making Hawklan start slightly.

Gulda went on. 'None the less, you *are* burdened by it and it does cloud your sight. For that, and many other reasons, you should know the truth.'

'Or at least what you and Andawyr consider to be the truth,' Hawklan said.

Gulda nodded and paused again as if to collect her thoughts.

'Among men,' she said after a moment. 'The Orthlundyn were Ethriss's greatest allies. Always they had stood against Sumeral, mistrusting Him from the first and seeing Him truly for what He was, before all others. They were flawed creatures as are we all, but they remained largely free of His taint, and came to form the heart of Ethriss's power.'

She looked around. 'They lived here, in this land, in a manner not greatly different from that of the present Orthlundyn, though there were many more and they were . . . bolder, if you like, more vigorous. As individuals they travelled far and wide across the world, seeking and rejoicing in knowledge. This was why it was they who sensed from the first the true nature of Sumeral. And having seen the truth of Him, this was why they were the first to oppose Him.'

She stopped and glanced at Andawyr, as if seeking relief from this task, but he offered none.

She went on. 'When finally, Sumeral launched war on those who opposed Him and in so doing woke the Guardians, it was to the Orthlundyn that Ethriss first gave Sumeral's own grim teaching. Then too, as now, they were apt pupils and learned well. Their captains and leaders went forth and fought with many armies, opposing Sumeral's will wherever it was known.'

Hawklan frowned slightly and looked from Gulda to Andawyr. 'How do you know all this?' he said. 'In everything I've read about the First Coming there's been virtually no mention of the Orthlundyn.'

Gulda did not reply, but Andawyr said simply, 'The Cadwanol know much more about the early days, Hawklan. Hear the tale out then ask your questions.'

Hawklan nodded reluctantly, and Gulda continued.

'By their conduct, the Orthlundyn became both a rallying point for those who opposed Sumeral – and there were many – and a target for His most savage cruelty. Sumeral gave little quarter to any of His enemies, and none to any captured Orthlundyn. Those who were not slaughtered on the field were taken for . . . later amusement.'

Hawklan turned his face away sharply, as if trying not to hear the words. Gulda hurried on.

'Eventually the war became total, with all the horror and injustice that that meant. Savage and vengeful marauders committed atrocities in Ethriss's name; wise and just nations found themselves led to fight by the side of Sumeral and his allies.' Gulda shook her head and her voice became impassioned. 'In those days, what tragedy could happen, did happen. Not a race existed that was not involved in the conflict in some way. Lands blighted, seas poisoned –' Andawyr reached out and touched her arm. She stopped speaking and looked at him.

'I'm sorry,' she said, recovering herself after a moment, and turning back to Hawklan. 'It's difficult to be orderly in telling so vast a tale.' Her hands fidgetted briefly with the top of her stick before she began again. 'The armies of the Great Alliance stood against Sumeral at all points, sometimes victorious, sometimes not. But Sumeral knew that the heart of Ethriss's will, the heart of all men's opposition to Him, lay in the Orthlundyn, and that they must eventually be destroyed if He was to prevail. At first he sought to cut off their heads and he succeeded in having one of their kings assassinated, and various Lords at different times –'

'Kings and Lords? In Orthlund?' queried Hawklan.

Gulda nodded. 'By then, yes. They it was who built Anderras Darion – with a little help from Ethriss. War needs and breeds leaders and hierarchies, you know that. But the Kings and Lords of Orthlund were chosen by the people for their worth, and remained close to them, closer even than those you've met in Fyorlund. The great strength of the Orthlundyn in battle came not only from each individual's belief in their cause and the trust they had in their leaders, but also, to a high degree, from the personal knowledge they had of them.' Then she waved the interruption aside.

'In any event, such deeds of individual slaughter availed Sumeral nothing, serving only to harden the resolve of the people to remain firm against Him; it was truly said of the Orthlundyn that when a leader fell, their army was but one man the less. Eventually, therefore, Sumeral's every manoeuvre was dedicated towards bringing His many armies together to attack Orthlund itself, even though He knew the cost of such an assault would be appalling.'

She paused, reluctant again. 'And He was aided in this intent by Ethriss.'

Hawklan frowned again as a memory flitted by. 'Stand your ground,' he said, echoing the words that had returned to him but minutes earlier.

Gulda nodded. 'We come nearer to your time, Hawklan,' she said. 'For Ethriss too knew that if he was to defeat Sumeral, then *he* must crush *His* army utterly. And seeing Sumeral's intention, he brought together a great council of the leaders of the Great Alliance. In secret conference they determined that Sumeral should be subtly allowed to gather His armies together and bring them to Orthlund's southern border. Once there, the Orthlundyn would retreat to draw Him between the mountains and the Great River, and then the armies of the Alliance would close behind Him, and drive Him into the spears of the Orthlundyn, entrenched and defensive.'

'Stand your ground,' Hawklan said again, emptily.

'It was a good strategy,' Gulda went on, gently. 'Well prepared, well laid, well executed.'

Hawklan nodded. 'I supported it,' he said, his voice distant. 'My army can hold off *any* attack. Let them come, they'll break like waves against the rocks . . .'

'Your army?' Andawyr said.

Hawklan's eyes narrowed as he struggled again for some elusive memory. 'My . . . father's army?' he said doubtfully. 'Did I beg for the command?'

Neither Gulda nor Andawyr answered and after a moment he gave up the fruitless striving and continued.

'They were glorious,' he said. 'All my friends, back from distant places and great deeds for this one final stroke. Years of secret planning and manoeuvring it had taken, but the Great Corrupter's army was at last to be crushed between the hammer of the Great Alliance, and the anvil of the waiting Orthlundyn. We waited, banners and pennants fluttering in the wind, swords and armour glinting in the sunlight; the horses, the soldiers, all restless and ready. Like a great celebration, a magnificent tournament.'

He gritted his teeth and leaned foward. 'A great array was to meet the enemy, then retreat, reform, retreat again, luring them ever deeper into our land. And then we would hold them. We had line upon line of traps and defence works laid for them. And line upon line of spearmen and archers and slingers and great artillery machines. Lines that seemed to stretch to the very horizon. The mountains guarded our eastern flank and the forest and the river our western.'

He looked earnestly at Gulda. 'We were not children and callow youths,' he said. 'We were battle-tried and hardened; all of us. We knew that for all the splendour of the sight and the hopes we held high, this would be a long and grim battle; one in which there would be no respite until the end, and one in which we could not falter or all would be lost. Even the initial retreats would take a sad toll. Each stand would have to be more desperate than the last, or Sumeral would sense the trap and retreat.

'Then they were there.'

He stopped and, gazing upwards, shivered. 'I remember a cloud passed over the sun and I felt a cool breeze on my face like a bad omen just as a look-out cried, "Enemy ho."' He turned towards the fire. 'We'd all seen them before, they were ever a foul, frightening sight, but they were even more so in the clear light of Orthlund. They seemed to bring their own ghastly night with them. The dust of their march, the forests of tall pikes, the awful carrion birds that flew with them. The mockery of their golden flag with its single silver star – the One True Light as they called it.' Hawklan's lip turned up in contempt. 'The pulsing rhythm of their stamping feet, and their endless chanting. The very sight of them had scattered armies in the past.

'But not us. We knew them for what they were. Men and Mandrocs and other fouler creatures of His inventing. Fearsome and terrible, but all of them fallible and none of them proof against sword and spear. And though we could see Him shining among their ranks we knew that Ethriss and the Guardians would be guarding us somehow from the awesome power that He and His Uhriel could use. Men must fight men. We would hold.'

He pointed his finger in emphasis. 'And we did. Day after

aching day. I've never seen such slaughter. We stood firm, taking few casualties at first while they kept walking forward into our volleys of arrows and shot, falling like corn under the scythe until they had filled up our trenches and pits with their dead and dying and could walk over them. Though He never ventured so close. Time and again the archers and slingers broke open their infantry and our cavalry smashed into it, but –' Hawklan shook his head, his eyes distant – 'they never truly broke, never scattered and ran. They retreated, taking dreadful losses, then another group would take their place while they reformed.'

He fell silent and for a long time sat motionless, staring into the fire. Neither Gulda nor Andawyr spoke.

'But we would have held them,' Hawklan continued eventually. 'We knew how they would fight, possessed by their Master's will, and we were prepared. Though we'd not truly realised the sickening weariness of it all. Night after night we'd sit and watch their distant camp fires and try to rid ourselves of the clinging horror of it all; try to cheer each other with talk of victory, and what we'd do afterwards. But it was to little avail; the nearness of His presence was like a miasma hanging sickly in the air.'

He paused again, then looked up at his listeners. 'And day by day we gained an increasing measure of His true nature. When His men died, they became . . . normal again . . . free of His firing spirit . . . free to die lost and bewildered on a foreign land far from their homes and loved ones . . .' His voice trailed off briefly. 'We didn't understand the Mandrocs,' he went on after a moment. 'They were just demented savages to us, but I suppose it might have been the same with them too.

'But we would have held them,' he repeated. 'We had the equipment and the will. Soon the army of the Alliance would smash into their rear and then . . .'

Half-heartedly he struck the palm of his hand with his fist.

His brow furrowed. 'Then, somehow, there was confusion and disarray on our left flank. Somehow it had been turned and they were pressing home a powerful cavalry assault.' He put his hand to his forehead and bowed his head, searching yet again for some memory. 'How could that have happened? I remember –' He looked up almost weeping. 'Ethriss! Where are all their names, their faces? My friends? My kin? Where are they? I remember . . . towards evening . . . the infantry

81

managed to reform and throw back their cavalry as night fell, but we'd taken heavy casualties and our left flank had been pushed far back.'

Some of the distress left his face, though now it was drawn and grim. 'No one knew what had happened. Suddenly they were there. A great force had come from nowhere and was driving through our flank guards. "Only the night has saved us," someone said. "They've broken a gap we can't defend. They could be moving through right now, to take us in the rear at sunrise, if not sooner." I could do no other than order an immediate retreat. The anvil had broken before the hammer had even struck.'

Hawklan stopped speaking, and showed no inclination to start again.

'What else do you recall?' Gulda asked gently after some time.

Hawklan's eyes opened, wide and weary. 'Riding, walking, encouraging, fighting endlessly . . . but always retreating; all the time retreating. We stood here and there, but they were too many for us, away from our entrenchments. I remember passing towns and villages; some were already deserted; some had thrown up rough fortifications manned by the old folk, and children . . .' His face became pained again. 'I wouldn't let any of the army join their kin in these towns. "We *must* keep together while we can. The Alliance army will strike soon and the enemy will have to turn to face them. Then we'll be on *their* rear."' He shook his head sadly. 'We told the people to flee to the mountains or to the river in the hope of crossing to Eirthlund.' He paused again.

'I remember Anderras Darion sealed and shrouded in mist as we marched past one dark day. It was raining . . . as if the whole sky were weeping for our plight.

'I remember red night skies to the south, vying with the sunsets, as the enemy sacked the towns and villages.

'And the Alliance never came.

'That dreadful army pursued us relentlessly, drawing ever closer. Only our total extinction would stop them.

'And I remember their terrible birds, swooping down on us, screaming, clawing.' He shuddered, then, unexpectedly, he smiled, and reached up to touch Gavor. 'But as we were driven into the northern mountains, some power sent us a rare ally.' Hawklan leaned forward, anxious to describe this brief triumph. 'When we woke one morning, the birds were waiting for us as usual, perched all about the high rocks and crags, flapping their ragged wings and shrieking to one another the way they did, as if they were goading one another on. The din grew and grew, and we took our swords and pikes to deal with them, but as they rose into the air, a great fluttering black cloud welled up high above them from the tallest of the peaks.' Hawklan raised his hands, suddenly the fireside storyteller. 'A great multitude of ravens. Without a sound, they fell out of the sky onto Sumeral's appalling creatures –' Gavor clicked approvingly. 'It had a strange beauty all its own. The ravens were smaller . . . but such fliers . . . swooping, diving, twisting . . . soon the air was full of clouds of feathers, falling like snowflakes, and splattering skeins of blood, and tumbling dying bodies.' His lips drew back in a triumphant grimace and his fingers curled. 'We dealt with those that were not dead by the time they hit the floor.'

He nodded to himself. 'They flew with us ever after, the ravens,' he went on. 'But Sumeral's carrion never returned. Not until . . . the end.'

Then, as sudddest as it had come, Hawklan's brief exhilaration passed and he sank back into his chair, silent again.

'And the end?' Andawyr prompted softly.

Hawklan turned his gaze to the fire again. 'We moved ever northwards into . . . Fyorlund,' he said, frowning uncertainly. 'Though it wasn't called Fyorlund then I'm sure. I doubt it had a name. It was an empty fertile land occupied by deer, horses –' He shrugged. 'All manner of harmless things living their peaceful lives. Until we arrived and brought *them* after us.

'We were exhausted in both spirit and body. We'd left our precious land to its most terrible enemy. The people had looked to our great army for protection with the same certainty that they looked to the sun for warmth and we'd had to tell them to flee like frightened animals before this predator. The darkness that was pursuing us still must surely envelop us and everything that we held dear.'

'You turned and stood,' Gulda said flatly.

Hawklan nodded. 'We'd no choice,' he said. 'They would have pursued us if we'd run forever, such was Sumeral's hatred of us. Our supplies were long gone. We were in little shape to forage. We had scores of wounded with us by then whom we may as well have dispatched as left behind. So we chose a site – a low hill in the middle of a plain – polished our weapons and shields, formed our battle array, and waited.

'It was a splendid, foolish sight. Weapons glinting in the sun, pale-faced men and women fearful yet resolute, flags flapping in the breeze.' He shook his head. 'That's a lonely sound,' he said sadly. 'We knew our cavalry would be wasted against so vast an army so we had released the horses to roam free, and formed ourselves into a single square. No one spoke. Each communed with his own heart and made whatever peace he could with his conscience. Whatever had happened to the Alliance, it would have been no betrayal. We knew that.' There was doubt in his voice. 'Just as our defence line had been breached, so some setback must have struck them also. All we could do now was what we had set out to do from the beginning: hold as long as we could and inflict as much harm as possible on our foe.'

Hawklan looked down at his hands. 'But I found no peace,' he said. 'I had sought the command, and it was mine. I had had the finest advisers and friends to guide me, and much of my own knowledge, but some vanity on my part had caused me to underestimate the power of our enemy, and all was lost as a consequence.' Abruptly, tears welled into his eyes, but he did not weep. 'Yet no one offered me any reproach.' For a moment, he could not speak. 'Ethriss, I knew too would forgive me, but I would not forgive myself. I would die unshriven, by choice.'

Andawyr slowly wrapped his arms about himself as if chilled by the pain and self-reproach in Hawklan's tone.

Hawklan looked up. 'When they came, they were vast even then. And He was still with them, but always keeping His distance from us. They paused awhile and made camp; to taunt us, I think. The birds were there again, but so also were the ravens, and their dark gleaming spirits were higher than ours by far. I doubt they lost *their* day.

'Then, after many hours watching, they attacked. Wave upon wave of them. The din was appalling. The screeching of the fighting birds, the rumbling chanting, the thunder of stamping feet, our own battle song and war cries. We slaughtered them in their thousands again; our archers and slingers were formidable. And those who reached us perished on swords and spears. But relentlessly, their endless, mindless sacrifice wore us down. Eventually all our arrows were spent and we'd sent back to them all their own. Our slingers were out of shot and there was little natural ammunition on that grassy hill. So we faced them with swords and locked shields . . .

'And then they fired the hill, and where their storming missiles and charges had failed, smoke and flame succeeded and our dwindling square was broken. Many of us reformed, but many fell alone, cut down as they staggered away from the fire, blinded by the smoke . . .' Hawklan wrinkled his nose. 'Whatever they used to fire the hill, the smoke was black and foul like nothing I'd ever smelt or seen before, it blotted out the sun and it burned and burned . . .

'And it was over. A handful of us were left, standing, slithering on the heaps of our own dead. One by one we fell, until there were just three.'

Hawklan's face was desolate.

'I remember the enemy falling back and standing silently watching us. I remember the sky, black with smoke, and flickering with fighting birds. There was a raucous command from somewhere, and the enemy lowered their long pikes – they were not going to close with us again. Then the figure next to me shouted defiance at them, hurled its shield into their midst and reached up to tear away its helm.' Hawklan paused and his eyes glistened as he relived the moment. 'Long blonde hair tumbled out like a sudden ray of sunlight in that terrible gloom.' He shook his head. 'I hadn't realised who it was. A great roar went up from the circling army. I called out her name . . .' He opened his mouth to call again. Both Gulda and Andawyr watched, lips parted, as if willing him this release, but no sound came from any of them.

'Without taking her eyes from the approaching enemy, she reached back and her hand touched my face briefly. "I am here," its touch said. "I am with you to the end." I threw away my own helm and shield and took my sword two-handed as she had. Then the figure at my back cried out in recognition. He too I had not recognised in the press. Thus by some strange chance, we three childhood friends formed the last remnant of our great army.'

He paused again and clenched his fist, as if around his sword hilt. 'A group of the enemy threw down their pikes and rushed forward to take . . . the girl. She killed three of them with terrible skull-splitting blows, but . . .

'So I slew her. I slew my friend. With a single stroke. I saw her head tumbling red and gold down the slope and into the darkness under those countless trampling feet.' He shook his head. 'Better that than that she be taken alive . . .

'The rest of her attackers fled back to their pikes and the enemy began its final slow advance. Back to back we held. Pushed aside and broke their long spears. Killed several. Then my last friend and ally fell and I . . .' He faltered.

'He said "I'm sorry," even as he fell . . .

'That last burden was my end and I too sank to my knees . . .'

There was a long silence, then.

'A hand took my shoulder.'

Hawklan looked up at Gulda. 'A hand took my shoulder,' he repeated. 'Then . . . darkness.'

He fell silent again and, for a long time, all in the room sat motionless as if not daring to move for fear that this might bring Sumeral's terrible army crashing down on them over the top of their protected, book-lined redoubt, so vivid was Hawklan's dreadful telling.

Gulda pulled her hood forward and her face was hidden in deep shadow. Andawyr's eyes were glassy with shock as he struggled to accept the reality of what he had heard, and the true nature of the teller.

It was Hawklan who eventually spoke.

'Is this the tale you'd have told me?' he asked, his face still drawn, but seemingly composed.

Gulda drew back her hood. Her face was unreadable.

'Yes and no,' she said. 'Yes, I'd have told you about the destruction of the Orthlundyn army and much of its people, but no, I could not know what you've just told us.' She reached out and took Hawklan's hand in an uncharacteristically feminine gesture. 'My poor prince,' she said softly.

Hawklan gripped her hand. 'My poor people,' he replied.

There was another long silence, then Andawyr said, 'Finish his tale, Memsa, unburden him.'

Hawklan looked at her. 'Do you know my name?' he asked.

Gulda shook her head. 'We know who you are,' she replied. 'But not your name, nor even the names of those who rode with you.'

Hawklan frowned. 'I don't understand,' he said. 'Do you know how I came here?'

Gulda shook her head again. 'That's an even greater mystery,' she said. 'But at least I can tell you that the Orthlundyn's sacrifice was not in vain.'

Hawklan leaned back in his chair, his face questioning.

'Then, as now, tó presume to match Sumeral in cunning was

an act fraught with hazard,' Gulda said. 'We don't know whether Ethriss's plan was betrayed or whether it was just seen for what it was, but Sumeral saw the trap, and laid His own, secretly moving an army into Riddin before he launched His direct attack on Orthlund's southern border. It was this army that fell on your flank.'

Hawklan looked at her intently. Riddin had been like Fyorlund then; empty save for some fishing villages on the coast and a few wandering shepherds. An army could have been moved in with ease.

'But . . . it would be almost impossible to bring an army through the mountains. Anderras Darion guarded the easiest route –' He stopped.

Gulda shook her head. 'It took great leadership,' she said. 'But Sumeral had many fine Commanders, and it was a deed you yourself would have honoured.'

Hawklan looked down, remembering Dacu's patient observations on their journey from Fyorlund. Even Ethriss had presumed the mountains and Anderras Darion would protect Orthlund's eastern flank. 'Go on,' he said softly.

'When the Alliance army entered Orthlund as planned, they found the enemy occupying your entrenchments,' Gulda continued. 'As you retreated northwards, the Alliance army was held fast for many days. I'll spare you the details, though they're heroic, but eventually the new defenders were overrun and they retreated to form a rearguard to the army that was pursuing you.'

'So the hammer did strike,' Hawklan said.

Gulda nodded. 'Ferociously,' she said. 'But, as you said, the anvil was broken, though it was no man's fault.' Her voice fell. 'The Alliance army pursued with all speed, driven on relentlessly at first by Ethriss's will and then by their own desperation as they realised what had happened. They passed gutted villages and scorched farmlands, groups of straggling, bewildered survivors, and the unburied bodies of countless less fortunate until they too passed into the empty northern land we now call Fyorlund.'

She paused and looked at Hawklan reflectively. 'However, such had been the fury of your defence, first in Orthlund and then, finally, on that lonely hill, that Sumeral's army was but a shadow of what it had been, and He Himself was much weakened. When news came to Him that the great host of the Alliance was approaching, it's said that He formed up His army to meet them, but seeing them so reduced, and fearing that Ethriss himself might in his rage be at the forefront of his army, He turned and fled. Fled up into Narsindal where once He had dwelt, with the victorious ravens taunting and harrying Him all the way.'

Gulda shrugged. 'Whatever the truth, He and His army were gone from the field when the army arrived. Only Ethriss stood amidst that carnage; come by some means beyond us. He held the Black Sword and the Bow of the Prince, and he wept as he wandered the battlefield. But he did not speak, except to name each of the dead as he came to them. Even those that no one could recognise.' Gulda turned away and pursed her lips to stop them from trembling. 'He knew them all,' she whispered.

'He sent the army in pursuit of Sumeral,' she went on. 'And while they were gone, with Theowart's help, he threw up a great burial mound for all the dead.'

'Vakloss,' Hawklan said, recalling suddenly the strange unease he had felt when first he had seen the City.

Gulda nodded. 'The army followed Sumeral as far as the borders of Narsindal and then returned, concerned about their extended supply line and the possibility that the enemy might turn and counter attack in the mountains.

'"We have Him caged then," Ethriss said. "He must never come forth again." And he gave charge of the land to the Fyordyn, his second most favoured people, whose own land had been despoiled beyond recovery by Oklar. Their task was to watch Narsindal and protect what was left of Orthlund and the Orthlundyn. And he gave the inner lands of Riddin to a great horse-riding nation who too had been cruelly dispossessed by the war. Their task was to aid the Cadwanol in guarding the Pass of Elewart, the only other route out of Narsindal. Then he returned to Anderras Darion.

'There, however, surrounded by so many beautiful memories of his finest friends, his grief and remorse were appalling and it was a dark place for a long time. The people of the Alliance wandered Orthlund, seeking out survivors and helping them to rebuild their homes and restore their lands. But it was a cruel task, so broken were the Orthlundyn, so cast down.

'Then one day, Ethriss came out of his inner chamber and, wandering the Castle, subtly touched all the likenesses of his friends, so that they were different. And he removed all mention of their names also. "As you love me, I beg you, speak none of these again, lest you disturb the true obeisance I must do them in my heart," he said. "Those who remain I shall repay as well as I am able.""

Hawklan grimaced at Gulda's obvious pain. 'What of their prince?' he asked.

Gulda looked at him. 'Ethriss said no more. He remade the prince's Black Sword and Bow to be his own, and the legend grew that, horror-stricken at fate of his beloved Orthlundyn, he had risked all by venturing into the heart of the battle and snatching away the prince at the very point of death, laying him to sleep in a secret place against some future need.'

'And nothing more?' Hawklan asked.

Gulda shook her head. 'Nothing more,' she said. 'But from our knowledge and yours, can you doubt who you are?'

Hawklan did not answer, but rested his head on his hand and lowered his eyes pensively.

Tentatively, Gulda went on, 'Then there was a period of great peace for many years. Sumeral and His Uhriel were weakened in every way, but so were Ethriss and the Guardians and neither could assail the other with any hope of victory. So Ethriss and the Guardians moved back out into the world, mending what could be mended, and slowly easing the rifts that Sumeral's words had torn between its many peoples. But always Ethriss returned to Orthlund to add some further wonder to the countryside and to Anderras Darion so that perhaps subtler forces than man might protect it should Sumeral venture forth again.' She raised a warning finger. 'And venture forth He did, many times. Unhindered in Narsindal, He grew in knowledge, and His armies grew in strength, particularly the Mandrocs. Gradually His Uhriel and many other agents seeped out into the world to undo the work of Ethriss and cause yet more havoc and chaos. Then He too led His armies out of Narsindal, and though the horse people of Riddin always held Him at the Pass of Elewart, and the Alliance kept Him from Orthlund, He dragged war to and fro across Fyorlund times beyond number for generation after generation, until that last terrible battle, when both He and Ethriss fell.'

Gulda stopped, and there was another long silence.

Eventually, Hawklan looked up. 'I feel no different,' he said. 'I am as I was when I found myself in the mountains – no prince, no great leader – though events have reminded me I am

89

a warrior as well as a healer. I hear and feel the truth of your words, and the truth of my few memories, but in some way they bind me to here and now.' He looked up, his face concerned. 'I am of *this* time utterly, not some time long gone. Why does the absence of the names and faces of my . . . friends . . . my kin . . . and their terrible fate pain me so little? How can I have lost so much and known such horrors and yet still be so at peace with myself?'

Andawyr reached forward and took his hand. 'Ethriss's ways are beyond us, Hawklan,' he said. 'Grief reforges us, you know that, whether we will or no. Perhaps there lies your answer. Perhaps in the aeons you must have lain in silent darkness, the ties that bound you withered, while those which held and supported you grew strong.' He released Hawklan's hand and made a small gesture of helplessness.

Hawklan looked at Gulda. Still her face was unreadable, but when she spoke, her tone was certain.

'You're at peace now because you were at peace then,' she said. 'For all the pain, you accepted what was, and your actions and thoughts were true to what you saw, or as true as any man's can be. That's why you sense no silent horde waiting vengefully for you in the darkness of your mind.'

'And I'm wakened now to do as I did then?' Hawklan asked, almost angrily.

A small spasm of irritation passed across Gulda's face. 'You're wakened now to be yourself and to act as you see fit,' she said.

'And if the end is the same?' Hawklan said, his face anxious.

'What end?' Gulda replied coldly. 'There was no end, there is no end. There are only steps along a journey. The step the Orthlundyn took was not the one they had anticipated, but none can see the future, and though they were destroyed, in their destruction they ensured the removal of Sumeral from this world for countless generations.'

'You understand what I mean,' Hawklan said.

'And *you* understand what I say,' Gulda replied sharply. 'You know you must choose right thoughts, and perform right acts – but the choice is wholly yours.' She leaned forward, her face suddenly passionate. 'If you would look for guilt at the heart of all this, don't look to your own puny failings or waste your energies reproaching the Guardian who created you and then slept. Look to Sumeral and only to Sumeral. He had the choices that you have, that we all have, and he chose to destroy what others had created to replace it with some vision of his own. *He* brought this on us, wilfully and willingly, and what we do now with His choices is up to us.'

Hawklan nodded, but made no reply. Instead, he said, 'I'd expected something different. A sudden surge of old memories probably; faces, places, happenings. Certainly not this . . . handful of recollections that I seem to have stumbled on by accident. The only emotion I seem to have is surprise – surprise that I feel so unchanged.'

'You are of this time,' Andawyr said. 'Perhaps Ethriss intended you to remember nothing, but to just . . . be here, ready armed with the blessings of your great understanding and experience. Perhaps the few memories you have, he left you as a token so that you might know your worth.'

Gulda shook her head. 'There are depths in humanity that are beyond Ethriss's reach, even though it was he who created us,' she said. 'Did he not tell the Cadwanol that they were to go beyond?'

Andawyr nodded.

Gulda went on. 'Hawklan can send now into those depths the knowledge that the terrible price his people paid was not in vain, nor was it through some failure or weakness on his part. It was paid because a great evil had to be opposed. Now he's been given the chance to oppose that evil again – should he choose.'

'It's of no matter why I am what I am,' Hawklan said simply. 'I *am* here, I have such memories as I have, and I have no alternative but to oppose Sumeral.'

He leaned back in his chair and looked at his two friends thoughtfully. Andawyr, the strange little man who exuded an almost childlike innocence yet who was the powerful and tested leader of an order that had preserved the knowledge of long gone times intact, and with it, skills in the use of the Power that had perhaps formed the world itself. Then Gulda, a dark deep shadow of a person, with a staggering breadth and depth of knowledge. Who was she? He remembered the indistinct figures he had seen shimmering around her in the mist at their first meeting. Figures calling out to Ethriss. Something had drawn them to her, for all she claimed to know nothing of them. Then there was her grip and the way she handled his Black Sword – a swordswoman for sure, but . . . ? And was it true what Loman said? That she never slept?

And on his shoulder, Gavor. Stranger by far than the two

91

opposite, with his hedonistic and irreverent ways, and the black spurs that had come to Loman's hand in the Armoury as mysteriously as had the Black Sword to Hawklan's. Spurs that even fitted around an irregularity in the wooden leg that Hawklan had made for him. He it was who had taunted Dan-Tor at that grim silent stalemate at the Palace Gate in Vakloss and exposed Oklar.

Ravens had fought at that dreadful battle, and seemingly won their day, surviving to harry Sumeral into Narsindal.

Who are you, my faithful companion? Hawklan thought. To save your life I struck a first blow and pinioned an Uhriel.

His eyes drifted around the room. It was elegant and beautiful, though the carvings and pictures that decorated it were simpler than in most of the rooms and halls of the Castle. Andawyr's small torch and the glow of the radiant stones threw jagged shadows of the stacks of books onto the walls, to form a further dark mountain range beyond that which the books and documents themselves formed.

It came to him that he had lied. He *was* different. He was more whole, more sure in his balance in some subtle way. That most of his earlier life was gone from him pained him no more than the sight of some old, long healed wound. As Andawyr had said, he was armed with the blessings of the understanding and experience that that life had given him, and to these were added all the richness of the last twenty years among the Orthlundyn. Such memories as he did have were like flowers rising up from the dark rich earth that held and nurtured their roots. Even the vivid memories of his final terrible moments held no crippling sadness. If anything they would be a spur to his future actions.

Abruptly, his euphoria evaporated as Andawyr's earlier remark returned to him with chilling clarity. 'Our position may be more grave than I feared.'

'If I'm not Ethriss,' he said quietly. 'Then who is? And where is he?' He leaned forward. 'And if he can't be found, then who in the end will oppose Sumeral Himself?'

His words hung ominously in the silence.

'We've no answers, Hawklan,' Andawyr said. 'Only questions.'

After a moment, Hawklan stretched out his legs and then stood up. 'I came here to talk about what we should do next,' he said. 'Now I know.'

# *Chapter 7*

The sound of Eldric's own footsteps echoed behind him as he strode purposefully along the corridor. With so many conflicting memories around him he still felt slightly ill at ease in the Palace. There were distant and deep memories of happy, reliable times when his father had been alive and when Rgoric's father had reigned, and he, Eldric, had been a young trooper on Palace secondment facing a future that was as true and straight as the past. Then came the memories of the double blows of the King's early death and the Morlider War to be followed by the creeping lethargy and uncertainty that had grown relentlessly through the years of Rgoric's cruelly blighted reign. And finally and most vividly, the memories of the terrors and triumphs of the last months, with his imprisonment and rescue, the miraculous recovery and brutal slaying of Rgoric, the exposing and routing of Oklar, and dominating all, the gradual realisation of the true nature of what had come to pass in Narsindal.

Automatically he acknowledged a cheery greeting from a passing official and, somewhat to his surprise, the involuntary smile that had come to his lips remained. This is an ancient building, he thought. Many others in the long distant past must have walked this way and pondered similar thoughts, and indeed faced worse problems. He was not alone, nor ever would be. Somehow, Fyordyn society had acquired a great momentum through the ages, and it was even now righting itself, recovering from the blows that Dan-Tor had inflicted on it over the years. And though it was still sorely hurt and weakened, it *would* become whole again.

Eldric felt his step lighten a little. Later, he knew, this optimism would be plagued by doubts and worries; about Dan-Tor and his Mathidrin in Nardsindalvak, about the banished Lords, the continuing trials, the great bitterness and anger that could taint all the country's affairs for many years to come; these and many others would conspire to bear him down and make him look to a bleak and wearisome future.

His smile became at once a little grimmer and more amused. These moods were as much to do with his liver as the state of the country, he decided pragmatically. There was a path to be trodden that was for the most part quite clear. How he felt about it was irrelevant.

His brief inner discourse ended as, passing through an elaborate archway, he reached his destination; the Crystal Hall.

He stopped and gazed around, immediately glad to be in this remarkable place with its shimmering inner carvings that flickered and changed endlessly to some mysterious rhythm seemingly beyond analysis. Around him, farmers ploughed their fields and harvested their crops, scholars sat and debated, soldiers fought, castles and cities fell, craftsmen worked at their trades, great boats sailed majestically on sun-sparkling seas – a source of some puzzlement to the land-locked Fyordyn – mountains filled horizons and great skyscapes billowed to the heights and welled over onto the elaborate vaulted ceiling.

It was not a place he visited very often, but each time he did, he regretted his neglect and promised resolutely that in future he would spend more time here. Circumstances, however, seemed to be conspiring to ensure that that particular future was slipping further and further away from him.

'Lord Eldric,' said a voice. 'Will you join me?'

Eldric looked across the hall towards the glittering image of the great tree. Sat in front of it was the Hall's sole occupant, Dilrap. Eldric brought his mind to the matter in hand, and walked over to him.

'I was looking for you, Dilrap,' he said, sitting down next to the Secretary with a little grunt of effort.

Dilrap smiled. 'You catch me malingering, Lord,' he said, turning his attention back to the tree. 'I make a deliberate point of coming to this place every few weeks to just sit and watch. It's a place that holds very special memories for me.'

Eldric laughed gently. 'You're a stronger man than I, Honoured Secretary. I'm afraid I too easily allow the urgent to displace the important,' he said, adding anxiously. 'But am I disturbing you?'

Dilrap shook his head. 'No, Lord,' he said. 'Nothing can truly disturb me now.'

Eldric looked at the portly figure beside him. Dilrap looked the same as ever, yet in some way he was utterly different. For one thing, Eldric had noted, with an untypical awareness for such matters, someone had 'done something' to Dilrap's formal robe of office, and it was no longer necessary for the poor man to be eternally twitching and tugging at it to ensure that it remained on his shoulders. But that was superficial. The man was changed from the inside.

Almost as if sensing his thoughts, Dilrap turned to him and answered his unspoken question.

'I've known such terrors these past months, Lord,' he said. 'It was frightening enough when he was just Dan-Tor the schemer, but after he stood exposed in his true form . . .' He shivered.

Eldric nodded. Hitherto he had always felt sorry for Dilrap, seeing him as a man thrust by tradition into a role for which he was totally unsuited. Now, however, he saw him as a man who had been forged by circumstances and who had transcended that role heroically.

And, to crown this with dignity, Dilrap had quietly declined all the honours that the Geadrol woud have granted him for his silent and relentless opposition to Dan-Tor.

'Lords, I am the Queen's Secretary' he said. 'That is honour enough for any man and to be allowed to retain that post and fulfil my duties is all I ask for.'

Reluctantly the Geadrol had bowed to this wish, and Dilrap had set to with relish repairing the damage that Dan-Tor had wrought to the elaborate machinery of Fyorlund's government. He was well suited to the task, not least because he had been an unwilling party to much of it.

It was not unfair to say that Eldric stood in some awe of Dilrap's achievement. On an impulse, he said, 'It defies me how you were able to stand so close to . . . Dan-Tor . . . Oklar . . . for so long without him sensing your defiance. I always found him alarmingly perceptive.'

Dilrap raised his eyes so that he was looking at the topmost branches of the tree. Despite the overcast and chilly weather outside, the Crystal Hall had found a grey winter brightness against which to set the tree, now a sharp, black, many-veined silhouette waving slightly in response to some breeze unfelt by the watchers.

'I sometimes think my constant terror confused him,' he said. 'I don't think he could see through it.' He turned and looked straight into Eldric's eyes. 'Forgive my interfering, Lord,' he said. 'But I've seen how the Goraidin work, and should you ever think of sending a man secretly into the Mathidrin with the intention of coming close to him either to deceive or assassinate, rid yourself of the notion now. I was fortunate. I was of some use to him but he despised me and presumably didn't see me as a threat so he never asked the questions that would have made me betray myself. He cannot be lied to. And, as I said, I think my constant terror blurred his vision. I fear a braver man would fare far less well.'

'And I fear you see straight through me, Dilrap,' Eldric said. 'That was indeed an idea that Yatsu and I had considered.'

Dilrap shook his head slowly to confirm his absolute rejection of the idea.

'However,' Eldric went on. 'There are other related matters that I'd like to discuss with you. Could I ask you to join me and Commander Yatsu in a leisurely ride about the City while we talk.'

Dilrap started. 'Ride, Lord?' he exclaimed, briefly his old twitching self. 'I'm an unhappy horseman; a poor specimen to ride in such company. I'd hinder you.'

Eldric laughed and the branches of the tree seemed to sway in approval. 'I'm not proposing a tournament, Dilrap,' he said. 'Still less a cavalry charge. Just a gentle ride through the City. I need some air, some space, and some blunt company about me to clear my mind. Besides' – his voice became a little more serious– 'I think it's important that you be seen in my company. Not everyone in the City understands why you remained as Dan-Tor's adviser.'

'*You* understand, Lord,' Dilrap replied. 'That's sufficient for me.'

Eldric stood up and held out his hand. 'It's not sufficient for me, Honoured Secretary,' he said. 'And it would be a sorry happening if some cringeing oaf who'd spent his time cowering in his cellar sought to redeem himseelf by stabbing you for aiding the enemy.'

Dilrap eyed him uncertainly. There had been such attacks against individuals immediately after the battle, and though Eldric had dealt with them with uncharacteristic ruthlessness, they still occurred from time to time. And it was true, he knew, that despite the widespread proclamation of his help in opposing Dan-Tor, there would be some who could not or would not understand.

He heaved himself to his feet. 'Well, I suppose I should do more riding,' he said. 'Had I been able to ride better, I could have fled with you and your son in the first place and spared myself much pain.'

Eldric laughed again.

A little later saw Eldric and Yatsu accompanying an anxious Dilrap mounted on a sturdy chestnut mare, carefully selected for her placid demeanour. As promised by Eldric, their pace was indeed leisurely but it was some time before Dilrap eased his tense-knuckled grip on his reins and stopped looking down nervously at the ground far beneath him.

Eldric looked round with approval as they rode away from the Palace. The broken and exposed buildings lining the two great avenues of destruction that Oklar had cut through Vakloss in his assault on Hawklan, had gradually begun to deteriorate and crumble under the effects of the weather, the many rescue operations, and various half-hearted attempts at repairs. The resultant aura of neglect and decay had earned them the inevitable epithet of 'the rat-runs' and it had been an almost unanimous decision by the Geadrol that these tangible signs of Oklar's will should be obliterated as soon as possible.

It was an idea that for the most part chimed with the will of the people and now, despite the fact that winter would soon bring it to a halt, work was proceeding apace on replacing the smashed buildings with new ones. These were to be as similar to the originals as memories and the none-too-comprehensive archives of the Rede's office would allow.

Work too was well under way with the new Palace gates, and the great gap that Oklar had torn in the wall was filled with a cobwebbed archway of scaffolding, alive with clambering figures and ringing with the clamour of their work.

Thus as the trio rode through the streets they found themselves amid the City's normal bustle, greatly swollen by craftsmen, labourers and apprentices, together with carts and wagons loaded with all manner of building materials, and no small number of idly curious spectators.

In his quieter moments at his stronghold and in his castle, Eldric had pondered sadly the seeming ease with which the Fyordyn had fallen under Dan-Tor's dark spell. At such times it shook him to his heart that so strong and just and ancient a people could succumb so quickly and silently, and he was sorely tempted to let the sword slip from his own hand in despair.

Now he found himself amazed at the speed with which the people seemed to be recovering. In his mind, it was as if for twenty years, Dan-Tor had slowly lulled the Fyordyn into a waking sleep and then lured them into a grim mire. Then, some chance, if chance it was, had made him falter in his moment of triumph and, as the mud had closed about them, the people had reached out and clasped the roof of some ancient tree. Now, after a desperate struggle they stood on firm ground again; battered and shaken, but wide awake and very angry.

Eldric looked at his companions and smiled. 'The City's recovering,' he said.

'It's *crowded*,' Dilrap replied with a worried frown, anxiously tightening his grip on the horse's reins.

'Don't worry,' Yatsu said, grinning, but pulling closer to the nervous Secretary. 'There's no room to fall off here.'

Dilrap was not consoled, and showed it.

Gradually however, they moved away from the heart of the City, into quieter streets, and thence into one of the great parks. The lawns and shrubberies looked damp and jaded under the overcast sky, but Eldric's mood took him above such trivialities. He reined to a halt and took in a deep breath.

'Cool and damp,' he said, patting his chest. 'Not a time of year that poets wax lyrical about, but every now and then I remember the claustrophobic smell of those miserable little rooms in the Westerclave, and then a single breath in the open air reminds me of what's to be valued in life more vividly than any of our greatest works of art.'

His two companions remained silent. Both had known too many terrors in their own lives to intrude on his reflections.

Then Eldric clicked his horse forward again. 'Winter Festival soon,' he said. 'It's not something we normally make much of, but I think perhaps we should this year. Lights, music, dancing, a beacon in the middle of the winter darkness. After all, the Grand Festival was spoiled somewhat, wasn't it?'

'It's a nice idea,' Dilrap said. 'It'll serve to mark the end of a great unhappiness and the beginning of a new resolve.'

Yatsu nodded in agreement but added more sombrely. 'It may also mark the beginning of cruel and hard times.'

Eldric looked at him. 'You're right,' he said. 'But Dilrap's word says all that must be said. Resolve. That creature Dan-Tor poisoned our hearts for twenty years before we saw him for what he was. Now at least we have the opportunity to turn and face him – our true selves to his true self.' He raised a hand to forestall Yatsu's interruption. 'I know. There are countless details to be planned out, much information to be gathered; difficult, perhaps dreadful decisions to be made, but you know as well as I do that we've no true choice in the matter.'

Yatsu smiled broadly and spoke to Dilrap. 'It's easy to see the Geadrol's back in session isn't it?'

Dilrap allowed himself a chuckle.

'You're impertinent, Commander,' Eldric said, though none too seriously.

'And long may he remain so,' Dilrap said. 'When Lords would lead us into war.'

Eldric looked at the two men and then out across the chilly park. Then he raised his hands in surrender and laughed. 'Well, you may choose not to accord me my lordly dignity, but I shall be using my lordly authority to ensure we have a Winter Festival the like of which we haven't had in years, whatever its social significance. Defy me in that, if you dare.' He offered them a jovial clenched fist.

They rode on for a little while in companionable silence, coming to a halt eventually on top of a small rocky tor at the centre of the park. The view away from the City was to the south, but the distant horizon was lost in the damp wintry gloom. At their backs, the lines of the Palace too were softened by the faint mist but the occasional torchlit window shone out to heighten the impression that the whole edifice was staring out as intently into the grey vagueness as they were.

'So Hawklan is with us again,' Eldric said, echoing all their thoughts. 'And Sylvriss safe with her father. Causes for celebration in their own right. And some stories to be told, I suspect, for all the fullness of Arinndier's messages.'

'Many stories indeed,' Yatsu said. 'Creost and the Morlider, the Orthlundyn arming, the Cadwanol of all things, myth upon myth. And these strange Alphraan he refers to. Many strange threads are pulling together.'

Eldric nodded thoughtfully. 'We must ensure that we're ready to take our own place in the patterns that are being woven,' he said. Then, brusquely, 'We must hurry and finish the cleansing of our house so that we can turn resolutely to the north.'

Dilrap frowned slightly, unhappy about Eldric's tone. 'That cleansing involves the judging and punishing of our country-men, Lord,' he said with some reproach in his voice. 'It's not a matter for haste, but for careful assessment and consideration of all relevant facts.'

Eldric looked half surprised, half annoyed at Dilrap's criticism, but meeting the Secretary's gaze, he lowered his eyes.

'You're right, Honoured Secretary,' he said. 'They were ill-chosen words. I'm sorry. It's just that it's such a wretched business, and I long for the time when it'll all be finished.'

He turned his horse and urged it forward down the small hillock. The others followed him.

'It was bad enough with the Lords and the High Guards,' he went on. 'But at least it was clean-cut for the most part and the major offenders have gone north to join their erstwhile ally.' He cast a quick glance at Yatsu, who at the time had forcefully expressed his views on sending to the enemy soldiers and leaders who were trained in the ways of the High Guards. The Goraidin, however, made no response and Eldric continued. 'It's dealing with all these pathetic specimens who were in the militia and the like that I find distressing. I honestly don't know who's the worst in some cases, the "criminals" or the petty minded and self-righteous creatures who are giving evidence against them. It's very hard.'

Neither Yatsu nor Dilrap commented. Both were bystanders in this saga while Eldric was at its heart, being one of a group of senior Lords who had to decide on those difficult cases that the courts felt unable to rule on. Both sympathised with him.

'Still,' he went on awkwardly, 'it's nearly over now and nothing worse will happen to most of them than a few months working on the re-building. I'm glad we've done it strictly by the Law and not in secret under some harsh military Edict. There's been enough done in the shadows of late. There'll be anger and bitterness about for years yet; those who suffered under Dan-Tor's minions, those who were maimed or lost loved ones in the battle . . .' He paused. 'Openness and debate should give us some understanding and that's probably our best hope for turning all that . . . torment . . . towards dealing with its true cause.'

Both Yatsu and Dilrap nodded in agreement.

So that's why we came out, Dilrap thought. Eldric needed to ease his burden a little; to grieve a little.

'I apologise for my reproach, Lord,' he said. 'Another's load is always lighter.'

Eldric did not reply but nodded his head in acknowledgement of the apology. Then he looked at Yatsu and saw the icy spectre that rode by the Goraidin's elbow whenever this subject was touched on. He reached out to banish it.

'Your own words will come to pass, Commander,' he said, almost gently. 'Those who were at Ledvrin will be pursued without mercy and pursued for ever. They may have fled with the Mathidrin, but they'll be found and brought to justice eventually. No place nor passage of time can shelter them from that and the task will never be laid aside until it's completed.'

Yatsu inclined his head slightly. 'I know, Lord,' he said, his voice enigmatic.

Dilrap looked at Yatsu. Quiet and self-effacing, with his wry humour, the Goraidin was invariably excellent, reassuring company. He exuded gentleness and great strength at one and the same time, yet . . .

Unexpectedly, in the presence of the man, calm intellectual knowledge became cold visceral understanding, and Dilrap realised truly for the first time that Yatsu had within him a more efficient, cold-blooded and ruthless killer than Urssain, Aelang or any of those demented souls who had descended on Ledvrin. Where he differed from them was in the vision he had which enabled him to see this truth in himself; in the strength of spirit which enabled him to accept it; and in the wisdom which told him why and when such grim skills were needed.

Impulsively he leaned over and took Yatsu's arm sympathetically.

The gesture provoked no sudden response, although Yatsu turned, a little puzzled. The two men's eyes met. Yatsu, whose years of training and experience had taught him to channel his fear into the execution of deeds which would carry him silently to the heart of his enemy's camp; and Dilrap who with his inner terror screaming constantly, had faced Oklar, stood his ground, and wilfully chosen to tangle his way with a web of deceit and confusion. A brief flash of understanding passed between these two opposite yet kindred souls. He smiled in acknowledgement.

Then Yatsu chuckled, as if, like Eldric, he had had some burden lifted. 'Shall we canter a little?' he suggested.

Dilrap's eyes widened. 'No thank you,' he said hastily but firmly, before Eldric could reply.

His alarm overrode Yatsu's enthusiasm and the three continued their ride through the park at walking pace. Their conversation wandered over various topics but was drawn inevitably back to the weighty matters of the moment.

'It grieves me that he holds Narsindalvak,' Eldric said. 'He can come and go about Narsindal as he wishes.'

Yatsu shrugged. 'Narsindalvak's not much fun at the best of times,' he said. 'And full of those scheming Mathidrin, treacherous Lords and malcontent High Guards, with winter coming on . . .' He smiled broadly. 'I doubt they're going to be in a mood for celebrating the Festival. And as for those who've been billeted to some camp in Narsindal itself or given the job of holding the approaches! Narsindalvak's going to seem pleasant to *them*! I'd say that Oklar's going to have some severe morale problems before long. What we'll have to watch for is the possibility of him sending out raiding parties precisely to ease such problems.'

'You've changed your mind about our sending the renegades to their chosen master have you?' Eldric said, half smiling.

'No,' Yatsu replied. 'But the arguments were closely balanced and a decision either way carried its own hazards. I'll not deny I didn't relish the idea of imprisoning them and tying up a great many men to act as guards, but it goes against my nature to give an enemy information unless it's specifically to deceive them.'

Eldric let the matter lie. As Yatsu said, it had been thoroughly argued and the decison made. Whatever consequences arose from it, he knew that Yatsu and his like would make the most of them without reproach.

'You think raiding parties are a possibility,' he said after a moment, taking up Yatsu's passing comment.

The Goraidin nodded. 'They may need the supplies, they may need the diversion,' he said. 'Yes. I think they're a distinct possibility. In fact I've increased the border patrols already. It'll give us an opportunity to toughen up some of these flower guards a little more quickly.'

Dilrap watched the two soldiers share a brief moment of amused professional malice as they laughed at the term 'flower guards'; one coined by the traditional High Guards for those whose Lords had allowed them to become more decorative than effective. He felt momentarily isolated.

'And we must decide soon what to do about the mines,' Yatsu went on. Eldric nodded, his face suddenly darker. Whatever Arinndier decided with the Orthlundyn, the mines were a matter that should be attended to as soon as possible.

Following the battle, Idrace and Fel Astian had told of their own secret war against Dar-Tor since their return from Orthlund. Working as labourers they had moved across the country, listening and watching, until they had found their way to the heart of Dan-Tor's corruption, becoming workers in his workshops. There they had learned of the dangerously inflammable material that was prepared in one of the work-shops, ostensibly for use in the manufacture of many of Dan-Tor's artifacts. Unclear in their thoughts but concerned that the vast and growing quantity that was being held in storage was for no good purpose, the two High Guards had not hesitated to direct Yatsu and his Goraidin towards its destruction when the opportunity presented itself.

When questioned, Dan-Tor's workers had revealed that they knew nothing of the true nature of the material, other than that it was dangerous and that Dan-Tor's instructions in its preparation were best obeyed to the letter. It was derived, it seemed, from ores and minerals that came, 'from some place up north somewhere'.

It needed no tactical genius to realise the potential of such a substance. The discipline of the phalanx pikemen had saved them during the battle, when they had parted to allow the blazing wagons to pass, but had the material been launched by catapults then no amount of evasion would have served and the day would have been lost, with appalling casualties to boot.

Eldric reined his horse to a halt thoughtfully. No one knew why Dan-Tor had chosen to make and store the dreadful stuff in Vakloss, but presumably he could make it elsewhere. That could not be allowed. But workshops and warehouses could be built anywhere; the only way its manufacture could be prevented for sure would be to destroy the mines from whence the raw materials came.

He grimaced as a vision came to him of great catapults hurling balls of flame against crowded infantry and cavalry.

'Start preparing detailed plans for an assault,' he said tersely, clicking his horse forward.

Yatsu nodded, and the trio rode on for a while in a slightly more sombre mood.

Eventually, they came to a narrow bower at the edge of the park. In the spring and summer it would be ablaze with colour, and redolent with many scents, but now it was damp and bedraggled, and as the riders stopped to pass through, it splattered them with copious flurries of cold droplets.

They emerged from the bower, damper, but a little more cheerful, to find themselves in a wide, tree-lined avenue. Their conversation began again, though still it was dominated by the battle.

'It was a shame we didn't take that creature during the battle,' Eldric mused at one point.

'You'd neither have held him nor killed him,' Dilrap said.

Both Yatsu and Eldric looked at him, surprised at the cold certainty in his voice.

'Only a very special person could do either,' Dilrap emphasised.

'He fled fast enough when he was threatened,' Eldric said, rather defensively.

Dilrap nodded slowly. 'I doubt he fled because you menaced him personally, Lord,' he said. 'He simply retreated in good order to preserve what he could of his Mathidrin in preference to paying whatever it would have cost him to use his . . . power . . . on your whole army. He'd have used it on anyone who came too close, have no doubt about that.'

Yatsu smiled at this brief but accurate military dissertation and Eldric affected an injured indignation. 'It was only a winter daydream, Honoured Secretary,' he said. 'You don't have to be so stern.'

Yatsu laughed out loud at the Lord's expression, causing his horse to start a little.

'Commander, aren't you going to protect me from such assaults by armchair tacticians?' Eldric said.

Still laughing, Yatsu shook his head. 'No, Lord,' he said. 'Your position's not tenable. I'm afraid I too will have to retreat in good order and yield the field to the Honoured Secretary.'

Eldric sighed massively, then laughter erupted out of him too like a sudden burst of sunshine through the damp grey gloom.

Dilrap joined in, not isolated this time, but truly part of the body of warriors who had set their swords and their wills against the evil of Oklar and his master.

# *Chapter 8*

Agreth's expression was pained as he turned to Arinndier.

'It's very difficult,' he said. 'They're so . . .' He searched for a word. ' . . . vague in their introductions. I've really no idea who's related to whom, although I can work some of them out from their features. And as for where they come from . . .' He threw up his hands in despair. 'How they cope, I do not know.'

Arinndier could not help but smile at the Riddinwr's discomfiture. 'I don't think they follow bloodlines as intently as the Riddinvolk, Agreth,' he said, looking round the hall, crowded with Orthlundyn elders, senior officers, Helyadin, and all the newcomers. 'As for me, I'm ashamed to admit that I've forgotten a lot of their names already, let alone their relationships.'

The confession seemed to amuse Agreth, and he leaned back in his chair, chuckling. 'Ah well,' he said. 'We're strangers here, I suppose, but more holds us together than holds us apart.' He became confidential. 'And, to be honest, I'd rather be with these people than some distant cousins I can think of whose lineage I know for ten generations.'

Arinndier laughed, but any further conversation was ended by the entrance of Hawklan, preceded by a swooping Gavor and followed by Gulda and Andawyr. The general hubbub lessened as all attention turned towards them.

The hall chosen for the meeting was simple and functional, its relatively few carvings and pictures being abstract and calm in character as if to help the focusing of concentration. Comfortable bench seats and desks had been laid out in spacious semi-circles to achieve a similar effect, and it was to a group of seats at the centre of these that Hawklan and the others moved.

As he sat down, the remaining murmur of conversation faded and there was a sudden uneasy silence.

Hawklan looked at the waiting people and, cocking his head on one side as if having difficulty hearing, smiled, and said, ironically, 'Ah, a goose has walked over my grave.'

It was the phrase that Dan-Tor had used during a similar silence when he had visited the green at Pedhavin in his guise as a travelling tinker. For those who had been there on that day, Hawklan's wilfully casual use of the phrase acted both as a release and a reminder. For the others it was merely a mildly humorous opening to what must surely become a serious, perhaps even grim, meeting.

The tension vanished and the atmosphere in the hall became quietly expectant.

Hawklan made no preamble.

'It's time to decide, friends,' he said simply. 'We've spent the last weeks talking, learning, thinking. Bringing together all the knowledge we have of both recent and long past events so that when we reached this point we'd be able to speak to some purpose. Now we shall see whether this will indeed prove the case.'

He turned to Arinndier. 'We're indebted to you for your stern control of our ramblings. You've managed to teach some of us the value of *listening*.' He cast a significant look at a group of elders earnestly occupied in a whispered conversation. 'And if such an impossibility can be achieved, then perhaps others can be as well,' he concluded pointedly.

There was some laughter at this remark and Arinndier nodded his head in acknowledgement.

Hawklan continued: 'The Lord Arinndier, as you know, both speaks and listens with the authority of his people, as does Andawyr, as do we Orthlundyn here.' He smiled at Agreth. 'The Riddinvolk, being wiser, or more foolish, do not entrust such authority to any one man, but we know that Agreth will report our discussions faithfully to them when he is able to return. In the meantime, our thanks to you for the help you've already given with the training of our cavalry squadrons, and be assured that when the Morlider arrive we shall help your people if it is possible. We can but hope that they're not assailed while the mountains are still impassable.'

Agreth bowed and thanked him.

Hawklan looked round his audience. Again he was direct. 'I'll waste no time discussing further the many different . . . adventures . . . that have happened to us all recently, and I'll waste none debating how it could have happened that such an evil – so long presumed dead as to be known to most of us only as a myth – could so suddenly be alive and whole and as intent on its purpose as it was millennia ago. Suffice it that it *is* alive, and that it *does* threaten us, and if we choose to take no action, then it *will* destroy us utterly.'

'You have no doubts about this, Hawklan?' one of the elders asked. 'In all that has been discussed over these weeks and months, there seems to have been a presumption that we can come to only one conclusion, namely armed conflict; war against Sumeral. One of my sons died over in Riddin, fighting against the Morlider, and we must remember that when we reach this "inevitable" conclusion, it is our young people who will bear the consequences of this decision, while many of us here will remain safe in our homes. Do you find no other interpretation that can be placed on these happenings that might avoid such a conclusion?'

Hawklan lowered his eyes briefly. 'None,' he replied after a moment. He shook his head sadly. 'None of us here would strike before we would talk. Indeed, few of us here would wish anything other than good fortune to our neighbours or even passing strangers for that matter. Sumeral however, without provocation, sent Oklar secretly into Fyorlund to destroy it, and but for the King, he'd have succeeded. Indeed so near this success did he consider himself that he'd ventured forth and was spreading his evil amongst *us* here, even as his foothold in Fyorlund was beginning to falter. As it was, he did them terrible harm. Now we hear, again by chance, that a second of the Uhriel is abroad, intent upon leading the Morlider against Riddin.'

The elder nodded, but did not yield. 'I know all this,' he said. 'Indeed from what I've heard, I can deduce too that Sumeral may even have had some hand in the making of the Morlider War so that Creost could be carried to the islands, and so I could have greater cause to see Him brought down than many other Orthlundyn. But still we can't send our young people into such dangers without assuring ourselves that this . . . creature's . . . needs can't be met by debate or perhaps just by the threat of force.'

Gulda fidgetted impatiently. 'You can't threaten force without being prepared to use it, and in any case you can only treat with an aggressor when you've stopped him,' she said bluntly.

The man met her gaze almost angrily. 'Maybe so, Memsa,' he said determinedly, then waving his hand around the listeners, 'But I'll stand against this tide until I have an answer which satisfies me that we've really thought about this and aren't simply assuming that this . . . war . . . is a foregone conclusion, because that was what happened the last time.' He raised his voice passionately. 'Our young people will give us the protection of their courage and vigour. We in return must give them the protection of our wisdom and experience.'

The two protagonists stared at one another for a tense moment, then with a slight nod, Gulda leaned forward and rested her chin on her hands.

'You're right,' she said. 'I'll be silent.'

The man turned expectantly to Hawklan who looked at him almost helplessly.

'All I can give you from my personal knowledge is what I've already given you,' he said. 'My every experience with Oklar's agents in the form of the Mathidrin has been marked by the foulest treachery and the most brutal disregard for life. The appalling trap laid for me at the Gretmearc, the kidnapping of Tirilen, the slaughter of Jaldaric's men, the slaughter of innocent men and women in the streets of Vakloss, the slaughter and mutilation of Lord Evison's men, the terrible destruction he wrought across Vakloss in his rage. These and other things you've been told of, and know that their truth can and has been testified to by others. For my . . . contact . . . with the Uhriel and Sumeral Himself you have only my word, weigh that how you will without fear of *my* reproach.' The old man nodded. 'Oklar himself radiated an evil . . . a wrongness . . . that I can't begin to describe to you,' Hawklan continued, 'and the mere nearness of Sumeral's Will was cold . . . alien and terrible beyond my comprehension. My heart tells me that Sumeral works only for our destruction, and that negotiations, treaties, would be but pieces on the game board for Him, until He achieved that end. Pieces to be adopted, or discarded as His need dictated. My whole being tells me that He is a disease beyond all treatment save excision.'

'And what does your reason tell you?' the elder asked.

Hawklan lowered his gaze again. 'Less,' he said uncomfortably. Then he turned to Andawyr. 'The Cadwanol hold the greatest knowledge about Sumeral. Knowledge gathered during the First Coming and for generations afterwards. Knowledge tested by relentless scholarship ever since. Weigh his words too as you see fit.'

Andawyr started slightly at being unexpectedly drawn into this debate. 'I've little I can add,' he said. 'Hawklan's right. In the past Sumeral has made treaties, alliances, promises, beyond number, but all vanished like smoke in the wind when they'd served their purpose; *His* purpose.'

The room fell silent, and the questioning elder rubbed his cheek fretfully. 'I hear you all, and I trust your hearts, and your pain, but . . .' He frowned and shook his head unhappily. 'I know my own thoughts are dominated by my grief for my son, for all it's twenty years or so old. I'd do much to spare any other having to bear such a burden. Yet, setting this aside, I still feel we need to come nearer to the heart of this . . . this· . . . whatever He is.' Then, in some anguish. 'It eludes me utterly *why* all this should be.'

'It eludes us all,' Gulda said gently. 'As the answer to the question, "why?" always must, in the end. All our reasons falter eventually. But not being able to answer questions such as "why the rain? Why the wind?" doesn't prevent us knowing their joys and discomforts, does it? And consider even your carving, carver. You may have filled a lifetime debating this and that subtlety and refinement of expression and technique, but still you don't know *why* you carve, do you? Whatever needs drives you, your *only* answer is to carve. And whatever need drives Sumeral, be assured, *His* only answer is to destroy the works of Ethriss and the Guardians.'

The old man nodded slowly. His face was pained. 'I see that you've thought the same thoughts as I have, and come to no wiser answers. Yet I still dread what we're going to ask of our young people.' He lifted his hands a little and dropped them on to his knees in a gesture of resignation. 'I can ask no more,' he said sadly. 'Except that we, in the safety of our years, remember always, those to whom will fall the lot of implementing our wills.'

Someone behind him leaned forward and laid an affectionate hand on his shoulder.

Hawklan looked round the room again. He knew that the old man had spoken the hidden thoughts of many of those present but he could see that Gulda's simple statement had also answered the predominant question in so far as it could be answered. He was glad the man had spoken. It was good to admit that such questions had been asked but had remained unanswered.

He smiled. 'You've opened our discussion well,' he said kindly. 'Now we're left only with practicalities, and there I think we *can* reach some answers.'

The atmosphere in the hall changed quite suddenly, and there was a modest outbreak of coughing and shuffling as the further release of tension found expression in changes of posture.

Gavor flapped his wings noisily and hopped up on to Hawklan's shoulder.

'Motivation aside, I have my own views on what Sumeral's immediate intentions are and how we should deal with them,' Hawklan went on. 'But I'd rather hear all yours first.'

He extended his hand towards Arinndier and nodded to him to begin.

Arinndier cleared his throat and sat up very straight. 'I would imagine that Sumeral, and Oklar, are assessing the extent of the damage they've suffered, why they suffered it, and where *our* weaknesses and strengths lie now that we've been exposed in battle. We here have been doing the same, of course, as I'm sure they have back in Vakloss. The only real questions that I can see are: *when* will He venture forth again, and at the head of what kind of army? This time we fought men – sadly for us, many of them our own kind, sorely misled. But twice to our knowledge He's used Mandrocs and by tradition they were always the mainstay of His armies. And there were those dreadful blazing wagons, the like of which I've neither seen nor heard of before.'

No one seemed inclined to disagree with these observations, but Arinndier himself looked uncertain. 'The most critical of these two, is the "when?" We can debate the probable constitution of his army in due course, but I think we can safely assume that it'll be very large, disciplined and well armed, and that accordingly it will have to be met by a similar force; one requiring perhaps all our High Guards and as many of yourselves and the Riddinvolk as are prepared to help us.'

The dilemma then became that which had faced both Eldric and Dan-Tor. The maintenance of a large inactive fighting force for any length of time presented difficult morale and supply problems, but worse than these were the social consequences of removing so many young men and women from their homes and crafts and the consequent burden that must fall on the more elderly. Yet to have no such force ready was to court defeat.

Hawklan stayed silent as the subsequent discussion moved to and fro, intervening only occasionally as it drifted too far into the vague and general, or into inappropriate detail.

Suddenly, a strange, excited whistling filled the hall and brought all debate to a bewildered conclusion.

Andawyr smiled broadly and stood up. There was a scuffling at the door of the hall, then an oath, then the door lurched open and the sinuous brown figure of Dar-volci tumbled in. There was a little more profanity about the design of the doors 'in this place,' as the felci rolled over and scrabbled to regain his balance on the polished floor, then, righted at last, he scampered across to Andawyr, who bent forward, arms extended, to receive him.

'Where've you been all this time?' he said, not without a hint of the anxious parent in his voice, as he struggled to contain the wriggling felci which was now clambering all over him and chattering noisily.

Dar-volci began an elaborate whistling, apparently in reply. It was so piercing that most of the watchers grimaced and several put their fingers in their ears.

Andawyr frowned in exasperation and, over-balancing under the impact of Dar-volci's attentions, flopped down into his chair again.

'Dar, you're talking felci,' he shouted above the noise. 'And loud enough to send to Riddin. Talk properly.'

The felci stopped wriggling abruptly and the whistling sank through a brief glissando into a dying fall. He stood for a moment on Andawyr's lap, his head cocked on one side.

'Properly?' he said. 'I was talking properly. Only a cloth-eared human would confuse this rumbling cacophony with real speech.'

'Of course, of course,' Andawyr said hastily. 'You're right, as always. But where've you been?' he repeated. 'And what have you been doing?'

He took hold of the felci. 'You're thinner,' he went on, anxiously. 'And your coat's a mess.'

Dar-volci began to scratch his stomach vigorously with his forepaws, sending up a cloud of dust, then, balancing precariously, he brought his back leg up to reach more inaccessible places. This sent up more dust, and the vibration of the scratching made Andawyr clutch the edge of his seat. Finally Dar-volci shook himself violently.

'Off my knee, if you're going to do that,' Andawyr said, coughing. He stood up and dumped his friend unceremoniously on the floor.

'Dar-volci, you're so thin. Where've you been?' The felci mocked Andawyr's anxious tone reproachfully.

Andawyr glowered at him as he beat the dust off his robe.

'You're so inconsistent, you humans,' Dar-volci went on, with the infuriating manner of a teacher yet again repeating an old lesson to a particularly obtuse pupil. 'Always have been. One minute you're all fuss and concern. The next – boom – you're dropping us on the floor.'

'Which is where you belong, you furry dustheap,' Andawyr snapped, still dusting a fair cloud from his robe.

Dar-volci sneezed, then blew a loud raspberry.

'I *like* this rat,' Gavor whispered in Hawklan's ear.

'That's the last time you call me that, crow,' said Dar-volci, levelling a menacing clawed forepaw at his flatterer.

Hawklan felt the impatient tap of Gavor's wooden leg. Sensing the beginning of an acid and acrimonious exchange, he cleared his throat conspicuously.

'My friends,' he said loudly. 'This is Dar-volci, the brave *felci*' – he nudged Gavor with his head – 'who gave us much needed assistance at the Gretmearc. I've thanked him once, but I'm happy to thank him again, in front of you all. Welcome to our conference, pack leader.'

The felci sidled over to Hawklan and, placing his forepaws on Hawklan's knees, stared at him intently.

'Thank you,' he said simply, after a moment. Then he looked at Gavor, who craned his neck forward and met his stare like a jousting knight.

'Truce . . . raven,' the felci said, with a significant hesitation.

Gavor's eyes narrowed, then he said. 'Truce . . . felci,' in like vein.

'Come here, creature.' Gulda's voice interrupted the uncertain peace-making. Her face was screwed up in puzzlement, and she was beckoning the felci. Dar-volci dropped down onto all fours to sidle over to her, and then sat up on his haunches and examined her as he had examined Hawklan and Gavor.

'Where do *you* come from?' Gulda asked eventually.

Dar-volci laughed a deep and rumbling laugh. 'From long ago and far away,' he said with a lilt. 'Just like you, old one, only more so . . . much more so.'

Gulda started slightly, but she made no attempt to pursue her question. Instead, she reached out and stroked him. 'You *are* a mess,' she said.

Dar-volci shrugged. 'Nothing that a good scratch and shake won't deal with. When I can have one without interruption,' he added, looking significantly at Andawyr.

'What have you been doing all this time?' Gulda asked.

Dar-volci's excitement returned. 'Meeting the Alphraan again. Singing, playing, telling the old tales, but mainly clearing their lesser ways. You think *I'm* a mess, you should have seen those! But all will sing to all again soon. And their heartplace . . .' His voice tailed off into a series of ecstatic flutings.

'What do you mean, lesser ways, all singing to all?' Hawklan asked, remembering the remarks the Alphraan had made as they had talked during their journey from Fyorlund.

'It's beyond your understanding, Hawklan,' Dar-volci said, though not unkindly. 'Suffice it to say that the scattered families are coming together again, re-born and full of hope. Their song is echoing from here to the Caves of Cadwanen, healer, and they are eternally in your debt for your guidance and the epic slaying that freed their heartplace.'

Hawklan frowned. 'I want no heroic songs about that,' he said coldly. 'I slew that creature by good fortune and out of grim need. And it was old and beyond its time.'

'It would have seen all of you off without any difficulty,' Dar-volci said defensively.

'That's why I killed it,' Hawklan said, an edge to his voice. 'But make no songs and legends of it. It's not a matter for pride.'

Dar-volci chattered to himself for a moment uncertainly, then laughed. 'Songs and legends make themselves, warrior,' he said. 'Consider yourself fortunate if they come anywhere near the truth.'

Hawklan did not reply.

'What did you mean, Dar, the ways are open as far as the Caves?' Andawyr said, apparently satisfied with the state of his robe, and holding out his hands again.

The felci clambered back up on to the Cadwanwr's lap and, circling twice, curled up into a relaxed bundle.

'What I said,' he murmured. 'And I'm worn out. It's a long way. Still, the others are here now so they can carry on. I'm going to sleep for a week.' Then he yawned massively and brought his head down wearily on to his forepaws. 'But carry on talking,' he said, faintly. 'I'll be listening.'

Hawklan looked at Andawyr who shrugged helplessly.

'He'll tell us when he's ready,' he said, stroking the sleeping felci. 'But he *has* been working very hard. He's thin and exhausted.'

Hawklan nodded, then, on an impulse, looked around and said, 'Are you ready to join our conference also, Alphraan?'

A soft, elusive, sound filled the hall like a myriad tiny bells, and at its heart a voice said, 'Thank you, Hawklan, you have brought us from the darkness, and we are yours to command. We wish to serve until He is no more.'

Arinndier, Jaldaric and Tirke, looked round in amazement, as did some of the Orthlundyn elders. Hawklan smiled. 'I doubt you'll see anything,' he said. 'For some reason they're reluctant to show themselves.' Then, looking around again in spite of himself, he said, 'Won't you join us in person now that we're friends and allies?'

'No,' came the simple and immediate reply. There was no animosity in it, but the word was surrounded by subtle shades of meaning that conveyed an absoluteness to the answer which placed it quite beyond debate. There would be no explanation of their conduct.

Hawklan bowed. 'As you wish,' he said. 'Nevertheless you are at all times welcome to come and go through Anderras Darion as you please, and to listen and speak at our debates.'

'Thank you,' said the voice.

An awkward silence descended on the hall as the Alphraan's voice faded, but a sudden explosive snore from Dar-volci ended it abruptly.

'Let us return to our debate, then,' Hawklan said, laughing. 'Has anyone else anything to add to the remarks already made about the problems of billeting a large army in Fyorlund for any length of time?'

'Without some idea of when an attack might occur, nothing can be determined, however much we talk,' Dacu said.

'Is it possible for the Goraidin to move into Narsindal and perhaps get some idea of what's happening?' Athyr asked.

Dacu shrugged slightly. 'Very difficult,' he said. 'The seeing stones in Narsindalvak are extremely powerful. That means night travel. And the mountains beyond the eyes of the tower are effectively impassable at the best of times.'

'It could be done though?' Athyr pressed.

Dacu nodded. 'Oh yes,' he said. 'It could be done, but not quickly. And it would be dangerous. And I doubt it would serve any useful purpose. The natives are Mandrocs, and it's simply not possible to pose as one of those. And we know far too little about the Mathidrin to risk infiltrating them except at

114

the lowest levels. The best we're going to be able to do is establish look-out posts and report what we see. And even that's going to be difficult.'

Athyr let the matter rest. He had trained enough with Dacu over the past weeks to respect his judgement.

Then Dacu cut across all the debate about the problems of maintaining a standing army. 'We can't just sit around and wait for an attack,' he said simply. 'It'll destroy us as effectively as any army He could send against us.'

Hawklan looked around at his friends as the debate wilted.

Yrain looked tentatively at Gulda, then raised her hand to speak. Hawklan nodded to her.

'If we can't risk waiting, then that leaves us no alternative but to take the initiative ourselves,' she said.

The elder who had opened the discussion looked up and stared at Hawklan, his expression saying clearly that this was what he had feared.

Such is the power of Sumeral's teaching, Hawklan thought, though it occurred to him, not for the first time, that humanity provided singularly apt pupils.

He dismissed the thoughts; they were neither helpful nor relevant.

'Are you suggesting that we should attack *Him*?' he asked, his voice neutral.

Yrain hesitated. 'From what's been discussed so far, I don't see that we've any alternative,' she said. 'It seems that negotiation isn't worth serious consideration. And in any event, as Memsa said, we need to be able to stop Him by force even if we'd rather talk.' She leaned forward, her voice intent. 'We know definitely that the longer the delay, the greater will be *our* problems. We accept that this might be the case too with the enemy, but we know *nothing* of their society, nothing at all – except that it's produced a large number of disciplined and, by all accounts, brutal, troops. There are the Mathidrin. We don't know how hardened they really are, but seemingly they faced the High Guards outside Vakloss quietly enough, and retreated only when their leader retreated; and then in good order. Then there are the Mandrocs. We know they travelled in stealth across Fyorlund and into Orthlund to destroy Jal's patrol, and we know they slaughtered Lord . . .' She paused to recall the name. ' . . . Evison's entire company of High Guards; no small feat of arms I'd imagine. We also know, from

115

Andawyr, that armed bands of them led by Mathidrin are wandering Narsindal where once only their tribal hunting parties roamed. I'd say that all this betokens a harsh military society and as such, one that will benefit from delay by building up its strength.'

Hawklan looked at Andawyr.

The old man looked pensive. 'The Mandrocs are tribal and territorial, with a . . . warrior culture, I suppose you'd call it,' he said. 'A tribal leader selects himself by the simple expedient of killing anyone who opposes him, and their system of justice consists of retribution – usually violent. I've seen the results of one of their tribal "settlements". It was horrific – an entire community destroyed – males, females, young, animals even, all slaughtered, and the village razed utterly. But while their fighting's fierce, it's primitive and wild, and they've no concept of strategy and tactics. It's just a matter of charge in and kill the enemy until there's no one left or until you're dead or incapacitated. I'm afraid that Yrain's right. We can only conjecture about how it's been done, but it looks as though their natural savagery has been . . . harnessed, channelled in some way. It's not a happy prospect.'

'It's a chilling prospect,' Arinndier said. 'The Annals of the Watch from only a few generations back are full of tales of seemingly arbitrary attacks on patrols along the lines you describe. Primitive weapons, primitive tactics, but terrifying ferocity. But the armour that came back from Evison's was anything but primitive, and from what Jaldaric can remember their behaviour was anything but undisciplined. Sometime, somehow, a powerful will has stamped its mark on the Mandrocs and, on balance, I have to agree that delay may only enable the enemy to increase His strength.'

Gulda intervened. 'If we march into Narsindal then *we* are the aggressors. But setting that small point of morality aside, *we'll* be the ones with the lines of supply extended through hostile territory, and *we'll* be the ones battering ourselves against an enemy who only has to hold its ground until we're sufficiently worn down for it to ride out and mop up the remains.' Her tone was caustic.

Yrain answered her immediately, her face flushed slightly. 'By His conduct, Sumeral's given notice of His intention to attack both Fyorlund and Riddin without any provocation from either of them. There's no immorality in ambushing an ambusher.'

There were some murmurs of approval from her listeners. Gulda raised a menacing eyebrow.

Yrain faltered for a moment, then she clenched her fist and ploughed on. 'And another thing. The Morlider touch many lands in their journeying. If Creost controls them, who knows how many other countries have been swayed to His cause? For all we know, we could already be encircled. Mandrocs to the north, the Morlider to the east, and who knows what to the south and perhaps even the west?'

A buzz of alarm rose up from the listening group. A faint flicker of a smile passed over Gulda's face and she sat back in her seat without commenting.

Dacu caught Hawklan's eye.

'Perhaps we should consider ourselves from the enemy's point of view,' he said. 'If He wants a delay, for whatever reason – building up His army or acquiring allies – then He'll wait. If then we wait, we lose, while if we attack, we catch Him perhaps less prepared than He'd choose. If, however, He doesn't want a delay, then it's in His interest to lure us to Him so that He can fight a defensive war as Memsa's outlined. He's not strong enough yet to invade us, or He'd have done it. So if we attack, then unfortunately, we do His bidding, but if we don't . . .' He paused. 'I fear He'll lure us forward with some atrocity like Ledvrin. And He'll commit further atrocities until we say "Enough". On balance, I don't think we've any real choice. To delay is to risk certain defeat or the death of innocents.'

The Goraidin's analysis was like the closing of a terrible trap, and a bleak silence followed it. Hawklan, Gulda and Andawyr exchanged glances.

'Alphraan, you're silent,' Hawklan said.

'We've nothing to add,' the voice said flatly and simply, as if trying to quell the awful regret and fear that resonated around it.

'Has *anyone*, anything further to say?' Hawklan asked.

There was some head shaking, but no one spoke.

Hawklan lowered his head. 'Sadly, nor have I,' he said. He indicated Gulda and Andawyr. 'The conclusion you've reached is that which we three reached independently. I wish truly it could have been otherwise, but . . .'

He left the sentence unfinished, and silence seeped back to fill the hall like a cold mist.

When he spoke again, Hawklan's voice was distant.

'It seems we have no choice,' he said. 'We must levy our troops and take the battle to the enemy. We must do what even Ethriss did not do. We must assail Derras Ustramel itself.'

# *Chapter 9*

As Hawklan's voice faded, the silence returned, colder than
ever, seeming to freeze the entire group into immobility.

'Will you lead us, Hawklan?' Athyr asked eventually, his
voice sounding strained.

Hawklan looked down to avoid his gaze, then he stood up
and drew the Black Sword.

'There are forces at work here of which we know nothing,'
he said. 'This Sword,' – he looked around at the austerely
decorated walls and ceiling – 'this whole castle fell to my hands
by some mystery beyond my understanding and, I suspect,
beyond all our knowing. I will lead you if you wish, but you
must know that since my journeyings and my encounter with
Oklar I have learned much about myself, including memories
of a time when I was other than I am now. Of a time before
when I led a great Orthlundyn army. When I led it to a defeat
so total that not one of its fighters survived.'

The atmosphere came suddenly alive again. Agreth leaned
across to Arinndier and whispered to him. The Lord nodded,
and the two men rose quietly, Arinndier beckoning to the
other Fyordyn as he did so.

'This is an Orthlundyn matter,' he said to Hawklan. 'We
will leave you.'

'Stay,' Hawklan said, sitting down and laying the sword
across his knees. 'I thank you for your courtesy, but if the
Orthlundyn choose me, then I fear the Fyordyn and the
Riddinvolk will gravitate to me also, whether I will it or no.'

Arinndier met the green-eyed gaze squarely. It was free from
pride and ambition, and free from spurious regret and false
humility. It was the gaze of a man who saw the truth and knew
he could not turn from it.

'Hear what has to be said,' Hawklan went on. 'So that in
your turn you can decide when the time comes. I'll take this
burden willingly if it is thrust upon me, but thrust upon me it
must be. I have its measure and I'll neither seek it nor avoid
it.'

Slowly, Arinndier sat down.

Then, briefly, Hawklan told his listeners the history of the

119

Orthlundyn as he recalled it and as it had been completed for him by Andawyr and Gulda.

There was a strange, deep, quietness when he had finished. Although obviously intrigued and curious, Agreth and the Fyordyn remained silent out of courtesy. The Orthlundyn, however, remained silent because most of them seemed to have been profoundly moved by the tale. Some were openly weeping.

Hawklan nodded. 'Your minds say "How and why did we not know this history?" That, seemingly, was Ethriss's choosing. But your hearts acknowledge its truth. It's a tale that makes you . . . us . . . more whole.'

No one questioned him.

'Choose your leader now,' Hawklan said quietly.

The first to speak was Aynthinn, the elder from Wosod Heath. His manner and tone were emotional, but at odds with the prevailing solemnity. 'I think we've had this conversation before, healer,' he said, shaking his head and chuckling. 'And it seems to be more for your benefit than ours. With your every word you confirm what we know about you. I always suspected you were an Orthlundyn deep down, for all you're rock blind. Now you've come to us at a time of need, armed with a knowledge of Him from another age –'

Hawklan interrupted him. 'My memories offer me no guidance or support that you yourselves have not offered,' he said. 'The enemy is of *this* time, *I* am of this time, and your decisions must be of this time, strengthened perhaps by the knowledge of time past,' – he held out the Sword – 'but untainted by mysterious portents, the true meaning of which are beyond us.'

Aynthinn looked at him patiently, his face becoming more serious. 'The portents you speak of do affect us deeply, it's true,' he said. 'How could they not? And the tale you've just told us enriches us in some way beyond immediate fathoming; we are truly in your debt. But *you* are the one who's beginning to cling to the past, not we. We have no choice but to be in the present,' – his face brightened again, – 'and no one could accuse the Orthlundyn of being obsessed by history. I say again, you come armed with a true knowledge of Him from another age. And knowledge is everything. We choose you not because of your Sword and your castle, or because of the value that Sumeral seems to place in you, though these things weigh with us. We choose you because we've known you for twenty years and we know you're our best man.'

120

The simplicity of Aynthinn's conclusion shook Hawklan, and he looked around, uncertain what to say next.

Arinndier could not forbear chuckling at his surprise. 'I've known you for only a matter of months, Hawklan, but I've seen enough to recognise your worth. The High Guards must choose their own leader as need arises, but you have my sword and those of Eldric, Hreldar and Darek.'

Dacu too smiled, then he made an almost imperceptible hand signal. Hawklan caught the gesture and nodded an acknowledgement. 'You have the word of your companions?' he asked.

'If you saw the gesture, yes,' Dacu replied smiling.

Hawklan laughed, then looked at Agreth. The Riddinwr bowed. 'I ride with you, Hawklan, if Urthryn will release me,' he said. 'I shall tell the Moot all that I've heard and seen. I shall tell them of my own judgement, and that of the horse you ride, which is a judgement shrewder than mine by far, and I've no doubt that Sylvriss too will speak about you, if she hasn't already.'

Hawklan thanked him and stood up to return the Sword to its scabbard.

As he did so, another voice spoke. 'We are with you too, Hawklan.' It was the Alphraan, and though their voice was soft, it filled the hall with echoing subtleties of loyalty, obedience, friendship, and many other images of support and aid. Hawklan felt the Sword come alive in his hand, and looking at the hilt he saw its myriad stars twinkling and the two intertwined strands glittering brightly into its unfathomable depth. He felt Loman and Isloman looking at him.

'Thank you,' he said simply, as the Alphraan's voice faded.

Then he looked back to his audience. 'I accept the burden that the Orthlundyn wish me to carry,' he said quietly. 'Because I know that if I fight amongst such people then I am but one man, and if I fall, the army will be but one man less.' There were some protests, but he silenced them with a wave of his hand. 'It must be thus,' he said firmly. 'You, above all, know this. Nothing less is acceptable if we are to face Him.'

Then he turned to Agreth and Fyordyn. 'I accept now your personal loyalties and I offer you mine,' he said. 'As for your armies . . .' He shrugged. 'There's no haste for such decisons. Let's see how events unfold.'

Dar-volci interrupted the proceedings with a noisy splutter, and rolled over on Andawyr's lap until his legs were in the air.

Andawyr supported him carefully to prevent him rolling off, and gave Hawklan an apologetic look.

'Dar never did have any sense of occasion, I'm afraid,' he said.

Hawklan smiled. 'He's only missing humankind planning one of its greater follies,' he said. 'I doubt he'd be other than dismayed at the spectacle.'

Andawyr did not reply, but looked down at the sleeping felci, with its tight closed eyes and incongruously gaping mouth. Gently he stroked its stomach.

Hawklan sat down and looked round at his gathered friends and countrymen. Am I about to betray you all again? he thought, but almost immediately the answering thought came that though he had led the Orthlundyn to defeat, he had not betrayed them. It was little consolation, and his original thought simply transformed itself into, am I going to lead you all to defeat again?

He crushed the futile inner debate. Now was now. He must learn from the past, but be uncluttered by it. Now he must tell the Orthlundyn and the others how he intended to lead them.

He leaned back in his seat.

'My first task as your leader should be to discuss with you what strategy we must use against this powerful foe,' he began. 'However, I shall not do that. Instead I shall tell you what the Orthlundyn must do and I shall ask you to do it as I know you can do it . . .' He paused. ' . . . but without me.'

There was a brief, stunned, silence, then a babble of questions filled the hall. Even Gulda and Andawyr turned to look at him in some surprise.

Hawklan raised his hand for silence.

'This is indeed a man we go to meet,' he said. 'In that lies perhaps our greatest hope. But He is no ordinary man. He is, in truth, an unbelievably ancient and powerful force. A force well beyond our understanding, that has chosen to appear as a man because only thus can it conquer the world of men. And even though His three Uhriel were once human, they are now barely so, so corrupted by power are they.

'When the Lords of Fyorlund decided that they must attack Oklar, just as we've decided we must attack his Master, they knew a little of Oklar's power and they devised field tactics that they hoped might offer them some protection. The worth of those tactics will never be known because Oklar, as we know, was bound in some way, and not permitted the full use of his power.'

He paused, and his face became grim. 'However, I am told that the power Oklar used against me was' – he made a dismissive gesture – 'a mere fraction of what he might have done. Put another way, no field tactic, however ingenious, could have saved the Lords from Oklar's power had it been truly launched against them.

'Now we propose to send a similar army of men against Oklar *and* his Master, *and*, in all probability, Creost and Dar Hastuin. How can any mortal army face such power?'

The hall became very still.

'It cannot,' he said quietly. 'Sumeral could destroy our vaunted armies with precious little effort. Yet He does not use that power to achieve His ends. Instead He moves silently and with cunning as He builds up a great mortal army of His own.' He paused and watched the effect of his words on his audience.

'Perhaps He fears Ethriss and the Guardians,' he continued after a moment. 'Perhaps not. Perhaps equally it is all some horrific lure, to draw our might to Him so that our destruction will be both easier and more complete.' He paused again.

'We don't know,' he went on. 'We *cannot* know. But we can't take such a risk.'

He became more casual. 'This we've known since my return from Fyorlund,' he said. 'But it's something we've not dwelt upon, having chosen instead to concentrate, quite rightly, on preparing ourselves to meet mortal enemies.'

'Now however, we've come to the sharpening of spears and swords, to the burnishing of armour, to the deciding of the orders of marching, and this knowledge must be faced squarely.'

His green eyes became intense as he looked at his motionless listeners.

'Orthlund, and such allies as come to its side, will march directly against the enemy, and prosecute the war with all their skill up to and through the gates of Derras Ustramel, and to His very throne. You will be led by Loman and, if she is prepared, by Memsa Gulda. I will not be at your head. Andawyr and I, with others, will go another way. To levy the forces that must be levied if you are to be protected from the power of Sumeral and His Uhriel.'

The silence disintegrated again.

'No,' cried several voices.

Gulda raised an eyebrow and Loman shifted uncomfortably in his seat.

'We mean no disrespect to Loman or to the Memsa, but . . .' was the gist of the protests. Hawklan raised his arms to silence them.

'You forget too easily,' he said coldly. 'With the Memsa's guidance, Loman's skill and his sight into truth made an arrow that struck down Oklar; that would have killed him had I been more worthy. And you, you carvers become fighters, did *I* craft you into an army, or did they? Did *my* insight protect any of you from the Alphraan, or did *theirs*? No. I was elsewhere fighting the same war in another place.'

He held out his hand to prevent further debate and turned to Gulda. 'Are you willing . . . ready . . . to do this now?' he said. 'To move against Dan-Tor?'

Gulda, watching Hawklan intently, nodded, but did not speak.

'Very well,' Hawklan said, turning back to his still shocked audience. 'Then that is how it must be. The army under Loman and the Memsa will assail Narsindal while I go another way.'

'What do you intend to do?' someone asked through the silence.

Hawklan hesitated. 'That you must not know,' he replied.

'*Must* not?' his questioner echoed. 'Are we not to be trusted with your intention.'

Two needs vied within Hawklan for dominance: the commander's need for obedience, and the healer's faith in knowledge. But both would have to be met.

'I trust *you* with the duty of destroying Sumeral's army,' he replied gently. 'You in your turn must trust me with the duty of destroying Sumeral's other power.'

'But –'

Hawklan raised his hand again. 'The details of what I intend are as undefined now as are your tactics for dealing with some unknown army on some unknown terrain at some unknown time in the future. *That* much I *can* tell you. I can tell you also that with others more powerful than I, I shall be striking to the heart of Sumeral's Old Power, just as you will be striking to the heart of his armed might. Between those two tellings, *no one* knows what I intend, not even Andawyr and the Memsa. Should the merest whisper of what lies there reach Him then it would be my downfall. And if my venture fails then we are all

124

doomed, just as surely as we are if yours fails. Do you still wish to know my intention?'

The man looked at him for some time then slowly shook his head. 'No,' he said simply.

This brief exchange seemed to have silenced most of the questions that had bubbled out when Hawklan had made his announcement, though he now found he was the focus of the entire hall's silent attention; not least that of Andawyr and Gulda.

He stood up and walked to one of the decorated panels that lined the hall. For a moment he studied its uncharacteristically simple patterning, then he touched a raised lip that protruded from the sill.

Slowly the pattern dissolved to reveal a window scene carried to the hall by the Castle's many mirror stones. It was a view over the Orthlundyn countryside as seen from just above the main wall, and the winter hues of the landscape were oddly heightened by a heavy grey sky. Both landscape and sky merged into a common greyness well before either reached the horizon.

There were several expressions of surprise, Hawklan's included.

'Well, for all the indications we've had of an early winter, it seems it's going to snow sooner than we all imagined,' he said. 'And heavily, by the looks of it.' He looked at Arinndier and Agreth. Riddin had been inaccessible for some time due to snow in the higher mountains, but now it seemed that Fyorlund too was likely to be cut off very soon. He pursed his lips and shook his head.

Isloman made reassuring noises. 'I doubt anyone will start a campaign in this weather,' he said. 'Certainly the Morlider have no love for snow. We suffered badly when the winter came early during the war, but they suffered worse.' He turned to Agreth. 'If they've any choice about it, I think it's unlikely they'll attack until the winter's showing signs of easing.'

'Thank you, Isloman,' Agreth said. 'But I'm afraid I'll just have to live with the uncertainty. I doubt Urthryn will allow any relaxation of the coastal watch so at least my people won't be taken by surprise if the Morlider do come.'

Arinndier too seemed undismayed. 'If the winter's early here then almost certainly the northern mountains at home are well blocked already. Only the most desperate would try to bring an army through them, and of the many things we've seen from Oklar, desperation was not one. Besides' – he indicated Agreth – 'as in Riddin, our people will be watching, regardless of the snow.'

Hawklan turned round, a dark silhouette against the grey backdrop. 'So, circumstances determine our plans for us,' he said. 'The northern reaches of Fyorlund snowbound and, presumably, Narsindal also; while to the east, the mountains that prevent us helping the Riddinvolk also protect us should any harm befall them. The winter comes like a benevolent besieger to confine us safe in our nests, pending a call to arms in the spring.'

'Take care, Hawklan,' Gulda said.

Hawklan nodded. 'Indeed,' he said thoughtfully, then, quietly, but very positively: 'Loman, start general winter training immediately, and speed up the Helyadin's – Dacu, will you help with that? And make sure the villages along our southern and western borders are on their toes – Yrain's point was sound. I don't think anything serious is going to happen in the next few weeks, but having determined our strategy, we must tell the people and have them prepare to mobilise at a moment's notice. The sooner they get used to the idea, the better.'

He turned back to the wintry scene and went through the order of the levy agreed by the Orthlundyn.

The army was to consist first of those unmarried men and women who wished to serve in it. Those who were married but with no children were to be the first reserve, and those with children, the second. The remainder, the old, the young, and the infirm, were to form a militia for the defence of their homeland should all fail, and they were also to share the re-distribution of work that would occur due to this great upheaval. In this latter, as with the cavalry training, Agreth's advice had been invaluable, the Riddinvolk being long used to the disruption of their ordinary lives caused by the demands of the Muster.

Hawklan smiled as he remembered an acid comment by Loman about the Riddinvolk being more concerned over the disruption to their Muster activities by the demands of home and hearth, than vice versa, but its brief light dwindled to nothing in the great blackness that surged up within him abruptly.

Ethriss, this is appalling, he thought. Even if they defeated Sumeral, what was to happen was an abomination, an insanity, and its necessity offered little consolation. The face of the elder who had questioned him at the beginning hung in his memory. Sons and daughters were to be separated from their parents, husbands and wives from each other. What cherished loving bonds were to be torn asunder there? Even for the lucky ones it would be months of fretful worrying during which a portentous future would cloud all present doings. For others there would be the nursing of loved ones who had been smashed physically or mentally by what had been done to them, or worse, what they themselves had done. And finally there would be those for whom the parting embrace would be the last. So much delicate patient toil to be destroyed so casually.

Unconsciously, he laid his left hand on his sword hilt. Damn you, Sumeral, he thought savagely. Damn you back into the darkness that you've come from. I'd have forgone the past twenty years with all their light and joy, had I known this was to be the price. He felt the ancient, mocking, spectre of vengeance rise within him and he faced it. I have your enemy's sword now, and I'll cleave you from neck to hip with it if we meet. And relish the deed.

His mood lightened as suddenly as it had darkened and he turned and moved away from the window.

'Grim times for us all,' he said. 'But we're as ready as we can be and there's no reason why we should make them grimmer than necessary. How long to the solstice, Gulda?'

She told him.

'Good,' he said. 'Then we'll make this year's Winter Festival one that will warm and sustain us through *anything* the future has chosen for us. Loman, make sure that that too goes out with the other orders.' He clapped his hands and smiled broadly.

The sound of the clap echoed round the hall and the listening Alphraan caught it and spun it into a glistening, brilliant, rhythm, to counterpoint Hawklan's declaration. Clapping and laughter rose up from the audience to complement it, and with a wave of his hand, Hawklan dismissed the meeting.

As the people began to leave, Hawklan felt a powerful grip take his elbow. He did not need to identify the owner.

'Memsa,' he said, cautiously.

'Young man,' she replied neutrally, ushering him discreetly to the door. He cast about for an escape route, but Isloman, Loman and Andawyr, with Dar-volci still draped in his arms, appeared beside him suddenly, like solicitous flank guards.

'Are *you* in trouble, dear boy,' Gavor said, chuckling maliciously.

'Well, at last I can rely on the support of my faithful ally, can't I?' Hawklan replied.

Gavor looked around and sucked in his breath noisily. 'Not against these odds,' he said. 'I suggest you surrender immediately.'

In silence, Gulda propelled Hawklan steadily towards the room which she had commandeered as the central command post for the Orthlundyn army. It was a large, spacious room, at one end of which was a window that occupied virtually all of the wall. The view through it was similar to that to be seen from the meeting hall, and normally sufficient light flooded through it during the day to illuminate every part of the room. Now however, the premature winter greyness dominated the room, and as the party entered, the torches burst into life. Their warm light made the scene outside even darker and filled the window with a faithful, if dim, echo of the room and its occupants.

Gulda ushered Hawklan to a low settee and, signalling Isloman to close the door, waved the others to whichever seats they might choose.

She herself sat down heavily on a seat behind a desk which gave her a commanding view of Hawklan's position. She placed her stick on top of the desk with ominous slowness and leaned forward to rest her head on her interlinked hands.

'"Andawyr and I, with others, will go another way,"' she began, quoting Hawklan's words faithfully. '"To levy the forces that must be levied if you are to be protected from the power of Sumeral and His Uhriel."'

She looked at Hawklan narrowly. 'Explain,' she said, quietly but with a purposefulness that made the three other men in the room sit very still.

Hawklan looked at his interrogator, then stretched out his legs and relaxed on the settle.

'How can it be otherwise?' he asked. Gulda's eyes widened at his replying with a question, but he continued before she could give vent to her feelings on the matter. 'A few days ago, you and Andawyr told me who I am –' He smiled. 'Who I had been, I should say. Equally importantly, you told me who I was not. I was not Ethriss. That was not something I'd ever had serious doubts about myself, nor can I pretend to any regrets about it, but it begs the real question, "Where is

Ethriss"?' He turned and fixed Andawyr with a penetrating stare.

The Cadwanwr tried to avoid the gaze by setting Dar-Volci more comfortably on his knee.

'You've been very silent about parts of your own adventures, Andawyr,' Hawklan went on. 'You've told us of your journey into Narsindal, and of your subsequent escape. And you've been honest in admitting that your Order has been remiss in its duties. But something's missing.'

Andawyr did not speak.

'You're Ethriss's chosen,' Hawklan continued. 'To you alone he gave knowledge about the Old Power. Consider. Someone, somewhere, with far less knowledge than you, I imagine, woke Sumeral and the Uhriel. Yet we hear nothing about you, with your great power and knowledge, trying to wake Ethriss and the Guardians, without whom we are probably doomed. What has happened, Andawyr? Why are Sphaeera, Theowart, Enartion, and above all, Ethriss not walking amongst us even now, determining the order of our battle?'

Andawyr looked down at the seemingly oblivious felci draped across his lap.

'I don't know, Hawklan,' he said hesitantly. 'I've made no mention of this before because I needed to know for certain who you were. And I've made no mention these last few days because I've been thinking. My knowledge is not for those who haven't the wisdom to withstand it.'

Outside, a few large snowflakes meandered down out of the greyness, casual vanguard to a mighty host.

Uncharacteristically, Andawyr sighed. 'Ask me no details, because I can give you none that you'll understand,' he said, addressing everyone. 'But Hawklan's right. On my return from Narsindal, I was . . . greatly changed. My brothers saw this and saw the truth of our danger and together we sought to contact the Guardians.' He looked up and stared at his distant reflection in the darkening window.

'It took great faith.' His voice was suddenly quiet and his remembered sense of wonder and awe overflowed to fill his listeners. 'But by some miracle we succeeded. Redeemed ourselves a little, perhaps, for our neglect.' He shrugged. 'For a moment the Guardians shared their being with us. I . . . we . . . *became* the Guardians. Knew and understood them.'

He fell silent.

'What did you learn?' Hawklan prompted gently after a moment.

Andawyr looked at him, his face slightly surprised as if expecting to find himself somewhere else.

'I'm not sure,' he said then, though no one reproached him, he added. 'It was an experience beyond ordinary words. No simple, clear-cut conversation . . .'

'Speak what comes to you, Cadwanwr.' Gulda's voice was hauntingly gentle and patient.

'They know of the danger,' Andawyr said, his face rapt with concentration. 'They too seek Ethriss, for they fear that alone they are not enough.' His eyes narrowed. 'I think they are . . . scattered,' he said. 'I think they are one with their creations. It is a great strength and a great weakness. I don't think they will ride among us in Narsindal.'

'You *know* this?' Gulda said, again with great gentleness.

Andawyr shook his head. 'Their awareness of the danger, and their search for Ethriss, yes, beyond doubt,' he said. 'But the other, the scattering, has only just come to me.'

'What do you mean, a great strength and a great weakness?' Hawklan asked uncertainly.

Andawyr frowned a little. 'If they pervade the earth, the air, and the water,' he said, his voice distant and pre-occupied. 'That would be a strength because they could not be defeated without great, perhaps total sacrifice by the Uhriel. A sacrifice I doubt they'd be prepared to make, for they are the way they are because of their all-too-human lust for being.'

Dar-volci stirred restlessly.

'And the weakness?' Hawklan pressed, gently.

Andawyr's voice was still distant when he answered. 'They will have lost their ability to . . . move, or to move quickly. To place their power wherever the Uhriel threaten. If my feeling is right, then while perhaps they cannot readily be overwhelmed by Sumeral, I fear they cannot readily come to our aid in battle.'

Hawklan frowned. 'Why would they have become this way?' he asked.

Briefly, a look of irritation passed over Andawyr's face. 'I don't know!' he said sharply. 'I . . . we . . . touched their hem; at their gift became them for some timeless moment. I couldn't interrogate. I told you it was beyond words . . .'

Hawklan raised his hand in apology and Andawyr's tone softened.

130

'Perhaps they thought Sumeral and the Uhriel truly died at the Last Battle,' he said. 'And that all that would be left to oppose would be the remains of Sumeral's teachings that lingered in men.' He shook his head. 'Perhaps they needed peace. Who can say how *they* suffered in that conflict? I've no idea, Hawklan. Perhaps it's no more than their true nature.' He finished with a shrug.

'But they look for Ethriss?' Hawklan said.

Andawyr nodded.

'Then they fear Sumeral, for all He may not be able to overwhelm them easily?' Hawklan said.

'They're not invincible. Given time, and humanity out of His path, He could do anything,' Andawyr replied.

Hawklan looked at the snow falling increasingly heavily outside, white in the light from the window. The path ahead of him seemed to be growing narrower and narrower.

'If the Guardians are searching for Ethriss, then obviously they don't know where he is,' he said, his expression apologising for the triteness of his remark. 'But where can we begin to look if they can't find him with their power and wisdom? Could he not, in fact, be dead; slain by Sumeral's last throw?'

The flakes outside twisted and swirled as a breeze moved round the tower like the wake of a silent eavesdropper.

Andawyr nodded slowly. 'Yes,' he said quietly. 'That's possible, but I doubt it. That, I'm sure the Guardians would have known. And Sumeral certainly would have felt it. No, he's alive, somewhere. Don't forget, there are many places that lie beyond the writ of both the Guardians and Sumeral; both deep underground and, it would seem, deep inside the hearts of men.'

Hawklan turned away from him. 'So even if he is alive, we've no way of finding him?' he said, his voice chillingly final.

The room became very silent. Andawyr looked at the healer's motionless figure.

Hesitantly, he said. 'I don't think that matters. I think that you'll be drawn to him, just as you were drawn to this time and this castle, and towards his ancient enemy. You are the closest of all of us to the heart of this mystery.'

Hawklan frowned. 'That's no answer,' he said angrily. 'And you know it. That's a protestation of faith.'

The room became silent and still again, filled with Hawklan's frustration. When he spoke again however, his voice was apologetic. 'Not that there's any harm in that if it sustains you, but it's not enough. Certainly not enough to risk the lives of all our finest young men and women for – not to mention the Fyordyn and Riddinvolk who'll be riding with us in due course, I've no doubt.'

'Which brings us back to where we started,' Gulda said. 'Horses and men, swords and spears. What do *you* intend to do?'

Hawklan looked round at his friends and then at their images hovering in the deepening darkness beyond the window.

For a while, he did not speak then, softly, he said, 'Loman's arrow injured Oklar profoundly. I saw it for myself and according to Arinndier's account of what that Secretary . . .' He hesitated, at a loss for the name.

'Dilrap,' Gulda provided.

Hawklan nodded. 'Secretary Dilrap said the arrow remained in his side, bleeding continuously.' He laid his hand on his sword. 'There's a blade for every heart,' he said. 'And if Sumeral has come amongst us again as a man, and surrounded Himself by mortal armies, then He is not invulnerable, and He can look to face judgement, or die again as a man.'

'*You* would call Sumeral to account?' Gulda said, her eyes widening, almost mockingly.

'If the opportunity presents itself, yes,' Hawklan replied. 'But I'd lose no sleep if I had to slaughter Him unshriven.'

Gulda wrinkled her nose disdainfully. 'And presumably you intend to ride to the gates of Derras Ustramel, like Eldric rode into Vakloss to confront Dan-Tor,' Gulda said acidly.

Hawklan ignored the jibe. 'I intend to enter Narsindal, quietly, while His attention is on the approaching armies,' he said. 'Move across it, equally quietly. And yes, enter Derras Ustramel and confront its tenant.'

Gulda opened her mouth to speak, but Hawklan raised his hand.

'I would take with me on this journey, if they wish to come, Isloman, Andawyr and our best Helyadin,' he said. 'And *none* must know of it.'

Gulda stared at him, her expression changed by Hawklan's manner from almost contemptuous dismissal to one of concern.

'Well, I suppose you've enough skills there to get you part way across Narsindal,' she said, after a long silence. 'But as for even reaching Derras Ustramel, let alone entering it and facing Him . . .' She left the reservation unfinished.

Hawklan met her gaze. 'What alternative have we?' he asked simply. Gulda did not reply.

Hawklan turned to Isloman.

'I'd rather die looking Him in the eye than hacked to pieces in some anonymous battle mêlée, or suffocating under a mound of bodies,' said the carver. 'Or worse, living to see those I love slaughtered while I stood by helpless. At least this time we'll know what we're walking into.'

Gulda shuddered involuntarily. 'Not remotely,' she said.

Isloman looked at her uneasily, and Hawklan frowned.

'What alternative have we?' he repeated, though more strongly than before.

Gulda looked at Andawyr.

'I'll go,' said the Cadwanwr, though his face was grey with fear. 'Hawklan's right. We have no alternative. In all our talking and conjecturing, you and I have contrived to avoid this truth most assiduously.'

Gulda looked down at her hands, toying idly with her stick.

For the first time since he had met her, Hawklan saw her truly uncertain.

'But to go into *His* presence . . .' she muttered.

For a moment Hawklan thought he saw her face flushed, but before he could remark it properly she had pulled her hood forward and leaned back in her chair.

'Gulda . . .' he said, concerned.

She lifted a reassuring hand. 'Have you decided how you intend to achieve this . . . confrontation?' she said out of the darkness of her hood.

Hawklan shook his head. 'No,' he said. 'Not in detail. The idea itself has only recently become clear. I thought we'd travel to the Caves of Cadwanen, learn what we could of the terrain of Narsindal from the Cadwanol, and then enter Narsindal through the Pass of Elewart. After that . . .' He shrugged. 'That's why I want to take our best Helyadin.'

Gulda nodded. 'Do you have such information?' she said, the hood turning towards Andawyr.

'Some,' the little man replied. 'Mainly of the south and south-east.' He spread out his hands in an apologetic gesture. 'The interior's very poorly mapped. No one knows even where Lake Kedrieth is exactly, other than it's in the middle of a marshy and treacherous region.'

Gulda nodded again, and turned back to Hawklan. 'And after your encounter with Oklar, you feel you can beard his Master in His own den?' she said.

Hawklan shook his head. 'After my encounter with Oklar, I have some measure of my inadequacy for such a task,' he said quietly.

'Then what do you hope to achieve?' Gulda asked simply.

'I don't know,' Hawklan said. 'But all the travelling I've done these past months has been without clear direction. To the Gretmearc, to Fyorlund, to Vakloss. All vaguely motivated, yet all apparently serving some fruitful end.' He rested his hand on his sword. 'Perhaps I'll be able to kill Him. Perhaps I'll be no more than a . . . focus . . . of some kind, for greater powers . . .' He shrugged his shoulders.

'Perhaps you'll die,' Gulda said.

Hawklan nodded in acknowledgement. 'But not easily, I hope,' he added.

Gulda eased her hood back and leaned forward again. Her face was calm once more, and slightly amused. 'So this is an act of faith then?' she said.

Hawklan glanced repentantly at Andawyr. 'Yes, I suppose it is,' he said awkwardly. 'But it's still the only alternative,' he added defensively. 'Our army will meet His. The Cadwanol will contend with the Uhriel, but someone must do battle with Sumeral Himself.'

'And you are that one?' Gulda enquired, not unkindly.

'Not by my choice,' Hawklan said with a grimace of distaste. 'But who else should it be?'

Gulda levelled a finger towards his sword. 'That sword could indeed slay Sumeral,' she said. 'Perhaps your hand could wield it truly enough. But He has many weapons, and you haven't the remotest skill with the Old Power. If He senses you coming, and He may well, with *that* by your side, then He'll dispatch you with a thought wherever you are.'

Hawklan looked at Andawyr. 'That's why I wanted Andawyr to come with us,' he said. 'He could offer us some protection.'

'He can't oppose Sumeral,' Gulda said, raising her voice.

'I didn't ask him to come with us to do that,' Hawklan replied, his own voice rising in response. 'That task, whatever it proves to be, is mine. Andawyr has hidden from Sumeral's vision before – perhaps he could do it for us.'

Gulda took a deep breath as if to launch into a prolonged onslaught, but Hawklan struck first.

'Sumeral is not what He was at His height,' he said. 'Nor, thus, His Uhriel. Had he been, He'd have swept out of Narsindal years ago instead of all this plotting and scheming.'

'Don't seek to understand His intentions,' Gulda said warningly. 'Didn't we agree that?' Her manner became severe. 'And know this. Sumeral at one tenth His strength is far beyond anything that this Cadwanwr could attain, leader of his order or not.'

Andawyr nodded.

Hawklan turned to him. 'Strength is of no avail against nothing,' he said. 'You hid from Sumeral by not opposing Him, didn't you? You avoided Him because you had the knowledge to stay silent. That's why I want you to come – your knowledge is the greater part of your true strength in this battle.'

'I'm not arguing,' Andawyr said, nodding towards Gulda. 'I've already volunteered. But you're right; silence is probably the only thing that will bring us to Derras Ustramel safely.'

Dar-volci yawned and stretched on Andawyr's knee. 'I'll come as well,' he said. 'Sounds fun.'

Gudla ignored him and turned her attention to Loman and Isloman. 'You think this is a good idea I suppose?' she said.

'No,' Isloman said. 'I think it's an appalling, terrifying idea, but I doubt there's any other, and I can't do anything other than go.' He leaned forward and spoke earnestly. 'Apart from the atrocities that have been committed to people, there's no true peace for me anywhere now if I do not oppose the . . . creature . . . who opened those mines and so defiled those ancient, resting rocks. All the work I've ever done; the knowledge I've gained; indeed, my whole life; would count for nothing if I did not set it in the balance against the worker of such an abomination.'

Gulda turned to Loman. He returned her gaze steadily.

'Stop dithering, Gulda,' he said impatiently. 'There *is* no alternative. Sumeral and His Uhriel have to be killed. Wherever Ethriss is he's beyond our finding, but we have his sword, his bow, his castle and not least his Cadwanol with us. Hawklan's the only person remotely capable of doing the job, and one way or another our Helyadin will get him to Derras Ustramel so that he can do it. All we need to discuss now are details.'

There was an ominous silence. Gulda's face had darkened

135

as Loman had spoken. Gavor whistled a vague tuneless dirge softly under his breath and looked at almost everything in the room except the two protagonists. Even the snowflakes outside the window seemed to hover.

Gulda's face contorted, at first in anger, then in an almost girlish mixture of amusement and distress.

'It's Memsa to you, young Loman, and don't forget it,' she said with a peculiarly unsteady chuckle. 'On the whole I preferred your brother's more poetic commitment, but you're not without some mastery in simple communication. I commend the clarity of your vision.'

She laughed softly, but it was an uncertain sound, and her hand came to her face to wipe away tears.

'I don't know why I should laugh,' she said. 'Ethriss knows, I can't think of anything more devoid of humour than what we're talking about.'

She sniffed noisily and, retrieving a kerchief from somewhere, finished wiping her eyes. 'When do you intend to go then?' she said.

Hawklan looked at her uncertainly for a moment. 'It *is* the only alternative, isn't it?' he asked.

'I'm afraid so,' Gulda replied, almost casually. 'And the smith's right. All we have to debate now are the details.' She stood up and stumped over to the window. As she stood there, her reflection stared relentlessly through her as if she did not exist.

'How will we keep in contact with you?' Loman asked.

'You won't,' Hawklan said. 'You'll have no idea where we are, and we'll have no idea where you are. That way neither can inadvertently betray the other.' He leaned forward. 'No one, save us here, is to have any inkling of what we intend. It's going to be a perilous journey at best, and if He's forewarned . . .' Hawklan left the sentence unfinished. 'To all enquiries your answer must be: "They've gone to seek and waken Ethriss." Neither of us can afford to waste time fretting about the other. Have no illusions; we must *both* succeed or we'll both perish. Is that clear? Commitment must be total at all times.'

Loman nodded.

'When are you going?' Gulda asked again.

'As soon as we can get over the mountains,' Hawklan said. 'And as soon as you wish after that, you can make preparations for the army to march.'

Gulda turned back from the window. 'You'll not leave before the Winter Festival, then. Or for some time after, if I'm any judge,' she said, inclining her head towards the steadily falling snow.

Hawklan smiled. 'I'd no intention of doing that anyway,' he said. 'This Festival is important; a beacon of light in the midst of the darkness in every way.'

He stood up and walked over to the window. The snow was falling very heavily now and, all around, the lights of the Castle were shining out to illuminate its silent, graceful, dance. It was a comforting and reassuring sight.

A little later, Andawyr lingered with Gulda after the others had left.

'You were suspiciously quiet, sage,' Gulda said with some irony.

Andawyr replied with dismissive airiness. 'Far be it from me to venture amongst such incisive debaters,' he said.

'*Can* you protect them?' Gulda said abruptly, brushing aside his facetious shield.

'I can help them remain hidden, I think,' Andawyr replied. 'Providing He's not actually looking for us. But at the end –' He raised his hands in resignation. 'Who can tell? I've risen to some trials recently that I'd have thought overwhelming only a year ago.' Still holding Dar-volci, he hitched himself up on to her desk. 'And the Order has changed too – remarkably. I'll send who can be spared to you when we reach the Caves. If they can bind the Uhriel, then perhaps Hawklan and I between us . . .'

He finished with a vague gesture. Conjecture about such a meeting was pointless.

Gulda's eyes narrowed. 'You and Hawklan may prove to be the best we can offer, but . . .' A look of realisation spread across her face. 'You still think he's Ethriss, don't you?' Her voice was almost a whisper.

Andawyr hesitated, as if searching for a denial, then, stroking Dar-volci thoughtfully, he said, 'I believe he carries the spirit of Ethriss within him, yes.'

'But –'

'But everything indicates he's the last Prince of Orthlund,' Andawyr continued across Gulda's interjection. 'Yes, I know that too, and I accept it. He *is* the last Prince. But I believe he also carries Ethriss.'

'You cannot know this,' Gulda said.

Andawyr nodded, agreeing with her doubts. 'But it's not completely an act of faith,' he said, looking at her intently. She raised her eyebrows questioningly.

Andawyr swung down from the desk and laid Dar-volci gently on a nearby chair. 'I've told no one here how we tried to make contact with the Guardians, and what happened,' he said.

'Would anyone have understood?' Gulda said.

Andawyr ignored the question. 'We made a great . . . silence . . . a stillness . . . the like of which I've never known,' he went on. 'In it, as I told you, we became for a little while, the Guardians themselves.' Andawyr's face twisted, and his hands fluttered with uncharacteristic uncertainty as he searched for words. 'As our . . . joining . . . with the Guardians faded, we seemed to be drawn to something; something that was either bound . . . or hidden. And as we touched it, it stirred.'

'Hawklan. In the cave,' Gulda said. 'The silence that woke him was of your making? The silence that quelled the Alphraan and so impressed that Goraidin, Dacu.'

Andawyr nodded. He pulled a chair forward and sat down beside Gulda. 'But our silence was an . . . absence . . . of conscious thought,' he said earnestly. 'It wasn't something that could impose itself on others. What Dacu and the others felt was not of our making, it couldn't have been, by its very nature.'

Gulda frowned.

'It was something from Hawklan himself,' Andawyr said, taking Gulda's hand, as if for reassurance. 'Some part of him responded to what we were doing and did the same, like the playing of one instrument will cause another lying idle, to sound. Only this was a far deeper, more intense echo of our actions if it could reach out to others like that. Especially others in such a state of agitation and fear.'

Gulda's face was tense. 'I understand,' she said softly.

'Somewhere inside that man lies Ethriss,' Andawyr concluded. 'Of that I'm certain, though it's beyond my reaching.'

Gulda's blue eyes fixed him. 'And your hope is that Sumeral's touch will rouse him?'

Andawyr met the gaze without flinching. 'Yes,' he said simply. 'Mine can't. Oklar's didn't. Sumeral Himself becomes our only hope.'

Gulda let out a long breath and shook her head. 'We hang by

slender threads,' she said. 'You may be right or you may be wrong, but Hawklan mustn't even guess at this. He must know to the depth of his being that ultimately it is he, and he alone, who must face and defeat Sumeral, mortal frame to mortal frame. The slightest hint that some other may appear to take the task from him could well destroy us all.'

Andawyr nodded vigorously, but Gulda's gaze did not release him. 'And you too must travel in the knowledge that you are probably wrong, or that you too will falter at the moment of need. Do you need my help in that? I'm not without some skill in the Old Power myself.'

Andawyr showed no surprise, but nodded an acknowledgement of this revelation. 'No thank you, Memsa,' he said. 'Like Hawklan I can only face Sumeral with hope if I'm aware of the true nature of my burden.'

Gulda reached out and took his hand.

Outside, the snow fell, its legion soldiers patiently transforming the Orthlundyn countryside.

# Chapter 10

'Live well, and light be with you all, my friends,' Eldric said, raising his glass. 'Let it shine in our hearts brighter than ever this year to see us through the darkness that threatens us.'

The hall was lit only by a few subdued torches and by the great mound of radiant stones crackling and singing in the large fireplace. They threw dancing shadows of the motionless people on to the decorated walls and ceiling.

'Light be with you, Lord,' echoed Eldric's guests.

There was a brief, expectant silence as all eyes turned towards the large fir tree which had been chosen as the centre-piece of the Festival decoration.

Then, in gold and silver, and glittering reds and oranges, wound about with blues, greens, and yellows, and all manner of colours, the countless tiny torches that bedecked the tree burst into life, starting slowly at the lower branches, and rising teasingly upwards, mingling and changing as they did so. Some danced around and through the boughs, others swirled hither and thither, until with a sudden rush they came together at the top in a dazzling circle of white light.

There was a gasp from the children and happy applause from the adults. Even the paternal condescension affected by the younger High Guards, struggling with genuine surprise, faltered into open pleasure as Commander Varak beamed broadly.

'Splendid, splendid,' Eldric shouted, clapping his hands and then extending an arm to direct his guests' appreciation towards a group of servants and retainers standing nearby. 'I haven't seen a display like that since I was a boy. Well done. It's heartening to see that such skills have been kept alive all this time.' He paused and looked again at the sparkling tree. 'Our marred Grand Festival seems to have been almost a generation ago, rather than a matter of months. Let's make amends for that by celebrating this Winter Festival as it should be celebrated, and –'

Impulsively, he took up his glass again. 'I give you another toast,' he said. 'To the next Winter Fesitival. And the one after that, and the one after that, and . . .'

His voice disappeared under a great cheering, which faded only when he sat down and waved his hand over the burdened table.

Following their lord's example, and mindful of his order, Eldric's guests sat down and began the daunting task of eating their way through the extensive Festival fare that his kitchens had laid, or more correctly, constructed before them.

For a moment however, Eldric sat back, one hand toying idly with the carved animal head that decorated the end of the chair arm, the other equally idly tilting his glass to and fro. He looked at the lights of the tree reflected in the bowl of the glass. Then, silently, and almost imperceptibly, he nodded a small salute towards a group of figurines standing on a raised dias in the middle of the table. They were not likenesses, but they represented absent friends; the tallest was meant to be Isloman, and against his legs, like a discarded shield, rested the circular disc that he had given to Eldric as a parting gift. On it was carved the picture of Hawklan riding Serian. The Queen was there too and, more sombrely, a miniature of the Warrior, the ancient statue of the exhausted soldier that stood in Vakloss to commemorate those who had fallen in battle. Here he served the same purpose.

Eldric glanced around the table. He had just completed an extensive tour of the troops guarding the approaches to Narsindalvak and found their morale excellent but, he reminded himself, there were morale problems for him here also and he must remember to keep a special watch for the tears that would surely come to some of his guests during the evening as their minds turned inevitably to loved ones who were lost forever in the battle for Vakloss.

Darek caught the movement and laid a hand on his arm. Eldric started gently out of his reverie and turned to him. Darek's eyes flicked to the figurines and his eyebrows arched significantly.

Puzzled, Eldric followed the gaze and after a brief search, chuckled to himself. Some one had unearthed a tiny model of a hen and painted it black. It stood next to Isloman in solemn representation of Gavor.

'Light be with you, dear boy,' Darek mimicked.

'Light be with you,' said the young High Guard as the duty Sirshiant loomed up out of the shadows.

The Sirshiant came to an ominous halt in front of him, and

looked down at him with exaggerated sternness.

'And with you, trooper,' he said slowly, his breath fogging the air between them. 'But let's have the correct challenge in future. Suppose I'd been a Mandroc.'

The trooper stamped his feet in the well-trodden snow. 'Well, I'd have wished him The Light, and then whacked him with my pike, Sirsh,' he replied.

The Sirshiant's mouth curled slightly at the edges and one eyebrow went up.

'Very festive of you, trooper,' he said. 'Very festive. I like my troopers to be thoughtful in their ways.'

'Thank you, Sirsh,' the trooper replied, executing another small dance and turning his gaze back to his duty, northwards.

The snow-covered landscape was radiant in the brilliant moonlight, but in the distance dark clouds shadowed the mountains and hid them from its touch. It seemed as though they were waiting, brooding, darker even than the black, moon-washed sky.

'What are we making such a fuss about the Winter Festival for this year, Sirsh?' the trooper asked. 'Lord Eldric and all coming round ordering us to enjoy ourselves.'

The Sirshiant did not answer immediately, but put his hands behind his back and blew out a long steaming breath to the north.

'Because the Lord Eldric's got a lot of sense, lad,' he said eventually. 'As you'd have heard, if you'd listened to him. Him and the others are doing their best to bring the country together again. Sooner or later we're going to have to go up there' – he nodded towards the mountains – 'and winkle those beggars out of Narsindalvak. Then, if I'm any judge, we're going to have to go into Narsindal itself and find *Him*, if we're not going to be looking over our shoulders forever. We can't do any of that unless the country's ready and with us, and the Winter Festival's part of that.'

The trooper nodded dutifully. 'Would it help if I went back to camp and did my bit for steadying the country right now?' he suggested. 'I can't see any hordes teeming out of the mountains tonight.'

The Sirshiant turned and eyed him. 'You're not here to look for teeming hordes, lad,' he said. 'You're here to look out for me, in case, bewildered beyond repair by having to deal with incorrigible jesters such as your good self, I wander off, howling, and, falling down, do myself a hurt.'

'Ah,' said the trooper, nodding sagely and dancing again.

The Sirshiant continued. 'Bearing Lord Eldric's injunction in mind, however, I *will* allow you to sing a Festival Carol to yourself, as you march conscientiously up and down. But not too loud. People are trying to enjoy themselves back at camp and I don't want them thinking we're being attacked.'

The trooper contented himself with a reproachful look and, hugging his pike to him, slapped his gloved hands together.

'On the other hand,' the Sirshiant continued. 'It *is* the Festival, and a certain member of a certain group has just come back to say that the pass is still well-blocked, and all our . . . neighbours . . . are busy celebrating themselves after their own fashion, so –' He nodded towards the camp.

The trooper grinned and set off without any further comment, but he had scarcely gone five paces when he stopped. Turning back to the Sirshiant, his face was serious. 'I've been watching, Sirsh,' he said. 'But I didn't see anyone coming back.'

The Sirshiant nodded. 'Don't worry, trooper, neither did I. That's why he's Goraidin, and we're not. Enjoy your party. Light be with you.'

'Light be with you.' Oslang held his hands out in front of himself and then snapped his fingers.

A small star of light appeared just above his outstretched palms. It hung motionless in the soft, subdued torchlight that filled Urthryn's private chamber.

'Take it,' he said.

Sylvriss cast an uncharacteristic 'should I?' smile at her father, who shrugged a mighty disclaimer.

'Is it hot?' she asked.

Oslang laughed. 'No,' he said. 'Go on. Take it.'

Sylvriss's tongue protruded between her teeth and, hesitantly, she reached out to take the glittering star.

As her hand closed about it, it slipped between her fingers at the very last moment. She gave a little cry of surprise and drew her hand back.

'Try again,' Oslang said, encouragingly.

Sylvriss, her face glowing in the torchlight, and her eyes sparkling in this newly made starlight, looked at Oslang in friendly suspicion, then reached again for the twinkling light.

As before, it floated quietly and smoothly away from her curling fingers and then from the second hand which was lying

143

in ambush. There followed a brief flurry of increasingly frantic arm waving by the Queen, but the light moved through it all with unhurried calm.

Urthryn laughed at his daughter's frustration, as her hands eventually fell back into her lap.

'No,' Oslang said, his eyes teasing. 'Like this.' And his hand came out and gently wrapped itself about the waiting light. As he held out his gently clenched fist, the light shone out from between his fingers with seemingly increased brilliance.

When he opened his hand, the star rose into the air and floated towards Sylvriss.

She looked from her laughing father to the smiling Cadwanwr, then abruptly, her hand shot out and seized the light.

However, she was so surprised at catching it that with another cry of surprise she immediately opened her hand and released it again.

Urthryn roared, provoking a look of indignation from his daughter.

Oslang smiled, then taking hold of the hovering star he placed it gently on Sylvriss's still outstretched palm, closing her fingers around it gently as he did so.

'Now clap your hands,' he said.

After a slight hesitation, Sylvriss did as she was bidden.

A brilliant cascade of twinkling lights burst out from between her fingers and rose up to dance in front of her face. As she reached out to them, they swirled and danced around her hand.

'Beautiful,' she said.

Oslang bowed, then waved his hand. The hovering sparks scattered and spread themselves through the cellin boughs that traditionally decorated the walls of the Riddinvolk homes during the Winter Festival.

There they glittered and shone, amongst the prickly dark green leaves and bright red berries.

'A fine trick, Oslang,' Urthryn said. 'It's a pity the Old Power can't be confined to such uses.'

'Indeed,' Oslang replied, leaning back into his chair and closing his eyes. 'But who would confine the confiner?'

Urthryn nodded and let the debate die.

For a while, the three sat in companionable silence. Sylvriss, large now with Rgoric's child, exuding a gentle, enigmatic calm which seemed to fill the room; Urthryn, content that the shores of Riddin were guarded as well as they could be, was as pleased to be spending the Festival with his daughter as he would have been celebrating with his line; and lastly Oslang, luxuriating in the lavish hospitality he had received from his hosts. He patted his straining stomach. Such over-indulgence, he thought. But there was barely a whiff of true contrition to mar his satisfaction. He must have a word with Andawyr when he got back about the Cadwanol being a little more . . . enthusiastic about the Winter Festival in future.

Gradually Oslang felt himself falling into a doze. He was vaguely aware of distant revelry seeping into the room, and Urthryn and Sylvriss bestirring themselves to go and join it.

'Will you join us, Oslang?' said a voice, also somewhere in the distance.

'Later,' he managed to reply, but he heard his answer being greeted with laughter, and a reassuring hand was laid on his shoulder.

Roused a little, he felt Sylvriss moving past him on the way to the door. Turning, he made a gesture that would have sent stars shimmering through her hair for the rest of that evening, but as he looked, the radiant stones flared up and the sheen of her black hair made him lower his hand.

Best confined, he thought. You'd paint a rose, you donkey.

'Light be with you truly, lady,' he mumbled as he slipped deep into a happy slumber.

'Light be with you, Girvan Girvasson.'

The Line Leader turned and peered into the darkness at the approaching rider. The figure increased the light of his torch a little to illuminate his face as he came alongside.

Girvan smiled. 'Brother,' he said in some considerable surprise. Then he leaned across to embrace him.

'What's drawn you from your relentless pursuit of idle leisure down at Westryn,' he said, still holding him.

Girven laughed. 'Our Festival Helangai, brother,' he said. 'I saw your Line had volunteered for coast watch duty to avoid being soundly beaten again so I decided to seek you out and offer you yet more instruction in the subtler arts of the game.'

Girvan smiled and shook his head. 'You're quite right,' he said. 'Avoiding your Line in the Helangai is always uppermost in my mind, as it is with anyone else who's survived so far in life without being kicked in the head by a horse.'

Girven beamed, and his brother ploughed on.

'However, I'd happily have my people trounce them, were it not for two facts. Firstly, we're on duty, and secondly, as you may have noticed, it's pitch dark. Though I appreciate that most of your Line can't tell night from day.'

Girven grinned broadly and then peered intently out across the shore towards the lights of the distant look-out boats extending to the horizon and beyond.

'Ah,' he said, after a moment, in mock surprise. 'You're right. I suppose that means we'll just have to share your watch and our meagre supplies with you.'

Girvan bowed graciously, partly to hide his face; it was a generous gesture on his brother's part. 'How meagre are your supplies?' he asked.

Girven looked at him significantly. 'As meagre as usual,' he replied.

Girvan cleared his throat. 'Have you got any of grandfather's . . . liniment . . . with you,' he said, affecting casualness.

'A little,' Girven answered, in the same vein.

Girvan smiled expectantly. 'Then welcome to the coast watch brother,' he said. 'And Light be with you and your wondrous Line too.'

'And grandfather,' Girven added reproachfully.

'Oh yes,' Girvan chuckled. 'Light be with Grandfather especially.'

'Light be with you, Ffyrshht,' burbled the drunken Mathidrin as Dan-Tor appeared unexpectedly around the corner.

The trooper's two supporters, marginally the better for drink, sobered abruptly and closed ranks quickly, if unsteadily, to support him; a griping fear returning control of their minds to them for the moment. Their suddenly pale faces heightened the flush of the wine in their cheeks and made them look like ghastly marionettes. Wide-eyed, they managed to salute their Master.

Dan-Tor strode past, and the two men, almost unable to believe their good fortune, desperately dragged their oblivious colleague away with much fearful hissing for silence.

Dan-Tor's face was unreadable, but the old and unexpected greeting had struck him as powerfully as Hawklan's arrow, and he found himself unable to deal out the punishing response that such insolent familiarity would normally have earned. The scuffling sibilance of the departing drunkards mingled in his ears with his own tightly drawn breath.

Strangely uncertain and disorientated, he turned off the broad curving corridor and ascended the long stairway that would take him to his private quarters. No Mathidrin trooper guarded this part of the tower fortress, nor even any invisible snare woven from the Old Power. Both precautions were unnecessary; the aura of an Uhriel was protection enough.

With an angry wave of his hand he doused the globe that dutifully attempted to light as he entered. As its brief glimmer faded sulkily, an ancient, dreadful memory bubbled up from the dark and awful depths of the well of his history.

'Light be with you, daddy,' piped the childish voice. Dancing in its wake came other memories; a cherished face, glistening dark hair, opened arms, trusting eyes and, worst of all, the touch of a trusting heart.

His eyes opened wide in horror as this tiny flame rose from the grey ashes of his long crushed humanity to shed its cruel, penetrating light. Instinctively his every resource leapt to defend him, with a ferocity that would have served to protect him from an assault by Ethriss himself.

For a moment he swayed uncertainly, his whole being tense with the centuries of guilt and remorse that this small light threatened to illuminate. Wilfully he extended his Power into the arrow in his side until a physical agony so possessed his body that all else dwindled into significance.

Then it was over. As he withdrew the Power, his pain faded, and all that remained of the desperate memory was a livid afterglow. He sat down awkwardly.

Light be with you! The greeting raked across him. Damn the man, he thought. He should have consigned him to darkness where he stood, but . . .

He breathed out irritably. His natural inclination had been to forbid all celebration of the Winter Festival, but Urssain and Aelang had prevailed upon him.

'Morale is low enough, Ffyrst. It would be a needless provocation unless it served some clearly visible purpose.'

Now, a quieter part of him mused, his response to this small incident had been a salutary demonstration of his vulnerability, and a reminder that his armours could not be too many.

Vulnerability. To have been brought so low by the mindless ramblings of some drunken oaf after surviving the giving of the news of the loss of Fyorlund to Him was a disconcerting irony.

For at Derras Ustramel, there had been no mighty outburst;

no sudden black extinction. Only a brief, slow glance from those eyes, and a briefer touch of that chilling will. You are my Uhriel, it said. You must ever learn. Then, a silent, icy, dismissal.

Looking up, Dan-Tor peered out into the darkness over the mist-shrouded land to the north, doubly hidden now by the heavy snow-burdened clouds.

Learned? What was to be learned? That these inconsequential humans were poor material for His work; always dangerously flawed and unreliable? The face of Rgoric came to him. He needed no lessons there. And how could he protect himself from the vagaries of random chance? Then, blasphemously: and we would have held Fyorlund if You would have unbound me.

Dan-Tor looked round, as if this treacherous thought alone might have brought Him there to deliver a belated retribution.

When he turned back again to the window, the darkness outside was at one with the darkness inside, and for a moment he felt his extraordinary loneliness.

As if responding, a dim, hesitant glow came from the globe.

As the images of the room began to form under its cautious touch, Dan-Tor found something blurring his vision, some cold, unfamiliar irritation in his eye.

Then, sustaining this time, came, 'Light be with you, daddy.'


'Light be with you all,' Loman half-shouted, with a dismissive wave of his hand as the last few sentences of his speech disappeared under a mounting roar of cheers and applause.

'Bravo, bravo,' cried Hawklan and Isloman, applauding ironically as the red-faced smith flopped down onto his chair between them, laughing. 'A most moving final toast to our feast,' Isloman added with heavy graciousness.

Loman had no time to reply to his false praise, however, as, slapping him on the shoulder, Isloman said, 'Duty calls,' and stood up and wandered off, threading his way through the many guests who were now bustling around clearing the long rows of tables and pushing them to the sides of the hall.

'Wait a minute. Wait a minute.' Gavor's agitated voice nearby rose above the mounting din. He was hopping along pecking desperately at a plate that Tirilen was dragging across the table in an attempt to remove it.

'You'll never fly again, you feathered barrel,' she said.

'I enjoy walking,' Gavor replied without looking up, as he placed his wooden leg resolutely on the plate to impede its further progress.

Tirilen conceded defeat and relinquished the plate. 'Good,' she said. 'You can join in the dancing then.' And with that she began clearing various other dishes from round around the raven, though not without some anxious sidelong glances from him, and a great deal of fretful wing flapping.

'Gavor must have eaten three times his own weight,' Andawyr said, leaning over to Hawklan.

'Gavor has many and capacious appetites,' Hawklan replied.

Andawyr frowned. 'I think cavernous might be a better word,' he said.

Further comment about Gavor was curtailed, however, as the entire table on which he was sitting was pushed aside by a crowd of enthusiastic guests.

With the same abandon, the crowd shooed Hawklan and the others back until the middle of the hall was clear. Then a clapping, foot-stamping, chant began.

'Is-lo-man. Is-lo-man.'

Just as it began to involve virtually everyone in the hall, Isloman appeared through a wide arched doorway.

'Good grief,' Arinndier exclaimed. 'What's he carrying?'

Isloman was carrying a large circular stone held high above his head, while behind him a small procession of apprentices carried other stones of various sizes.

'It's a traditional hearthstone,' Hawklan replied to the Lord, smiling. 'Watch.'

At the centre of the hall, Isloman cautiously bent down and lowered his burden to the floor. Despite his gentleness, the floor shook as he released the hearthstone. Then the apprentices filed forward and laid their own burdens on it. As they did so, the torches in the hall gradually dimmed, and the babble of the onlookers died away almost completely.

When the last stone had been placed, there was a considerable pile, and after making one or two adjustments, Isloman took something from a pouch at his belt and struck one of the largest stones with it.

Immediately, the stone glowed white, and as Isloman stepped back, the whole pile burst into a brilliant incandescence, sending a great shower of white, orange and yellow sparks of long-held sunlight cascading upwards into the high vaulted ceiling, where they swirled and fluttered like wind-blown stars.

The light from the stones sent the shadows of the watchers dancing all across the walls, and a great cheer went up, not least from Agreth, Andawyr and the Fyordyn.

'Magnificent,' Arinndier shouted to Hawklan above the noise as he clapped his hands high.

Hawklan took the Lord's arm and pointed towards the large fir tree that stood at the far end of the hall. That was a symbol the Fyordyn were familiar with and, as Hawklan pointed, the countless tiny torches that decorated it burst into life, as at that same moment similar torches flared up in Eldric's castle far to the north.

Arinndier's noisy approval faded into a broad but slightly sad smile.

'I haven't seen anything like that since I was a boy,' he said, shaking his head. 'I don't know how we've come to celebrate the Winter Festival in such a half-hearted manner over the years, but I'll do *my* best to see we bring it back to its old splendour when all this is over.'

Hawklan nodded and urged his friends forward as the rest of the guests in the hall made their way to the blazing stones or to the glittering tree as fancy took them.

Andawyr looked up through the ornate streamers that had been hung across the high ceiling like a great, colourful spider's web.

'May I?' he asked, looking at Loman and casting another glance upwards.

Loman smiled and held out his hands in a silent invitation to his guest to do his will. Gleefully, Andawyr clapped his hands, then taking the cord from around his waist he flicked it out and upwards. As the cord straightened, a cloud of brilliant white sparks appeared around it. Unlike those that had burst out of the radiant stones, however, these rose slowly up into the darkness, spreading out gracefully as they did, until they covered the vaulted ceiling like the stars on a sharp frost-clear night.

The sight was greeted with an awed silence.

Even Andawyr's glee faded, as he looked at his hands and then up at his handiwork. 'Anderras Darion is a holy and wonderful place, Hawklan,' he said, very softly. 'More wonderful than I could ever have imagined.'

Then applause and shouts of approval rose up from the

guests and, fastening his cord about himself again, the Cadwanwr beamed. 'It's a long time since I've done a party trick,' he said. 'But they should see the night out.' Then placing his tongue between his teeth as an earnest of his concentration, he squinted narrowly upwards again, and snapped his fingers. Immediately, one of the stars streaked a bright white line across the ceiling.

A gasp came from the watchers and Andawyr laughed and clapped his hands again.

'Show-off,' came a deep voice from by his feet.

Andawyr laughed again. 'Nonsense, Dar,' he said. '*This* is showing off.' And he shook his extended hand over the felci. A small cascade of sparks fell from it and spread themselves over the felci's fur.

'They're not hot,' he said, by way of reassurance to the spectators. 'They're quite harmless.'

And certainly, Dar-volci seemed unperturbed by the event.

'Ratty, dear boy, you look splendid,' Gavor said, flapping down to land in front of the felci. 'They go with your eyes.'

Dar-volci looked at him steadily for a moment and then inclined his head slowly to look up at his benefactor. 'Very droll, Andawyr,' he said. 'Very droll. But you should know better by now.' Then, returning his attention to Gavor, his mouth bent into a sinister smile. 'Light be with you, crow,' he said, and, like a wet dog, he shook himself vigorously from nose to tail. The sparks flew off in all directions, showering most of the people standing nearby.

The main recipient, however, was Gavor, and as Dar-volci ended his impromptu display with a vigorous scratching to dislodge a few more sparks from behind his ear, he looked at the raven critically.

'Very fetching, Gavor,' he said. 'I think I'll keep a few after all.' And he rolled over in the sparks that were scattered over the floor.

Gavor extended a wing and peered along it. Its blackness shimmered now not only with its natural iridescence but with brilliant silver lights, that shone and glinted in the flickering glow of the radiant stones.

'You're right,' he said. 'They're most attractive.' And spreading his wings he rose boisterously into the air with a raucous cry.

Hawklan watched his friend swooping and diving about the hall in great silver streaked arcs, then he looked down at

151

Andawyr. There was a slight frown on the Cadwanwr's face.

'What's the matter?' Hawklan asked.

Andawyr shook his head. 'Nothing,' he said.'Nothing important. It's just . . .'

He stopped and Hawklan raised his eyebrows by way of encouragement.

'It's just that I wonder how he can do that,' Andawyr finished.

'Do what?' Hawklan asked.

'Shake off the lights,' Andawyr said.

Before Hawklan could speak, Andawyr turned to him. 'You try it,' he said, indicating the lights that were now decorating Hawklan's trousers. Hawklan looked down and then, balancing on one leg, began dusting the tiny lights away. But they did not move. Instead, they seemed to pass through his hand. Carefully he tried to pick one up between his finger and thumb, but again, without success.

'I can see them but I can't feel them,' he said. 'I don't understand. They just fell off Dar-volci.'

Andawyr grinned. '*You* don't understand,' he said. '*I* don't understand. He's always doing things like that. Things he shouldn't be able to.'

Dar-volci looked up at him and blew a slow gurgling raspberry. 'You mean like this?' he said, and reaching out he picked up one of the lights from the floor and placed it fastidiously in the centre of one of his incisors.

'How's that for an infectious smile?' he said, standing on his hind legs and beaming malevolently. The star twinkled mockingly at Andawyr whose face crumpled in frustration.

'*How* do you do that?' he complained, offering Dar-volci his two clenched fists.

Dar-volci ignored the plaint and dropped back on to all fours again. 'Do excuse me,' he said, smiling again. 'I must mingle.' And with a sinuous wriggle, he was gone.

Hawklan could not help but laugh at Andawyr's discomfiture.

'He's right. I should know better than to play tricks on him by now,' the little man said, unsuccessfully trying to brush the splashed lights from his own robe. 'I always come off worst.'

Suddenly, above the hubbub of the milling guests, a drum beat sounded; a single steady beat. The noise in the hall fell and the guests began to move away from the centre of the floor expectantly. Hawklan took Andawyr's arm and led him aside.

From the same doorway through which Isloman had entered, came a solitary drummer, clad in a traditional carver's smock, simply decorated with designs of the cellin plant with it spiky green leaves and its red berries. He was stepping out a leisured march to his own slow beat.

Several paces behind him, moving at the same stately pace and similarly dressed, came a man and a woman playing a low, nasal, droning ground bass on long pipes.

As the little procession moved into the hall, two more pipers emerged, playing a slow, jerking melody that bobbed and jigged over the drum beat and ground bass like the flames that danced from the radiant stones. Higher pitched than the other pipes and also double-reeded, their sound was strangely harsh, but far from unpleasant, and drivingly powerful in its rhythm and intensity.

Some of the audience began a soft clapping to the drum's beat.

Then came two more drummers. With drums clamped under their left arms, their short, double-headed drumsticks flickered rippling embellishments to the pulse of the first drummer.

The clapping increased and the playing became louder.

Agreth, Arinndier and the other Fyordyn, captivated by the sight and sound of the players, began to join in with the clapping, and then found that the crowd around them was beginning to sway from side to side. Nods and smiles from their neighbours encouraged them to join in that also.

The music grew louder still, though without changing tempo, and on every fourth beat the audience began to add a resounding foot stamp to their clapping. One or two shrill cries went up.

Arinndier felt his arms tingle with excitement at the sound, and into his mind came the thundering Emyn Rithid that the Fyordyn had unexpectedly sung in acclamation of Sylvriss at Eldric's mountain stronghold. It seemed to him that the two tunes were in some way the same.

Then, abruptly, it ended and he almost lurched forward into the sudden silence. Another great cheer went up.

'What was that, Lord?' Jaldaric asked Arinndier, his face also flushed with exhilaration.

'I don't . . .' began Arinndier, but the remainder of his admission was lost as the drummers began again, this time with a bouncing rhythm that would make any foot tap. More

153

musicians ran into the hall and whoops and yells rose up from the guests, as couples began to run into the middle of the hall to line up for what was obviously to be a boisterous dance.

Arinndier tried to play the old man and turned discreetly to seek sanctuary with Rede Berryn who was seated at the edge of the hall; but a female form intercepted him.

'I have no one to dance with, Lord,' Tirilen lied, smiling and holding out her hands to him.

Jaldaric and Tirke too had little time to ponder the etiquette of selecting a partner as they were cut out from the mêlée by two girls moving like skilled sheepdogs.

Even Dacu and Tel Mindor failed to merge into the background sufficiently to escape yet two more swift and sharp-eyed predators.

Dacu turned to a grinning Isloman and flickered a plaintive hand signal to him as he was led away. Isloman looked at his brother earnestly. Loman furrowed his brow in concentration then, pursing his lips, shook his head like a death judge. Isloman looked back to Dacu and clamping his fist to his heart, pronounced sentence. 'Think of Fyorlund, soldier,' he shouted.

And thus the celebration continued; under Andawyr's starlit sky, faces, happy, mischievous, besotted, moved in and through the lights and shadows of the firelight and the glittering tree, bound in a swirling mosaic of music and dance and laughter. At the touch of the Spirit of the Winter Festival, rivalries and differences, fears and ambitions, all disappeared; the old became young as they swung through the dances, and the young became sage and sober as they viewed such transformations – though not for long. Anderras Darion was indeed a holy and wondrous place, but it was Ethriss's greatest creation that was celebrating his greatest gift to its full.

Escaping the dance, Hawklan flopped down by Gulda. She was chuckling to herself about some splendid confusion that Tirke had caused by moving left when he should have moved right. In common with everyone else, her face was flushed and happy. It had a haunting quality.

How old are you? Hawklan wanted to ask. How beautiful were you once? But the questions laughed at him. She was as great an enigma as he, but like him, whatever she was, or had been, whatever strange mysteries lay beneath her relentless personality, she was here *now*; whole and unencumbered.

As if reading his thoughts, Gulda turned to him and smiled

radiantly. 'A happy thought this, healer,' she said. 'You have a sure touch.'

Hawklan bowed in acknowledgement of the rare praise. 'No spectre would dare visit this feast,' he said.

Gulda nodded and then looked around at the guests. Agreth was in earnest, hand-waving conversation with a rather large, well-hocked, lady. Arinndier, red-faced, and mopping his brow, had reached the sanctuary of Rede Berryn's altar and was clinging to it for the time being, though he exuded some gameness still. Dacu and Tel Mindor were back to back, facing overwhelming odds, and Jaldaric and Tirke had been taken captive somewhere.

Overhead, in the gold-tinted darkness, a star-bedecked Gavor glided hither and thither like a silver, moonlit kingfisher, swooping down incessantly to encourage or torment the dancers as the whim took him, or to offer trenchant observations to some of the many debates that were proceeding amongst the watchers. Mirroring him on the ground, Dar-volci rolled and scampered, occasionally standing on his hind legs and emitting hoots and whistles which seemed to betoken considerable approval.

All around, figures moved, shadows flitted, and the wall carvings danced and changed at the touch of the flickering firelight.

Gulda took Hawklan's hand and squeezed it affectionately.

Later, Hawklan slipped quietly out of the hall. As he walked away down the long corridor, it seemed to him that the laughter and the music was ringing through the whole castle.

The impression did not leave him even as he stepped out into the cold night on top of the great wall. Myriad coloured torches all about the towers and spires lit the snow-covered roofs and transformed the castle into a strange and magical landscape. And though the silence was as deep as the night was black, the whole seemed to vibrate with some irrepressible inner energy.

Hawklan closed the door behind him gently and, pulling his tunic about him tightly, stepped forward through the crunching snow towards the edge of the wall.

Peering out into the darkness he could see lights in Pedhavin below where those villagers who had not come to the castle were celebrating the Festival.

Then, very softly, as if to greet him, but reluctant to disturb the night stillness, a mellow carillon of bells began to ring out somewhere in the darkness overhead. Hawklan turned and looking up, smiled. No one knew what power rang the bells of Anderras Darion.

A silvery giggle drew his attention down again, and something struck him lightly. Looking down, he saw it was a snowball. Children, he thought as he peered intently into the shadows to seek his assailant. But he could see nothing until a tiny figure came forward a little, a slight, indistinct silhouette.

'Light be with you, Hawklan,' said voices all around him.

Hawklan started and then smiled again. 'And with you, Alphraan,' he said. 'Won't you join our celebration?'

More giggling surrounded him. 'We have and we are,' came the reply. 'It is such a raucous and unholy din, we can hear it in our heartplace. But it is joyous beyond measure. Thank you. We seem to be ever in your debt.'

Hawklan laughed. 'I feel no debt and I waive such as you feel there might be,' he said. 'That is my Festival gift to you.'

'You burden us further, Hawklan,' the voices said, though full of laughter. 'But as part repayment we shall bring the song from our heartplace to your Round Dance.'

Hawklan bowed graciously, and there was more giggling, but when he looked up, the tiny figure was gone.

Overhead, the bells were continuing their soft carillon.

Hawklan stepped back inside again, kicking the snow from his shoes and slapping his arms about himself as the winter cold began to make itself felt.

'Ah. You're there,' said a voice as he closed the door. 'I wondered where you'd sneaked off to.'

It was Isloman. 'Come along,' the carver went on. 'They're waiting for you to start the Round Dance.'

Hawklan's entry into the hall was greeted by loud and ironic cheering which he received with wide open arms. As he strode forward the crowd parted and reaching the glowing fire, he stretched out his arms sideways and placed his hands on the shoulders of his neighbours. They did the same, and very quickly the inner ring of the dance was formed.

Then, like ripples from a pebble thrown into a still pond, further outer rings were formed until almost everyone in the hall was standing holding his neighbour, and waiting.

Hawklan nodded and the lone drummer began the steady beat with which he had begun the celebration. With each beat, the dancers took one step, to form a simple pattern of three in one direction and one back. Adjacent rings moved in opposite directions.

As the pipes and the other drums began to play, the steps became higher, and the foot stamping louder. Sturdily supported by their neighbours, Andawyr, Agreth and the Fyordyn were borne to and fro, though they eschewed the increasingly elaborate steps being executed by some of the Orthlundyn. Once again Arinndier felt the surging power of the Emin Rithid ringing through his mind over the jerking rhythmic tune of the pipes.

They *are* the same, he realised.

As the dance reached its final stage, the sound of the drums and pipes seemed to change, to swell out and rise up to ring round the vaults of the star-strewn ceiling. Without breaking the step of the dance, Hawklan looked up, and as he did so, a sonorous chorus of voices filled the hall, weaving around and enhancing the pulsing rhythm of the musicians.

And wordless though the chorus seemed to be, it was a great paean of thanksgiving and joy. Mingling somewhere in its depths, beyond simple hearing, Hawklan thought he heard the poignant happy calls of the wolf cubs he had orphaned.

'Alphraan, Alphraan.' The word whispered around the hall and rose up to be woven into the texture of the song.

Gulda leaned forward and twining her hands over the top of her stick, rested her chin on them.

She smiled at the happy, colourful spectacle circling the hall.

'You do not dance, Memsa,' said a soft voice close by.

'My heart does, Alphraan,' she said. 'My heart does. And so does Anderras Darion's. Thank you for the gift of your heartplace.'

'Ah . . .'

'And light be with you, Sound Carvers,' she added softly. Then, looking again at the laughing, singing guests moving in concert around the hall, she said, 'Live well, and light be with you all, my friends.'

# Chapter 11

The storm was appalling, and had been for several days. The watch boats had long been driven ashore and, shortly after they had returned, the Line on coast watch had given up any pretence at patrolling as the screaming wind sweeping in from the sea had made it difficult for even the horses to keep their feet. Besides, the rain and spray which were being hurled horizontally across the shore were so dense that it was almost impossible to see the next rider, let alone the distant horizon.

Girvan laid his writing stylus on one side and looked around the fisherman's cottage that was serving as his temporary headquarters. It was echoing with the muffled sounds of the storm raging outside, but it was warm and friendly though, with its low open-beamed ceiling and enormous clutter of seafaring relics and ornaments, it was very different from the traditional Riddin dwellings he was used to being billeted in. Then again, it only reflected the fisherfolk themselves; they too were warm and friendly, but different; in some ways not Muster people at all, though they pulled their weight fairly enough. There was always that reserve about them; a quiet, inner strength. Ironically, it made them particularly good with horses, but they didn't seem to have the relish for the animals that the Riddinvolk normally had.

After his several weeks watching the sea and sharing a little of the lives of these seafolk, Girvan felt he was beginning to understand this stillness. A rider had a partnership with his horse, and a knowledge and regard for his land. But the sea was different. True, there was respect and knowledge, but there was also fear – no, not fear . . . more a dark, deep insight. There could be no partnership of equals between man and sea. It was brutally indifferent to those who rode and harvested it, and its power was awesome. Yet it was this very indifference that gave the seafolk such a grim measure of their true worth.

Girvan glanced covertly at his host and hostess. They were sitting on either side of the wide fireplace which was aglow with clucking radiant stones. The wife was working patiently at a delicate embroidery, while the husband sat sucking on a long-dead pipe, staring into the fire. Strange habit, smoking, Girvan thought. It was no horseman's habit for sure, yet somehow it added to the fisherman's aura of calm preoccupation.

As if sensing the Line Leader's observation, the man spoke, without turning from the fire. 'This is a bad storm, Girvan Girvasson. It has an unnatural feel to it.'

Girvan sat up and looked at the man intently, noticing as he did so that the wife had stopped her sewing. 'What do you mean?' he asked simply.

The man did not reply immediately, but took his dead pipe from his mouth and stared at it as if for inspiration. He shrugged a little unhappily. 'It has an unnatural feel to it,' he repeated. 'It blows too long, too hard. It has no . . . rhythm . . . no shape.' He looked up at the watching Line Leader. 'It carries the wrong smells,' he concluded.

Girvan looked down at the note he had just been penning. It was a routine report to Urthryn at Dremark. ' . . . This pounding storm has an oddly unnatural quality about it . . .' he had been on the point of deleting this eccentric and seemingly irrelevant observation, but if this man, with his deep knowledge of the moods of the sea, had sensed something untoward, then he too must be content to let his instincts guide him.

The name Creost hung unspoken between the two men.

'I agree,' he said. 'I'll send to Urthryn immediately and tell him our feelings. Let him and Oslang make of it what they will.'

The fisherman nodded, then stood up. 'Where are your men?'

Girvan looked a little surprised. 'In their billets I imagine,' he replied.

The fisherman nodded again. 'Come along,' he said, reaching for his voluminous waterproof coat that hung behind the door.

'Where?' Girvan asked.

'To rouse your men, and our own,' the fisherman answered. 'We must go to the high banks and cliffs and do our duty.'

Girvan hastily scribbled a note to complete his report and, sealing it, placed it in his pocket. 'What can we possibly see in this weather?' he said.

The fisheman shrugged. 'We belong out there, Line Leader,' he said. 'Not in here. We should be listening to what the storm tells us.'

Girvan cast a longing glance at the fire, then reluctantly stood up. The fisherman smiled as he followed Girvan's gaze. 'Keep the hearth warm, my dear,' he said to his wife, laying an affectionate hand on her shoulder then, throwing the Line Leader his cloak, he beckoned him towards the door.

Outside, the storm was fully as bad as it had seemed from the inside, the wind being all the more cutting for the near-freezing water it was carrying. Underfoot squelched the chilly remains of the earlier snowfalls which refused to thaw fully under this icy onslaught. Used though he was to many weathers, Girvan could not forbear grimacing. The fisherman did the same. 'I've ridden out some foul weather in my time, but never anything like this. Come along.'

Soon a small crowd of fishermen and Muster Riders were huddling in the lee of the village's meeting hall. There was little cheery banter. Girvan used his authority with the Riders.

'Yes, I know we'd all rather be sat by these kind peoples' firesides, but if both Cadmoryth and I feel something's amiss, then we must get out into the storm and listen. We *are* on duty, and we maintain the discipline of the Line, for all we're on our feet. Is that clear?'

There were some desultory murmurs of agreement which Girvan knew was as near as he was going to get to enthusiasm that night. He felt in his pocket for the report to Urthryn.

'Lennar,' he said, peering into the group. The girl shuffled forward, a shapeless dripping mound of unwillingness, and Girvan thrust the document out to her. 'You're duty runner tonight if memory serves me. Mount up and get this to the Ffyrst as quickly as you can. Move inland. Don't take the coast road. And I want you to tell the Ffyrst when and where this weather changes. It's important. Do you understand?'

'No, but I'll do what you say,' the girl replied, brightening a little at the prospect of riding away from this benighted and chilling place where the land seemed to be almost as wet and cold as the sea. She took the report from Girvan and, with a brief farewell to her friends, scuttled off into the storming night.

'Where should we go?' Girvan said, turning to Cadmoryth.

The fisherman answered without hesitation. 'Out along the cliffs,' he said. 'It's an onshore wind, there's no danger, and there's the best view by far.'

Girvan nodded. 'Not that there'll be much to see,' he said.

'Nevertheless, we'll see whatever's there,' the fisherman replied.

The path to the cliff top was steep, though not very long, and the untidy procession slithered up it in comparative silence. Once at the top, they spread out in a ragged line, fishermen and riders paired off and staring into the howling wind.

'I can scarcely keep my feet,' Girvan shouted, catching hold of Cadmoryth for balance as a powerful gust struck them both. More used to keeping his feet under such conditions, the fisherman smiled and took hold of Girvan's arm to sustain him. But his concentration was out to sea. 'This is wrong,' he said, his face close to Girvan's. 'I feel it more than ever now. This is no natural storm.'

'Then it's Creost's work,' Girvan said, though the strangeness of his own words made him feel disorientated. 'Could the Morlider sail on us under cover of this kind of weather?'

Cadmoryth shook his head. 'I wouldn't think so,' he said. 'Certainly, no one would choose to sail when it's like this. It's different if you're caught in it by accident, then you *have* to sail, but only from wave to wave, enough to keep afloat. You can't look to sail to any greater purpose than that.'

Girvan scowled, painfully aware that he could not begin to think in terms of sea warfare. If Creost could indeed cause such a storm, what would be the reason for it. Was it simply to clear the sea and the shoreline of watchers? If so, it had been singularly effective, but then, as Cadmoryth had indicated, who could bring boats ashore and land men in such conditions?

A shout interrupted his reverie. Turning, he was surprised to see the lights of a rider cautiously negotiating the steep path. He stepped forward to meet the newcomer. It was Lennar.

'What's the matter?' he shouted, half concerned, half angry that his messenger had returned.

Lennar bent forward, water cascading off the hood of the large cape that some fisherman had lent her. 'The storm faded away, barely a mile inland,' she said. 'I thought you'd want to know before I rode on.'

Girvan patted her arm. 'Wait,' he said, then, placing his fingers in his mouth, he blew a penetrating whistle and gesticulated to the nearest watchers. 'Get back to the village, mount up and head north to where the cliff drops straight into the sea,' he said to one pair. 'And you go south,' to another. 'Take care, but be as quick as you can.'

'What are we looking for?' one of the men asked.

'Just find out what's happening to the weather,' Girvan answered. There was an urgency in his voice that forbade any further debate, and the riders left quickly, like Lennar only too happy to be away from this awful blustering watch.

Within the hour, both parties were back, however. The weather in the north and south was calm.

Girvan showed no emotion when he heard the news, but he felt his stomach churning as if he were about to vomit. 'Give me the report,' he said to Lennar. Dutifully, she handed it to him.

Crouching down to shelter the document from the rain, Girvan wrote for a few minutes, then re-sealed it and returned it to Lennar.

'Take someone with you,' he said. 'Full speed, maximum care. Take remounts.' Then, turning to the newly returned riders, he said, 'Raise the local Lines.'

'What's happening, Girvan?' said Lennar, her face pale in the torchlight.

'Just ride, girl,' Girvan replied. 'As well and as quickly as you can.'

As Lennar and her companion made their way carefully back down towards the village, Cadmoryth turned to Girvan. 'Behind the storm comes the Morlider?' he asked.

'I can see no other reason,' Girvan replied. 'This is the only stretch of shore for miles where boats could land. And where the cliffs become too steep, north and south, the storm abates.'

Cadmoryth wrapped his arms about himself and moved forward towards the cliff edge.

Abruptly, the storm was over. Girvan and the other watchers stood motionless on the cliff top. Tentatively the Line Leader lifted his hand to his head, as if unable to believe that the awful noise had indeed ended.

Below them, the sea, its recent demented fury forgotten broke prosaically over the long shoreline of the broad bay, and to the east, a clear cloudless sky lightened. But where a dark sea should have met the watery yellow sky with a sharp, clear, edge, ominous ragged silhouettes waited. Girvan felt his chest tighten with fear. He screwed up his eyes in an attempt to see more clearly.

'It's them,' he heard Cadmoryth say needlessly. Morlider islands! Swept close inshore under cover of the storm.

Girvan looked at the fisherman. 'How far away are they?' he asked, reaching out for something normal.

Cadmoryth frowned. 'Perhaps only half a day,' he said softly after a long silence.

Girvan's body was shaking and uncertain with the ceaseless battering it had received through the night, but Cadmoryth's simple statement started a trembling moving through it that was quite another response. Half a day! He pushed his hands deep into the pockets of his bulky waterproof cloak, and turned to one of his men nearby.

'Take two riders and make full speed to the Ffyrst. Tell him the Morlider are here, perhaps half a day off-shore. The local Lines have been roused and we'll start evacuating the local villages immediately. We'll be ready to give them a welcome, but . . .' He left the sentence unfinished.

As the man ran off, Girvan turned to Cadmoryth. 'Your people had best get to horse, fisherman,' he said gently.

It was not unusual in Orthlund for the days following the Feast of the Winter Festival to be characterised by widespread inactivity.

This year was only different in that lethargy reached almost epidemic proportions, with further snowfalls conspiring with over-indulgence to impede all forms of physical effort.

Orthlund's great healer fared little better than his charges for the first few days, but towards the end of the week the relentless clump of Gulda's stick prowling the corridors of Anderras Darion began to remind him, and others, of the virtues of diligent application to useful tasks.

It was not, however, the immediate threat of Gulda's caustic presence that galvanised Hawklan abruptly, nor the knowledge that the spectre which had avoided the feast was still there to be faced. It was an Alphraan voice speaking softly in his ear.

'Hawklan, come quick,' it said, simple and clear, though in a tone filled with nuances of terrible urgency.

Hawklan jerked into wakefulness and screwed his eyes tight as the torches, sensing his awakening, burst into life.

'What is it?' he managed, swinging out of bed, almost without realising it, and sleepily groping for his clothes.

'Come quickly,' the voice said, more urgently than before.

'Where?' Hawklan said, as he began to struggle with buttons and buckles.

'Follow. Bring your Sword,' came the reply, and the sound

163

that had guided him and his companions through the tunnels in the mountains rang out again in his small, spartan room.

'Where?' Hawklan insisted, a little more firmly.

There was a brief pause, then: 'Into the mountains. Come quickly.'

'Into the mountains,' Hawklan muttered to himself in some exasperation as he pulled off his tunic and reached for several layers of more appropriate clothing.

'What's the matter?' he asked. 'Are we being attacked? Has someone been hurt?'

'No, but come,' said the voice. 'Before the wind changes. It is most important.'

Hawklan stopped dressing and scowled at this enigmatic reply. 'I can *feel* that,' he said, his exasperation mounting. 'But I need to know where I'm going, and for what, so that I can take supplies. I don't know how you survive in the snow, but humans tend to die very easily.'

The sound faltered. 'Supplies are being prepared,' the voice said after a moment.

Briefly, Hawklan considered further interrogation but rejected the idea; urgency was humming all around him. He nodded and began dressing again. 'Waken Loman and Isloman,' he said.

'They have,' came the voices of the two brothers simultaneously. Hawklan started and glanced around involuntarily to see if they had both entered his room unheard, although he knew they had not. Carrying their voices thus was a device the Alphraan had not used before, but he chose not to remark on it; the unspoken sense of urgency was growing.

'What about Gavor?' he said, dragging on his boots.

There was a slightly embarrassed pause in the sound. Hawklan looked up.

'*Wake* him!' he demanded. 'A little profanity won't hurt you.'

Before any reply came, there was a knock on his door.

'Come in,' Hawklan shouted, irritably. The door opened and Isloman walked in, fully dressed for a long trek through the mountain snow and looking not dissimilar to a large jovial animal. 'Loman's packing supplies,' he said by way of greeting.

Barely a minute from his bed, Hawklan rebelled. 'What in thunder's going on, Isloman?' he said.

Isloman shrugged. 'I know as much as you do,' he said.

'They woke me and Loman up and just told us to start getting things ready. Two or three days they said – perhaps. But they seemed so anxious about something we didn't feel inclined to argue.'

Hawklan's irritation could not sustain itself. Something serious had happened beyond a doubt. He nodded. 'Are we going to be allowed to eat before we start on this errand?' he asked, buckling on his Sword.

Isloman grinned and patted his pocket. 'Apparently we must eat as we walk,' he said. 'Although the amount you put away at the Feast should keep you going for another three days at least.'

Hawklan raised a menacing forefinger. '*That* is a calumny, carver,' he said. 'Delicate and discerning are the words you were searching for to describe my appetite.'

Isloman gave a nod of agreement. 'Would you like some help with that belt?' he said.

Within the hour, the three men had left the village and were heading up into the mountains following the Alphraan's guiding sound. Daylight was easing its way through a uniformly grey sky, and as it became brighter, so the snow-covered mountains came increasingly into view. They were magnificent, spreading into the misty distance like a jagged frozen ocean, though all three travellers knew that for all their beauty the winter mountains held dangers far greater than those to be encountered in summer.

The sound pulled them forward relentlessly, but Hawklan reproached their unseen guide. 'We're travelling as quickly as we can,' he said. 'The going's difficult. Too fast and we'll be exhausted very quickly, and if one of us fails and is injured then we'll never reach wherever it is you want to go. We're trusting your guidance; you must trust our pace.'

There was no reply, though the guiding note seemed to become a little more patient.

Some while later they were joined by Gavor, who landed clumsily on Hawklan's head.

'I hope someone's got a reason for all this,' he said in the manner of a strict school teacher roused from a clandestine slumber.

'Ask your little friends,' Loman said.

Gavor studied the grey sky. 'We're not speaking at the moment,' he replied with haughty indifference. 'Their intrusion was most . . . inopportune.'

165

All three men laughed. 'They can't be all bad, then,' Loman said.

Gavor glowered at him indignantly and then gave a martyred sigh. 'It's very difficult coping with people so lacking in delicate sensibilities,' he said. Then, thrusting a wing in Hawklan's face, he said in an injured tone. 'Look, dear boy. All my stars have gone.'

'Thus passes the glory of the world,' Hawklan commiserated insincerely. 'But I'm sure all your friends love you for what you are, not your vulnerable exterior.'

Loman gave a snorting chuckle but Gavor ignored him. 'Thank you, dear boy,' he said to Hawklan. 'I see there's some hope for humanity yet.' Then, he leaned forward towards Loman. 'You might take some solace in that yourself, smith,' he said. 'Coming into the mountains looked like a bear, with your fur coat and all.' He paused and peered intently downwards. 'And what in the world have you all got on your feet?'

'Snowshoes,' Loman said, warily.

Nearly falling off Hawklan's head in his anxiety to examine the footwear, Gavor flapped his wings to regain his balance and then laughed loudly. 'You *do* cheer up a deprived soul, dear boys,' he said. 'I really don't know why you don't practise a little harder and learn to fly. It's not difficult. I've done it since I was barely an egg. Walking does seem to present an awful lot of strange problems, and some *very* strange solutions.'

Hawklan interrupted Gavor's merriment. 'Walking presents even more problems when there's a large over-fed bird standing on your head,' he said. 'Would you like to fly on and see if there's anything unusual ahead?'

'Delighted, dear boy,' Gavor said, still laughing, and he glided down to land on a small stretch of exposed rock some way in front of the party. There he took three or four painstaking high-stepping strides in cruel imitation of his friends, prompting Loman to bend down to gather up a snowball. Before the smith could implement his intent however, Gavor stretched out his great black wings and flapped up into the cold winter air, laughing raucously.

'Game to the bird, I think,' Isloman said, banging his snowshoe against a rock to clear it of clogged snow.

No one disagreed.

Gavor's arrival seemed to have lessened the unease that had been pervading the three travellers but, on his departure, the urgent note of the guiding sound returned to dominate their thoughts.

Abruptly it changed direction and led them from the Riddin path they had been following and up a narrow gulley that could only lead them higher and higher.

Hawklan looked at his friends questioningly. 'Alphraan,' he said. 'You'll make our journey easier if you'll tell us where we're going.'

The note faltered and became full of apology. 'None may know, yet,' said a voice suddenly, very softly. Then it was gone and the guiding sound returned.

'That's all we're going to be told,' Isloman said, adjusting his pack. 'Let's just watch where we're going and keep putting one foot in front of the other.'

This they did, for the remainder of that day. Gavor returned, but with no news, and their steady walking took them further and further from the normal tracks of the mountains, and progressively higher.

As the light began to fade, they found themselves on top of a wide ridge. Hawklan stopped and looked round. Everything was still and calm and beautiful. Unusually, there was not even the slightest breeze blowing. He remarked on it.

'It's a good job,' Loman said prosaically. 'This can be a cold place even in summertime when the wind's blowing.'

'You know where we are?' Hawklan asked.

Both Loman and Isloman nodded. 'It's been a long time,' Isloman said. 'But we've both been up here when we were young, and the only place this ridge leads to, is there.' He pointed ahead to a distant peak disappearing into the clouds.

Hawklan found he was looking upwards. 'It looks high,' he said.

'It *is* high,' Isloman said, looking concerned. 'The highest local peak by far. And we can't go a great deal further.'

'Is it difficult to climb?' Hawklan asked.

Isloman shook his head. 'No,' he replied. 'At least I don't think so. Though neither of us ever reached the top; the air's too thin. What can they want of us here? Are you sure this is safe?'

'I feel no danger,' Hawklan replied. 'All I feel is their urgency. But I don't see that we've any alternative but to continue, do you?'

Both men shook their heads. 'No,' Loman said. 'But we'll have to camp soon, the –'

167

'There is no time for rest.' The Alphraan's voice interrupted him. 'Hurry. We will guide you, have no fear.'

The three men looked at one another. There was a note in the voice that could not be denied. Loman looked up at the darkening sky and checked his torch.

'Come on,' he said resignedly. 'I doubt any of us would be able to rest anyway.'

Hawklan glanced at Isloman, who nodded, and the three set off again. As they moved slowly forward, the ridge became progressively steeper, and the cloud covering the mountain moved down to greet them.

Soon they were climbing through the mist, guided by the Alphraan's urging note and stepping carefully by the light of their torches. Increasingly they stopped to rest. It had been a long day and the way was becoming not only steeper but rougher, obliging them to relinquish their snowshoes to scramble over the rocks. The Alphraan allowed them little respite, however, their guiding tone if anything becoming more urgent still.

'Enough,' Loman said eventually, flopping down on a rock and breathing heavily. 'This is madness. We're going too fast and we're getting too tired. One of us is going to have an accident. Look, even Gavor's looking seedy.'

Hawklan turned his torch on Gavor. The raven did indeed look subdued, standing in the snow with his head bent forward as if he were listening for something.

'What's the matter,' Hawklan asked him.

Gavor did not reply. Concerned, Hawklan bent forward and picked him up, but still he made no response.

'Alphraan,' Hawklan said, an edge to his voice. 'Is this your doing?'

But the question was ignored. 'Come quickly,' said the voice. 'It is only a little further. They need you, but they doubt.'

Hawklan scowled. 'Enough,' he said, echoing Loman's plaint, his voice grim. 'I asked: Is this your doing?'

The guiding note stopped abruptly. Hawklan looked around. In the sudden silence, it seemed that the darkness beyond the torchlit dome of mist was closing in upon them, as if some great weight were pressing down. Somewhere, he heard . . . sensed . . . a sound. A vaguely familiar sound.

Suddenly, Gavor stirred in his arms, then wriggled free violently. 'This way,' he said hoarsely, and flapped off into the darkness.

Hawklan swore, and all three turned up their torches. But Gavor was gone, swallowed up in the night and the mist.

'Come on,' Hawklan said, turning to the others. But Loman seized his arm.

'Where, Hawklan?' he asked. 'We've nothing to guide us now. We've been walking steadily uphill since before sunrise.' He slapped his chest with his hand and took a deep breath. 'It's already getting difficult –'

Abruptly, Hawklan held up his hand for silence. 'Douse the torches,' he said. Loman scowled at the interruption but after a brief hesitation did as he was bidden. The darkness closed around them like some ancient predator.

'What is it?' Loman whispered.

'I thought I saw something,' Hawklan said. 'But –'

'You did,' Isloman interrupted. 'Look.'

Gradually, as his eyes adjusted to the intense darkness, Hawklan noticed a hazy glow some way ahead of them. Cautiously he started to move forward.

'Careful,' Isloman said. 'There are . . . figures . . . moving about.'

Hawklan screwed up his eyes, but his vision was not that of the Orthlundyn carver and he could distinguish nothing but the faint glow. He wondered for a moment if Isloman could be seeing the figures that he, Hawklan, had seen gathered around Gulda at their first meeting. But there was no driving compulsion here as there had been in the cold, damp, glen.

'Who are they?' he asked softly.

He sensed Isloman shrugging. 'I can't see clearly enough,' he said. 'But I presume they're whoever the Alphraan wanted us to meet, let's go and see.'

Carefully, using only a single dimmed torch to show them the ground, the three men moved slowly through the crunching snow towards the glow. As they neared it, Hawklan began to distinguish the figures to which Isloman had referred, though for some reason they seemed to become no clearer as he drew nearer. The effect was strangely disorientating, especially when he saw also that prowling up and down in front of them, stark and clear-cut, was Gavor.

Hawklan screwed up his eyes again to make some sense of what he was seeing and realised abruptly that the mist around the figures was denser by far than the mountain mist that surrounded him and his friends. It was as if it were contained

169

in some way. Further, it was the source of the light. It seemed almost as though it was a vague doorway into some bright, private mansion.

'This is he?' said a voice. It was soft, gentle, and slightly muffled and it came from one of the figures.

'This is he,' replied the Alphraan, their voice, as ever, clear and disembodied and without any direction.

'Who are you, and what do you want?' Hawklan said, moving towards the figures.

'Come no closer . . . Hawklan,' said the voice. 'The mist you see keeps our worlds apart. We have moved as deep as we dare and need it for our protection. If you pass through it you may perish, as would we if we came to you.'

Hawklan stopped. 'Who are you?' he repeated.

One of the figures stepped forward, and Hawklan could see the others reaching out nervously to restrain it.

'I am Ynar Aesgin,' it said. 'One of the Soarers Tarran of Hendar Gornath, Margrave of this land. These are my companions in flight. 'We are –'

'Drienvolk,' Hawklan completed the sentence. The memory of the great cloud land he had seen floating through the spring sky over Riddin returned to him vividly. Involuntarily, he glanced upwards as if expecting to see the huge bulk of the sky island towering above him, but all was darkness.

A flood of questions surged into his mind, but all that he could voice were, 'How did you come here?' and 'What do you want?'

'We came here because that was the will of Sphaeera,' said the figure.

'But . . . Viladrien have never come to Orthlund before,' Hawklan said, still uncertain what he should be saying.

'Not in countless generations,' Ynar said. 'But many things are not as they were. Not now that *He* is awake again, and His Uhriel are turning to their old devilment.'

Hawklan put his hand to his head. Were not even the citizens of the skies to be allowed peace? 'Does He assail you also?' he said.

Ynar nodded, but before Hawklan could ask any further questions, he said, 'The Alphraan tell us you are a great prince, wearer of the Black Sword of Ethriss and key-bearer to Anderras Darion. They say you have made whole their shattered family and struck down Oklar himself with an arrow from Ethriss's bow. Is this true?'

There was an unexpectedly plaintive, almost desperate note in his voice.

'It may be that I was once a prince,' Hawklan answered quietly. 'The prince who led the Orthlundyn to their doom, if you know the tale. But now I am a healer and the Orthlundyn know no ruler, nor have since that time.' There was no response from the Drienvolk but Ynar was leaning forward slightly as if listening intently, Hawklan continued. 'It's true that I carry Ethriss's sword and hold the key to his castle, but how that has come to pass is beyond my knowledge. As for the Alphraan, it was they who brought their own family together, and while it was I who fired the arrow that wounded Oklar, this was the smith who made it,' He indicated Loman, then Isloman. 'And this the man who saved my life by bearing me on a Muster horse from the horror of Oklar's wrath.' And finally Gavor, still pacing fretfully up and down at his feet, 'And this the friend who made Oklar show his true nature.'

The figures in the mist milled around, seemingly in some excitement. 'What of Oklar now?' asked one.

'I don't know,' Hawklan replied. 'He is pinioned in some way. It seems he could not free himself of the arrow, and he did not use his Power when the Fyordyn launched their army against him. Now he skulks in the tower fortress of Narsindalvak. The Fyordyn watch him, and we are preparing an army to ride into Narsindal and face Sumeral Himself.'

There was more agitation amongst the Drienvolk.

'In our pain and distress we doubted you, Alphraan,' said Ynar. 'But this man – these men – are fired by Ethriss's spirit beyond doubt and their telling seals the truth of your own words. Forgive us. How can we atone?'

'The pain of our own ignorance is all too near for us to offer you any reproach, old friends,' came the Alphraan's voice. 'And the music of your great land echoes now through our Ways to put *us* eternally in *your* debt.'

As Ynar turned back to him, Hawklan repeated his earlier question. 'Who assails the Drienvolk, Ynar?' he said.

'Dar Hastuin assails us, Hawklan,' the Drienwr replied simply. 'He rides the Screamer Usgreckan again and has been amongst us for many years.'

'Amongst you?' Hawklan said, instinctively resting his hand on his sword hilt. He felt Loman and Isloman becoming suddenly alert behind him. Was this, after all, another subtle trap, with the Alphraan as innocent dupes?

'Amongst some of our people,' came the reply, hastily, as if noting the concern the remark had caused. 'He has corrupted and possessed the minds of many of our kind on other lands, but not yet ours.' Suddenly there was defiance in the voice. 'Nor will he, though he hurl us to the depths of the ocean.'

Hawklan flinched from the passion in the voice; it betrayed the desperation of a man prepared to lose all in order to destroy his enemy. Yet it was uncertain. Childlike almost?

'Your voice tells me you're sorely pressed,' Hawklan said. 'I know nothing of your . . . lands or your people, but we are allies against a common foe; tell me how you will be attacked and how we can help.'

There was a mixture of gratitude and gentle amusement in the Drienwr's reply. 'We are both at some extremity here, Hawklan, and we cannot even touch let alone help one another,' he said. 'But you help us more than you know by your very presence. And your news that Oklar is harmed and that the peoples of the middle depths are rising to oppose Sumeral will bolster us in our last days.'

Hawklan looked round at Loman and Isloman in concern, then he stepped forward towards the strange mist. 'Your *last* days? Do you go to war looking only to your defeat?' Suddenly, and somewhat to his own surprise, his voice became angry. 'War is chance run riot. Where the merest gesture, the shifting of a pebble, the braying of a horse, may tilt the balance. You cannot wield your sword while your hearts and minds are so bound.'

Except for Ynar, the figures in the mist retreated a little. 'Hawklan,' he said. 'You admit to knowing nothing of us or our lands. We will be attacked in ways you cannot begin to understand. It is –'

Hawklan cut across him. 'I understand that if you are defeated, then Dar Hastuin will own the skies and will be free to add his power to that of Oklar and Creost which is already ranged against us.'

The Drien bridled. 'You do not *understand*, Hawklan,' he said, his voice rising. 'Like Creost with the Morlider Islands, Dar Hastuin has committed the ultimate blasphemy. *He moves the lands to his own will*. He can command the higher paths and destroy at his whim any land that opposes him. Either binding them with his legions or . . .' He hesitated, as if having difficulty speaking. ' . . . crushing them in the depths. So far chance has kept us from him, but he knows of us and even now

172

is seeking us out. When he finds us . . .' He left the sentence unfinished.

Hawklan hesitated. He did not indeed understand, he realised, but the word blasphemy hung in his mind. He recalled Agreth's telling of the interrogation of the Morlider Drago by Oslang. To Drago, the moving of the islands had been a matter of mystery and awe; to these Drienvolk however, it was a blasphemy, and blasphemy implied choice.

'Can you not move your own land?' he said quietly.

There was no reply.

He repeated the question.

Still there was no reply. Gavor flapped his wings noisily in the cold air. At the sound, Hawklan suddenly felt as if he were one of the figures on the other side of the glowing mist, looking through at this strident black shadow of a man from the choking middle depths, who had had the affrontery to stand in judgement over them.

'You are right,' he said contritely. 'For all we are both human, we are too far apart for us to understand one another truly. I should not intrude. You have your own choices to make in the light of your own ways and your own needs.'

He bent down by Gavor, who stopped fidgeting and looked up at him. 'But war tests many things. It is the horror of Sumeral's gift that we must accept it to oppose it. Healer though I am, I know that I must be as He, to defeat Him. If I am fortunate I hope I will stay my hand from excess in victory. That tiny hope is all that will distinguish me from my enemy when we finally meet. So it may have to be with you. Many valued things have to be set at hazard.' Then, Andawyr's conclusion about Creost returned to him unexpectedly. 'But remember,' he said. 'If Dar Hastuin uses his Power to move your lands then he is that much weakened in himself.'

Ynar moved as if to speak, when suddenly there was a small commotion behind him. Hawklan caught ' . . . the paths move . . .' spoken urgently.

'We have little time, Hawklan,' the Drienwr said. 'Sphaeera wills us away, and it is already dangerous for me and my companions to stay here; we have been too deep too long. We will ponder your words. We will ponder your heart. But we have not your strength. Wish us . . . good fortune . . .'

'Light be with you,' Hawklan said impulsively.

'Ah,' came the response. 'So we are as much alike as we are different.' Then, shocked. 'But this is of no import. In burdening you with our cares I'd forgotten. We came to warn you that –'

Ynar staggered suddenly before he could finish, and the mist shifted and swirled violently. Some of the figures in it seemed to be disappearing – upwards, Hawklan thought, though he could not see their passing. He felt a cold breeze on his cheek. When he looked at the hazy figure of Ynar again, he saw anxious hands reaching out to draw him away. The Drienwr, however, was resisting their pull and extending his arms out towards him.

Again on impulse, Hawklan drew his Sword and, taking hold of the blade, thrust the hilt towards the reaching figure. There was no resistance when the Black Sword entered the mist, but it became white, brilliant and shining. So bright that Hawklan had to turn his eyes away.

The Drien's right hand closed around it, and the air was suddenly filled with the sound that only Hawklan and a quiet Riddin child had heard on a sunny spring day months ago; the song of the Viladrien. Now, however, it was vast and joyous and seemed to fill the entire sky.

'Wait!' It was Gavor. Abruptly, his great wings started to thrash violently, throwing up flurries of snow, and slowly he rose and flew into the mist. As he did so, he too became white, and the movement of his powerful beating wings seemed to become infinitely slow, their great pulse matching that of the song of the cloud land. As Hawklan watched, he saw Ynar extend his left hand and Gavor alight on it. They were talking, Hawklan thought, but the scene was almost dreamlike and it seemed to Hawklan that Ynar was moving upwards with Gavor, although he could still feel the Drien's light but strangely powerful grip on the sword.

Then the mist was gone though, like the moment of the onset of sleep, none of the three watching men noted the moment of its passing.

Hawklan found himself holding the blade of his Sword, its blackness glinting in the subdued torchlight that had illuminated the last part of his journey. He was flanked by Loman and Isloman, gazing uncertainly upwards into the darkness.

For some time, no one spoke, as if fearful of disturbing even the memory of what had just passed. Then the mounting breeze that had presumably carried the Viladrien away, buffeted them, and Hawklan started out of his reverie.

'Gavor,' he cried out. 'Where's Gavor?'

His cry galvanised his friends, and both of them set up a great shouting.

Hawklan clenched his teeth in anxiety as he thrust his Sword back into its scabbard. What had happened to his friend? Then, following in the wake of that question came the memory that the Drienwr had said that he had come with a warning.

For a moment Hawklan was overwhelmed by an appalling sense of loss. His friend taken; some warning unheard; who knew what allies were perhaps lost now? And all through his angry impetuosity. He did not dare to look at Loman and Isloman for fear of the reproach that might lie in their eyes.

'Look.' Isloman's voice reached into his darkness. He was pointing into the sky.

Hawklan drew his hood about his face to protect himself from the cold wind. The sullen clouds that had covered Orthlund for the past days were now scudding across a sky tinged yellow with moonlight. In the distance, and high above them, marked by Isloman's pointing hand, was the dark form of the Viladrien; vast among the breaking clouds, and with its upper surface glittering with countless lights.

The three men stood spellbound at the sight.

'Such things we've seen, Hawklan,' Isloman said after a long silence. 'I'd be a rare carver if I could catch one tenth of that vision.'

Though buoyed up briefly by the majestic sight, Hawklan lapsed again into angry self-reproach.

'And a rare captain I'd be if I'd listen to people instead of lecturing them,' he said. 'Gavor's gone who knows where, and whatever the Drienvolk had to tell us is gone too.'

Before Loman and Isloman could speak however, something struck Hawklan's head a glancing blow, and fell into the snow a few paces away. A familiar voice swore out of the darkness, then came: 'Sorry, dear boy.' Loman turned up his torch to reveal Gavor struggling to right himself in the soft snow.

'At last,' he said churlishly. 'You might have done that sooner. 'I'm not an owl you know.'

'Where've you been?' Hawklan said, crouching down and holding out his hand for the bird. 'I thought you'd gone with Ynar.'

Gavor's truculence vanished. 'I did, in a way,' he said distantly. 'He took me where all Sphaeera's creatures should go. I saw it, Hawklan. Saw it. Sphaeera's . . . Anderras Darion. Great mansions and halls, towering and open . . . and

175

the lights and colours – such a land . . . and such people . . . soaring everywhere –'

Hawklan picked him up gently. 'But you were gone only a few minutes,' he said.

'No, I was there for hours,' Gavor replied.

Hawklan looked at him thoughtfully and then abandoned his interrogation. 'Did you hurt yourself when you landed?' he asked.

'No, no,' Gavor answered.

'I'll carry you anyway,' Hawklan said. The two friends looked at one another, and Gavor nodded.

'We'd better leave and find a camping place lower down before this wind gets any stronger,' Loman said. 'This is a dangerous place.'

'We shall be with you,' came the Alphraan's voice, as the three men turned up their torches.

Their descent was slow and cautious, each knowing that tiredness and gravity were treacherous downhill companions. Gavor remained silent and warm inside Hawklan's cloak, and when they finally made camp they ate a simple meal and lay down to sleep with barely a word.

The next morning a clear blue sky and brilliant sun displayed the white peaks and valleys surrounding the three travellers, and they broke camp and continued their descent in good spirits. Gavor in particular seemed unusually boisterous and was soon floating high above the sweeping valleys.

Despite the beauty of the scene however, Hawklan's thoughts were dominated by his conversation with the Drienwr. It seemed that Dar Hastuin had power over the Drienvolk as Creost had over the Morlider. Of the Uhriel, only Oklar so far had been successfully resisted. But what did it mean? Creost's intended assault on Riddin could be understood, but what did Dar Hastuin's power in the air mean for the Orthlundyn and Fyordyn armies?

With difficulty Hawklan managed to set his concerns aside. Ynar had been right, he didn't understand; indeed, he *couldn't* understand. He knew nothing of the Drienvolk, nor, he suspected, did anyone else, perhaps not even Gulda. Gavor probably did, but could he explain it? Such little as he had mentioned was strangely confused.

But he could not set aside the knowledge that the Drienvolk had sought him out to warn him of something and he had thrust it from Ynar's mind with his unexpected anger.

176

Eventually he voiced his concern. 'Alphraan, do you know what Ynar tried to warn us of?'

'No, Hawklan,' replied the Alphraan. 'When our ways met there was great happiness, but we came to you when we felt their pain. They gave us no warning, we –'

'Oh, I know about that, dear boy,' Gavor interrupted, landing softly on Hawklan's shoulder. 'I thought you'd heard Ynar telling me. You should've asked.'

Gulda had been told by the Alphraan about the sudden departure of Hawklan and the others the previous day, but on questioning them had received no answer other than, 'We may not tell,' overlaid with sounds of reassurance.

Unable to interrogate the Alphraan, she had taken the rebuff with an ill grace, and had eventually retreated to the deserted wall where she had stood defying the ubiquitous whiteness like a rock in the ocean.

Motionless and seemingly oblivious to the cold wind that was blowing over the snow-covered landscape, she stood for a long time rapt in who knew what thoughts.

Suddenly she started. Hawklan was speaking to her.

'The Alphraan carry my voice, Gulda,' he said. 'We are needed in Riddin. Begin the levying of the army and select those who can march across these mountains.'

Gulda cocked her head on one side, as if testing the sound she was hearing then, without speaking, she turned and walked towards the door that would lead her down into the Castle.

# *Chapter 12*

Pandemonium was well established when Hawklan and the others returned to Anderras Darion on the day following their meeting with the Drienvolk, and it continued steadily for the next few days. On receiving Hawklan's strange, disembodied instruction, Gulda had immediately sent messages to all parts of the country and gradually the chosen contingents were beginning to converge on the great Castle, bristling with arms and supplies, and with just enough enthusiasm and curiosity to keep their alarm at bay.

At a brief council of war, Hawklan told of the strange meeting and of Ynar's message; the Morlider islands and a great armada were gathered off the northern shore of Riddin.

'It'll be a difficult journey,' Loman said. 'A forced march across the mountains and right across Riddin.'

No one disagreed. 'I don't think we've any alternative,' Isloman said. 'If what that Morlider – Drago – said about his people being united and learning to fight with some semblance of discipline is true, then the Muster's going to be hard pressed especially in this weather. Good infantry can stand off cavalry and defeat it if their nerve holds. And if the Morlider have numbers *and* Creost . . .' He left his conclusion unspoken.

By now familiar with the open speaking of his hosts, Agreth was only mildly defensive at the suggestion that the Muster was anything other than invincible. 'It's a fine infantry that'll stand long against our charges,' he said. 'But I agree, if they have the advantages you suggest, then we'll be hard pressed.'

Later, alone with Andawyr and Gulda, Hawklan mused on the route that the Morlider Islands were apparently taking.

'Why would they come so far north?'

'They probably think they can establish a good base before the Muster catches wind of them,' Gulda suggested unconvincingly. 'It'll also give them the mountains to their back. Make it harder to flank them.'

Hawklan pulled a wry face. 'It also gives them the Pass of Elewart at their back, and it cuts off the Cadwanol,' he said, looking at Andawyr.

Andawyr shrugged. 'I doubt Creost knows the Cadwanol

178

still exists, let alone where,' he said. 'At least I hope so. More importantly, it occurs to me that they might be expecting reinforcements down the Pass.'

It was a grim thought. Hawklan scowled. 'It's also an escape route into Narsindal for Creost if anything goes wrong,' he said. Then, slapping his knees impatiently, he stood up. 'Still, I think we'll be wasting our time worrying about Creost's strategic thinking. If he's expecting reinforcements then all the more reason we get over there quickly, and if he's got any escape routes planned let's make sure he can't use them.' He looked at Andawyr darkly and his voice was suddenly cold. 'He's your province, Andawyr. According to Dar-volci, the Alphraan have their . . . ways . . . open as far as the Caves so presumably you can send a message of some kind. Rally your people's every resource. I want Creost bound or dead at the end of this venture.'

With difficulty, the Cadwanwr held Hawklan's menacing gaze, but he did not reply.

Hawklan walked to a window and stared out. 'If Riddin falls then not only do we lose a massive cavalry force, which will be vital in Narsindal, we'll have to tie down most of our own army simply guarding our borders. We'll just have to meet Creost and the Morlider head-on and crush them utterly. Whatever the cost of success it can't begin to compare with the cost of failure.'

Gulda grimaced. 'What about your own plans?' she said, turning away from Hawklan's cruel summary.

'They're unchanged,' Hawklan said. 'In fact, moving to oppose the Morlider gives us a legitimate reason for being in that area if Sumeral has spies there. We'll have to judge the situation as we find it, of course, but if all goes well, we should be able to slip away to the Caves and thence to the Pass at some juncture.'

Then the uproar faded and a substantial part of the Orthlundyn army stood ready at a temporary camp just outside Pedhavin, fired by Hawklan's determination and anxious to begin its desperate trek across the mountains.

'You have our best there,' Gulda said quietly as Hawklan prepared to mount Serian. He nodded but did not speak. Instead he looked up at the Castle Wall towering high above him, massive and solid against the grey sky. It was snowing a little and a few flakes settled on his face and slowly melted. For a moment a terrible pain showed.

'The Alphraan will tell you of our progress while we're in the mountains,' he said hoarsely. 'I leave the disposition of all the other troops with you and Lord Arinndier. See what reply Eldric sends to our news then head into Fyorlund as soon as you can. The people know what to do if things go wrong. The castle's well stocked and self-sufficient . . . if . . .' His voice faded.

Gulda smiled a little and shook her head. 'We've been over this ten times, Hawklan,' she said. 'We all know what to do. Take care.' Then she stepped forward and embraced him. As she released him, Hawklan felt his arm held in a merciless grip and his eyes pinioned on her blue-eyed stare. 'Ethriss go with you, prince,' she said. 'You and I will meet again at Derras Ustramel. We'll end this horror either dead or with His head impaled on your Sword.'

Then, without further comment, she turned and stumped back towards the Castle Gate. Hawklan watched her go, shaken by the terrible passion of her unexpected declaration. He was uncertain how long he stood there but suddenly he found Tirilen standing in front of him. She had been saying farewell to her father and her uncle and she was weeping, though not pettishly or with a clinging heart. A healer herself, she knew it was the only release she had for the measureless sorrow and pain she felt, and she knew not to deny it.

Hawklan wanted to say something, but he found no words that would do anything other than rattle vainly in the cold winter air. Instead, he leaned forward and kissed her forehead. She placed an arm around his neck and held him for a moment.

'Take care,' they both said simultaneously. Then Tirilen turned to follow Gulda, and Hawklan swung up onto Serian.

'Carry me to my army, Muster Horse,' he said. 'My legs unman me.'

The journey through the snow-clogged mountains proved to be quite as difficult as had been envisaged. The path to Riddin was not designed to accommodate an army, and the several thousand troops were soon spread out along valleys and ridges in a thin, rambling line.

'I'm glad we don't have to guard our flanks in this terrain,' Hawklan said to Isloman as he reached a prominence and stared back at the great winding procession.

Necessarily, progress was slow and careful as they had brought no carts and for the most part each individual was carrying his or her own equipment and supplies, although the few hundred horses they had brought for the use of scouts and skirmishers served as useful pack animals also.

For the first few days the weather confined itself to bright sunshine and occasional light falls of snow, and the natural good spirits and camaraderie of the marchers lessened the effects of the cold and the discomfort. As they climbed steadily towards the heart of the mountains however, the weather deteriorated markedly and the wind began to whip the snow into a dense, obscuring blizzard.

For a while the long twisting line eased forward, but as the light began to fail, Hawklan brought it to a halt, and gradually a thin, blurred skein of beacon torches began to thread its way through the white-streaked darkness as the army gratefully pitched camp.

In the command tent, Hawklan was not too concerned at the change in the weather. 'We've made good progress so far,' he said. 'Very few accidents, no animals lost, and morale good.'

Loman was less sanguine. 'A situation that could change very quickly if we get stuck here for any length of time,' he said.

Hawklan nodded. 'There's no question of that,' he replied unequivocally. 'This weather won't be keeping the Morlider away. We rise early tomorrow and we move forward, regardless. Everyone's well-equipped and fit, and we can't afford to dawdle. If anyone objects, remind him that we haven't the supplies and our friends haven't the time to wait the weather's whim.'

And move they did, for all the wind was screaming its relentless opposition. The way was too narrow and the line of march too long for Hawklan and the others to move to and fro offering encouragement, so each section had to maintain its station by the simple expedient of shouted or whistled signals. Hawklan expressly forbade the Alphraan to help. 'You won't be with us on the plains of Riddin,' he said. 'These disciplines must be well learned from the start.'

The blizzard blew for several days but, driven both by Hawklan's will and his example, the Orthlundyn army plodded slowly and defiantly on, each individual, limbs aching with fatigue and head bowed against the pitiless wind, concentrating on the person immediately in front, trying not to wait for that precious instruction to halt and camp that would eventually drift out of the whirling din ahead.

Finally the wind seemed to lose heart and, subsiding, allowed distant peaks to come into view once more.

It was with no small relief that Hawklan clambered up onto a ridge and confirmed for himself that his army was still intact, he remained on the ridge as the long column wound slowly past him, then he walked its length from rearguard to vanguard, bringing his healing touch to bear where the blizzard had torn into the will of his people.

'You're quiet,' Isloman said that night.

Hawklan chuckled ruefully. 'I'm exhausted,' he said. 'That's a long, thin army we've got out there.'

Surprisingly, more injuries occurred during the subsequent fine weather than during the blizzard. The worst was the loss of a young man in an act of foolish bravado on an icy ridge. His flailing, sickening progress down the steep cliff face was watched in silent, impotent horror by a thousand eyes until he finally disappeared from view. Then there was uproar and ropes were lifted down from horses.

'No,' Hawklan cried in distress. 'He's beyond our help now.' But it was the gentle whispering voice of the Alphraan that stilled the noise.

'We will find and tend his body,' it said. 'Go on your way. Greater needs drive you.'

That same day, another had a leg broken trying to help a struggling horse up a slithering icy slope. Thence came a flurry of sprains, dislocations and bruises caused by falls, together with cases of frostbite, exposure and even some snow-blindness that had kept silent through the blizzard. Few of these reached Hawklan however, Tirilen and Gulda having ensured that each contingent had someone versed in healing. The consensus in the ranks was that some of these healers left a great deal to be desired, but equally this proved quite an effective incentive to staying careful and uninjured.

Along the journey, Hawklan noted the landmarks he had seen when he had travelled to Riddin during the spring: the hollow where he had been surprised by Loman and Isloman on his return; the high knoll where he had encountered the strange brown bird and, unknowingly, the Alphraan; the valley where he had met Jareg and the ailing Serian. Then finally they reached the long steep ascent where Gavor had mocked him as he came perspiring to the top and looked for the first time out across the Decmilloith of Riddin.

Now, of course, the scene was very different. The forests and farmlands, the hedges and roads, were buried beneath a great whiteness, soft and deceptive under a pale yellow sun. And behind him was no mountain silence, but the rumbling clamour of his labouring army. Some way below, he knew, was the place where he had seen the Viladrien. How strange, he thought, that one of those great cloud lands had reached out and drawn him hither again.

He turned and looked at his toiling people and then back at the white expanse of Riddin. Once he had held out his arms to receive this country's harmony. Now, black on the skyline, he drew his Sword and holding it high let out a great cry of defiance. Gavor, sitting on his head, flapped his powerful wings like a living helm. As Hawklan's cry echoed around the valleys, it was taken up by the army who sent it ringing out until it seemed to fill the whole sky.

As they moved down through the gentler foothills fringing the mountains, the Orthlundyn encountered none of the Riddinvolk. The few small hamlets and farms they passed seemed to be deserted, though there were fresh hoof prints in the snow to indicate that they had been visited recently.

'Where is everybody?' Hawklan asked Agreth.

The Riddinwr looked puzzled. 'Urthryn must have called a General Muster,' he said. 'That means everyone has been mobilised.'

'Everyone?' Hawklan said.

Agreth nodded. 'Even the sick and the incompetent have a task in the General Muster,' he said. 'The people from these farms and small villages will have moved to one of the bigger villages nearby. The livestock will be being tended by runners in rota. They'll all be helping, planning . . . it'll be a great sharing . . .' Though he was trying to affect a casualness, he could not keep the emotion from his voice.

'This is not usual?' Hawklan said.

Agreth shook his head slowly. 'Not even in the War was the General Muster called.' Almost as if he could not help himself, he swung up on to his horse and, standing in the stirrups, stared out over the white landscape.

'My people,' he whispered softly to himself, then dismounted.

'What does it mean?' Hawklan asked.

Agreth shook his head again. 'It means that Urthryn's committed the entire nation to the destruction of this enemy. It

183

means total and utter war. But as to what's happened, I just don't know. We'll have to wait until we meet someone.'

Hawklan nodded. 'Well, let's march,' he said. 'If we're needed, we're needed now. If we come upon a Morlider victory celebration then we'll give your people vengeance. If we come upon your own victory celebration then so much the better.'

Agreth looked fretful and Hawklan laid a hand on his shoulder. 'You'll be with your people soon,' he said. 'And you'll have our swords by your side. Lead on.'

Agreth frowned in self-reproach. 'I'm sorry,' he said. 'Don't think me a churlish guest. It's just that all this . . . has taken me by surprise. I –'

He stopped and with an effort quelled the turmoil inside himself. 'Until we find out what's happened I suggest we send out Dacu and the Helyadin as scouts,' he said, his voice calm and purposeful. 'The rest of us can follow the route we've discussed previously.'

Hawklan smiled and nodded to Loman to transmit this advice as an order. 'As you command, Line Leader,' he said.

Riddin was criss-crossed with wide, well-made roads and though these were for the most part snow-filled, the Orthlundyn found themselves making excellent progess after the legaching toil through the mountains.

Together with Loman and Isloman, Hawklan rode up and down the line, encouraging the marchers, looking at the few sick and injured and subtly assessing the conditon of the whole army. As the light began to fail, Dacu returned with the Helyadin.

'There's no signs of hostile activity,' he announced, dismounting and walking alongside Hawklan. 'In fact the only place we've seen any activity at all is in the village about an hour's march down the road.'

Hawklan looked up at the darkening sky and then at Agreth. 'Ride ahead and announce us, Agreth,' he said. 'We don't want to be attacked in the dark by some startled militia. Go with him, Dacu, Athyr, in case there's news we need to know quickly.'

As the three men rode off into the gloaming, Hawklan turned to Loman. 'Strike the torches, but hood them,' he said. 'There's no point announcing our numbers until we find out what's been happening here. And take a small vanguard forward.'

Loman frowned slightly. 'Dacu would've told us if there was any risk,' he said.

'Do it,' Hawklan said peremptorily. 'We're all tired and we're none of us battle-ready yet.'

Hawklan's precautions proved unnecessarily, however, as within the hour Agreth returned. He was accompanied by an elderly man seated straight and tall in his saddle.

'Hawklan, this is Fendryc, second son of Fendarek, from the Haron branch of —' Agreth stopped and rubbed his nose with a rueful smile. 'Fendryc is the Elder to the village ahead,' he said briefly, with a quick look of knowing apology to his new companion. 'It's his runners whose tracks we've seen at the farms.'

Hawklan smiled and extended his hand to the old man. Fendryc leaned forward and took the hand. Hawklan's eyes narrowed slightly in dismay.

'Don't dismount,' he said gently. 'Your joints pain you. You shouldn't have come to greet us in this cold.'

The old man looked from Hawklan to Agreth, his stern expression fading into one of profound surprise.

'I told you the Orthlundyn was no ordinary man, Elder,' Agreth said simply. 'Tell him your news.'

Hawklan mounted Serian to bring himself level with Fendryc. The old man was recovering his composure. 'I thank you for your courtesy, young man,' he said. 'But to be in action again sets my discomfort well aside.'

Hawklan made to reply, but Fendryc continued: 'My people are ahead marking out a good site for your night's camp and we'll let you have such fodder and radiant stones as you might need, but I have to ask you: why are you here?'

Hawklan raised his eyebrows. 'The Morlider, Fendryc,' he said. 'The Drienvolk told us of their attack.'

The old man shook his head. 'Drienvolk,' he muttered, his voice a mixture of awe and disbelief.

'Drienvolk,' Hawklan confirmed. 'They saw the islands and the great flotilla of ships, and good fortune gave them the chance to warn us.'

Fendryc lifted an unsteady hand for silence. 'I don't doubt you, Orthlundyn,' he said. 'The Morlider are indeed coming. They were sighted many days ago sneaking towards us in the wake of a great storm. Urthryn called the General Muster and almost all the Lines will be gathered there now.' He clenched the waving hand. 'A host the like of which has never been gathered before. We'll destroy them as they land.' He looked at Hawklan and repeated his question, 'But why are you *here*?'

'I don't understand,' Hawklan said.

The old man pointed into the darkness. 'They are gathered in the south, not here. It's several days hard riding by fast horse even in summer. It would take weeks on foot.'

Urthryn slapped his gloved hands together as much in frustration as to warm them. With his knees he guided his horse to Girvan's side. His face was concerned. 'What does the fisherman say?' he asked. 'What did the watch boats see?'

Girvan shrugged. 'Nothing new,' he said. 'And they were chased off like all the others. There's a lot of activity going on out there but they couldn't get close enough to see anything in detail.'

Urthryn shook his head and let out a long steaming breath. 'Why should they delay like this? It makes no sense. The weather's good. They had the benefit of some surprise when they arrived, but they must surely know we've gathered our strength by now.'

Girvan could offer no help. The waiting was not doing the morale of the Lines any good, not least because no one could see any reason for it. And it had been extensively discussed by Urthryn, his advisers, the Goraidin, and all the senior Line Leaders, not to mention Oslang and the other Cadwanwr who had arrived. He glanced around. The duty Lines were strung out across the cliffs and row upon row waited along the shore. Behind him the massive temporary camp dwarfed the small fishing village. He had never thought to see so many riders in one place at the same time. It was a logistical triumph: the Muster – the Riddinvolk – at their very finest.

But the enemy did not come.

Urthryn lifted his hand to his face and removing a glove, rubbed his eyes wearily. 'Oslang,' he said, turning to the Cadwanwr. 'Has a night's rest given you any great inspiration?'

Oslang shook his head. 'None, Ffryst,' he replied. 'We detect no use of the Old Power. I'd like to think that they've decided not to attack having learned about your force in some way, but that's hardly realistic. I can only imagine they're hoping to destroy your morale by a prolonged delay.'

Urthryn grimaced. Same old thoughts treading a weary round. But he could scarcely reproach the Cadwanwr – they were not, after all, fighters, and couldn't be expected to think as such. Even the Goraidin could offer little, though something was being missed and everyone knew it.

'It's a feint,' Olvric had said after the first few days of waiting.

'Cadmoryth's boats have seen hundreds of ships moored by those islands, and swarms of men,' Urthryn had replied.

'Before they were conveniently chased away,' Olvric retorted. 'And why didn't they capture your boats, or sink them?'

'Because we took your good advice,' Urthryn replied with some heat. 'We've built boats like theirs. We were too quick for them.'

'Cadmoryth?' Olvric said, looking at the fisherman enquiringly.

Cadmoryth had looked opologetically at his Ffyrst. 'I can't be certain,' he said. 'But it's a possibility that our boats were allowed to escape. At least two of our captains said they didn't think the Morlider were trying very hard.'

Urthryn scowled again as he remembered the conversation. Still, the Goraidin usually talked sense and at least restarting the coast watch to a couple of days' riding north and south had helped with morale by giving the otherwise idle Lines something to do.

'Ho!' A loud cry cut across his musing.

Girvan seized his arm and pointed to one of the fishermen standing in a precariously rigged look-out tower on top of the cliff.

'Ships ho!' came a second cry.

Urthryn urged his horse up the steep path followed by Girvan and the two Goraidin. Oslang followed cautiously, one eye on the nearby edge of the cliff, the other on the silent ranks of patiently waiting riders watching him pass with some amusement. Cadmoryth did not move but stared out at the ragged horizon, his eyes narrowed.

When Urthryn reached the look-out tower, its occupant was clambering down with alarming agility. He was red-faced as he jumped down the last section making Urthryn's horse start a little.

'Hundreds of them, Ffyrst,' he said, pointing out to sea. Urthyrn reached into his pocket and retrieved a seeing stone. No sooner had he lifted it to his eyes than he drew in a sharp breath.

'Signaller,' he said. A young boy stepped out of the waiting ranks. Urthyrn walked his horse to the edge of the cliff and looked down at the riders on the shore far below. 'Sound the alert,' he said to the boy.

'Ffyrst!' the boy shouted excitedly then, licking his lips, he lifted up a curved brass horn and blew a simple but piercing call.

The ranks lining the cliffs maintained their station, though a noticeable tremor ran through them. On the shore below and in the camp behind the cliffs, a purposeful surge of activity began.

'Messenger!' Urthryn shouted. Another figure stepped from the ranks. 'Go down to the Line Leaders on the shore. Remind them that these brigands are not to land. They die in the water. We've arrows enough to sink their damned islands; see that they're used well.'

Involuntarily, Oslang grimaced at Urthryn's tone and for an instant the Ffyrst looked angry at this implicit reproach. His anger however, did not reach his voice. 'Your friends will be brought up as part of the alert,' he said. 'Are you prepared?' His voice was unexpectedly gentle.

Oslang gave him a grateful and slightly apologetic nod. 'As far as I know,' he said. Then, more reassuringly: 'We'll fight to our limits if Creost manifests himself, have no fear about our resolve. We know the cost of failure.'

Urthryn nodded.

'Shall I recall the coast patrols?' Girvan said. Urthryn looked at the distant islands and at the riders on the shore below. Then, as he looked up, his eye fell on Yengar. The Goraidin was looking upwards. Urthryn followed his gaze. Clambering nimbly on to the swaying platform of the watch tower high above, was Olvric.

Still watching the Goraidin, Urthryn said: 'No. Tell them what's happening and tell them to be on the alert in case it is some kind of elaborate trick.' Then, to Olvric, he shouted, 'What do *you* see, Goraidin?'

'Ships,' came the reply after a moment. 'Maybe four hundred or more. In ranks and files as neat as your squadrons.' Olvric's voice was uncertain.

'Your friend seems doubtful,' Urthryn said to Yengar.

The Goraidin nodded. 'So am I. They must know by now what they're sailing into. I can't imagine how they expect to land and establish a bridgehead against what they must surely see arrayed here. Your archers alone may destroy them.'

'That's my fervent hope,' Urthryn said. But the Goraidin's

doubt disturbed him. What could possibly overwhelm the massive forces waiting on the shore?

Creost, came the thought.

He looked at Oslang, now greeting Ryath and the other Cadwanwr who had arrived over the past few weeks. They sit on horses like ill-tied baggage, he thought, in spite of himself, then he crushed the ungracious thought ruthlessly. He could not feel comfortable about the role these strange people were to play. Would they indeed fight to their very limits when need arose, as Oslang had promised? And what would those limits be? What power did this Uhriel command? He remembered Drago, knocked to the ground seemingly by a mere thought from Oslang. Then there was the power that Oslang had exerted over the Morlider's mind. But these thoughts gave him no solace when he remembered a rather awkward Girvan telling him of the strange 'unnatural' storm that had blown so terribly before the islands appeared and when he recalled Sylvriss's tale of the destruction of Vakloss by Oklar.

Again, he set the thoughts aside. He had no alternative but to prepare his people to face a large and vicious army about to launch an unprovoked war of conquest. He would simply have to trust that the Cadwanwr knew what they were doing.

The approaching ships were clearly visible now. They were a magnificent sight, large colourful sails billowing to catch what slight breeze there was, white foam protesting around their bows, oars beating the waves rhythmically. Briefly, Urthryn felt a twinge of regret. How many good men and horses were to be killed and maimed today? Why were these people not content just to sail their beautiful ships and ride the oceans' paths on their wondrous floating islands? Why must they seek always to destroy and ravage?

He let the thought pass by unhindered by debate. Perhaps the Morlider had their own answer to such questions, but now he had time only for killing strokes until those same ships were heading back from whence they came.

The riders on the shore could now see the ships and were manoeuvring to ensure that no part of the shoreline would be unprotected. As the ships neared the beach, the riders would move to the sea's edge and launch volley upon volley of arrows into them. Any who survived that onslaught would then have to wade through the water for perhaps a hundred paces or more through the same intensity of fire. Yet, they *must* know this, Urthryn thought again, as some ill-formed unease rumbled deep within him.

'Ffyrst.' It was Oslang. Urthryn turned.

'Creost is putting forth his power,' the Cadwanwr said, his face intent as if listening for some distant sound.

'I feel nothing,' Urthryn said, uncertain how to respond.

Oslang paused. 'I think it drives the ships,' he said. 'But there's something else as well that I can't identify. It's subtle. Shall we oppose the ships?'

Urthryn looked at the approaching fleet again. To his eye, nothing was untoward. He was distracted by a sharp whistle. It was Yengar signalling to Olvric, giving him Oslang's news. High above, the Goraidin lifted his hands to shade his eyes.

'No,' said Urthryn, turning back to the Cadwanwr. 'Let them come. Let's settle this affair blade to blade.' He looked down again to the riders on the shore. They were beginning to move forward, but something was different, though precisely what eluded him.

For a while there was silence except for the sound of the sea and the distant cries of the riders on the shore, then: 'Ffyrst. Something's wrong.' It was Cadmoryth; he had followed Urthryn and the others up the cliff path slowly, on foot. He reached up and took Urthryn's wrist in a powerful grip. His other hand was pointing to the shore. 'The tide's ebbing,' he said.

Urthryn frowned. That was the change he had seen but not recognised – but what was the significance of a receding tide?

Cadmoryth answered the unspoken question. 'It's too fast and it's not the time,' he said. 'I was so occupied, I didn't notice. Get your people off the shore now!'

Urthryn snatched his hand free and took in at once the fisherman's nervous face, the advancing ships, and the riders, walking their horses after the now rapidly retreating water.

'I don't understand –' he began.

His voice disappeared under a great cheer from the riders around him as the archers on the shore released their first volleys into the leading ships. Even on the cliffs, the rush of the arrows could be heard.

'Ffyrst –' Cadmoryth seized his wrist again desperately. 'For pity's sake.'

But a more urgent cry caught Urthryn's attention. It was Olvric. Looking up, he saw the Goraidin clambering down the watchtower. Uncharacteristically, he was shouting – shouting frantically. 'The boats are empty. And there's something out there, coming in fast. Get those people off the shore. Now!'

From the beach came the sound of yet more volleys of arrows, and the crunching rattle of the ships beaching in the shallows. The riders were advancing relentlessly, following the receding water almost at the trot now and eagerly waiting for the first sight of the enemy that had chosen to threaten their land.

But Urthryn scarcely registered the unfolding saga beneath him. He was transfixed by Olvric. Normally emotionless and laconic, the Goraidin's face was now alive with fear and he was staring out to sea. Urthryn followed his gaze. The distant islands were no longer visible. Instead, a blur now separated sea and sky.

Then a figure surged past him and went right to the edge of the cliff. It was Oslang, his hood thrown back and his arms extended.

Ryath and the others followed him.

'Do as they say, Ffyrst,' Oslang cried, without turning round. 'I think we can give you a little time. But hurry!'

Urthryn's hesitation vanished. 'Signaller, sound retreat,' he shouted.

'Retreat, Ffyrst?' the youth enquired uncertainly.

'Retreat, boy!' Urthryn thundered. 'As you've never blown it.'

Shaken by his leader's sudden anger, the boy's mouth dried and made him falter with the first notes. From some hitherto unknown depth of patience, Urthryn found a nod and a strained smile of encouragement for the boy, and the call to retreat eventually burst out of the curved horn, clear and determined.

'Louder, lad,' Urthryn whispered to himself, as the nature of the advancing blur in the distance began to become apparent. It was a great foaming wave.

As the strident horn call reached the ordered ranks on the beach there was confusion. Battle-ready and on the verge of facing their enemy, the sudden urgent call to retreat was not heard by some, doubted by most others, and blatantly ignored by a few.

Urthryn's eyes widened in horror as he saw the hesitation. Then, suddenly, a powerful wind struck the watchers on the cliff. The signaller faltered again as his horse shied, but Yengar caught its reins and steadied it. 'Keep blowing, boy,' he shouted above the noise of the wind and increasing roar of the oncoming wave.

It seemed to Urthryn, as he watched, that the squadrons below, still confused, were blundering and floundering with infinite slowness, and that the dreadful wave was lingering like some taunting hunting animal waiting its pleasure before launching its final, speeding, attack.

Everywhere was dominated by its distant thunder carried on the wind, but somewhere in the din he heard his own voice rising up to join with those around him in shouting fruitless encouragement to the riders below.

On the shore, Muster discipline was beginning to assert itself, aided in no small degree by the eerie silence that greeted the attack on the grounded ships. Arrows had flown over their sides and thudded into their capacious interiors, but not a sound had emerged. No cries of pain, or rage, or fear, no rattle of arms; nothing. And as more ships crunched into the shallows the silence seemed to deepen. The only sound that emerged from the ships was the flapping of their impotent sails in the sudden wind. It had a mocking quality about it.

Then the other sounds began to impinge on the riders; the desperate clamour behind them and, worse, the deep and ominous rumble rising out of the now spray-obscured sea like a massive cavalry charge.

'Too late. Too late,' Urthryn whispered to himself as the squadrons below began to wheel and turn to gallop up the beach. He saw through their eyes – they were much farther out than they had thought. It was a long way back to the village. His horse shifted restlessly underneath him, responding to his inner turmoil.

On the cliff edge, Oslang and the other Cadwanwr stood motionless, faces set in profound concentration. Suddenly, the wind faltered and the advancing wave rose and fumed as if it had struck some unseen barrier.

They *are* giving us time, Urthryn realised. Though how it was being achieved, he could not tell. Below, he saw the leading riders at last reaching the village and turning to head up the cliffs towards the sound of the horn.

Urthryn held his breath as the wave continued to be held by the unknown skills of the Cadwanwr. His riders were streaming off the shore. But the ramps and walkways up into the village were narrow and the great mass of riders were slowed virtually to a halt. For a moment Urthryn was almost overcome with emotion as he watched the impeccable discipline of the Muster holding. Fear and urgency surged up to him from the waiting riders, but no panic.

Then, one of the Cadwanwr sank slowly to his knees. The others ignored him. Another fell; heavily. Urthryn's gaze moved from his riders to the fallen man. Without examination, he knew the man was dead. Whatever these men were doing it was taking some grim toll. A third faltered, his folding body feeling to Urthryn like the curling finger of a cold hand closing about his stomach.

'Hold, Oslang!' he shouted. 'Hold!'

Below, a great black mass of riders oozed slowly towards the constricting exits from the beach.

'Hold, Oslang!' he whispered.

But he could see that all the Cadwanwr were nearly spent. Not from their actions, for they stood as silent and stern as before, but from the beached ships now being lifted by the nearing tide, and beginning to jostle one another like a crowd of excited children at a party.

Then the rest of the Cadwanwr yielded, slowly and painfully. Oslang was the last. He alone remained standing at the end, though he staggered back, exhausted. Urthryn leaned forward in his saddle, and caught him. Oslang looked up at him, his face full of a great weariness and a terrible remorse and grief.

'I'm sorry,' he said faintly. Urthryn put a protective arm around him, and held him firmly against the horse for support and comfort.

Looking up, Urthryn confirmed the scene that he knew would be unfolding. The wave was moving forward again. Even from above, its size and speed were terrifying. The colourful ships were jigging and rolling in anticipation. Immediately below him, the dark crowd of riders became darker as instinctively they urged their horses forward to reach the safety of the higher ground.

Abruptly, the horn call stopped and the signaller, overcome by his exertions and by the now obvious futility of his actions, let the instrument slip from his hands as his head slumped forward. He was sobbing.

The shouting crowd lining the cliff tops fell silent too as, gathering up the bobbing ships, the wave reached its destination and, crashing over the crowded Muster squadrons, roared angrily up the cliff face as if it would not be sated unless it overwhelmed even the high watchers.

Urthryn watched in empty helplessness as, in seconds, thousands of his charges were destroyed. Some were crushed in the great rolling mêlée of men and horses, some were smashed against the rocks, or by the empty, charging ships; others were drowned as they were towed out to sea by the retreating wave, and some were suffocated in the clinging sand made suddenly soft and quick.

Yet, it transpired, there were miraculous escapes also. A father and son, swept up onto a narrow rocky ledge, a woman who awoke bruised and shaken to find herself in one of the empty Morlider ships. And many others found themselves thrust to the surface where they could swim ashore or cling to debris until the villagers, manning such boats as were undamaged, were able to rescue them.

Despite his agony, some reflex of leadership galvanised Urthryn even as the wave was foaming around the foot of the cliff. 'Yengar, Olvric, help the Cadwanwr,' he shouted then, shaking the signaller, had him blow 'Stand Firm'. If all the riders present descended on the beach in impromptu rescue missions, who knew what further harm might ensue in the crush?

As Urthryn turned and galloped off down the cliff path to take personal command of the rescue, Oslang reached out and took Yengar's arm to steady himself. 'Ryath,' he said, none too gently prodding his prostrate friend with his foot. 'Ryath, get up. We must still the water before it retreats too far and returns again. Get up! And we must find the Creost and the islands before they move beyond us.'

Olvric and Yengar exchanged a glance. 'Find the islands first, then still the water, Oslang,' Olvric said. 'We need to know whether to move north or south. Riddin is defenceless while we wait here. The Morlider may be landing and moving against us at this very moment.'

# Chapter 13

Dacu swung down from his horse. He was breathing heavily and his face was flushed.

Hawklan did not alter his steady pace through the snow, and Dacu fell in with him.

'Well?' Hawklan asked.

'They're there,' Dacu said, between great breaths. 'Right where the Drienvolk said they were heading. There must be forty thousand and more landing while we watched. And they've been there for some time. They've established a large camp and a lot of it's being fortified.'

Hawklan did not try to keep the relief from his face. After the old man's news that the Muster was gathering in the south to face the Morlider, there had been a considerable debate about where the Orthlundyn army should go.

Agreth had wanted to march south, hoping to find some Muster outpost still manned that could ride to Urthryn with news of their arrival and arrange for supplies to carry them over the long journey. Others had suggested dividing the army, with one section moving south and the other continuing across Riddin to the sea.

Hawklan's instinct had been to heed the Drienvolk's warning. Tactically it made more sense and, according to an unyielding Gavor, it had been unequivocal. 'Their greatest islands have come north, carrying many men, and such numbers of boats as we have never seen – a great and powerful host. We watched them for much of their journey. They defied the ways of Enartion.' This observation, Gavor declared, had distressed Ynar greatly and for a little while the Drien had been unable to conclude his warning. 'But now they are waiting.'

Waiting for what? Hawklan had thought. A feint to the south, or an attack? Or had the Drienvolk been subtly deceived in some way, looking down from their great advantage? *That* was a doubt he had carried all the way from Orthlund, but about which he could do nothing other than trust his intuition.

In the end he had over-ruled the suggestions. They could

not possibly leave the north without knowing what was happening on its shores. Dacu and the Helyadin would ride to the bay where the Morlider were supposed to be, and the Orthlundyn would march after them until they returned with definite news.

Now it was here, and his relief faded as quickly as it had bloomed. The number and seemingly well established position of the Morlider was appalling. 'Have they any scouts out?' he asked.

Dacu shook his head. 'None that we saw. Not even perimeter guards in fact. They're not expecting anyone.'

Hawklan looked puzzled. 'Any horses?' he asked after a moment.

'Very few that we could see,' Dacu replied. 'Probably difficult to transport.' He shrugged. 'Besides I doubt they're going to risk facing the Muster on its own terms.'

Hawklan agreed. This was true, and with the absence of guards was a stroke of fortune. The Morlider had effectively contained themselves. Though they had considerably superior numbers and it would not be possible to prevent reinforcements and supplies arriving by sea, the Orthlundyn could perhaps stop them breaking out until the Muster could be roused.

*If* the Muster could be roused!

Hawklan's doubts returned. What if the Morlider indeed had a second army attacking to the south? It was a grim thought, for if it were true, then the Orthlundyn would have to attack the Morlider ahead of them immediately, or risk being caught between two armies themselves. He set the thought aside. It was not a realistic choice unless circumstances changed radically. The Orthlundyn were in good heart but they were tired and would fight well for only a limited period. They could not expect to overwhelm such a substantially larger, well entrenched force easily, and even if they were victorious, what would they do next? A forced march south after such a battle, carrying their wounded and the subtler burden of battle-fatigue would be impossible. They would probably have to retire to Orthlund, leaving who knew what confusion behind. For a little while he had no alternative but to wait and watch and move as his enemy did.

He looked at Agreth, who had run up at the arrival of Dacu and listened intently to his report. Taking the Riddinwr's arm, he said, '*Now* you go south, Muster rider. Take the horses and supplies you need, and ride with this news until you come to someone who can carry it faster.'

Agreth nodded. 'And what will you do?' he said anxiously. 'You don't have the resources to face such numbers.'

Hawklan looked at him squarely. 'One horseman in our ranks isn't going to make any difference,' he said. 'Do what you do best – ride. Our actions here will be decided by those of the Morlider, the state of our supplies, or any news that comes from the south. If we have to engage them we'll stand and hold for as long as we can.'

Suddenly granted his wish, Agreth found himself torn between his desire to ride over the snow-covered countryside to his own kind and his strange new loyalty to these people who, unasked, had undertaken this long exhausting march to defend *his* country, and who now found themselves in such a perilous position.

Unexpectedly, Hawklan smiled. 'Don't worry,' he said. 'They don't seem to be in hurry to move. We'll just wait until they do. Besides, *we* have the advantage of surprise,' he added. 'You heard Dacu. They think they're alone up here. They're waiting for a message from Creost probably. The last thing they'll be expecting is an army waiting for them if they leave their camp. Now go. Straight away. Find out what's happening to your people and tell them that we're here.' He paused, then: 'Tell Urthryn I trust implicitly the judgement of a man who could father such a Queen as Sylvriss.'

As Agreth strode off, Gavor's head appeared out of Hawklan's cloak. 'Rather glib, dear boy,' he said. 'My own assessment of the situation is that we're in a mess.'

Hawklan pushed the raven back under his cloak without replying.

'It was an act of monstrous folly, and we've paid a terrible price for it,' Bragald shouted, his face livid. 'I spoke against the General Muster and the manning of the beach at the time, and I was right. Step down and face the judgement of the Moot, Urthryn.'

Angry cries filled the great tent, both in favour and against the Riddinwr's outburst.

Urthryn stood up and raised his hands. The din faded. He looked at his accuser.

'Yes, Bragald,' he said, uncharacteristically omitting the man's formal address in his irritation. 'You spoke against it, but you offered no alternative.' There were more cries from the gathered riders. 'You'd have let them sail in and build a camp on the beach unhindered –'

'We could've attacked them as they built it,' Bragald interrupted.

Urthryn's temper snapped. 'Rubbish,' he shouted. 'We went through all this before. Had those ships been full of men, how could we possibly have got sufficient squadrons down there fast enough? And do you seriously think that we could have held the village and all those steep winding pathways up the cliffs against determined infantry?'

'But the ships *weren't* full of men!' Bragald shouted in reply.

Hiron, sitting next to Urthryn, reached up and laid a restraining hand on the Ffyrst's arm. Urthryn sat down.

'Bragald, your ability to state the obvious never ceases to astound me,' Hiron said, coldly. 'Urthryn's tactics were both right and wrong. Right because there *was* no other way to defend that beach, and you know it, but wrong because he did not foresee the nature of Creost's attack.' He stood up and leaned forward to the audience. 'And who of you here could have foreseen such an assault?' he said, almost viciously.

'What about these Cave dwellers you set such store by?' Bragald spluttered. 'Couldn't they have foreseen it?'

Urthryn glowered at him. 'I know nothing of their skills,' he said. 'But they it was who discovered the threat to us, and they paid a price amongst their own, holding back that . . . demon's . . . wave.'

'One old man,' Bragald sneered.

'Number for number, they lost as we did,' Urthryn said angrily. 'And their efforts saved hundreds of our people. Could you have stayed that wave, Line Leader? And it's infamous that you should abuse such allies when they may not speak here.'

For a moment a sullen silence filled the tent.

'More to the point,' Hiron said, 'we waste time with these fultile recriminations. Even while we talk, the Morlider might be landing somewhere –'

'And thanks to Urthryn's General Muster, our coastal watch has been effectively abandoned,' Bragald said.

'The coast is watched for two days' riding both north and south,' Urthryn said, defensively. 'Have you forgotten already the numbers that the Morlider came in last time, when they were fragmented and disunited? We needed the Orthlundyn and the Fyordyn to defeat them then. Now we know they're united under Creost. How could we do other than put the greater part of our power where they threatened to land?' He frowned and shook his head. 'But Hiron's right. What are we sitting in Moot for? Why aren't we –'

'We're sitting in Moot to choose our Ffyrst,' Bragald shouted. 'My house lost kin in that –'

'We all lost kin, Bragald,' Urthryn thundered, standing up and stepping forward. 'You can burden me no more than I already burden myself.' His voice fell suddenly. 'Do you think I'm unaware of how it might all have been otherwise? Not a moment seems to pass when I don't see that dreadful destruction sweeping over our people . . . or walk through that wreckage again, and those . . . broken bodies . . . men, women, strewn about the shore like . . .' He faltered. 'But that scene will be repeated endlessly if we waste further time in futile debate. We can only honour our dead by performing our duty to the living.'

'You can honour our dead by relinquishing your office, before the Moot votes you out,' Bragald said.

Urthryn's face set. 'You do not listen, Bragald,' he said grimly. 'You never listen and you never think.' Bragald bridled at the sudden quiet menace in Urthryn's tone. 'We are attacked. We are at war. A war which, at the moment, we're losing. We've lost a day with this nonsense of yours, and who knows what else we've lost in the way of unity through your clattering rhetoric and petty ambition.' He swept up his cloak from the chair and fastened it about himself. 'Our Law aside, the office of Ffyrst ceases to exist when its holder doesn't have the hearts of all the Lines. If you seek those, Bragald, then set yourself before the Moot here and rant to *your* heart's content, but know this.' He raised his voice. 'Know this all of you. Cadmoryth's people – the fishermen – are not here, talking. They've patched the enemy's boats and gone in search of them. Oslang's people too are searching in their own way to find and face this . . . Uhriel. I will not do less. The House of Urthryn will waste no more time in pointless debate. We ride to find the Morlider, and we ride *now*. Follow me who will.'

# *Chapter 14*

Hawklan stood at the entrance to his tent and looked up at the grey sky. It seemed to be strangely oppressive and the air around him felt as though a summer storm were pending. Andawyr joined him.

'Shut the door,' came Dar-volci's deep voice from within the tent.

Hawklan glanced back through the opening. Dar-volci was curled up in front of a small fire of radiant stones and Gavor was asleep with his claw clutching the back of a chair.

With a smile he sealed the flap, and then pulled his cloak about himself.

'What's the matter?' Andawyr asked.

Hawklan shrugged. 'The weather,' he said looking around. 'It's still snowing, but it feels like a thunderstorm building up.' He shook his head. 'And my ears are ringing.'

Andawyr looked puzzled. 'It feels odd for sure,' he said. 'But I can't hear anything.'

'It's rather like the song of the Viladrien,' Hawklan said tentatively. 'But . . . harsher in some way.'

Andawyr looked up at the featureless sky and shrugged. 'It's probably a thunderstorm building up, as you say. I wouldn't worry about it.' Then, taking Hawklan's arm, he said, 'It's very peaceful. Let's walk.'

And peaceful it was. The two men walked slowly down the ranks of snow-covered tents, largely silent except for the occasional muffled conversation, and the odd individual pursuing some duty.

'This weather's opportune,' Hawklan asid. 'It keeps us as well hidden as we can expect in the absence of any convenient forest.'

He rubbed his arms uncertainly.

'What are we going to do?' Andawyr said abruptly.

Hawklan stopped and turned around. 'I don't know,' he said after a moment. 'But we haven't much time. They're not showing any signs of moving out, but they're growing in strength daily; we've only got limited supplies and now that we're rested a little we're likely to have a morale problem.'

'And we've no idea what's happening in the south.' Andawyr completed the list.

Hawklan shook his head. 'Nor are we likely to have for several days, even if Agreth doesn't run into any difficulties.'

Hawklan looked at the sky again. 'Something's happening up there,' he said.

Andawyr followed his gaze, but the snowflakes falling towards him, dark against the greyness, told him nothing. Casually he took hold of the cord around his waist.

'You're right,' he admitted. 'It's been going on for some time. Someone somewhere is using the Old Power. But it's a long way away.'

Hawklan looked at him anxiously. 'Creost?' he said.

Andawyr shook his head and cast a knowing glance upwards.

'Dar Hastuin?' Hawklan said, lowering his voice as if afraid of being overheard.

Andawyr hesitated. 'I can think of no other,' he said. 'The Power's being used for no good, that I *can* tell. And it seems to be . . . up there. But it's way beyond anything *we* can influence.'

The memory of Ynar-Aesgin's pain and fear returned to Hawklan, but further discussion was ended by the appearance of Gavor. He landed on Hawklan's shoulder and shook the snow from his feathers. 'Jaldaric and Athyr have just got back,' he said. 'They want to see you right away.'

The two Helyadin, still wearing their white camouflage, were pacing up and down outside Hawklan's tent when he and Andawyr returned.

'What's happened?' he said, motioning them inside.

'They've started to send out foot patrols,' Athyr said, loosening his coat and throwing his hood back. 'They nearly spotted us.'

'It's about time,' Hawklan said, then, anxiously, 'What about Tirke and Yrain?'

'They should be all right if they keep their wits about them,' said Athyr. 'But I don't think they'll be able to move until nightfall.'

'Gavor, find Loman and Isloman will you?' Hawklan said. 'Ask them to come here straight away.'

'And Dacu, dear boy,' Gavor added.

'And Dacu,' Hawklan confirmed.

Within minutes, the bulk of the two brothers was filling the small tent. When Dacu arrived, Dar-volci reluctantly yielded his place at the fireside and clambered on to Andawyr's lap.

'Decision time I think,' Hawklan said when Athyr had given his news to the new arrivals. 'Presumably it's only a matter of time before they find us if they're sending out patrols, and we can't lose the one advantage we have – surprise.'

No one disagreed, though the atmosphere in the tent seemed to become suddenly heavy.

Dacu crouched down and stared into the small fire.

'When shall we attack?' he said.

'Unless Tirke and Yrain tell us something different when they get back, we'll have to make the first raid tonight,' Hawklan said, without pause. 'And be ready for a major encounter tomorrow or perhaps the day after.'

Dacu closed his eyes. 'With no cavalry worth speaking of,' he said.

Hawklan nodded. 'But such as we have is better than theirs,' he said. 'And they've almost certainly been training to face cavalry and not infantry.' He waved the conjectures aside. 'It's of no importance anyway. We're going to face the reality of it all soon enough, and our people are as well prepared as they can be.' He looked around the tent. 'Does anyone want to change any of the battle plan?' he asked. Dacu smiled wryly. 'Other than to march back to Orthlund,' Hawklan added in reply to the unspoken suggestion.

But the mirth could not survive in the stultifying atmosphere of the tent. 'Come on,' Hawklan said understandingly. 'We've no choice, you know that. There's nowhere we can hide or seriously disguise our numbers out here, and if they find us they'll move out to meet us and against such numbers we'll have a real problem on our hands. Added to which we're going to start running into serious supply problems very soon.'

He looked round at his friends again. All, except Dacu, were looking at him. The focus of all their attentions, he felt a great loneliness rise up inside him like a black, engulfing shadow. The familiar, terrible images that had so often returned to haunt him, images of war and defeat in a long gone time, came with the darkness, and for a moment it seemed that the tent and the waiting people were receding into an unreal distance.

But his mind would not allow it. He rested high on the shoulders of these people, like a mountain peak on its broad base, yet, paradoxically, he alone must support their entire weight now. He knew that if he faltered then all would fall. Many things may sway a battle, but the resolution of an army was paramount and this was merely a measure of the resolution of its leader. Wilfully he looked into the ancient darkness and then scattered it with the light of his twenty years at Anderras Darion. Whatever the Morlider had been, they were His creatures now. They must be defeated utterly; crushed. The only choice that he, Hawklan, could give them was flight or death.

The atmosphere in the tent changed palpably. Andawyr inclined his head and looked at Hawklan narrowly. Dacu turned from the fire as if someone had spoken to him.

Hawklan stood up. His presence was suddenly almost frightening and, despite the softness of his voice, everyone in the tent held their breath.

'Dacu.' The Goraidin stood up. 'Extend our perimeter guards and double your observation patrols. We need to know exactly where they are at all times if they're going to move about. If any come near this camp, destroy them totally. Act on your own initiative if Tirke and Yrain run into difficulty, but jeopardise nothing, you understand?' Dacu nodded and turned to leave.

'Loman,' Hawklan continued. 'Rouse the company commanders. Tell them what's happened and issue the battle orders. Isloman, Athyr, get your group ready to move tonight. We'll meet in the command tent and go through the final details at sunset or whenever Tirke and Yrain get back.'

As Dacu and the others were leaving, a sentry appeared outside the tent escorting a slouching figure wearing a bedraggled and over-sized fur coat, and carrying a large pack.

'What's this?' Hawklan asked, looking at the vision with some amusement.

'It just wandered in from the north and asked for Andawyr,' replied the sentry.

Hearing his name, the little Cadwanwr stepped forward, setting aside Hawklan's cautionary hand. He peered into the deep hood. The figure extended its arms, and two gloved hands eventually appeared from the long sleeves of the coat.

'Atelon,' Andawyr said in a mixture of delight and concern. The hands flicked back the figure's hood to reveal the tired but smiling face of the young Cadwanwr.

Andawyr embraced him and then ushered him quickly into Hawklan's tent.

'What are you doing here?' he said, removing the young man's snow-clogged coat busily. He stepped outside before Atelon could answer and Hawklan could hear the coat being shaken vigorously. Atelon gave him a nervous smile and Hawklan introduced himself. The Cadwanwr looked at him uncertainly as he took the offered hand and gave his own name.

'Sit down,' Hawklan said. 'You look very tired.'

The young man needed little bidding and he was warming himself in front of the radiant stones when Andawyr returned.

'What are you doing here?' Andawyr repeated, sitting down beside him.

Atelon looked mildly surprised. 'The felci brought your message,' he answered. 'We didn't know what to think. Oslang had sent the Muster to take us down south when the Morlider islands appeared.' He cast a glance at the seemingly sleeping Dar-volci and lowered his voice to a whisper. 'And the felci have been behaving most peculiarly lately. Rambling on about the Alphraan, and opening the ways . . . all sorts of things. We didn't know what to make of it. But they were adamant about what you'd said. The Morlider were landing in the *north* – here. And the Orthlundyn were coming. So, in the end we decided we'd better find out. It was all we could do.'

Andawyr nodded and patted his arm. His face was concerned. 'We?' he said. 'Where are the others?'

'There was only Philean and Hath left, of the Senior Brothers,' Atelon said. 'And they're far too old for such journeying. I was the only one who could possibly –' He stopped; Andawyr was gaping.

'Only Philean and Hath and you!' he said, his voice rising. 'How many went south?'

Atelon gesticulated vaguely. 'All the senior brothers who were still there, except we three,' he replied. 'But most of the students and junior brothers are still at the Caves,' he added reassuringly.

Andawyr stood up. 'What's the matter?' Hawklan asked.

The Cadwanwr frowned a little. 'The Caves are . . . vulnerable,' he said.

'All the defences are sound,' Atelon said, a little reproachfully. 'And the seals to the lower levels. We checked them thoroughly before I left.' He met Andawyr's gaze. 'The Pass has been as quiet as ever since we put the watch stones out.

And while Philean and Hath mightn't be up to a winter hike they're –'

Andawyr raised his hand. 'Yes, I'm sorry,' he said. 'I'm sure you've done everything that was necessary. It's just that your news startled me. It's a long time since the Caves have been so empty.' He shrugged and smiled broadly. 'But it's good to see you. To be honest, I had my doubts about whether the message would even arrive and I didn't seriously think that anyone would venture out in this weather if it did. I'm indebted to you.'

Atelon returned the smile, but his face too was concerned. 'Is it true?' he said. 'Have the Morlider come north as well as south?'

Hawklan interrupted. 'Take him to your tent, Andawyr,' he said, laying a hand on the young man's shoulder and easing a little of the strain and fatigue he felt there. 'Tell him what's been happening while he eats, and then let him have a rest. He might be needed soon.'

As the two Cadwanwr strolled through the falling snow, with Dar-volci loping along behind, the camp was coming alive. Well-wrapped figures were moving purposefully hither and thither through the greyness as Hawklan's battle orders began to be implemented. Atelon kept glancing upwards nervously.

'He's a strange man, Hawklan,' Atelon said. 'Very powerful. More even than I'd imagined from your description of him.'

Andawyr nodded. 'He's changed,' he said. 'Very much changed. And you've caught him at a . . . crucial moment. But I'll tell you about that shortly. Tell me about *your* journey.' He looked at the young Cadwanwr solemnly. 'It was hardly an act of wisdom to venture out on your own in these conditions.'

Atelon shrugged. 'It wasn't much fun,' he conceded. 'And I got lost a few times. I know this area a little but I'd forgotten how the snow changes the countryside. That sentry frightened me to death appearing out of nowhere, but I'll admit I was glad to hear that Orthlundyn accent when he challenged me –' He glanced upwards again.

'What's the matter?' Andawyr asked.

Atelon looked awkward. 'I thought it was because I was tired,' he said hesitantly. 'But it's still there, coming and going, and not pleasant.'

'What is?' Andawyr persisted.

'The Old Power,' Atelon said, rather hastily, as if to get an anticipated reproof over with quickly. 'I think. No, I'm sure it is. It's faint and distant and –' He extended a finger upwards. 'It's . . . up there . . . but . . .'

Andawyr did not let him continue. 'Did you use the Old Power yourself to get through your journey?' he asked.

Atelon shook his head. 'No. Except once, a little, to light some bad radiant stones – I'm sure they'd been baked you know,' he said with mild indignation. Dar-volci cleared his throat conspicuously but Andawyr said nothing, and Atelon returned to his answer. 'I'd no idea what I was walking into. I didn't want to attract the attention of anyone – anything – I couldn't cope with. Especially after I began to feel *that*.' He looked upwards again.

'Sound judgement there, anyway,' Andawyr said approvingly. '*That*,' – he imitated the young Cadwanwr's gesture – 'is Dar Hastuin.'

Atelon's eyes widened in fear and, unconsciously, he cowered a little as if to avoid the attention of the sinister presence far above him.

'Viladrien are nearby,' Andawyr went on. 'And from what Hawklan's told me I suspect some battle's afoot up there which may be as vital to us as anything that's happening down here.'

'Viladrien?' Atelon said in amazement. 'And fighting?'

Andawyr nodded, but did not amplify his remarks.

'What can we do?' Atelon said after a moment, rather from want of something to say than anxiety for an answer.

'Nothing,' Andawyr replied, shaking his head. 'Except hope, and be aware.'

He stopped at a tent and unsealed the entrance. Dar-volci scuttled in and headed for the radiant stones. 'Here's my tent,' Andawyr said. 'Let's obey our leader's orders and talk while you eat and rest.'

When Andawyr and Atelon left his tent, Hawklan threw on his cloak and, gesturing Gavor on to his shoulder, strode out into the snow.

Until the time of his meeting with Isloman and Athyr, he knew that he must wander the camp, talking, laughing, encouraging, commiserating, but, above all, quietly inspiring the Orthlundyn army – *his* army – with the deep resolution that alone could bring it against the superior numbers of the Morlider with any chance of success.

His pilgrimage took him through tent after tent, each

standing dark and sullen in the fading winter light but inside glowing with subdued torchlight and filled with men and women, honing edges, testing bow strings, checking shields, armour, belts and buckles. Some were quiet and thoughtful, others were talking more loudly than usual and laughing more easily. But few needed his words. The Orthlundyn *know* what they face and what they need to meet it, he realised. It heartened him. Who supports whom? he thought with a smile. Perhaps, after all, he *was* no more than one man in the Orthlundyn army.

The camp's small administrative centre was frantic with activity, as were the stores, and a mere glance told him he was not needed in either place. The kitchens were pursuing their normal routines uncertainly, but there he could be of no help anyway.

Only towards the end of his brief journey did he feel his resolve tested: twice.

As he entered the hospital tent, the two duty healers rose to greet him. They were smiling, but a subtle reproach hung in the air. How can you be both healer and warrior, Hawklan? it said. You know the scenes that will be enacted here soon, as smashed and broken bodies are dragged in from the battlefield in hope of repair or solace, or at worst, an easier death; bodies that have walked and run, slept, eaten, loved. And *followed you*.

There was no answer other than that he and those with him were there by choice and knowing at least *some* of the truth.

It offered little comfort.

He placed his arms around the shoulders of the two women. 'Don't be afraid of your anger,' he said. 'You'll need it to mend some of the ills that you'll see soon. Use it.'

Leaving the hospital tent he wandered absently for a few minutes before finding himself by the stables. Someone inside was singing softly. Entering, he saw that the singer was a lanky youth grooming one of the horses. At the sound of Hawklan's footsteps in the straw the youth turned and, recognising him, smiled awkwardly.

But as their eyes met the youth looked away suddenly.

'What's the matter?' Hawklan asked.

The youth's hand fidgetted with the grooming brush, then, suddenly he said. 'I'm frightened, Hawklan.'

'Good,' Hawklan replied, almost automatically. 'Your fear will help keep you alive.'

The youth looked at him suspiciously. He put down the brush gently on a nearby stool and twisted from side to side, his whole body denying Hawklan's words.

'It's not the same, Hawklan,' he said fearfully. 'Not the same as training and talking at home.' Then, abruptly, 'I don't want to die,' he said. 'Or be . . . maimed. And I don't want to kill anyone. I don't think I can. I . . . don't want to be here – freezing, frightened and days from home.'

The brief flow stopped and the youth turned round and began to stroke one of the horses nervously. Hawklan looked at him, his own conscience made flesh.

'You're not alone in that,' he said quietly, after a pause. 'What else are you frightened of?'

The youth turned back to Hawklan sharply, oddly unbalanced by the question. 'Isn't that enough?' he said.

'Speak *all* your fears,' Hawklan said, ignoring the question.

For a long moment the youth stared at him, then he seemed to become more composed. 'I don't want to see my friends killed,' he said. 'I don't want to be responsible for their deaths. Suppose I . . . fail them in some way; slip, stumble, forget a drill when I'm in the line, and break it . . .'

Hawklan looked down. Something in the youth's manner touched him deeply. These last remarks were only a hastily snatched garment to cover the naked truth of the previous outburst. But it did not matter. The youth's fear taunted him. He had many skills he could use to lift the morale of his people when it proved necessary; skills that would ease burdens and carry the bearer boldly into battle. But now they had a hollow ring to them; Hawklan recognised the mocking residue of their original creator's teaching.

Here he could use none of them.

Reaching out, he stroked the horse as the youth had been doing. 'You won't,' he said simply. 'Will you?' It was all he could offer.

Leaving the stable, Hawklan continued on to the command tent. Tirke and Yrain were there with Isloman and Athyr, poring over a plan of the Morlider camp. Both radiated a mixture of relief and exhilaration at their first silent encounter with the enemy. Their mood lifted some of the darkness from Hawklan that his encounter with the youth had left. He smiled and as he had with the healers, laid a hand on the shoulder of each as a token of welcome and understanding.

Yrain was marking on the plan the extent of the latest

fortifications. Hawklan looked over her shoulder.

'They're nearly completed,' he said unnecessarily when she had finished.

Isloman ran his finger over the plan. 'Apart from this uncompleted end here, there are four openings,' he said. 'None of which is gated so far. The ground's well compacted by now. We should be able to get in and out quickly in the confusion.'

Hawklan frowned uncertainly.

'They're not expecting anything,' Isloman went on persuasively. 'They've still not got guards out. They haven't had any all the time we've been watching them.'

Hawklan nodded, and tapped his finger on the plan thoughtfully. 'This uncompleted end is cluttered with tents and stores of some kind,' he said. 'Access is out of the question there. Then these gaps are a long way apart and none too wide. And for all they've no guards that we can see, we've no idea how quickly they'll respond once things start to happen. You could find yourselves trapped in there and our hit and run attack could easily turn into a slaughter.'

The entrance of the command tent opened to admit Dacu and Loman.

Hawklan turned to Yrain. 'Tell me about these patrols,' he said. 'Size, number, uniforms –' There was a little laughter at this last. The Morlider might perhaps be united in spirit and intent but they were as individually and eccentrically dressed as could be imagined.

'Single patrols, about twenty men strong, uniforms – well-wrapped, but casual,' Yrain replied, with a smile. 'So far they've come out at irregular intervals and they seem to be following different routes. I think they're just finding their way around.'

Hawklan thought for a moment. 'Is there a patrol out now?'

Yrain nodded.

'It'll be dark when it returns?' Hawklan continued.

Yrain nodded again.

Pitch-soaked torches burned smokily along the wooden palisade, throwing uneasy dancing shadows on to the nearby line of tents. Near to one of the four gaps in the long defensive paling a large fire burned. Four figures crouched around it. The sound of waves breaking over the shore in the near distance formed a constant bass harmony to their conversation.

'What's he doing down there any way?' said one irritably. 'Why've we all got to sit up here freezing our backsides in the snow while he and his fancy guards swan around down south somewhere.'

His neighbour kicked him, none too gently. 'Shut up, you blockhead,' he said, looking around anxiously. 'This place is full of those big-eared Vierlanders, and a comment like that could see you discussing your complaint with him face to face.'

The first speaker rubbed his leg and made a disparaging noise. 'So what?' he muttered.

His companion looked round hastily then seized him roughly and pulled him forward. 'I'll tell you so-what, fish-brain,' he said, through clenched teeth. 'He'll boil your blood in your veins with a look, that's what. I've seen him do it.' He shuddered and released his charge. 'Personally I don't give crab's fart about that, but he's liable to do it to us as well for not skewering you on the spot. Now shut up.'

Chastened, the first speaker stirred the fire with his foot. A shower of sparks rose up through the falling snow.

'I meant no disrespect,' he said awkwardly and more as if for the benefit of any listeners in the darkness around the fire than out of genuine regret. 'But I came to kill Riddinvolk, not sit shivering behind a wooden fence at the top end of nowhere.'

'There'll be plenty of time for killing, don't you fret,' replied another, older than most of the others. He drew a long knife and turned it over longingly. 'The Chief knows what he's doing. That's why we've got decent tents, clothes, food; so that we *can* wait. Not like last time. Men's feet and hands turning black. Dying screaming in the night, or worse, just going . . . quiet – and lying down in the snow waiting to die. Trying to fight those damned horse riders and those poxed inlanders from over the mountains with your hands too cold to feel your sword; the chiefs quarrelling like old women and everyone fretting in case the islands moved off along the ways too soon.' He spat into the fire and bared his teeth. The firelight bounced menacingly off his twisting knife. 'None of that this time. This time we take this land.' He paused and nodded reflectively. 'I've some rare scores to settle I can tell you, and I intend to enjoy them. I've waited twenty years – a little longer's neither here nor there.'

Any further debate was precluded by the arrival through the opening of a group of men heavily muffled and hooded in furs.

The man with the knife looked up. 'About time,' he said unpleasantly. 'Where the devil have you been? We've been freezing to death waiting for you.'

The new arrivals moved towards the fire eagerly, with some hand rubbing and foot stamping. The man watched them as they approached, then he leaned forward a little, his eyes narrowed, trying to peer into the darkness of the leader's hood.

Suddenly his hand curled around the handle of his knife and he started to rise. 'You're not –'

Before he could finish, a sword emerged from the leader's fur coat and ran him through. There was not a flicker of hesitation in the deed, nor in the hand that shot out to silence any cry he might make and, before his knife had tumbled onto the snow, others from the group had killed the remaining three guards with the same ruthless expedition.

'Guards after all,' Athyr said. 'I hope the others are all right.' He looked down at the dead men. 'Still, first and last duty for this lot. Prop them up quickly and gather round as if you're warming yourselves.' He wiped his sword on the dead man's coat and looked at Tirke. 'See what's happened to the others,' he said.

The young Fyordyn hesitated. The blood-stained sword in his hand was shaking.

'Tirke!' Athyr hissed angrily.

'I'm sorry,' Tirke said starting. 'When I pulled my sword out, his –'

'Later.' Athyr's voice was both understanding and grimly unequivocal. 'You did well. You killed him before he knew what was happening, quickly and quietly; that's all that matters here. Keep it that way and we'll be get back to camp safely.'

Tirke nodded awkwardly. 'By numbers,' he said.

Athyr patted him on the arm. 'By numbers,' he confirmed. 'Now, signal.'

Tirke ran to the palisade and looked up and down its length intently. Producing a small signalling torch he sent a brief message in both directions.

The Morlider patrol had been ambushed, and groups of Helyadin, suitably disguised, had arrived simultaneously at all four entrances in an attempt to ensure deep and silent penetration into the camp. Hawklan had told them to prepare for guards, but nonetheless they had been an unpleasant surprise.

'Groups one and three are all right,' he said, returning to Athyr. 'But group four's met some resistance.'

Even as he spoke the faint sound of raised voices in the distance reached them. The entire group stood motionless and silent. The commotion mingled with the sound of the sea but showed no immediate signs of stopping.

Athyr ran through the anticipated options quickly. Three groups into the camp without disturbance was one of the better ones. Isloman's group would now act as diversion by holding for as long as they could before retreating.

'Three are going in a hundred paces,' Tirke said.

Athyr nodded. 'We'll go a hundred and fifty, tell one to go two hundred at their discretion.'

Tirke sent the message and then, without speaking, the group set off towards the sound of the breaking waves. They made no effort to quieten their footsteps, knowing that to the sleeping army around them a stealthy footfall would ring like a clarion call while the crunching indifference of their passing comrades would warrant no more than a mumbled oath.

The group encountered only two solitary wanderers and both met the same sudden and cruel fate as those at the gate.

Occasionally the distant sounds of Isloman's encounter drifted to them over the sound of the surf.

As they walked over the frozen sand and snow, churned up by the traffic of the camp, Athyr found flickering fireflies of sympathy beginning to dance in his mind. The layout of the camp was a bizarre mixture of imposed order and personal idiosyncracy; all the tents were different and, for the most part, crudely made out of animal skins and various fabrics. Pitch torches and the remains of camp fires glowed and guttered everywhere. Athyr could not avoid feeling the personal endeavour and the fulfilment of modest skills that radiated from these details and his carver's soul could do no other than respond in some degree. He tried to scatter the thoughts, but they reformed. These people were trapped in and by their own ignorance, he saw. Blazing torches for light! Open wood fires for heat! Presumably they had the same inside their tents; tents that would let that meagre heat escape into the winter night with scarcely any hindrance; they had no conception of collection, or re-use; small things, but they typified the state of these benighted, misled people. They knew so very very little . . . it was tragic that—

His foot caught an extended guy rope and only the quick

response of his neighbour prevented him from sprawling headlong.

Athyr nodded his thanks and cursed himself darkly for a fool. Whatever had made the Morlider into what they were, they *were* what they were and, misled or no, they were numerous, dangerous, and more than capable of over-running the Orthlundyn army if they were given the opportunity. More urgently, they could destroy this tiny infiltrating force if they were roused by some such further act of carelessness. The Morlider could not now be retrieved by knowledge, especially as they had been welded into some semblance of a whole by Creost. That salvation might await them some other day, but . . .

One hundred and fifty.

His training and his wiser instincts cut across his thoughts. This was far enough. The intermittent noise of the distant fighting had faded; Isloman must have done what he could and retreated. Would the Morlider rouse the whole camp, or would Isloman have been able to preoccupy them with the lure of pursuit?

Conjecture was irrelevant.

'Time to go,' Athyr hand-signalled to his group. 'You know what to do. Keep to your pairs, keep quiet, keep moving, and cut down anyone who gets in the way.'

The group spread out silently.

Athyr reached into his pouch and withdrew one of the specially prepared radiant stones. He placed it on the ground against the wall of a tent then, nervously and with a well extended arm, he struck it. Almost immediately it glowed a dark sinister red and he stepped back hastily. Quickly he moved to the next tent.

In a few seconds the stone would begin to release its stored energy; not in a steady hearth-warming flow, but in a great uncontrollable surge of heat that would continue for many minutes. In addition to his concern at being in the heart of the enemy's camp, Athyr's nervousness was aggravated by the fact that once struck, such stones were unstable and there was no indication how long it would be before this release occurred.

He was crouching down striking a fourth as the first one began to flare. He paused momentarily to watch it and suddenly a blow sent him sprawling. As he fell, the stone he had struck blazed up dazzlingly in front of him.

Momentarily blinded he rolled away from the heat, eyes

213

closed. When he opened them he saw a blurred figure silhouetted against the glaring light. It was bending over him, arm extended. Reflexively Athyr tightened his grip on his striker to use it as a dagger against this assailant but, with unexpected speed, a foot pinned his wrist onto the frozen snow-filled sand.

'It's me!' the figure hissed, its voice a mixture of alarm and exasperation. 'I had to knock you away, you weren't looking and your stone was going. Get up for pity's sake!'

It was Tirke. The foot released Athyr's arm and he allowed himself to be dragged to his feet. Tirke was looking at him anxiously and was about to speak.

Athyr forestalled him. 'Come on,' he said urgently, seizing his arm. He had recovered most of his composure as soon as he had recognised Tirke's voice but his heart was beating at a rate that he knew would not now diminish until he was clear of the Morlider camp.

Against the background of growing flames and mounting clamour, the Helyadin moved silently and swiftly between the crooked rows of tents, leaving the glowing red stones that would spread that clamour even further.

As they neared the palisade and the unguarded opening, a man came running towards them, sword in hand.

'The Gate watch have all been killed,' he said, a murderous fury in his voice. 'Those stinking horse riders must be in the camp.'

Athyr gripped his sword under his fur coat but before he could strike, three more armed figures came running in the same direction. Too many and too angry to kill either quickly or quietly. He had to get his group out urgently now.

He gesticulated frantically towards the sea. 'The ships! The ships! Fire!' he gasped hoarsely, as if he had been running desperately.

The words could not have been better chosen. The merest glance at the flickering skyline galvanised the four men who ran off shouting and banging tent ropes as they passed.

Athyr and Tirke ran on desperately until they reached the fire by the opening in the palisade. Two of the dead guards had tumbled over, and were staring upwards wide-eyed into the still falling snow. Tirke paused as he passed by, then wiping his hands down his sides as if they were dirty he moved to join Athyr who had slipped through the opening and was waiting in the shade beyond.

Four figures emerged from between the nearby tents, their rapid stealth identifying them as Helyadin. Athyr stepped forward and ushered them through the opening. They vanished into the darkness.

Almost immediately, others appeared. Athyr dismissed them after their companions. Tirke found himself examining faces and counting, just as he knew Athyr would be. So near the end of this mission he found his fear rising almost uncontrollably. Four more left! Come on! Come on! Yet Athyr seemed quite calm.

The din in the camp was now considerable and there were signs of waking activity in the nearby tents. Shadowy figures were emerging everywhere.

*Where in Sumeral's name are you?*

Tirke's agonised but silent question was answered by angry voices and the clash of arms nearby. Athyr ran towards the sound and, without thinking, Tirke followed him. As they reached the aisle from which the noise had come, two figures emerged, one supporting the other. Behind them two others were walking backwards holding their swords double-handed and keeping a group of about six hesitant Morlider at bay. In the gloom beyond them, Tirke thought he saw two figures sprawled on the ground. That would account for the Morlider's caution.

Athyr seized the free arm of the injured man and lifted it around his shoulder.

'Run,' he shouted unnecessarily, to his fellow bearer.

Tirke joined the two men forming the rearguard. Abruptly three of the Morlider disappeared behind a tent.

'Watch your flanks,' one of the Helyadin cried, followed immediately by the cry, 'Run for it.'

Tirke and the other Helyadin needed no such injunction and, turning, they dashed for the opening. A figure came briefly into the edge of Tirke's vision and he lashed out at it wildly with his sword. The sword made contact with something and there was a cry of pain. Tirke did not pause in his flight; he suddenly had the impression that the entire Morlider army was being drawn towards him personally.

Outside the palisade, the ground sloped upwards slightly and the snow became increasingly deep, making both flight and chase awkward and lumbering. However, unburdened by any injured companions, the Morlider soon caught up with the retreating group. There was a brief untidy skirmish which left two Morlider bleeding and groaning in the snow, before they in their turn withdrew a little to surround the Helyadin comfortably beyond sword's length.

Rather to his surprise, Tirke saw that there were in fact only about a dozen or so, and that not all were armed.

Without command, the Helyadin formed a circle.

'Tend to your ships, Morlider,' Athyr shouted, waving his sword towards the now roaring flames, but the lure did not have the effect it had had before.

Instead, one of the Morlider threw a small axe. Its blade glittered briefly in the flickering light, and somehow, Athyr managed to strike it with his sword and destroy most of its momentum. It travelled on, however, to catch Tirke a glancing blow on the shoulder. The impact made him stagger forward and two or three of the Morlider started towards him. The pain of the blow broke through Tirke's fear and released a darker creature. As he recovered his balance he took one hand from his sword hilt and drew a long knife. The attackers faltered, though it was as much the look on his face as the extra blade that made them hesitate.

Athyr glanced towards the camp. More Morlider were emerging; delay would be fatal. He hitched his injured companion into a more comfortable position then, speaking in the battle language, said, 'Into the darkness.'

Abruptly the five men and their burden were running through the hindering snow. The surrounding circle burst open as, surprised, by Athyr's alien command and this unexpected charge, the Morlider scattered to avoid the slashing blades of the Helyadin. The surprise was only momentary, however, and a grim pursuit began again in earnest as yet more Morlider poured out of the camp.

Rage and terror mingled equally in Tirke as, gasping for breath, he forced his legs high to carry him through the deep snow and tried to keep near his companions in the deepening darkness that lay beyond the reach of the light from the blazing camp.

Very soon, however, he fell, almost bringing down a close pursuer. Turning as he fell he felt rather than saw a descending weapon. Some reflex twisted him from its path and he let out a startled cry.

As his attacker raised his weapon for a second blow, Tirke lashed out at him wildly with his sword. The blade raked across the man's thighs and Tirke felt it scraping along bone.

He had a sudden vision of Loman patiently and caringly teaching him how to use a sharpening stone. The Morlider gave an agonised cry and hurled himself backwards in a frenzied and belated attempt to avoid his terrible injury.

Tirke saw him rolling away frantically, still screaming, but he had little time to assimilate this scene, as he could also see Morlider closing in on him from all sides. He had a fleeting impression of his companions similarly assailed.

A blow from somewhere knocked the sword from his hand and he swung his knife in the general direction of this attack. He sensed a pair of legs leaping away, but in front of him appeared a looming figure lifting a spear high for a blow that must surely pass through him as easily as through the snow beneath him.

In the instant that it took for the spear to reach its zenith, Tirke felt his body futilely bracing itself for the dreadful impact, and the welling up of a great surge of cringing terror inside him. Yet even as the terror took shape, another emotion rose up and twined around it like a strangling serpent; a consuming fury, blazing from who could say what fire in his soul. Somehow he would kill this man even as he died.

This resolve had scarcely begun to reach his hand when the shadow of his doom went staggering backwards violently. The man took several flailing, unsteady paces and then crashed to the ground. Against the light of the blazing camp, Tirke saw him struggling to pull an arrow from his chest. After a moment he became still, though the arrow still swayed from side to side a little.

Then Tirke realised that he was also watching the other Morlider running away.

He struggled into a sitting position and looked behind him. As he did so, a long row of swaying lights appeared in the blackness; the second phase of the attack on the camp was beginning.

Relief almost as powerful as his terror overwhelmed him briefly, and he found his legs were shaking violently as he staggered to his feet.

Suddenly he was with his companions and there were horses all around. Someone was carrying the injured man away, and hands were reaching down to help the others.

'Come on, Tirke,' a voice said. 'Shift yourself, you're frightening the horses standing gaping like that.'

It was Jaldaric. Tirke looked at him vacantly for a moment

and then taking his proffered hand, swung up behind him clumsily.

'Just a moment,' he said, as Jaldaric clicked to the horse.

Jaldaric paused.

Tirke looked back through the gently falling snow at the Helyadin's handiwork.

The gentle slope he had just scrambled over was lit orange and yellow by the flames rising from the camp. Three substantial areas were ablaze, figures could be seen running in all directions and the noise of the flames and the shouting and screaming rose above the sound of the distant surf.

It was a grim, tormented sight, yet he knew it had been a good start to the night's work.

Now the cavalry would take over. Already their line was beginning to gather speed and Tirke could see that few of the Morlider who had ventured out of the camp would return. The thought reminded him of the rest of his own companions.

'Did everyone get back safely?' he asked.

'Some injuries I think, but no one killed as far as I know,' Jaldaric replied. 'You and the others were the last out.'

Injuries. The word brought back to Tirke the memory of the hurts he had caused that night and, in its wake, one of Hawklan's injunctions: 'Take no risks, but, if circumstances permit, wound rather than kill. An injured man is more trouble to the enemy than a dead one. He absorbs resources and he saps morale.' Then he had paused. 'And it'll burden you less at some happier time in the future.'

Tirke and Jaldaric watched as the cavalry caught up with the fleeing Morlider. There would be little wounding in *that* melée.

From a higher vantage point, Hawklan, Andawyr and Loman watched the same scene.

While some of the cavalry, yelling raucously, were dealing with the Morlider, others were flinging ropes and grappling hooks over the palisade. Very soon, large gaps had been torn in the defensive wall.

Hawklan nodded approvingly. The Orthlundyn were not natural horsemen by any means, but they had absorbed fully such teaching as Agreth had been able to give them and were mastering the necessary skills competently enough.

The first wave of cavalry retreated and for a moment a strange stillness pervaded the scene. Hawklan ran his eye along the still extensive remains of the palisade. Here and there groups of Morlider seemed to be forming in some semblance of order. Then, as though the night itself were moving to assault the camp, the second wave of cavalry surged forward. Silent this time, in tight formation, and without illumination, they were suddenly there, riding through the flame-lit night.

As they rode they shot volleys of arrows deep into the camp, arrows carrying the same radiant stones that the Helyadin had used. Some of them glowed white so quickly that they consumed the arrows that carried them, to fall fluttering and flaring out of the air; others fell dully into the ranks of tents and flared up only after the riders had passed.

Hawklan saw a movement in the nearest group of Morlider. He leaned forward. 'Wheel!' he muttered urgently. The leader of the riders saw the danger at the same time and, as if Hawklan's will had reached out through the night, he turned the line back towards the darkness. But it was almost too late. The Morlider stepped forward and released a small but accurate volley of arrows at their assailants.

Two horses went down immediately and a third stumbled trying to avoid them. Both Andawyr and Loman breathed in sharply and Hawklan felt Serian trembling underneath him. He laid a hand on the horse's neck and watched, his face unreadable. Now was the first of many real testing times, for both him and the Orthlundyn.

The sound of shouted commands came faintly to the watchers.

Two riders broke off to pursue the third horse, which had recovered itself almost immediately. Other riders picked up their unhorsed companions while the remainder returned the Morlider's fire, causing them to scatter for shelter behind the palisade. Then, as quickly as they had appeared, the riders merged back into the darkness.

Andawyr turned to speak, but Hawklan held up his hand for silence. Again there was an almost eerie stillness in front of the camp. The Morlider archers re-formed.

Suddenly two adjacent groups of archers further along broke up rapidly. Hawklan could not see what was happening, but he knew that the Orthlundyn were standing back and firing from the cover of darkness. As soon as the defenders were routed, albeit temporarily, the cavalry rode in again to fire further volleys of flaming arrows into the camp. Hawklan nodded approvingly.

The harassment continued through the night and for much of the time the Morlider camp was in considerable disarray.

'If only we had the numbers, we could drive them into the sea,' Loman reflected.

Hawklan nodded slightly. 'A good word to choke on, *if*,' he said. 'But even if we drove them to their boats, they'd be back, wouldn't they, Andawyr?'

The Cadwanwr started. He had been watching the unfolding saga with mounting distress. No amount of knowledge, he realised, could have fully prepared him for the frightening ordinariness that framed this reality. The horse shifting underneath him, the creaking of harness, Loman softly clearing his throat, the occasional snowflake landing cold on his now clammy face. Hawklan still Hawklan. The crackling flames and the terrible tactical games being played before him should have meant . . . more than they did. But they were outside his protective cocoon of darkness, and they were so . . . distant . . . unreal.

Hawklan's voice reached out and brought him to the present with a jolt.

'Yes. Yes,' he stammered, catching the vanishing gist of the question. 'I doubt they'll leave until Creost abandons them.'

Hawklan turned and looked at him. As their eyes met, Andawyr said, almost shamefacedly, 'Thank you. I couldn't have helped.'

Hawklan did not reply, but the understanding and compassion of both warrior prince and healer showed in his eyes, and comforted the Cadwanwr. Earlier, as the details of the attack were being discussed, Andawyr had asked if he could help: he had devices of his own that would not extend him; a breeze to fan the flames, some fires of his own, something to tear out that palisade? Hawklan had shaken his head. 'Another time,' he had replied gently. 'Your Power's for another purpose, you know that. Men must fight men. Here particularly, the Orthlundyn must learn those final lessons which can only be learned in combat. To ease their way with weapons they themselves can't wield would be to mislead them and betray them in some future battle.' Then, practical as ever: 'Besides, you don't want to betray your presence to Creost if he's there, do you?'

'He isn't,' Andawyr had replied positively, but Hawklan's silent green-eyed gaze had said, 'Can you take that risk?'

As time passed, however, the Morlider began to recover

from the initial impact of the Orthlundyn assault.

'They've realised we're not intending an all-out attack,' Hawklan said, as gradually the fires were doused and the archers defending the gaps in the palisade became both more cautious and more effective. 'Pull back. We can do no more tonight. We'd be risking riders and horses needlessly if we persisted.' Loman nodded in agreement. 'I doubt they'll venture out,' Hawklan continued. 'But leave pickets out in case, and have the army deployed by first light. They'll come out then with a vengeance.'

In the command tent, Hawklan looked purposefully at his friends. 'We've done them some harm,' he said. 'And shaken their nerve. Have we learned anything that would make us change our basic tactics?'

'Loman tells me their archers are more organised than they used to be,' Isloman said. 'But that crowd we ran into were the same as ever – wild and dangerous.' Old memories of close-quarter fighting rose like vomit to mingle with the new, but with an angry grimace he dismissed them. 'I think if we can crack their discipline, they'll revert to type – individual warriors looking to fight and kill. Then we're in with a chance. I see no reason to change anything.'

No one disagreed. The conduct of the Morlider that night had shown the veterans enough to confirm that their enemy was both the same, and profoundly changed.

Hawklan reached up and touched Gavor's beak absently. 'The tactics stand, then,' he said. 'Tomorrow –' He smiled ruefully. 'Today. We *will* drive them into the sea. They'll have been training to deal with cavalry and they'll expect to meet cavalry not disciplined infantry. We still have surprise on –'

Andawyr stood up suddenly. 'Wake Atelon,' he said, cutting across Hawklan. 'Quickly. Bring him here.' His voice was strange and distant.

There was a brief pause then Dacu ran out.

'What's the matter?' Hawklan said, concerned by Andawyr's manner.

A distant roll of thunder sounded softly through the tent.

'Dar Hastuin,' he said, his voice strained. 'He's above us. And putting forth great power.'

Hawklan looked alarmed. 'Against us?' he said.

Andawyr shook his head. 'No,' he answered. 'I think he's found the Drienvolk.'

Gavor flapped his wings restlessly and Hawklan reached up

221

to him again. 'There's nothing we can do, old friend,' he said. 'We touched briefly, but the Drienvolk must fight their own kind in their own way. Stay here and guard my back.'

Before Gavor could reply, the entrance to the tent burst open and Atelon staggered in, supported by Dacu. His young face was haunted and fearful, and his mouth was working though no coherent sounds were emerging.

'He was like this when I found him,' Dacu said, his own face riven with concern.

Andawyr looked at his student for a moment and then walked over to him very calmly and took his hands. Hawklan saw again the man who had destroyed the lair of the Vrwystin a Kaethio at the Gretmearc. Dacu released his charge.

At the touch of his master, Atelon seemed to recover some of his composure.

'Don't be –' Andawyr froze, and his words of solace faltered. Atelon's legs buckled and Dacu stepped forward quickly to catch him.

'Andawyr, what's happening?' Hawklan said, his eyes now wide with anxiety.

Andawyr lifted a hand for silence but kept his attention on Atelon. The young man's eyes opened and with an effort he straightened up. Hawklan winced inwardly as the healer in him felt Atelon's pain and fear.

'You feel it all?' Andawyr said.

Atelon nodded.

'That's good,' Andawyr said, his voice gentle but filled with a great resolve. 'I'll not exhort you to be brave, I'll ask you only to be a Cadwanwr, and do what must be done. Can you accept that?'

Atelon nodded again. 'Yes,' he said faintly, but clearly.

Andawyr turned to Hawklan.

'Very shortly, you'll lead the Orthlundyn against the superior numbers of the Morlider army, and fight to very limits of your skill and strength to destroy them,' he said. 'Atelon and I will accompany you to do the same against their new leader.'

Hawklan's eyes narrowed with an unnecessary question.

Andawyr answered it. 'Whatever his purpose was in the south, it's ended; for good or for ill. Creost is here now.'

# *Chapter 15*

The long flight of stone steps led down from one of the Palace's many side doors. It was a little-used entrance and the steps had not been routinely swept clear of snow, thus ensuring that such use as they had received had trodden a ragged pathway down the centre that had the texture of uneven, but polished alabaster.

It glistened treacherously in the sunlight as Eldric emerged from the doorway.

Blinking in the sudden brightness, he eyed his proposed path suspiciously. Then, pulling his large cloak about his shoulders, he began a cautious descent, using his gloved hand freely on the stone banister rail to retain his balance.

Reaching the bottom without mishap or excessive loss of dignity, he made a note to return by another route and then crossed a narrow courtyard to bring himself out into the Palace gardens.

It had not snowed for several days and though the extensive lawns and shrubs were brilliant in the winter sunshine they had lost that silent perfection which the first falls had given them. Untidy heaps of snow lay around the trees where the wind and the fluttering birds had dislodged it from the branches; human footsteps respectfully marked out the now hidden pathways, while the imprints of claws and padded feet showed no such restraint and were strung out purposefully across the lawns in an intricate tracery. Here and there a riot of destruction in the snow indicated the activity of the Palace children, not all of whom were particularly young.

Eldric took in the scene and smiled, then stepped forward to add his own marks to this great marring.

As he walked, he turned his mind to the message he had just received from Arinndier. Viladrien! Alphraan! Cadwanwr! Creost moving the Morlider against Riddin, and Hawklan leading half the Orthlundyn army into the snow-filled mountains to meet them while the other half was preparing to move north to join the High Guards for an assault on Narsindal!

Arinndier had laid out the facts simply and clearly. Indeed,

Eldric could almost hear him speaking as he read the Lord's characteristic hand.

He looked south. The Orthlundyn armed and ready for war! And with an army that was good enough to impress Arinndier! But for half of it to venture across the mountains at this time of year! Could even Hawklan bring his people through such an ordeal in a condition fit to fight a battle, or worse, a series of battles against the savage and numerous Morlider? By all accounts the journey north had been difficult enough for the two men who had brought Arinndier's message; how much more so then for an army? And if Riddin fell, what then? What of Sylvriss and her child; the heir to Fyorlund's throne? And what of Fyorlund's southern and eastern borders?

Eldric weighed the thoughts briefly then, with some difficulty, let them go. He could do nothing about these matters, he knew. Nothing except wait for further messages – tend his crops and keep his sword sharp as his father would have said. Urthryn would surely protect his daughter, no matter what happened. And if the rest of the Orthlundyn army was moving north then presumably they had made their own arrangements for the defence of their land should Hawklan be lost. As for Fyorlund's border with Riddin, a few regiments of High Guards could always be left to protect that if need arose. Whatever force might come over those mountains certainly wouldn't come quickly, winter or no.

It was too vague and untidy a resolution to be satisfactory, but it would have to suffice for the time being, though Eldric found that even the thought of Hawklan being lost in battle was deeply unsettling.

He reacted to his unease almost immediately. 'We must stand on our own,' he muttered into the cold air. To look to one man, however remarkable, as some kind of saviour, someone who would bear the responsibilities and fulfil the duties of others, would be a profound error. 'Another betrayal of the people and our trust,' he concluded.

He could allow himself to cling to the fatherly concern that he had felt on reading that Jaldaric was now training 'with the Orthlundyn Helyadin – similar to our Goraidin,' but apart from that he must continue to occupy himself with his own duty; with stern practicalities. Send messengers to welcome the approaching Orthlundyn. And find somewhere to put them all! Send the news to Hreldar and Darek currently out in the field, training and co-ordinating the different regiments of

High Guards; this new army would radically affect the plans being laid for the assault on Narsindalvak and thence Narsindal. And to Yatsu, busy in the east with some of the Goraidin and their new recruits, preparing to assault Dan-Tor's mines.

He straightened up and took a deep breath. As always, when he did this, the cold air felt as if it were a light shining inside him, seeking out and exposing the lingering, stagnant memories of the imprisonment that returned to haunt him in his darker moments. It was a small, personal reaffirmation.

Remembering the treacherous stairway, he turned and set off briskly towards the front of the Palace.

With Gavor perched awkwardly in front of him, Hawklan walked Serian towards the top of the long slope that led down to the Morlider's camp on the shore. Andawyr, on his smaller mare, rode by him, accompanied by Atelon. Loman, Isloman and a group of Helyadin maintained close station around the three. They were an unprepossessing sight, as Hawklan had told them to cover their light mail armour with rough cloaks to give the impression that they were a hastily levied local defence group.

A faint roll of thunder reached them. Several such had echoed down through the darkness since Andawyr's announcement of the arrival of Dar Hastuin. Each time, Hawklan had looked at the Cadwanwr who had simply nodded helplessly in reply. Both knew that while the Morlider and the Orthlundyn were waiting for their battle, the Drienvolk were probably fighting theirs.

The slowly lightening sky, however, was an unbroken mass of grey, lowering cloud and gave no sign of this strange and alien combat.

'Our tasks are here,' was Andawyr's final comment. 'We mustn't burden ourselves with their pain when we can't alleviate it.'

Reaching the top of the slope, Hawklan reined Serian to a halt. In the far distance, the vague, misty horizon was broken by three islands which only the local Riddinvolk could have denounced as being unnaturally there. Nearer, on the shore, the rope-strewn masts of beached ships canted this way and that, and in front of them ragged columns of smoke rose from the camp. Hawklan viewed the scene with some satisfaction, though how much of the smoke was due to the previous night's attack and how much due to the Morlider's crude cooking and heating fires he could not tell.

Not that it was of any great moment now. The attack had doubtless done some useful damage to both materials and morale but its primary purpose had been to draw the Morlider out of their enclave to join battle. The only question taxing Hawklan as he gazed through the morning greyness was, had this been successful? If the Morlider simply repaired their defences and stayed behind them then the Orthlundyn would have to continue their harassing attacks, and while the previous night's had cost them only two horses and various relatively minor injuries, future forays, being expected, would necessarily take a far greater toll.

It was with some relief therefore that he saw a large column of men forming up outside the camp, and he urged Serian forward to ensure he stood clear and bold on the skyline. At his signal the others joined him.

'Careful,' Andawyr urged softly to Hawklan. 'I can feel Creost's presence all around.'

'What's he doing?' Hawklan asked.

Andawyr looked at him impatiently. 'How could I know?' he said, a little more sharply than he had intended. 'He's not attacking us for sure, you'll not need me to tell you when he does that.' Then, repenting a little: 'He's exerting Power in some way . . . wrongly, but not . . . against anyone . . . not destructively.' He shook his head as if trying to clear it. 'It's probably to do with preventing the islands from moving . . .' He paused thoughtfully, then leaned across to Atelon and spoke to him softly.

Another, loud, roll of thunder interrupted this conversation and made everyone look upwards. Hawklan suddenly felt his flesh crawl. He had not felt such a sensation since he had approached Vakloss to confront Dan-Tor, but this, though fainter, was in some way far worse.

'The Drienvolk are suffering,' he said to Andawyr.

'We can do nothing,' Andawyr reiterated. 'Look to your front; to the enemy you *can* fight.'

Hawklan pulled his mind from the invisible torment high above him and looked again at the smoking camp and the gathering men. As he had expected, the appearance of riders on the skyline had caused some commotion, and angry voices were now reaching him above the ubiquitous sound of the sea.

'Have your bows ready,' he said, nudging Serian forward.

226

'Let's see if our estimate of their temperament – and range – is correct.'

The small party began moving down towards the camp, two of the Helyadin discreetly falling in on either side of Andawyr whose horsemanship would be decidedly uncertain if, as they anticipated, they were obliged to leave quickly.

As they neared someone shouted an order and the abuse that had been directed at them died down unexpectedly. Abruptly, some of the Morlider broke ranks and spread out in a line to face them. They were archers, silent and waiting. Their bows were lowered, but their arrows were nocked; and the man-oeuvre was executed with some efficiency. Hawklan redirected his group a little to approach the other side of the column. There was another order and archers appeared on that side only.

Hawklan stopped and examined the watching men. 'Loman. First impression: How do they compare with the Morlider you fought?' he said.

'Badly,' Loman answered tersely. 'From our point of view. Somebody's really knocked them into shape. The ones we faced would have been charging at us in a mob by now.'

Hawklan nodded. 'Stay here. We have to make sure they keep coming after us. I'm going forward to see if I can provoke them a little. Be ready to run quickly.'

Gavor flapped his wings in anticipation but as Hawklan was about to move forward Tybek rode past him, and at the same time Loman surreptitiously leaned across and took Hawklan's reins.

Caught unawares by these movements, Hawklan looked from Loman to the retreating Tybek open-mouthed. Loman casually handed him his reins back. 'Don't make yourself conspicuous, *Commander*,' he said, his tone slightly mocking. 'You have a bodyguard now.'

In spite of the mounting tension in the group as Tybek neared the silent column, Isloman, riding on Hawklan's other side, chuckled at the sight of the expression on Hawklan's face. 'We thought it was best not to tell you,' he said.

Hawklan was about to answer when Tybek stopped. He was some distance from the archers but, Hawklan judged, within range.

Hawklan found he was making himself breathe quietly and deeply.

Tybek stood in his stirrups and slowly looked over the

227

waiting column. His manner was arrogant and he offered them no preamble.

'We visited you last night, Morlider, to let you know what will happen if you choose to stay,' he shouted. 'Go back to your islands. We want no fighting but there'll be nothing but pain and death for you if you remain.'

For a moment there was no response, then a short, stocky figure stepped forward out of the front rank. He cocked his head on one side and looked at Tybek narrowly.

'We'll put up with the pain and death, horse rider,' he responded. 'After all, it's going to be yours, not ours.' Jeering laughter rose up from the waiting column. The man continued. 'We're not here to debate, we're here to take this country ourselves. If you'll take my advice you and your scruffy mates'll turn your nags round and not stop riding until you're on the other side of the mountains. It'll be a month or two before we get over there.' His followers endorsed this remark with vigour and obscenity.

Tybek waved the din aside airily. 'Don't mistake us for what's waiting for you out there,' he said, pointing back up the slope.

The stocky man clapped his hands and then folded his arms. 'That wouldn't be . . . *horses* . . . would it?' he said, laying a mocking and ponderous emphasis on the word. 'It's nice to know you've got one or two left. We thought they'd all gone south.'

More laughter greeted this remark. Someone shouted. 'Fresh meat at least, lads!' The stocky man smiled and gave Tybek an apologetic shrug.

'It seems that horses don't worry us like they used to,' he said. Then his face changed, the smile vanishing. 'Anyway, my men are getting cold standing about like this. We'll have to be on our way. We've a camp to find and burn; a murdering sneaking night thieves' camp. If there's horses – or riders – in it, so much the better.' His voice rasped with a viciousness that was like the drawing of a sword. Tybek made his horse shy and prance as if it were startled, surreptitiously using the movement to edge it backwards and preparing it to turn and run.

'Get Andawyr out of here, now,' Hawklan said urgently. 'The rest of you get ready to move in and help Tybek.' Before the Cadwanwr could protest, the two Helyadin were quietly leading him away.

Still affecting to be having difficulty in controlling his horse, Tybek was continuing his debate. 'You've been warned. If you're too stupid to learn from a little warning like last night's then take your chances against a full Line of the Muster.' He pointed back up the slope again. 'We could use the practice.' He paused and curled his lip. 'And if anyone should know about sneaking, murdering thieves, it's you, you fish-stinking scum.'

'Shoot him down,' roared the Morlider, rising more to the sneering contempt in Tybek's voice than to the words. But as the Helyadin turned his horse again, he brought his bow up and released an arrow at one of the extended lines of archers. Then, urging his horse forward up the slope with his knees, he turned in the saddle and released a second arrow at the other line.

It was an ineffective assault, both arrows falling short, but it was so sudden that it caused a brief hesitation in the two lines and when they had recovered and released their volleys, Tybek was at the limit of their range.

'Our bows have a longer range,' Loman said with some considerable satisfaction as Tybek caught up with the now retreating group.

Tybek glowered at him, his face flushed. 'Wonderful,' he said caustically, adding, rhetorically, 'Did I *volunteer* for that?'

Loman laughed and patted him on the back. 'You did, and you did well,' he said.

As they rode on, one of the Helyadin galloped ahead with the information about the approaching column and its archers while the others maintained a pace that drew them away from the Morlider only slowly.

Hawklan looked at Tybek. A mixture of exhilaration and disbelief lit the young man's face, but there was also a new, stark, knowledge, in his eyes. The knowledge of the awesome reality of facing someone who was seeking to kill him. Tybek would be different ever after.

The sight and the thought took Hawklan's mind back to the conspiracy that had silently provided a bodyguard for him and sent Tybek out on the dangerous impromptu mission that he himself had casually been about to take. The Orthlundyn army was also changing, beginning to become an autonomous whole. It had learned what it needed of him and it would protect him whether he willed it or not; within certain limits it would not hesitate to constrain him for its greater good.

It occurred to him briefly that perhaps, after all, what he imagined to be leadership was no more than the pressure he exerted against such constraints. It was an uncomfortable thought and he did not dwell upon it for, rather to his surprise, in thinking about the army, he found himself experiencing the unexpectedly turbulent emotions that he had seen in many a parent's eye as they watched their offspring grow. Happy to see their child learning and achieving, yet sad to see it moving out and away on paths of its own choosing, increasingly less dependent on that which had been for so long the centre of its life.

He smiled at the whimsy of the thought, but was surprised again to find a parental fear swimming in its wake. What if I've not taught this child well enough? What if it should wander too far and become not a source of hope and light for the future, but some fearful monster.

The intermittent cries of the following Morlider, abusive and savage, ended his reverie. He looked around at his companions, their breath steaming and streaming behind them as their horses carried them through the cold morning air. It had *better* turn into a fearful monster, he concluded acidly. That was what it had been born for.

They rode on in silence for a while, with the Morlider column following them steadily and in good order. Eventually the Helyadin who had galloped ahead, returned. 'Dacu has the message,' he said to Hawklan.

Hawklan thanked him and looked around the white landscape. He could see nothing untoward other than the dark scar of the Morlider column, but he knew that Dacu and the other Helyadin would be watching their progress and relaying the information back to the waiting Orthlundyn army. In confirmation of this, Isloman hissed, 'Message,' and inclined his head towards a small cluster of trees in the distance. Hawklan looked up in time to see a torch flickering briefly.

'What did it say?' he asked.

Gavor sighed conspicuously. 'Flashing lights,' he muttered loudly with monumental contempt. 'I don't know why you don't let me do all this message carrying.'

Hawklan had placed Gavor under the same injunction as Andawyr; faced by men, the army must learn from the start to fight and live without the peculiarly valuable aids that those two could offer. 'Soon you'll have to leave them, then what will they do,' he had said, adding by way of consolation, 'Your time will come, have no fear.' But the raven had taken the restraint with an ill grace and for the most part had been in a profound sulk ever since.

Hawklan's jawline tightened at Gavor's tone. 'We've had all this out as you know full well,' he said, in spite of a promise he had made to himself earlier not to rise to Gavor's goadings, adding, a little petulantly, 'Besides, we have Creost and Dar Hastuin nearby somewhere and, if you remember, you tend to make a bad first impression on Uhriel.'

Gavor met the sarcasm with a dignified inclination of his head then, muttering something profane under his breath, he related the message, though with great distaste.

'"Two more columns leaving the camp. Same size as first", flash, twinkle, flash,' he said.

Hawklan favoured Gavor with a malevolent look, then threw a mute appeal to Isloman. Unsuccessfully trying not to laugh at this exchange, the carver nodded a confirmation.

Hawklan thanked him over-courteously, while Gavor whistled tunelessly to himself and looked with exaggerated interest about the snow-clad countryside.

A rumbling series of thunderclaps sounded an end to the interlude and once again Hawklan found himself gazing upwards into the concealing blank greyness of the sky. He felt an unreasoning anger at his ignorance about the Drienvolk. Had he had known more about them, perhaps he would have been able to offer Ynar guidance at their brief and perhaps crucial meeting.

With his anger, however, came a deepening of his resolve. The Drienvolk were fighting the same war. The only help he could give them was to win his own battle. The Orthlundyn had resources beyond his reckoning and they looked to him to use them to the full. With that trust came the obligation to commit himself as fully to them as they had to him. They would not falter unless he did and, outnumbered or not, he must lead them forward until Creost and the Morlider were defeated, whatever the cost.

'Riders ahead,' Loman said.

They were Athyr and Yrain. Both were as unkempt as Hawklan and the others, though under their ragged clothes Hawklan knew they too would be armed and armoured for the task ahead.

Athyr's face was stern and determined, and he waited on no invitation to speak. 'I think the only way we'll draw enough of them out of the camp is to bring the three columns together and then attack them with just enough infantry to make them send back for reinforcements. If we keep increasing our infantry and gradually easing them back, then they'll probably send for more and more until –' He banged his fist into his open palm.

Hawklan looked thoughtful for a moment, and then nodded. 'Loman?' he said, turning to the smith.

'I doubt the Memsa could have done much better,' Loman said, smiling a little. 'I certainly can't. We'll have to think as we go, anyway.'

'Battle stations, then,' Hawklan said simply. 'Take command, Loman. Isloman and I will ride as observers with Andawyr and Atelon and . . . my . . . their . . . bodyguard. You know the final dispositions. Wait for my signal if we don't meet again.'

Reaching forward, he took first Loman's hand in both of his, and then Athyr's and Yrain's. 'This will be our day,' he said looking intently at each in turn.

As the three galloped away, Andawyr said quietly, 'I wish I shared your certainty.'

Hawklan turned to the Cadwanwr. 'You do, Andawyr,' he said. 'You do.'

Andawyr started a little as the force of Hawklan's personality seemed to become almost tangible around him. Whatever power lay in this man, he realised, was freely given to all who had the will, the courage, to accept it; its light illuminated his own resolves and, more alarmingly, his own dark skills with a fearsome clarity.

'Why didn't you take command yourself?' he heard himself saying.

Hawklan eased Serian forward and Andawyr fell in beside him. 'The Army's a weapon of Loman's forging,' he said. 'Loman's and Gulda's. He understands its heart far better than I ever could. He belongs here. I – we – belong elsewhere.'

Gavor flapped his wings noisily and then shook his wooden leg violently. 'Can I at least go and watch, dear boy?' he said, with forced politeness. 'I'm getting cramp standing here.'

Hawklan looked at him suspicously and then said, 'Go on,' with reluctant indulgence. 'But take care.'

Released, Gavor launched himself from Serian's head, and after dipping briefly began to climb purposefully until he was high above the cold landscape and the insignificant dots that were moving about it in their deadly game.

To the east the grey sky dwarfed the hazy Morlider Islands,

and even the ugly stain that was the huge camp along the shore was diminished. A little to the west of the circling raven, the Orthlundyn camp blended with the terrain to become almost invisible.

It irked Gavor to be just a spectator to these momentous happenings, though he understood the wisdom of Hawklan's judgement. However, free now to travel the ways he knew, it soon occurred to him that sooner or later Hawklan would be the focus of trouble and that there would be plenty to do then, with no reproach to be offered. The thought made him chuckle conspiratorially to himself and in an excess of glee he tumbled over and, shaking his wooden leg threateningly at the clouds above, laughed to himself.

Hawklan looked up at the black dot gliding in smooth sweeping arcs and occasionally faltering and dropping vertically. He smiled. It was good to have such a friend, whoever he was.

'Let's find a high place of our own,' he said to his companions.

As the morning proceeded, Hawklan moved his group to and fro for reasons that Andawyr could not always discern but which seemed to keep them fairly clear of the increasingly heated activity while enabling them to observe much of it. He began to see the truth of Hawklan's comment about Loman and the army. No messages came to Hawklan asking for advice or help, yet frequently Andawyr saw Hawklan nodding approvingly at some manoeuvre by the skirmishers who were harrying Morlider columns.

Groups of mounted archers attacked from first one direction then another, then from various directions simultaneously. Carefully they avoided betraying the superior range of the Orthlundyn bows, but it was dangerous work and while it took a constant toll of the Morlider in dead and wounded, it also took some toll of the Orthlundyn, several being wounded.

'They're very different from what they were twenty years ago,' Isloman remarked at one point. 'Their discipline under fire is far superior.'

Hawklan nodded. 'They're certainly keeping their stations well and using their shields to some effect,' he said. 'I think Loman should send in some foot slingers now, that should –'

Isloman caught his arm and pointed. A group of figures had dismounted and were approaching one of the columns on foot. Hawklan left his sentence unfinished and leaned forward intently.

At Dacu's suggestion, the slingers were armed with lead shot rather than the shaped stones that their natural inclination drew them to. With these the range of the slings was markedly superior to the Morlider bows and, coupling their expertise with jeering abuse, the slingers exploited it fully.

Almost immediately the Morlider column wavered as shields were used indiscriminately for protection against the rain of fast and almost invisible missiles. The slingers moved forward and pressed home their attack, at first randomly, then concentrating their fire at the centre of the column. The assailed Morlider faltered initially then crouched behind their shields and stood their ground. To relieve their comrades, the archers began to fire at the slingers, only to find their arrows falling short.

Standing next to Hawklan, Andawyr watched as the archers began to edge forward cautiously to bring the slingers within range, and slowly the whole column began to curve markedly. At this distance it was like watching an unusual board game, and, almost deliberately, he kept his mind from thinking of the grim reality that the participants were facing.

Abruptly the slingers changed their point of attack, leaving the centre and turning on a large group of archers at the front of the column who had ventured forward too far. Several of them went down under this unexpected and sudden assault, but the main damage resulted from the disordered retreat of the remainder. Seeing this, the slingers redoubled their efforts, at the same time moving forward towards the confusion. Andawyr noted a change in the tone of the angry cries that were reaching across the white expanse that separated him from the scene.

'Retreat,' he heard Hawklan whisper.

A tremor seemed to run through the whole column, and then the far end began to fragment and swing around as the goaded Morlider began to break ranks and charge the slingers in both an excess of fury and an attempt to relieve their comrades.

Andawyr found he was gripping the edge of his saddle fiercely, and preparing to shout out, 'Run!'

But his advice was unnecessary. The slingers were already retreating rapidly, and riders were coming forward with horses to collect them.

Just as the Cadwanwr began to let out the breath he had been holding, one of the slingers, trailing the others, staggered and fell. Andawyr could not see what had happened but presumed the man had been struck by an arrow. A rider, a woman, galloped forward urgently to help him, leaping down from her horse as it came to a halt amid a great flurry of snow. For an interminable moment, she struggled desperately to help the injured man into the saddle. Finally succeeding, she prepared to mount behind him.

However, startled by something, the horse darted forward unexpectedly and she fell heavily into the snow.

Standing up quickly but unsteadily, she looked around. Behind her, her horse was bolting away carrying the injured slinger slumped across its neck. In front, Morlider were converging on her.

It needed no military skills to see that her companions could not reach her before the enemy.

Instinctively, Andawyr reached out to strike the approaching Morlider and protect the woman as she stood watching them, uncertain which way to run.

Before he could act, however, a hand took his extended arm and tightened round it powerfully. Looking up he met Hawklan's haunted face.

'No,' the healer said. His voice was quiet and full of torment, but quite implacable.

Andawyr tugged at the grip ferociously, but it held him inexorably and pitilessly. After a brief, futile struggle, he found his gaze drawn inexorably to the distant tragedy about to be enacted.

The lone woman had seen the hopelessness of her position and turned to face the Morlider resolutely. Slowly she drew her sword with her right hand and a long knife with her left, then raising the sword above her head she began running to meet her foes. The advancing Morlider paused. Andawyr's hand closed into helpless fists as he heard her high-pitched cry of defiance.

She had not taken four paces when arrows began to hit her. The Morlider archers were taking their first true revenge.

The stricken woman staggered forward a little further until another volley of arrows brought her to her knees. With her last strength she lifted her sword high and then fell forward into the snow. The impact of her fall broke some of the arrows and drove others right through her, but for a moment her body lay slumped across them until she slumped over incongruously sideways.

The hesitant Morlider rushed forward and in a convulsive spasm of vengeance-taking, began hacking the body frenziedly.

Andawyr turned away from the scene and Hawklan released his arm.

'Why?' Andawyr said accusingly after brief silence.

'You know why,' Hawklan replied, his voice icy with a terrible restraint. 'Do you think *my* grip could curb *your* power?'

Andawyr bared his teeth as anger surged up inside him. 'Damn you,' he said viciously.

'Don't damn me, damn *Him*,' Hawklan said, his voice still cold. 'There'll be worse than that done before we're free again. *We all learn today* . . .' His rebuke ended abruptly with an indrawn breath and Andawyr saw that he was looking again at the distant field.

The column had largely disintegrated as an ordered force after the fruitless pursuit of the riders, and the slaughter of the woman, and while a few individuals were dashing to and fro obviously trying to re-form it, most of the Morlider were wandering about aimlessly or standing around in small agitated groups. This had been precisely the object of the slinger's attack but now a group of them had discovered the fate of their companion and were circling round to return to the field.

Hawklan's brow furrowed. Victory over the Morlider depended largely on breaking their discipline, but implicit in this intention was the assumption that the Orthlundyn would maintain theirs. Now, as the riders began to charge forward, Hawklan felt his great resolution falter.

Even as his doubts began to form, however, the cold voice within him spoke. You're standing too close, it said. Doing as Andawyr did. There are many currents in the sea, large and small, but the tides are inexorable, break the waves how they will. So also is your purpose.

*We all learn today.* His own words returned to him.

With an effort he set his fears to one side and turned as cruelly observant an eye as he could on the unfolding events.

Some twelve riders were heading straight for the broken body as fast as the snow would allow, gradually coming into close wedge formation. Their line of approach was for the most part bringing them through the disordered Morlider from the side and they were largely unnoticed for much of the way, except for those who were trampled underfoot and cut down by slashing blades.

Despite his enforced coldness, Hawklan felt part of him surging forward in this attempt to recover the body of a fallen comrade.

As the riders reached the woman's body, one of them dismounted and picked it up quickly with a strange gentleness while his companions circled wide around him in pairs using bows and swords to prevent the Morlider from reforming. Hastily he threw it over his saddle and remounted, only to dismount almost immediately to pick up a severed limb that had tumbled into the snow.

Then they were fleeing, holding the same close formation until they reached their waiting companions.

Hawklan weighed the incident in the balance. It had been impulsive and wrong; it may have given some shrewd-eyed Morlider commander a measure of their attacker's worth that Hawklan would not have preferred; but it had been well executed and successful and would have done much for the morale of those involved. If circumstances allowed that day, he would offer them commiseration and perhaps qualified praise.

As he made this cold command judgement the mingled emotions of the recovery party reached out to him. Dominant was anger; anger at the Morlider; anger at themselves, that their comrade had fallen unnoticed as they fled the field; anger and horror at the dreadful damage that had been wrought on the body. And, for the moment the most painful of all, guilt at their own swirling exhilaration at their deed.

Briefly too he felt other, different, emotions, almost too painful to be borne? A lover? A brother? The healer in him *would* seek these people out and ease what pain he could.

But circumstances did not allow him that healing visit. The tactics used to break up the Morlider column proved equally successful on the other two, and by judiciously continuing the harrying, Loman kept them all in some disarray and eventually succeeded in bringing all three within sight of one another.

This done, he launched an infantry attack against one of them.

At the sight of the orderly lines of Orthlundyn approaching on foot the Morlider, angry and frustrated, broke ranks completely and began to move towards them in disorder, shouting abuse and threats, and waving their weapons in

237

anticipation of the close quarter fighting that had been denied them so far that day.

Riding inconspicuously with the rearguard to the Orthlundyn Hawklan heard other cries amongst the hubbub; the cries of officers trying to regain control of their men. After a while they faded away. It was another useful measure of the Morlider's discipline.

The second column, a little further away, also began to break up, and men came running across to help their comrades mete out justice to this taunting, elusive enemy.

The third column, however, was of a different mettle. It had been the least affected by the skirmishes, and now it maintained its ranks as it turned and began to move rapidly towards the closing antagonists.

Loman watched it carefully. Whoever was in command had assessed the events of the day more accurately than the others and was trying to interpose an ordered defensive line between this dangerous enemy and the loose-knit mob that the other Morlider had become.

Loman signalled the phalanx commander to slow the Orthlundyn's approach, then he turned and spoke to Athyr. The Helyadin nodded and then galloped off to join the small contingent of cavalry that was guarding the infantry's left flank.

Hawklan noted the incident with approval. Loman's response had been his own. By surreptitiously slowing the Orthlundyn, he was ensuring that the third column would be able to move into position but almost certainly would not have time to form up properly or deploy their archers. Had they been left outside the conflict they could have moved to attack the Orthlundyn from either flank or rear; Hawklan judged that their discipline would carry them through any assault the cavalry could offer.

Good leader, Hawklan thought. But not good enough. In his anxiety to protect his fellows from their folly the Morlider was walking into Loman's trap. It was a mistake that would probably cost him his life. Even now Hawklan knew that Athyr would be passing Loman's order to the Helyadin among the cavalry. 'Identify the leader and kill him; and any rank and file leaders.' A glance confirmed it; several of the horsemen were preparing their bows.

A peculiar, almost snarling clap of thunder rattled overhead as if giving special sanction to this incisive and deliberate surgery that would occur amid the random butchery.

Damn you, Sumeral, Hawklan thought bitterly as the sound rumbled into the distance. Would that it were in my province to return to you all the pain you create.

A shout brought him back to the cold wintry Riddin countryside. It was an order from the phalanx commander and it echoed across the Orthlundyn as the file commanders took it up.

Almost as one man, the front rank of the Orthlundyn swung up their shields to form a continuous wall and the first three ranks lowered their short pikes.

Then they moved from their leisurely march to a jogging trot.

Loman's timing had been good. The third column was moving into position, amid resentful shouts from their fellows at being apparently deprived of their prey, when the approaching men were suddenly transformed into a single armoured unit carrying a serrated row of death before it.

Several of the Morlider made a valiant effort to form their own shield wall, but it was too late and the Orthlundyn pikes drove into them, killing and wounding many on first impact.

The dark part of Hawklan calculated as it watched the destruction of the best of the three columns.

Then the Orthlundyn's progress faltered as they tried to push through the dense mass of shouting and screaming men.

Push! thought Hawklan grimly, willing himself amongst the heaving pikemen. Push! Remember your drill. Watch your neighbour. Listen for your file commander. That way you'll live. Push!

For a moment, he was free. Free of doubt and debate. Now Sumeral's will would be tested at sword point. It was a good feeling for all that the events before him were horrific.

Briefly the Morlider held, as their disordered rear ranks, unaware of what was happening, continued to push forward. Then, though retreat was against the very heart of their fighting code, they broke as those at the front turned and crashed through those behind in a desperate attempt to avoid the relentless, terrible rows of jabbing spear points.

An attack now by the mounted archers could rout the Morlider entirely, sending them scattering across the snow at the mercy of the pursuing cavalry. But the destruction of one small group was not what was wanted. Today the entire invasion must be crushed. Today the Orthlundyn must overwhelm a vastly larger army and one of Sumeral's terrible Uhriel.

Loman let the Morlider retreat, slowing down the advance of the phalanx and then stopping it altogether once contact had been broken.

The Morlider had taken heavy losses, as was evidenced by the corpses and untended wounded decorating the blood-churned snow, yet they were still conspicuously more numerous than the unscathed Orthlundyn, and as they saw their smaller enemy faltering in its advance, the unspoken shame at their flight was redoubled. Cautiously, they began to move forward again.

Loman watched their confusion carefully, noting with satisfaction four men breaking away and heading back rapidly towards the camp. He took the phalanx forward again before the enemy could re-form properly and then he confined himself only to such manoeuvres as were necessary to maintain this modest disorder.

Outnumbering their troublesome opponents and yet unable to assail them because of their impenetrable shield wall with its lethal hedge of spear points, and the small but menacing cavalry flank guards, the Morlider's frustration grew apace. The odd individual would charge forward, roaring and screaming, and hurl an arcing spear or whirling axe at the silent, waiting, ranks, only to see it brought down by waving pikes, or bounce ineffectually off raised shields. The same fate befell the occasional arrow.

Hawklan watched as Loman's tactics inexorably destroyed whatever ordered discipline the Morlider had acquired under Creost's tutelage. It was a good sign.

As the seemingly stalemated skirmish moved uneasily to and fro, Gavor dropped silently out of the sky and landed lightly on Hawklan's shoulder. 'Time to go, dear boy,' he said softly, 'There are two more columns leaving the camp – at the double.'

Hawklan read the same message from a distant flickering signal. 'Gavor, I thought I told you –'

'I haven't told a soul, dear boy,' Gavor interrupted petulantly. 'I just thought *you'd* be interested.'

Hawklan let Gavor's injured tone release the smile that was in reality for the day's bloody success so far.

'I'm glad to see you enjoyed your flight,' he said.

'Oh yes,' Gavor said, with an enigmatic chuckle.

Hawklan turned sharply at this response. 'What have you been doing?' he asked suspiciously.

Gavor hopped up on to his head. 'My, this is going to be fun,' he said. 'We're going to drive these beggars into the sea, aren't we, dear boy? And that fish-eyed creature Creost.'

Hawklan started and looked up, causing Gavor to tumble off with a squawk. 'Steady on, dear boy,' he said flapping up awkwardly onto Serian's head.

'Gavor, where've you been?' Hawklan asked urgently.

Before Gavor could reply Loman was by Hawklan's side. 'You saw the message?' the smith asked rhetorically. 'Two more columns coming. It's working. I've sent skirmishers out again and I'm bringing up a second company.'

Hawklan abandoned his interrogation of Gavor and nodded. 'Take care,' he said. 'We don't know how these people are organised. There was a marked difference in discipline between the third column and the other two. Judge each one on its own. Disorder and confusion are more important than damage at this stage. Take no risks, there'll be plenty of those later.'

Loman gave him a mildly reproachful look, but Gavor was more direct. 'He knows all this, dear boy,' he said bluntly. 'As does everyone else. Let's get on and leave them to it.'

Leaving the small, bloodied battlefield, Hawklan returned to Andawyr and the others waiting nearby.

He repeated Loman's comment when he reached them. 'It's working.'

If the relief columns were leaving at the double, then the messengers who had carried news of the ambush back to the camp had carried with them a useful note of alarm and confusion. All that remained now was to see how far that would spread and how many troops would be lured out before Creost or his senior commanders realised fully what was happening.

Watching the movements of both Morlider and Orthlundyn, and reading the signals that flickered to and fro between the concealed Helyadin, Hawklan and his group returned to their silent overseeing of the battle plan.

Several more columns came out from the Morlider camp to be harried and taunted by skirmishers and then confronted by Orthlundyn infantry. As Hawklan had noted, they varied in discipline, but those that stood firm were attacked ruthlessly and eventually all were broken.

Suffering considerable losses, the Morlider were gradually eased back towards their camp, shepherded by smaller but unbroken ranks of Orthlundyn.

Hawklan rode up on to a small hill from where he could see most of the separate but converging conflicts. A rumble of thunder greeted him. He looked at Andawyr; the thunder, if thunder it was, had been increasing steadily for several hours. Andawyr met his gaze with open anxiety, but with an inclination of his head redirected him yet again to the earth-bound battle.

Hawklan nodded an acknowledgement then gazed around: at the sky, still grey and ominous, though lighter in places as if the sun were struggling to break through; at the clusters of fighting men, black scars against the snow; at the small portion of the Morlider camp that he could see from that vantage. His mind and his intuition told him that the first part of the assault against the Morlider was ending; that a pivotal point had been reached beyond which the balance could only swing to the enemy if he did not now commit the entire army.

He hesitated.

Memories of Orthlund and its people, sunlit, peaceful and glorious rose to stand against the stark, bloodstained, winter greyness of the present.

He reached up and touched Gavor's beak. 'Forgive me,' he said softly. 'And guard Andawyr as you'd guard me.'

Gavor bowed his head and looked at him beadily like an old schoolmaster. 'Now, dear boy,' he said purposefully. 'Dar Hastuin and Creost foul my air.'

Hawklan frowned a little and then patted Serian's neck. 'Now, Hawklan,' the horse said, with the same resolve as Gavor. 'This is my land, and I would ride to save it.'

Hawklan nodded and turned to one of his Helyadin bodyguard. 'Signal to Loman, "Now",' he said.

The young man spurred his horse clear of the group to obey the order.

Hawklan watched him for a moment and then took off his gloves and reached up to unfasten the laces that held his ragged cloak.

They were stiff in the cold air and gave him a little difficulty, but he eventually freed them and with a broad gesture swung the cloak from his shoulders to reveal a black surcoat covering the fine black mail armour that Loman had made for him. It bore no emblem. Ethriss's sword hung by his side.

Isloman looked at him, his face impassive. The sight brought back vividly to the carver the memory of Tirilen prinking out the healer for his trip to the Gretmearc; of his shock at the sudden appearance of a figure that might have stepped down from one of the many carvings that decorated Anderras Darion. Now, however, the presence of the man set all such comparisons at naught. Hawklan was here, now, powerful as much because of his doubts as his certainties; a whole man.

Who masters one art masters all, Isloman thought as, with quiet gentleness, Hawklan folded his old cloak and placed it in his saddle bag.

Then with the same calm, Hawklan lifted up the grim black helm that Loman had also made. As he held it up he looked round at his companions.

'To the light, my friends,' he said quietly.

Serian lifted his head and shook it as Hawklan urged him forward, and with a powerful beat of his wings, Gavor launched himself into the air to glide, black and stark, against the white Riddin snow.

# *Chapter 16*

Dan-Tor stared out into the greyness that encompassed Narsindalvak. The garish light from the globes illuminating the room turned the slowly swirling mist outside the window a pallid white. At the Ffyrst's feet was a small constellation of dull red stars where his blood had dripped from the barbed end of Hawklan's arrow still protruding from his side.

Behind him, Urssain and Aelang stood silent and watchful; like the Mathidrin as a whole, loath to be there but bound to him more than ever.

'How serious is this?' Dan-Tor asked eventually, without turning round.

The two men exchanged a glance. 'Very serious, Ffyrst,' Aelang said. 'We think that commanders Faron and Groniev are committed to it – and most of their senior officers. Their men will follow them almost certainly, of course.'

'Of course,' Dan-Tor echoed softly. 'And the other commanders?'

'They'll wait,' Aelang said awkwardly, after a dangerously long pause.

Dan-Tor's lips parted to reveal his white teeth in an expression that was neither smile nor snarl. His own image stared back at him from outside, faint and transparent, and seemingly surrounded by the glowing white mist. It taunted him. Great Uhriel, where is your power now? Your vaulting ambition? Bound and blind, and surrounded by ants who think themselves ravening wolves. Will you still be here when Creost and Dar Hastuin are fawning at His feet and receiving His favours? Toying with your remnant soldiers and bleating over the ill-chance that took Fyorlund from you and stuck you like a hunted pig?

'No,' Dan-Tor muttered.

'I beg your pardon, Ffyrst?' Aelang said, leaning forward intently.

'No!' came an awesome, cavernous, voice in reply.

The two Mathidrin froze. The voice was the voice of Oklar. His presence, his malice, filled the room, filled their bodies and their minds leaving space for nothing but himself.

244

'It will not be!'

Both Urssain and Aelang had seen the anger of the Uhriel rise up within the Ffyrst before, and even though its terrible purpose had never been directed towards them, they found it terrifying beyond words. It was as if they were falling into the infinitely deep maw of some flaring, malevolent, volcano.

Neither dared to move. Both knew that if one had committed some inadvertent folly, then for the other to seek to aid him would be to do the same, and meet the same fate.

But, as quickly as it had come, the awesome presence faded until it was like a thunderstorm in some far distant valley. Both men remained silent.

'Why do you bring this to me?' Dan-Tor said eventually, his voice and presence normal again. 'You're more than able to attend to such . . . administrative . . . problems without my aid.'

'With respect, Ffyrst, this is more than a minor problem,' Urssain said, speaking for the first time. 'We knew something was being plotted, but we presumed it was against us, as usual. It was only when two of our informants in Faron's company met with "accidents" that we even began to suspect how serious it was . . .' he paused.

'And?' Dan-Tor prompted.

Urssain looked quickly at Aelang, who nodded.

'They intend to seize the tower and attempt to make a peace with the Lords.' Urssain concluded his denunciation more hurriedly than he had intended.

There was a long silence. Eventually Dan-Tor raised a hand delicately. 'And where am I in this . . . new peace?' he asked quietly.

Urssain hesitated momentarily. 'You are to be . . . assassinated, Ffyrst.'

Dan-Tor frowned a little at his mist-shrouded double hovering outside, as a long forgotten sensation stirred within him. It took him some time to identify it. It was amusement.

Its rebirth however, was brief, as Dan-Tor's black corrosive scorn choked its faltering sunlight.

He turned to his aides, then moved to a chair and sat down.

'And you are concerned for my welfare, commanders?' he enquired, looking first at Urssain and then Aelang.

Urssain had stood next to the Ffyrst too long to even attempt the lie that the question seemingly sought. He could however risk an oblique statement of the stark truth.

'You destroyed half of Vakloss with a gesture of your hands, Ffyrst,' he said. 'You have powers beyond our understanding. No one could assail you and hope to live. It's a measure of Faron and Groniev's folly that they should even contemplate such an idea. But if their treason is allowed to take too strong a root in the men before it's torn out then we could find ourselves fighting our own, and that would be disastrous for our cause.'

Dan-Tor appreciated Urssain's attempted subtlety, especially the reference to 'our cause', but suddenly he felt irritated. It was as if Dilrap was buzzing about him again with his eternal mind-clogging swathes of regulations, procedures, 'respected traditions', and who knew what other petty restrictions that he deemed necessary for the quiet, subtle overthrow of Fyorlund.

Here, however, on the borders of Narsindal, Dan-Tor's vision and purpose were clearer and he refused to have either clouded by such pettifogging human trivia. Yet Aelang and Urssain were correct. A major upheaval amongst the Mathidrin and the renegade High Guards would risk destroying them as a fighting force, especially if it occurred within the claustrophobic confines of Narsindalvak. It might be a measure of Faron and Groniev's folly that they imagined they could eliminate him as though he was just another Mathidrin officer standing in their ambitious way, but it was also a measure of the seriousness of their intention that he had not detected it himself.

In dwelling too long on the fate that had brought him here and on the deep, silent, purpose of his Master, he had allowed himself to drift too far away from these unreliable and fickle creatures upon whose backs he must necessarily ride to achieve victory.

It was a salutary reminder, he realised. Now, it seemed, others too were in need of the same.

'Come with me,' he said, standing up abruptly.

Faron and Groniev were holding an officer's meeting when Dan-Tor entered with Aelang and Urssain in his wake. On the wall behind the two conspirators was a large map showing Narsindalvak and most of what had been Dan-Tor's estates in northern Fyorlund. Marked on it were the dispositions of the watching High Guards.

The two commanders came smartly to attention and there was a great scraping and clattering of chairs as their officers hastily stood up.

'Sit down,' Dan-Tor said tersely. 'I have something to show you which it will be in your best interests to take full note of.'

Aelang and Urssain kept their faces impassive, though Aelang's eyes gleamed at the tone of the Ffyrst's voice.

'Ah, you're still studying our position, I see,' Dan-Tor went on. Walking to the map he turned his back on Faron and Groniev and began to study it thoughtfully.

'What's your assessment of our position, gentlemen?' he said after a moment.

Faron's eyes flickered uneasily to Aelang and Urssain. He was visibly disconcerted by this unexpected appearance of the Ffyrst, so long ensconced and distant in his eyrie. Groniev however, answered calmly and immediately.

'It's adequate for our present needs, Ffyrst,' he said. 'But leaves much to be desired if the High Guards move against us in force, as they probably will when the snows have cleared.'

Dan-Tor continued examining the map. 'This tower fortress is the symbol of the High Guards' faith and strength, commander,' he said. 'It's generally regarded as being unassailable. Do you think it can be lightly taken from us?'

Urssain quailed inwardly at Dan-Tor's reasonable tone.

Groniev shook his head. 'No, Ffyrst,' he said. 'But I don't think it has to be. Narsindalvak's a watch tower and barracks. Enemy movements can be seen at great distances, and forces launched against them, but until we join up with the Mandroc divisions *we're* in no position to venture out against numerically superior forces. And if we don't venture out, we'll be besieged and by-passed, and the Lords will be able to march into Narsindal to find the Mandrocs leaderless.'

Dan-Tor nodded. 'You think that superior force in an enemy is everything, commander?' he said.

Groniev looked at him uncertainly. 'Not *everything*, Ffyrst,' he said. 'Though it depends on the extent of the superiority. Knowledge of the enemy, leadership, terrain, are also important factors.'

'Vastly superior force, then,' Dan-Tor offered, turning slightly.

Groniev nodded. '*Vastly* superior force *must* triumph, Ffyrst,' he said.

'And vastly superior force together with knowledge of the enemy, leadership, etc?' Dan-Tor continued.

Groniev, relaxing now, shrugged a smiling concession of the obvious.

'What would you call a leader who knowingly led his men against an opposition so armed, commander?' Dan-Tor said.

Groniev frowned a little, uncertain about the direction of this conversation. He searched for an answer. 'Insane,' he decided. 'Or suicidal.'

'Yes,' Dan-Tor said quietly, as if wearying of the subject. 'Of course.'

A whirring silence filled the room.

Then, turning to Faron, Dan-Tor said, 'What insanity prompted you to move against such odds, commander? Or are you, as your co-conspirator suggested, suicidal?'

Urssain felt a faint twinge of sympathy for the assailed commander.

Faron did not reply, but gazed back at Dan-Tor like some timid animal held by the gaze of a predator. Groniev, spared Dan-Tor's gaze, understood their position immediately. Urssain watched in disbelief as the man drew a knife.

With seemingly timeless slowness however, Dan-Tor turned and, before Groniev could lunge at him, seized his tunic, dragged him forward and hurled him into the paralysed Faron. The two men staggered across the room and crashed brutally into the wall.

Urssain found himself almost gaping at the spectacle. He had stood and quaked before the Ffyrst many times, in fear of some terrible, if unknown, retribution, and he had seen others worse affected; but he had never seen him resort to actual personal violence. Strangely he felt the action should have demeaned the man in some way; but it did not. Both Faron and Groniev were heavy and powerful men, well used to dealing with physical assaults, but Dan-Tor had hurled them across the room as effortlessly as if they had been some child's playthings. Urssain noticed that he was not even breathing heavily.

Groniev slithered to the ground, stunned, but Faron lurched forward from the impact. As he did so, some desperation broke him free of whatever fear had restrained him. With a cry of pain and anger he bent forward, snatched up the knife that Groniev had dropped and in one smooth movement hurled it at Dan-Tor.

It was a swift and powerful throw and the knife struck Dan-Tor squarely on the chest.

Then it clattered to the floor.

He doesn't wear armour, Urssain thought, but his momentary bewilderment vanished as Dan-Tor stepped forward and taking hold of Faron, lifted him clear of the floor and hurled him against the opposite wall of the room. Again the deed seemed to be effortless.

Urssain needed to feel no pulse to realise that this second impact had killed Faron, but it was Dan-Tor's casual indifference that chilled him. It was far worse than any callousness or wild-eyed cruelty.

Dan-Tor looked down at the fallen knife. He opened his hand and the knife rose up into it.

Then he extended his other hand, palm upwards, and drove Groniev's knife into it. It did not penetrate. No scratch appeared, nor blemish. He repeated the attack several times but the hand remained uninjured. '*You* could not wield the weapon that could injure *me*, commander,' he said, then, as if bored, he tossed the knife away idly.

Groniev meanwhile had struggled to his feet. He was leaning against the wall, his eyes wide with terror and rage.

Dan-Tor cast a brief glance at the broken body of Faron, then turned to Groniev. 'Superior force, commander,' he said quietly. 'Indeed, vastly superior force.'

Groniev did not reply.

'And I know my enemy, commander, do I not?' Dan-Tor went on. 'I know his very heart; his *darkest*, *closest*, fears.' The tone of his voice made Urssain shiver. Dan-Tor held out his arm to the stunned audience. 'As for leadership, let your men choose now who they wish to follow.'

No one moved.

'What was your other point?' he said thoughtfully. 'Ah yes, the terrain. Well' – he paused – 'I know and understand that better than you can begin to imagine.'

Groniev, still leaning on the wall, looked hastily from side to side, seeking an escape from his plight. Urssain felt again a brief sympathy for this fellow creature caught in the path of a force he could not begin to understand, but it faded rapidly. The man had seen the destruction of Vakloss; if he chose to dispute with its perpetrator then let him take the consequences.

Dan-Tor raised his right hand towards Groniev as if he were about to offer a blessing. With a flesh-crawling screech of protest, a wide and jagged crack appeared in the wall immediately behind the commander and, with a surprised cry, he tumbled backwards into it.

Several of the watching officers moved forward instinctively, at this, but a wave of Dan-Tor's left arm froze them all where they stood.

Groniev managed to regain his balance, but even as he did so, the crack closed a little, wedging him tight and he let out a brief but unexpectedly fearful shout.

Urssain remembered that Groniev had a morbid and abiding fear of enclosed places. He felt Oklar's spirit filling the room.

'I know and understand my terrain, commander,' Dan-Tor repeated. Then, slowly, as if to a foolish child: 'And I am master over all that shape and form it. From the weather-blasted peaks of the highest mountains, through the choking, suffocating dust of the southern deserts, to the rocks that lie bound helpless and airless in the dark, crushing, depths far below us; the rocks from which this tower is built.'

As he spoke, the crack slowly began to close and Groniev began to struggle desperately.

'Do you doubt this, commander?' Dan-Tor continued.

Groniev opened his mouth as if to reply, but all that merged was a choking cry; a cry of terror that began to rise rapidly in pitch and intensity, until it was a howling, pleading scream.

Urssain then saw that the crack was not crushing Groniev as he had imagined, but closing around him so that soon he would be entombed. Groniev's scream became one of primeval, inhuman terror. Urssain tried to swallow, but could not; the scream seemed to resonate with every tiny, unreasoned fear lurking in the dark unknown reaches of his own spirit. And it went on and on and on . . .

Then the crack was gone, closed utterly, and the last shrieking note of Groniev's nightmare rose into the dank silence of the room and died.

All that could be heard then was a faint and distant stirring as of some tiny burrowing rodent scuttling behind a panel, though it seemed to Urssain that the whole room was vibrating with the frenzy of Groniev's demented struggling.

Dan-Tor stared pensively at the wall for a moment. Urssain noted that he was leaning slightly towards his wounded side as if it were troubling him.

The officers, somehow released from their paralysis, seemed unable to look at each other. All were pale and visibly shaken. Some sat down heavily, as their legs refused to support them. One man vomited.

Dan-Tor remained standing, staring at the wall for a long

time, as if awaiting some event then, though he made no movement that Urssain could see, the crack opened again, silently and suddenly, and Groniev slithered from it. As he crawled clear, the crack closed with what, it seemed to Urssain, was almost a sigh.

Groniev lay at Dan-Tor's feet and made no effort to rise. His choking breaths were as inhuman as had been his scream.

Dan-Tor signalled to two men at random. 'Take him and leave him in the valley somewhere,' he said.

Wrinkling their noses, the two men hoisted Groniev into a standing position. He was unable to walk so they placed his arms roughly around their shoulders and hauled him hastily from the room. His feet dragged lifelessly.

Urssain stepped aside as they passed. Groniev's finger nails were torn and bloody. And he stank! Urssain's stomach heaved as the smell wafted past him, but he fought down the spasm. Worse than that was the slack-jawed mouth and the dreadful blankness in Groniev's eyes. Whatever he had been, he was that no more. The Ffyrst had weapons far worse than death ready to hand.

Dan-Tor watched the departure of the would-be usurper impassively and then turned his attention to the shocked officers, awaiting their own sentence in silence. Those who had sat down, stood again, as inconspicuously as they could.

'As for you, gentlemen,' Dan-Tor began. 'I own to a mistake.' His voice, however, lacked the self-reproach of the words. 'A mistake in trusting in your loyalty, a mistake in imagining that you knew where your best interests lay, a mis –'

'No, Ffyrst,' began the cries before he could continue.

'We were lied to and misled; threatened; forgive us, Master,' was the gist of the ensuing babble.

Dan-Tor watched impassively. Then he stepped forward and walked among them. Tall and straight, and the desperate focus of all there, he was like a hunter surrounded by his fawning dogs.

Abruptly, he was almost avuncular. 'Gentlemen,' he said, smiling. 'I think perhaps you persuade me. These . . . misunderstandings . . . are the inevitable consequence of our confinement here. Men such as yourselves – warriors – fretful at such inactivity when a treacherous enemy lies so near, can easily fall pray to the corrupting forces that pervade these times. But you are officers, leaders, you must be vigilant. Doubts and lies can be as deadly weapons as swords and spears.'

He looked around at his audience. 'Sit down,' he said, making a signal to Urssain and Aelang to remain standing. 'I reproach myself a little for allowing this to arise. I've been too long away from you, occupied with matters of wider strategy. Tell me now your fears and concerns so that I can undo the work of those traitors.'

Despite his seeming warmth and charm, the stark images of the recent violence were still far too clear in the minds of all present for them to rush into sudden camaraderie with their enigmatic leader; but equally, a silence would be just as dangerous.

'Why are we here, Ffyrst?' came a hesitant voice eventually. 'Why did we flee when we could have held and defeated the High Guard?'

Urssain could hear his pulse throbbing in the silence that followed.

But there was no explosion. Dan-Tor's smiling reasonableness remained.

'You did not have my view, captain,' he replied eventually. 'Neither of the battlefield nor . . . of the conflict on other planes.' He paused as if searching for a simple explanation. 'It's true, you could well have held the field, but the Fyordyn were aided in ways which I was unprepared for. Aided by powers that you know nothing of.' He paused again briefly. 'As you know, they had been inspired by the Orthlundyn, Hawklan, a strange fanatic who had already attempted to kill me at the very gates of my palace. What you could not know, and what I learned almost too late, was that he has dabbled in certain ancient arts and has somehow acquired a skill in them; a skill far beyond his understanding – a child wielding a great and powerful sword.' He leaned forward confidentially. 'Had I resisted him as he rode secretly amongst the High Guards then, in his flailing ignorance, he could have unleashed forces that might have destroyed us all. It was no easy decision for me to quit that field, but I had no choice. I had to let slip what we had won together to save my best men for another time.'

A long silence greeted him, the first coherent explanation of the retreat from Vakloss that had been offered to the Mathidrin. Very cautiously, the original questioner pursued his enquiry. 'But what of Hawklan, Ffyrst? He lives still. Will his . . . power . . . be any the less in the future?'

Urssain, deeply sensitive to Dan-Tor's moods, felt the

distant rumbling of the Uhriel, and held his breath in anticipation. But it faded, or was restrained, and Dan-Tor smiled – almost laughed – again. 'Hawklan offers us no threat now, captain,' he said. 'Nor in the future. His strength lay in surprise only. I have his measure, and should he choose to ride against us again I'll demonstrate to him what skill in his chosen art *really* means.'

There was just enough barrack-room bravado in his voice to set his listeners alight; he had caught their mood and their needs exactly. Clapping his hands together, he straightened up; his tall lank frame dominated the room.

'Don't let the narrowness of our confinement here make you forget that this is no small venture we're employed upon,' he said. 'You mustn't take to heart the loss of a few petty privileges in Vakloss, and a little . . . sparseness . . . here. One day, not too long away, you'll look back on this time and smile at yourselves for fools. The One that *I* follow, is bringing together the many threads of His intent. Soon, *you* will be leading our vast Mandroc army out of the interior. An army that will sweep through the waiting Lords like an icy winter wind through dead autumn leaves. An army that will move irresistibly down through Orthlund and Riddin and out into the world beyond where all will fall before you and where His bounty will give you power and wealth such as you would hesitate to dream of now.'

Urssain recognised the rhythms and inflections that he had heard echoing across the torchlit crowds in front of the palace at Vakloss and he felt the thrill of the other listeners as Dan-Tor's words reaffirmed his own ambitious intent.

However, Dan-Tor finished this harangue with a dark and, for some of those present, familiar warning. 'Remember this day above all others, and the fate that has befallen those who defied me. The choice is yours; be you my faithful servants and you will be rewarded as my power grows. But recall. You are bound to me and by me. You can be expunged at my whim and others found. Serve me well.'

As they walked away from the now crushed rebellion, Urssain keeping a respectful pace behind his master, noted again that the Ffyrst was leaning slightly to his injured side.

It occurred to him briefly to make some sympathetic enquiry, but no sooner did the thought arise than others rose hastily to silence it; the demon in the Ffyrst was far too close to the surface for such a risk.

'Do you want the companies broken up, Ffyrst?' Aelang said.

Without pausing in his long strides, Dan-Tor shook his head and replied, 'No. They'll be no more trouble now. Besides, things will be happening shortly – we've no time for re-organising our company structure. Promote Castarvi and Mendarran and put them in charge. Tell them it's a field commission – provisional – that'll encourage them to stamp out any lingering problems those men are having with their loyalty.'

The two Mathidrin exchanged a brief look. It was a good choice and also a small lesson for themselves; it told them that the Ffyrst had not distanced himself from his troops as far as he affected. Castarvi and Mendarran were both young, capable, and ruthlessly ambitious, and both had conducted themselves well on the field at Vakloss and in the subsequent retreat. Urssain and Aelang would be able to claim credit and thus loyalty for their promotion, but at the same time Dan-Tor had pointed up his warning – 'Others can be found.' They would both need to be watched.

A salutary lesson, Urssain thought later, alone in his own quarters. In a few brief minutes Dan-Tor had not only quelled the incipient rebellion, he had fired the whole force occupying the tower with a new resolve; the tale of the destruction of Faron and Groniev and Dan-Tor's subsequent speech would have been retailed to everyone in the tower within the hour. The terrifying physical strength, hitherto never suspected, had been grim surprise enough, but his antics with the knife and the horrific destruction of Groniev had told everyone in the Mathidrin exactly who commanded them in terms they understood. And the promotion of Castarvi and Mendarran would send ripples down through every rank as the jockeying to replace them began.

Yet above all this had come the mention of Him; and His plans. That had been more than a surprise. Urssain could not remember when he had last heard Dan-Tor refer to these world-spanning intentions, and certainly he had never heard them aired so freely.

He felt excitement, ambition and fear – terror, even – fighting within him. Part of him wanted to flee; flee back to a life of petty thieving in the old unchanging Fyorlund of Rgoric and the Geadrol, of village Redes and their Pentadrols; but even had he not participated in the destruction of that order, he had been shown too much now for such thoughts to be ever more than fleeting distractions on his journey forward in the wake of his master.

Yet what kind of a man could it be to Whom even Dan-Tor would bend his knee? And what kind of a place was Derras Ustramel, His great fortress, whose very name was whispered nervously, if it was mentioned at all? No one that Urssain knew of, save Dan-Tor himself, had ever been there, and even his visits were rare.

In front of Urssain glowed some of the genuine radiant stones he had had the foresight to ensure would be stored for him here in preference to those concocted in Dan-Tor's workshops. But even their sunlight could not reach the inner chill that possessed him when he thought about the dank mists that for most of the year pervaded the outer reaches of Lake Kedrieth and the great Mandroc barracks that lay there. And beyond the mists . . . ?

Involuntarily, Urssain wrapped his arms about himself and gazed into the glowing stones.

Mimicking his aide, Dan-Tor too sat still and silent in his eyrie, high in the mist-shrouded tower. The arrow in his side ached dully through his use of the Old Power in dealing with Groniev, but he scarcely noticed it. The very triviality of the events had heightened his growing inner turmoil at the bleak impotence of his position.

Silence.

All was silence. Here, in Narsindal, His will could reach out and touch His servant, but . . .

Silence.

And darkness too. The seeing stones of Narsindalvak saw the surrounding mountains and valleys, even, to some extent, through the mist, but what of Fyorlund and Orthlund and Riddin? Where was that silent, elusive demon, Hawklan? Had that horse witch Sylvriss truly reached Dremark and perhaps raised the Muster to seek vengeance for her husband's death? These were matters of no small tactical importance.

Then, thoughts that had not come to him for eons. How fared his detested comrades, Creost and Dar Hastuin? Sent forth as he had been, to seize the peoples of their old domains, had they returned in triumph while he languished in this prison, bound and blind, and contending yet with these feckless and inadequate humans? Was that why He sent no word? Was Oklar, first and greatest of the Uhriel to be the butt of their mockery because chance had wrenched Fyorlund from him? Was he to place his hand beneath the feet of Creost and Dar Hastuin? The thought was unsupportable.

He stood up and turned to the window; a circle of dark grey in the darkness of his room. No double mocked him here. Nor would any mock him, ever, save Him . . . until . . .

Red glaring eyes blazed in at him from the mist.

It was his own gaze. He turned away from it suddenly as if, even at this great height, some unseen observer might read this last, dangerous, scarce-formed thought, in his face.

He must have his true sight again! The thought burned inside him as never before. The bird held by the Cadwanol must be torn free so that the Vrwystin a Goleg could see again! But with this accursed arrow in his side he could not use the power, and if he could, there still lingered the fear that such use might inadvertently awaken Ethriss.

The thought of the Guardian, terrible and vengeful, rose before him, yet even as it formed, other, quieter, thoughts came with it. The Cadwanol, alerted now to the wakening of Sumeral must surely be putting forth their greatest power to find and waken their erstwhile master. And their power was not trivial if it could bind the Vrwystin a Goleg.

Yet Ethriss slept still.

Wherever he was, he was beyond their reach! And beyond the reach of any casual disturbance.

New patterns formed in the Uhriel's dark mind. Calm resolve entwined itself around his mounting rage to form an unholy duo. The bird must surely lie at the heart of the Cadwanol's stronghold. Released, it would not only give Dan-Tor his eyes again, but it would show where that heart lay, and with that the destruction of the Order could be assured. For destroyed they must be. At best they were an unknown factor in any impending conflict, while at the worst they might yet awaken the Guardian; their very survival through the ages betokened a patience and will not to be ignored lightly.

And with his eyes and his power restored, he would once again have the true vision of an Uhriel. He could tolerate the cloying masquerade that he was obliged to maintain to fire these creatures about him, and no enemy could stand against him; not the Muster, the Lords, that seeping, corrosive sprite, Hawklan, nor those upstarts for His favour, Creost and Dar Hastuin.

Dan-Tor nodded to himself. Several ends could be served here.

His surging passion burst through its restraint and he reached out his power deep and distant; under the cold mountains and across the plains of Fyorlund until, reluctantly, it shied away from the touch of the Great Harmony of Orthlund. For an instant he felt an almost overwhelming urge to shake this, *his* domain, and tumble these irksome creatures into oblivion, though it shatter his mortal frame utterly.

He would tolerate this impotence no longer.

He would wait His will no longer.

He would do that which had never been done.

He would go to Derras Ustramel. He would seek an audience.

# *Chapter 17*

A great cheer spread through the waiting ranks of the Orthlundyn as Hawklan's message flickered from its last sender and was read directly by many of them.

The day had been chill and tedious; a day of foot stamping, arm beating, and endless last-minute checking of equipment and weapons as the Orthlundyn waited and watched, gaining relief only from the relayed messages detailing the successes of the companies assaulting the Morlider columns.

But now, *the* message had arrived and the myriad irritations of the long wait were ended. All doubts and fears dissolved, momentarily at least, in a wave of exhilaration as shouted orders penetrated the din, and the advance began.

Hawklan, Isloman and Andawyr together with their Helyadin bodyguard took station at the top of a small rise that lay in the army's path.

'A fine sight but a sad one,' Isloman said, as they waited.

Hawklan looked at him. 'Remember your mines, carver,' he replied. Much of his face was hidden in his helm, but his voice bore a stern reproach and the will behind it struck Isloman almost like a physical blow. 'We're here out of necessity and now we're committed totally. Sadness is for another time and will be the greater if we ponder it here. Now, there is only this moment, and victory. All else are traitors to our true need, old friend.'

Still the healer, warrior, Isloman thought, as he felt the last two words seal the small wound to his pride that the rebuke had offered. He bowed slightly in acknowledgement, then put on his own helm.

Hawklan turned to Andawyr and Atelon and looked at them both intently. Much rested on this strange couple, he knew. They it was who must resist the Old Power that Creost would inevitably send against them before the day was through. If they failed, then the Orthlundyn would fall like corn before a scythe at this terrible touch. It was an awesome burden for such seemingly frail creatures.

'You are prepared to oppose and destroy Creost,' he said. It was not a question and for all its simplicity it carried the same will that would soon fire the entire Orthlundyn army.

Like Isloman, both inclined their heads in acknowledgement.

Loman galloped up. His face was flushed, and showed a grim satisfaction. 'I threw two more companies in on your signal, and attacked. You should have seen them scatter.' He laughed. 'They're running back in total disorder,' he went on. 'Athyr will pursue them as far as possible and then do what he can to lure out the rest of the camp.'

'Good,' Hawklan said, smiling. 'I think we've done enough to make them angry, and while they're angry, their training won't stick, and we have them.' His mailed hand reached out and patted Loman's arm. 'Come on, let's join our army, commander,' he said. 'We'll ride with you until we see the enemy's response.'

It took them only a few minutes to reach the advancing army and as they did so, another spate of cheering broke out. Spontaneously the front rows began lowering and raising their long pikes in salute, making waves ripple along the entire front, so that it looked like a field of tall grass ruffled by a summer wind.

Gavor and Serian caught and responded to the mood of the people immediately, Gavor letting out a cry of delight and rising up into the air, Serian prancing a little, and then shying and kicking out his forelegs to throw up great flurries of snow.

Hawklan too could do no other than respond. He drew the Black Sword and holding it high above his head, trotted Serian along the rows of bobbing pikes. Gavor flew to and fro around his head.

The cheering echoed along the line as they passed.

Then Hawklan rode amongst the various companies, satisfying himself that all were prepared, and quietly ensuring that his implacable determination pervaded the whole army.

As Hawklan was being greeted by the advancing army, Athyr was walking to the top of the long slope down to the shore and the Morlider camp. As Loman had reported, the Morlider columns, having suffered heavy losses, were fleeing in complete disarray back to their camp. Had Athyr launched even his small cavalry units against them, their losses would have been magnified appallingly. Instead, however, he withdrew the riders, and dispatched them back to join the army. The Morlider had prepared themselves to face the Muster; if they saw cavalry cutting down their fleeing companions, there was a strong chance that they would either stay where they were, or form up into the disciplined phalanxes they had obviously rehearsed. Neither of these alternatives was desirable. If, on the other hand, they saw their comrades being pursued simply by the now superior numbers of *foot* soldiers, it was probable they would continue to come out as a disordered and vengeful mass.

To tempt the Morlider further, and to some extent to protect the Orthlundyn from the Power of Creost should it be brought against them, Athyr had the several companies break ranks before they came in sight of the camp so that they would appear to the majority there to be no more than a large but disorganised group of raiders.

It was thus this seemingly motley group that appeared on the skyline behind the fleeing Morlider. Maintaining the charade, Athyr had the Orthlundyn straggle a long way down the slope before halting.

Almost immediately, large numbers of Morlider began to emerge purposefully from the camp. Athyr smiled in satisfaction as he watched them.

Slowly however, his smile began to fade. The number of Morlider coming from the camp was unexpectedly large, and while many of them were heading towards the Orthlundyn in an angry mob, a substantial proportion were lining up in ordered ranks and files.

The smile became a frown. Athyr had little doubt that if need arose his companies could form up and hold the undisciplined charges of the mob, but the group forming up outside the camp, he noted, were already substantially larger than his own force and were armed with long pikes. They were a different matter. They could destroy his people in a single leisurely charge.

For a moment he began to wonder who was luring whom. Had Creost been aware of their presence all the time? Did he have his own Helyadin moving silent and unseen through this chilly landscape, or did he have a Gavor amongst the seagulls that squabbled noisily around the camp? Had he allowed so many of his troops to be sacrificed just to lure the Orthlundyn into full battle? It occurred to Athyr that because *he* would not be prepared to countenance such savagery he should not have assumed that his enemy would be similarly constrained.

Angrily, he dismissed the thoughts, knowing they were no more than the corrosive products of his own fear and self-doubt. Circumstances had dictated Hawklan's strategy and the probability was that Creost, or his commanders were simply reacting. In any event, such considerations were irrelevant. No matter at whose behest, battle was about to be joined. His task had been to lure out the enemy if possible and in this he had been successful; too successful, he thought ruefully looking at the growing mass of Morlider outside the camp. Now his task was to protect his companies and perhaps do some further damage to the enemy in the process.

The intention had always been to retreat, but now came the question of the manner in which this should be done. His people had been marching and fighting for several hours; if he ordered a retreat from their present disordered positions there was no guarantee that they could outstrip the Morlider whose greater freshness was being amply demonstrated by the speed of their advance.

He must bring his people together.

But if he left it too late, the Morlider would be running berserk amongst them, and if he did it too soon, the very suddenness of the manoeuvre might perhaps give too much information to the calmer minds forming the phalanx in front of the camp.

As he watched the advancing crowd he realised that the choice had been made for him. The Morlider were too many and coming too quickly. Suddenly he seemed to see them very clearly and as if from some other place. His fear had slipped away, and been replaced by a dark and terrible resolve.

He would have to engage and destroy them if he was to be able to retreat.

'We will kill every one of you,' the resolve said silently to the Morlider. 'Every death will weaken your army further and help draw forth your massing companions below.'

Then the strangeness was gone. But everything was changed.

Athyr placed his fingers in his mouth and blew the penetrating whistle that his friends had been willing from him for some time past. Faster than for any drill they had ever performed, the Orthlundyn converged on him.

The angry Morlider misunderstood the sudden movement, taking it for a headlong charge, and with a great roar they ran even faster in their desire to close with this treacherous and elusive enemy.

Few survived to benefit from the realisation of this mistake.

The scattered, scurrying Orthlundyn became, very suddenly, a long, solid, armoured mass protected by a jagged row of glistening pike heads.

Like many of their compatriots that day, most of the Morlider either perished directly in the first impact between the two forces, or in the subsequent mêlée as the front ranks struggled frantically to escape the relentlessly thrusting pikes.

Athyr saw the exercise fulfilling his cold resolve though, perversely, he was pleased that the voice of his conscience made itself heard briefly, railing at the profound pity and futility of such carnage.

As the Morlider broke and began running back to the camp, the archers who were guarding the flanks of the phalanx killed and injured many more.

Again, the Orthlundyn had taken no losses.

As the remnants of the Morlider fled, Athyr turned his attention back to those gathering outside the camp. The sight made his stomach leaden with fear. In exaggerated mimicry of his own force, a huge swaying forest of pikes stood silent and waiting. What appeared to be massed ranks of archers guarded the flanks, and archers and shield bearers were strung out in front of this terrifying vision.

Too successful, he thought again with dark irony. This must be their entire army. Once they start to move, they'll pursue us for ever. How can even Hawklan . . . ? His legs started to tremble and this time no stern resolve came to aid him.

Then, faintly, there was a distant cry. It echoed along the waiting line and, slowly, as though a soft breeze had blown through it, the great forest wavered and began to move forward.

'Time to leave,' Athyr heard himself saying, in a voice whose quiet calm almost had him searching for some other speaker. 'Break ranks and retreat at the double.'

The Orthlundyn needed little urging and were soon energetically widening the distance between themselves and the advancing enemy.

As they ran, a solitary figure on horseback appeared on the skyline ahead of them, black and forbidding. Then, one on each side of him, came two others, armoured, helmed and grim. Athyr started, his mind suddenly flooded with thoughts of the three Uhriel and the terrible unknown powers that they could bring to bear on these insignificant humans who had had the temerity to take up arms against them.

Then a familiar voice intruded. 'Come along, dear boy, this is no time to be dawdling. You seem to have made yourself distinctly unpopular.'

The voice was Gavor's, and Athyr's vision cleared to identify the three riders as Hawklan flanked by Loman and Isloman.

Hawklan took off his mailed glove as Athyr ran towards him. 'You've done well, Athyr,' he said, leaning forward and taking the man's hand. 'Tend to your people. Take them to the rear so that they can get a little rest, then get your horse and come back here.'

As Athyr shouted orders to his companies, Hawklan turned to look at the advancing Morlider.

'Many of these will die today,' he said, his voice cold with distaste. 'Send a herald out with a flag of truce. Tell them we want to talk.'

Both Loman and Isloman looked at him in disbelief. 'They'll kill him,' they said in surprised unison.

Hawklan smiled a little at this unexpectedly positive and unanimous advice. 'Very well,' he said. 'Get *me* the flag. Andawyr and I will go down – with our bodyguard,' he added reassuringly.

A loud clap of thunder rolled over the two brothers' replies.

'Good,' Hawklan said, wilfully misunderstanding their unheard protests. 'I'm glad you agree. There may yet be a chance to talk our way out of this. You two stay here. Bring the cavalry and the front ranks into sight on my signal.'

His manner was so authoritative that Loman and Isloman could only exchange a brief look of resignation. However, as Hawklan turned away, Loman flicked out an emphatic hand signal to the Helyadin bodyguard.

'Language, dear boy,' Gavor tutted reproachfully. 'A simple "Take care," would have sufficed.' Then he was flying after the already retreating party.

Holding the green flag of truce himself, Hawklan led his small entourage towards the approaching Morlider. He stopped just in front of the scattered bodies that were the remains of the crowd that had fallen before Athyr's force.

'Halt!' His voice, commanding and powerful rose above the clatter of the moving army.

Another voice repeated the command and rapidly it passed from officer to officer through the extended ranks and the great line came to a lumbering stop.

There was another command and the file in front of

263

Hawklan opened to make a broad pathway. Along it came one man on horseback flanked by what appeared to be either advisers or bodyguards. The rider was a large and imposing man, untypical of his fellows to the extent that his heavy-boned face was beardless. He exuded a menacing physical power, and he sat his horse as if defying it to disturb him in any way.

Hawklan felt Serian react in some way, but it was too subtle for him to understand.

The man stopped some way from Hawklan and looked at him appraisingly. Then, almost surreptitiously, he glanced at Andawyr.

'Who are you that chooses to stand in our way, horse rider?' he called out. 'And what do you want? We're anxious to settle some debts today.'

Hawklan gave his name. 'I am one of the defenders of this coast who've cost you so dear so far,' he said. 'I come under a flag of truce to speak to your people.'

The Morlider curled his lip and bared his teeth viciously. 'Speak to me then,' he replied. 'I'm Toran Agrasson. I command this . . . little patrol. But hurry, we're impatient to try *real* knocks with you.'

Hawklan pointed to the distant islands. 'Do you speak for *all* the peoples of your united lands?' he asked.

The Morlider's eyes narrowed slightly, but his voice showed no uncertainty. He glanced from side to side at the waiting army. 'I speak for *these*,' he replied. 'That's all you need to concern yourself with.'

Hawklan shook his head. 'I speak for all my people,' he said. 'And I must speak to the one who speaks for all of yours or terrible harm will be done here today. Send a messenger for Karios.'

Agrasson started visibly and an alarmed murmur rose up from the army.

'Isn't he with you?' Hawklan asked, before Agrasson could answer.

Agrasson recovered himself. 'Our chieftain is where he wills to be,' he replied. 'But don't seek to meet him too soon, leader of your people.' His tone was sneering. 'Aside from your deeds of last night and today, each careless mention of his name will cost you a year's torment when he has you in his thrall . . .' He looked up at the lightening sky overhead. Thin skeins of bright blue sky were appearing in the greyness. '. . . Which will be long before the sun sets today – if you survive.' This brought some laughter and jeering from the nearby ranks.

Hawklan looked down for a moment then, straightening up, he took off his helm and gazed slowly over the vast expanse of the waiting army. Finally he looked again at Agrasson. 'Very well, Toran Agrasson, I'll speak with you, but know first that if you speak only for these gathered here, you speak for a doomed and betrayed people.' He waved again towards the distant islands. 'If your leader is too timorous to face the consequences of his own deeds, then let *us* at least, as true men, as warriors, not degrade this place further with lies and deceit. Let us call your chieftain by his true name.'

Agrasson frowned angrily and for a moment seemed inclined to ride forward.

Hawklan raised a hand to stop him. 'Creost,' he said, his voice becoming more powerful. 'Creost. The Uhriel. One of the creatures of Sumeral who is risen again and seeks once more to spread his evil over the world.'

This time Agrasson backed his horse away from Hawklan, as if fearful of being caught in some awful retribution. He pointed an unsteady hand at Hawklan. 'You weave a terrible doom for yourself with such words, horse rider,' he said. 'Seek earnestly to die today. It's the happiest of the futures now before you.'

'No!' Hawklan roared. 'I weave nothing. I come here to cut the threads that bind you all and that have led you to this folly. I come here to tell you the truth.'

'Enough!' Agrasson shouted, but Hawklan waved his protest aside.

'Do you truly think that this . . . abomination . . . from another time . . . will lead you to glory, to wealth, to whatever it is he has promised you?' he said, projecting his voice out over the now silent army. 'This creature who has already slaughtered so many of your kin and torn your islands from the ancient ways of Enartion. You are a brave people. People of the sea. You, more than I, must know the price that will have to be paid for such folly.'

'Archers!' Agrasson roared. But his men, held by Hawklan's voice, hesitated, and the Helyadin had drawn and aimed their bows at Agrasson and his companions before the nearest Morlider archers could bring theirs to bear. Hawklan held up his hand.

'No,' he said, gently. 'You'll die before us, and our deaths will not kill the truth; they'll serve no end but his. Like the Fyordyn you've been cruelly misled by forces beyond your knowledge. They're free now, and arm against Sumeral himself, though they have paid a terrible price. You –'

'You're lying,' Agrasson burst out, though seemingly more for the benefit of his own men than for Hawklan. 'Our chieftain's brought us unity and strength –'

'He's deceived you in every way,' Hawklan shouted, cutting across him. 'Even here. Did he not tell you that the Muster would be far to the south? That there would be no one here to oppose you?'

He turned and signalled to Loman.

There was a brief silence, then slowly, a long row of points began to rise from the skyline like tiny shoots of grass. Hawklan watched the faces of the Morlider soldiers carefully as the front ranks of the Orthlundyn infantry marched forward. Behind them a forest of pikes waved gently, indicating an unknown strength to the rear; two close-ranked formations of cavalry appeared on the flanks.

As they halted, the sun broke through a gap in the clouds and the unfamiliar sunlight danced and sparkled on bright surcoats, and polished shields and helms and weapons. It was a daunting spectacle, made all the more intense by the dark grey winter sky that formed the backdrop.

'*Nice* timing,' whispered Gavor into Hawklan's ear with untypical awe.

Hawklan ignored him. 'Turn away from this,' he said to the Morlider. 'Go back to your islands and the true ways of the sea. Make no widows and orphans for this cold land that you do not belong to. If truly you did not know his deceit, then see it writ large in glittering edges and points waiting for you up there, and in the blood and gore of your companions right here.' He waved his hand over the carnage that lay between himself and Agrasson.

The sunlight faded as the clouds closed again and a cold breeze ruffled the clothing of the waiting men. Hawklan felt his faint hopes shrivel at its touch. Such doubts as he had seen stir in those Morlider near to him, were gone, and only a savage, driven intent remained. Here, as in Fyorlund, the heart of the disease would have to be excised before peace could be found.

What Agrasson thought, he could not tell; the man's face had become a mask.

'You don't reply,' Hawklan said after a long silence.

Agrasson indicated the army with a nod of his head.

'They're reply enough,' he said impassively, adding scornfully, 'It was thoughtful of you to bring your army to us, it'll save us a great deal of searching.'

Hawklan nodded sadly. 'Then carry a message to Creost for me,' he said. 'Tell him that Hawklan, the Key-Bearer of Anderras Darion, has pinioned Oklar and now comes to seek out the lesser Uhriel for an account of his misdeeds. Look at me, Toran Agrasson.' His voice was soft, but extraordinarily commanding and, reluctantly, Agrasson's eyes met his. 'Tell Creost there is no escape from the forces that have been set against him and that today he will be killed or bound.'

With an effort, Agrasson broke free from Hawklan's gaze. 'He'll hear your message, horse rider, have no fear,' he said. 'And I'll repeat my advice; seek earnestly to die today, Hawklan, Key-Bearer of Anderras Darion and speaker of fine words. Seek earnestly to die.'

Hawklan bowed slightly and, replacing his helm, began to walk Serian backwards. The Helyadin did the same, keeping their bows levelled at Agrasson and his companions until they were beyond bow shot.

'I could have told you that would happen,' Gavor said. 'So could Loman and Isloman. All that lot understands is fighting.'

Hawklan nodded, as he handed the green flag to one of the Helyadin. 'I could do no other than try, Gavor,' he said. 'Besides, I've left some darts of self-doubt stuck in some of them, and every little helps.'

Gavor condescended a cluck of mild approval.

Hawklan turned to Andawyr. 'What did you learn?' he asked.

Andawyr shrugged a little. 'He's there somewhere,' he said. 'But not truly exerting himself. I doubt he's any idea of the threat we can pose.'

Hawklan nodded. 'Good,' he said. 'Let's keep it that way for as long as possible. But we have to face him today no matter what else happens, and I'd like to know where he is.'

'He's on that boat there.' The voice was Gavor's. He was nodding towards a small boat anchored off shore, well away from the other vessels that were plying to and from the islands.

Hawklan frowned at him. 'I thought I told you –' he began, then with a resigned shake of his head, 'Never mind . . . A seagull told you, I suppose,' he said.

'No,' Gavor replied with some scorn. 'They're a very dim

lot. Not a thought in their heads except family squabbles and *fish*. I found him on my own.'

'They're coming.' One of the Helyadin ended this exchange. Glancing back, Hawklan saw the great mass of the Morlider army moving forward again. He galloped Serian up to Loman who was waiting anxiously with a group of company leaders.

'Are Dacu and all the Helyadin back?' Hawklan asked.

'With the cavalry on the left flank,' Loman replied, pointing.

Hawklan nodded. 'Isloman, Andawyr, Atelon and I will join them,' he said. 'We'll stay there unless we're needed. Have you worked out your battle plan?'

Loman looked around at the company leaders. 'Yes,' he replied. 'Unless you saw anything special down there.'

Hawklan shook his head. 'They're as nasty looking as you always told me. And strong, but nothing your rock heavers can't handle. Their pikes aren't as strong as ours by the look of them – and they've got a motley assortment of close quarter weapons so I doubt they've learned how to fight in phalanx other than with pikes.'

'Good,' said Loman, signalling his companions back to their posts.

Then he took Hawklan's elbow and led him aside a little way. When he turned to speak, his eyes were fearful and his face grim, 'Look how many there are,' he whispered. 'Can we truly win against such numbers. Can I . . .' His voice faltered.

Hawklan reached down to his quiver and drew one of the black arrows that Loman had made for Ethriss's bow. He held it out in front of the smith.

'In this, you made a weapon that brought down an Uhriel,' he said. 'A deed none other could have done.' Then, with a nod of his head towards the army: 'And in them, you, Gulda and all the others have made a weapon just as fine. You've talked and debated together, trained and shared hardships together, sought out and corrected flaws together just as you would at a Guild meeting. You're many and yet one.' He smiled. 'Unlike me, your whole army's already been told your battle plan by now and they'll implement it because they'll see its soundness.' He raised an emphatic finger. 'Or they'll change it as need arises. And that change will accord with your will – you *know* that, don't you?'

He paused and looked back at the approaching Morlider. 'Unlike them. People who fight because they're driven by fear or who fight for fighting's sake. They understand nothing of the true purpose of combat; or why they're here. Our cause, our understanding, our discipline, our training, our will; all these are superior to theirs.' He turned back to Loman; his face was purposeful and implacable. 'Destroy these invaders, Loman, we've other battles to fight.'

Loman reached out and gripped Hawklan's hand powerfully then, without speaking, he spun his horse round and trotted back to Isloman and the others.

Hawklan remembered Loman's concerned face as they had parted once before, outside Anderras Darion. Referring to the decision to train the Orthlundyn, Loman had said unexpectedly, 'I've never had a tool on my bench that I haven't used eventually.'

A perceptive and tragically accurate remark, Hawklan thought, as he watched Loman embracing his brother and exchanging battle farewells with the others.

His own reply returned to him.

'All choices . . . carry responsibility . . . Having seen what we've seen and learned what we've learned can we do anything other than tell the people the truth and teach them what we can?'

He looked at the ranks of the Orthlundyn.

The people *had* chosen. Chosen to learn, chosen to face the truth, and chosen to defend what they valued.

Then a great certainty rose up inside him to shine like a dazzling summer sunrise.

*And they had chosen to win this day!*

Hawklan drew Ethriss's Black Sword and held it high. Gavor rose powerfully into the air with a raucous, laughing cry, and Serian reared and screamed his own challenge to the invaders of his land. Then overtopping both, and ringing out across the waiting people, Hawklan's voice was heard, crying,

'To the light!'

The cry spread through the army, washing to and fro like a great roaring wave.

Then, Hawklan and the others were galloping to join the Helyadin, Loman was shouting orders and the whole army began to move forward.

The long phalanx, sixteen men deep, moved forward very slowly, but the cavalry squadron guarding the right flank set off at the trot, leaving behind only a small flank guard. As they advanced, they gathered speed and took up a column formation as if to launch a direct charge against the centre of the Morlider front. The Morlider halted and their vanguard of archers prepared to greet this folly with the destruction it deserved.

Abruptly, however, while still out of range, the column swung round and half of the riders dismounted. Within seconds, the defending archers found themselves under a hail of lead shot. At first there were few casualties as the Orthlundyn tested out the archers' shield bearers. Then they began to concentrate their fire and casualties began to mount rapidly.

The Morlider began to move forward again; the skirmishing slingers were comparatively few and to remain stationary under their assault would have been to incur far more losses than if they kept moving.

The slingers held for a little while, still concentrating on the destruction of the archers, then quickly retreated and remounted. The squadron, however, did not withdraw immediately. Instead, the second half charged forward and released three volleys of arrows in rapid succession.

Many of the arrows were brought down by the waving pikes or deflected by shields, but many too found more effective marks.

Watching the foray, both Atelon and Andawyr started suddenly.

'What's the matter?' Hawklan asked, concerned.

'I think he has your message,' Andawyr replied, a little breathlessly.

'I feel nothing,' Hawklan said, remembering the sensations he had experienced when approaching Oklar.

'You will, healer,' Andawyr said knowingly. 'And very soon, I imagine.'

'Look,' said Isloman pointing. 'There's someone coming out onto the deck of the boat.'

Hawklan looked at the solitary boat then abruptly he felt the presence of the Uhriel. Even at this distance, the figure seemed, like Oklar, to be a rent in the reality around him. A great wrongness. Unconsciously Hawklan's left hand moved to the hilt of the Black Sword.

'What will he do?' he asked, but neither Andawyr nor Atelon were listening. They were moving forward from the group and looking fixedly at the distant figure. Hawklan signalled to the Helyadin. 'Protect Andawyr above all, then Atelon, then me.'

Quietly a group of the Helyadin positioned themselves behind the two Cadwanwr.

Hawklan turned his attention back to the advancing Morlider. The first cavalry squadron was riding to and fro in loose formation, generally harassing the enemy's centre with bursts of slinging, while the second had advanced and was using the same tactics as the first further along the Morlider's left wing.

Several times this sequence was repeated, with the squadrons concentrating their assaults on the Morlider's centre and left.

At the rear of his army, Toran Agrasson looked puzzled. 'These aren't the Muster I remember,' he said to one of his officers. 'Archers, stone throwers and spear carriers, with only a handful of horsemen.' The frown deepened, then a realisation dawned. 'They're *not* Riddinvolk,' he exclaimed. 'I knew that big fellow's accent was funny. They must be those northerners.' He snapped his fingers. 'Fyordyn. That's it, they're Fyordyn. I'll wager the horse riders had asked them for help and they've come on us by accident.' He laughed loudly. 'And look at what they're doing. Outnumbered more than two to one and trying to break our centre. They always were arrogant bastards. This is going to be fun. Pass the word, keep some of them alive for sport afterwards.'

Hawklan watched Loman's battle plan unfold gradually. Because of its great length and with the centre and left constantly faltering under the attacks from the cavalry, the Morlider's line had become distorted. In particular, the unhindered right was moving forward rapidly and pivoting inwards. At the same time, largely hidden by the confusion of galloping horsemen, the Orthlundyn phalanx was marching and counter-marching but drifting slowly, inexorably to its left – towards the Morlider's pivoting flank.

Then the second squadron was charging forward as if to repeat its two-pronged assault yet again. The archers and shield-bearers at the centre prepared themselves for the anticipated assault and once again the line slowed a little.

But the assault did not occur. Instead, the cavalry, keeping comfortably out of range, thundered past at full gallop, hooves pounding and throwing up flurries of snow.

The Morlider pikemen and archers at the centre relaxed and began to move forward again, warily watching the retreating spectacle. Soon the riders would break formation and return again, but they'd have to come to grips sooner or later.

This time however, the cavalry showed no signs of dispersing. And sweeping round in a great curving arc the first squadron galloped down to join them.

Still to some extent obscured behind them, the Orthlundyn phalanx quickened its pace.

'They're going for our right flank,' Agrasson said in growing disbelief.

'Shall I order the left to swing round?' asked the officer by his side.

Agrasson shook his head. 'No, not yet. They might have more over the hill. There's no danger. The flank archers will bring them down by the netfull once they're in range.'

The cavalry however, did not move within range of the Morlider archers. They remained carefully beyond it, and for the first time that day demonstrated the longer range of the Orthlundyn bows; demonstrated it with volley upon volley into the massed archers guarding the right flank of the Morlider line.

The Morlider held for only a short time under this lethal rain, then they began to scatter in disorder. As they broke, the cavalry abandoned bows for swords and charged into them to complete the rout and expose the flank of the Morlider line utterly.

During this assault, the Orthlundyn phalanx demonstrated a skill of its own. With parade-ground elegance it changed formation, making itself eight men deep instead of sixteen, and doubling its length to the left in the process. Then, as the cavalry tore away the flank guard, the extended phalanx increased speed and with a great shout, charged the Morlider's right wing.

As the five rows of lowered pikes crashed into those of the Morlider, Hawklan ruthlessly quelled the reproaches that were rising up in him as loudly as the terrible noise of the battle. Now all were to be tested. Would the will and discipline of the Orthlundyn overcome the wild fighting frenzy of the Morlider?

The thinning of the phalanx had been a risk, but it seemed that the speed with which it had been executed had justified it. The Morlider on the right flank, assailed by the cavalry hastily discarded their now ineffective long pikes, and resorted to their traditional swords and axes. But though they fought bravely they took little toll of the cavalry and the disintegration and destruction of the right wing accelerated relentlessly.

'Hawklan!'

It was Andawyr, and his voice was taut with fear. He was pointing to the distant figure of Creost. Hawklan followed his gaze. The strange unreality that pervaded the Uhriel seemed to have intensified. Serian whinnied uneasily. Without realising why, Hawklan drew the Black Sword. Then suddenly, he began to feel an unnatural warmth, a warmth that rose inside him with a choking menace, as if a ravening fever had just seized him. Serian started to shiver.

This was the touch of Creost. The touch of death. Hawklan's eyes widened in helpless terror as sweat broke out all over him.

Andawyr extended his arms as if both defying an enemy and welcoming an old friend. Atelon, beside him, bowed his head slightly and lifted his hands to his temples in concentration. Neither spoke, but Hawklan could feel their ringing opposition to Creost's Power. As suddenly as it had come, the nauseous warmth that had pervaded him passed away, and he saw the figure on the boat stagger slightly.

Looking round, he saw that Isloman and the Helyadin were wide-eyed and flushed, and their horses restless.

A strange quiet had come over the battlefield.

'He would have destroyed half his own to destroy us,' said a soft voice laden with horrified disbelief. Hawklan turned. It was Atelon. The Cadwanwr still sat with his head bowed but his face was riven with effort. He began to speak further but his voice was inaudible. Hawklan bent forward.

'We hold him,' came a faint whisper. 'Fight, Hawklan!'

Hawklan put his free hand on the young man's shoulder in an involuntary gesture of comfort. At the touch, the Cadwanwr's pain and torment crashed over him like a great icy wave. For a timeless moment he was no more; he was the least mote caught up and whirled around by forces beyond imagining. Yet, too, he was not; the deep stillness at his centre was beyond all such turmoil; it embraced and accepted the pain in silence, and in so doing rejected it utterly. Then it gave him his name again and showed him himself as healer and warrior.

Through his outstretched hand, it told Atelon, and listened; and through the other, it told the Sword, and listened.

And it showed Hawklan the balance of many futures that the

touch of Creost had brought to the bloody, snow-covered field.

Warrior and healer heard and, standing high in the stirrups of the great Muster horse, Hawklan raised the Black Sword of Ethriss, and roared his will to his people.

'Orthlundyn. To the light!'

As his cry sounded over the faltering warriors, it reached out and brought each back to the fray, and it was a mighty roar that returned to the Key-Bearer of Anderras Darion.

Still bemused by the unseen assault from their leader, the Morlider gave way before the Orthlundyn's onslaught, and the right wing, after retreating for some way, broke and became a rout as men abandoned their long pikes and turned to flee from the swords of the cavalry and the relentless pointed hedge of the phalanx.

The watching Helyadin cheered, but Hawklan himself was watching the motionless Andawyr and the distant scar that was Creost. The battle being waged there was beyond his understanding, but he knew it to be as terrible as that between the two armies. He could do no other than watch and wait, and act as his heart bade him.

The battle between the two armies, however, he did understand, and he knew that for all the success of the Orthlundyn against the right wing of the Morlider, the army as a whole was far from defeated. Indeed, he noted that the Morlider's left wing was beginning to wheel round to outflank the Orthlundyn and, of more immediate danger, the archers from the left flank were running along the line.

In addition, small groups of Morlider were beginning to break ranks and attack the small cavalry contingent guarding the right flank of the phalanx.

These were not unexpected manoeuvres, but Isloman came to Hawklan's side anxiously.

Hawklan raised a hand before he could speak. 'Loman's seen it,' he said. 'Look.'

As he pointed, part of the cavalry broke off from the destruction of the Morlider's right wing, and began galloping to intercept the approaching archers and to relieve their companions protecting the phalanx's right flank.

Without thinking, Hawklan drew off his mailed glove and wiped his brow. His fingers glistened with perspiration and he looked again at the two Cadwanwr. Andawyr seemed unchanged, sitting motionless on his horse, his arms still extended. His oval, battered face was quiet and oddly dignified, but Hawklan could sense a terrible strain in the man. It was as if he were facing a great wind that no other could feel. Atelon, on the other hand, was wilting visibly.

Hawklan reached out and taking Atelon's hand, thrust the Black Sword into it. 'Feel the spirit that used the Old Power to make this blade, Cadwanwr,' he said. 'It will unmake Creost's vile abuses and hurl him back into oblivion if you will it.'

Atelon made no response, but slowly straightened up. Gently, Hawklan took the sword from his hand and sheathed it.

He looked again at the distant figure of Creost.

'Dacu,' he said. The Goraidin eased his horse forward. 'Can we get out there and attack him directly.'

'No,' replied a familiar deep voice emphatically. Dar-volci emerged from Andawyr's stout coat. 'His Power is divided. It assaults you and it holds the islands. If you threaten him with death – and *you* could – he might let slip the islands and destroy you and all these in his extremity.'

Hawklan opened his mouth to speak, but Dar-volci had retreated into Andawyr's coat again.

Dacu finished the idea. 'We could only reach him by boat, and there's too many people still in that camp for us to do that,' he said. 'We'd better leave him to Andawyr and concentrate on what we know about.' He pointed to the battle.

The Morlider left wing was moving purposefully round, its pikemen maintaining a disciplined formation, and the archers had spread out making themselves difficult targets for the volley fire which had destroyed the others. The cavalry however had succeeded in fighting back the assault on the right flank of the phalanx, though the Morlider who had abandoned that assault were now acting as shield bearers to the archers. More numerous than the cavalry, the archers were gradually easing forward and would soon pose a threat to the phalanx.

Suddenly, a brilliant light lit the whole battlefield, glaring white off the snow and transforming the dark mass of the two armies into grey smudges. Then it was gone and in its wake came a terrible thunder clap. Though there were no mountains or cliffs nearby, the sound seemed reluctant to fade, rattling and echoing to and fro across the sky.

All started violently at this din save Andawyr and Atelon, though Atelon turned to with a look of consternation on his face. Andawyr merely nodded his head in the direction of their lone enemy.

The Helyadin were struggling to control their horses and even Serian was showing signs of alarm. '*That* wasn't thunder,' he said.

'No, it was someone else's battle I fear,' Hawklan replied, leaning forward and patting his neck. 'But it's done us no favours.'

Nor had it. Their horses frightened by the lights and the noise, the cavalry were in some considerable disorder while the Morlider archers had recovered quickly and were using the confusion to advance rapidly.

The Morlider left wing too was closing round inexorably.

Suddenly a hand grabbed Hawklan's arm and twisted him round. It was Dacu. He was pointing to a group of about fifty riders galloping round the Morlider's left wing.

'A large part of their cavalry, I suspect,' Dacu said. 'And not coming to discuss a truce by the look of it,' he added, as the riders turned and headed directly towards the Helyadin.

'Striking to the heart of the enemy, as they think,' Hawklan said, nodding in agreement.

'Or as they know,' Dacu said, looking significantly at the Cadwanwr.

Hawklan felt an ancient force stirring inside him. He singled out some of the Helyadin. 'Tybek, Jenna, you . . . six, stay here,' he said. 'Protect Andawyr and Atelon at all costs. If things turn against us, get them to Fyorlund as we've arranged. The rest of you, come with me.' Then turning Serian before Dacu could speak his inevitable protest, he took up two of the lances that had been stuck into the ground nearby in readiness for any defensive action the Helyadin might have to take. 'Line abreast, then into wedge formation just before we hit them,' he shouted.

Serian reared up without any apparent command, and started off towards the advancing riders. Dacu hesitated for a moment, then Isloman galloped past him on one side and a lance was thrust into his hand from the other.

'Come on, Goraidin,' shouted Yrain. 'Shift yourself. He's going to get himself slaughtered.' And with a yell she was off after Isloman and Hawklan.

Hawklan's brief tactical instructions were only partially successful. Though barely seconds behind him, Dacu and the Helyadin could not hope to match the speed of the great Muster horse as it thundered towards the approaching Morlider at full gallop.

To the few in the marching Morlider ranks who lifted their eyes briefly from the figures in front of them, it seemed that Hawklan, galloping on alone, his cloak streaming, and his great horse wild-eyed and pounding, was like a boulder crashing down a mountainside, while behind came the avalanche; Dacu, Isloman and the Helyadin, in a wide ragged line, shouting and screaming, with the polished points of their lances cold and final in the Riddin snowlight.

The advancing Morlider horsemen, in loose formation, saw the tumult coming but did not waver. Instead, four of them split off to deal with this black-helmed apparition, charging at it in defiant echo of its challenge. The Morlider understood the berserk fighter.

But though Hawklan had the all-consuming fury of the berserker, it was guided by his cold inner vision that saw always the true need and thus it was that the first two Morlider who met him were not impaled on the shining lances from Anderras Darion, but unhorsed.

Seeming to have selected the two riders on the left for his first assault, Hawklan swerved Serian at the last moment to attack the two in the centre. Surprised by the suddenness of this manoeuvre, both riders flinched away from the inexorability of Hawklan's driving lances only to find their points passing narrowly by and the shafts guiding them effortlessly out of their saddles. Both men fell heavily.

Dacu felt himself gasp at the sight of this superlative fighting technique and even as it happened, the memory returned to him vividly of Hawklan galloping through the sunlight to unseat the demented Ordan Fainson on their flight from Vakloss.

Briefly he felt the ambivalence of motives in Hawklan's actions; not to kill, through caring and compassion; not to kill, to burden the enemy with wounded. He swept the thoughts aside as the Helyadin moved into their wedge formation. Such choices were not his. Hawklan's skills were as far from his as were his from the average High Guard; here he needed all his own just to survive, and a mind elsewhere would see him killed. Part of him however marvelled again as at the edge of his vision he saw Hawklan beat down an attacking sword with his lance, then bring it up to strike his assailant under the chin, unseating him.

Dacu closed with his chosen target but, scarcely realising what he was doing, he swung the point of his lance away suddenly and swung the aft end round to strike him in the face.

As the Helyadin struck the Morlider, Hawklan was swinging his lance around to deliver a ringing blow to the head of the fourth rider who was struggling to turn his horse to face this explosive assault. The man tumbled out of his saddle, stunned, but a fifth rider joining the fray was less fortunate; Hawklan drove the aft point of his lance into his throat. As the Morlider crashed, choking into the snow, Hawklan turned with a great roar to the entangled mass of fighting riders.

The initial charge by the Helyadin had killed several of the Morlider and injured or unhorsed several others. It had not, however, scattered the attackers and, lances having been discarded, swords, axes and clubs were being used in savage close-quarter fighting.

The Helyadin's greater skills, both in riding and fighting, were prevailing against the Morlider's numbers and brute power, but barely, and it was obvious that the Morlider were neither going to yield nor flee.

With one lance, Hawklan impaled an axe-wielding giant who though badly hurt and on foot was about to hamstring Isloman's horse. The second lance he drove into the ground between the legs of a horse to bring it down. Its rider, however, rolled as he fell and, coming upright almost immediately, ran forward as if to drag Hawklan from his saddle. Serian hit him broadside, but it took a powerful kick from Hawklan to end his part in the skirmish.

Hawklan drew the Black Sword and urged Serian into the middle of the mêlée.

No sooner had he done so than he found himself in another place.

# Chapter 18

'In the name of pity, Hawklan, help us!'

The voice was that of Ynar Aesgin. It rang in Hawklan's head and possessed his body, though the images in his eyes were still those of the Helyadin and Morlider locked in savage and bloody combat.

A great rage and fear surged through him.

'What have you done?' he roared, though no sound was heard in Riddin. 'Release me. I will die here, or others will die protecting my helplessness. Release me!'

'This is not my doing,' came the reply.

'Release me!'

'I do not bind you, neither can I release you,' said Ynar. 'Would I had such skills at my command, I'd have sought you before this extremity.'

Faint and distant voices impinged on Hawklan, calling his name frantically as the images of his friends battling the Morlider around his helpless frame came before him with fearful clarity. An ancient part of his mind struggled desperately for release, but none came.

'Help us, Hawklan,' intruded Ynar again. 'Hendar Gornath understood the great truth of the Sword you bear and he has held firm. The Soarers Tarran have repelled Dar Hastuin's terrible hordes . . . at great cost . . . but now he takes his tormented land to the higher paths . . . He will crush us . . . Destroy us utterly. Help us.'

The despair in the Drien's voice appalled Hawklan.

'I cannot help you, Ynar,' he cried.

'He will destroy us!'

'I cannot help you!'

Ynar's pain filled Hawklan. 'What do you want of me?' he said.

'Your strength, your knowledge, your wisdom, to guide us.'

'If you understand the Sword you are wiser than I am. You have what you need. Search your hearts.'

Ynar's despair did not abate.

'But tell us what to –'

Hawklan screamed. 'Do what you must, Drien. I know

nothing of your ways. You sought no conflict. *You have the right to be*. No one, no thing, can deny you that. Do –'

Ynar was gone.

The din of the battle broke over Hawklan deafeningly; Isloman's voice roaring his name, others screaming and shouting, swords and shields clashing.

He tightened his grip on the Black Sword but something struck his helm a ringing blow and the impact toppled him from Serian's back to leave him rolling in the cold damp snow beneath the flailing hooves of friend and foe alike.

A figure crashed down beside him, screaming and clutching a partly severed arm. The screaming stopped as a horse's hoof struck the man's head.

Hawklan rolled away to avoid the same fate and then, leaning on his sword, staggered to his feet and shook his head to still the roaring in his ears that the blow had left. A horse buffeted him, and only some ancient reflex twisted him away from a descending sword blade. The same reflex cleared his vision and drove the Black Sword upwards under his attacker's chin then tore the blade free from the ghastly grip of the man's skull.

Then Serian was there, rearing and prancing to keep his foes away.

As Hawklan swung up into the saddle he gave out a great howling cry of rage at his impotence before Ynar Aesgin's terrible agony and then there was a brief frenzied whirl of movement. A single thrust of the Sword killed a Morlider pressing Jaldaric; a high lashing kick from Serian smashed the thigh of another, and a whistling cut scythed through the shield of a third, leaving him unscathed but unmanned before the black-helmed vision of his death. His flight from the field drew the few surviving attackers after him like water from a fractured bowl.

The skirmish was ended.

'What happened to you?' Isloman was wide-eyed as he took Hawklan's arm.

Hawklan released the grip gently and raised his hand slightly to forbid any further questions. He looked around at his companions. They were a grim sight, bloodstained and steaming in the cold air, but they were all there even though some were injured. Their faces reflected Isloman's question.

'Later,' he said, turning the Helyadin's gaze back to the battle with a nod of his head.

The Orthlundyn phalanx had turned and was driving along the Morlider line, but was coming under attack from the Morlider archers. The cavalry had withdrawn and was regrouping, presumably with a view to attacking the Morlider archers before the circling left wing outflanked the phalanx.

Once again, Hawklan felt the battle come to a balancing point. The Morlider were fearsome and brave fighters and, despite their dreadful losses, they were beginning to slow down the phalanx, even holding it in places, as some of wilder spirits among them actually seized the ends of the long pikes and hacked at them with swords and axes in an attempt to reach their foes.

Hawklan had no doubt that the phalanx would hold and that the mounted archers could do great harm to the approaching Morlider wing: but would it be enough? He sensed perhaps not; their position was becoming increasingly defensive. And, despite the considerable panic in certain places, the Morlider's mood seemed to have shifted from surprise and anger into indiscriminate battle fury. Thus fired and uncaring about their fate, their sheer weight of numbers could give them the day.

*Would* give them the day, if action was not taken.

He led the Helyadin back to Andawyr and the others. The Cadwanwr were still motionless, both now with arms extended, but it seemed to Hawklan that the unseen wind which buffeted them was taking a toll.

It came to him that if their conflict was not ended soon then Andawyr and Atelon must surely crumble, standing alone against this terrible Uhriel. Out on his solitary vessel, the sinister figure of Creost stood, equally motionless.

Hawklan frowned as his gaze took in two approaching ships. Reinforcements, he thought.

He looked again at the disposition of the Orthlundyn forces. He could have done no better, he saw. Loman's command had been sound and shrewd but–

Reinforcements. What other forces still lay on those distant islands?

A horse-pulled sled galloped past, swaying ominously. It was one of several that the Orthlundyn had made for carrying supplies about the battlefield, and it was stacked high with bundles of arrows. Riding the horse was a young boy.

Drawn from his thoughts by the sled's seemingly reckless progress, Hawklan pointed.

'Who –?' he began.

'He's from the village,' said one of the Helyadin. 'Fendryc's village. There's a few knocking about. They just turned up and started helping with the horses.'

Hawklan swore. The Riddin village with its population of the too old and the too young left to tend the surrounding farms! The Riddinvolk had thrown their every able resource into meeting this enemy. Now even the frail were stepping forward.

How could he do less? Now, more clearly than ever he saw that he too must commit his last resource to try and tilt this battle. If the Morlider were bringing in reinforcements . . .

He set the calculation aside, and his resolve, buried by the sudden burden of Ynar Aesgin's fears, reasserted itself.

Turning to the Helyadin he said quietly, 'String your bows, friends. We're going to stop that Morlider left wing.'

Despite himself, Isloman expressed the immediate response of the group. 'It's not possible,' he said, his voice full of alarm. 'There's not remotely enough of us.'

Hawklan looked at him for a long moment and then smiled slightly. 'Since when is the possible so easily measured, carver?' he asked. Then he patted Isloman's arm affectionately. 'Tirke, Athyr, keep our quivers filled. We've a battle to win.'

Turning Serian, he began walking towards the ordered ranks of advancing Morlider. Except for those trusted with the protection of the two Cadwanwr, the others rode after him.

As they rode forward, Hawklan glanced upwards. The sky had been silent since the lights and thunder that had panicked the cavalry, but as he looked at the grey, mottled clouds he felt a strange sense of foreboding.

What extremity had the Drienwr been in to have reached out, unknowing, to seize him thus? He remembered how Andawyr had appeared before him as he sat drowsing in the library at Anderras Darion and in that dusty sunlit storeroom in Vakloss. But here he had been about to enter battle.

He set the questions aside. If even Andawyr did not truly understand how such things had happened, how could anyone else? But still the foreboding persisted, and the lingering regret that perhaps yet again he had turned away the Drienvolk when they had sought his aid. That he could have done no other in such circumstances offered him little consolation.

'Here,' he said, reining Serian to a halt. 'Dismount. Line abreast. Pick your targets and take your time. If they break and charge us, maintain your aimed fire into the leading ranks until my command, then remount and move down line.'

The Helyadin obeyed Hawklan's order in silence, and their flimsy line stretched itself out in front of the dark mass of the Morlider and their waving pikes with the easy leisure of companions about to enjoy an afternoon's friendly archery practice.

Their assault did not have the immediate morale-breaking impact of the massed volleys that had shattered the Morlider's flank guards, but the Helyadin were expert shots and almost every arrow struck its target. Very soon a length of the approaching wing was in complete disarray.

Eventually, as Hawklan had envisaged, a section of the assailed infantry began to charge forward in desperate fury in an attempt to end this peculiarly dreadful attack.

He watched them come. 'Keep firing,' he said unhurriedly. 'Take your time. Three more shots at least. Aim for those still holding their stations.'

Nearer.

'One more.'

Nearer.

'Mount up.'

And the Helyadin were gone, leaving the charging Morlider to hurl axes, swords, and abuse after them with equal futility.

Twice more the group reformed and attacked the relentlessly advancing line, doing great harm.

As they pulled away for the third time, Hawklan looked at the frayed and straggling line that had marked their assault.

It was not enough. The whole wing had slowed a little as a result of the attack, but much of it was still intact. The Helyadin's attack was having an effect quite disproportionate to their numbers, but they were still very few.

For the first time that day, Hawklan's mind turned to Agreth. A single Muster squadron could smash the unprotected flanks and rear of the Morlider line . . .

Had the Riddinwr reached an outpost that might carry his news swiftly south? Had he been able to draw away the Muster from whatever treachery had led them there? Despite himself, Hawklan found his eyes looking to the misty horizon in the hope of seeing the quivering movement that would be riders approaching.

But all was still.

'Riders.' The urgent voice was Dacu's. Hawklan took in a

sharp expectant breath. But Dacu was not pointing to the horizon, he was pointing to another group of riders emerging from behind the Morlider line. Fewer than before, but galloping again towards the Cadwanwr and their small guard.

Still attacking the heart, Agrasson, Hawklan thought.

Quickly he dispatched half the Helyadin to intercept them.

'Don't close with them,' he shouted. 'Shoot the horses, then the men. I want no survivors. Then get back here as quickly –'

His orders froze in his throat as the foreboding he had felt before suddenly returned, though far worse, doubling and redoubling, as if a great power were descending from above to crush the whole loathsome field and all on it.

Then the sky ignited.

A dazzling incandescence flooded the two armies and the snow-covered arena with a light so bright that it seemed that no matter could stay its flow sufficiently to cast a shadow.

Yet even as hands rose to cover tormented eyes, there came a noise that swept such concerns into nothingness. It filled the sky and enfolded the battling peoples in an embrace so powerful that not one there could hear his own screams. The swaying lines of pikes wavered and fell like corn before hail as Morlider and Orthlundyn alike tumbled to the ground vainly trying to avoid this overpowering and terrifying onslaught.

Hawklan fell forward and clasped his arms around Serian's neck. Faint but sure, an inner light held firm amid the tumult within him and showed him that now above all times, the outcome of this battle lay in his hands.

He tightened his grip around Serian's neck. His voice would not be heard, but the healer in him would reach the horse.

'Hold, Serian,' it said. 'Listen to the sires within you who know me and who know the truth. This is the doom of another world, not ours. Who rises first from this, carries the day.'

The great horse reared and screamed unheard as its spirit fought against the fears that would have its body flee from this horror, but Hawklan entered into it and for a timeless moment the two sustained each other, moving beyond the light and the noise.

Then, as the dreadful brilliance lessened and became a shifting, ghastly, bloodstained iridescence, and the sound dwindled into a cascade of tumbling thunderclaps, Hawklan leapt down from Serian.

'Quiet your own, before they recover their wits enough to flee,' he shouted, then he ran among the stunned Helyadin, dragging them to their feet, staring into shocked eyes, slapping faces, thrusting unsteady forms on to equally unsteady horses, and roaring his will at all of them.

Two others were doing the same, he noted. One was Isloman; the great carver, though patently terrified, was unceremoniously dumping the Helyadin into their saddles. The second was Dacu. Fleetingly the memory returned to Hawklan of the great silence that had awakened him in the mountains and how it had so moved the Goraidin. 'A gift to guide me forever,' he had said. The memory eased his own pain in some way.

'Through the archers and rally the phalanx!' he shouted to the two men, signalling at the same time.

Both nodded and mounted their own horses.

Hawklan spun Serian round in front of the recovering group, and drew the Black Sword. He was an ominous figure, cutting as starkly into the minds of his shaken troops as he did through the baleful, shifting, red light still pouring from the blazing sky.

'To me, Helyadin, to me!' he shouted, his voice still lost in the dying din from above, but his meaning unmistakable. The Helyadin started forward, first at the trot then at the gallop, as their leader drew them forward and as the rhythm of their movement began to displace the terrible possession of the noise.

As they rose, Hawklan's own vision cleared. The Morlider who had been riding to attack Andawyr were scattered, most of them unhorsed by their panicking mounts, but so too were the Orthlundyn cavalry. The great blocks of infantry, both Orthlundyn and Morlider, were motionless.

He could not bring himself to look up, as if fearing to see some awful livid wound torn into the very fabric of the sky. Whatever had come to pass in the Drienvolk's conflict, this battle here had to be won, and Creost defeated.

The thought took his gaze briefly to Andawyr and Atelon and thence to the Uhriel. Though their bodyguards were gone, both the Cadwanwr were seemingly unmoved by the happenings around them, as was the distant figure of Creost, still jagged and awful in Hawklan's sight.

At the edge of his vision, he saw the two ships bearing reinforcements for the Morlider. In the eerie stillness of the fallen armies and the whirling confusion of the demented horses, the smooth purposeful movement of the two vessels seemed strangely grotesque.

Soon the enemy's reinforcements would be ashore.

Then the Helyadin were crashing through and over the Morlider archers, swords rising and falling, arcing red in the reflected cloud light and the blood of their hapless enemy. The swathe they cut, however, caused no great panic as most were too occupied with the terrors still shaking the sky above them.

Nearing the Orthlundyn infantry, Hawklan saw that, like his brother, Loman, though unhorsed, had recovered quickly from the ordeal. The smith was running along the ranks of fallen and crouching figures as desperately as Hawklan had run amongst the Helyadin. Under his exhortations, individuals were rising to their feet and struggling to help their neighbours.

'Spread out. Get these people moving,' Hawklan thundered, leaping down from Serian at the run and dashing forward to join Loman.

Then, as the infantry climbed up from its knees, he and the Helyadin were through to the broken front line of the Morlider, a thin strand of frenzied, hacking, skirmishers spreading out before the recovering Orthlundyn like a ripple precursing the arrival of a great wave.

The rumbling above continued to fade, but as it did so, the Orthlundyn filled the incipient silence with their own thunder as once again they began their relentless advance.

Hawklan and the Helyadin retreated through the phalanx and remounted.

'We'll not re-form the cavalry,' Dacu said anxiously. 'There's hardly anyone mounted and the horses are scattered everywhere.'

Hawklan did not answer immediately, but looked upwards slightly. Through the residual rumbling, he thought he heard a thin, flesh-crawling screeching high above, but it disappeared under the mounting pandemonium of the battlefield and he dismissed it.

He turned back to Dacu and his concerns. 'Most of them have still got their bows,' he said. 'Get them guarding this flank, and skirmishing. Then do what you can with the horses; we need them.'

As the Helyadin dispersed to execute this command, Hawklan turned and rode back towards Andawyr. On the way he passed the sled that the Riddin boy had driven by him so apparently recklessly but minutes ago. It had overturned and the horse was struggling white-eyed and foaming in its harness.

Hawklan drew his sword and reaching over, cut the animal free. Serian backed away as, with much kicking and stumbling, the terrified horse stood up.

'Calm it, Serian,' Hawklan said.

'Tend your own, Hawklan,' the horse replied with an inclination of his head towards the far side of the sled.

Hawklan looked where Serian indicated, and saw a small form lying in the snow. He dismounted quickly and ran to the boy, but even as he bent over him, he knew that the child was beyond any aid he could offer. From the impressions in the snow, it seemed that the sled had rolled over him when it overturned.

A surge of memories swept through him. Memories of the children of Pedhavin, shouting, running, silently watching, as they played their eternally secret games about the winding sunlit streets of the village, and around the courtyards and halls of Anderras Darion. And somewhere was the glow from his own golden childhood in another age.

He let the vision unfold without restraint until he found his vision blurring, then colder, adult needs made him lay it aside; though gently.

The freed horse came and stood beside him. It lowered its head and touched the boy.

'Not *your* fault,' Hawklan said, stroking it. Then, to the boy, he whispered, 'I'm sorry,' very softly. 'Fear no more.'

Remounting Serian, he turned again towards the Cadwanwr.

As Hawklan approached, Andawyr moved slightly as if he had been struck, and Hawklan felt again the choking warmth rising up inside him that had marked Creost's entry into the fray. He turned and looked over the battlefield.

The right wing of the Morlider was being routed as its bewildered and shocked fighters struggled to escape the renewed advance of the Orthlundyn pikes. The left wing, disarrayed to some extent by the Helyadin's quiet but savage assault, had stopped its advance and was faltering in some confusion. Dacu and the Helyadin were rallying the broken cavalry to protect the Orthlundyn's vulnerable flank on foot.

Hawklan felt both the exhilaration of the Orthlundyn and the terror of the fleeing Morlider. If the attack could be sustained, the Morlider would soon break utterly.

Creost was acting now not to destroy his enemy, but to save his army! From somewhere, the Uhriel had found a resource to beat back the opposition that the two Cadwanwr had offered him. For a chilling moment, it occurred to Hawklan that pehaps this foul agent of Sumeral had only been toying with these irksome creatures that scuttled irritatingly about its feet. But the moment passed. The seizure of Riddin must surely be vital to Sumeral's strategy and while the fate of the Morlider army as men doubtless meant little to Creost, as a tool for implementing the will of Sumeral, it was well wrought and powerful, the work of many years; it would not lightly be broken and destroyed if it fell within its creator's remit to prevent it.

'He would have destroyed half his army to destroy us!' Atelon's shocked words came back to Hawklan vividly. Had there been any doubt in his mind about that first assault by Creost, there was none now. Better to lose half the army than to lose all of it.

Hawklan urged Serian forward. He knew nothing of the ways of the Old Power, but he knew that he was the chosen of the Sword of Ethriss and that both he and the Sword now belonged to the battle against Creost.

The cloying warmth ebbed and flowed as he galloped through the snow to bring this aid to the struggling Cadwanwr. A quick glance showed him that the Helyadin bodyguard had recovered, but all, save two, had lost their horses. He jumped down from Serian and, drawing the Black Sword, stepped forward to join Andawyr and Atelon.

Looking out over the battlefield, he saw the figure of the Uhriel, now more disturbing than ever in the aura that surrounded it. Should he place the Sword in Andawyr's hand as he had in Atelon's? Should he hold it in front of himself as he had when Oklar had stood revealed before him? No instinct guided him, though something drew his gaze down to the Sword itself. As he looked at it, he saw the twining strands in the black depths of the hilt shining and flickering triumphantly as they wound their way through countless brilliant stars into some unknown, unimaginable, distance.

A touch on his arm returned him to the field. It was Jenna, white-faced and shaking, but in control. She was pointing out to sea.

One of the two ships bringing reinforcements was heading towards the shore. Hawklan could not make out how many were on board, but the danger lay not necessarily in the quantity of troops but in their quality. Could these perhaps be an elite like the Goraidin and the Helyadin? Such a group, fast, powerful, determined, could turn this battle even now. But Jenna shook him and redirected his attention to the other ship.

His eyes widened.

Oars plunging into the waves at what must have been a body-wrenching rate for the rowers, the ship was heading at great speed towards the boat on which stood the malevolent figure of Creost.

Then it struck.

Its bow reared out of the water as it rode up over the smaller vessel, then it seemed almost to pause before crushing it under the waves as if it had been some child's toy. Hawklan saw the Uhriel hurled into the sea to be submerged as the rowers appeared to redouble their efforts and drove their ship over the splintering remains of the boat in a fury of thrashing destruction. Then, at the same frenzied pace, the ship turned towards the shore.

Before Hawklan could even react, however, a great dome of water swelled up and burst under the stern of the retreating ship, upending it totally. Hawklan saw men tumbling out of the ship to fall into the sea under a hail of oars and tackle. Then the ship itself fell on them in a great cloud of spume and spray.

He would have turned his face away from the horror of the sight, but a greater horror held him. Atop the crashing wave stood Creost, his rending presence tenfold what it had been. Instinctively, Hawklan raised the Sword in front of himself.

There was a cry from both Andawyr and Atelon; a cry of both pain and triumph.

'We have you, demon!' Andawyr cried out.

Joining his triumphant shout came a terrible cry from the distant figure; a cry that Hawklan recognised; a cry that he had heard from the wounded Oklar. It filled him with the same nameless terrors, but he passed through them unmoved. The creature had been sorely hurt by some hand; now he must be destroyed. He felt dark forces of his own gathering within him.

'The Sword, Hawklan, the Sword!' It was Andawyr. His face was alive with both triumph and fear and Hawklan had the impression of a dazzling brilliance beneath the prosaic clothing, as he had once before at the Gretmearc. 'We have torn the islands from him. His army is lost but his rage in his agony may be far beyond our containing.'

The Cadwanwr's words briefly disturbed Hawklan's terrible focus and he looked at him uncertainly, then at the distant islands. They seemed to be unchanged, but even as he watched, a ragged white began to blur their edges.

Waves, Hawklan realised. Huge waves, to be seen at this distance. The long frustrated will of Enartion was asserting its ancient sway once more.

Hawklan's purpose focused again, the clearer still for this new knowledge. With a cry he willed Serian forward at full gallop towards the still unbroken Morlider.

As he neared them he pointed his sword towards the sea.

'Look to your homes,' he roared repeatedly, galloping along the line. 'Creost is downed. Look to your homes.'

Few heard him over the din of the battle, but to their knowing eyes the merest glance confirmed the truth of his words and the news sped through the ranks faster even than the galloping Serian.

The Morlider army, ferocious and dangerous even in rout, was no more. Now the Riddin shore was filled with frightened men running desperately to reach the boats that alone could take them back to their lands.

For a moment, Hawklan's heart ached at the pity of the transformation, but his mind did not turn, even briefly, from the true enemy on that field, and his dark, focused forces became a sinister battle fever.

'Ho! Creost!' he shouted. 'Come. Face your destiny. Face the justice of the Black Sword of Ethriss for your crimes.'

As he rode to and fro, wending his dangerous way through the fleeing crowd, and shouting his challenge, he thought he heard again a distant screeching high above, but when he looked up, nothing was to be seen but the brightening sky and high circling sea birds.

Some strange freak of the air carrying a dying creature's tormented cries, he thought. Yet it was a sound the like of which he had never heard before.

He thrust it from him and returned to his search for Creost. Now he could feel the creature's presence all around him; but where was its heart?

Then, abruptly, the crowd parted, and he was there; malevolence and rage pouring from him. Serian reared.

Hawklan surveyed his foe, the true architect of this day's horror. The Uhriel was smaller and broader than Dan-Tor and his skin had a pallid lustre that reminded Hawklan of his own arm after it had been seized by the Vrwystin a Kaethio at the Gretmearc. Worse though, were his eyes. Cold, black, and dead they were, but far beyond Gavor's contemptuous epithet, fish-eyed. And, like Oklar, facing him at the Palace Gate in Vakloss, Creost seemed to intrude into this time and place with an appalling wrongness.

Despite the crush of the fleeing Morlider, none stepped near their erstwhile leader. It was as if his raging aura would destroy any who came too near.

Hawklan jumped down from Serian and walked towards him. Taking off his helm he stared, unblinking, into the Uhriel's eyes. At Vakloss there had been ignorance and doubt, but here was knowledge and certainty. Here, no debate was needed; this creature must die, and this sword would kill him.

Yet, just as he was about to stride forward, Hawklan hesitated. The healer in him felt Creost's pain.

'We have torn the islands from him!' Andawyr's words returned to him. Now Hawklan understood the consequences, if not the nature, of this . . . victory. The Uhriel was indeed sorely hurt. Some part of it reached out to Hawklan and cried for rest and peace to recover from this pain.

The warrior in him set aside the healer, gently. The hurt was of his own making, it said. He is still malevolent and powerful, perhaps more powerful in his intent towards us, than before. He is beyond all help. He must die.

Hawklan gripped the Black Sword and strode forward.

Creost did not move but, abruptly, Hawklan felt the awful warmth that had seized him before become a burning horror all over him.

Creost's mouth opened to reveal a cavernous blackness as cold and dead as his eyes.

'So you are the bearer of the heretic Ethriss's Sword; the sender of arrogant messages, the one who would slay me.'

The voice's withering contempt and certainty chilled Hawklan's heart, even as he felt his body burning.

'Whatever chance threw that bauble into your hand, did you an ill turn. See how you wilt at the least of my touches, and see how your vaunted sword protects you. Now stand aside, I have true foes to seek and punish for this day's work.'

'No,' Hawklan managed to gasp out. 'You will not pass me, Uhriel. You *cannot* pass me. I pinioned your loathsome soulmate with a lesser weapon than this. You, I will kill for sure; for this day's work, and many others.'

Still Creost did not move, but his black eyes seemed to expand. Though he made no sound, his demented fury

291

screamed at Hawklan like a scarcely chained predator. He raised a pale hand towards his adversary. Hawklan forced his legs to move forward.

'Hold, creature!'

The Uhriel's gaze left Hawklan, and he felt his pain ease a little, though some power still held him back from his purpose.

Andawyr came to his side. A pace behind him stood Atelon.

Cadwanwr and Uhriel stared at one another in some unseen conflict of wills; a strange enclave of stillness in the midst of the whirling tide flowing across the battlefield.

'Know this, pawn of the great Corrupter,' Andawyr said, his voice powerful and clear even above the clamour of the fleeing Morlider. 'While you slept, we waited. While you lay in the darkness, we searched in the light, and we learned. We are not the Cadwanwr of old, and you are not the Uhriel of old. Our knowledge and skill are greater by far and your vaunted Power is weaker by far. Turn from this awful road. Nothing but your doom lies at the end of it. *He* will deceive and desert you now, as he did aeons ago.'

Hawklan felt the Uhriel's fury screaming, and his own grew in unholy harmony with it.

'You blaspheme, old man,' Creost said. 'And you misjudge both your skill and my Power grievously.'

Then, there were no more words. The Uhriel's fury burst forth to assail the Cadwanwr. Hawklan felt it swirl around him, but both Andawyr and Atelon stood unmoved.

For a moment, Hawklan saw and understood the Cadwanwr's great skill. Even with Atelon's aid, Andawyr did *not* have the power of this awesome creature now that it was freed from the burden of the islands; but while Creost's fury ran unfettered and uncontrolled, his strength could be redirected against himself and his pain and injury made the worse.

He saw too, however, that Andawyr could not kill this thing. That task was his alone.

He took the Sword in two hands and tried again to move forward, but still some force held him where he stood.

He was a mote, held motionless in some terrible deadlock of wills and powers.

Yet he was the mote that would tilt this great balance and topple the monstrous enemy.

'I will not be bound,' he roared, though no sound came from his mouth.

But still he could not move forward; could not measure

those few paces that would bring him within reach of the end of this horror.

Then the screeching came again. Thin, skin-tearing, and frightful, it shimmered through Hawklan's resolve like a bright ringing crack in a fine glass.

It was not the sound of any wholesome creature. It had the quality of desecration about it that hallmarked His work.

With appalling suddenness, it grew until it overtopped both the commotion of the battlefield and the grumbling sky.

Creost's black eyes turned upwards, drawing Hawklan's with them. A black bird was there. Gavor? But something was amiss. Hawklan screwed up his eyes as they refused to focus clearly on the descending form, dark against the clearing sky.

It seemed that Gavor was coming too close, too quickly, but–

The screeching became unbearable.

It was not Gavor! It was some other bird. A huge bird. And someone was astride its back!

The awesome deadlock between Creost and the Cadwanwr shattered suddenly. Hawklan's gaze returned to Creost and he felt his arms lift the Sword high as they obeyed his long restrained will. As his legs prepared to carry him forward, however, someone seized him about the waist and sent him crashing to the ground.

Rolling over, he brought a mailed fist round to deal with this assailant, only to find that it was Andawyr.

Before he could speak however, the air was full of the sound of the beating of great wings, and the descending creature landed in front of Creost.

Hawklan gaped. The creature was a grotesque travesty of a bird. Its body was larger than Serian, its feet were taloned, and a serpentine neck supported a long pointed head that swayed to and fro menacingly. Astride its back, however, was a worse sight. Gaunt and deathly pale, with long tangled white hair that writhed as if it existed in a wind-blown universe of its own, sat the white-eyed figure of Dar Hastuin.

Hawklan recognised the Uhriel, though no name had been spoken; nothing else could so offend the time and place by its very presence.

Come in triumph to aid your ally, and gloat over your victory, you obscenity? he thought.

Anger rose up through him like a sudden blazing fire as he struggled to his feet. Freed from whatever had held him, he knew he must slay these abominations while chance allowed. The Black Sword seemed to draw him onward, singing, to the deed.

As he dashed forward, he saw Dar Hastuin's clawlike hand reach out to take Creost's.

'No!' he cried. They must not escape the reach of the Sword.

He aimed a savage blow at the head of the frightful bird, but it pulled away from him with unexpected speed and, curling its long neck, struck at him like a serpent, screeching horribly as it did so.

Hawklan staggered as his reflexes moved him away from the blow, but he did not lose his footing.

Creost was astride the flapping creature now. Hawklan moved forward to strike again, but the bird struck first, making him fall over this time. As he rose to his feet, the bird began beating its wings so ferociously that he could scarcely keep his balance in the wind it created. Then it charged at him, making him dive desperately to one side.

As he rolled through the trampled snow he brought himself upright, sword still firmly gripped. But the bird was in the air, carrying its loathsome cargo.

'My bow,' he roared. 'Serian.'

The horse was by him in the instant, but even as he reached for the bow, Hawklan knew that the Uhriel were beyond even its range. Quickly he swung up into the saddle. Serian could surely outrun that bird!

Before he could move however, Andawyr stepped in front of Serian and laid a gentle hand on his muzzle.

'Stand aside, man,' Hawklan shouted angrily. 'We can have them yet.'

Andawyr shook his head sadly. 'No,' he said. 'In the confusion of the moment we might indeed have slain them. But not now. Not together, and riding Usgreckan. They would slay us if we challenged them. Let them flee if they themselves haven't realised that.'

'No!' Hawklan shouted, urging Serian forward to push Andawyr aside. But the horse did not move.

Hawklan's anger foamed up into his eyes then drained away abruptly as it broke against Andawyr's stillness. He leaned forward and looked into the old man's face.

'No,' he said again, quietly, and in some despair. 'It cannot be, Andawyr. Not when we've been so close.'

'It *is*, my friend,' Andawyr said gently. 'It *is*. But the day is ours. Creost hurt, and his mortal allies broken and fleeing should give us the Muster by our side when we march into Narsindal. And we know that Dar Hastuin too was hurt, hurt at least as sorely as –'

'How, hurt?' Hawklan said, looking at him sharply.

Andawyr shrugged and looked upwards. 'Whatever happened up there, he too was defeated.'

Hawklan looked up. Inland, the sky was dark and heavy with winter, but overhead and out to sea the cloud had been breaking up for some time as the tide turned. Now much of the sky was blue, and filled with tiny blowing clouds. Directly overhead, and very high, a large white cloud moved slowly out to sea.

Though he could hear nothing above the noise around him, Hawklan felt the presence of the great cloud land. He raised his sword in salute. 'Live well, and light be with you, Ynar Aesgin, and with your soarers, riders of the high paths. May you find the peace to heal all your pains,' he said, quietly. 'Forgive me if I failed you.'

He swung down from Serian and gazed at the passing Viladrien for a moment in silence.

As he turned back to Andawyr, Isloman galloped up. His face was flustered and anxious. 'Hawklan! Quickly!' he shouted pointing to the south.

Hawklan followed the direction of his hand. There in the distance were horsemen; hundreds of them, spreading out as they approached.

'Muster,' he said softly, smiling as he remembered the call of the old lady he had met on his sunlit way to the Gretmearc. 'Haha! First Hearer again,' he heard her say.

But his smile faded almost immediately, and with a shout he remounted Serian and drove him forward. The Muster were heading towards the fleeing Morlider with lances and drawn swords. Their intention was unequivocally clear.

'I will take you to the Line Leader,' Serian said as he gathered speed. 'But sheathe your sword or neither of us will live to reach him, they're in full cry.'

Hawklan gave the horse his head, marvelling again at his speed and power as he galloped forward towards the approaching horsemen.

Looking at the Muster, Hawklan saw the wisdom of trusting to the horse. He could not have stopped the impending massacre single-handed, and he could not have found the leader amidst so many.

Indeed, in Hawklan's eyes, the grey-bearded man before whom Serian eventually halted was scarcely distinguishable from any of the other riders, in his heavy clothing and helm.

'Hawklan,' cried the man riding next to him. The voice was Agreth's and its tone was full of both pleasure and relief.

Hawklan returned him no courtesies, however.

'Call your men back,' he said urgently. 'Call them back.'

Agreth hesitated and looked uncertainly at his neighbour. Urthryn took off his helm; his face was grim, and strained with great weariness.

'Take care,' Serian said softly.

'You are the man Hawklan,' Urthryn said appraisingly. 'I should have known you from your demeanour without Agreth's calling your name. We are greatly in your debt. A matter to be honoured in due time. But we've ridden as the Muster has never ridden before to find these murderers, and nothing will stop us meting out due punishment.'

Hawklan glanced over his shoulder and saw the Muster reaching some of the stragglers.

'Call them back!' he shouted furiously. 'They're retreating. Let them go.'

Urthryn recoiled from Hawklan's outburst, then his face darkened. A rider next to him, misunderstanding his movement, brought a lance up protectively towards Hawklan's throat.

Almost off-handedly, Hawklan seized the shaft as it moved forward, and with a barely perceptible movement unbalanced the man so that he toppled from his saddle. Another rider reached for a sword, only to find Hawklan's newly acquired lance resting heavily across his hand. Other swords were drawn rapidly.

'No!' shouted Agreth, holding out a hand before his own angry leader. Then, to Hawklan, 'What are you doing, threatening the Ffyrst? These invaders slaughtered thousands of our kin mercilessly. They must be punished.'

Hawklan struggled with his anger. 'Whoever fought your people in the south, it was not these. They've been on this shore for weeks and the only people they've killed have been Orthlundyn, and that only today. Call your riders back.'

'Hawklan, they swept our people away like so much . . . dung out of a stable.' Agreth's face was pained. 'Smashed and drowned them all as they waited on the beach –'

Hawklan's brow furrowed. 'Drowned?' he said.

Agreth faltered, 'A wave. A great wave . . .' he said, his voice fading as his gaze turned to the sea, sparkling now golden and grey, and alive with fluttering sails and bobbing vessels.

Hawklan turned to Urthryn. 'If your people were slain by the sea, then their murderer is Creost,' he said, his voice now urgent and pleading. 'And he has fled this field, injured and robbed of his mortal army.' He swung his arm over the retreating masses. 'These people were deceived and misled. They've taken a hundred losses to our one and now their very lands are drifting from them. Let them go. Call your riders back. Your true foe – *our* true foe . . . lies yonder.'

He turned and pointed to the north, but as he did so, he froze. Serian whinnied uncertainly. Low over the horizon and black against the distant clouds was an unmistakable silhouette. Usgreckan and its unholy burden were returning.

Andawyr's fears returned to Hawklan. *Together* the two Uhriel might yet reverse this rout. A great silent cry of denial rose up within him and he swung Serian round, scattering the gathered Muster riders. 'Break your heart, prince of horses,' he said, his face savage. 'We must kill these before they reach our peoples.'

And wild though Serian's charge had been to intercept the Muster, it was as naught before the tumultous black wind of his race to greet the Uhriel, with Hawklan carrying high the bow of Ethriss and the ranks of friend and fleeing enemy parting before him like the sea before a surging prow.

'Hawklan, no! You'll be killed! Stay by us!' came Andawyr's voice as the great stallion sped by, but nothing could stay such purpose, and Andawyr and Atelon spurred their horses after him like flotsam in his wake.

The sound of Usgreckan came ahead of him, bearing the Uhriels' rage like a foul wind. It mingled with the cry rising in Hawklan's throat as he nocked one of Loman's black arrows onto the glistening string of Ethriss's bow.

But as the two foes closed, a third figure appeared; a small black dot falling precipitously from high out of the sky.

As it seemed set to fall past the screeching Usgreckan, its wings spread wide and it arced down to strike the ghastly white head of Dar Hastuin a punishing blow.

'Gavor!' Hawklan shouted in alarm and distress. 'No!'

But the battle was far from his reach and Serian's pounding charge slowed as both horse and rider found themselves helpless specators to Gavor's lone assault.

The two Uhriel struggled and flailed their arms to repel Gavor's frenzied attacks while Usgreckan twisted and swooped, but all was to little avail against Gavor's consummate flying until eventually a fortuitous blow struck the raven full square.

Even as his friend fell, Hawklan released an arrow, and then another and another. The first glanced off Creost's hand which was reaching out to deliver some final blow to the falling Gavor; the second and third did no hurt, but passed close by, causing Usgreckan to tumble and almost unseat its riders. Then Andawyr was by Hawklan's side, his bright eyes blazing and his arms extended, adding his own menace to Hawklan's assault.

Usgreckan shrieked and fled, its fearful cry echoing over the whole field. Gavor struck the ground.

Hawklan galloped desperately to his stricken friend.

The black form looked fragile and broken in the deep Riddin snow, and there was blood all around him. As Hawklan knelt by him, Gavor opened his eyes weakly and said, very faintly, 'Sorry, dear boy.'

Then his eyes closed and he lay very still.

# *Chapter 19*

The snow-covered landscape was yellowed by a low, watery sun as it peered fitfully through the wintry haze. Vague patches of grey shadow picked their way over the fields uncertainly as, high above, unseen clouds formed and changed and drifted slowly by.

'Thaw coming soon,' Eldric said, feeling the cold dampness in the air.

A few heads nodded indifferently. No one relished the raw, blustering interregnum between the paternal tyranny of winter with its white, biting certainty, and the usurping anarchy of spring with its irreverent, unassuageable energy.

Eldric did not pursue his foretelling. It had only been a nervous twitch to break the silence which had enfolded the waiting group as they watched the distant Orthlundyn army winding its way through the brightening morning towards the City. Turning to Hreldar and Darek, he became prosaic.

'Come on,' he said. 'I'm freezing to death here. Let's go and meet them.'

The two lords exchanged a brief smile. Eldric intercepted it and scowled enquiringly.

'We had a small wager that you wouldn't wait,' Darek said, smiling unrepentantly.

Eldric snorted and clicked his horse forward. His entourage fell in behind him, noticeably more cheerful for being on the move again.

'I wonder what this Gulda's like,' Hreldar said.

'*Memsa* Gulda,' Darek said sternly. 'If Arrindier's underlining is anything to go by.'

'Remarkable I should imagine,' Eldric said. 'All our messengers come back looking slightly stunned, and delivering her messages with great precision.' He laughed. 'And I swear Arin's hand was shaking every time he wrote her name.'

As the troop rode on, the road became more and more crowded with people walking the same way for the same purpose. Gulda had politely declined the Geadrol's suggestion that the Orthlundyn march through Vakloss to receive a formal welcome.

'. . . We are an army, but we are not soldiers, Lords. We are a people come to aid in the destruction of Sumeral, not to tourney. Your good will and a place to pitch our shelters will be welcome and honour enough . . .'

'I *did* tell you!' Arrindier wrote.

But nothing could prevent the people of Vakloss providing their own informal welcome, muffled and gloved though they might be.

Eldric was pleased to see the crowds. Dan-Tor's rule and his bloody deposition had left many scars on the Fyordyn; scars which ached and throbbed from time to time and some of which might take generations to heal fully. But the Uhriel's leeching corrosion had destroyed none of the vital threads which bound the people together. The re-establishment of the Geadrol and, above all, the open meting out of justice in the traditional courts, proved too rich a fare for the ranks of malcontents that had thrived on Dan-Tor's diet of envy, vindictiveness and secretive treachery. The recovery had gone on apace.

It had been helped, too, by the news from Orthlund. With old enemies threatening Riddin, and the Orthlundyn – the quiet, gentle Orthlundyn – marching through the winter mountains to their aid, the Fyordyn's own sufferings could be seen as part of a wider torment. A combination of guilt at their failure to fulfil their ancient duties, and anger at Dan-Tor's personal betrayal swept away many lesser grievances.

Now the Orthlundyn were here. And soon the winter would be ended. Then the creator of this long nightmare would feel the wrath of his victims!

The Fyordyn were optimistic.

Except for the news from Riddin, Eldric thought. Or, more correctly, the absence of news. According to messages from Arrindier, the Alphraan had reported that the army had left the mountains to enter Riddin in good heart, but since then there had been only silence. What had happened there? What had happened to the Muster? the Orthlundyn? Hawklan? And, not least, Sylvriss? And, though heard only in Eldric's heart, Jaldaric?

It had been suggested that some of the Goraidin be sent through the mountains to find the answers to these questions, but Yatsu calmly, if regretfully, stated the obvious. 'Men could die on such a journey,' he said. 'That's probably why they've not sent any news themselves. And at the worst, what information could such a venture bring us that we can't already make preparation for? The Goraidin should be used where they'll be of greatest benefit. They must stay in the north, preparing for the assault on the mines.'

Nobody had seriously disputed his comments, but still the silence from Riddin lay across all considerations like a small cold hand.

Distant cheering brought Eldric out of his brief reverie and he saw that the road ahead was blocked by a milling crowd. Beyond the bobbing heads he could see wagons and horsemen, prominent among the latter being Arrindier.

Eldric reined to a halt and smiled.

'Commander Varak,' he said. 'Take a few troopers and see if you can gently open up a way for us . . . and our allies.'

Varak saluted smartly and signalled to a group of High Guards. Their offices, however, were not required. Even before they had moved forward, the crowd ahead parted to reveal a black, stooping figure leaning on a stick.

'Gulda,' said Eldric and Darek simultaneously.

'Memsa!' Hreldar reminded them raising his eyebrows in mock warning.

Gulda moved purposefully towards them, Arrindier and other horsemen following in her wake. Eldric and the party dismounted to greet her.

For the first time in many years, Eldric felt young again as the black figure bore down on him; too young. He had the distinct feeling that he was a child again and standing in front of one of his old teachers. There was quality about Gulda that belied utterly the stooped form and the stick she seemed to lean on.

'Lord Eldric,' she said – a statement, not a question, he noted. He took the offered hand. Her grip was like a man's; indeed, not unlike Hawklan's in the feeling it gave of great power finely and totally controlled. He found his balance being subtly tested. A brief appreciative smile passed over Gulda's face, then her piercing blue eyes looked into his and reduced him unequivocally to the schoolroom again.

The word 'Gulda' formed in his throat, but 'Memsa' came out as he scrabbled back to his true age and dignity. 'Lord Arrindier has written much about you. It's an honour to meet you.'

'I deduce from what he's told me that you conducted a fine

campaign,' Gulda said, without preliminaries. 'You and your Goraidin. Well done. *Bravely* done, against such a foe.' Then, before Eldric could speak, she moved to Darek and Hreldar, gave them their names and tested them similarly.

As she did so, her gaze took in the other waiting dignitaries and their High Guard escort.

'Commander Varak,' she said.

'Yes, Memsa,' the startled commander replied, clicking his heels and bowing slightly.

Gulda nodded and grunted non-committally. 'Thank you for the escort you sent us,' she said warmly. 'They've been most efficient and helpful. Disciplined but with lots of initiative. You and I will get on well.'

Varak's mouth opened, but no sound came.

Eldric moved to rescue his flustered aide. 'Memsa, we've come to greet you and your people and to escort you and your senior officers to the Palace for a *small* ceremony of welcome.'

Gulda pursed her lips. 'These people are all the welcome we need, Lord,' she said, looking at the surrounding crowd. 'That and a place to camp.'

'That's all arranged, Memsa,' Eldric said. 'These Guards and your escort will attend to it.' He looked at her intently. 'Join us please. We see the value of our small ceremonies much more since the passing of Dan-Tor.'

Gulda looked at him intently and then gave a conceding nod. 'A perceptive observation, Lord, I commend you,' she said. 'Give me a little time to see the people settled first – we've covered a good distance today and they're tired, cold and hungry – then, with your permission I'd like to walk your city again; alone; see for myself the damage that Oklar wrought on it.'

'Alone, Memsa?' Eldric queried awkwardly.

'I'm well acquainted with the place, Lord,' Gulda replied, mildly indignant. 'You needn't fear for my getting lost.'

Eldric began to flounder. 'Memsa, there are a small number of disaffected elements in the City –' he began.

'They'll not bother a harmless old woman,' Gulda said, turning away from him and heading back to her army. 'Have no fear, I shall join you before noon.'

Arrindier dismounted. He was smiling broadly as he greeted Eldric and his friends warmly. 'Welcome to the ranks of the intimidated,' he said. 'If it's any consolation, the Memsa gets worse as you get to know her.'

Eldric looked at him uncertainly. 'That's most reassuring,' he said.

'I can see you don't believe me,' Arrindier went on, laughing. 'Well, if I were so inclined, I'd wager that you'll be discussing strategy and tactics with her before sunset, welcoming celebration or not.'

Arrindier was correct. At noon, Gulda presented herself at the Palace where, in one of the great halls, and together with a few senior company commanders, she patiently accepted an official welcome in the form of a rather long speech from the City Rede, and a hastily shortened one from Eldric. This was followed by what was to have been a feast of welcome, but Gulda took the initiative.

'Lords, I thank you for your welcome, but now we've much to discuss. We'll eat as we work,' she said, but with an unexpected graciousness that disarmed even the cooks and chefs.

Thus, to Arrindier's amusement, and well before sunset, the Fyordyn found themselves retailing the history of Fyorlund from the Morlider War to the present; retailing it in great detail under Gulda's gently incessant interrogation. At times it seemed she was allowing the discussion to ramble aimlessly; the Mandroc found in Lord Evison's castle, the brief use of the Old Power, if such it was, by Dan-Tor prior to the Lords' assault on Vakloss, the terrible fire wagons that had been launched against the infantry, the gradual deterioration of the High Guards over the years, Hawklan's confrontation with Dan-Tor and its consequences, the illness and recovery of the King; an apparently endless list of topics were touched on and then left until, quite abruptly, Gulda clapped her hands.

'Good, good, good,' she said. 'This has been most helpful. As I expected, we shall *all* get on splendidly. However, I must return to camp now; we all of us have duties to perform. I shall come back tomorrow and we can begin in earnest.'

As she reached the door of the hall, she stopped and turned round. 'You didn't falter in your duty, Fyordyn. You were foully brought down by an infinitely subtle hand. A hand that has led astray wiser than you by far before now.' Her face became stern and the stick came up. 'Your tellings are full of self-reproach. That must end. Cling to your past only in so far as you can learn from it. All else will cloud your vision – and get your throats cut.'

Eldric started at the unexpected harshness in her voice as she made this last comment, but before he could respond, Gulda and her small company were gone.

He slumped back into his chair and slapped the table with his hand. A nearby goblet chimed out in protesting harmony. 'Good grief, Arin, is she always like that? Where does she come from? The way she takes charge of things she reminds me of Dan-Tor.'

Arrindier laughed. 'No one seems to know anything about her,' he said. 'And she won't tell you, rest assured. I *did* tell you about her in my letters.'

'I presumed you were exaggerating,' Eldric said ruefully. Then he looked affectionately at his old friend. 'Still, it's good to have you back. And whatever that woman is I'm glad she's on *our* side. From what little I saw, the Orthlundyn have sent as fine a body of men as you said.'

'Men and women,' Arrindier corrected off-handedly, reaching across the table for a piece of bread.

Eldric frowned. 'Women?' he said as if he had misheard.

'Women,' confirmed Arrindier. Then catching Eldric's eye he raised his hand hastily to forestall the impending outburst. 'And, if you'll take my advice, you'll accept it without comment.'

Despite the seriousness in Arrindier's voice however, the observation was to little avail. 'Women can't wield axes and swords, draw bows, fend for themselves in the field,' Eldric exclaimed.

'The Riddinvolk do,' Arrindier said.

Eldric waved a dismissive hand. 'Cavalry's not infantry,' he said rather peevishly, unexpectedly stung by this immediate riposte from someone who should have been an ally. 'Besides, they're a different people.'

Arrindier smiled but his voice and manner were uncompromising. 'So are the Orthlundyn,' he said. 'Very different from us and very different from what we, or for that matter, what *they* thought they were. Accept it, Eldric. I've learned a lot about them these past weeks, they're a strange and powerful people. It's as if the whole country was waking from some long sleep. It behoves us all to take Gulda's advice and *learn*.'

A flurry of remonstrations came to Eldric's mind, but they fell to nothing against Arrindier's resolution and he blew them out in a reluctant growl. 'Very well,' he said, nodding. 'After all that's happened of late I suppose we should be beyond being surprised. But . . . women . . . fighting . . .' He shook his head and sighed resignedly. 'I can't see it myself. But tell me about them anyway.'

After leaving the impromptu command meeting, Gulda stood pensively on the Palace steps. 'Go on ahead,' she said to her companions. 'You're tired, and there's still a lot to do. I've some things here I need to attend to.'

As the Orthlundyn left, Gulda turned and went back into the Palace.

Walking through its many corridors and halls, she was inevitably an object of some curiosity to the servants and officials that she encountered. Few, however, lingered to question her, finding that her stern enquiring eye invariably reminded them of duties to be fulfilled elsewhere.

As she entered the deserted Throne Room, its many rows of torches burst into life, and the great stone throne glittered and sparkled as if in welcome.

She looked along the deserted arches and galleries that lined the room, and at the solitary window at the far end, now pale with the uncertain winter twilight. Then she walked the long carpeted way to the steps that led up to the throne. Pausing before she reached them, she turned and stared at the floor. Though no stain existed to mark it, Gulda was looking at the place where Rgoric had met his cruel end.

She stood there, still and silent, for a long time, then slowly she turned her back on the throne and returned to the great double doors through which she had entered. Gently closing them she set off again on her solitary pilgrimage around the Palace.

Eventually her footsteps carried her through an elaborate archway and into the Crystal Hall. It was apparently deserted, and the subdued light was tinted with a rich redness that the Hall had drawn from the setting sun outside.

Gulda gazed around at the flickering sagas being silently enacted in the depths of the strange walls. Slowly she moved around the hall, her stooped form carving its own deep and subtle darkness through the shadows. Occasionally she reached out and touched the translucent, gold-threaded wall, and the scene behind it would shift and flurry in surprised agitation, sometimes seeming to flow out along her arm to hover briefly in the warm darkness.

She smiled and the whole wall rippled with celebration.

As she stopped before the great tree, its stark, wintry

branches seemed to reach out to greet her, becoming alive with the eyes of countless glittering insects.

She chuckled in response, then she paused. There was another presence in the hall.

Gulda nodded. 'Honoured Secretary,' she said, without turning.

'Memsa,' came the acknowledging reply.

Gulda turned round and looked at the figure of Dilrap, sitting motionless in the shade. 'Forgive me, I'm intruding on you,' she said.

Dilrap shook his head. 'No, Memsa,' he replied. 'There's few who appreciate the splendour of this place in its quieter moods and such as there are could not, by their nature, intrude.'

Gulda bowed slightly.

'Rather, I suspect it's I who intrude on you,' Dilrap went on. 'The Hall pays homage to you. I've never seen it so . . . alive . . . not even in bright sunshine.'

Gulda smiled and sat down beside Dilrap. 'No,' she said. 'It pays me no homage, nor anyone. I understand it, that's all. I used to play . . .' Her voice tailed off and Dilrap's eyes narrowed as a terrible loneliness washed over him. Impulsively he reached out and took her hand. It closed around his, strong and powerful, yet almost unbearably plaintive.

'They're all here still, for those with the eye to see them,' she said, after a long silence. Her voice was a throaty whisper. 'Sunlit, glowing times, full of laughter and joy. Captured by hands and skills long, long, gone. Times before . . . before *He* came. Before His taint sought out the weaknesses . . . seeped into them . . .'

She fell silent again and Dilrap folded his other hand around hers; no words, he knew, could reach into such darkness.

Neither moved nor spoke for some time, and the redness around them slowly deepened and faded, to be replaced by the paler, quieter, stillness that came from the night-covered winter landscape outside.

Slowly Gulda withdrew her hand from Dilrap's gentle clasp.

'You have strangely powerful hands, Memsa,' he said. 'Like the Queen's.'

'Ah. Your Queen. Sylvriss. The horsewoman,' Gulda said, looking down at her hands, her voice still uncertain. 'Another mote in Dan-Tor's eye.' She paused briefly. 'I went to the

Throne Room,' she went on. 'Her love sustained Rgoric to the very end.'

'I know,' Dilrap said simply.

Gulda nodded. 'Of course you do,' she said. 'I forgot who I was talking to.'

She turned to him. Dilrap met her gaze, but as he looked at her his eyes filled with bewilderment and uncertainty.

'You are not what you seem, are you, Gulda?' he said simply. 'Why do you choose to be thus?'

Gulda started very slightly when she lowered her eyes. 'You have great silence around you, Dilrap,' she said. 'You stood at the right hand of Oklar and deceived him. Looked into his dark blazing soul and hid your deceit behind the truth. And you lived. And remained a whole man. It has given you a sight rarer than you can know . . .' She hesitated. '. . . But where you cannot aid, perhaps you should not look too closely. Thank you for your sharing, though. You are rich and blessed, Honoured Secretary.'

Dilrap made no response, but Gulda's mood seemed to lighten markedly. She looked around the Hall, and gave a short ironic chuckle. 'This place could have destroyed Dan-Tor, you know. He never came here, did he?'

Dilrap shook his head. 'Never,' he confirmed. 'It would have shown his dark, tormented soul to whatever was still human within him.'

Gulda drew in a long hissing breath. 'Rich and blessed indeed,' she said. 'Such strength we find, in such unexpected places.'

Urssain shivered despite the layers of clothing he was wearing. He pulled the heavy muffling cloak tight about himself, and began walking up and down again, over the well-trodden snow, stamping his feet occasionally in a vain attempt to repel the relentless penetration of the damp coldness that pervaded everywhere.

Nearby stood the heavily armed Mandroc patrol that had escorted Dan-Tor across Narsindal to this awful place. They were motionless, as was their leader, though he was standing easy, with his muscular, hairy arms folded across his chest. A large powerful-looking creature, markedly less heavily clad than Urssain, he seemed oblivious to the temperature. His upper lip had snagged on a lower canine tooth, giving him a scornful sneer, and his unreadable, grey-irised eyes were following the fretful Commander relentlessly.

No breeze stirred the scene, and the steaming breaths of the group gathered around them, thickening the pale mist that rolled over them from the still, grey waters of Lake Kedrieth.

'Wait,' Dan-Tor had said as they had reached one of the approaches to the great causeway that swept out across the lake and disappeared into the mist.

That had been hours ago. Urssain cursed inwardly. To have been chosen as escort to the Ffyrst across Narsindal was an honour he had both sought and feared. On the one hand it confirmed him indisputably, together with Aelang, as Dan-Tor's closest adviser; a vital step along his chosen path. But on the other, Narsindal was a soul-draining place; a place from which his chosen path was intended to lead him. Its decaying desolation seemed to seep into his body, but worse than that was the pervasive sensation of watching malice; a feeling that had worsened since he had last been there and one which he found now almost tangible in its oppressiveness.

His gaze moved upwards involuntarily as if to confirm the awesome presence of Derras Ustramel: His great fortress. Torn from the living rock by some unknowable Power, its towering, ramping heights were said to see all that moved in Narsindal, even through the mists; while its roots, spread wide and deep far below the icy lake, were said to house dungeons enough to hold all His enemies for all eternity.

But there was nothing to be seen. Only the perpetual mist. Though for a chilling moment, Urssain felt his prying gaze held as if by some unseen power, and it was only with a massive effort of will that he tore his eyes away.

Shaken, he looked along the causeway. It was crowded with groups of slaves wearily hauling wagons and sleds under the supervision of Mandroc guards. As he watched, a Mandroc patrol marched on to the causeway along one of the other approaches and he stared at it until it too disappeared into the mist.

Save for the slaves, no humans walked that road, though it was said that He was surrounded by men of His own choosing; men whose cruelty would –

No! Urssain dashed the thought aside. Rumours, rumours, rumours. That was all that ever came out of the mist. To question either Mandroc or slave who had been there would be to meet only wide-eyed terror. *If* any chose to serve Him, let

308

them serve Him; he was content to pay the price of serving Dan-Tor.

Every part of him cried out: Let me be away from this place.

Then, as if echoing this silent plea, a piercing, inhuman, scream rang out over the lake. It cut thorugh the mist like a glittering spear thrust, and Urssain's eyes widened in horror as the sound unmanned him. His motionless, ordered, Mandrocs and their leader, however, reacted more violently, throwing themselves on the ground in seemingly blind terror.

'Amrahl protect us. His will be done,' came the gabbling chant of their guttural voices. 'Great is His name.'

Somewhere in the mist a bird called out in alarm and the sound of its desperate, unseen, flight chimed with Urssain's racing heart.

The scream faded, but so slowly that, in Urssain's mind, it seemed to become a bright teeth-grating whine that might dwindle for ever, but neither die, nor leave him. Die it did, however, and in its wake came a deep and ominous rumbling. Lapping waves rose in alarm on the surface of the grim lake and the ground under Urssain's feet shook.

The Mandroc chanting redoubled in intensity.

'Black Lord, intercede for us,' said the leader, clutching at Urssain's feet.

Urssain did not reply – could not reply; his throat was too tight with terror. He stood motionless.

Then all became silent save for the fearful babbling of the Mandrocs and the slap of the wakened waves on the lake. From somewhere, Urssain recovered his voice.

'Be silent, and stand up,' he said to the still prone Mandroc leader, pushing him none too gently with his foot. 'Do you think that such grovelling would hide you from the will of Amrahl?' His tone was contemptuous. 'Re-form your escort. The Groundshaker is His greatest servant and he will return soon. Would you greet him with this childish folly?'

At the reminder of this more imminent threat, the Mandroc hastily scrambled to his feet and began shouting orders to his quaking patrol. Most of them stood up and took their positions again, but a few responded neither to their leader's words nor his subsequent brutality.

Urssain released a sigh of relief, disguising it as one of loud irritation. It was some time since he had dealt with Mandrocs but a little straightforward disciplinary action would vent his own fears admirably.

Drawing his sword he walked over to the nearest Mandroc still on the ground, bent down and yanked the creature's head back.

'Why do you disobey your leader, *hadyn*?' he said, staring into the whitened eyes and using the Mandrocs' own expression of contempt. 'Do you forget the punishment for such actions?'

The Mandroc's trembling increased. 'Amrahl, Amrahl,' he stammered.

Urssain placed the edge of his sword against the Mandroc's throat. 'Listen to me, worthless one,' he said through clenched teeth. 'That you're not skewered to the ground is a measure of my mercy. But it's ended. Get up, now, or I'll send your spirit on the Dark Journey to face Amrahl's true Greatness with your cowardice about your neck and the curse of your tribe and your lodge bellowing at your heels for bringing such dishonour on them.'

The threat galvanised the terrified Mandroc and in a great trembling flurry he struggled to his feet, as did the few others still cowering on the ground.

'Black Lord.' It was the Mandroc leader. Urssain turned to find him pointing out over the lake.

Moving on a scarcely felt breeze, the mist was thickening rapidly. Very soon it was possible to see only a few paces along the causeway and the world for the waiting group became a small grey enclave of damp silence.

Urssain sheathed his sword. He tried not to speculate on the scream and the shaking of the ground. Both had emanated from Dan-Tor, he knew; he had heard their like before, many times worse, when Hawklan had treacherously struck down the Ffyrst. But what had caused them now? Had Dan-Tor, like Faron and Groniev, attempted some coup against his Master, and failed? The thought shrivelled almost before it formed; it was ludicrous. Whatever strange world Dan-Tor dwelt in, it was far beyond such squeaking ambitions. And whatever had happened, Urssain could do no other than wait to find out. If someone had ended Dan-Tor, then he would serve them just as willingly. He pulled his cloak about himself again.

For a long time there was no sound other than the lapping water, then came angry Mandroc voices, muffled by the mist, and the sound of the shuffling slaves and the creak of their carts began again.

It had scarcely begun however, when it stopped suddenly.

'He comes,' whispered the Mandroc leader.

Urssain peered vainly into the mist. He could neither see nor hear anything but he too knew that Dan-Tor was returning. Unconsciously, he straightened up.

Then a vague shape appeared in the greyness. Urssain's eyes narrowed, but the mist, swirling now, disorientated him and he could not focus clearly. Indeed, he found he could not even discern whether he was looking straight ahead or up in the air, and the shape seemed to become many different things as it came forward; tall and straight at one moment, then swaying and hovering like some strange bird, then, impossibly, far below him, large and bulky.

Gradually it resolved itself into a horse and rider. Urssain identified the rider as Dan-Tor, by his hazy silhouette. But he had had no horse. All the horses had been left behind at the Mandroc camp half a day's march south; no horse would come near Derras Ustramel, not even those that would bear Dan-Tor.

Yet, now, Dan-Tor was riding, without a doubt.

Urssain moved forward to greet his Lord.

As the figures neared, so the mist's deceit fell away and horse and rider stood clearly exposed.

Urssain took in a deep breath. It *was* a horse that Dan-Tor was riding, but one such as Urssain had never seen before. Its shape was oddly angular and almost obscenely muscular, and at the back of each leg rose a curving bony spur. But it was the head and, above all, the eyes that made him shiver. Narrow and serpentine, the eyes glistened green through the mist, radiating a malevolence that seemed to confirm the impression of malign intelligence which was given by a bulging forehead. Held low below the great hunched shoulders, the head swayed slowly from side to side as if searching. As Urssain took in the vision, it turned towards him and slowly opened its mouth to reveal the tearing teeth of a predator. Then came a rasping and unmistakable noise of challenge which froze Urssain to the spot. It stopped only at a cold word from its rider.

Urssain tore his gaze away from the creature and looked up at Dan-Tor. He too was different, though in what way Urssain could not tell.

'Ffyrst,' he said, saluting. The head of the horse creature swayed towards him again as if attracted by the movement of prey.

'Commander,' Dan-Tor acknowledged. His voice was both

pained and triumphant, and he was clutching his side.

Urssain searched for something to say into the misty silence. 'Are you hurt, Ffyrst?' he ventured.

Dan-Tor turned to him slowly and shook his head. 'All hurts are as nothing now, Commander,' he said, his white smile chilling in the gloom. 'See. I am whole again.'

As he spoke he removed his hand from his side.

Urssain leaned forward.

Hawklan's arrow was gone.

# *Chapter 20*

Cadmoryth stirred uneasily. Hawklan leaned forward and took his hand. Urthryn and Girvan watched the healer anxiously, but looking at each in turn he gave a slight shake of his head.

It was a confirmation of what he had said earlier when, found on the beach as the Muster rounded up those Morlider abandoned by their fleeing compatriots, Cadmoryth had been brought to the hospital tent, unconscious and broken.

Girvan turned away briefly in distress, but Urthryn bared his teeth in angry frustration. He turned to leave.

'Ffyrst.' Cadmoryth's voice was weak, but lucid, and audible even above the commotion filling the hospital tent.

Urthryn turned and looked down at the fisherman. The man's eyes were open and clear.

'I'm here,' Urthryn aid.

'Ffyrst,' Cadmoryth said again. 'Forgive me. So many good men dead. I . . .' His voice faded.

'Hush, rest, fisherman,' Urthryn said, but Cadmoryth shook his head and beckoned him closer.

Urthryn knelt down beside the bed and bent forward to catch the failing words; his travel-stained tunic soiled the white sheets that covered Cadmoryth's broken frame.

'I saw the evil, Ffyrst,' the fisherman whispered. 'I could do no other than . . . hurl myself at it. I forgot my duty as captain of my vessel, forgot my crew, now –'

'Hush,' Urthryn said again, looking helplessly at Hawklan. 'You forgot nothing, fisherman. Sometimes a leader leads, sometimes he is simply a tool of the will of his people. Your whole crew saw the evil. You held the helm, but *they* rowed their hearts out to crush that abomination. The Orthlundyn saw the truth of it all.' He indicated Hawklan with a nod of his head.

Cadmoryth's eyes followed the movement. Hawklan nodded. 'It was the will of your crew,' he said. 'Your boat leapt at Creost like a hunting animal.'

A brief smile lit the fisherman's face as he remembered that last surging charge to avenge the treacherous deaths of so many on that southern beach. 'It did, it did,' he said. 'The Morlider

313

know how to make a fine ship. But so many dead . . . it burdens me . . .'

'Many survived Creost's wrath, Cadmoryth,' Hawklan said. 'And you brought him down with your deed. Gave us the day. Broke the Morlider utterly. Who knows how many lives you've saved? A good day's haul, fisherman, a good day's haul . . .'

But Cadmoryth was not listening; he was clutching Hawklan's hand urgently. 'Who lived, healer, who lived?' he asked.

'I don't know their names,' Hawklan replied. 'But they've been fretting about outside all the time you've been unconscious. They –'

'Bring them here,' Cadmoryth said, interrupting him and trying to rise. The effort however was too much, and he slumped back, gasping. 'No, wait,' he said. 'Wait a moment.' He lay still for a little while then, momentarily, he grimaced in distress.

'There's no landfall from *this* journey, is there, healer?'

Hawklan bent forward and spoke to him softly, placing a hand on his forehead. Slowly the fisherman's breathing became quieter.

'Girvan,' he said after a moment. The Line Leader crouched down by him. 'Girvan . . . Tell my wife . . . I'm sorry . . . I didn't mean to leave her. Tell her . . . thank you . . . for the light she's given me . . .' His face became pained again. 'You'll find the words, Girvan. She liked you.'

Girvan nodded, but could not speak. Cadmoryth patted his hand reassuringly. 'Ffyrst,' he said. 'You'll look to the needs of my wife?' His tone was anxious.

'It's ever our way, fisherman, have no fear for that,' Urthryn replied.

Cadmoryth closed his eyes briefly. 'Thank you,' he said, then, smiling a little: 'That was a rare ride you made, Ffyrst. A fine yarn to tell your grandchild when it arrives.'

'It was fair,' Urthryn replied. 'But as nothing compared with your great journey.'

Cadmoryth gave a brief breathy chuckle than he lay back and looked up at the roof of the tent.

A timber post with ropes lashed about it, rose up by his bed like a mast. Radiant stones filled the tent with their stored summer warmth and the slowly billowing fabric of the roof faithfully held and returned it, but Cadmoryth's eyes narrowed a little and his face tightened as if he were facing a cold, spray-filled wind, and revelling in it.

'Send my crew in,' he said to Hawklan, faintly. 'They'll tend me now.'

As the three men moved away from the dying fisherman, Urthryn took Hawklan's arm. 'You must rest,' he said. 'Our healers and yours are sufficient. You've done enough.'

Hawklan looked at him, and then around the tent. It was filled with long rows of wounded. They were lying on a hotch-potch of beds; a few had been hauled over the mountains by the Orthlundyn, and some had appeared silently in the wake of the Muster, but most were rough and ready creations salvaged from the remains of the Morlider camp. It was fitting; most of the wounded were Morlider. They had taken appalling casualties in both dead and wounded at the hands of the Orthlundyn, and the tent was filled with the sound of their collective despair; a dark, disordered chorus of cries and groans, shot through with muffled screams.

Worse to Hawklan, though, the place reeked of fear and horror. A spasm of anger ran through him.

'A healer *can't* rest while such pain cries out,' he said, more severely than he had intended. Then, thus triggered, the anger came out as unhindered as it was unjust. 'But you can, and must. You're wearier than I am. You have younger officers who should be doing much of what you're attempting. Let them do it, they'll do it better and quicker. *We've* serious problems to discuss when these poor souls have been eased. It's you who should rest, Ffyrst, not I.'

Girvan took a discreet step backwards.

Urthryn frowned furiously. 'You're powerfully free with your orders, Orthlundyn,' he said barely restraining his own anger.

Hawklan reflected the frown. 'Fault my logic, Ffyrst,' he said. 'Better still, accept the wisdom of your people. Most of them are sleeping.'

Urthryn bit down his reply. 'Sylvriss said you were a remarkable man,' he said. 'We'll talk later. When *both* of us are rested.'

As Urthryn left, Girvan paused briefly by Hawklan. 'Your remarks were unnecessary, Orthlundyn,' he said bluntly but without anger. 'Think about swallowing them later. The Ffyrst is a wise and patient man, but he's more than tired, he's exhausted in every way. The journey we made might have been epic, but it was also grim and he left behind much quarrelling and bitterness. Then to find the Muster could offer so little at the end . . .'

Hawklan nodded. 'I know,' he said regretfully. 'Time and rest will see us all at greater ease. See him settled if you can, then rest yourself.'

When Girvan had gone, Hawklan cast a brief glance towards the group sitting silently around the peaceful form of Cadmoryth. He could do nothing there. He knew that, fisherman all, they were waiting for the turn of the tide that would take their comrade away.

Leaving them to their vigil, Hawklan strode off down the long aisle between two rows of beds. All around him were men, young men for the most part, suffering from fearful injuries. Those with lesser injuries were being treated in other places. Here were severed and broken limbs; bodies, crushed and mutilated; the terrible gaping gashes and stab wounds made by swords and long bladed pikes. And, like a grim harmony note underlying everything, the thought of what must lie ahead of those who were healed. Maimed, abandoned and alone amongst their enemies.

He caught the eye of a man who in Orthlund might still have been an apprentice carver. He was bearded, but the fluffy blond mass merely served only to accentuate his fresh-faced youth. From his skull emerged the shaft of an arrow. Hawklan went to him and placed his hands about his face. The eyes slowly looked up at him, but they were blank.

The boy would live, Hawklan knew. Perhaps for a long time, but . . .

Rest, he thought? Would he could. His body ached with fatigue after the gruelling hours of fighting and then the even more gruelling hours of clearing the battlefield. But he had not lied to Urthryn; he *could* not rest while so much pain cried out. At their extremities, the warrior and the healer in him had little love for one another and their mutual anger marred him.

'May I help?' came a voice as he stood up from the young victim.

Turning he saw first Yengar and Olvric, then the speaker. All three looked desperately tired. Hawklan sensed the third man for a healer, and his face, was elusively familiar.

'Marek,' said the man, answering Hawklan's questioning expression. 'Healer with the Lord Eldric's High Guard. We met, or rather, I saw you, when you were . . . unconscious . . . at Lord Eldric's. It's good to see you whole again.'

'You were sent with Queen Sylvriss to Dremark,' Hawklan said, smiling, as he recalled both the memory of Marek's face

316

from that strange interlude following Oklar's assault on him, and Agreth's account of the Queen's journey. 'When did you arrive?'

'An hour or so ago,' Marek replied. 'But everything's so confused we had difficulty finding you.'

Hawklan's smile broadened. 'Came with one of the baggage trains, did you?' he said.

'Yes, and even that was hard going,' Yengar said ruefully. 'We didn't last two days with Urthryn's riders.' He seemed distressed by this failure.

'Set it aside, Goraidin,' Hawklan said. '*That* journey will go down ever in Muster lore. It took no small toll of their own. Is the Cadwanwr with you . . .' He cast about for the name.

'Oslang,' Yengar said. 'Yes. And the others are following. He's with Andawyr now, but he's worse than we are. I doubt he'll wake up before the rest arrive.'

Hawklan nodded. 'You two find Dacu then rest awhile, there's nothing for you to do here. Marek; you see how things are, do as your heart moves you, you're the best judge of your own worth at the moment.'

The Fyordyn looked around the tent and then back at Hawklan. 'I'm tired through travelling uncomfortably and sleeping badly,' he said. 'But I'm sound, and fresh from tending Sylvriss, who in her present condition gives more than she receives.' Hawklan felt Marek taking charge of him. 'You on the other hand are almost spent. In a little while you'll just be another burden. Go and rest.'

Hawklan frowned at Marek's bluntness, but the healer's words cut through his weariness and both cleared his vision and gave him the little strength he needed to accept what he saw. He looked about the noisy tent once more and, feeling the awesome weight of pain and fear in the place, realised he had been trying to carry it all in reparation for the part he had played in creating it. That was not healing.

'You're right,' he said simply. 'I've stayed too long. I'll go for a walk then I'll sleep – as instructed.' He tilted his head towards the far end of the tent. 'The Duty Healer's over there if you're going to stay.'

The cold struck him as he stepped out of the warmth of the tent. It was snowing; large damp flakes floating silently and leisurely down through the grey sky. The two Goraidin strode off purposefully towards the Command tent in search of Dacu, and Hawklan turned towards the sea.

As he walked, he let the countless unrepeating patterns of the swirling snowflakes fill his mind. Better they than the tangled mass of the thoughts he was still clinging to. He had not started this appalling juggernaut on its life-crushing journey; who knew what butterfly's wings had? Such threads as he could unravel went back only to that spring morning when a bent and crooked tinker had appeared on the green at Pedhavin; and he could not see even those being woven into any other pattern. Nor, truly, was that pattern an ill one, despite the miasma of pain emanating from the sad heart of the hospital tent. His own words to the dying Cadmoryth returned to comfort him: 'Who knows how many lives you've saved?'

Now, at least, Sumeral's malice and intent stood plainly exposed; the Morlider were gone, leaving the Muster free to help in the struggle; the Orthlundyn had been tested in battle and their discipline had given them the day against fierce and overwhelming odds. The Cadwanwr too had met some great trial and survived; they would be the wiser for that. A good day's haul indeed, he thought, even though much of him cried out still at the tragedy that such nets had had to be cast.

The sound of the sea brought him to a halt and he realised that he had walked further from the camp than he had intended. He was at the top of the slope that led down to the remains of the Morlider camp.

The falling snow was already obliterating many of the scars of the battle, though in so doing it was hindering the groups of Riddinvolk and Orthlundyn charged with the task of cleansing the area. Rows of bodies, already covered to protect them from the scavenging seabirds were slowly disappearing under a further, cold, shroud. Stacks of weapons and supplies too were merging anonymously with the whitening terrain.

He became aware of Serian standing by him. The horse had followed him from the camp.

'How are the horses?' Hawklan asked.

'Better than the humans,' Serian replied. 'They forget more quickly. They did well.'

Hawklan patted the horse's neck. 'Indeed they did,' he said. Then, on an impulse: 'Do you wish to return to the Muster now that you're home again?'

The horse lifted its head and shook it, throwing a spray of snowflakes into the air. 'I'm no longer a Muster horse, Hawklan,' he said. 'Touched by His evil at the Gretmearc, then redeemed by you. Facing the wrath of Oklar with you.

Listening to the sounds of the Alphraan and the song of Anderras Darion. And now all this; charging against Dar Hastuin and Creost as they rode Usgreckan. I am not what I was. And I am possessed by the demon that possesses you. I ride next against Sumeral. Do we ride together still?'

Hawklan looked out over the battlefield again. The snow was not falling quite as heavily, and an onshore breeze was beginning to blow. In the distance the sky was lightening, and here and there small golden swashes of sunlight were glittering on the sea. The horizon was true and straight, undisturbed by any unnatural intrusion. 'Winter's ending,' Hawklan said, swinging up into the saddle. 'And we ride together still, Serian, to His very throne.'

Returning to the camp, Hawklan made straight for his tent. As he approached, Andawyr came to the entrance. He too looked tired, but his eyes seemed to be brighter than ever.

'I've been chased away from the hospital tent with orders to rest,' Hawklan said.

'Rightly so,' Andawyr said unsympathetically. 'You should listen to your own advice more.'

Hawklan pulled a wry face. 'Perhaps,' he said. 'But while I'm confined to quarters will you arrange a meeting of all senior officers – a Council of War – first thing tomorrow morning. And gently with Urthryn, please, Andawyr. My brief meetings with him so far have been . . . a little fraught, to be generous about it.'

Andawyr opened his mouth to reply but a low, pitiful moan from inside the tent interrupted him. He turned to let Hawklan enter.

Inside, resting in a small makeshift hammock slung off four poles, lay Gavor. His eyes were closed and he was very still. Curled up on the floor nearby was Dar-volci.

Hawklan looked at his old friend sadly. Andawyr came to his side.

'It's bad isn't it?' Andawyr said.

Hawklan nodded. 'Yes,' he said, soberly. 'I don't think I've ever seen anything like it before.'

A single black eye flickered weakly, and Gavor uttered another low groan.

'It's the complications that are doing the damage,' Hawklan went on, crouching down to be closer to the listless form. His face was lined with concentration, and when he spoke his voice was heavy with concern.

'You see, Andawyr, after the fall, he began to develop symptoms of malingering, but I suspect now that it's turned into severe and chronic hypochondria. I think it could be terminal.'

The eye opened wide and glared malevolently. Hawklan and Andawyr smiled in reply.

Gavor groaned again – loudly. 'I don't know which hurts the most,' he declaimed. 'The pain of my terrible injury or the cruel indifference of my friends.'

'I told you. You've only sprained one of your chest muscles a little,' Hawklan said, flopping down onto his bunk. 'Your pectoral muscle to be precise. A couple of days and some exercises and you'll be good as new.'

'You weren't so callous when you pulled me out of that snowdrift,' Gavor said, his tone injured.

'I thought all that blood was yours, that's why,' Hawklan answered, closing his eyes and turning his back on the raven.

Gavor chuckled at the memory of his attack on the two Uhriel, then he groaned again. 'It hurts when I laugh,' he said.

'Go for a walk,' Hawklan said curtly. 'The amount you're eating, you'll soon be too fat for your wings to carry you, sprain or no sprain.'

Gavor's head shot up indignantly. Then, turning to Andawyr, he said, 'Would you be so kind as to give me a wing down, dear boy, I'd hate my suffering to disturb our great leader.' As Andawyr lifted him out of the hammock he added plaintively, 'I'll be out in the cold if anyone needs me.'

'Gavor, clear off, I'm trying to get some sleep,' Hawklan replied.

Gavor muttered something under his breath and stumped over to Dar-volci. 'Come on, rat, let's go round to the kitchens; see if they've anything for sprains.'

Dar-volci uncoiled himself, stretched languorously, then sat on his haunches to scratch his stomach. 'Good idea, crow,' he said, dropping down on to all-fours again. 'I'm feeling like something medicinal myself. You can do your bird impressions for me as we walk.'

Hawklan turned his head and stared in disbelief.

Slowly through the day, the camp changed, becoming quieter and more ordered as time pushed the nightmare of the battle inexorably further away. Cadmoryth died as the tide began to ebb, as did several of the Morlider. Others lived and died to different rhythms. The snow stopped, and the sky cleared, and the day ended with long sunset shadows cutting obliquely through the ranks of tents.

Hawklan slept.

The following day began as the previous had ended, with a clear sky. A brilliant sun shone low into the camp and the snow-covered landscape echoed its light stridently.

A gentle shaking awoke Hawklan and he smiled as he opened his eyes to see Gavor tugging at his sleeve and, beyond him, the sky, blue and unblemished, visible through the slightly opened entrance of the tent.

Then he closed his eyes and lay back, his face pained momentarily.

'I thought I was at home,' he said, sitting up and swinging his legs off the bunk. 'A summer's day ahead . . . with fields to walk, flowers and blossoms to smell . . .'

'Sorry, dear boy,' Gavor said repentantly.

Hawklan reached out and a laid his hand on the raven's iridescent plumage. 'Hardly, your fault, old friend,' he said, smiling again, then, more matter of fact: 'How's the wing this morning?'

Gavor extended it gently. 'Creaking,' he said. 'But better. I think the knees are going though, with all this walking.'

'Knee,' corrected Hawklan.

'Spare me the pedantry at this time of morning, dear boy,' Gavor said, jumping down from the bunk and landing with a grunt. 'Just because it's not there doesn't mean I can't feel it. *And it's stiff.*'

The statement was definitive and Hawklan did not pursue it.

'Well, can you manage a walk to the mess tent?' he asked, standing.

Gavor inclined his head pensively, then with an awkward flapping, bounced up on to the bed and thence on to Hawklan's shoulder.

He was still sitting there an hour later when Hawklan rode across to the nearby camp that the Muster had established. As they approached, a small crowd began to form at the edge of the camp. Gavor started to preen himself.

The crowd, however, seemed to be interested predominantly in Serian, Hawklan himself being greeted with an uneasy politeness.

As on the battlefield, Serian led him to Urthryn.

321

The Ffyrst's tent was larger and more elaborate than the undecorated field tents that stood in ranks around it, but not ostentatiously so. An officer of some kind stood outside it; no mean fighter, Hawklan judged, probably a bodyguard, and vaguely familiar.

He dismounted and introduced himself.

'I saw you on the field, Lord,' replied the officer eyeing Gavor narrowly.

Hawklan looked at him. 'Ah,' he said diffidently after a moment, 'I remember. I pulled you off your horse, didn't I?'

The man nodded, then the question burst out of him. 'You *lifted* me out of the saddle as if I was a child! I've been thinking about it ever since. I've never felt anything like it. How did you do it?'

Hawklan laughed at the man's unrestrained curiosity, though not unkindly. 'Don't concern yourself. You handled your lance well. I've had remarkable teachers in my time.' Then, more seriously: 'If your wish to learn overrides your sense of indignity at being unhorsed by an Orthlundyn, then you're half-way there already. If time allows we'll talk further.'

Before the man could pursue the matter, the entrance to the tent opened and the figure of Urthryn appeared. He started a little at the sight of Hawklan and Gavor.

The officer saluted and Hawklan bowed.

'May we speak before the meeting, Ffyrst?' he said.

Urthryn looked at him enigmatically for a moment, then he nodded to the guard and with a slight bow ushered Hawklan into the tent.

Inside, Urthryn offered Hawklan a plain wooden seat, taking a similar one himself. The two men looked at one another in awkward silence for a few moments.

'I came to thank you for recalling your people from the pursuit of the Morlider,' Hawklan said eventually. 'In the heat of the moment, my asking . . . lacked tact . . . as did my conduct in the hospital tent. I know now that you and your people suffered dreadful losses at Creost's hands in the south. Losses that cried out – still cry out – for vengeance.'

Urthryn was silent for a moment, watching his unexpected guest carefully. He seemed to be struggling with some inner debate. 'You have a gift for understatement, Orthlundyn,' he said at last, his voice angry. 'You charge through our ranks – on one of our own horses, I note – disarm two of my best men as if they were fractious children, order me to call back the

Line from full pursuit. Then you chase me to my bed when you can scarcely stand yourself. Your conduct lacked tact indeed –' He stopped suddenly and looked down at his hands. The sound of bustling activity outside filtered into the silence.

When he looked up, his face was distressed but his manner was calmer. 'Every time I close my eyes, I'm walking through the mangled corpses on that beach. Corpses as far as you can see. Young and old, men and women. And horses. And seagulls everywhere, screeching and squabbling, I hear them too.' He put his hands to his ears gently. Hawklan resisted the temptation to reach out to him. Such a man, he knew, understood his own pain and needed to face it unaided.

'If it's not that, then it's the relentless pounding of the journey we made, shaking my whole body even yet. Pushing myself beyond all pain and hurt and pulling the others behind me to avenge all that. Riding as Muster riders have never ridden before. And then to arrive and find we were . . . too late . . .'

His face contorted and he leaned to one side slightly, swinging his arm low as if seizing something. He clenched his fist tight as if to stop the gesture. 'I'd like to use those Morlider prisoners in the Helangai,' he said savagely. 'Smash and crush them. Let them suffer as we and our kin suffered.'

Hawklan's eyes widened in distress at this outburst but he said nothing.

The spate ended as abruptly as it had begun. 'I'm sorry,' Urthryn said. '*You* understand, don't you? To have such things happen to those in your charge can hardly be borne.'

Hawklan nodded.

Urthryn looked at him intently. 'You owe me no thanks for stopping the pursuit,' he said quietly. 'It's I who should thank you for interceding and preventing an atrocity that would have stained us forever. As for the hospital, well, we were all sick at heart there. I'd hoped, twenty years ago, to have seen the last of such handiwork.'

Hawklan relaxed into his hard chair. Urthryn caught the movement and, for the moment eased of his burden, smiled slightly. Hawklan responded and raised his eyebrows enquiringly.

Urthryn's smile widened and he scratched his head, another small homely gesture to distance further his recent painful outburst. 'I've never seen an outlander who could sit on one of our camp chairs and look comfortable before. But then I've never seen anyone – *anyone* – ride like you did towards that,' – he shook his hand as he searched for a word – 'that screeching *monstrosity* and those abominations riding it.' He warmed to the subject. 'It was a pity your arrows didn't bring them all down. As for your crow . . . Gravy, here . . . well . . .'

Gavor leaned forward indignantly.

'No,' Hawklan said quickly, laughing in spite of himself, and shaking his head. 'Some wiser impulse guided my aim. If I'd killed their steed I'd have deprived them of the option of fleeing and they'd have destroyed us all for sure. *Gavor*'s attack panicked both them and Usgreckan into flight. We were fortunate that calmer counsels didn't prevail.'

Urthryn looked doubtful but did not pursue the matter. His earlier rage seemed to have ebbed totally. It would return from time to time, Hawklan knew; that could not be avoided. But each time, it would be less.

'Sylvriss was right,' Urthryn said suddenly. 'You're a remarkable man.' He leaned forward confidentially. 'Are you sure you don't have Riddinvolk stock in you somewhere? The Orthlundyn are notoriously careless about their bloodlines, you know.'

'So Agreth has mentioned,' Hawklan replied, then, deflecting the conversation: 'Is your daughter well?' he asked.

Urthryn smiled contentedly. 'She was when we left,' he said. 'Blooming, in fact.' His smile became sadder. 'Despite the news we'd had to bring from the beach.'

'Perhaps when one of your messengers returns to Dremark, you'd tell her I'm whole again and that I'll be ever in her debt, and in the debt of her child,' Hawklan said.

Urthryn looked puzzled and a little suspicious, but he nodded. 'Well, I can't pretend to understand what you mean by that,' he said. 'But bewilderment is also becoming my normal condition these days. Of course, I'll send her any message you want.' Then, standing, he held out his hand. 'Now we've made *our* small peace, shall we ride to the Council of War together? See if we can make the future better than the past?'

The tent used by the Orthlundyn as a Command Centre was barely large enough to accommodate the many people who gathered at Andawyr's behest, but eventually everyone found somewhere to sit, stand or lean.

Andawyr, Hawklan, Urthryn and Loman sat at one end

facing the others. By common consent, and to the quiet mockery of his countrymen, Dacu found himself given charge of the meeting.

Unexpectedly, Urthryn asked to speak first. There was a profound stillness in the tent as he told of the great gathering of the General Muster and of the terrible destruction wrought on it by Creost's cunning.

'Cadmoryth and the fishermen repaired two of the Morliders' own boats and sailed northward on who knows what impulse. They offered no reason, nor made any debate, they just hoisted sail and left. I haven't the words to honour them sufficiently.' He looked down, unable to proceed for a moment.

'Then Oslang told us we should travel north, and within days we met Agreth.' He looked across at his adviser. 'An epic journey also, Line Leader, to be honoured in due time,' he said, then, turning back to his audience: 'All else, you know.'

He paused again. 'Save this.' He straightened up. 'Our loss on that beach all but tore the heart from our people. While the fishermen showed us the way by pursuing the enemy, we celebrated our grief in petty bickering.' He turned to Hawklan, his face pained. 'Only one in six of our houses rode to this field; forty or so squadrons. And, thanks to our debating, even we arrived too late to spare some of your people. Others may join us, I don't know. I've sent the news of the happenings here to all, but travelling's difficult and we left the Moot in great disarray.' He shook his head sadly. 'I'm sorry.'

'You reproach yourself too much, Ffyrst,' Andawyr said before Hawklan could reply.

'I'm no longer Ffyrst,' Urthryn said. 'I doubt the office can exist in such turmoil.'

Andawyr waved the comment aside. 'Names, titles, offices,' he said, almost contemptuously. 'You are here, Urthryn of the Decmilloith of Riddin, Son of the Riddinvolk. You came to fulfil the duty of the Muster and defend your land, and none could have done more from what I hear. That circumstances prevailed against you was none of your doing. You owe yourself no reproach. We've all failed in different ways and paid our different prices before we came to this place. The only crime we can commit now is to drag these failings behind us instead of moving forward. You command the loyalty of your forty squadrons and they've been spared for a future time.'

Urthryn opened his mouth to speak, but Andawyr's hand came up to silence him.

'With Dar Hastuin by his side, hurt though he was, not ten, fifty, a hundred times your forty squadrons would have prevailed against Creost if Cadmoryth hadn't struck him down and given us the chance to tear the control of the islands from him. Atelon and I were almost spent when that happened. The fisherman and the bird tipped the balance and gave us the day.' He leaned back in his seat and spread out his hands in a gesture of resignation. 'And if you'd been with us, how would even your horses have fared when Dar Hastuin's Viladrien was destroyed?'

Urthryn nodded reluctantly. The Muster's only casualties had occurred in the panic that ensued when the sight and sound of that awful destruction had reached them. He stood silent for some time.

No one sought to speak.

'Very well,' he said eventually. 'You're right, Cadwanwr, though the rightness quiets my head more than my belly. Perhaps time will attend to that.' He turned to Hawklan. 'I place myself and my riders at your command. Those who come after must make their own decisions.'

Hawklan bowed. 'Place them at the command of Loman,' he said. 'The army is his. My task is to find and waken the first of the Guardians, Ethriss.'

Urthryn gaped, 'How –' he began.

'I can answer none of your questions, Ffyrst,' Hawklan said, interrupting him. 'That would be to destroy us all. Our army will oppose His army, the Guardians and the Cadwanwr will oppose the Uhriel, but only Ethriss can oppose Sumeral and only I can find and waken him.' He looked at Urthryn intently.

Urthryn turned to Loman who returned his gaze steadily.

'Loman built this army, brought it through the mountains, fought this battle,' Hawklan went on. 'If you'd help us, then you must go with him to Fyorlund and join with the Lords to assault Derras Ustramel itself. If not, then perhaps you'd give us supplies to help us on our way – we're already woefully short.'

Urthryn swayed, momentarily disorientated by the urgency and strangeness of Hawklan's words set against the endless, pounding familiarity of his recent journey and the sight of the man-made carnage on the battlefield. Then other, stranger, scenes came to him: the colourful flotilla of empty boats eerily approaching the shore, and the great wave that swept away so many riders and divided the rest into squabbling bands; then the glaring brilliance and tumult of the dying Viladrien, and the fearful screaming of Usgreckan. In some way he could not fathom, he knew that all true choices were gone. And these people had saved his land.

He saluted Loman. 'Together to Fyorlund and Derras Ustramel then,' he said.

Loman smiled broadly and, standing up, wrapped the startled Riddinwr in a powerful embrace. There was some laughter after Urthryn disentangled himself and rubbed his ribs ruefully.

As though a cloud had moved from the sun, the atmosphere in the Command Tent became more relaxed and the discussion turned quickly to practical matters.

It transpired that the Orthlundyn's supplies were indeed now dangerously low. Nor were the Muster much better placed, they also having come there in haste. Such food as was found in the remains of the Morlider camp had been destroyed either by fire in the Helyadin's attack or by the Morlider themselves as they charged through all that stood in their way to reach their ships.

And there were prisoners, sick and well, to feed and to dispose of.

Hawklan cast an anxious glance at Urthryn as the topic arose, but the Ffyrst gave no sign of a return of his earlier rage. 'We'll tend to the prisoners fittingly,' he said. 'If the islands are truly gone then it may be a generation before they return but what we do now may determine what happens then.'

Andawyr and Hawklan exchanged glances. 'What will you do with them?' Hawklan asked.

'I don't know,' Urthryn admitted. 'For now we'll have to make a camp for them of some kind, then slowly settle those that want to stay into different Houses.'

'And those that don't?' Hawklan asked.

Urthryn blew out a noisy sigh. 'Take them to the south or let them make their own boats and sail away.' He shrugged. 'Don't worry. The smell of that beach and the noise in that hospital tent will be with me forever. We'll do nothing that might have the seeds of such happenings in them for the future.'

'And if the Moot has other ideas?' Hawklan said.

'The Moot only has authority over the Houses when the

conduct of one threatens another in some way,' Urthryn said off-handedly.

'This is all we can do now, Hawklan,' Dacu said, cutting across Hawklan's next question. 'We've more pressing problems to discuss, not the least of which, after supplies, is how we're going to get the army and Urthryn's squadrons up into Fyorlund.'

It was a timely point. The traditional route through the mountains from Riddin to Fyorlund, that taken by Sylvriss and Rgoric's wedding party many years ago, entered the mountains far to the south and west of their present position. It would be a long dispiriting journey for the weary Orthlundyn.

'The route we followed when we came through with the Queen could be used,' Yengar volunteered. 'It's due north from here. It won't be easy, but it'll be a lot shorter. We have it detailed in our journals.'

The journals were produced and the meeting slipped easily into discussing the considerable logistical problems associated with moving the army and the Muster through the mountains.

Despite his concerns about the disarray amongst the Houses, Urthryn had no doubts about the willingness of the Riddinvolk to provide adequate supplies for the expedition and the ability of the Muster to carry them at least as far as the mountains, thereby considerably easing the Orthlundyn's burden. It would be no easy task, he conceded, but it could be, and it would be, done.

The mountains, however, presented other problems.

'This route might be manageable by your infantry and their few horses, but it'll be too difficult for so much cavalry, especially as there'll still be a lot of snow about when we get there,' was Urthryn's conclusion after Yengar's notes had been carefully studied.

'And it concerns me that we know nothing of what's going on in Narsindal,' he went on. 'After what's happened, we've no alternative but to assume that there's a substantial army up there – or armies – and for all we know, they could be marching down the Pass of Elewart right now. Perhaps the Uhriel didn't flee, perhaps they simply went for reinforcements.'

'I doubt it,' Andawyr said. 'The Pass is being watched along almost its entire length. We'd have received news if anything untoward had happened.'

Urthryn looked at him paternally. 'Always assuming that

the . . . brother . . . carrying the message hasn't got lost walking through the snow,' he said. Andawyr pursed his lips and sniffed.

Urthryn beckoned Agreth forward. 'Get two patrols out straight away. One to the Pass and the caves to find out whether anything's happening and to establish a message line, the other to mark out the best route to the mountains for the army. And make a start on this supply problem right away.'

As Agreth departed, Urthryn shot a broad, conciliatory smile at the slightly discomfited Andawyr. 'Give the patrol whatever messages you need to send to your people,' he said.

Then he sat back and stared pensively at the charts that had been produced during the discussion.

'What do you want to do?' Hawklan asked, knowing the answer.

'"Want" isn't the word I'd have chosen,' Urthryn replied. 'I don't think we've any choice. We'll have to go through the Pass and along the southern edge of Narsindal to the Tower to meet the Lords' army.'

Hawklan nodded.

'It's a long journey, through territory that's hostile enough without having an actual enemy in it,' Dacu said. He indicated Yengar and Olvric. 'One of us will have to go with you. We're the only ones here who've ever ridden the Watch.'

'And one or more of us,' added Andawyr.

Urthryn smiled and bowed in acknowledgement. 'All we need now are more riders,' he said resignedly.

The following day marked, for most, the true end of the battle on the unnamed beach. The dead were buried. More correctly, they were honoured; burial of the Morlider dead had been under way almost continuously since the actual fighting had ended.

They were laid in great pits just below the storm line of the beach. Toran Agrasson, shocked at the betrayal of his people by Creost, and bemused by the treatment he and the other prisoners were receiving at the hands of the victors, organised the grim work. 'We give our dead to the sea,' he said, sweating as he hacked at the frozen ground. 'But so many so close to the shore . . .' He shook his head. 'They'll rest easy enough here, touched by the sea when the winds blow fierce and strong.'

Apart from Cadmoryth and his crew, the only Riddinwr to perish was the young boy who had died under his sledge. He was carried back to his village by Hawklan and Urthryn, and laid to rest under a snow-laden tree. 'He used to sit in it with his friends for hours in the summer,' said his distraught grandmother. 'What am I going to tell his parents, Ffyrst?'

Urthryn took her hand. 'I've no words for the death of a child,' he said, shaking his head. 'For whatever comfort it gives, the healer here tells me he didn't suffer. And he was helping Riddin's true friends fight a cruel and treacherous foe. There are worse ways to die. In due time we'll honour his name in the Lines, but . . . I'm sorry.'

He was very silent as he rode back to the camp, speaking only once. 'For all I know Creost may have killed his parents too,' he said bitterly. Hawklan did not reply.

The Orthlundyn chose a small hillock overlooking the sea for the burial of their few dead. Isloman recovered a large rock from the shore and polished it smooth to serve as a simple, unmarked headstone in the Orthlundyn tradition. Hawklan stood for a long time staring down at the stone after the others had left.

'There's no answer,' Gavor said into the long silence.

Out of the many expressions of sadness and grief that day, that for Cadmoryth and the other fishermen was the most formal. Usually a fisherman was buried as the Orthlundyn had chosen, in some spot overlooking the sea. However, those who died at sea were, like the Morlider, given to the sea.

'But they should not be slid quietly into the cold waves, they should be sent the old way,' was the will of the surviving fishermen. In the lore of the fishing communities it was said that before they had come to Riddin they had been a great seafaring race and that the greatest among them in those times were sent to their final resting places in a blazing ship. Practicalities however seemed set to confound them, turning their grief into angry frustration. There was no pitch, little kindling and, above all, no boat to tow the burial ship away from the landward embrace of the tide.

'I knew him a little,' Oslang said. 'Will you accept my help?'

Thus the Orthlundyn, Riddinvolk, Cadwanwr and Morlider gathered in ranks on the shore to watch the funeral of the men who had pitched themselves against Sumeral's cruel agent and both won and lost.

Gently, the fishermen laid out the bodies of their comrades in the remaining ship, each saying such farewells as moved him.

Girvan Girvasson helped them.

As he stood looking down at Cadmoryth's pale dead face, the memories of his time with the fisherman and his wife flooded over him. He wanted to say 'thank you' for the quiet welcoming warmth that had pervaded almost its every moment, but his throat tightened around the words. His face strained, he took something from his pocket and looked at it for a moment, turning it over gently. Then he bent forward and placed it between Cadmoryth's stiff fingers. It was the fisherman's pipe.

Saluting, Girvan turned and left the ship. He was the last.

As the Line Leader joined the others, two of the fishermen removed the gangplank and cut through the mooring ropes. Then Oslang stepped forward and opened his arms as if to embrace the vessel.

Slowly, from no wind that any other could feel, the pennant at the ship's masthead began to stir, the sail began to fill and, as if some unseen crew were manning it, the ship started to move slowly forward, its timbers creaking and its sail flapping, almost joyously, like a freed bird.

There were no other sounds save the sea itself. Even the gulls were silent.

As the ship moved out to sea, a flame flickered into life amidships, then one at the stern, then another and another. Soon it was blazing from end to end.

But the flames consumed nothing, nor would they until the time was fitting. This was the gift of the Cadwanwr. The Morlider ship would carry its brave and cruelly killed crew out across the endless ocean and into legend.

As it dwindled into the distance, its bright beacon flame shone like starlight in the tears that ran down Girvan Girvasson's cheeks unchecked.

# *Chapter 21*

A brilliant sun made the snow-covered fields dazzling, and a sharp wind tumbled clouds across the blue sky. It also tumbled anything light enough through the whirling confusion of activity that was the Orthlundyn camp.

Tents and shelters were being dismantled and wrestled with in the chilly buffeting breeze; people were running hither and thither – it was too cold to stand still; food, weapons, clothes were being packed vigorously, and a wide-eyed Ffyrst stared on in some amazement.

'You brought all this on your backs?' he said.

'Most of it,' Loman said. 'But the horses carried the bigger items.'

Urthryn dismounted. 'I commend you,' he said. 'I can't avoid the feeling that some of my people would fall over if they had to travel more than a hundred paces without a horse.'

Loman laughed. 'I think we can call a truce on that,' he said. 'I'll not mock your walking if you don't mock our riding.'

Urthryn drew in a long, bargaining, breath through pursed lips. 'You're asking a lot, Orthlundyn,' he said.

Loman was unyielding. 'Exigencies of war, horseman. Exigencies of war,' he pronounced.

Before the debate could continue however, Hawklan came between the two men.

'None of your people are on patrol, are they?' he asked Urthryn.

The Ffyrst nodded. 'None,' he said. 'As you asked. Are you leaving now?'

'Yes,' Hawklan replied. 'All of us as we agreed. Separately and quietly. The fewer see us, the better.'

Several days had passed since the funeral. It was an interlude which had given both Orthlundyn and Riddinvolk the opportunity for a much needed rest. Urthryn's galloping messengers had brought no grim news from the Cadwanol of approaching armies and, as he had promised, supplies began to arrive. Also, to his undisguised relief and pleasure, so did further fighting squadrons.

Yet it was also a hectic time as the various travellers

exchanged their histories, and officers from the two armies began to learn about the intricacies of each other's forces and make detailed plans for the intended journeys.

Urthryn however, was still troubled at times by Hawklan's pointed refusal to explain his own intentions further. Now he tried once more.

'I'd feel much happier if I knew more clearly what you're going to do, Hawklan,' he said. 'This business about Guardians and Ethriss and suchlike still feels odd to me.' He raised a hand to fend off the inevitable reply. 'Yes, I know, I've seen what I've seen and I've heard what I've heard, but I can't help thinking that a good arrow storm would have brought those two Uhriel and that damned bird thing down, and they bled easy enough when Gravy laid into them.'

Hawklan laughed and put his arms around the shoulders of the two men.

Urthryn looked at him suspiciously. 'You're just going to say "Trust me", aren't you?' he said.

Hawklan shook his head. 'No,' he said, smiling. 'I wouldn't dream of asking that. You said it yourself; you've seen what you've seen, and you've heard what you've heard. Trust your eyes and your ears if you can't trust the seat of your trousers.'

Urthryn scowled. 'You're worse than a Fyordyn to argue with,' he said.

'I try,' Hawklan said. 'I try.'

Then he became more serious, tightening his grip on the two men affectionately. 'Loman, you know my heart. Take care in the mountains. I imagine Gulda will have the Fyordyn either in order or rebellion by now. Urthryn, you know more than you realise. Pay heed to Oslang and the Goraidin. Take great care in Narsindal, and *plenty of arrows*.' He looked from one to the other. 'Make no great scene of this parting. We'll all meet again at Derras Ustramel.'

And with a brief embrace he was gone, striding off into the camp's busy traffic.

From the top of a nearby tent, Gavor launched himself after the retreating form. His landing was not one of his best.

'Whoops, sorry, dear boy,' he said thrusting his wooden leg down Hawklan's collar to gain his balance.

'How's the wing?' Hawklan asked unsympathetically, straightening his collar.

'Better,' Gavor declared, hopping up on to Hawklan's head. 'Better. I'm well known for my great powers of recovery.'

Hawklan sniffed. 'You're still yawing I notice,' he said.

Gavor bent forward and stared indignantly into Hawklan's inverted face. 'Don't get technical with me, healer,' he said. 'You stick to your potions, I'll do the flying.'

Hawklan laughed, but Gavor maintained a stern, figurehead dignity until they reached Serian.

'All farewells made?' Hawklan said as he mounted his horse.

'I'd none to make,' Serian said. 'Let's start this journey now.'

Hawklan patted him. 'Forward then,' he said. 'We'll head south and then circle out of sight of the camp.'

Within the hour, Hawklan found himself approaching a small group of riders heading north. A quick glance told him that he was the last to arrive and as he joined them, the group began to move forward at an easy trot.

They maintained that pace for the rest of the day, and when they finally stopped to camp, Hawklan pronounced himself well pleased. Andawyr was less so, slithering down from his horse with shameless indignity.

'I'm really going to have to put more effort into this,' he said.

Hawklan laughed. 'You're going to have to put *less* effort into it,' he said.

Andawyr growled sulkily.

Later, in the warmth of their shelter, Hawklan eased the pain in the Cadwanwr's rebelling muscles. When he had finished, his hands were glowing, and he rubbed them together slowly and gently, examining them as he did so.

'What's the matter?' Andawyr asked.

'Nothing,' Hawklan replied reassuringly. 'It's just nice to be able to heal simple aches and pains again after the . . .' He hesitated. '. . . After the hospital tent.'

Andawyr nodded understandingly, and stretched his small frame out luxuriously but cautiously. 'I think you're going to have plenty of simple aches and pains between here and the caves,' he said, yawning.

Hawklan smiled. 'I doubt it,' he said. 'You've not got this far by refusing to learn, and you'll be wiser by far in a day or so.'

Andawyr, however, was asleep, and Hawklan's prophecy was greeted with a snore.

Hawklan's eyes narrowed at the sound and he leaned forward and gently closed the Cadwanwr's mouth.

Over the next few days the wind became less strong, but it was occasionally blustery, and thoughout had a raw, damp, edge to it that the fitful sun did little to allay. The snows were beginning to thaw.

As the group rode steadily on, well muffled and wrapped, and speaking little, the northern mountains gradually came into view, their white jagged peaks rising eventually to dominate the entire horizon like the teeth of some monstrous trap.

Occasionally Dacu consulted the map that he had been given by Urthryn, but this was usually only to add some note of his own. The route they were travelling was all too clear. Being that which would be followed by both the Orthlundyn and the Muster, it had been well marked by the Muster riders who had been preparing supply caches to ease the marching army's burden. The tracks of these riders and the slow thawing of the snow also served to disguise the group's own progress.

Steadily they moved further away from the combined army unknowingly following them. Reaching the point where the Orthlundyn would leave their route to follow the one along which the Queen had been brought, the group stopped briefly.

'Are you sure that those High Guards can find their way back?' Hawklan asked, momentarily concerned as he looked at the desolate, unwelcoming mountains.

Dacu laughed. 'Yes,' he said. 'And so are you. Almost everyone in the army has a copy of the route, and they're not exactly devoid of intelligence, are they?'

Hawklan raised an apologetic hand and the group continued northwards.

Eventually one point in the scene ahead of them began to displace the dominance of the cold magnificence of the mountains. It was the bleak maw of the Pass of Elewart.

'Well over a day's ride,' Dacu estimated as they paused to look at it.

There were doubting murmurs from some of the others, but Andawyr nodded. 'We'll not even reach the caves by tonight,' he said. 'School yourselves for another night in the shelters.' His manner was cheery, and somewhat at odds with the sombre mood that the sight of the Pass had induced in the others. With unexpected enthusiasm he clicked his horse forward. 'And do you think you could do something about whoever's snoring, Hawklan, he keeps waking me up,' he shouted back.

Both he and Dacu were correct. As night fell, the Pass seemed little nearer, and they were obliged to make camp again.

The following day greeted them with whirling showers of sleet, damp snowflakes and large cold raindrops. Tirke, still cautious of Dacu and his unequivocal wakening technique, was as usual the first awake. He opened the entrance of the shelter, peered out groggily, and broke the news.

'My favourite weather,' he said heavily as he crawled out and peered around.

The Pass, the mountains, everything beyond a few hundred paces, was gone, hidden in a dull greyness.

'Welcome to the mountains,' Andawyr said, his unwarranted cheerfulness persisting.

Quieter than ever, the small procession of grey silhouettes set out again, Andawyr taking the lead and the horses picking their way carefully through the damp, treacherous snow.

Hawklan gazed around. Even in the mist, he could feel the mountains nearby, huge and oppressive. It was a sensation quite different from that of the mountains which bordered Orthlund and couched Anderras Darion. Remembering Isloman's response to the mines, he looked across at him anxiously. The carver however, seemed more intrigued than distressed. He caught Hawklan's glance and brought his horse alongside. His expression was amused.

'I do believe you're hearing the rock song at last, Hawklan,' he said. Then he laughed, and the sound echoed from somewhere. 'Mind you, you'd be deaf not to. These rocks have a powerful song indeed. Like nothing I've ever heard before. There'll be some rare carvings to be found here; rare carvings.' He fell silent for a little while. 'We must come here one day,' he said softly, apparently to no one in particular.

'Doesn't the Pass disturb you?' Andawyr asked.

Isloman shook his head. 'I can feel some distress there, but nothing can disturb me after the mines,' he said. 'And this isn't the same. The mines were like a . . . deep . . . purposeful, malevolence. What I feel here is more like an echo – an echo of a long dead rage. Long, *long* dead. Something whose effects are well buried under eons of rain and wind. I look forward to seeing the Pass. I think it'll have a strange song all its own.'

Andawyr looked at him approvingly, but did not pursue the discussion.

Gradually the sleet became a fine soaking drizzle and the mist cleared a little. Coming to the top of a small incline, Tirke was about to ask, 'How much further?' when Andawyr pointed towards a cluster of buildings which were just becoming visible.

They stood at the foot of a rock face which rose sheer above them to disappear into the mist, and their apparently indiscriminate positioning over the tumbling ground reminded Hawklan immediately of Pedhavin.

The resemblance ended there though as, unlike those on the Pedhavin houses, the roofs were very steep, with eaves that swept down past the walls as if anxious to usurp their function and fasten themselves to the ground. So steep were the roofs in fact, that little or no snow had stuck to them and even from a distance, the travellers could see ornate patternings laid out in the green and blue slates that covered them.

'Home sweet home,' Andawyr said, smiling broadly.

Most of the party tried to look enthusiastic, but whatever they had been expecting, a quaint hamlet of stone cottages was not it.

Inevitably it was Tirke who paved the way for the virtuous to follow. 'Where are the caves?' he asked Andawyr, almost querulously.

Andawyr fought off a smile and waved a casual hand in a direction well to the left of the village.

'You surprise me, Helyadin,' he said. 'I'd heard you had quite an eye for such things. That's a bit bigger than an Alphraan's cave, isn't it?'

Tirke followed the pointing hand and then cleared his throat awkwardly.

Looming through the rainswept greyness was a dark shape in the rock face. It was so large that it made the village seem like a cluster of children's toys, and several of the group closed and opened their eyes in an attempt to accommodate the sudden change in perspective.

Isloman threw back his head and laughed. 'Never mind, Tirke,' he said, laying a great hand on the young man's shoulder. 'If it's any consolation, I didn't see it either.' And as he laughed again, the sound spread over his companions like sunlight bursting from behind a dark cloud.

Despite the enormous cave mouth nearby however, Hawklan still could not avoid a sense of anti-climax in finding that the home of the Cadwanol was no more than a mountain village, albeit with rather unusual architecture. He made no outward sign however, continuing to smile at Isloman's merriment.

Unexpectedly, Dar-volci peered out from Andawyr's robe. He gazed around for a moment, twitching his nose, then, grunting gruffly to himself, slithered down from the horse and lolloped off across the snow. 'See you later,' he shouted back over his shoulder, and suddenly, with a joyous whistle, he was gone.

Andawyr shook his head and smiled, but said nothing.

As they drew nearer to the village, Hawklan saw that the streets were empty, but quite suddenly, without any bell or other alarm apparently being sounded, people, hastily pulling on cloaks and capes, began to emerge from the houses and gather in the main street.

Andawyr dismounted as they reached the first houses, and was immediately surrounded by the villagers. He shook the hands of some, embraced others, and generally talked to several people at once; there was much laughing and excitement. Guiltily, Hawklan found that his sense of disappointment was not lessened by the very ordinariness of these people.

Gradually, Andawyr managed to bring about some semblance of order then he gestured the others to follow him and set off up the winding main street through the village. Hawklan and Isloman exchanged glances as they set off again; despite the haughty appearance of the strange high-pitched cottages, and the towering proximity of the great rock face, the village at close quarters was even more like Pedhavin.

The villagers walked alongside the group like smiling flank guards, though none made any attempt to speak to the new arrivals.

Andawyr eventually stopped outside a building which, like others nearby, was built hard against the looming rock. Some of the villagers ran forward to drag open two large wooden doors, and Andawyr gestured his companions inside.

As the doors closed behind them, Hawklan and the others dismounted and looked around. It was a large barn, high roofed and airy, with one side occupied by a great haystack which filled the air with a characteristic mixture of freshness and mustiness. Along the other side were stalls for the horses, and an assortment of rakes, pitchforks, ropes and harnesses, and many other pieces of farming paraphernalia.

Gavor thrust his head out from Hawklan's cloak, and with a

cheery croak, flapped up to one of the high roof beams. As he landed he disturbed a small flurry of dust which floated lazily down through the still air.

Hawklan looked up at him, and noticed that though the place was well lit, he could see no lights of any kind.

'Unsaddle your horses and rub them down,' Andawyr said, taking a host's command over the hesitating group. 'There's plenty fodder and water for them here and there'll be plenty for us when we've finished.'

'Are we going to walk to the caves?' Isloman asked, gesturing vaguely towards the doors. 'It looked to be quite a distance.'

Andawyr looked puzzled for a moment, then, realisation dawning, he shook his head. 'Ah, you mean *the* cave, just outside the village,' he said, his two hands drawing out a great arch through the warm, comforting, air. 'No,' he went on, disparagingly. 'That's just to impress visitors. The Caves proper are well hidden. Don't worry, you won't get wet reaching them.' He laughed a little to himself than set about unsaddling his horse. 'Come on, I'm hungry,' he said.

Though none the wiser, his guests followed his enthusiastic example. It took some time to dry off the horses, but no one seemed inclined to hurry. It was the first time that any of them had been in a building other than a tent or shelter since they had left Orthlund and, humdrum though the place was, its large, warm space gave it a distinctly luxurious aura.

The task eventually done, and the horses feeding contentedly, all eyes turned to Andawyr expectantly. He gestured to a small battered door at the rear of the barn. It looked as if it might be the entrance to a disused storeroom.

'Don't worry about the lights as you step through,' he said, struggling with the latch. 'They're rather bright and you may have difficulty seeing clearly. They need adjusting. Just walk straight ahead to the far door and go through it, I'll be with you in a moment.' The door creaked open and a brilliant light flooded through the opening, causing some gasps of surprise from the watchers. The barn around them was plunged into gloomy unreality by contrast, and Gavor's black shadow expanded across the roof space as he glided silently down to join the others.

'They certainly *do* need some adjusting,' said Isloman, laughing, as he lifted a hand to shield his eyes, but Andawyr made no acknowledgement other than to shepherd them all urgently through the doorway. As Hawklan passed behind the others, Andawyr stepped after him and pulled the door shut. The barn became real again; rich with warm odours and silent except for the occasional clatter of a horse's hoof on the stone floor.

After a few short paces through the dazzling brightness, the group passed through a second door and emerged into a long corridor, blinking and laughing like bewildered children. A soft echoing ring sounded as each came through the doorway.

Waiting to meet them were two old men, dressed in simple white robes such as Andawyr wore, but noticeably less untidy.

'Philean, Hath,' Andawyr said, smiling broadly as he stepped forward and took their extended hands. 'It's good to see you both manning the fort so well. And it's good to be back. Have you water and soaps and warm towels for your beloved leader and his guests?' He closed his eyes rapturously.

The larger of the two Cadwanwr looked at him sternly. 'You were ever a hedonist, Andawyr,' he said. 'But in deference to the rigours your brave companions have been through, we've prepared a modest greeting for them which we hope will meet with their approval.'

'Lead on, lead on,' said Andawyr unrepentantly, waving his arms urgently. 'I'll introduce everyone as we go.'

Later, lounging back into a soft, supporting chair, Isloman stared up at the ceiling. It was undecorated, like the few other rooms and corridors he had seen, but it was delicately curved and lit by torches very similar to those that lit Anderras Darion. He smiled in appreciation of the subtle shadows that they threw, then he blew out a long, sated, breath. 'I had no idea I'd become so disgusting after all those weeks marching and camping,' he said. 'And I'd forgotten completely what good food tasted like. Andawyr, you have a slave for life.'

A few grunts from his neighbours confirmed that this was the opinion of them all and that further discussion would be superfluous.

'Don't thank me,' Andawyr said. 'Thank Philean and Hath and the other brothers who prepared everything.' He chuckled. 'Mind you, I suspect the baths were as much for their benefit as ours. We've become used to one another, but I shouldn't imagine any of us were too fragrant, and Philean was always very fastidious.'

'Your wisdom remains undimmed, Andawyr,' Philean said, bowing, and smiling broadly.

The room fell silent again and apart from the soft undefined noise of occasional activity outside, the only sound that could be heard was that of Gavor's wooden leg as he clumped about the table in search of uneaten morsels.

Slowly the euphoria passed and the needs of the times began to reassert themselves. Andawyr levered himself upright and stretched. Philean and Hath were seated on either side of him. He looked from one to the other.

'Now we must talk,' he said. 'The essence of the battle I put in my message. Do you need to know anything further about it before we begin?'

Both shook their heads. 'Your message told us everything,' Philean said. 'A terrible affair. It needs no immediate amplification. Only the future matters now.'

Andawyr nodded. 'Creost and Dar Hastuin came north,' he said. 'Did you see them?'

'They flew along the Pass,' Hath replied, grimacing. 'Our seeing stones brought the sight to us, and the sound of Usgreckan seems to echo yet around the peaks.'

Andawyr folded his hands in front of himself and shook his head pensively.

'What's the matter?' Hawklan asked.

Andawyr squeezed his nose between his fingers. 'I'm finding it difficult to think that we're succeeding,' he said. 'Sumeral's Uhriel have all been returned to their Master, wounded and demeaned. Yet it has the feeling of having been too easy. Almost as if it were intended to be thus. It concerns me.'

'Dismiss your concern,' Hawklan said coldly. 'Only a little while ago we were tired, hungry, and dirty; now the discomfort's all forgotten. Days ago you and Atelon were faltering, facing death or worse, before Creost's assault, yet your agony was forgotten almost as soon as Cadmoryth's ship struck him. Months ago I floundered across Riddin, Orthlund and Fyorlund and was swept into . . . who knows what world . . . by Oklar's anger; yet all that confusion and pain is forgotten now. It's the nature of the creatures we are to forget the totality of the horror of such things. If we're lucky, we remember enough to learn from. Think, Andawyr, think. You *know* that *nothing* so far has been easy. We've all been tried to new limits in our different ways and any of us could have fallen at any time. Suffice it that we're all here now, as whole as we've

341

ever been. Wiser by far, and set to continue on our journey.'

He leaned forward and stared into Andawyr's face. 'And remember this. We decided that we wouldn't concern ourselves with Sumeral's intentions. His mind is beyond us. We can't use cunning and treachery as He does, we must use simplicity and directness.' He waved a hand round his listeners, almost angrily. 'Tell them why we're here.'

Philean and Hath seemed disconcerted by this public rebuking of their leader, but Andawyr just nodded thoughtfully.

'Yes,' he said. 'I'm sorry. You're right. The debating's long ended.'

He looked round the room hesitantly, then cleared his throat.

'When you were asked if you wished to accompany us on this journey, we told you what we told everyone else,' he began. 'Namely, that we were going to search for Ethriss and waken him. Our army – and the Muster, and the Fyordyn – go forth in the belief that they will face only soldiers – men, Mandrocs – whatever, but mortal creatures, capable of being brought down by the sword. They believe that my brothers will protect them from the dreadful Power of the Uhriel, and that Ethriss will be brought forth somehow to oppose Sumeral Himself.'

Despite the warmth and comfort of the room, his tone seemed to bring a chill to everyone.

'But –?' Tirke anticipated, seizing on the doubt in Andawyr's voice.

Andawyr nodded, as if thanking him for his help with this telling.

'But,' he echoed, 'we do not know where Ethriss is.'

There was a long silence, and when he spoke again, it was slowly and apparently with great reluctance. 'The Guardians themselves do not know where he is. We could wander for generations and not find him. And even if we found him, there's no guarantee that we'd have the skill to waken him.' He looked around at everyone again. 'We cannot assume that Ethriss will aid us. We must be prepared to face Sumeral alone.'

Though no one moved, Hawklan felt the emotions whirling round through his companions; disbelief, doubt, fear, anger – mainly anger.

He spoke before it found voice.

'You may ponder all these matters as I have done, endlessly, but you'll find nothing that could have been done to keep us from the path which has led us here.' The pending questions spent themselves unheard against the rock of his presence.

'But this is *not* the time of the First Coming,' he went on. 'Things are not as they were. Now Sumeral is known for what He is *before* He has spread His corruption throughout the world. The Cadwanol is wiser and stronger by far than in those times, while the Uhriel are weaker. And some power has given us the great armoury of Anderras Darion to arm the awakened Orthlundyn, and the Black Bow and Sword of Ethriss –'

'And you, Hawklan,' Andawyr said, before he could continue. 'We have been given you, with your strange skills learned and honed in another age.'

Hawklan did not answer.

'What are we here for, if not to find Ethriss?' Yrain asked. Her voice was calm but her face was strained.

'We're here to go quietly into Derras Ustramel, and kill Sumeral.'

The voice was Dacu's. All eyes turned to him and then scattered back to Andawyr and Hawklan.

Both nodded, unsurprised by the Goraidin's correct deduction.

There was a sudden babbling upsurge of questions, but Hawklan lifted a hand and it died as quickly as it had come.

'This *can* be done,' he said. His voice was final. 'Andawyr, Isloman and I go because we cannot do otherwise. Yrain, Jenna, Tybek, you were chosen because you're amongst our finest Helyadin. Athyr, you also, and because you're a Morlider Veteran. Dacu, because you're Goraidin and a Veteran. Jaldaric, Tirke, because you bring special qualities of your own; you, Jaldaric, from your imprisonment, you, Tirke, from your journey through the mountains.'

'We haven't the skills of Yrain and the others,' Jaldaric said awkwardly.

Hawklan nodded. 'I know,' he replied. 'But you're more than good enough to hold your own and you bring old Fyordyn skills with you, as does Dacu.'

There was a brief silence. Gavor's head appeared from behind a bowl of fruit. 'What about me, dear boy?' he asked.

'You're coming to guard my back and to watch our way,' Hawklan said, turning to look at him.

Green eyes and black met; old friends.

'Ah,' Gavor said, after a moment. 'And as a conscript I see.'

Hawklan nodded.

Gavor gave a soft 'Humph,' of injured resignation and disappeared behind the fruit bowl again.

The brief exchange eased the confused tension that had filled the room.

'This venture was kept from the people for fear of its inadvertently coming to the ears of the enemy,' Hawklan said. 'The journey will be hard enough without their being warned of our coming. However, I'll admit that the deceit distresses me . . .'

He fell silent and stared absently at the table. A nearby torch was shining through a clear glass goblet and throwing a splash of multi-coloured light on to the heavily grained surface. He gave a slight sigh, and Gavor's head came inquisitively over the fruit bowl again.

The brief introspection faded quickly, however, and he looked round again at his companions. 'Our chances of success at the end are not calculable,' he said. 'They're probably very small . . . I don't know. If any of you wish to leave, then do so without any reproach from me. Ride back and wait for the army, and hold your peace.' Then, in contrast to these words, his voice and manner became grimly purposeful. 'However, if you wish to stay, understand this: I value Orthlund and my life there, and however small the odds, I intend to return to both in due course. *I have no intention of winning this cause by dying for it.* I have a memory of advice from someone, somewhere: "You win by making the other poor devil die for *his* cause." It's advice I intend to follow. Indeed, I commend it to you all.'

He sat back. 'Now,' he concluded. 'Who rides with us?'

'I do,' said Dacu quietly. His reply was echoed unanimously round the table. The healer in Hawklan rose to reproach him at his success in engineering the loyalty of his chosen group, but the warrior rose too and laid the reproach aside. 'They are as trapped as we are,' he said, 'and their vision is clear enough for them to see it.'

'Good,' Hawklan said simply.

'Er . . . ?' said Gavor tentatively.

'Silence in the ranks,' someone said, and the last vestiges of tension disappeared in laughter.

'When do we leave?' Tirke asked.

'Fairly soon,' Hawklan replied. 'Within the next few days. We need to study whatever maps and charts are to be had here, and plot out a route as well as we can. We need to learn what we can about the ways of the Mandrocs, and we have to replenish our supplies and also learn enough about Narsindal to be able to survive when they run out.'

There was much head nodding at these observations and Yrain started to ask a question.

Hawklan raised his hand. 'Tomorrow,' he said gently. 'Tomorrow, we begin properly. But for the rest of this evening, let's just talk and enjoy this peace.'

Yrain tried not to frown.

Hawklan smiled. 'Very well,' he said. 'Just this one last thing. And let me anticipate your question. We have no specific plan of campaign. We are Helyadin and Goraidin, doing one of the things that such troops are intended to do; entering the enemy's territory like shadows and doing as much harm as possible. In this instance, striking to its very heart. Our tactics will be to put one foot in front of the other . . . *very carefully*.'

Over the following days, the group studied the documents that the Cadwanwr produced for them and, amongst other things, decided upon the route for the first part of their journey. It was not one they had anticipated, and it left Hawklan with a sad task which he postponed until the end.

'You cannot come with me,' he said to Serian, laying his hand on the horse's muscular flank. Serian shifted, his feet clattering on the stone floor, but he did not speak.

'We have to go through the caves to reach Narsindal,' Hawklan went on. 'Andawyr fears that the Pass itself may be watched, and any news of our arrival could prove disastrous.'

Serian shifted again. 'This is not the way it should be,' he said eventually. 'You and I should ride against Sumeral together.'

Hawklan pressed his forehead against the animal and closed his eyes. 'So our hearts say, horse,' he said. 'But circumstances dictate otherwise.'

Serian's hoof scratched at the floor fretfully.

'I go where I must, Hawklan,' he said. 'Set me free to find another destiny.'

'You've always been free, my friend,' Hawklan said. 'I've already told the Cadwanwr that your door is to be open so that you may leave when you please.'

Serian bowed his head low. 'Farewell, then, prince,' he said. 'Until we meet again.'

Hawklan put his arms round the horse's neck and embraced him, then he turned and left without speaking.

'At Derras Ustramel,' Serian said softly as the battered door closed and the light in the barn became dim again.

Returning to his companions, Hawklan found them fully laden and anxious to start. Their enthusiasm drew him from his introspection and he smiled as Dacu helped him fasten his heavy pack.

'Everything checked?' he asked. The Goraidin grunted a terse confirmation.

'Who's carrying *my* food?' Gavor asked suddenly, in great alarm.

Each looked at the other and shrugged a wide-eyed disclaimer.

'Don't worry, Gavor,' Tirke said. 'We'll see you get well fed. You're the emergency ration.'

There was some laughter at this, but a small circle cleared expectantly as Gavor walked slowly across to him.

'Very droll, Tirke,' the raven said darkly. 'Very droll.' Tirke cringed a little in anticipation of some form of retaliation, but Gavor turned as if to move away. 'Oh,' he said, turning back again casually. 'I was sorry to hear about your sore leg.'

Tirke, mildly relieved at escaping so lightly after such an indiscretion, gazed at him in some surprise, and shook his head. 'I haven't got a sore leg,' he said.

'Really?' Gavor said, then his black beak shot forward and struck Tirke's shin with a resounding thud. 'I could have sworn you had.'

While Tirke was executing a small hopping dance to renewed laughter from his friends, Gavor flapped up on to Hawklan's shoulder. 'And another thing, Tirke, dear boy,' he said. 'It's not wise to talk about eating one's companions when one's made out of meat oneself, is it?'

'Peace,' said Hawklan, trying not to laugh. 'There'll be plenty to fight about before we've reached the end of this journey. Andawyr, lead on if you would, please.'

Andawyr wriggled about underneath his pack until it was comfortable then set off down the long stone corridor. Though it was deep below ground it was well lit by the window stones which brought bright, daylight scenes from the surface. Since Andawyr's return, the seeing stones had been readjusted, and at least half of them gave a view of some part of the Pass. This had been done throughout the whole cave system thus ensuring that in addition to a formal watch being maintained, a substantial informal one was kept also.

Occasionally they passed through an arch decorated with strange glowing symbols, and the same soft echoing ring that had greeted their entry to the Caves sounded again.

'What is that?' Athyr asked.

'The Caves are on Full Watch,' Andawyr said. 'They're riddled with traps and devices to protect us from the many strange foes that have beset us through the ages. Had you carried His taint, you'd not have survived so far. The chime celebrates your wholeness.'

The matter-of-fact tone of his voice was more chilling than any threat could have been and Athyr let the topic lie.

Then Andawyr led them through a short dazzling passage like the one through which they had passed from the stable.

As Isloman stepped out, blinking, he found himself in another long corridor. It was brightly lit, but by torches not window stones. He gazed around, his head back like an animal scenting some subtle change carried on the breeze. 'We're much deeper,' he said. 'Very much deeper. How can that be?'

Andawyr nodded appreciatively. 'How did *you* know we were so deep, carver?' he said by way of answer. Then, relenting a little, 'We call them the slips,' he said. 'They spare us the toil of endless flights of stairs but they're really a part of our defence system. Each entrance has many exits and some are into regions which are far away from here, and far from pleasant.'

Again his matter-of-fact tone was chilling.

'We could use them at Anderras Darion,' Isloman said ruefully, remembering the endless stairs of the Castle.

Andawyr laughed. 'You *have* them at Anderras Darion,' he said. 'But they'll only work when they're needed. If the Castle were to be attacked, for example.' He laughed again. 'Ethriss always did have a bit of the stern puritan about him.'

They walked a little further in silence until, rounding a corner, they came upon Philean and Hath, waiting by an open doorway.

Andawyr unslung his pack and spoke to the two men quietly for a moment. Then, seemingly satisfied, he turned to Hawklan. 'This is where the bird is kept. The eye of the Vrwystin a Goleg that you brought to my quarters at the Gretmearc.' He paused and looked a little apologetic. 'In my heart I abused you for a profound fool at the time, but now I marvel at the slender threads that brought it to us, to waken our Order and blind our enemy.' He shook his head. 'We do right to be simple and direct,' he said. 'Who can say what ends any act may lead to?'

Hawklan peered into the room. Behind a large central column a blue radiance tinted the torchlight. He made to step inside, but Andawyr laid a hand on his arm. 'No,' he said quietly. 'I came this way just to satisfy myself that it was soundly held. No one knows the true powers of the creature. I'd rather it didn't see you.'

Hawklan nodded and stepped back as Andawyr entered the room.

The Cadwanwr was scarcely in the room, however, when the blue radiance flared up abruptly and an ominous rumble shook the room and the corridor. Andawyr faltered, and even as he hesitated the blue light flared brilliantly then vanished, and the air was filled with a hate-filled shrieking that Hawklan recognised at once.

The bird was free.

Strange, strident chimes began to echo along the corridor.

Hawklan watched spellbound as Andawyr's arms rose up and a brilliant white light shone from them and wrapped itself around the wide column. The shrieking intensified.

'Hide yourself!' Andawyr's voice, speaking unexpectedly in the Fyordyn battle language, seemed to come infinitely slowly to Hawklan's ears as he felt other reflexes taking command of him.

The Black Sword was in his hand almost before he realised his intention to draw it, but as he stepped forward, a figure moved in front of him and struck him a blow on the chest that sent him staggering. 'Hide yourself,' came the slow command again. Hawklan saw that it was the old Cadwanwr, Hath, and even as he fell backwards he wondered at the old man's speed and strength.

Both Philean and Hath were now in the room; wild struggling silhouettes against a demented flickering brilliance which seemed to resonate with the appalling screeching of the bird.

Briefly, a hint of blue returned to the light, but almost immediately the room and the corridor shook violently, and with a cry all three men were sent sprawling back through the doorway.

Scarcely yet on balance, Hawklan had a vision of a flitting brown shape and two malevolent yellow eyes seeking for him. Into his head came the terrible cacophony that had tormented him at the Gretmearc, but now it was thunderous and triumphant, like the song of a pack of predators converging on its prey.

He could see the Cadwanwr reaching out to him, but they would be too slow, he knew. Then his arms were swinging high and the Black Sword struck the demented creature an appalling blow in mid-flight.

There was a bright, blood-red flash.

Days before, a far lesser blow had cleaved a stout Morlider shield effortlessly, but instead of the bird falling, broken and destroyed, it merely flew on, still shrieking. Hawklan felt the Sword torn from his grasp by the impact.

He heard it clattering to the floor somewhere, as he himself was falling over, raising his arms to his face to shield himself from the screaming bird.

Before the baleful eyes turned to him, however, a long, brown shape interposed itself and with a powerful twisting leap, Dar-volci closed his massive teeth around the swerving bird. The tone of the shrieking changed immediately; not to anger, Hawklan noted, but to a mixture of surprise and fear.

As Dar-volci landed, he gave his head a blurring series of neck-breaking shakes. The bird's screaming wobbled incongruously and with a final shake, Dar-volci released it and sent it crashing back into the room.

The door slammed shut behind it untouched, with a deafening crash, and the three Cadwanwr threw themselves against it. The rumbling that had shaken the cave before redoubled itself, but it faded as the three Cadwanwr passed their hands over the thin line that marked the edge of the door.

Finally all was still, though the strident ringing still clattered along the corridor. Turning round and leaning against the door, Andawyr slid gracelessly to the floor. His two companions looked at him but made no effort to lift him up. All three looked shocked and drained.

Someone retrieved the Black Sword and thrust it into Hawklan's hand. He became aware of the sound of running feet, and knew that Cadwanwr from all over the Caves were converging on this one small room. When he spoke, his voice seemed to echo strangely in his head, 'What happened?' he asked inadequately.

Andawyr did not reply, but began struggling back to his feet. Dacu and Tirke stepped forward to help him. He nodded a cursory thanks then turned again to face the door, at the same time reaching out to take hold of Philean and Hath.

The three stood for a moment in some strange, silent, communion, then Andawyr stepped back. 'We can do no more,' he said. 'It would do too much harm.' He looked at the gathering crowd of brothers and acolytes. 'We've been massively assailed,' he said. 'But the creature's held and the immediate danger's over. I commend you all on the speed with which you answered the call, but no help is needed now. Brothers Philean and Hath will tell you exactly what's occurred shortly, in the meantime, return to your duties. Maintain the Full Watch.'

Reluctantly the crowd began to disperse.

'I'll come with you to the last door to ensure the seals are sound,' Hath said to Andawyr. 'But we mustn't delay.'

Andawyr nodded and, picking up his pack, began urging Hawklan and the others forward. 'Quickly,' he said. 'We must leave immediately. If the Vrwystin tries to free the bird again, the Caves may be sealed automatically.'

Hawklan postponed his questioning in the face of Andawyr's urgency. Hastily the little man hustled them along the corridor and then through another slip.

They emerged into a wide circular area with a low, domed ceiling. Around it were several arches, though what they led to could not be seen as beyond each lay darkness.

'This way,' Andawyr said, striding towards one of them.

As they passed through, torches burst into life to illuminate a long corridor. It was markedly smaller than any of the others they had been through and the walls were more roughly hewn and less well polished. There was also a sense of oppression about the place that the torches, with their dimmer, yellower light, did little to alleviate.

The corridor took them steadily downwards, and ended in a small flight of steps. At the bottom of these was a heavy wooden door secured by three great iron bolts. Hath went down first and, after passing his hand over them, slowly drew the bolts.

Isloman clenched his fists as he watched the Cadwanwr pull on the door's ornate handle. It seemed that the door would be far too heavy for such a frail soul to open.

But it opened smoothly and easily and with a faint, sighing

movement of air. Hath beckoned the watchers down quickly and pointed to a further flight of steps beyond the door.

'You'll need your lights now,' he said. 'Go down the steps and wait. Light be with you all.'

Cautiously the group obeyed him, Dacu going first and Hawklan last, save for Andawyr himself.

Hawklan paused at the foot of the steps and looked up at Andawyr and Hath standing on the other side of the door. Andawyr hesitated on the threshold then turned and embraced his friend.

Their brief conversation drifted down the steps to Hawklan.

'Light be with you, Andawyr,' Hath said shakily. 'We'll remember your teachings and your courage, and hold this place no matter what transpires.'

Andawyr did not reply, but just nodded, then he turned away quickly and came down the steps.

The door closed with a booming thud that echoed away into the cavernous darkness beyond the torches of the tiny group.

# *Chapter 22*

As the reverberations of the closing door dwindled into silence, all eyes turned to Andawyr descending the stone steps.

'What happened back there?' Hawklan tried again.

'Show me your sword,' Andawyr said.

Frowning a little at this reply, Hawklan drew the Sword and handed it to the Cadwanwr, who examined it carefully and then squinted along it knowingly, humming slightly to himself as he did so.

'Did it hurt you when you hit it?' he asked.

'A little,' Hawklan replied. 'I didn't expect such an impact.'

Seemingly satisfied, Andawyr handed the Sword back and took hold of Hawklan's arms in a grip that Hawklan recognised.

'Well, healer?' he asked.

Andawyr smiled. 'Well indeed,' he said. 'Both of you are unscathed. I'd no serious doubts about the Sword. But you could've been hurt badly.' He shook his head in relieved surprise. 'You wielded the Sword well. You are indeed much changed.'

'For the third time, Andawyr,' Hawklan said slowly and purposefully. 'What happened back there.'

Andawyr nodded, invoking patience from his questioner; despite their unprepossessing surroundings he seemed much more relaxed. 'We'll talk as we walk,' he said. 'Keep together. Keep the torches low, we've a long way to go. Two will suffice; one front, one back. That'll make sure no one starts to fall behind.'

The group found themselves walking along a wide, apparently natural tunnel. Strange rock formations threw grotesque shadows in the moving torchlight and patches of water running down the walls glistened coldly. Apart from the echoing sound of their own walking, they could hear only the occasional splashing of drops of water.

'Dan-Tor is whole again,' Andawyr said bluntly. 'The Vrwystin a Goleg is his creature and only he could have used the Old Power thus to free the bird. It's fortunate it happened when it did. Had it escaped and an acolyte, or even me for that matter, opened the door unsuspecting, the consequences could have been appalling. That thing loose in the Cadwanol –' He shuddered.

'What does it mean?' Hawklan asked.

Andawyr grimaced. 'We must assume that Creost and Dar Hastuin will be made whole again at Derras Ustramel, so for my brothers with the army, Dan-Tor's recovery means they'll be stretched to their very limit. For the army, the release of the Vrwystin means that the extent and disposition of all our forces will be known to Dan-Tor at all times.'

'But it's not free,' Hawklan said. 'It's trapped in that room.'

Andawyr shook his head. 'It's trapped, true, but it's free,' he said. 'The blue light you saw, was a manifestation of a great binding that restrained the whole creature. It could see nothing. Now, the room merely confines the one bird. Merely blindfolds one eye in perhaps . . . thousands . . . who knows?'

Hawklan's face was now as grim as Andawyr's.

'Then he'll see us, too,' Dacu said, speaking Hawklan's thoughts.

Andawyr stopped walking. 'Yes, I'm afraid so,' he replied.

'Our only hope lies in surprise,' Hawklan said. 'Sumeral must know nothing of our intention until we march into His very throne room.'

No one spoke, and the silence seemed to press in on the waiting torchlit faces.

'Could Gavor and Dar-volci perhaps hunt them down for us?' Yrain suggested hesitantly.

Gavor shot her an alarmed look.

Andawyr shook his head. 'Gavor can't fly either quietly or quickly enough,' he said. 'And if he caught one, it would kill him. You saw what it did to Hawklan when he struck it with the Sword.' He looked earnestly at Yrain. 'And that was a blow that would have cut down a horse and rider. No. The Vrwystin's a formidable creature, and its eyes are not what they seem.'

'Dar-volci caught it,' Yrain persisted.

'Dar-volci's a felci,' Andawyr replied. 'They're strange creatures. They can do many things that are beyond our understanding, but in any case, even if he could destroy the occasional bird that wouldn't destroy the Vrwystin and the merest glimpse of us sneaking around Narsindal would bring Dan-Tor down on us. Or worse.'

'I'm sorry,' Yrain said.

'Don't be,' Andawyr said, more positively. 'Your idea has at least clarified the matter. I'm afraid that we have a task to perform before we can hope to attack Him. We must find the heart of the Vrwystin and kill it, if we're to be safe from discovery.'

Hawklan remembered the power of the blow that had wrenched the Sword from his hand, and the desperate struggle he had seen Andawyr fighting with the bird, both at the Gretmearc and now here, in the heart of his own citadel. And if Andawyr was to be believed, the birds had each but a fraction of the Vrwystin's true power.

Andawyr looked at him and read his doubts. 'We have no choice,' he said simply. 'To venture out on the surface now would be to announce our presence to Dan-Tor within hours.'

Hawklan shrugged, his face pained. 'I don't know enough to dispute the matter with you, Andawyr,' he said. 'If you say it's necessary then it's necessary. Just tell us where we can find it and what we'll have to do, and let's get on with it.'

Andawyr started walking again. 'I don't know where the heart is,' he said. 'But we're heading in the right direction. To Narsindal. And it will be underground somewhere, that much is known about the creature.'

He hitched up his pack as if he were shaking off the problem. 'Anyway, we'll have to concern ourselves with that later. There'll be none of the eyes down here, and right now we've got a great deal of walking to do, followed by who knows what problems when we come into unknown territory.'

The group plodded on for several hours, moving through narrow, claustrophobic tunnels, through spacious caverns whose ceilings and walls extended beyond the reach of the torchlight, through smaller caves where the torches drew brilliant rainbow colours from the rocks. Not infrequently their progress was slowed by Isloman who was constantly stopping to examine rocks, to peer into shadows, and generally allow his carving instincts to obscure the true object of their journey.

'Some day,' he kept muttering.

Considerable alarm was caused at first by the occasional appearance of bright green eyes gleaming through the darkness, but these were invariably followed by a whistle and a shouted greeting from Dar-volci, which was returned in kind by the owner of the eyes.

'Felcis abound down here,' Andawyr declared. 'And there

are lots of other small animals and insects as well.'

'Are you sure that's all?' someone asked.

'Oh yes,' Andawyr replied. 'There's been nothing nasty in this part of the caves in generations.'

There was a hint of reservation in his voice which prompted the question. 'How many generations?'

Andawyr shrugged. 'Later on, we may have some . . . problems,' he conceded.

Further debate was ended by their arrival at another wide cavern. On one side, the floor sloped away down to a wide, fast-flowing stream. It came out of the darkness and disappeared into it.

Isloman stood for a moment looking at the slope, then he walked across to the edge of the stream. Small waves reached up from the surging flow and flowed gently over the smoothed rocky floor to lap at his feet. He frowned slightly.

'What's the matter?' Hawklan asked.

'This stream's normally lower than this,' Isloman replied. 'Now it's in spate, and I'd say it's risen only recently –'

'It's the thaw,' Dar-volci interrupted, pointing upwards to the craggy ceiling that supported the snow-covered mountains above them. 'Don't worry. The water will only rise slowly. It's the summer storms that cause the real flooding.'

'Flooding?' came an anxious voice.

Andawyr glared at Dar-volci. 'This part *of* the caves doesn't flood – even in summer,' he said quickly and with some force.

'Meaning other parts do?' Isloman said.

Andawyr shot another dark glance at Dar-volci. 'Nowhere that we're going,' he said. 'Our most serious problem would appear to be a wilfully provocative rodent.'

Dar-volci chuckled then, with a gleeful whistle plunged into the stream and disappeared from view.

Later, he returned as the group was preparing to camp. Andawyr gave him a reproving look as he wriggled into the shelter and curled up in front of the radiant stones.

However, the felci spoke before Andawyr could begin.

'I think we have an ally in our search for the Vrwystin,' he said, closing his eyes.

Andawyr's face became serious. 'No more of your antics, Dar,' he said. 'My sense of humour's not at its best, and none of the rest are happy underground.'

Dar-volci opened his eyes and looked up at Andawyr. Then he unwound himself languorously and wriggled round the glowing stones until he was at the Cadwanwr's feet. Andawyr reached down and stroked him.

'Dar-volci is not joking,' said a voice.

Involuntarily, everyone in the shelter looked around.

'Alphraan,' Hawklan said, part question, part statement.

'Hawklan,' came the reply.

'How long have you been with us?' Hawklan asked.

'Since you came from the silent place.'

Hawklan's forehead furrowed. 'The silent place?' he echoed.

'The place of the Cadwanol,' said the voice, its words filigreed around with subtle meanings full of wonder and awe. 'We cannot enter there. All is echo. It is a mighty fortress.'

Hawklan nodded. 'What do you want?' he asked.

'We wish to come with you,' replied the voice. 'We wish to help and guide you.' Then an unexpected harshness came into the voice, nerve rending, like a myriad tiny glittering edges. Everyone in the shelter winced. 'We wish to seek out the Vrwystin a Goleg . . .'

Hawklan raised his hands as if to protect himself from an assault, so full of hatred was the sound whose glowing centre was the words 'Vrwystin a Goleg'. He was not alone. Everyone in the shelter was reacting in distress.

'Take care, Alphraan,' Hawklan cried out. 'You forget the power of your speech.'

Immediately the shelter was filled with sounds bearing the images of regret and remorse.

Hawklan smiled and shook his head. 'Alphraan, quiet yourselves, and remember the . . . crude simplicity . . . of our speech and our hearing.'

'We are sorry,' said the voice with an obvious effort. 'But the Vrwystin is an ancient and dreadful foe whose waking is an abomination. You will need our help both to find and to slay it.'

Hawklan looked at Andawyr, who nodded.

'Come with us then, sound weavers,' Hawklan answered. 'We welcome your help.'

Tiny dancing sounds of excitement and happiness rang round the shelter. As they faded, Hawklan said, 'But do your . . . ways . . . come so far north? Soon we'll be into regions uncharted and unknown to both men and felci.'

The sounds returned, full of laughter, and with faint hints of some far distant age, long gone. 'It's true that not all the ways are easy, Hawklan,' the voice said. 'But they are everywhere, everywhere.'

Hawklan opened his mouth to ask another question, but Andawyr laid a hand on his arm. 'Leave it,' he said, shaking his head. 'Even if they could explain, I doubt we'd understand. Just accept their help and be grateful.'

'Gratitude is not necessary, Cadwanwr,' the voice said. 'Nothing we can do would repay what Hawklan and the Orthlundyn have done for us . . .' The voice trailed off into sounds which told of their heartplace and of the renewal and rejoining that was there. And light and the Great Song . . .

Hawklan looked at Andawyr and raised his eyebrows in amused resignation. 'Good nght, Alphraan,' he said. 'We must rest now.'

'Good rest, all of you,' the voice said.

Hawklan slept well through what his body told him was the night, though once he woke, disturbed by something. He glanced around the shelter, lit by the subdued light of the radiant stones. Nothing was untoward, but Dar-volci was gone. He closed his eyes again; he felt no sense of menace, and the felci came and went as he pleased. As he felt sleep closing over him again, he heard the sound of ringing laughter far in the distance; laughter and song? and the fluting, whistling of felcis?

The journey continued uneventfully for several days through the endlessly varying and complex cave system. They found themselves fording swollen streams; scrabbling over tumbled heaps of rock such as might be found strewn across a mountain face; walking through echoing caves that were like great columned halls where massive stalactites and stalagmites had met and fused; wandering, more unhappily, through spaces which, for the taller, were less than head height but whose walls were beyond the reach of their brightest torchlight.

On one occasion they were held silent and spellbound by a chamber that was filled with billowing outcrops of white rock poised like a great frozen ocean.

'Douse the torches,' Isloman said suddenly. With some reluctance this was done after a little further urging, and for a few moments the group stood motionless in the total blackness. Then, as eyes adjusted, the huge wave formations began to appear again, now not only white, but shot through with many colours, and shining as if from intensely bright light

357

buried deep below. They were hauntingly beautiful. 'One day . . .' Isloman was heard to mutter softly again before he struck one of the torches.

Several times they heard great torrents of water nearby but though they came across many streams, they found no rivers. They did however, come upon a massive waterfall, tumbling from some unseeable height above into some unfathomable depth below.

All the larger chambers that they passed through provided them with several exits, and in the narrower tunnels they encountered innumerable side tunnels and elaborate junctions and branches. Dacu supervised the marking of these and the recording of them in the journals.

His concern amused Andawyr who twitted him gently about it.

'There's no point coming back this way,' he said. 'Believe me, *no one* is going to answer a knocking at *that* door.'

'They'll open it for you, and you'll be with us,' Dacu replied, giving him a ferocious scowl and striking a bold mark defiantly on a nearby rock. Andawyr laughed.

Eventually however, his sure choice of route began to falter until finally he stopped and shook his head.

'From here it's only my rock sense that's going to guide us,' he said. 'And Dar-volci's.'

'And ours,' said the Alphraan.

'And yours,' Andawyr confirmed then, turning to Dacu, he grinned. 'Make sure the marking and the journals are kept well, Goraidin. I'll want this route well recorded when we get back,' he said.

Dacu gave him a look of theatrical disdain.

That night, however, the atmosphere in the shelter was subdued, though, ironically, the sense of the awesome weight of the great mountains looming above them was less inside the close confines of the shelter than outside.

'We could wander about down here forever,' Tybek said eventually. His tone was unemotional, but he voiced the fear lurking in all of them.

Andawyr looked at him. 'We walk towards danger whatever path we take,' he said gently. 'You know that. It's been so since we decided on this errand.' He leaned forward. 'But understand this, all of you. Whatever fate is waiting for us, it will not be a lonely dying of starvation down here. Aside from the Alphraan and Dar here, I'm a Cadwanwr; born to dwell under mountains as easily as above them. I came out of Narsindal, walking exhausted through the endless unlit darkness, through ways I could not possibly know, and afraid to use the Old Power which should have sustained me. And I came through whole. So will you all. We've good lights, and supplies to take us well into Narsindal, and if need arises we've many other resources between us.'

'There's fish,' Dar-volci interposed, helpfully.

'And some most unusual plants,' Gavor added.

Andawyr looked at them both. 'True,' he said unenthusiastically. 'But I think short rations might be preferable.'

'Nonsense,' boomed Dar-volci, chattering his teeth ecstatically. 'They're delicious. I'll bring you one tomorrow – as a special treat. I can –'

'No fish!' Andawyr said definitively.

Dar-volci chuckled malevolently.

Andawyr's forceful declaration seemed to sweep aside the concerns that had been mounting, but nevertheless, progress over the next few days became slower and more fraught, with Andawyr walking some way in front of the group and pausing longer wherever alternative routes offered themselves. Dar-volci occasionally ran ahead and the group would have to pause until he returned with a simple nod or shake of the head for the Cadwanwr.

'Why don't these Alphraan help more?' Yrain whispered to Hawklan at one point.

'It is not the time,' came the reply before Hawklan could speak.

Yrain jumped, and looked about awkwardly. 'I'm sorry,' she said. 'I –'

'Do not doubt the deep wisdom of the Cadwanwr and the way-maker,' said the voice. '*We* are wise in this lore, but even we learn with his every step.'

Then the route began to move steadily downwards, sometimes quite steeply. The temperature, which had been for the most part cool so far, began to grow very cold, and an unpleasant staleness began to pervade the air. Once or twice Hawklan caught the anxious look in Andawyr's eyes.

'What's the matter?' he asked discreetly as they were making camp later.

'We're very deep, and getting deeper,' Andawyr replied quietly. Then, hesitantly: 'We've moved well beyond the reach of Oklar and even the writ of Theowart . . .' His voice had fallen to an awed whisper and he caught Hawklan's sleeve nervously. 'I'm beginning to doubt . . .'

Hawklan raised a hand gently, to stop him. 'No,' he said. 'You've always doubted. Now you're beginning to fret. Your people have been deep before. Wasn't it Ethriss himself who told you to go beyond? You'll guide us through safely.' Before Andawyr could reply, Hawklan signalled Dacu.

'Go a little way away, beyond our chatter here; sit in the darkness and be still,' he said, looking at Andawyr intently. 'Dacu, you go with him. Remember the Great Silence that roused me. Alphraan, share this as you need.'

A soft voiceless whisper of thanks floated around him briefly.

Dar-volci jumped up into Andawyr's arms unbidden.

As the two men walked off into the darkness, Hawklan motioned the others in the shelter.

'I sense some kind of trial ahead for us,' he said. 'What it will be I don't know, but you're Helyadin and you'll cope with it whatever it is. Stay aware and, above all, don't cling to your fear. We must keep to a minimum the burden we impose on Andawyr.'

It was a long time before Andawyr and Dacu returned, and most of the others were asleep when the two men quietly entered the tent. Andawyr did not speak, but he smiled at Hawklan before he lay down and apparently went to sleep immediately. Dar-volci curled up beside him.

Dacu looked at Hawklan. His manner was relaxed and his eyes were alive with some silent animation. 'This is a strange . . . alien . . . place,' he said, enigmatically, to Hawklan, then he too lay down and fell asleep.

During the night, Hawklan woke twice. On both occasions he thought he heard the dying notes of a faint, howling, cry, far in the distance. It chilled him.

The message had been brought to Eldric's mountain stronghold by two exhausted but triumphant Orthlundyn. While they rested after their difficult journey, posts of High Guard riders carried it rapidly across Fyorlund to Vakloss.

Now, Eldric pushed it away angrily, and looked up at Gulda. 'You knew about this?' he said.

'About what?' she replied.

'About Hawklan not leading the army. Wandering off somewhere on this wild . . . expedition. No one knowing where he is, how he's faring, anything.' Eldric struggled to keep his feelings under control.

'Yes,' Gulda replied simply.

Her calm did little to help Eldric's restraint and his colour rose noticeably. Before he could erupt, however, Gulda continued, as calmly as before. 'It needs no great knowledge of strategy to see that his mission is necessary,' she said. 'Nor any great insight into affairs or people to know that he alone can undertake it.'

Eldric tapped the table in mounting frustration, trapped utterly by Gulda's brief yet all-encompassing, remarks.

'But . . .' he spluttered out eventually.

Gulda raised her eyebrows, like a school teacher at an intelligent but too presumptuous pupil. Eldric breathed out noisily and, sagging into his chair, reached out and picked up the message again.

'I should have thought you'd be a little more pleased at the news, Lord,' Gulda said.

Eldric nodded. 'I am, I am,' he said genuinely. 'I can't pretend to understand what the escape of Creost and Dar Hastuin implies, but the Morlider defeated and Riddin secured; that's good news indeed. As is the approach of the rest of your army, though I'm concerned that Urthryn's taking the Muster into Narsindal.'

Gulda looked pensive. 'He'd little choice, presumably,' she said after a moment. 'The route that Loman's taking was the nearest but if what the Goraidin told Urthryn made him decide it wasn't suitable for a large cavalry force, then . . .' She shrugged. 'Besides, he couldn't leave the Pass undefended. It'd be a threat both to his country and his supply lines. He'd want to sweep and secure it properly before he left.'

Eldric turned to Arrindier and the others, silently watching this exchange.

'I think it forces the issue,' Hreldar said. 'Dan-Tor will see them coming days before they reach Narsindalvak. And he's not going to assume they intend to ride straight past.'

There was general head nodding in response to this. 'He'll see them as an attempt to cut off his retreat,' Hreldar went on. 'I don't see that he's any alternative but to attack them.'

No one disagreed. There was no indication what portion of his force, if any, Urthryn intended to leave at the head of the Pass, and there was little doubt that the Muster could not be deployed at its best in the rocky terrain through which they had to travel. A force of Mathidrin and the renegade High

Guards the size of that occupying Narsindalvak could do them great damage.

'He must realise this,' Darek said.

'Maybe, maybe not,' Eldric replied. 'Urthryn's an experienced leader. And he's got Yengar and Olvric to advise him, but he was thinking on his feet after a bitter journey by all accounts, and with several contradictory needs to be met. We can't take the risk of his force being harried excessively, perhaps even defeated. I think we'll have to move against the northern estates and Narsindalvak, if only to occupy Dan-Tor's forces.'

'Commander Yatsu, what's your view?' Gulda said as Eldric paused after this conclusion.

'I agree,' the Goraidin said. 'There's little else we can do, but I've a feeling that Dan-Tor may choose neither alternative. I think he may simply abandon Narsindalvak.'

Eldric looked at him questioningly.

Yatsu returned his gaze. 'The real army. *His* army, are Mandrocs. And they're in Narsindal; waiting for who knows what signal, but waiting certainly for their officer corps.'

'The Mathidrin,' Darek said.

Yatsu nodded. 'I think they've been using Narsindalvak as little more than a winter barracks in which they could recover from their defeat,' he said.

'So much the better then,' Arrindier said heartily. 'If they're there and venture out to face either us or the Muster, then we can engage them. If they're not, then we can join up with the Muster and go after them.'

The room fell suddenly silent as the implications of Arrindier's almost off-hand remarks became clear.

Darek brought his finger tips together and tapped them on his chin.

'Thus casually we slip into war, gentlemen,' he said quietly, looking around at his friends. His eye came finally to Gulda. 'Memsa, what say you?'

Gulda also scanned the watching Lords. Then she closed her eyes and sat very still for some moments.

'It is the time,' she said eventually. 'Winter will pass this year into a bloody and dreadful spring, but our brief respite is ended. We know nothing of His intentions, but delay will work against us, beyond doubt. We must ride to meet Sumeral before He rides to meet us.'

'But who will face Him when we meet?' Eldric

asked, harking back to his earlier concern.

Gulda looked at him. 'It matters not,' she said. 'The army must face the army, and the Cadwanol must face the Uhriel.'

There was a long silence, and the quiet buzz of the activity of the Palace gradually seeped into the room.

'So be it,' Eldric said eventually. 'The Geadrol gave me this authority against my wishes; now, against my dreams and hopes, I must exercise it. Arin, call a meeting of the senior Lords and their commanders to finalise our battle plans. Darek, Hreldar, help him. Yatsu –'

The Goraidin stood up.

'Destroy those mines.'

Yatsu saluted.

As the Goraidin prepared to follow the two Lords, Eldric spoke again. 'Commander, if opportunity allows you to understand more of this . . . substance . . . that Dan-Tor used against us, then seize it.'

The Goraidin's normally calm features wrinkled momentarily in distress. He remembered all too vividly the terrible heat on his back as he and his companions had fled away from the warehouse that they had fired with the help of Idrace and Fel-Astian's special knowledge. He remembered too the sudden appearance of his frenzied shadow leaping fearfully ahead of him as all before him blanched in the blistering light of this brief new sun they had created.

Eldric turned away from the involuntary reproach. 'Those who would use such a weapon must understand fully what that use implies,' he said.

Yatsu bowed slightly, and left without speaking.

As the door closed, Eldric stood up and walked over to the window. Gulda watched him; a dark shadow in the fading afternoon light.

He looked out over the city with its snow-covered roofs rising untidily above the dark black and grey streets lined with sodden, well trodden, and slowly melting snow.

Here and there the snow had slipped rakishly down a roof, to expose it like a flaunted shoulder.

He watched the people pursuing their various errands, huddled against the cold thaw wind; each movement part of the great momentum of the City's life.

Then it started to rain, and very soon the view became blurred and distorted as rivulets of water began to flow down the window like uncontrollable tears.

363

# Chapter 23

The following day, Andawyr led the group forward with seemingly greater confidence, scarcely hesitating as they continued to wend their way through tunnels and chambers and past innumerable junctions and branches. The route, however, still took them inexorably downwards, the temperature remained chilling, and the staleness in the air became almost tangible. Thus the journey which, hitherto, had been marked by the banter and mutual encouragement of companions in mild adversity, became for a while an introverted, almost sullen, procession.

Strange sounds began to drift through the stagnant air; scratchings and scufflings. Occasionally one of the walkers would turn sharply in an attempt to catch the tiny pin-prick lights that might have been eyes, glistening red in the torchlight; but they were always gone.

And then a soft, scarcely audible sound, like an in-drawn breath, would sigh through the gloom, and twice Hawklan thought he heard a distant wailing howl.

On each occasion, his hand reached out hesitantly to catch Andawyr's shoulder, but was equally hesitantly withdrawn.

'There. I saw it,' Yrain cried. 'Look.'

A torch flared up and all eyes followed her pointing hand. Something at the edge of the darkness scuttled away.

Hawklan turned to Andawyr.

'I don't know,' the Cadwanwr said, answering his question before he could ask it. 'But this is not our place, we mustn't linger.' Then he was moving again.

Some of the group started to draw their swords, but Hawklan signalled them not to. 'The light alone will probably frighten anything that lives down here,' he said. 'Let's not be too anxious to kill things that we don't understand.'

There was quality in his words that helped to dissipate the mounting unease in the group, but surreptitiously he loosened the Black Sword in its scabbard.

They continued in silence for some time until once again the walls and roof of the tunnel began to disappear beyond the torchlight and they felt themselves to be in some open area.

The air became fresher though there was still a strange quality about it.

Faint scurryings in the darkness marked their entry, but beyond these was an echoing emptiness in the silence that was like nothing they had encountered so far.

Isloman gazed around and then gave the instruction he had given once before. His voice was excited.

'Douse the torches,' he said.

This time no one demurred and once again the group was plunged into darkness.

Gradually a faint light began to manifest itself. Not, as before, coming from some particular rock formation, but from above, like the vanguard of dawn. Around the silent watchers, the silhouettes of great rock formations began to appear.

'This is no cavern,' Isloman whispered, as if even the slightest sound might dispel the faint and pervasive light. Darvolci started chattering and whistling softly then Hawklan felt him brush past his legs.

'Take care –' he began.

'This is a . . . landscape we're looking at.' Isloman's awe-filled voice cut across Hawklan's warning.

As the words faded, Hawklan felt the shadows around the group assume a new perspective. Though he could not distinguish any details, he knew that some of the shapes he was looking at were a great distance away. His eyes moved upwards. Somewhere, high above, faint lights sparkled.

'Look,' he said, pointing upwards though he knew the others could scarcely see him.

'Stars,' someone said softly.

Almost reluctantly, Andawyr intruded into the ensuing silence. 'They'll be insects of some kind,' he said. 'I've heard about them. Creatures that live underground and which glow in the dark.'

To give substance to his words, some of the lights began to move, very slowly. Others, Hawklan noted, were winking in and out of existence, though not rapidly like stars, but in a leisurely, fading way.

'Where are they? How high?' someone said. 'It's too dark to judge distances.'

'They're far above us,' Isloman said. He rubbed his eyes and pointlessly stood on his toes as he peered upwards.

'I think they're whole clusters of . . . insects . . . or

whatever,' he said. 'Clusters that keep breaking up and reforming again.'

Dar-volci interrupted any further discussion. His low excited whistling came out of the darkness then he said, 'Come here, carefully. Use a dimmed torch to see where you're treading.'

Following his instructions, the group slowly made its way towards his voice, Isloman leading.

'Careful,' said Dar-volci urgently as Isloman neared him. The great carver stopped, gently extending his arms to stop those following him. Very cautiously he eased himself forward and then abruptly drew in a sharp breath and dropped onto his knees.

'It's a cliff edge,' he said, before anyone could speak. Carefully he crawled forward a little.

'Give me a torch,' he said, reaching back. Dacu thrust one into the extended hand. Isloman struck it alight. It revealed him to the others, kneeling on a rocky edge, immediately beyond which lay darkness. He leaned forward and, lowering the torch over the edge, peered after it.

Cautiously the others joined him. There were murmurs and gasps of surprise.

Isloman swung the torch from side to side, and turned up its light. The ensuing brilliance at once shrank and expanded the world around the group. Shrank it by destroying the subtle radiance that had gradually increased as eyes had adjusted, but expanded it by showing that they were at the top of a craggy rock face which fell precipitately away from them into the darkness far below.

Tirke flicked a stone over the edge. It fell whitely through the torchlight and then was gone. The listeners waited silently, but no sound came back to record the end of its journey.

Tirke swallowed nervously.

'Keep your torch alight, dear boy,' Gavor said to Isloman, hopping to the edge of the drop. Then, before anyone could speak, he had launched himself into the darkness.

There was another long silence until he returned. 'It's a long way down, and very wide,' he said.

'Did you reach the bottom?' Tirke asked enthusiastically.

Gavor shook his head. 'I'm not a bat, dear boy,' he said with mild irritation. 'And flying in the dark's not much fun you know.'

Dar-volci ended the discussion. 'Come back,' he said. 'And turn that torch off.'

As the group retreated a little way back from the edge, Isloman did as he was bidden and once again they were plunged temporarily into utter blackness.

Slowly the faint glow and the subtle shadows came back to them. A murmur of questions came with them.

'Look now,' Dar-volci said over the growing hubbub. His voice was full of strange excitement.

All eyes turned again to look out into the darkness beyond the cliff edge. But nothing was to be seen. Nothing except more shadows within shadows, perhaps far below, perhaps far away.

'It *is* a landscape,' Isloman said. 'We're looking out over a huge area. It's like being high in Anderras Darion.'

From somewhere in the dark distance came a faint noise that might have been the call of an animal.

'*Where* are we, Andawyr?' Hawklan said, his voice a mixture of curiosity and concern.

'I don't know,' Andawyr replied. 'But we must move on. It's not our place.'

'Some day . . .' said Isloman, before Hawklan could pursue his question.

'Some day quite possibly, carver,' Andawyr said. 'But this day and until we see Him perish, we must keep moving forward.'

He waved his hand for silence; it was a faint white blur in the shimmering darkness.

No one either spoke or moved until eventually Andawyr said, 'This way,' and, striking his torch, moved off again.

The others fell in behind as before, but Hawklan strode alongside Andawyr.

'What do you mean, it's not our place?' he asked. 'I don't understand.'

Andawyr cocked his head on one side as if he were still listening to something while he answered. 'It's just not our place,' he said again. 'It's . . . old . . . very old. From before –' He waved his hand again. 'Ask me no more, healer. I can't answer you, and it's . . . difficult for me here . . .'

Hawklan laid a reassuring hand on his shoulder and stepped back.

'Dacu,' he said. 'All of you. Make sure our route is well marked.'

Encased within the dome of their own torchlight, the group continued on in comparative silence for some time, the main disturbance being Dar-volci, who kept chattering and whistling to himself.

Suddenly Jaldaric, who was carrying the rear torch, cried out in annoyance.

Hawklan turned to see the Fyordyn flailing his free arm as if to beat off some irritating insect.

'Douse the torches!' The command was loud, urgent, and unequivocal, and it was Dar-volci who gave it.

It was also effective, and the group found itself in darkness yet again. But this time the soft diffuse radiance did not return. Instead they found themselves almost immediately underneath a cloud of vague, fluttering lights.

'Sphrite!' cried Dar-volci, his voice a bizarre mixture of surprise and delight mingling with a concern that verged on panic. 'Don't touch them!' he shouted. 'Get down on the ground. Get down! Right down and stay still.'

'Do as he says,' Hawklan shouted, unnecessarily.

As he himself crouched down, someone pushed him off-balance and fell on top of him as he went sprawling. He heard a scuffle nearby and an oath from Andawyr. He was about to push the offender away when he realised that whoever it was, was deliberately protecting him with his own body. Loman's amused taunt returned to him. 'You have a bodyguard now,' together with its unspoken corollary, 'Whether you like it or not.'

He lay still.

Glancing upwards he saw that the fluttering lights were flying insects of some kind. He could hear the sibilant thrum of countless tiny wings beating as the creatures pursued whatever errand it was they were on.

'They're like butterflies,' Yrain said.

'Andawyr –?' Hawklan began.

'I don't know,' replied the Cadwanwr, his voice muffled and irritable.

Abruptly there was a grunt of effort nearby, and Hawklan became aware of Dar-volci leaping high in the air, his sinuous body twisting dark against the flickering lights. As he reached his peak there was the resounding snap of his jaws closing on something, and he was chewing audibly and with relish as he thudded back onto the ground.

Hawklan noticed that the shifting cloud scattered and rose a little at Dar-volci's intervention.

'Ssphride!' said the felci, speaking with both satisfaction and his mouth full. Then, more clearly, and still urgently. 'Keep down. Keep still.'

Twice more he leapt, each time catching something, and each time with the same effect of the hovering insects, then quite suddenly, they were gone. Hawklan looked up to see a hazy cloud of yellow golden light receding into the distance. He displaced his protector and rose into a kneeling position.

Out of the darkness came a loud belch. 'Oops, sorry!' Darvolci said repentantly.

Someone struck a torch.

'Put it out,' hissed Dar-volci furiously.

The torch flickered out instantly.

'I'll tell you when it's safe to strike it again, but when you do, keep it *very* dim,' Dar-volci went on.

'Dar, what's going on?' Hawklan and Andawyr asked the question simultaneously.

A further, stifled, belch and a mumbled apology precursed the felci's reply. 'They were sphrite, they were sphrite, they were sphrite,' he babbled, excitement overriding his alarm. Hawklan could hear him running about and bumping into people.

'Dar!' Andawyr shouted ferociously.

Regardless of the felci's injunction, he clocked his torch into life. 'Dar!' Andawyr shouted again. Shadows etched out the lines in his mobile face as he waved his torch about angrily. 'What in thunder's name is going on? What were those things?'

'Turn that damn thing out,' shouted Dar-volci.

'No!' Andawyr replied equally loudly, though at the same time he dimmed it.

'Look, they *are* like butterflies,' Yrain said again, cutting across the brewing quarrel. 'There's one on the ground here.'

The torchlight revealed her bending forward towards a small fluttering red shape on the ground. She had removed her glove and was reaching out gently to touch the insect with an extended finger.

'No!' cried Dar-volci.

In almost the time of a single heartbeat, Hawklan saw Yrain's smile begin to change to a look of horror as the sphrite clambered onto her finger and closed its wings rapturously; saw Dar-volci leap forward and knock away the ecstatic insect with an extended claw; then saw him seize the woman's wrist in his powerful claws, and close his dreadful teeth around the finger end.

He was spitting the bloody stump out and shouting, 'Seal the wound, seal the wound!' before Yrain's piercing scream reached her lips.

Hawklan snatched the torch from Andawyr and, turning part of its dim yellow light into a glowing red heat, held it against the spurting finger end. The acrid smell of burning flesh rose up into the cold subterranean air. Yrain's scream of fear and pain rose past its peak and descended into one of monumental anger.

Quickly handing the torch back to Andawyr, Hawklan reached out to put his arm around Yrain's shoulders but, with a snarl, she brushed him aside, and snatched a knife from her belt. Her eyes turned, gleaming, towards Dar-volci but, recovering her balance, Hawklan seized her wrist and, spinning swiftly on his knees, twisted round, to take her gently but inexorably face-down on to the ground.

Yrain struggled briefly, but Hawklan pinned her shoulder with his knee, and quietly slipped the knife from her already loosening grasp. Yrain beat her free hand on the ground in frustration for a moment, and then lay still.

'Are you quiet now, Helyadin?' Hawklan said softly.

'Yes,' said Yrain, her voice breaking.

Hawklan released her and gently helped her into a sitting position. She pushed him away, forcefully but not angrily, and began to nurse her injured hand. Tears were running down her face, glistening in the dull torchlight; but she was not sobbing and, though shocked, her expression was one of anger and bewilderment.

Hawklan swung a menacing finger round to Dar-volci, standing by the crouching Andawyr. 'Explain,' he said, his own shock showing as anger.

Unexpectedly, Yrain reached out and touched his arm. 'No, no,' she said, still breathing heavily. 'It wasn't his fault. I think he's saved my life. There was something on that . . . thing . . . and it was doing something to me.' She shuddered.

Hawklan looked at her and then turned back to Dar-volci. Andawyr had placed his arm protectively around the felci.

'Turn the torch down, Andawyr,' Dar-volci said. 'As low as it will go. And the rest of you keep a look-out in case any more come back.'

Andawyr reduced the torchlight to a dull glow and the group drew closer together.

'Explain,' said Hawklan again, more quietly.

'We must get away from here, Hawklan,' Andawyr said, before Dar-volci could reply. 'We must get away while I've still some semblance of rock sense in this place.'

There was an urgency in his voice that Hawklan had not heard before. He nodded reluctantly. 'Can you walk?' he said to Yrain, standing up and extending his hand to her.

This time she took it. 'Yes,' she said. 'I'll be all right if I keep moving.' Hawklan felt her shaking as he helped her up and as they walked he supported her inconspicuously. He felt a grateful squeeze on his arm.

The group moved slowly in the low torchlight. At Andawyr's request, they walked in silence, though Dar-volci kept muttering to himself and occasionally whistling.

At one point, the terrain they moved over was strangely flat, and Isloman bent down to examine it. He made no comment when he stood up, though Hawklan sensed some turmoil in him.

Eventually, Andawyr stopped, and began turning from side to side like weather vane in a blustery breeze. His face was concerned.

'Alphraan,' he said.

There was a long silence, then, 'This place is beyond us too, Cadwanwr,' said the voice. 'We follow you.'

The voice was full of awe and the words were surrounded by an aura of profound regret and self-reproach.

'There are dangers in all the ways,' it went on. 'But do not fear your doubts. You are better armed than you know.'

Andawyr looked round at the group, patient silhouettes in the faint torchlight then, his face unreadable, set off again.

The ground became increasingly more uneven and after a while they found themselves scrambling carefully across a rocky plain. Again Andawyr cast about, then Hawklan caught the faint Alphraan whisper, 'Here, Cadwanwr,' and a hint of the guiding note that had led him once into the Alphraan's heartplace.

Andawyr turned to follow it and within a few minutes the group was entering what appeared to be a large cave. Andawyr stared into it and nodded to himself. His manner became noticeably more relaxed.

Isloman stopped and peered back regretfully into the hazy darkness through which they had just travelled. As he did so, he rested his hand on the wall of the cave. At once, he started, almost violently, and again Hawklan felt his turmoil.

'What's the matter?' he said.

Isloman struck a torch and held it close to the wall without speaking. He inclined his head significantly, and Hawklan followed his gaze. The wall was rough and uneven, but here and there, even in the small patch of torchlight, thin, straight, joint lines could be seen.

He gasped and turned to Andawyr. 'This is man-made!' he said.

'As was part of the pathway we trod,' Isloman added, his voice almost shaking.

Andawyr looked at them. Though his manner was easier, his face was still agitated and Hawklan could sense that he was wilfully crushing some inner turmoil of his own.

'Another time,' he said eventually, his face becoming impassive. 'Another time.'

Hawklan noted the phrase's ambiguity.

Then, before anyone could speak, Andawyr turned and began walking into the cavern, turning up his torch a little.

'There's no danger from the sphrite, now, is there, Dar?' he said.

The felci seemed preoccupied and Andawyr repeated the question.

'No, no,' said Dar-volci, starting a little. 'No danger to you now from the . . . sphrite.'

He hesitated over the last word and then began chattering excitedly again.

'When can we stop and get some proper light on Yrain's hand?' Hawklan asked, sensing that Andawyr's own crisis had passed.

'Very soon,' Andawyr replied, and within a few hundred paces he stopped and turned up his torch.

'Sit down, all of you,' Hawklan said. 'Just relax for a moment.' He crouched down by Yrain and gently took the offered hand.

'Tell us what happened,' he said to Dar-volci as he studied the injury.

Andawyr nudged the felci, who jumped again, and Hawklan repeated the request.

'They were sphrite, Hawklan, sphrite.' Dar-volci's answer babbled out, almost uncontrollably. 'They still exist. After all this time –'

'Slowly!' Hawklan said sternly, without looking up. 'Tell us what happened. What were those things?' He glanced at the felci. 'And don't say "sphrite" again.'

Dar-volci trotted over to him and stood up to look at the damage he had wrought on the woman's hand.

'I'm sorry,' he said, both to Yrain and to Hawklan.

Yrain reached out and stroked his head. 'It's all right,' she said. 'I'm sorry I drew my knife on you, but –'

Dar-volci whistled softly and flopped down gently on to her lap. Yrain left her plea unfinished.

'They *were* sprite,' Dar-volci said to Hawklan, his voice much calmer though it was obviously with some effort. 'They're part of our . . . most ancient lore. In our games we tell of times when great swirling clouds of them swept down to the lure lights, and the deeplands would fill with leaping kin, feeding . . . gorging.'

Hawklan became aware that the rise and fall of the felci's words were echoing strangely around the cavern. 'Alphraan?' he said, on an impulse. 'What's your part in this?'

There was no answer, but the air was alive with some inaudible dancing.

Dar-volci looked around and tilted his head on one side as if he were listening. 'Yes,' he replied to some unheard question. 'The ways will be as never before. Can you carry back the news?'

The atmosphere changed. 'No,' said the voice sadly. 'We are bound to the humans and we are too far beyond.' Then, more optimistically, 'But the ways are known. We shall return.'

'Dar! Alphraan!' Hawklan said as he began bandaging Yrain's hand. 'I don't understand what you're talking about but you'll soon be too far beyond my patience.'

Dar-volci shook his head vigorously, as if to clear it. 'The sprite used to be our . . . food,' he said. 'Long, long ago. Before the Alphraan, before Him, before even . . .' He stopped.

'. . . Before . . .' he said softly, almost to himself.

An ancient silence hung in the cave.

Dar-volci returned to his listeners. 'Then, later, *He* came. With His digging and delving, and his foul poisons, first seeping through the rocks, then reaching down to corrode the ways. Reaching even the deeplands and destroying the sprite's great breeding colonies.'

There was such venom in the deep, powerful voice, that Hawklan stopped his careful bandaging and stared at him wide-eyed. Andawyr too seemed taken aback by the felci's passion.

'And destroying us,' Dar-volci went on. 'Or those that didn't flee and learn about the lesser ways.'

'But I thought it was His creatures that drove you from your homes after the First Coming,' Andawyr blurted out, unable to contain himself.

Dar-volci clicked his teeth and shook his head. 'You know what we tell you,' he said. 'His creatures were the last straw. Drove us into the society of humans for our protection.'

There was a bitterness in his voice that made Andawyr wince. 'Has that been so unpleasant for you?' he asked, his tone genuinely injured.

Dar-volci did not answer at first, but seemed to be occupied again with some other memories.

'We lived in the deeplands for a reason,' he said almost off-handedly. 'And it served us.' Then, apologetically: 'But we are all of us different now. And none of us would have chosen finer companions than your many brothers through the ages.'

He wriggled off Yrain's lap and began trotting off into the darkness.

'Dar,' Hawklan cried. 'Where are you going? Finish your tale. Why did you do this?' He held out Yrain's bandaged hand.

The felci turned and stood on his hind legs, extending his tail as a counter-balance. 'She knows,' he said nodding to Yrain, and idly scratching his stomach. 'The pain alone was reason enough.'

Hawklan looked at Yrain, who nodded. 'But –' he began.

'No buts, Hawklan,' said Dar-volci dropping back onto all-fours and walking off into the darkness. 'Be content that I recognised them and that you escaped them with so little hurt. Trust me. You don't want to know anything else about what the sphrite do to your kind.'

Hawklan made to stand up, but Andawyr laid a hand on his arm. 'Leave him,' he said. 'I've never seen him like this. He's had some massive shock; something that we can't begin to understand. Let's take his advice and be glad he was with us, whatever it is those things do.'

Hawklan stared into the darkness after the felci, then, reluctantly, nodded.

Andawyr took Yrain's bandaged hand from him and examined it professionally. 'Neatly done, healer,' he pronounced eventually, his tone bringing some normality back to the scene. 'But you're no great weaver yet.'

'Let's move,' Hawklan said tersely.

For the rest of that day, they walked through tunnels and caverns such as they had encountered previously, Andawyr again leading them with at least a superficial confidence.

Dar-volci returned to them after a while, seemingly his old self, though he would occasionally pick up a pebble or a small rock and crunch it in his jaws with a sound that soon began to draw groans of agonised protest from everyone.

Nevertheless, for all that their progress seemed to be good, Hawklan still sensed a strangeness about the place that he could not define; and distant sounds still came to them through the echoing tunnels.

Towards what they felt to be evening, they came to a small chamber with a single exit, which a brief exploration by Dar-volci confirmed was going upwards quite steeply for some considerable distance.

The prospect of moving upwards again, brought the first smiles to the group for some time.

'We'll make camp here,' Hawklan said. 'It's been a strange day amongst strange days and Yrain needs to rest. She's in pain, and still shocked.'

He waved aside Yrain's protests before they formed. 'That's an order, Helyadin,' he said. 'We can use the extra rest to check all our supplies and to make sure that your journal accounts are made up correctly.'

As the others erected the shelter, Isloman wandered around the chamber pensively, touching the walls.

Hawklan joined him. '*This* is natural, surely?' he said softly, looking around at the uneven walls and roof.

Isloman nodded hesitantly and took Hawklan over to the entrance to the tunnel they were intending to use the following day.

'There are some strange marks here,' he said. 'Look.'

He bent down and brought his torch close to the floor. Its light revealed a mass of scratches scarring the floor. Some were quite deep and long, but the majority were shallow and short. All of them were running roughly parallel with the direction of the tunnel.

'There are some on the walls and ceiling too, but not as many,' Isloman said.

Hawklan ran his finger along one of the scratches and

shrugged. 'They mean nothing to me,' he said. 'What do you think they are?'

Isloman shook his head. 'I've never seen anything like them,' he said. 'They're not chisel marks for sure, and some of them are quite new.'

Hawklan stood up and peered into the gloom of the tunnel.

'I think we'll post a watch tonight,' he said. 'We've been far from alone for a large part of this journey and after those sphrite, I don't think we should risk being caught unawares again.'

Isloman nodded.

No one disputed Hawklan's decision, but it was not received with any great enthusiasm. The caves were still very cold, and while this was tolerable when walking, it was not conducive to standing about idly for any length of time.

Tybek won the first watch as a result of a highly suspect drawing of lots that Tirke organised. Jenna drew the second.

Eventually, all tasks completed, Tybek, with a menacing gesture towards an innocent Tirke, left the shelter, and one by one the others fell asleep.

Hawklan, however, found some difficulty in catching his sleep. After a little tossing and turning, he lay back and, relaxing, stared up at the roof of the shelter, dimly lit by the radiant stones. Yrain too, was a little restless, turning over frequently, and muttering in her sleep, and Hawklan knew that his own wakefulness was in response to her continuing distress at her sudden, explosive, mutilation – and whatever unknown torment her brief contact with the sphrite had brought her.

He dozed fitfully, waking occasionally for no apparent reason, sometimes drowsily, sometimes with a start.

He was vaguely aware of Tybek rousing Jenna, and the change in the weight of the measured tread outside the shelter as the young woman took over.

Then he was lying somewhere in Orthlund, breathing in the cool air and looking into the soft light of a burgeoning summer dawn. Outside the wind was rustling through the trees, and someone was knocking at his door, and calling his name.

Urgently!

He was not in Orthlund! He was –

The knocking was coming from outside.

It was Jenna. She was banging frantically on the shelter and shouting, 'Hawklan, Hawklan!'

Suddenly wide awake, Hawklan seized his Sword and a torch and; stepping nimbly over his wakening companions, moved to the entrance.

Outside the shelter, Jenna was standing with her sword drawn, peering into the darkness. Echoing round the cave was the strange hissing that had intruded into Hawklan's dream. It was growing steadily louder.

'It started a few minutes ago,' Jenna said. 'It's coming from the tunnel.'

Hawklan strode forward to the mouth of the tunnel. The noise was indeed markedly louder there. He pointed the torch into the darkness.

At first, it showed him only the upward sloping floor, but then, somewhere beyond its apparent reach, a jostling mass of red, glinting eyes blinked into life.

# Chapter 24

The galloping hooves threw up great showers of melting snow as the horsemen rode down the hill. At the bottom, they slowed as the road turned sharply to lead them into the village.

The single street that wound through it was deserted, the drizzling rain keeping everyone indoors who had matters to attend to that could safely be left for a day or so.

The riders halted and held a brief, arm-waving, discussion. Then, with a snort of annoyance, the leader swung down from his horse, strode up the short path of a nearby house, and banged urgently on the door. A small patch of snow on the roof gave up the uneven struggle against winter's demise and slid down suddenly to land noisily on the wet ground a pace or so away from the man.

He turned to look at it, then stepped into the shelter of the doorway. As he did so, the door opened suddenly to reveal a large man. He was leaning with his left hand on the door frame and his right behind the half-opened door.

He peered intently into the hood of his visitor then seemed to become more relaxed in his manner. The rider spoke and the man nodded and then, ushering the rider forward, he stepped out with him into the rain.

In his right hand was a large axe.

Holding it close to the head he extended it towards the far end of the village and then tilted it first to the right and then the left, at the same time talking earnestly to the rider.

The rider waved out the same instructions with his right hand, then, thanking his guide, he returned to his horse. As the group prepared to ride off, he gave the man a further brief salute and received an acknowledging wave of the axe in return.

One of the riders glanced back as they gathered speed down the empty street. Shoulders hunched, the man was scuttling back into the warmth of his home.

'Is that a tradition in these parts, Lord?' he asked. 'Greeting strangers at your door with the threshhold sword in your hand?'

'After Ledvrin, I'm afraid it is, Sirshiant,' replied the leader.

The Sirshiant grimaced.

The Lord caught the expression. 'You're from the west,' he said. 'You had burdens of your own, I appreciate, but they weren't those of the people around here. Take no offence at such actions. It grieves me to know why they happen, but it causes me no distress to see people willing to guard their own. Besides you know well enough that an object's a weapon only when it's used as such.' He laughed, unexpectedly. 'In this case, that axe wasn't an axe, it was a signpost.'

The group splashed out of the village and followed the road through the sodden countryside for some way until they came to a crossroads. Turning right they rode a little way and then hesitated at a narrow gateway. Beyond it was a rough-surfaced cart track leading to an isolated farmhouse.

The Lord nodded and one of the riders dismounted and opened the gate. The others passed through and galloped on towards the farmhouse as he closed the gate and remounted.

As they clattered into the farmyard, the door of the house opened and a woman appeared with a cloak cast hastily over her head.

'This way, Lord,' she said. 'Your men can go into the barn over there. I'll send someone over to help them straight away.'

The Lord and one of the other men dismounted and followed the woman into the house.

They found themselves in a broad hallway, its ceiling supported by heavily carved wooden beams and its walls bearing a homely mixture of pictures, outdoor clothes, and various bits of harness and tackle. Behind the door hung a short sword, its blade dark and pitted with age – though its edge was recently sharpened.

The woman threw her cloak on to a peg and with a brief 'excuse me,' trotted along the hall to a room at the back where she could be heard giving instructions to someone.

As the two men waited, the steady drips from their clothes formed large spreading pools on the tiled floor. The Lord fidgetted impatiently as he waited.

A door opened and a young girl came out. As she saw the two men, she stopped in the doorway and smiled pleasantly. The Lord, however, was looking over her head into the room. Gently, but hastily he eased her to one side and stepped inside. The other man held out a tentative hand as if to restrain him, but did nothing.

'Lord Eldric,' said Sylvriss, looking up at the mud-stained and soaking figure who had just entered.

'Majesty –' he began.

'Lord!' came a stern voice from behind him. Eldric started. It was the woman of the house. 'You can't go in there in that state,' she said witheringly. 'You must get out of those wet clothes and muddy boots immediately.'

Sylvriss lowered her gaze and smiled as the discomfited Senior Lord of the Geadrol retreated in disorder.

'I'm sorry, your Majesty,' said the woman leaning in and closing the door. 'You know what men are like.'

Within a few minutes the woman returned, leading a marginally drier and more presentable pair of visitors.

'Lord Eldric, Hylland,' Sylvriss said, smiling broadly and holding out a hand to the two men.

'Majesty, are you all right?' said Eldric, kneeling down by the side of the bed and taking the offered hand.

'Yes, Lord Eldric, we're both of us well,' she replied inclining her head to the other side of the bed.

Eldric looked across. Hylland was bending down and reaching a playful finger into a simple crib. The tiny sleeping figure lying there moved its head from side to side, frowned, and smacked its lips contentedly.

Eldric stood up and moved round to the crib. Looking down at the heir to Fyorlund's throne, he smiled with grandfatherly wonder and fatherly memory.

'How did you come to be here, Majesty?' he asked after a moment. 'We came as soon as we heard, but –'

'Lord,' Hylland interrupted. 'Will you excuse us? These questions will wait awhile. Now, her Majesty and I must talk alone for a moment.'

Eldric looked at him impatiently then nodded with awkward understanding, and once again retreated.

He was pacing the hallway and affecting to look at the pictures when Hylland emerged some time later.

'Is everything all right?' he asked anxiously. 'You were a long time.'

The healer smiled. 'Healer's privilege, Lord, to play with the baby first,' he said, then he laid a reassuring hand on the Lord's arm. 'They're both fine. Mother and son. She's a little tired and he's a bit small, but that's only to be expected. He'll soon catch up. The birth caught everyone by surprise but went well enough seemingly, and I couldn't have tended them better

380

at the Palace than these people have here. Our concerns were needless.'

Eldric let out a long breath. 'Can I go in?' he asked, unconsciously casting a glance towards the rear room that housed the Queen's new protector.

Hylland opened the door for him. 'Yes,' he said. 'She's waiting for you. I'll go and give the men the news.'

Eldric nodded, and stepped inside.

He paused for a moment as he closed the door behind him, taking in the atmosphere of the room. It was clean and spruce, but only a little more so than it would be normally, he felt, and it held a subtle mixture of scents: old ones, rich and solid, deep sunk into the floor and walls, and echoing the lives of generations; and newer, sweeter, ones, dominating for the moment, but ephemeral, and due to pass away soon, like the melting snow outside.

But perhaps not totally, he thought. Perhaps they too will add a small lasting note to the room's old chorus.

He looked at his Queen. Her face was as rich in tales as the room. A little fuller than it had been, it told of a tiredness, both from old trials and new, yet it was lit from the inside by a joy and a vigour that could not be touched by a mere passing physical weakness.

She was beautiful. Unexpectedly Eldric felt his knees go weak . . .

He cleared his throat noisily and stepped forward carefully on his momentarily uncertain legs.

Sylvriss indicated a chair that had been placed by her bed.

'Sit down, Lord Eldric,' she said. 'You look tired.'

Eldric sat down. 'Not as tired as I was only minutes ago, Majesty,' he said. He looked across at the crib.

'A fine baby, Hylland tells me,' he said. 'Our Queen back amongst us, and an heir. It'll do much for the people.'

Sylvriss looked at him in silence.

'It'll do much for us all, Majesty,' he added, meeting her gaze.

Sylvriss smiled and laid her hand on his arm. 'It does much for me, to be back,' she said. 'Back in my other home. My husband's home.'

Despite her smile, Eldric caught a note in her voice that made him look at her uncertainly.

'I've shed all the tears that I need to shed for his absence from this precious event,' Sylvriss said, answering his unspoken doubt. 'Besides, he's here with me now more than he's ever been and I intend to honour *his* life by the quality of both my own and our son's.'

Eldric nodded understandingly, then a slight anxiety came into his eyes. 'You *are* well, Majesty?' he asked. 'And the baby? Hylland said it was a little small, and it . . . he . . . did come much earlier than we expected.'

Sylvriss laughed. 'He came earlier than *I* expected, Lord,' she said. 'But it's hardly surprising after what's been happening. However, be assured. We are *both* well.' Her face became mischievous and she patted his arm. 'I dropped him like a well-seasoned mare,' she said confidentially.

Eldric coloured and cleared his throat again, turning away from the Queen's laughing eyes.

Eventually she released him. 'But we have to talk, Lord,' she said, more seriously. The hand on his arm became purposeful. 'I've no words adequate enough to thank you and the others for what you did in freeing Fyorlund from Dan-Tor and his evil. I wish I could have ridden with you. In due course you must tell me everything, but for now there are more pressing matters. Do you have any news of my father? Are there any problems with the Orthlundyn and the High Guards working together? When do you intend to move against Narsindalvak?'

Eldric held up a hand to end this stream of questions.

'Majesty, you must not concern yourself too much with these matters,' he said. 'Your task is to tend your child, Rgoric's heir. Fyorlund's future king.'

This declaration was a mistake, as the grip on his arm, and the tautened jawline told him.

'Lord Eldric. I shall tend my child, have no fear, but I am your Queen, by both right and by acclamation, as you may recall, and my other task is to tend my people.' She levelled a finger at him, and for a moment Eldric thought he heard Rgoric speaking. 'And there'll be no Fyorlund for *anyone* to rule if I fail in that, will there?'

Eldric opened his mouth to speak but the Queen's look silenced him. 'I didn't follow in my father's hoofprints, rallying the houses that Bragald's ranting had undermined, nor chase over the mountains and halfway across Fyorlund after the Orthlundyn army, to spend my time surrounded by maids and soft perfumes,' she said. 'We are at war, Lord. My small party managed the journey over the mountains, but my father had no other choice than to go the way he did and he'll need help, perhaps right now. Narsindalvak will have to be taken if –'

'Majesty, majesty,' Eldric said in some alarm, as the Queen looked set to leave her bed and gallop off to Vakloss. 'I meant no harm by the remark. I was concerned. First the winter kept news of you from reaching us, then came word of Creost and the Morlider invading Riddin. We've spent much of the time of your absence fearful that we might have sent you into danger instead of safety.'

Sylvriss looked a little repentant. 'I understand, Lord,' she said, more quietly. 'But until Sumeral and all his minions are brought to account, there'll be no true peace for Fyorlund . . . or for any of us.' She reached out and laid a hand on the crib. Her voice became stern. 'And I'll no more sit idly by like a helpless stable maid while these matters are decided, than Rgoric would have.' She paused and lowered her eyes. 'And I *am* concerned about my father.'

Eldric raised his hands in surrender. 'Majesty. Even now, we're preparing plans to assault Narsindalvak in order, at least, to occupy Dan-Tor's forces while your father approaches.' He looked at her gravely. 'We can't protect him on his journey through Narsindal, though, Majesty, and we've no news of how he's faring.'

Sylvriss nodded and a spasm of concern flitted briefly across her face. 'I realise that,' she said. 'But he knew what he was doing and he'll be riding in close defensive order.'

'And he has Yengar and Olvric to help guide him,' Eldric added. 'They're no ordinary men and they've both ridden the Watch.'

'And Oslang,' Sylvriss said, then she nodded again and let out a small sigh. It seemed for a moment that the chill mists of Narsindal had entered that warm room. The baby whimpered a little and Sylvriss rocked the crib gently.

The mood passed however, and Sylvriss gave a tight smile. 'Still, that's beyond us,' she said. 'We can't let it hinder us here. Our main concern must be with Narsindalvak. Give me an outline of your intentions if you would. I'm afraid Hylland's forbidden me the saddle for a little while, so I'll have to stay here until he says otherwise, but –'

'Majesty, there's a coach and your attendants following,' Eldric said. 'We can –'

He stopped in mid-sentence as Sylvriss's eyes widened in a

mixture of shock and disbelief. 'A coach!' she said. Her voice became measured. 'Have you ever known me to ride in a coach, Lord Eldric?'

Eldric's hands fluttered vaguely.

'I am a Muster woman, Lord,' Sylvriss went on, quietly and slowly, but with inexorable resolution. 'By tradition, we dismount only long enough to give birth, then we remount.'

Eldric sank into his chair a little for protection as Sylvriss continued. 'In deference to your Fyordyn ways I will accept Hylland's over-cautious stricture, but I will not be towed back to Vakloss in a cart like a sack of farm produce. Very shortly, I will ride. With my son for all the people to see. And you will ride by my side. In the meantime you will tell me of the plans for the intended assault on Narsindalvak.'

'Majesty,' said Eldric, bowing.

Hawklan stood motionless, hypnotised for a moment by the mass of red eyes glinting in the darkness ahead of him. Hypnotised until he realised they were moving towards him.

'Against the wall!' he shouted, scrambling back to the shelter. 'Gloves and knives!'

'And torches!' Jenna added, overtaking him.

There was a momentary delay amongst the drowsy watchers who had crawled out of the shelter after Hawklan, then the creatures emerged out of the tunnel like a streaming black river, and a flurry of knives, blankets and clothing were dragged out of the shelter with wide-eyed midday wakefulness, and great speed.

Gavor extended his wings in agitation and Dar-volci drew back his lips to reveal his own terrifying teeth.

The creatures were like rats, but bigger, and with large glittering round eyes. The hissing that in Hawklan's dream had become the rustling of distant trees, was a combination of their high-pitched squeaking and the scrape of their taloned feet as they scrambled across the rocky floor. They were tumbling over each other in their haste to enter the chamber.

In the brief seconds it took the travellers to arm and position themselves against the wall, the black tide spewing out of the tunnel spread to occupy over half the floor.

All of the watching group had faced different and dangerous trials in their lives, and faced them with courage, but none showed anything other than rank fear at the sight before them. Its seething activity was made the more horrible by contrast with the many days they had spent seeing only motionless rock and stone about them. Gloves were donned, and blankets hastily wrapped around exposed arms, but their few blades seemed pitifully inadequate against such savage, scurrying, numbers.

They watched dry-mouthed and gaping, as the tide flowed into the chamber; squeaking, scratching, clambering.

They watched for an interminable, unmeasurable, interval.

Then, slowly, the realisation dawned that the flood was passing them by unheeded.

And then it was gone.

As silence returned to the chamber, the cohesion of the warriors disintegrated. Almost all of them slithered down to the ground as their legs gave up the uneven struggle between terror and stability.

Hawklan tried to sheathe his Sword, but his hands were trembling too much.

'All right,' he managed, wiping his hand across his clammy face. 'Breathe easy. Whatever they were, they'd no interest in us, apparently.'

'This time round,' Yrain said, wrapping her arms about herself and shivering. 'And what if we'd been walking along that tunnel when they came through?'

Hawklan looked at her helplessly, then at Andawyr.

'It's the way we must go, Hawklan,' said the Cadwanwr, shaking his head.

Hawklan nodded. 'We'll think about it in a moment when we've all got over the shock a little,' he said.

He tapped the Sword idly against a rock. 'Is there any point my asking you what they were, Andawyr?' he said, though not unkindly.

'They were rats,' Tirke declaimed definitively, before Andawyr could declare his ignorance.

'I've never seen a rat with eyes like those,' Jenna snapped viciously. 'Nor that size.'

'Peace!' said Hawklan angrily before Tirke could reply. 'It's not that important what they were. Let's bend our minds to Yrain's problem. What do we do if we run into them when we're fully loaded with packs and moving along that tunnel tomorrow?'

He walked across to the tunnel, peered casually into it and then turned to look along the route the creatures had taken.

Dar-volci chattered his teeth. 'It mightn't matter what they were,' he said. 'But what they were doing might.'

'Why?' Hawklan said. 'That was probably a feeding frenzy or a mating frenzy, or something.'

Dar-volci made a disparaging noise. 'They were running away,' he said categorically.

Hawklan looked at him doubtfully. 'Running away?' he said. 'From what?' He stepped forward.

Scarcely were the words out of his mouth than two long arms swept out of the tunnel mouth, and grasping three-fingered claws snapped together where he had been standing.

Hawklan spun round at the sound in time to see a large triangular head surging towards him. He had a fleeting impression of large bulbous eyes focusing on him and two waving antennae, but dominating his attention was a wide gaping mouth which split the head in two with a grotesque and malevolent grin.

He jumped backwards to avoid the apparition but as he did so, one of the creature's misshapen arms struck him a glancing blow and sent him sprawling.

The Black Sword clattered out of his hand.

He became aware of a great commotion as screams and shouts rose up to fill the cavern. Vaguely, at the edge of his awareness, he sensed his companions rushing to his aid, but the two arms, obscenely articulated, were drawing back to strike again.

Gavor came from nowhere and struck the great head, but it tossed him aside effortlessly.

A large rock hit one of the poised arms with great force.

Isloman! Only Isloman could have thrown such a rock so hard.

But it too bounced off ineffectually, and the creature's eyes did not flicker by even a fraction from their intended prey. Somehow Hawklan jerked himself backwards as the arms lunged forward. He was not fast enough however and he heard himself cry out as the two clawed hands closed painfully about his body.

Worse than the pain though, was the terrible strength of the arms and the casual, callous, indifference of the creature's feeding intent as the arms drew him rapidly forward. Somewhere his name was shouted, and the Black Sword was thrust into his hands as his feet left the floor.

Without thought, he swung the blade down and struck the creature on the centre of its head.

The impact of the massive blow shook through his entire frame, and the creature too paused momentarily but, to his horror, Hawklan saw that the great Black Sword of Ethriss had done virtually no harm to the strange head.

The creature was still whole, and still intent on its simple resolve.

He felt the arms bracing to draw him further forward.

Suddenly everywhere was filled with a blinding light. A torch at full brightness, Hawklan thought irrelevantly as his eyes screwed up reflexively. The creature emitted an eerie screech and great membranes flickered over its bulbous eyes. Hawklan felt its arms grow slacker, but its grip did not change. He sensed the creature preparing to flee – with him!

Desperately he swung the Sword at one of the arms, but again it had little effect. Then, through the brilliance, he saw Dar-volci, his back legs swinging free and his foreclaws clinging to the creature's arm. Almost before Hawklan could register the fact, the felci's mouth opened wide and his formidable teeth closed around the creature's bony wrist.

Even through the clamorous din of his own terror, Hawklan heard the fearful crunching of bones.

The creaure let out another screech then, abruptly, released him. As he hit the ground, Hawklan was bowled over by the creature as it charged forward.

He was aware of rolling across the rocky floor for some way and of legs and a long torso passing over him, then the brightness faded and all that was left were the fading cries of the fleeing creature.

A circle of anxious and fearful faces formed around him, chief amongst which was a businesslike Andawyr, Gavor flapping on his shoulder.

'Don't move him!' Hawklan heard Andawyr say, the voice distant, buried somewhere beneath the noise of his own breathing.

Bright eyes peered into his intently, and expert hands probed his ribs. He winced. The eyes looked again, and the hands tested his arms and legs. He recognised the technique.

'I'm all right,' he said, weakly, trying to rise.

Andawyr's hand held him down. 'You're all right,' he said, waving aside the patient's own correct diagnosis as being merely fortuitous. 'Pick him up gently and put him in the shelter.'

'No,' Hawklan said, with an effort. 'Just help me up.'

Andawyr seemed inclined to dispute this, his face assuming a wearied 'healers make bad patients' expression.

'Please,' Hawklan said, holding out his hand.

Reluctantly, Andawyr's eyes flicked their permission around the watching circle, and Hawklan was hauled gently to his feet. Gavor alighted softly on his shoulder and he reached up to touch the raven's beak. Then, pausing for a moment to test his balance, he ran his hands over his ribs.

'Just bruised?' he said, grimacing and looked at Andawyr.

The Cadwanwr nodded. 'I think so,' he said. 'You were lucky.'

'I've been luckier,' Hawklan replied sourly as he started moving gingerly towards the shelter. He looked round at his companions. 'Was anyone else hurt?' he asked.

There was a general shaking of heads. 'Good,' he said. 'It seems we were all lucky. Alphraan, were any of you hurt?'

'No,' came the disembodied reply after a brief but alarming delay. 'We are well.'

Hawklan frowned unhappily. 'Will you not join us, after all, Alphraan?' he said. 'Such as I've seen, you're small and fragile, and I fear for you with such creatures about.'

A shimmer of grateful amusement twinkled through the small cavern. 'We cannot join you, Hawklan,' said the voice. 'But have no fear for us. We already walk under your protection, and we are not as fragile as we were when you cleansed our heartland, by any means.'

Hawklan looked around the cavern for a moment until his gaze fell on Dar-volci. The felci did not speak, but his manner said: 'Accept them as they are, healer.'

Hawklan shrugged resignedly. 'Whatever you wish, my friends,' he said.

Then he held out his hand to Dar-volci. 'Thank you,' he said. 'I don't know –'

'Hawklan, look.' Unusually, the interruption came from Jaldaric, and there was a note in his voice that made Hawklan stop and turn to him immediately. The Fyordyn was holding out the Black Sword to him, his finger pointing to its edge.

Hawklan took the Sword with a nod of thanks, and lifted the blade closer to his face to examine where Jaldaric was indicating. The edge had been blunted! The edge which had destroyed the Vrwystin a Kaethio at the Gretmearc, cut down Mandrocs in Orthlund, slain one of Sumeral's ancient creatures under the mountains, done service against the Morlider, and yet would still part a falling hair without disturbing its downward, floating, progress, had been turned by a single blow against this strange dweller in this strange world.

He showed it to Andawyr.

The Cadwanwr looked shocked at first, then he grimaced and gazed around the cavern. 'Too old,' he muttered. 'I never dreamt . . .' He left the sentence unfinished and turned to look at Dar-volci enigmatically. 'How did your teeth cut through that creature's bones where this blade failed?' he said.

Dar-volci stood on his hind legs and scratched his stomach idly, then he put a large pebble into his mouth. Various among the watchers put their hands to their ears to avoid the teeth clenching crack as he crushed it with gleeful relish.

'It's just a knack we have,' he said, spitting out fragments. 'We learnt it a long time ago.'

Andawyr looked almost angry at this response and seemed inclined to pursue the matter, but Dar-volci dropped down on to all-fours, turned away and began lolloping back towards the shelter. 'More importantly,' he said over his shoulder. 'I think it would be better if we all left as soon as possible, don't you? It seems our luck is turning.'

Andawyr snorted, then nodded in reluctant agreement. He looked at Hawklan. 'Do you feel up to walking?' he said.

'I'd rather walk than rest,' Hawklan said. 'I think all of us would. I'd certainly like to put some stern effort in before facing my next dreams. And I agree with Dar-volci. If there's one thing down here that's prepared to eat people, there may be others. I think we should leave right away.'

No one argued with this suggestion and the group stripped and packed the shelter with unprecedented speed.

When they moved off, the front and rear torches were brighter than before and each was flanked by two drawn swords.

They walked in silence for some time, the only sounds being the rustle of clothing, the muffled padding of footsteps and the heavy breathing as they laboured up the steep incline.

Eventually the slope became less severe, and Hawklan moved next to Andawyr. 'Was that one of His creatures?' he asked. 'From the First Coming?'

The Cadwanwr shook his head. 'No,' he said definitely. 'I don't know what it was, but it wasn't one of His, I'm sure. Had it been, the Sword would have cleaved it in half. As it was, only the sunlight from the torch and Dar-volci's teeth affected it.'

'I was hardly on balance,' Hawklan said thoughtfully. 'Perhaps it was a bad strike.'

Andawyr was shaking his head again even as Hawklan spoke. 'The blow was sound enough, Hawklan, and the creature felt it, but –'

'But what?' Hawklan prompted.

'Look at the grip of the Sword,' Andawyr said.

Hawklan drew the Sword and examined the grip. The twisting threads that ran through it, and the strange distant universe of twinkling stars that permeated it, were dull and flaccid, reduced to a clever patterning that might be found on any well-made sword.

'What's happened?' he asked.

Andawyr looked distressed. 'This place is . . .' He hesitated and his voice fell as if he did not wish to speak the words. 'This place is . . . from before the Great Searing. It's from a time before time.'

'What do you mean?' Hawklan asked.

'I don't know,' Andawyr replied, as if he was profoundly fearful of the question. 'We thought that such depths might exist. We've even, perhaps unknowingly touched upon them in our own searchings. But we never in our wildest conjectures imagined . . .' His voice fell even lower. '. . . living creatures . . .'

He seemed desperately reluctant to continue.

'Are the felci from here, then?' Hawklan pressed. 'Dar-volci knew about the sphrite.'

Andawyr did not answer for some time then, in a resigned voice, he said again, 'I don't know. These questions have taxed and fretted us through generations, Hawklan. It's no good asking Dar either, you'll get no sense from him. Nor any of them. They just laugh and run away if you ask them about such matters – as if we were children.'

He shook his head as if to rid himself of the problem. 'It's a matter for another time, Hawklan,' he said brusquely. 'But I fear even then it'll be utterly beyond our understanding. It serves no purpose here, other than to cloud our judgement with needless . . . academic . . . concerns.'

Hawklan looked down at the little man, bent slightly as he walked up the incline. He had never seen him so lost and hesitant.

'It affects your faith in the Old Power,' he said softly, with sudden realisation.

Andawyr seemed to turn away from him, as if an icy breeze had blown in his face. 'Faith is nothing without doubt,' he said bleakly, then he waved his hand to end the discussion finally.

Hawklan's every inclination was to pursue the question. Something important lay there, he felt, but he feared the consequences of the inner distress that it was patently causing Andawyr. He nodded and fell silent to allow the Cadwanwr to recover his composure. Tentatively he felt his ribs again and winced a little.

'Are you breathing all right?' Andawyr asked, his voice louder than necessary and reflecting his anxiety to return to matters of the moment.

'Yes,' Hawklan replied. 'It hurts a little, but there is nothing broken and time will ease it. I'll be better walking than resting.'

'If you're certain,' Andawyr said.

Catching Andawyr's solicitous tone, Gavor leaned forward. 'I'm still getting the odd twinge from my wing, dear boy,' he said. 'My *sprained pectoral*, you know. Certain parties have been really quite off-hand about it. And I think I've bruised my beak on that thing, as well.'

Andawyr gave him a sidelong look. 'Rest is what you need for a beak injury,' he said. 'Keep it closed. Less food, less talking.'

Gavor looked at him beadily for a moment and then, with an injured snort, returned to his sentry vigil, peering into the darkness ahead.

They came across no more strange creatures as they marched steadily on through the remainder of the night, though occasional cries reached them, and the walls and floors of the various tunnels and chambers they passed through were scratched and scarred.

There was little conversation as each individual concentrated on putting both distance and time between the present and the frightening events that had come in such rapid succession to disrupt their journey.

Eventually, Isloman and Andawyr looked at one another and stopped.

'Dawn,' they said simultaneously. 'Let's rest and eat.'

No one disputed the command, but as they settled themselves down on the hard floor, and began delving into their various packs, Tirke said, 'I don't believe this double act of yours, you know. Dawn, sunset, etc. My stomach says we're at least six meals behind.'

Gavor agreed.

Andawyr shook his head in a leisurely manner. 'That's because you're young and hasty, Tirke,' he said.

'As opposed to being old and greedy, like Gavor,' someone said. Gavor looked up from his food indignantly, but was unable to identify the offender amongst the laughing faces before his appetite drew him back again.

'What you have to understand, Tirke,' Andawyr went on as the applause died down, 'is that older people such as Isloman and I are naturally far wiser than callow youths such as yourself. Not only that, we have greater self-discipline, superior powers of concern –'

His eulogy ended abruptly as several large gloves and other articles of clothing arced towards him through the torchlight, in a spontaneous, noisy, and widely supported rebellion.

The torches seemed to flare up at the laughter as it carried away much of the tension that had accumulated in the group since they had been attacked by the sphrite.

When they had eaten, they rested for some time. Hawklan examined Yrain's finger and as he did so, Dar-volci clambered over the sprawled bodies and curled up beside her. She put her other arm around him.

Pronouncing himself satisfied with the wound, Hawklan redressed it and then leaned back against the tunnel wall. It gave him great solace to be a healer again.

The conversation fell to their position and their progress.

Andawyr announced that he felt they were now past the deepest part of their journey, but necessarily he could give no clear indication about where they were.

'I think we're beyond the Pass, however,' he said, to exclamations of considerable surprise. 'I think we're somewhere under the southern border mountains.'

'We must head upwards as soon as possible, then,' Dacu said. 'Too far west might bring us within sight of the seeing stones at Narsindalvak.'

'I know,' Andawyr said, a little shortly. 'But we're searching now not just for a way out, but for the Vrwystin a Goleg if you remember. With *that* free, *any* appearance on the surface is liable to be seen.'

The reminder of the reason for their hasty departure from

the Caves of Cadwanen, dampened the spirits of the group a little.

'What kind of a creature is it that lies in one place and has its eyes everywhere?' Dacu said, frowning. 'How can such a thing be?'

'More to the point, how can we find it in this endless maze?' Tybek added. 'And if we do find it, how do we know we'll fare any better than we did against those . . . things . . . down there?'

Andawyr looked at Dacu. 'It's *His* creature, Goraidin, an abomination, and like all his creatures, it does what it does at some great cost – either to someone or something, or both. Destroying it will do far greater good than just protecting us.'

He turned to Tybek. 'And we'll find it through knowledge,' he said.

Tybek looked at him owlishly.

'No, but *I* know about it,' Andawyr said, answering his unspoken question. 'I've faced it, wrestled with it, and made it know fear. For a timeless blink of the eye, I *was* it, and it, me. My knowledge of our needs will bring me to it just as they've brought us through these caves.'

'I won't pretend to understand,' Tybek said. 'But I've followed you blindly so far and I suppose I'll continue to do so.' He pounded his leg in emphasis. 'But this thing *could* be anywhere.'

Andawyr smiled. 'Oh no,' he said. 'Not anywhere. It will be deep below ground. Bedded to a certain kind of rock. A rock that I fear you carvers will feel before I do. And thus it can only be in these southern mountains. As for destroying it, well, rest assured, we'll have a greater chance than we had against the sprite and the other denizens of these caves we've met.'

Hawklan looked at Tybek and the others. They were none of them wholly satisfied by what Andawyr had said, but the brief exchange had made them easier simply by voicing their hidden fears.

After they had rested a little longer, the consensus was to move on and make camp at such a time as the 'elders' declared it was evening.

Thus they set off once again, following Andawyr into the darkness. They moved steadily through the day, meeting no animals, nor coming upon any vast open spaces, though the tunnels and caverns through which they passed still had an eerie aura about them, the more so as the walls were not infrequently riddled with numerous smaller openings.

The route they followed was generally upwards. Indeed, some of the inclines they encountered were both rugged and steep, though the relief at moving dramatically nearer the surface far outweighed the discomfort of the effort involved.

When finally they camped, it was in a wide cavern through which a small stream tumbled noisily. Its water was bitterly cold, but it was pronounced fresh, and after everyone had refilled their water bags, the hardier amongst them endeavoured to remove the excess grime that had accumulated on their journey.

Isloman caused no small stir by stripping to the waist and then both scrubbing and drying himself with rolling handfuls of small pebbles that he had gleefully spotted on the bed of the stream. Having witnessed such a sight many times before Hawklan laughed openly at the discomfiture of the others. When he had finished, Isloman was glowing. Beaming, he held out two great handfuls of the pebbles to the gaping watchers, a look of invitation in his eyes, but the curious circle widened suddenly with much head shaking, and, with a loud chuckle and an oddly gentle movement, Isloman returned the pebbles back to the stream.

As the small commotion died away, Hawklan's gaze fell on Yrain. She was drying her hands and looking at them closely: the bandaged finger, shorter than the others, the split and broken nails, the callouses and roughened skin that gloves had failed to prevent occurring, the dirt which the cold stream water could not move. They were like those of a man who had been toiling long in the field. Quietly she walked away from the camp and sat on a rock with her head bowed.

After a while, Hawklan went over to her. She looked up as he approached; her face was tear-stained. 'I'm sorry,' she said, streaking the tears across her face with the back of her hand.

'Don't be,' he replied simply. 'Do you want to talk about anything . . . your hand?'

Yrain held out her injured hand and turned it over once or twice, her face set. 'I'd rather be doing almost anything in the world than this,' she said, though her voice was quiet and calm.

Hawklan bowed his head. Yrain continued examining her hands.

'They cut that girl from Wosod Heath to pieces, didn't they?' she went on after a long silence, gently, curiously almost, massaging the end of her mutilated finger.

Hawklan frowned for a moment, until the memory of the fallen skirmisher charging alone against the enraged Morlider came back to him. 'Yes,' he said.

'I don't want that to happen to me,' Yrain said.

Hawklan could not find the words to answer her. 'She was dead when it happened,' he offered.

Yrain's eyes pivoted up to his though her head did not move. They were dark with scorn and anger. For a moment Hawklan felt a seething anger of his own rise in response, but he forced it down, and as he did so, Yrain's own expression changed. 'I'm sorry,' she said again. 'I suppose I'm in shock, aren't I?'

'A little, maybe,' Hawklan replied. 'But mainly you're just facing up to feeling lost and frightened. You'll be the stronger for it.' She looked doubtful, and Hawklan sat down beside her. 'Look at Isloman and Dacu, over there,' he said. The big carver, dressed now, but still apparently aglow, was wandering about with the Goraidin, showing him different rocks and talking earnestly. 'They seem so strong – they *are* strong – because they face their fears *all* the time, and they know that only fear of fear is the real enemy. They value everything and cling to nothing.'

Yrain watched the two men for a moment, then she turned to him, 'And you, Hawklan?' she said.

'And me, I hope,' Hawklan said, with a slight smile. 'Like you, I'd rather be doing almost anything in the world, than this.' He looked at her and sensed her easing away from her pain a little. 'But like them, I won't let that desire burden me.' He stood up and looked down at her. 'Nor will you, Yrain; you know that. Or when they move to cut you to pieces, they'll succeed, won't they?'

She grimaced as she nodded, then pulled her gloves on determinedly. 'Andawyr wants you,' she said, standing up and nodding her head towards the Cadwanwr who was gesticulating vigorously from one end of the chamber.

Hawklan looked at her for a moment.

'Go on,' she said. 'I'm all right now. It was just a little tiredness.' She held up her gloved hand. 'Look, five fingers,' she said, smiling ruefully.

As Hawklan walked over to Andawyr, he saw that the little man was signalling Isloman also.

'What is it?' Hawklan said, as both he and Isloman reached him.

'This way,' Andawyr said. 'See what you think.'

Turning up his torch a little, he led them away from the camp and around a rocky outcrop. Beyond it lay another chamber about the same size as the one they were camped in.

'Here,' he said, moving up a small slope along one side.

As the two men followed him, the shadows gave way to reveal a series of openings in the wall.

'What do you think?' he said. 'Which way?'

The two men looked at him uncertainly. Apart from the Alphraan at the depths of their journey, not once had Andawyr asked for advice on the choice of route, and these openings seemed no different from countless others that he had chosen between previously.

'Well . . . ?' he pressed.

Hawklan was about to protest his ignorance when Isloman stepped past him and walked to one of the openings. He stood there for a moment then stepped inside and, without turning, beckoned Hawklan.

As he walked forward, Hawklan faltered. Faintly, he felt something; something repellent. Then it was gone, like a distant cry carried by a powerful wind.

Isloman too was leaning forward, his face intent, as if trying to catch an elusive sound or scent.

Hawklan became aware of Andawyr by his side, expectant, but silent.

Isloman turned to the Cadwanwr. '*This* is the rock that this creature lives in?' he said.

Andawyr nodded.

Isloman blew out an anxious breath. 'It sings a *bad* song. If we must go this way we mustn't linger.'

Andawyr did not reply. 'Hawklan,' he said. 'What do you feel here?'

Hawklan walked slowly along the tunnel for a little way. The sensations came and went still, evading his full perception tantalisingly, but nevertheless, they were unmistakable. Here, was the corruption he had seen jigging a demented marionette on a tinker's hand at Pedhavin; the corruption he had seen in the aura that surrounded Oklar at Vakloss, and Creost and Dar Hastuin on the battlefield in Riddin.

'Him,' he said softly.

# *Chapter 25*

The Fyordyn had turned out to welcome the Orthlundyn army with some enthusiasm, but that was a mere fraction of the welcome they afforded to their Queen when she returned with her baby son.

The weather was the sourest-faced guest present at her reception, choosing to assail the crowd with a cold blustery wind, and occasional flurries of icy rain, but it could not prevail against so well entrenched an opponent as the genuine pleasure of the Fyordyn.

The city streets were alive with milling crowds, all waving flags and coloured ribbons. Weaving amongst them were lines of High Guards, once again in the formal uniforms of their Lords, and charged with the task of gently maintaining some semblance of order. From the houses and buildings hung all manner of buntings and other colourful decorations, swaying and dancing joyously in the peevish wind.

'The City looks as if it were in the middle of the Spring Festival,' Arinndier said, as he looked out from one of the Palace towers.

Darek joined him and stood for a moment surveying the scene. 'It *is*,' he said, smiling a little. 'It's the start of the rebirth of our country. The people see it more clearly than we do.'

Arinndier raised a mocking eyebrow at his stern friend's unwonted lyricism, but Darek's smile faded. 'Let's hope the coming frost is not too much for us all,' he said.

Sylvriss herself wept unashamedly at times as she rode through the cheering crowds with Eldric at her side, and her son wrapped snug and warm in the traditional shoulder sling of the Muster women.

Her tears, however, were for the most part tears of happiness and they were shared by many others in the crowd. Only when she saw the unrepaired remains of the damage wrought by Oklar did her face become pained, yet even then her anger enhanced rather than diminished her radiance.

Your smile lights the whole city, Dilrap thought, as he stood at the Palace Gate with the official welcoming party. Looking at the noisy crowd, he remembered others that had thronged the streets over the past months; the expectant crowd waiting for Eldric to call Dan-Tor to an accounting; the appalling, near-hysterical crowds that had gathered in the smoke-stained glare of blazing torches, to roar and cheer at Dan-Tor's bellowed lies and his violent hammering music; and, most tragic of all, the crowd that he had not seen, the crowd that had followed the Orthlundyn, Hawklan, to be crushed by the wrath of the revealed Uhriel.

And were these the same people? he thought, looking round at the upturned faces. The greater part of them must be, he concluded. How could it be otherwise? There were not so many people in the City that crowds of this size could be materially different. Curiosity and concern had taken the people to Eldric's accounting; fear had goaded them to Dan-Tor's harangues – and worse, darker, traits, he knew; had not he himself, with all his knowledge, responded to Dan-Tor's strutting martial theatre? And finally, self-righteous anger had drawn them after Hawklan on his fateful journey.

The crowd was a fearsome creature with a strange will of its own; capable of any extremity and quite beyond the control of its members . . .

'What a wonderful day, Dilrap, I'm so excited. It'll be so marvellous to have her back – and a baby too.'

Alaynor was responsible for all the female servants and officers in the Palace and her gleeful voice cut across Dilrap's darkening reverie. Dilrap turned to her with an indulgent smile only to find that her unbridled enthusiasm was immediately infectious and that he too was now one of the crowd.

Later, the Queen made a quieter, sadder, pilgrimage around the Palace, holding her child tight to her and facing the dreadful impact of familiar, once shared, objects and places. It was a journey she had made many times in her heart since she had fled the Palace, and she wept very little, but her face was pale and drawn when at last she came into the small meeting hall.

It was ablaze with torches and colourful decorations, but her few guests fell silent as she entered. She looked at them in silence for a moment, and then the strain eased from her face and she smiled warmly.

'I apologise if I'm not wholly myself,' she said. 'I'm afraid that my return to the palace and particularly to our old rooms, was more . . . taxing . . . than I'd envisaged. The potency of even the smallest item in evoking memories is not to be underestimated.'

She motioned them all to sit down, and then placed herself in the seat that Rgoric used to occupy.

As the scraping and shuffling of chairs faded, Sylvriss became the focus of all the watching eyes. When she spoke, her voice was strong and resolute.

'We've much to do, my friends, so I'll remove one obstacle immediately if you'll allow,' she said, Then, without waiting for this permission: 'I know of your feelings for my husband. But I'll not have any of you burdened with *my* special grief for him. It's an emotion you've all experienced in your time and it's one that must run its course, as you know. Over the coming days and weeks, I shall be easing your burdens by attending to many matters of state, both in connection with the rebuilding of Fyorlund and the prosecution of the war against the architect of this horror. My husband's name will occur frequently as will reminders of his more misguided deeds.' She looked round the table. 'I'd rather you discussed such matters simply and openly than have you dithering about uneasily in misplaced concern for my feelings. There is neither the need nor the time for such amongst friends.' She looked across at Loman and Gulda. 'And I count you both among my friends even though we've only met this day.'

Both of them nodded in acknowledgement.

'Now,' she went on. 'To business —'

Loman chuckled as, later, he and Gulda walked out into the chilly night and through the partly rebuilt archway of the Palace gate. 'I do believe you were impressed, Mesma,' he said.

Without breaking her relentless stride, Gulda gave him a sideways look and then nodded.

'Yes,' she said. 'She reminds me of someone I once knew; a long time ago.'

As was not infrequently the case, her tone seemed to prevent any further questioning.

'She's clever, capable, and savagely vengeful,' Gulda went on.

Loman turned sharply. 'Vengeful?' he said disbelievingly. 'Never! Even without having heard Isloman eulogising her I can tell she hasn't got a vengeful bone in her body. Besides, vengeance isn't a woman's way.'

Gulda stopped abruptly and her stick swung up to block Loman's path. He lurched forward a little over this seemingly immovable obstacle, and looked at her apprehensively. However, her face bore an expression that betrayed emotions far deeper than petulant annoyance, and there as no hint of any reproach against him.

'Neither you nor any man can have the slightest notion of Sylvriss's pain,' she said. 'True, you can probably understand her hatred for her husband's murderers. Perhaps you can even understand the pain of her grinding impotence at having to stand idly by for almost all her adult life while her lover was slowly degraded and destroyed. But such emotions are nothing against her real hatred. What has fired Sylvriss is her silent defiance of the Uhriel, Oklar. It has given her a sight she does not even know of, but which guides her every act.'

Loman's eyes narrowed. Was there a hint of uncertainty in Gulda's voice? He remembered how Sylvriss had stared searchingly at her when they had first met, and how Gulda had failed to hold the gentle brown-eyed gaze.

'It's the same with Dilrap,' Gulda went on. Suddenly, her eyes became distant and reflective. 'As it is with any who've stood too near to Hi–' She stopped in the middle of the word.

Then the moment was gone and her eyes returned to Loman again. 'Such people have seen into His true, awful intent, and they know the fate that will befall *all* of Ethriss's creatures if He is not destroyed. And now, to sharpen the edge of her own intent far beyond any man's understanding, Sylvriss – has – a child!'

She punctuated each of her final words with powerful jabs of her stick in Loman's stomach. Somewhat to his surprise, he found himself unbalanced; the old Gulda had returned.

'Listen and learn from such as Sylvriss, smith,' she concluded. 'Listen and learn.'

Then she turned and stumped off out into the still crowded Vakloss street.

As he ran to catch up with her, the memory of Gulda and Sylvriss's first meeting merged with that of their parting of a few moments ago.

The Lords were now familiar with Gulda's ways and merely bade her a polite farewell as she prepared to walk back to the Orthlundyn camp; but Sylvriss, concerned at such seeming discourtesy, had offered her a horse.

'I can find you one with a pleasant disposition,' she said.

The Lords held their breaths in wide-eyed alarm, but Gulda had merely smiled strangely, and said, 'A horse will be found when need arises, Majesty.'

Sylvriss had looked at her with an odd expression; surprise and . . . realisation . . . as if suddenly glimpsing something profoundly secret yet blindingly obvious. Then she too had smiled, and inclined her head in a graceful acceptance of this refusal.

The clear light of the newly restored street torches glistened up from the damp, well-worn stones, as Loman fell in beside Gulda's stooped black silhouette. 'Listen and learn,' he thought.

He had however, little opportunity for consciously doing either over the following days, as they were filled with a frenzy of activity. Somehow, the arrival of the Queen had been like the dropping into place of the keystone of an arch, and everything seemed now to be whole and stable.

One problem she dealt with before it arose was the matter of the command of the combined Orthlundyn and Fyordyn armies. It was a subject that hitherto had been tacitly, if uneasily, avoided by the principals involved, they being quite happy to immerse themselves in accommodating the many practical, operational, differences between the two forces.

'The army is mine,' Sylvriss declared without preamble. 'I rule the Fyordyn, and it is the Fyordyn who were charged by Ethriss with the watching of Narsindal and the protection of Orthlund.'

'That is certainly the Law, Majesty,' Darek volunteered hastily, ready to defend his Queen with learned argument should need arise.

But Sylvriss needed no such aid.

'There is no Law for a people who go to war, Lord,' she said quietly. 'Except survival.'

A grim silence spread through the listeners sitting around the table. Coming as it did from the Queen, this pronouncement had a chilling starkness that no warlord could have invested it with.

'However,' she continued. 'Our Law enshrines much wisdom, and imposes few restraints that an honest person would deem unnecessary or wish to see slackened and, while we're able, we will carry it with us. Being under arms makes for some cruel necessities, but it allows no licence.'

She looked at her audience, though apparently more to

ensure that they were listening than to invite questions. Then she bowed her head briefly. Her face was pained when she looked up. 'At least then at some future time we can account to ourselves as we might to some other authority.'

The atmosphere in the room eased a little. 'As for my command, have no fear,' she went on. 'I shall command as I intend to rule; with the consent, and after hearing the advice, of my various friends.'

She turned to Loman. 'Loman, you will be my second in command. You shall have all my authority save that you will obey *me*, and you will have the true responsibility for waging this war.' She smiled. 'I'm an untried horse trooper not a tactician.'

A small cry interrupted the proceedings. Sylvriss reached out and gently rocked the nearby crib.

'Lord Eldric, you shall be the next in command,' she went on. 'Beyond that you may determine for yourselves.'

Both Loman and Eldric opened their mouths to speak, but Sylvriss released the crib and raised her hand for silence.

'Loman, you'd affect to be just a shoer of horses from a quiet Orthlundyn village,' she said. 'But we haven't the time for such protestations. You're Goraidin; you led the Orthlundyn successfully against the Morlider; and you forged the arrow that struck down my husband's tormentor. These are qualifications enough but one more, above all, leaves you with no other road to travel; *you* are Hawklan's choice, and he would have commanded all without question had he so chosen.'

Before Loman could reply, Sylvriss turned to Eldric. 'Lord, does my decision offend you?' she asked.

Eldric, taken aback by the sudden question, answered frankly, 'Being honest, Majesty, I suppose it offends my . . . vanity . . . a little,' he said after a brief hesitation.

Sylvriss smiled, and then laughed softly. 'I find it heartening that you still possess such a young man's trait, Lord Eldric,' she said. 'I trust you have others. Rest assured, I want no surly elders about me.'

Her easy laughter spread around the meeting table like a ripple across a pond, and washed away much of the uneasiness. Eldric cleared his throat gruffly, went a little pink, and did his best to accept the compliment graciously. 'My vanity will survive the blow, Majesty,' he said. 'Especially if it's to be a requirement of my continued service to you.'

Only Loman seemed to be having difficulty responding to

the lightened atmosphere. He leaned back in his chair and stared downwards bleakly.

Sylvriss laid her hand on his arm. 'I'm sorry, Loman,' she said. 'Truly. We will help you bear your burden, but none of us can remove it, as, I fear, you're aware. That you didn't seek the leadership of the army and now would be free of it, is a measure of the correctness of my decision.'

There was an unexpected murmur of agreement at this remark that made Loman look up. As he did so, Eldric nodded approvingly and all the Fyordyn began slapping the table rhythmically. It was an acclamation.

Loman crushed his reluctance and turned again to face the task that he knew had been his ever since Hawklan asked him to prepare the Orthlundyn for war. He looked at the Queen and sought solace in practical matters.

'What about the command of the Muster, lady?' he said.

Sylvriss smiled. 'First, let's ensure they reach us safely,' she replied. 'Then leave my father to me.'

After that, attention turned to the final preparations for the assault on Narsindalvak.

Any form of surprise attack had been discounted at the outset. 'Nothing for days around can hide from Narsindalvak's seeing stones,' Eldric told Loman. 'Especially along the valley. They'll know our entire strength before we even see the tower.'

But Loman's main concern soon turned to Dan-Tor himself. 'From what I've heard and seen of the damage to your city, to be caught in a valley would not even leave us the dubious defence of dispersion against such a weapon.'

He looked at Gulda, who nodded.

'He was bound in some way when he faced us last . . .' Eldric said, though uncertainly.

Loman was blunt. 'Times change, Lord,' he said. '*I* was a smith, *now* I'm something else.'

He turned questioningly to Ryath, the most senior of the Cadwanwr who had returned with the Orthlundyn from Riddin. 'We held the sea that Creost's Power had sent against the Riddinvolk,' the Cadwanwr said. 'And Atelon here learned much from helping Andawyr in direct conflict against Creost. We can give you protection against Oklar.'

'Are you certain?' Loman pressed.

'Of being able to oppose him, yes,' Ryath continued. 'Of victory, of course not. But like you, we've survived one battle and learned from it, and our doubts are only the same as yours about your own army; straightforward and honest and not such as will corrode and impede.'

Loman bowed his head in acknowledgement of Ryath's openness.

Thus, within days, the people who had turned out joyfully to greet their Queen were thronging the streets once more. This time, however, their mood was more sombre as they bade farewell to the first companies of the allied army of High Guards and Orthlundyn leaving to reinforce the regiments already guarding the boundaries of Dan-Tor's northern estates.

Reluctantly, Sylvriss remained at the Palace. Despite her promise to stay and help with the rebuilding of the country, her immediate intention had been to sling her son about her neck and ride off with the troops. However, after a stormy clash of wills, Hylland had prevailed.

'You, madam, can go to Narsindal in a handcart for all I care,' he proclaimed furiously at the height of the fray. 'But your son came too early. He's stronger than he ought to be, by rights, but he needs both you *and* a quiet, civilised existence for a while. The last thing he needs is to be bounced up and down on horseback for hours, and then to spend the rest of his time roughing it in an army camp. Especially in this weather.' He flung his arm towards the rain-streaked window.

Sylvriss's eyes narrowed for a final counter-attack, but Hylland moved in to massacre his weakening opponent. 'I'm well aware of what the Muster women used to do, traditionally, Majesty,' he said. 'Drop their child behind a bush and then mount up and ride on! But I'll wager it's some time since any of them actually did it. And in any case, you're no tough old Muster wife with –'

'Thank you, healer,' Sylvriss said coldly and finally, through clenched teeth. 'We have weighed your advice and have decided to remain in the palace for a little while, for our son's sake. You are dismissed for the moment.'

Hylland bowed stiffly and retreated, victorious but battered and in some considerable disorder.

The army had fewer problems than the Queen's healer as it made its way across Dan-Tor's old estates. The new Goraidin that Yatsu and the other veterans had trained, had been reporting a marked lack of activity for some time, and as the army advanced it found only deserted campsites and abandoned villages.

The journey through the long, claustrophobic pass towards Narsindalvak was similarly uneventful, though they moved carefully and fortified their night camps for fear of ambush. On several occasions also progress was slowed by the need to contend with areas that were still blocked by snow.

Eventually, however, the top of the great tower fortress began to make fitful appearances through the mountain clouds.

Loman sought out Ryath and Atelon. 'You'd better prepare your people,' he said. 'Presumably where Oklar can see, he can act.'

The two Cadwanwr looked at one another and smiled. 'No,' Ryath said, shaking his head. 'It'll be easier for him, true, but he could have acted against us already had he wished. We've been prepared for him for some time now.'

Loman bowed apologetically.

Nevertheless, despite this reassurance, he found it difficult to prevent his gaze from drifting towards the watching fortress as they drew nearer.

'Why've they made no effort to harry us?' he pondered during one of his nightly conferences with the Lords. Their continuing easy progress had been concerning him increasingly. 'The terrain's ideal for it. Small parties raiding at night, or good archers high along the valley sides. They could do a lot of damage in spite of our defences.'

Eldric shrugged. 'Presumably he doesn't want to risk his precious Mathidrin,' he offered unconvincingly.

'Perhaps he hopes to meet us in force nearer the tower?' Arinndier offered.

'The Goraidin have reported no preparations being made,' Loman replied, shaking his head.

There were one or two further, tentative, suggestions then the meeting fell silent.

'Perhaps they've already moved against the Muster?' Hreldar said quietly.

It was a dark thought. Loman nodded slowly. Hreldar, he had heard, had once been fat and jolly. Now, though still heavy, he was solid and hard, and the change had etched lines in his face that gave him a grim aspect, though it vanished like mist in the sunshine when he chose to smile. Loman had already learned that though Hreldar did not speak a great deal, when he did it was usually to some purpose.

'I fear you may be right, Lord,' he said, after a thoughtful pause. 'It's certainly the most likely alternative.' He slapped his knees. 'Unless you've any objections, my friends, I propose we break camp early tomorrow, with a view to moving as soon as the light permits. We can leave a guard with the baggage train and the rest of us can proceed at forced pace. If Dan-Tor has gone to meet the Muster, then the reduced garrison at the tower can be easily contained and we can move to attack his army from the rear. If he's still in the tower, then we can prevent him leaving and keep the pass open for both ourselves and the Muster.'

After the meeting had broken up, Loman turned to Gulda. 'You're very quiet,' he said. 'You've scarcely spoken a word at any of these meetings.'

Gulda looked at him and smiled slightly. 'I'm only a teacher, young Loman,' she said. 'And there's little more I have to teach any of you now. I suspect I'll become even quieter as our campaign progresses.'

Loman looked at her silently, his eyes narrowing distrustfully. 'I don't know who or what you are, Memsa Gulda, bane and terror of my enterprising childhood, but you're certainly not just a teacher.' He tapped his fingers on his chest. 'I may not have the vision of those who've stood next to the Uhriel, but I know that even as I look at you I'm not seeing you truly. Nor ever have.'

Unexpectedly, Gulda's smile opened out into a laugh. It was a happy sound and it filled the simple tent with its rich echoing enjoyment. For an instant, Loman saw again the proud and handsome – no, beautiful – face he had glimpsed when he had burst in upon her at Anderras Darion, his mind whirling with terror and dismay after the labyrinth had rejected him. He found he was lifting his hand almost as if to protect himself from the sight, but it was gone, vanished in some timeless moment, as strangely as it had appeared. He shook his head as if to recapture it.

Gulda's laughter faded, and she stood up. 'Forgive me, Loman,' she said, laying an affectionate hand on his arm. 'I'm afraid my circumstances obliged me to develop a . . . way . . . with men, I make them stand in their own light for their own good.' The residue of her laughter bubbled out as a throaty chuckle.

'Who are you, woman?' Loman said, very quietly and very seriously.

The hand squeezed his arm powerfully. 'Someone who's

either reaching the end of a long, long, journey, or who's about to begin another one, smith,' she replied. 'I'll know which only when we reach Derras Ustramel.'

'No riddles, Memsa,' Loman said, almost plaintively.

Gulda looked at him again. 'What you choose to see is what I am, young Loman. Truly I can tell you no more than that.'

And then she was walking out of the tent before Loman could question her further.

For a moment, he considered going after her, but rejected the idea almost immediately. She would be doing some necessary work somewhere, and if he pursued her she would either chase him away ignominiously or let him trail after her like an uncertain puppy until tiredness got the better of him.

It came to him suddenly that the next time he saw her, he should say, 'Thank you.'

That thought however, was the furthest thing from his mind the following day when Gulda's stick poked him out of his leaden sleep.

'Come on, commander,' said a wilfully malevolent voice. 'Time to set a good example.'

When Loman emerged from his tent it was to a chilly, misty darkness filled with the clamour of the waking camp and the mixed smells of damp mountains and cooking.

With the brief vividness that only a scent can bring, Loman was back in the mountains of Orthlund with Isloman, on one of their youthful camping expeditions, full of ridiculous laughter in an infinitely larger world, and long before they became men and were both drawn to the same blonde tresses and blue eyes; long before they quarrelled and were reconciled; and longer still before the coming of Hawklan and the opening of Anderras Darion . . .

'There've been no incidents overnight.' Arinndier's voice scattered the memory, though it left a pleasant warmth in its wake that made Loman smile. Whatever the future, there was little wrong with the present, and the past had been good.

'Good,' he said, speaking his thought to serve as a reply to Arinndier. 'Just remind everyone to be especially vigilant today. The faster we move, the more careful we must be.'

It proved to be a needless injunction, however. Loman sent the Goraidin and the Helyadin ahead of the column in force, not with any pretensions to making a surreptitious assault on the fortress, but to secure the rocky flanks of the valley from ambush. They encountered nothing, however, and within hours signalled back the message that Narsindalvak itself seemed to be deserted.

'Tell them not to go any nearer,' Ryath said urgently. 'We can't protect them from here if they're attacked by Oklar.'

Loman nodded, then ordered the leading companies of infantry forward at the double, with himself and some of the Cadwanwr riding vanguard with the cavalry.

Thus, well before the day was through, the first contingents of the army approached Narsindalvak. Loman stared up at the great Fyordyn watch tower. Its broad, sprawling roots seemed, like Anderras Darion, to grow straight from the rocks before curving gradually into the body of the tower itself and soaring high above the neighbouring mountains. At the top, the walls flared out again to form the base of the high-domed Watch Hall. All around the tower, at every level, rings of windows stared out blankly, ominously, over the mountains. It was a dizzying spectacle and Loman found himself leaning backwards in his saddle as he looked at it.

Fyndal, one of the Helyadin, emerged from behind a tumbled mass of rocks.

'It looks empty,' he said. 'We've seen no movement of any kind since we arrived.'

Loman turned to Ryath.

The Cadwanwr sniffed, then half-closed his eyes as he looked up at the tower. 'I can feel no presence,' he said. 'Oklar isn't here.'

Loman looked at him intently. 'He's not here,' the Cadwanwr confirmed positively.

Loman grimaced. If Oklar was gone, then he could even now be leading the Mathidrin against the Muster. Could Oslang fend off the Uhriel on his own? Could Urthryn deploy his cavalry effectively in the unknown and mountainous countryside? Unanswerable and urgent questions, yet he could not gallop off in search of the answers until he had answered the other question – how many men remained in this seemingly empty fortress? He gazed up at it again; it could contain thousands, ready to surge out and cut his passing army in two, or fall on their rear as they marched to the relief of the Muster.

'We'll have to purge this place before we can move on, Lord,' he said to Eldric. 'And as quickly as we can.'

Eldric nodded and took charge. 'That's the main entrance,' he said, pointing to a wide ramp that swept up to a large double door. 'But it can only be opened from the inside. Seal the ramp with a shield line and archers, with pikes at the rear, then we'll send the Goraidin in through those two smaller doors at the side. We have the keys to those and they're the only other entrances.'

'I'll go with them,' Atelon said, his eyes widening excitedly, then, more seriously. 'There might be traps laid there that your men can't see.'

Eldric looked at Ryath who, albeit rather disapprovingly, nodded.

Eldric conceded suspiciously. 'This is no game, Cadwanwr,' he said sternly. 'Those are hard, tough fighters, who'll have to put themselves at risk to protect you. You can go if you're needed, but do exactly as you're told. And be alert.'

Loman watched the exchange in silence. He was well content to leave the whole operation to the Fyordyn; it was their fortress and they knew its layout.

Soon the archers were crouching behind their shields in anticipation of the double doors crashing open and some wild enemy charging out in force.

The Goraidin flitted to the side doors.

There was a sudden silence and then, at their own signal, the Goraidin threw open the two doors and charged inside.

Loman watched as they disappeared from view; he could see them moving left and right alternately as they passed through the doors, shields raised defensively. He saw Atelon stumble and an unkind hand drag him upright again.

Some shouting could be heard inside, then there was another silence. Loman became aware for the first time, of the sound of the wind moaning about the great tower. His horse shifted a little, its feet clattering slightly on the rocky ground.

Then, slowly, the double doors began to swing open. The archers prepared to fire, and a ripple went through the waiting pikes, but a solitary figure appeared in the widening gap. It was one of the Goraidin. He raised his shield in a beckoning gesture and shouted something. Only the word '. . . empty . . .' reached Loman.

The archers however, cheered and began moving forward.

Loman gazed around in admiration as he rode with the others into the huge ante-chamber that was served by the doors. Great ribbed walls arched high above him, wrapped by several tiers of balconies, and the space semed to reduce the entering army to echoing insignificance.

A raucous cry above made Loman start suddenly, but it was

only the Goraidin working their way methodically through the balconies and their adjoining corridors.

When the rest of the army arrived, the lower part of the tower had been searched and found to be empty, and the Goraidin, accompanied now by the Helyadin, were moving rapidly up through the many floors of the great building.

Finally they reached the Watch Hall itself and found it, too, deserted. Their relief at finding this, however, was marred by what they found there.

In the barracks and offices occupying the lower floors of the tower, the only sign of the previous occupants was the squalor and filth they had left. But in the Watch Hall they had made a determined effort to destroy everything that could be destroyed.

Many of the smaller seeing stones had been smashed, together with their ornate supporting frames, and the larger ones had been cracked and damaged.

Eldric walked around the Hall, his face ablaze with rage. 'We're blind,' he said bitterly. 'We haven't the craftsmen to repair these things. And we'll have to tie up men and resources in look-out chains now.'

Loman looked at him anxiously, then at the other Fyordyn, wandering aimlessly around the Hall. The wanton destruction seemed to be disturbing them all profoundly.

Abruptly, Eldric bent down, picked up a heavy fragment of a seeing stone, and hurled it violently at a temporarily rigged globe nearby. 'And get those damn things out of here!' he roared. 'Every one!'

The globe burst noisily, discharging a small cloud of unpleasant smelling smoke, and sending glittering shards tinkling across the floor. For a moment it sparked angrily then with a splutter it fell silent.

Eldric caught Loman's eye. He waved an angry arm around the scene, then the rage seemed to leave him abruptly and he slumped a little. 'I'm sorry, Loman,' he said. 'A childish outburst. But this place lies at the heart of our neglected duties. And this destruction is a measure of it even more than the damaged heart of Vakloss. If only we'd seen Dan-Tor's hand in the abandoning of the Watch. If only we'd opposed those who wanted this place closed and forgotten. If, if, if . . .' He picked up another piece of broken stone but this time he turned it over in his hand tenderly. 'It's as if we'd done all this ourselves.'

Loman did not attempt to console him. He knew that he could not truly understand the Fyordyn's distress. Instead, he ignored it and turned to a large wall bracket which had been badly bent out of shape. Wrapping his powerful hands around it he gave it one slow, twisting, heave, and restored it almost exactly to its original shape and position.

Then he did the same to its partner and stood back to examine his work with a narrow critical eye. Eldric watched him, his immediate grief being slowly set aside by amazement at this display of both strength and skill.

As he moved to repair other pieces of damaged metalwork, Loman threw a piece of seeing stone to Fyndal, standing nearby. 'I'm no hand as a rock judge, Fyn,' he said. 'But we should be able to do something about all this. Show that to some of the senior Guild members and get them up here quickly.'

'We might be able to help with those, too,' said Atelon, still breathless and flushed from his rampage through the building with the Goraidin.

With a grunt, Loman straightened another support. 'Your own smiths can attend to most of this work, Eldric,' he said. 'In the meantime, we command the heights and we have our Orthlundyn shadow vision and our own simple seeing stones. Set men to plain, old-fashioned watching and let's get the Goraidin and the Helyadin out looking for which way Dan-Tor has gone before we lose the light. If this place is empty then it means he's launched his full army against the Muster; Mathidrin, militia, and your renegade Lords with their High Guards.'

Loman's brutal summary brought Eldric and the others out of their preoccupation, and within the hour the Watch Hall was busy with stone and metal workers striving to undo the Mathidrin's orgy of destruction. At the large windows stood some of the keener eyed Orthlundyn, peering through seeing stones into the gathering Narsindal gloom.

Outside, standing on a high, rocky, outcrop, Loman waited for the return of the scouting patrol that had gone out in search of Dan-Tor's army.

He found it hard to be patient and kept slapping his hands together and pacing up and down. Now that his caution in moving along the valley had proved to be unnecessary, he began to reproach himself for the delay and to fret about the harm that the Muster might be suffering at the hands of Dan-Tor's army.

That he could have done nothing other offered him little consolation, though a small voice kept repeating it to him, adding, 'And you're too tired to think straight now.'

I should have stayed at my forge, came a counter-blast.

He kicked a small stone. Where was that patrol, he thought, yet again. It shouldn't have taken them this long to find the trail of an army. What were they playing at? Had they perhaps fallen into an ambush?

He shook his head. No, not those troops, it wasn't possible. But hard on the heels of this came an even darker thought: was perhaps this whole venture no more than an elaborate ruse by Dan-Tor to lure the allied army into Narsindalvak and trap them there?

He stopped pacing, and his stomach turned over. It was a thought that had not occurred to him before. Just as he had been prepared to seal up Dan-Tor's army, so also could Dan-Tor seal up his! That would leave him free to attack the Muster and to maintain command of the valley for a future invasion into Fyorlund.

Below him, he could see the almost chaotic activity swirling around the foot of the great tower as the army moved into its new barracks. His eye drifted upwards past the many windows, now lit and shining out brightly into the fading light. They also were bustling with activity.

The army was dispersed throughout the building and around the approaches to it. It was in no position to respond quickly to a surprise attack.

A determined charge up the valley would scatter most of those outside and drive the remainder inside.

Loman grimaced. He'd not been that careless, surely? He'd placed sentries and look-outs on such of the neighbouring crags as could reasonably be reached, but . . . ?

Distant shouts began to break into his tumbling thoughts.

Look-outs!

Their message reached him.

'Armed column approaching, fast!'

# *Chapter 26*

Hawklan stood motionless in the craggy tunnel for some time, then slowly drew his Sword. The hilt was alive in his hand again. As he looked at it, the twisting threads glittered and wound their way far beyond his vision into the twinkling oceans of stars.

Andawyr moved to his side. 'We're back in the depths of our own time now,' he said. 'Into dangers that we can at least, perhaps understand.'

'The Vrwystin a Goleg lies along here?' Hawklan said softly, inclining his head along the tunnel.

Andawyr nodded. 'Something of His does, and Isloman has heard the rock on which it lives.'

'Then tomorrow we go this way,' Hawklan said. 'What do you know of this creature?'

Andawyr looked at him unhappily. 'A great deal, and very little,' he said. 'A great deal from our library about what it can do and how it uses the Old Power. But very little – nothing – is known about its . . . heart, its centre . . . even what it looks like. And these creatures are like the Uhriel, they exist in planes not accessible to us.'

'Do you know how we can destroy it?' Hawklan asked.

The question did nothing to ease Andawyr's self-reproach.

'Like Sumeral Himself, it's mortal and it will fall to the right weapon, or if the force is great enough,' he said.

'It will fall to this, then,' Hawklan said, hefting the Sword.

'Or Isloman's arrows,' Andawyr said, nodding. 'Or the Old Power. It fears the Old Power turned against it; I know that since our encounter at the Gretmearc.'

'But –?' Hawklan prompted, catching the reservation in the Cadwanwr's voice.

'But I daren't use the Power for fear of Him,' Andawyr said. 'Even though we're deep here.'

Hawklan nodded. 'I understand,' he said. 'We must tread carefully, and make no plans?'

'I'm afraid so,' Andawyr replied.

Hawklan turned to Isloman. 'This rock that you hear,

Isloman, how dangerous is it? Is it what the Lords spoke of in their mines?'

Isloman nodded. 'I only know of it from my lore,' he replied. 'And from faint murmurs in some rocks I've found. I don't know how dangerous it is, but I do know that its power can't be seen or felt and that its effects linger and *will* kill us eventually if we stay near too long.'

Hawklan sheathed his sword and turned to walk back to the camp. 'So we must tread carefully, make no plans, and *hurry*,' he said ruefully.

The following day, however, they set off in good heart. The prospect of nearing the end of their underground journey and, to some extent, even the apprehension about the creature they were seeking out, added a new purposefulness to their march.

Progress, however, was not easy. As if through being nearer to the craggy surface of the mountains, the passages and tunnels that Andawyr led them through, were jumbled and disordered. Frequently they had to squeeze through narrow gaps and crawl on their bellies beneath rock ceilings that lowered over them with crushing oppressiveness.

And it was wetter. Small streams trickled down some of the passages, and damp patches glistened in their torchlight, like great eyes in the tunnel walls.

Gradually, Hawklan began to realise that he no longer needed to follow Andawyr. The aura of corruption that had come faintly to him the previous evening, was guiding him forward now as if it were a rope tied about him.

Isloman however, despite his best endeavours, was becoming increasingly nervous, as were the other Orthlundyn.

'Either it's my imagination, or those rocks are bad,' Athyr said eventually. 'I've never heard rock song like this before. It's . . . frightening, almost.' Tybek and the two women nodded in agreement.

'It's not your imagination,' Isloman admitted. 'And I think it's going to get worse before it gets better. Just keep moving.'

The brief exchange meant nothing to the Fyordyn, however, though the anxiety of their companions was necessarily infectious.

Then abruptly they were clambering into a long straight tunnel.

'This is not natural,' Isloman said immediately, his face pained.

He signalled Andawyr to shine his torch on the wall. As he

ran his hands over the rough surface he frowned. 'This has been torn out by uncaring hands a long time ago,' he said. He wrapped his arms about himself as if suddenly chilled. 'There's such pain here. Even after all this time.'

Hawklan took his arm.

'I'll be all right,' Isloman said. 'This is the same torment that I felt from the mines, but now I can accept it.' He turned to the other Orthlundyn who were beginning to look decidedly unhappy. 'As can you. Trust me. I know you hear only faintly, but you hear enough to sense truth.'

Suddenly the Guild's First Carver, Isloman opened his great arms as if to embrace the four Orthlundyn, like so many nervous children. Then he bent forward and spoke softly to them. Hawklan and the others sensing that their presence might be an intrusion, moved away a little, though Hawklan caught occasional words from the highly technical language that the carvers lapsed into when they were discussing their work.

When Isloman had finished, his charges, though still nervous, seemed to be greatly heartened. He looked at Hawklan and smiled reassuringly.

'That way,' he said.

'I know,' Hawklan replied. 'Dim the torches and move quietly.'

'We will go ahead.' The voice of the Alphraan made Hawklan start; they had been silent so long.

'I'll come with you,' came Dar-volci's deep voice in reply and, before anyone could speak, the felci bounded off into the darkness.

'I'll stay here with you, dear boy,' Gavor said, comfortingly to Hawklan.

They walked along the tunnel in silence for a long way. It was relentlessly straight and sloped very gently upwards. After a while, it seemed to Hawklan that the corruption in the air about him hung so thick that it was tangibly burdening his every movement. Andawyr too, seemed to be suffering in some way. The two men encouraged each other forward with an occasional shared glance.

The Orthlundyn also, were growing increasingly uneasy, although Isloman's words seemed to be sustaining them. The Fyordyn, however, were unaffected, though they were well aware that their companions were experiencing increasing difficulties which they could not share.

'Douse your torches, and wait,' came the voice of the Alphraan abruptly.

After a brief hesitation, Hawklan signalled to the two torchbearers, and once again the group was plunged into the profound darkness that pervaded this underworld.

Slowly, as they waited in silence, a faint glow appeared in the distance.

'Go forward quietly,' said the Alphraan.

The group did as the voice bid them, moving cautiously through the disorienting darkness, and keeping their eyes fixed on the distant glow.

As they neared it, the light gradually began to grow larger and take form. Soon they saw that it marked a sharp bend to the tunnel and that the light was coming from the far side.

The sense of corruption began to throb in Hawklan's head and he laid his hand on his Sword.

'No,' said the Alphraan softly. 'Look first . . . carefully.'

Reluctantly, Hawklan released the Sword and signalled the others to wait. They laid down their packs as he moved silently to the inner wall of the bend and cautiously peered round it.

The tunnel ended a few paces away, apparently joining some large well-lit chamber. At first the light was too bright for him to distinguish anything, but as his eyes adjusted he realised that the floor of the tunnel ended suddenly and that the light was coming from some source above.

Beckoning the others, he moved forward warily towards the end of the tunnel. It opened on to a narrow ledge and he paused and looked quickly from side to side before dropping on to his knees to peer over the edge.

With a sudden sharp breath he withdrew his head and made a hasty signal for silence. Then he motioned Andawyr to look.

As the Cadwanwr leaned forward cautiously, he started slightly, but made no other sign of surprise.

The tunnel had emerged about halfway up a large, roughly circular chamber. It was apparently natural though its walls were packed with numerous other tunnel openings and striped with ledges similar to the one they were lying on. These were joined in some places by steps and in others by precarious wooden ladders lashed together with ropes. Around the chambers, rows of Dan-Tor's globes shed their ghastly light.

Dominating the scene, however, were the birds. Hundreds of them, perched, silent and still, on the lower ledges and the rocks and boulders that strewed the floor of the chamber.

Their yellow eyes were blank and dead, yet somehow watchful.

However, Hawklan scarcely noticed the birds. Instead his gaze was drawn inexorably to the far end of the chamber. There, a shapeless, putrid yellow mass welled obscenely out of the rock wall. Around it, the rock was blackened and stained, and split by pallid white-edged cracks into irregular blocks, giving it a peculiarly diseased appearance. Fanning out around the mass and burrowing into the surrounding rock was a dense web of fine tendrils, and from its centre hung a single excrescence like a closed flower bud.

In Hawklan's eyes, the whole thing seemed to be rending its way into the present reality, just as had Oklar, Creost and Dar-Hastuin. He felt nauseous.

As Hawklan and Andawyr watched, the mass quivered slightly and Hawklan became aware of the cacophonous din that had filled his mind when he had pursued the bird through the Gretmearc. It was like a myriad alien voices full of hatred and venom and it rose to a climax that made him raise his hands to cover his ears, though he knew it would be pointless. Then, abruptly, it stopped, although Hawklan sensed a continuing tremor of disgust and loathing that was coming from some other source. It was the Alphraan, he realised. They too were reacting in some way to the creature and their reaction was so violent that they could not keep it hidden from him.

Slowly the bud began to convulse, and Hawklan saw that it was opening. With each pulse it opened a little further until finally it was spread wide, though the perfection of its shape was somehow disgusting where it should have been beautiful.

At its centre was curled a small brown mass. Suddenly, and without any other movement, two yellow eyes opened in the mass, and then with a violent wriggle it unwound to reveal itself as one of the birds. Hawklan felt cold as he noted that it bore none of the dishevelled incomprehension of a new-born creature. Indeed, with its wide open eyes it seemed to be obscenely whole. Then its beak gaped and, emitting a nerve-jarring screech, it flew up on to a nearby rock.

There was a flutter somewhere else in the chamber, and Hawklan knew that one of the birds had left as this had taken up its position with the others.

Andawyr edged away from the ledge and wiped his hand across his damp forehead. He motioned the others back around the bend in the tunnel. They looked at him expectantly, but he shook his head.

'I don't know what to do,' he whispered, his face haunted. 'I'll have to think.'

'We haven't much time,' Isloman said. 'This is a bad place.'

'I know, I know,' Andawyr replied crossly.

'I think I could hit it with an arrow,' Hawklan said, but Andawyr shook his head.

'I think those . . . tendrils . . . connect it to this world,' he said. 'We must cut them to destroy it, but how are we going to reach it with those birds there . . .'

'We will help,' came the Alphraan's voice. 'This is an old enemy and many debts are to be paid here.'

Though the voice was clear and distinct, there was an aura of rage permeating about it that made everyone present quail, though Hawklan detected also great fear.

'What will you do?' Andawyr asked hesitantly.

'Watch and be prepared to strike, when we tell you,' said the voice without further explanation, although again the words were full of meaning beyond their apparent content; this time they were indisputably commanding. 'We must join it to know it.' Then, a caution. 'Only Hawklan must go. Only he can wield the Sword truly. Use it as the Cadwanwr had said: sever the tendrils that hold it to the rock.'

Andawyr gave a resigned nod and motioned the others back to the edge.

'Make no sudden movements,' he whispered needlessly.

At first, nothing seemed to be happening, and Hawklan screwed up his eyes in the unpleasant globelight to scan the steps and ladders that would carry him to the chamber floor quickly. He pulled his gloves tight. Once or twice, out of the corner of his eye, he thought he saw tiny figures flitting about the chamber, but when he turned to look directly at them, there was nothing there.

Then the mass began to quiver again and Hawklan felt the beginning of the dreadful noise curling into his mind. But this time, as it grew, it changed. It was the same and yet different in some way that he could not identify. The hatred that filled it was in some way being sated, and filled with a deep, satisfied, lethargy. The quivering ceased but the noise continued like a foul lullaby.

Andawyr tapped him and nodded towards the birds. As he looked, he saw their eyes were slowly closing. Quickly he looked again at the route he must take should the Alphraan need him.

Then all the eyes were closed and Hawklan waited expectantly.

'The hold is tenuous,' said the Alphraan, very softly. 'And taxes us greatly. Strike now, Hawklan. The rest of you be silent and still.'

Before the voice had ended, Hawklan was on his feet and racing silently along the narrow ledge. He reached the first vertical ladder and almost slithered down it.

Dacu drew in a low breath and clenched his hands.

As he landed, Hawklan rolled over the edge of the ledge.

Despite the Alphraan's injunction, there was a gasp from the group.

But Hawklan was only lowering himself on to the ledge below; it would save him precious seconds.

Andawyr closed his eyes.

Then there was only one long ladder to reach the floor. Hawklan bounced down it four rungs at a time, silently and smoothly.

Landing, he turned and began the brief journey towards the loathsome heart of the Vrwystin a Goleg, drawing the Sword as he stepped delicately among the apparently sleeping birds.

As he reached the shapeless mass, the awful presence of the creature nearly overwhelmed him, and even though it had been changed by the Alphraan into an eerie sleep song, the Vrwystin's jabbering chorus still filled his head. Hawklan found himself struggling against an almost paralysing surge of anger and fear as he tried to lift the Sword to begin his assault.

Abruptly, and without a sound, the bud that had produced the bird, swung up and pointed itself at him like a blind serpent. Hawklan hesitated, hypnotised by this eyeless intelligence.

The chorus in his head changed. He sensed the Alphraan faltering but, out of the din, a tiny warning whisper darted towards him and, without thinking, he spun round, pressing himself flat against the wall. At the same instant the bud opened and spat out a stream of dark yellow fluid.

He watched in horror as the fluid landed on the floor. It hissed and bubbled for a moment and then sank out of sight into the hole it was dissolving. He tightened his grip of the Sword and looked back at the bud. It had closed again but was moving from side to side as if searching.

The Vrwystin's song changed again and Hawklan sensed a subtle stirring amongst the birds.

Still leaning against the wall, he raised the Sword to strike off the bud. As he did so, a fine tendril emerged from the wall and wrapped itself around his other hand. He started at the sudden contact and was about to bring the Sword down to sever it when he felt it begin to tighten.

With a frantic tug he tore his hand out of the glove. The tendril withdrew into the wall, cutting the glove in half.

Hawklan jumped away from the wall desperately, but when he turned he found himself staring into the mouth of the bud. It had a disgustingly voluptuous quality that both repelled and held him.

It was opening, he knew, but he knew also that his perceptions were racing far beyond the ability of his body to move. He would not be able to respond quickly enough. The image of the dissolving, bubbling rock, rose to cloud his vision and impede him further with its terror.

Suddenly, the bud juddered away from him. Something had seized it. Hawklan heard the familiar snap of closing teeth.

Dar-volci!

Hawklan's mind cleared. The felci had his powerful foreclaws about the stem of the bud and was trying to stretch it out and bite it. His fur was standing on end, his eyes were savage, and his lips were curled back to reveal his terrible teeth as Hawklan had never seen them before. It was an awesome sight.

For all its seeming dormancy, however, the Vrwystin was not defenceless. The stem writhed away from the felci's murderous attack and the bud tried to turn towards him. The movement jerked Dar-volci off his feet and it was obvious that the response was far more powerful than he had expected.

'The tendrils, Hawklan,' he shouted making another snapping lunge at the twisting stem. 'Cut the tendrils.'

The bud spat out another stream of fluid which Dar-volci only avoided by releasing the stem and leaping into the air. As he landed he seized the stem again just as it was retreating into the body of the Vrwystin. He tugged at it savagely, but as he twisted round to bite it, his grip slipped and it retreated again.

Hawklan lifted the Sword to help in the ensuing struggle, but the felci was twisting and turning with incredible speed, his jaws snapping savagely, while the bud was writhing and spitting in vicious counter-attacks as it tried to withdraw. The combat was one of instinctive animal responses and was far too fast for Hawklan to intervene without risk of injuring the felci.

'The tendrils, man!' Dar-volci shouted again angrily in a momentary pause.

Abruptly, the Alphraan's voice rang out in a plaintive cry. 'We are failing, Hawklan,' it said. 'It is too strong. We cannot maintain its awful dream. Strike now, in the name of pity –'

Hawklan lifted the Sword to hack through the quivering tendrils, but as he did so the Vrwystin's clamour changed again, and the sleeping birds suddenly rose up into the chamber in a swirling shrieking cloud, their blank yellow eyes wide, but oddly sightless.

The bud also seemed to gain new strength and Dar-volci, clinging onto the stem desperately, began to be drawn inexorably into the body of the Vrwystin. Some of the tendrils separated from the wall and began to wave about as if searching.

Hawklan swung the Sword. It cut through several of the tendrils, but Hawklan felt a resistance seemingly quite disproportionate to their thickness and number.

He hacked through another cluster. The screaming of the birds around him intensified, though mingled with it he could now hear the Alphraan's song. Some quality in it, however, told him that while they were still restraining the creature, some dreadful price was being paid, and soon they must fail utterly.

The birds in their erratic uncontrolled flight were beginning to crash into him painfully.

Dar-volci was still heaving on the steadily retreating stem, and swearing profoundly. Suddenly the stem flicked loose making him stagger backwards. As he scrabbled to recover his balance the stem flicked again and coiled a loop around him.

Several of the birds collided with Hawklan simultaneously, sending him staggering.

Dar-volci cried out as the coil began to tighten.

'Pull, Dar!' came a raucous shout from above, Hawklan looked up as he clambered back to his feet, flailing his arms against the blundering birds. Tumbling down from the high ledge was Gavor. He seemed to be falling like an untidy black bundle, but even amid the turmoil part of Hawklan soared at the consummate flying skill of the great raven as his seemingly disordered fall carried him unhindered through the swirling mass of yellow-eyed birds.

With a great cry of pain and fury, Dar-volci drove his back legs into the now pulsing body of the Vrwystin and heaved on the stem with one final effort. Slowly the stem was drawn out. Abruptly, Gavor's tumbling fall became a swooping glide. With his great black wings extended, he arced around steeply to avoid the rock face then, with his legs swung forward, he skimmed past Dar-volci like a rushing wind.

His glittering black spurs sliced effortlessly through the outstretched stem.

Dar-volci tumbled to the floor and, with a cry, scrambled to one side to avoid the gushing stream of venom that flowed from the severed stem. But suddenly the creature was awake and in mortal agony. Its appalling will filled the chamber. There was a terrible cry from the Alphraan, and then the eyes of the birds were bright, horrible, and focused, and their milling chaos malignly purposeful.

For a fearful moment, Hawklan stood motionless, paralysed by the dreadful clamour of the hateful language that came washing into his mind. But as the birds began to converge on him, their very movement seemed to break him free and with a great roar he slashed through the remaining tendrils with one single whistling blow.

The birds swept up the roof of the chamber, as if each part of the creature was seeking to avoid the death that was coming to it from the centre. The sound of their wings beating frenziedly against the unyielding rock filled the chamber, then there was silence, both in the chamber and in Hawklan's mind, and the birds began falling through the garish globelight like a ghastly, thudding, snowstorm.

Hawklan slid to the floor, shaking.

Slowly other, commonplace, sounds impinged on the silence. Looking up, Hawklan saw Dacu and the others scrambling along the ledges and down the ladders towards him.

Gavor landed on his shoulder. 'Splendid stuff, dear boy,' he said, poking him energetically with his wooden leg. 'Did you *see* that?' He extended his wings and uttered a gleeful, 'Wheee . . . And with a damaged pectoral as well.' Then, leaning forward: 'You all right, Dar?'

'I think so,' said Dar-volci standing up and running an anxious foreclaw over himself. 'That was timely intervention, crow.'

'My pleasure entirely, rat,' Gavor said headily. 'That was a rare piece of tulip wrestling you were doing, but I thought I'd better help when it got a little fraught at the end.'

Dar-volci gave a grunting chuckle, but winced as he

dropped back on to all-fours. Hawklan crawled forward and ran his hands over him gently.

After a moment, Dar-volci started to nuzzle his arm and rumble with pleasure. Hawklan smiled. 'You've got the same as I had,' he pronounced. 'Bruised ribs. They'll not be much fun, but they'll mend in a day or so.'

Then the others were around them, a panting Andawyr last. 'Are you all right, Dar?' he said, crouching down and taking the felci's pointed head gently in his two hands.

Dar-volci bared his massive teeth in a chattering grin of pleasure and triumph by way of answer, then clambered up the Cadwanwr and draped himself around his neck.

'Finish that thing, Hawklan,' Andawyr said savagely, nodding towards the leaking remains of the Vrwystin. 'I shudder to think what price has been paid to create and keep it, but it'll take no further toll of anyone or anything.'

With a few strokes, Hawklan hacked the remains of the creature to pieces.

Tybek looked at the pitted surface of the rock. 'These root things go right into the rock,' he said. 'Can it grow again from them?'

Andawyr shook his head. 'No,' he said. 'They're not roots. It's not a plant. It's a living, intelligent, creature. Or rather, was. Now it's truly dead and Oklar's greater vision is blinded. I doubt he'll consider it worthwhile to attempt to breed another. All we have to fear now are ordinary mortal eyes spying our travels.'

'Ah . . .' The faint sound echoed round the chamber. It was weak but it was full of relief at this unequivocal reassurance by the Cadwanwr. Hawklan grimaced in self-reproach at his forgetfulness. 'Alphraan,' he cried out. 'You're hurt. Let me help you.'

Even through the weakness in the voice, a hint of amusement could be felt. 'You cannot help us more, Hawklan,' it said gratefully. 'We take joy in your triumph over the Vrwystin. It is an old wrong righted and a small repayment for the return of our heartland. But we were too few and the battle against its will in that awful dream has spent us utterly. We must join the Great Song that will come to fill these mountains as the families spread forth.'

The words, however, were but a shadow of the true content of the Alphraan's speech. The sounds were rich with both sorrow and happiness, deep gratitude for deeds done, and stirring excitement for unknowable things yet to come. To the hearers it was almost unbearably poignant.

'Damn you, Alphraan, no,' Hawklan shouted, running forward towards the middle of the chamber. 'You mustn't die. Let me help.'

'You cannot,' said the voice, growing fainter. 'Go now to destroy Him, healer, we're beyond you. Our parting here is not your dying though it is both as sad and as joyous. We must go now to ensure that the way is truly marked.'

Fainter still.

'We could not have gone beyond the mountains, Hawklan. Grieve not. The Song prospers. Farewell Hawklan. Ethriss's chosen . . . Farewell sky prince . . . felci . . . blessed felci . . . light be with you . . . all.'

And, with a note like the infinitely dwindling resonance of a delicately struck bell, they were gone. Hawklan stood gazing round the silent chamber, his eyes glistening in the brightness and his face drawn and pained with the aching emptiness that the parting had left inside him.

No one spoke. For a while, ordinary words would be little more than a desecration of the subtle silence that the Alphraan had left.

Isloman was the first to move. He looked around the chamber, and rubbed his arms nervously. 'We must go,' he said in a throaty whisper. 'This place is bad.'

Hawklan nodded and, slowly sheathing his Sword, looked at Andawyr. The Cadwanwr wiped his hand across his eyes and then rubbed his forehead. He looked up at the dark mouths of the tunnel entrance gaping into the chamber.

'None of these tunnels are natural,' he said eventually. 'They run with no regard for Theowart's will. It's harder to understand the way.'

'Let's just go upwards, then,' Tybek said urgently.

Hawklan shot him an angry look, but Andawyr shrugged. 'It'll suffice,' he said. 'Far be it from me to dispute the worth of such promptings. You've been underground a long time.'

It took them quite a time to climb up to one of the higher tunnels, having first to retrieve their packs and then to negotiate several ladders which were far from safe. There were also various ledges which Andawyr, in particular, would have preferred to be substantially wider now that he was no longer driven by the combination of excitement and concern that had carried him downwards so quickly.

'Let me rest a moment,' he said, puffing with both relief and effort when they reached their destination. 'I think I'll know better where to go when I'm free of the light of those appalling globes.' He looked at Isloman. 'You say he filled Vakloss with those things?'

Isloman nodded.

Andawyr shook his head in pained disbelief. 'Your poor people,' he said to Dacu.

'I don't understand,' Dacu said, slightly perplexed.

'Nor do I fully,' Andawyr said, sitting down with a grunt. 'It's one of many things we'll need to think about when this is over.' He shook his head reflectively. 'Only He would think to use light as a weapon.' Then, more positively: 'Still, you're free of them now. I doubt their effects were permanent.'

Dacu did not pursue the matter, and a brief hand signal silenced Tirke before he began. Whatever Andawyr did not know, he could not tell. Questioning was therefore pointless.

After a brief rest, they moved on again. Once away from the globes, Andawyr did indeed become more confident in his leading, though it was still obviously harder for him than it had been, and although there were far fewer junctions and branches than before, he paused at each for much longer.

Anxious to be above ground now that their presence would not be so easily detected, the members of the group became increasingly fretful at these delays.

'It can't be helped,' Andawyr said eventually, cutting through the unspoken criticism. 'These tunnels follow the logic of the men who made them and they ring with pain. I need your help, not your foot-shuffling criticism. You Orthlundyn at least should –'

His protest was ended prematurely as a massive concussion followed by a rumbling roar suddenly thundered through the tunnel. Dust swirled up from the floor and fragments fell from the roof.

Instinctively everyone reached out to the solid rock walls for support, but they too were shaking, and when after a few seconds the rumbling faded away, one or two of the group were looking decidedly unwell.

'What was that?' Hawklan said breathlessly, looking at Isloman.

Before Isloman could reply, a warm acrid blast of air blew along the tunnel, carrying with it more dust and fragments.

Hawklan turned again to Isloman when the strange wind had passed.

'We must be near a working face,' Isloman said. 'That was an explosion, but . . . I'd have expected to hear people working.' He shook his head. 'And it was so powerful –'

More concussions interrupted his conjecture, though they were less severe than the first.

'Never mind what it is,' Tirke said. 'Let's get out of here.'

It was a sentiment shared by everyone, but Andawyr pointed in the direction the disturbance had come from. 'That's the way we have to go,' he said.

With mixed feelings they set off again. From time to time, further concussions and blasts of warm air struck them, though none were as severe as the first.

'Whatever it is. That's not rock winning that's going on,' Isloman said after a while. 'Something bad is happening.'

As he spoke, they came to the end of the tunnel and found themselves in an open space. The torchlight revealed that it was rectangular and, quite obviously, hand excavated. Several neatly circular tunnels entered it. The air was thick with newly disturbed dust, and the torches carved strange solid shadows through it.

Andawyr walked round pensively as he had at previous junctions. As he did so, two further small concussions shook the chamber, but they echoed so that it was not possible to determine which of the tunnels they emanated from.

'Come on!' Tirke said urgently, though half to himself. 'This place is beginning to crush the life out of me.'

'Shut up!' Andawyr said angrily. 'I'm trying to –'

Hawklan stepped forward suddenly, raising his hand for silence. 'Listen,' he said. 'Foosteps. Running.'

Scarcely were the words out of his mouth than a figure emerged from one of the tunnels at the far side of the chamber.

It was a Mandroc. Behind it, other figures were emerging into the dusty torchlight.

# Chapter 27

'Armed column approaching, fast!'

The shouted message chiming with his own alarmed thoughts, Loman turned towards the look-out.

'Confirm!' he signalled.

The look-out signalled back. 'Confirmed. Armed column approaching from the east.' A single finger directed upwards indicated that the message had originated from the Watch Hall high above.

Loman breathed out. Whoever was coming, must at least be some distance away. It was no ambush.

From the east, he mused. It must be Dan-Tor returning after his encounter with the Muster. He cursed himself again for his caution in travelling so slowly along the valley. What damage had that monster done?

He dashed the thought aside. Whatever Dan-Tor might have done to the Muster, he would find that he had no base to return to and a warm reception waiting for him.

He gazed down into the valley below. Hreldar was riding with some of his High Guard. Loman put his fingers in his mouth and blew a penetrating whistle.

The Lord looked up immediately.

'Get your duty companies along the valley at the double,' Loman signalled. 'Prepare a pike wall and archers to meet approaching column. Reinforcements to follow.'

Hreldar acknowledged the signal and began issuing orders to his Guards. Loman nodded, well satisfied. Hreldar's High Guard were not the most loved of the regiments in the allied army, but fired by their Lord's peculiarly special loathing for Dan-Tor, they were fierce and angry fighters.

He turned and saw that the look-out was receiving further news from another signaller. He intercepted it. The column had moved out of sight of the observers in the Watch Hall. He swore under his breath. Until the seeing stones there could be repaired, those laid out in the adjacent mountains would be ineffective and only straight line-of-sight observation would be possible.

He signalled to the look-out to find such companies as were

ready to hand and have them sent along the valley to join Hreldar. 'And some of the Cadwanwr!' he added as an almost frantic afterthought. Then he scrambled down the rocks, commandeered a horse from a bewildered trooper and rode off himself.

It did not take him long to reach Hreldar and his men at a narrow defile some way down the valley. The Lord was disposing his men in defensive order.

'What's happening?' he asked.

Loman told him. 'I don't know whether it's all or part of his army,' he said. 'Or what state they're in. And they're out of sight now. So we'll have to assume the worst. Is this the only way into the valley from this end?'

Hreldar nodded. 'As I remember,' he said. 'But I'm putting look-outs up on the top to make sure we aren't flanked.'

Loman glanced up approvingly. 'There'll be reinforcements here shortly,' he said.

Hreldar frowned slightly. 'It makes no sense,' he said. 'They must surely have seen the tower lit up, they'll know we're here and with a superior force to theirs. They must have realised that we'll be waiting for them.'

Loman shrugged. 'I'm not even going to try and reason this out, Hreldar, there isn't time. With the confusion back there, a company of cadets could cause havoc. We'll just have to wait and see. There's not much we can do wrong if we keep a strong defensive position.'

Hreldar nodded then rode off to supervise the continuing disposition of his men across the valley. As Loman waited, Atelon came galloping up. 'Ryath and some of the others are behind me,' he said breathlessly. 'Do you think this is Dan-Tor returning?'

Loman was about to repeat the answer he had given to Hreldar when there was an urgent whistle from above.

Loman gaped. It wasn't possible. The column was here already?

He looked at Hreldar's Guards. They would take a toll, but they were very few, even in this narrow part of the valley. This was going to be bad if the reinforcements didn't arrive soon.

He motioned Atelon to follow him then drew his sword and rode forward. Hreldar galloped across to join them.

As they reached the small line of pikemen and archers there was another whistle from above and abruptly the column came into sight.

It was cavalry, and moving fast.

The pikes came down and the archers drew their bows.

Loman peered into the darkening light, his Orthlundyn sight searching desperately into the approaching mass.

Suddenly he urged his horse forward.

'Put up your weapons!' he shouted to the Guards. 'Put up your weapons! It's Fyndal and the others with the Muster.'

Later, as the senior officers of the various armies gathered in one of the spartan rooms of the tower fortress, Loman found himself the butt of some considerable banter.

'A rare welcome, Orthlundyn,' Urthryn said, laughing as he settled into his chair. 'We ride down the Pass of Elewart and all through southern Narsindal unhindered, to be greeted by our allies with archers and pikemen.'

Loman raised his hands. 'You have my surrender, Ffyrst,' he said smiling broadly. 'But I'll not apologise again. I've been doing it since you arrived. I see now that this is a barrack-room version of your helangai; dragging the hapless defeated about from rider to rider.'

Urthryn laughed again, and slapped his legs. Loman saw Sylvriss's features written in her father's.

'Peace, then, Loman,' Urthryn said. 'I'll concede that when I saw your pikes waving in the gloom you gave me a rare fright. I thought that Dan-Tor had caught you napping and locked you in your own tower.'

'Their tower,' Loman corrected, nodding towards Eldric and the others.

Urthryn made a dismissive gesture. 'Still, I'd hate to think that our companions in this venture were so careless that they'd have let us arrive unnoticed.'

He became more pensive. 'It was a good response, indeed,' he said. 'Events are moving so fast these past weeks. Good and bad. So many of my people killed by that – creature's treachery. My countrymen squabbling like children in their pain. A great battle fought to defend our soil and avenge our dead and us not there.' He shook his head. 'Yet, on the other hand, we travel that accursed Pass and through the enemy's own land without hurt. My daughter rallies my people and then gallops off across the mountains to drop her foal in a Fyordyn farmhouse.' He gave a sombre chuckle. 'It's like something out of one of our old tales.'

Then his face became serious and, leaning forward, he held out his hands, cupped as if to help someone into the saddle. 'I accept my daughter's decision without reservation, Loman,' he said. 'The Muster will ride at your command.'

Loman bowed.

Urthryn relaxed and sat back in his chair. 'If it's possible I'd like to go to Vakloss and see my child and grandchild.'

'It isn't possible, Ffyrst.'

Gulda spared Loman the decision. He gave her a surreptitious look of gratitude.

'It'll take too long for you to get to Vakloss and back,' she said. 'We know nothing of our enemy's forces or intentions, but we do know that the three Uhriel are together in Narsindal again, and that Oklar's force has been gone from here for some time. Sumeral will gain strength from delay; we'll lose it. We must ride to meet Him as soon as the Muster and the army here can be integrated. That's going to mean hard, detailed, work. Work that can't be done without you, we can't afford any delay.'

Urthryn looked down, and passed his hand over his face briefly. 'Yes,' he said softly after a moment. 'I understand. There'll be other times.'

Gulda leaned forward and laid a sympathetic hand on his arm, and the room fell silent.

'Tell us about your journey,' she said after a while. 'Did you truly meet no opposition?'

Urthryn came out of his reverie. 'Yes,' he said, nodding, his manner mildly surprised. 'The Pass was grim and unpleasant. It's a forbidding place. I've never ridden along it before. I'd always thought the tales about the wind to be just that – tales. But it howls and moans almost constantly. You've never heard such sounds! I can see now why they call it the Discourse of Sumeral and Elewart . . .' He paused and became thoughtful again. 'The sound seems to seep into your very being. Even now when I lie down to sleep, I can hear it. I don't think I'll ever be truly free of it. And every now and then, there's this sudden silence and you know that one of the Sighs of Gwelayne is coming. It's an indescribable sound . . .' His eyes widened. 'Such pain. Such remorse. Such longing. It's a bad place.'

'Bad?' Gulda said, as if prompting him.

Urthryn frowned a little. 'No,' he said reflectively. 'Perhaps sad would be a better word, but it's a woefully inadequate one.' He looked at Gulda. 'Do you know the tale of Elewart and Gwelayne, Memsa?' he asked.

Gulda smiled. 'Yes,' she said simply. 'I know the tale of your first king, Urthryn. I know it very well. I know many old tales. I *am* a teacher.'

Her eyes became distant and her voice took on a storyteller's lilt. '. . . And Gwelayne's father, already bound to His evil, saw Sumeral's lust and plied his daughter with potions so that His true Self would be hidden from her and she would see only His beauty – for she was no foolish child. And thus besotted, she abandoned her true Elewart and went to Him. And they ruled together for generations as His power waxed and spread far and wide. And she became a haughty and terrible Queen. And as reward, He gave her father *his* desire and made him Uhriel, binding him yet further to His will. And to the grieving Elewart it is said that He gave great life, though this is debated by some. But, as a tiny seed roots unseen to become a great tree, so Gwelayne's true nature awoke and through the years took back her soul. And though she was held to Him still by her own lust, He knew she saw Him truly and that she would ever loathe Him. And in His wrath, He sought out and slew Elewart. Then, hearing of this, Gwelayne in her grief and remorse, turned from Him utterly, and for all His terrible power, He could not restrain her, for she knew His soul. And Gwelayne –'

'– wandered the bleak and blasted valley where she had pledged her truth to Elewart and, hearing ever the voices of her true love and her fiery desire disputing through the barren peaks, she pined and died. And Sphaeera, in pity, took her sighs and gave them to the mountains, that they might have some brief respite from the eternal Discourse of Sumeral and Elewart.' Urthryn's musical Riddin accent finished Gulda's tale.

Gulda nodded, and all the listeners smiled and applauded softly.

Then Gulda lifted a gently admonishing finger. 'And Gwelayne wandered . . . And her fate is not known,' she said slowly, finishing her own telling.

Urthryn bowed extravagantly. 'I wouldn't dispute with such a fine teller of tales, teacher. But I'm a romantic and I prefer the romantic ending to the mysterious one.'

Gulda smiled and looked round the room. 'But this isn't planning our campaign, is it?' she said. 'If all we encounter between here and Derras Ustramel is a sighing wind, then we can consider ourselves more than fortunate. Tell us of your journey across Narsindal, Ffyrst.'

431

Urthryn shrugged. 'There's little to tell,' he said. 'It was less disturbing than our journey along the Pass. Yengar and Olvric guided us. Oslang twitched his nose in search of demons.' He winked at the Cadwanwr. 'That's when he wasn't slithering out of his saddle. The weather was cold and unpleasant. The horses were unhappy, and the place felt bad. Except for our last little gallop, we travelled slowly, partly in deference to our guests and partly because fear of ambush kept us in defensive order; but we met no one, nor even saw anyone, let alone faced any attack.' He laughed again. 'Except, of course, at the end.'

Gulda raised her eyebrows. 'An admirably brief account,' she said. 'Yengar, Olvric, have you anything to add?'

The two Goraidin shook their head. 'No,' Yengar said. 'The place still gives me the creeps, but apart from finding the road, the whole journey was as the Ffyrst has said: uneventful.'

'Road?' Gulda said.

'It was new,' Yengar continued. 'It wound down out of the mountains and off across the plains, but we saw no one using it. I presume it's the one that Hawklan and the others saw after they'd ridden north from Lord Evison's. The one serving the mines. It's a considerable feat of engineering, whoever built it.'

Gulda frowned. 'Slaves will have built it, Goraidin, slaves. It'll be a tombstone for many of them,' she said, her frown deepening. 'We're already far too late for many poor souls.'

She was silent for a moment, then she turned to Oslang. 'What did you learn, Cadwanwr?' she enquired.

Oslang grimaced and shifted uncomfortably in his chair. 'I learned what I already knew,' he said. 'That I'm scarcely a horseman, let alone a Muster rider.' His rueful manner caused some amusement, but Gulda gave him a beady look and he shrugged apologetically. 'There's an awful presence pervading the place,' he said, more seriously. '*His* presence, beyond a doubt. But it was . . . passive . . . indifferent to us, almost. As if we counted for nothing. It wasn't what I'd expected.'

Atelon looked at him. 'Did you use the Old Power at all?' he asked.

'No,' Oslang replied. 'I would have done had need arisen. We were prepared all the time for sudden attacks and for Dan-Tor to come riding out to meet us, but to be honest I was too afraid to use it unnecessarily.'

Atelon nodded understandingly and sank back into his chair.

The discussion moved on to practical matters.

'We need to find out where Oklar has gone,' Arinndier said. 'If he's lurking somewhere in the west, he could move in behind us, cut off our lines of supply, and attack us in the rear.'

'Or move down into Fyorlund and Orthlund while we're wandering round in the mists,' Hreldar said.

Other voices began to speak.

Loman raised his hand for silence hastily. 'My friends,' he said. 'There are endless alternatives that our enemy might adopt, and all of them are beyond our calculating at this stage. It seems that He's quite willing for us to move into Narsindal, but whether it's to surround us, wear us down by fighting a defensive war, face us in one set piece action, by-pass us and attack the lands to the south –' He held out his arms. 'How can we possibly know?'

He leaned forward. 'Hawklan's advice was that we be open and straightforward, because we can't begin to oppose Sumeral, the arch-schemer, with cunning and craft. We must not look to fight Him with weapons which are so much His own.'

'We can't *not* debate what might happen,' Eldric said. 'We must have contingency plans prepared.'

'Of course,' Loman said. 'But our intention here is to march on Derras Ustramel and destroy both it and its occupant and anyone else who chooses to fight at His side. A straight thrust at our enemy's heart. We must have that foremost in our minds at all times.' Eldric looked anxious.

Loman turned to Urthryn. 'Ffyrst, Sylvriss tells me that she's set squadrons to patrolling the Pass. Can your people hold it against a large army?'

Urthryn pursed his lips. 'I see no reason why not,' he said. 'Though if any of the Uhriel attacked also –'

'The Cadwanol have laid many defences along the Pass of late,' Oslang said. 'It's better protected from the Uhriel than we are here.'

'Then is Riddin as safe as it can be made?' Loman asked.

The two men nodded and Loman turned back to Eldric. 'Can a large army move into Fyorlund over the mountains, Lord?'

'You moved over the mountains into Riddin when need arose,' Eldric replied tersely, a little discomfited still by Loman's apparent hastiness. 'And Mandroc raids into the northern estates are not uncommon.'

'Not to mention the attack on Evison's,' Arinndier added.

Loman let out a long breath. 'You know your own country, Lords,' he said patiently. 'Let me cut through the conjecture. What is the least that must be done to *prevent* a large force moving through the mountains at a place of its own choosing?'

'The repair of the Watch Hall,' Darek declared before Eldric could speak again. 'That at least would enable us to detect such an army. What would be needed to stop it would depend on the size, obviously.'

'Obviously,' Loman echoed thoughtfully. 'Otaff, how is work on the Watch Hall proceeding?'

Otaff was the most senior member of the Carver's Guild at the meeting. 'We're making steady progress,' he said. 'And the Cadwanwr are being very helpful. To be honest I think we'd be far more use working up there now than we are here, listening to you and the others talking logistics and tactics.'

Loman agreed and Otaff left, together with Atelon and other Orthlundyn and Cadwanwr.

Loman turned back to Eldric. 'If this work is done, then Fyorlund too will be as safe as we can make it,' he said. 'And will we have eliminated some of our more terrifying contingencies?'

Eldric nodded. 'It's a hasty Gathering, Loman, but yes,' he said.

Loman continued. 'This done then, I think what we should prepare to march north as quickly as we can, and protect our rear by a string of manned forts, patrols and posthorse messengers.'

He glanced quickly round his listeners to see what response this suggestion provoked.

'If we're going to thrust directly for His heart then I'd rather we used the army as a spear that we can withdraw than an arrow which we can fire only once,' said Darek. 'But I foresee a problem in manning all these forts. Leaving a duty garrison here, and who knows how many companies spread out across a hostile countryside in forts may leave us precious few at the front.'

'That will need serious, detailed, thought,' Loman conceded. 'But whatever we decide now, we can change our dispositions as the Goraidin and Helyadin obtain information about the enemy's strength.'

He paused and looked round at his audience again, then he stood up and began walking among them. 'I know we have a massive army here but, for what it's worth, I have a feeling that we'll find ourselves heavily outnumbered whatever form this conflict eventually takes. I think we must accept that now, and remember that numbers alone are not necessarily critical.' He paused briefly. 'Even with a cavalry force that was far too small, tactics and discipline gave us the greater part of the day against the far more numerous Morlider. Equally importantly, they brought us away with virtually no casualties.' He tapped out his conclusion on the pate of a carved eagle that decorated one of the chairs. 'And, all things being equal, it will be tactics and discipline that give us victory, not numbers.'

'But will they be equal?' someone said, amid the sage head nodding that greeted this remark. The speaker was Urthryn's adviser, Hiron and his question voiced a recurrent doubt. 'The Cadwanwr can perhaps bind the Uhriel, but who will bind *Him*, Loman? Can we be certain that Hawklan and the others will find and waken Ethriss in time?'

Loman turned to him. 'No,' he said, simply, and without hesitation. 'But it makes no difference to what *we* must do. If Ethriss is there, then he'll assail Sumeral in whatever manner such beings assail one another; the Cadwanwr will resist the Uhriel; and we'll pit ourselves against whatever mortal army He's collected about Him. And we must all prevail. If Ethriss is not there, then we and the Cadwanwr will hold as long as we can, and do what hurt we can, in the hope that, as in times past, it may stem His advance and give others, elsewhere in the world, a chance to prepare to face Him.' He bent close to Hiron. 'We have no other choice,' he said slowly, looking at him intently. 'For reasons beyond us, the creature is risen and come to great strength. He had brought death to all our lands already, and beyond – the Drienvolk, the Morlider. If He is not opposed now, then He will return again, again and again, to corrupt and destroy all of us, one way or another.'

Hiron looked away from the stern gaze in reluctant acceptance. It was a necessary question that he had asked, but it was the last time that the need to prosecute the war was mentioned amongst the leaders of the three nations and the Cadwanwr.

Two days later, Otaff and Atelon declared that the Watch Hall had been repaired as well as it could be under the circumstances, and the Fyordyn pronounced the work excellent. There were areas which were still beyond the reach of the tower's injured vision but, to much delight, there were also areas that could be seen more clearly than ever before.

The various officers of the army and the Muster spent much of the time learning about one another's forces and discussing tactics. Such rivalry as there was, was good-natured and drew them together.

Among the ranks, however, there were initially a few angry exchanges as some of the younger Riddinvolk chose to taunt the Fyordyn cavalry. Urthryn dealt with such incidents ruthlessly.

'Twenty years ago, when you were scarcely stirrup-high, these people came over the mountains to fight and die with us,' he thundered at the gathered culprits. 'Barely months ago they had to charge their own kind in massed infantry to drive Oklar from their land.' He jabbed his finger into the chest of the one he deemed to be the ringleader. '*You* need to understand what a debt is, young man, and to help you towards this, I'm grounding you until further notice.' Mouths dropped open, but Urthryn's stern gaze prevented any other form of protest. Grounding was a considerable disgrace in the Muster, and was usually used as a punishment for those who had ill-treated their horses. 'You and your equally witless friends here will help with the baggage train for a day or so and then you can spend some time with the High Guards,' he went on, 'in their infantry contingent. Then we'll see if your attitude's improved.'

'Bit severe, Ffyrst,' Agreth said quietly afterwards. 'They were only –'

'I'd ground Sylvriss if she behaved like that, in these circumstances,' Urthryn said, before Agreth could finish. 'I despise that . . . infantile behaviour, at the best of times.'

'They're only young,' Agreth protested tentatively.

'Then they should learn both humility and *true* pride from their horses if they look to get older,' Urthryn said angrily. 'This is no horse fair. The finest rosette any of us will come away with will be a head on our shoulders. Grounding those clowns will soon spread the word that *all* energies are to be directed northwards.'

Agreth bowed and let the subject lie.

Then the final plans were laid. The Goraidin and the Helyadin were gone ahead, the Watch Hall was manned, and the army stood ready to move.

There was no brash and raucous departing however, a steady downpour saw to that. Flags and pennants clung limply to their poles, and horses and hooded figures alike stood uncertain and dripping as Loman took one final look at the long column winding back out of sight along the valley, then he drew his sword and, holding it high, shouted, 'Duty Watch, forward.'

His voice echoed off the rocks and the walls of the tower. Eldric straightened up and glanced at his fellows. They too showed no outward sign, but he knew they were deeply moved by Loman's gesture. It was a long time since the traditional marching order of the Watch Patrols had been called out at Narsindalvak.

Watched by the duty garrison, the army slowly began to move forward on the first part of the journey that would carry it into the bleak, desolate heart of Narsindal and towards their terrible Enemy.

# Chapter 28

Sylvriss stood at the half-opened door to the nursery and looked at her son in his simple crib. His arms were thrown up over his head and he was lying very still.

The Queen was holding her breath and she did not release it until she saw the slight movement of the sheets that showed her son too was breathing.

Then, looking around rather self-consciously, she closed the door gently and, pulling her cloak about her, set off along the wide corridor.

As she walked past the hanging tapestries and the ornately carved panels that decorated the corridor, Sylvriss took out the message she had received from Narsindalvak and read it again. Her father was safe, but though he made little play of it, his regret at not being able to come to Vakloss and see his grandchild shone through his simple straightforward prose like a beacon.

She smiled indulgently, as children will at the folly of their parents then, carefully, she returned the letter to her pocket and turned down a broad curving flight of stairs.

Outside, she acknowledged the salutes of the guards and set off towards her private stables.

As she had throughout her bitter struggle to reclaim Rgoric from Dan-Tor's malign influence, she rode every day. Sometimes through the streets and parks of the City, sometimes around the extensive gardens of the Palace.

Her riding now, however, was not to assuage the seething emotions that had surged and roared within her in those times, but to ease the quieter, deeper, concerns that beset her now that her nation was recovering from its trial and turning to face its true foe.

As she neared the stables she heard the unsteady clatter of hooves and an anxious voice torn between coaxing and cursing. She quickened her pace.

Turning the corner she came into the smooth flagged courtyard that was bounded on three sides by buildings that Rgoric had had converted into stables suitable for her fine Riddin horses. The upper floors of the building protruded on to arched columns to form a covered walkway, and wandering in and out of the columns was the source of the small commotion. A High Guard cadet was trying to take the reins of a large horse, but the animal kept snatching its head away and then either walking round the columns or gently nudging its would-be captor sideways.

The boy was red-faced with frustration and despair, and an increasing amount of abuse was seeping into his language as he spoke to the animal. Sylvriss smiled at the sight: the boy must have saddled the horse for her and then tried to sneak a ride on it. Then her smile faded as the horse emerged calmly out of the shadow to avoid another lunge by the boy.

It was undeniably a Muster horse, but it was unkempt and thinner than it should have been, and it was not one of hers.

The cadet saw her and stopped his weary pursuit to salute; there was no guilt in his manner.

'I'm sorry, Majesty,' he said plaintively. 'It was here when I arrived. I don't know where it's come from, or who it belongs to and I just can't get hold of it.'

'It's all right,' Sylvriss said reassuringly, quietly walking up to the horse. It watched her, unmoving.

'It's a Muster horse like one of yours, isn't it, Majesty?' the cadet said.

Sylvriss nodded absently as she stared at the horse, her eyes widening with recognition. 'It's more than a Muster horse,' she said softly, almost to herself.

'You're Hawklan's horse, aren't you?' she whispered as she laid her hand on the great horse's neck. 'You're Serian.'

Serian dipped his head and shook it.

The question, *where is Hawklan?* rushed into Sylvriss's mind suddenly, but she set it aside with practicalities. 'And you're famished and filthy,' she said.

She signalled to the cadet. 'Open the big stable, move the other horses, get food and water and bring me a brush and comb,' she said. The boy gaped. 'Quickly!' she said urging him on with a wave of the hand.

Questions cascaded into her mind again as the boy scurried off. Hawklan had gone off with Andawyr and a small party according to Eldric. But what was he doing now, without his horse? And where was he? She looked at Serian carefully. Though untidy and obviously hungry, the horse bore no signs of injury, nor did he seem to be distressed. Indeed his eyes were calm and watchful. For an instant she felt a surge of driving purposefulness that she knew must be the horse's will.

'You've come over the mountains, haven't you?' she said. 'You're looking for him! No. You're going to meet him!' She clenched her fists in frustration. If only she could talk to the animal as Hawklan used to.

She reached up to take Serian's reins, then withdrew her hand. 'Come with me,' she said, walking away. 'The big stable has wide doors and I'll leave them open, have no fear.' She smiled as she looked back over her shoulder. Even in his present condition, Serian was a splendid horse. Have no fear, she thought mocking herself. You'd smash those doors with a single kick, wouldn't you?

Serian lowered his head and walked after her. Sylvriss spoke again as they walked. 'I'll clean you up and sort out your harness – if you wish – and when you've eaten, you can return to your . . . quest . . . unhindered.' Serian pushed her gently in the back, making her laugh.

Some while later, the cadet dismissed, she was putting the finishing touches to Serian and he was starting to toss his head restlessly.

'All right, all right, don't be impatient,' she said, slapping him with the brush. 'I know you feel better for it, but you'll feel better still if you'll let me finish.'

Serian looked at her reproachfully. Sylvriss laughed. 'Don't you make cow's eyes at me, horse,' she said. 'I'm a Muster woman, not some soft-hearted healer you can twist around your hoof. There. You're done.'

Serian bent forward and nuzzled her affectionately. Sylvriss stroked him. 'Oh, you're a wicked horse,' she said, laughing again, her lilting Riddin accent suddenly full and rich. Then, more seriously. 'On with your journey, Serian. Find Hawklan. And thank you for letting me help you.'

She patted him once more, and then walked through the wide stable doors into the courtyard. She did not look back, though she paused slightly and inclined her head when she heard his hooves slowly clattering after her.

Coming to a small flight of steps, she ran up them and turned as she reached the top to watch the horse leave.

Serian however, did not move. Instead he walked to the bottom of the steps and stood looking up at her. She stared at him, puzzled.

'What do you want?' she said after a moment. Serian shifted his feet and kept looking at her; there was a strange look in his eyes, almost as if he were annoyed at being kept waiting.

Sylvriss looked at him intently. 'You *are* looking for Hawklan, aren't you?' she said uncertainly, beginning to doubt the promptings that had given her the idea. But they were still there. The horse was journeying, he had stopped here simply for food and attention, she was sure, and now he wanted to be away again.

Sylvriss held out her hands. 'Serian, you can go. You're free, you can . . .'

Her voice faded as an unexpected and not totally welcome thought came to her. She moved down the steps and took hold of the horse's head. 'You want me to come with you, don't you?' she said, a little fearfully. Serian bowed and nudged her gently.

'But . . .'

Sylvriss looked around. Odd patches of snow lingered on the lawns and on the roofs of some of the outbuildings. The familiar walls of the palace towered over her protectively, grey and fatherly against the watery sunlit sky. There was much she had to do here in the Palace, in Vakloss . . . yet she was a Muster woman and the Muster were riding to war . . . and she was Commander of the entire allied army.

But her son . . .?

Serian shifted his feet again and Sylvriss felt some call within her that would not be denied.

'Wait,' she said, then she turned and ran back up the steps.

Minutes later, Hylland was bobbing in her wake as she swept through her rooms.

'No,' she said, casting a critical eye over her racks of clothes. 'You were right before, but now I must go.'

'Majesty –' Hylland protested.

Sylvriss looked at him, brown eyes unmanning him. 'It'll be all right,' she said. 'We're both of us growing stronger daily.'

'Majesty, you can't take a baby to war!' Hylland managed at last. 'You could be killed. He could be killed. There'll be all manner of hardship; disease, even.'

Sylvriss paused and looked from her packing to her child, still sleeping, despite the argument.

'Damn you, Hylland,' she said. 'I know that. But it makes no difference. If the war is lost then we could all be killed.' She went over to the crib. 'Or worse,' she said distantly. 'He could be turned into some poisoned puppet like his father, and who would there be to save *him*? I'd rather see him dead than that.'

Her voice cracked a little and tears sprang to her eyes though she did not weep.

She turned back to her work, easing Hylland aside as she moved towards a cupboard.

'Hawklan needs that horse, wherever he is, and the horse needs me – probably only to tend him – but he needs *me* nevertheless,' she said. 'Such few tasks as I've taken on here can easily be performed by Dilrap and his staff as before, but no one else can help Serian.' The memory of their tumultuous first meeting came to her, he carrying Isloman and the unconscious Hawklan from Oklar's wrath, she riding at Rgoric's bidding to rouse the Lords in the east. 'He and I have been one, albeit briefly,' she said.

The two antagonists looked at one another.

'Very well, Majesty,' Hylland said inclining his head resignedly. 'If you will allow me a few moments.'

Sylvriss's eyes narrowed. 'What for?' she said suspiciously.

'I too must prepare my travelling kit for the journey,' Hylland replied blandly.

Sylvriss's expression became both concerned and exasperated.

'You won't be needed,' she said hastily after an uncertain pause.

Hylland inclined his head again. 'As your Majesty wishes,' he said. 'In that case I must return to my Lord.'

Sylvriss drew in a noisy breath but Hylland went on formally before she could speak. 'I am Lord Eldric's Healer General, Majesty,' he said. 'An officer in his High Guard. Officially I'm on secondment to Palace duty to attend to you and the prince, but if that secondment has now been ended then I must –'

Sylvriss levelled a grim finger at him. 'Ten minutes, soldier. And I'll check your travelling kit – and pick your horses. You ride under Muster discipline if you ride with me.'

Gavor rose into the air, his flapping wings throwing dancing black shadows through the dust-filled torchlight.

The sound of swords being drawn hissed up after him.

Hawklan made to step forward towards the Mandroc, but Dacu and Isloman moved in front of him, flanked by Jaldaric and Tirke. Athyr, Tybek, Yrain and Jenna moved to protect Andawyr. Dar-volci chattered his teeth menacingly.

The Mandroc let out a surprised yelp and then drew a sword and dropped into a menacing crouch. The figures behind it

442

moved forward out of the haze and stood by it. There were three of them in Mathidrin livery and they too were wielding their swords purposefully.

Hawklan felt his stomach go cold at what he knew he had to do next. He pushed forward between Dacu and Isloman. 'No prisoners,' he said hoarsely.

'Wait!' Isloman said urgently, seizing his arm. Hawklan glanced at him quickly. His eyes were narrowed and his face was creased with uncertainty.

The Mathidrin stopped at the same command, then one of them reached up and removed his helmet. The other two copied his example.

A gasp of disbelief burst out from Dacu and the other Fyordyn.

'Yatsu?' Isloman said, stepping forward. 'Lorac? Tel-Odrel? What −?'

But his question disappeared under a sudden torrent of mutual welcomings as the Fyordyn began to greet their countrymen.

'What are you doing here?' was the common question of the two groups, but before it could be answered, a harsh, guttural voice intruded.

'We must go. This is a bad place. Too near the killing rocks.' It was the Mandroc and it was addressing Yatsu. Its eyes widened in fear as it pointed toward the tunnel from which Hawklan and the others had emerged, and its voice fell to a terrified whisper. 'And Amrahl's . . . creature . . . is down there. Hurry, hurry.'

'Lead on then,' Yatsu said, lifting his hand for silence. The Mandroc scurried through one of the tunnel openings and Yatsu beckoned the others to follow.

'Follow that?' Jaldaric said. Hawklan started at the snarling anger in the young man's voice. As he looked at him, however, the memory returned to him of Jaldaric standing alone in the spring sunshine and facing Aelang and the chanting mob of Mandrocs that was to massacre his friends.

Hawklan took his arm and felt his dreadful fear and rage. 'Yatsu is commander,' he said simply. 'We talk as we walk.'

Jaldaric turned to him, his face riven with torment. Hawklan urged him forward. 'As we walk,' he repeated.

They did little talking for some time however, the route being upwards and the Mandroc setting a fair pace, for all his rolling gait. The concussions and the blasts of air gradually became less frequent and more distant and eventually the pace slowed down. As it did, the questions emerged again.

'What are you doing here, and why are we following . . . *that*?' Jaldaric asked, nodding at the back of the Mandroc as he spoke.

Yatsu raised a conciliatory hand. 'That's Byroc,' he replied. 'He's one of the Ivrandak Garn tribe and he hates Sumeral more than we do.'

Andawyr looked intently at Yatsu as he spoke and then shot Hawklan a look of appreciative surprise.

'Call it what you want –' Jaldaric began.

'*Him*, Captain,' Yatsu said grimly. '*Him*. He's no more a *thing* than you are.'

Jaldaric's eyes blazed momentarily but Yatsu's stern gaze forbade any further remonstrance.

'Why are we followiong *him*, then?' Jaldaric managed.

'Because he's saved our lives half a dozen times already and unless anyone here knows any different, he's the only one who can get us out of here.' Yatsu's voice was angry.

Hawklan came between them. 'Are these explosions something to do with you?' he asked Yatsu.

A white grin displaced the anger in the Goraidin's grimy face. 'They certainly are,' he said. 'They're the funeral knell of those stinking mines.'

Mines! Hawklan thought in some surprise. Andawyr had been right, they had moved well to the west of the Pass.

'What happened?' he asked.

Yatsu confined himself to a brief operational summary. 'We've been studying them for weeks,' he said. 'Even managed to get right inside once or twice. When Lord Eldric told us to destroy them, we sent in a diversionary raid to draw out the guards, sneaked in a group disguised as Mathidrin to open the slave pens . . .' He faltered and his face became pained at some memory. ' . . . then we simply set fire to the storage silos. You've never seen anything like it. That stuff is appalling.'

'We?' queried Hawklan. 'You three and Byroc here?'

Yatsu's grin became a grimace. 'No,' he said. 'There were four companies of us altogether. Veterans and the younger ones we'd trained up. There was some hand to hand fighting with the off-duty guards as we were leaving, and we got separated. The others got away, but we were cut off by the fire, covering their retreat.'

'And Byroc?' Hawklan asked.

Yatsu frowned. 'We came across him in a special cage of his own when the fire drove us underground.' His voice fell as if he did not wish the Mandroc to hear. 'I think they had him lined up for something particularly nasty; he just fell on his knees and grovelled when we released him and he's no coward, believe me.'

'And you trust him?' Hawklan said.

'He led us to three underground storage units that we never even suspected existed, and helped us fire them safely and get away,' Yatsu replied. His eyes widened. 'And you should have seen what he did to the Mathidrin who tried to stop us! Yes, I'm well on the way to trusting him.'

Hawklan nodded. 'Will he speak to me?' he asked.

'Go and ask him,' Yatsu replied. 'He's got a mind of his own, to put it mildly.'

Hawklan strode forward to the Mandroc. He sensed many emotions radiating from the powerful figure as he fell in step beside him; suspicion, fear, anger.

He noticed markings of the Mandroc's face that he recalled having seen in a book at the Caves of Cadwanen.

'Why do you help us, Byroc, Chief of the Ivrandak Garn tribe, Plains Runner, Leaper of the Crags and Chosen Hunter?' he said.

The Mandroc's various emotions disappeared under a surge of surprise, but apart from a quick sidelong glance he gave no outward sign.

'Because they wish it,' he said, nodding back at Yatsu and the others. 'But keep the young one from me. He hates like the black ones.' His voice was harsh and unpleasant but Hawklan judged that to be because he was speaking in an alien tongue.

'The young one is Jaldaric,' Hawklan said. 'Son of a great warrior and chief. His friends were slain by your kind and he himself imprisoned by the leader of the Mathidrin – the black ones. He carries much pain inside, as you do.'

'Imprisoned?' Byroc said after a long silence.

Hawklan nodded. 'Why were you imprisoned, Byroc?' he asked.

Byroc looked back over his shoulder, his eyes whitening, then he opened his mouth and let out a great bellowing whimper of fear that echoed along the tunnel and made Hawklan wince in its intensity.

'Why were you imprisoned?' Hawklan pressed. 'And what

445

frightened you back there? There are few things you would flee from.'

'I would flee from Amrahl's creature,' Byroc said, quickening his pace, and speaking as if the words were being torn out of him. 'The all-seeing one.'

'The creature that sees through its yellow-eyed birds?' Hawklan asked.

Byroc nodded and quickened his pace.

'It is dead,' Hawklan said quietly. 'The raven, the felci, the sound carvers, and this Sword slew it. Amrahl's sight is as yours now.'

Byroc stopped suddenly, causing some commotion behind. He looked at Hawklan, and then at Gavor, and Dar-volci standing on his hind legs by Hawklan. Tentatively the Mandroc reached out towards the Black Sword. Hawklan drew it slowly and offered it to him, hilt first. Dacu and Isloman edged forward.

Byroc however, did not touch the Sword but withdrew his hand and stepped back a little, his mouth gaping to reveal his massive canine teeth. Then he looked at Hawklan again. 'You . . . and these . . . slew Amrahl's creature?' he said, the harshness in his voice softened by awe.

Andawyr stepped forward. 'Yes,' he said.

Byroc stared at the Cadwanwr and then stepped back again in undisguised fear. 'You are one of His kind,' he said. 'You wield the Great Harm, and the Sword possesses it too.'

'No, Byroc,' Andawyr said. 'I can use the same Power that He does, but it is like . . . fire or water. Whether I use it for harm or good is my choosing . . .' He screwed his face up with effort and began speaking hesitantly in a harsh, guttural, language.

The Mandroc replied uncertainly in the same language, and a short debate ensued. When it was completed he turned back to Hawklan.

'I do not understand all these things,' he said, shaking his head. 'Have you *truly* slain His creature? Do you truly come to oppose Amrahl's might?'

'Yes,' Hawklan said. 'The creature is truly dead. And many others than we move to oppose Him also.'

There was a low rumbling in Byroc's throat. 'I was to be given to it,' he said. 'My spirit was to be slowly torn from me and . . .' His voice deteriorated into a low, moaning, howl. Hawklan looked at Andawyr.

446

'The Vrwystin exists on many planes,' Andawyr said. 'Even we can feel Byroc's fear. Those parts of the Vrwystin's nature that are elsewhere feed on such emotions.'

Hawklan grimaced. 'And the part that was here?' he asked.

'That would feed on flesh and blood,' Andawyr replied reluctantly.

Hawklan remembered the tendril that had bound his hand and severed his glove. He shuddered.

'I owe you blood debt for ever,' Byroc said, suddenly stern. 'I will go with you even to Amrahl Himself and be your shield.'

Hawklan looked at him. Here was one of the creatures – the savage animals – that had massacred Jaldaric's patrol, that had cruelly butchered Evison's entire garrison, that he himself had cut down like so many unwanted weeds in the sunlit Orthlund forest. Here was one of the creatures that formed the heart of Sumeral's dreadful army during the First Coming; creatures so irredeemable that they had finally been abandoned by the Great Congress and condemned to live in Narsindal under the Watch of the Fyordyn. Yet here too was dignity and some form of honour and, above all, some form of opposition to Sumeral's domination of this land.

Many things are stirring, said a voice inside him.

'I release you freely from all debts, Byroc,' he said. 'I want no slaves, and your burden is ours. If it's your will, follow us and fight by us and welcome. All I'll ask of you now is that you take us from here. We also have been too long away from the sky.'

Byroc stood motionless for a long moment, his head inclined slightly, then he uttered a strange howl, bared his teeth, and began walking up the tunnel again.

The group fell in behind him, but their long underground pilgrimage was nearer its end than they had imagined. Within minutes, they found themselves walking towards a distant grey light that could only be daylight.

As they dew nearer, the light came and went a little as if there were clouds blowing overhead.

And then they were silently edging their way towards the ragged mouth of the tunnel. Cautiously, Isloman crept forward and peered out. In the distance, his carver's vision could just make out groups of tiny figures running down the rocky slopes towards the grey, mist-covered, sparseness of Nardsindal. Overhead, a cloud of dense black was blowing northwards.

He signalled the others to wait, and there was a long silence as they stood motionless, breathing in the cold mountain air and screwing their eyes tight against the brightness of the dull sky.

Crawling forward on his stomach, Yatsu joined Isloman who levelled a cautionary finger at the distant figures. Yatsu nodded, then looked up at the billowing smoke and smiled.

'Escaping slaves and the remains of the mines,' he said, and edging back from the entrance he sat up and leaned luxuriously against the rock wall.

The others followed his example.

Yatsu nodded. 'Now,' he said to Hawklan. 'Tell us how *you* come to be here.'

'In a moment,' Hawklan replied, turning to Byroc. 'I need to know first how the chief of the Ivrandak Garn tribe came to be trussed up as a meal for his great Leader's creature, and then fought and killed His soldiers, and helped destroy His mines.'

'He is not my leader,' Byroc replied immediately, his dog-like snout curling viciously. 'The Ivrandak Garn know no leader but whoever *they* choose. And I am their chosen, for all they are scattered and broken.'

Hawklan's eyes narrowed at the pain and bitterness in the Mandroc's voice even though it was masked by his harsh tone.

'What happened to your tribe?' he asked.

'We would not worship Him,' Byroc replied. 'As our fathers would not worship Him when *they* waked Him.'

'They?' Andawyr interrupted.

'The Dowynai Vraen,' Byroc's eyes widened and the fur ringing his face became rigid as he spoke. He was a fearful sight. 'They were ever corrupt and treacherous, a tribe of liars and thieves, who preyed on the terrors of the weak and foolish and who meddled in the Ways that should be forgotten –'

Hawklan raised his hands gently to stem the Mandroc's mounting anger. 'They woke Him?' he asked.

'They woke those who woke Him,' Byroc said, his voice still angry. He rasped several words in his own language, venomously.

'The Uhriel,' Andawyr translated partially.

A growl rose in Byroc's throat, but when it emerged it was a cry of pain. 'But for all their magicks we would not worship Him. The Ivrandak Garn worship nothing. Not the mountains, nor the rivers, nor the thunder. They have our fear and our respect, but not our spirits.'

He scanned his audience. 'Would you worship a mere mortal

448

creature?' he snarled. 'Or set his word above all things?'

No one answered.

'And the other tribes?' Hawklan asked.

'They worship Him. They have lost their true selves and placed their hands beneath the feet of the Dowynai Vraen,' Byroc said scornfully. 'A great madness possesses them. They fall down even before the black ones and cry out His name. They forget the wisdom and ways of their fathers, the ways of the plains and the mountains and the mist.'

'But in His name do they not become great warriors?' Andawyr suggested.

Byroc growled and struck his chest with his fist. 'Great warriors fight fearing the end of life, yet ready to face it,' he said. '*He* tells His *warriors* that there is a wondrous land beyond death to those who die in battle, where every desire is given without trial or strife. And *they believe Him* and rush to it in their blindness.' His tone was withering.

'And your people?' Hawklan said.

Byroc turned to look about at the grey daylight. 'Across the seasons, our lodges were burned, our hunting ranges poisoned, our wives and young taken to the slave pens,' he said. His manner was subdued, as if the pain were to deep to be encompassed by words. 'Then I was betrayed and captured like some animal, and though each took ten for his own life, the warriors with me were slaughtered while I stood bound.'

Hawklan looked at Jaldaric and noticed that even he was moved by the Mandroc's unexpected eloquence.

'An evil story, Byroc,' Hawklan said after a long silence. 'One that has been told in other lands now.'

'If *He* is not slain, it will not end until it has been told in every land, Sword Bearer, until the seas are dry, the mountains levelled, and the skies emptied – even of their stars.'

Hawklan felt a chill at his very heart as Byroc intoned this grim prophecy.

'Where will you go now, chief?' he said quietly.

Byroc looked at him. 'With you,' he said. 'On your journey to slay Him.'

There was an uneasy stir amongst his listeners and he made a noise which was eventually identified as a chuckle. 'Did you think that the chief of the Ivrandak Garn could not recognise hunters?' he said. 'And that was forged for only one prey.' He levelled a finger at the Black Sword.

Hawklan did not reply, but turned to Yatsu. 'Are you three

going back over the mountains to your company?' he asked.

Yatsu shook his head. 'Too risky from this side,' he said. 'We've no equipment and precious little food. Besides they won't have waited. They've no way of knowing that we weren't killed in that blaze.' He looked at Hawklan and then added, half-heartedly, 'We could head west towards Narsindalvak, I suppose. The army will be there by now, I imagine.'

Hawklan looked at Dacu. 'How are our supplies?' he asked.

'Sufficient as we are,' Dacu replied. 'But not so good if we have an extra four along; we'll have to live off the land much sooner. And the shelter's going to be crowded, to say the least.'

Hawklan thought for a moment then nodded. 'Very well,' he said. 'We all go. Yatsu, Lorac and Tel-Odrel are too valuable to be wandering back to join the main force, and Byroc knows the country.'

'No!' It was Jaldaric. 'We can't take a Mandroc for pity's sake, they're . . .' He faltered, remembering Byroc's tale; but the sight and wet-fur smell of the Mandroc evoked memories that surged through him and found voice despite himself. 'They're His creatures. They killed my friends. He'll betray us,' he said.

In an echo of his own meeting with the Goraidin many years ago in snowbound Riddin, Isloman drew his knife and offered it to the young man.

'*You* kill him, then. Now,' he said flatly.

Jaldaric looked at him and then, with an oath, turned away.

Hawklan intervened. 'If you remain standing on that Orthlund road, facing Aelang, *you'll* betray us, Jaldaric,' he said starkly. 'And if you ever meet the man he'll kill you, for the same reason; he'll be here and you'll still be there.'

Jaldaric glared at him but Hawklan offered no resistance to his reproach and anger, and Jaldaric felt it turning back upon himself. He opened his mouth to speak, but no words came. Hawklan watched him silently.

He continued. 'We'll live off the land whenever opportunity presents itself, starting now,' he said. 'Sentry duties will ease the accommodation problem.' He looked round at his companions intently. 'Be aware, all of you, all the time, as never before. We're very near the end now.'

After a short rest and a redistribution of their packs, the group set off again. Released from the confines of the tunnel, Gavor stretched his wings massively and launched himself into the air without a word. Hawklan smiled as he watched his friend climbing steadily into the pale sky. Soon Gavor was not more than a tiny circling dot.

'What do you know about Derras Ustramel and Lake Kedrieth,' Hawklan asked Byroc as they made their way down the rocky slope.

The Mandroc growled. 'Only that it is a bad place,' he said. 'The lake is as deep as the sky is high, and the marches around it are foul and treacherous, and full of dancing fires. And those who see His lair are changed forever.'

'Do you know of any paths through the marshes?' Hawklan asked.

Byroc shook his head. 'There are no paths,' he said. 'The waters shift and change. There is only the road. His road.'

He pointed. Hawklan followed his hand. Far before he saw a thin white ribbon meandering gently for a little way then straightening out and running northwards into the mist.

'We do not need it here, but at the end, only that can bring us to the lake,' Byroc said. 'If we are parted for any reason, follow it.'

The journey down the mountain from the cave was oddly euphoric for the group. There was little talking and each seemed to be looking around wide-eyed, as if permanently surprised at not seeing the rocky walls and roofs that had hedged them in for so long, and uncertain how to respond to the openness and the cold wind that was blowing.

They made good progress however, and towards evening the mountains were behind them. Dark and ominous against the gloomy sky, the disordered ranks of crags and peaks rose up forbiddingly to deny unequivocally any easy retreat back to the south.

As the light faded, so also did the euphoria, and the pervasive unease of Narsindal that it had kept at bay, began to seep into the group.

They were subdued as they made camp in the lee of one of the large patches of twisted undergrowth that dotted the rocky landscape.

Byroc watched as they unpacked and erected the shelter. Once or twice he took hold of the fabric and rubbed it between his fingers or sniffed at it. When the shelter was completed he peered inside cautiously and curled his lip.

'What's the matter?' Hawklan asked, standing by him.

'Bad smells,' Byroc answered. And without further explanation he lumbered off towards the dense undergrowth. 'I shall be near,' he said.

Hawklan was about to call after him when he suddenly felt the Mandroc's overwhelming loneliness. For a moment he saw the shelter as alien and unnatural, and his companions as flat-faced expressionless creatures hung about with angry and frightening memories.

'Whatever you wish, Byroc,' he said. 'But the shelter is yours if you need it.' The Mandroc, however, made no reply, and as Hawklan watched he quietly faded into the under-growth.

Inside the shelter, Hawklan told Yatsu and the others the tale of their journey from the Caves of Cadwanen and of his intention to confront Sumeral. It caused little surprise.

'I told you before that you were near to the player in this game, Hawklan,' Yatsu said. 'I'm glad you made the right decision.'

It was a remark that allowed no further comment.

Hawklan turned to Andawyr. 'This place has a bad feel to it,' he said, unknowingly echoing the words of generations of Fyordyn who had ridden the Watch.

Andawyr nodded. 'Few things have ever lived joyously in Narsindal,' he said. 'The fear from His First Coming still entwines the heart of everything. Now . . .' He paused. ' . . . He's all around again. Stronger than when I came only months ago. Watching, waiting, listening.'

'Watching?' Hawklan said, picking up the words in some alarm.

Andawyr shook his head. 'No, He can't see us now,' he said. 'He's watching for Ethriss . . . watching for those small signs that might presage his awakening.' He looked at Hawklan. 'If I use even a vestige of the Old Power,' he said. 'It would be like a clarion call to Him.'

'We knew that when we started,' Hawklan said.

Andawyr nodded. 'Yes,' he said. 'But now it begins truly. I'll need the help of all of you. I must reach out and be aware of Him, but I musn't oppose Him, not with so much as the weight of a falling leaf. Please keep what tranquillity you can in your own hearts, and protect me if you find me absent and withdrawn.' He found a smile. 'Treat me like a dotty grandparent.'

The brief flash of humour held little sustenance, however, and most of them slept fitfully through a night full of strange

452

animal calls, to wake just before dawn, ill-refreshed and reluctant.

After they had eaten a silent, and small, meal, they broke camp. Gavor came gliding down out of the grey sky. 'There are some strange-looking creatures in this place, but no people that I can see, though it's not easy with all this mist,' he said, settling on to Hawklan's shoulder. 'I suggest you go that way, dear boy,' he went on, leaning forward like a figurehead. Hawklan cast a glance at Byroc, who nodded.

As they walked, they found that the mist came and went in accordance with some mysterious law of its own and with scant regard for the damp wind. Sometimes they could see to the horizon, at others visibility was reduced to twenty or thirty paces. During such times, Byroc would raise his muzzle into the air and sniff rapidly and audibly at regular intervals.

The vegetation around them was stunted and seemingly deformed, as if it had fought some great battle just to struggle through to the surface. The dense patches of undergrowth that littered the plain and which loomed up out of the mist alarmingly on occasions, seemed to consist mainly of tangled brambles, as thick as tree trunks in places, and armed with vicious thorns.

From time to time, various animals bolted suddenly and startlingly in front of them causing a mixture of alarm and amusement. Hawklan frowned; for the most part the creatures were such as might be encountered anywhere in such wild terrain, but they were strangely altered. Teeth, claws and colouring betrayed powerful predatory needs, and eyes revealed constant watchful alarm. Occasionally he caught a brief snatch of speech, and that too was full of a mixture of menace and fear.

'Is there nothing here that hasn't been touched by Him?' he said softly to Andawyr.

'No,' Andawyr replied, adding enigmatically. 'Including us.'

Hawklan looked up into the grey sky. High above, Gavor was circling, spurred and watchful. Around him the Goraidin and the Helyadin were moving silently, armed and watchful.

*Did you think that the chief of the Ivrandak Garn could not recognise hunters?* Byroc's words came back to him.

He looked up again at Gavor. At least we have the eyes now, he thought. It gave him comfort. The combined skills of the group would keep them from the eyes of men, and Andawyr's silence would keep them from His sight. Their presence was unknown and thus unlooked for.

Dan-Tor dismissed the exhausted and quaking Mandroc messenger. He sat silent for some time, a strange sensation stirring inside. When it emerged, he recognised it as amusement, black and rich. It bloomed to enfold the vision that had been tormenting him since the eye of the Vrwystin he had been holding had shrieked and, impossibly, died; the vision, fleeting but vivid, of Hawklan wielding the Black Sword of Ethriss and destroying his precious creature.

Now, came the news that at the same time as the Vrwystin had been slain, the mines had been attacked by an unknown force of men and all the workings had been destroyed, and the shafts and adits sealed utterly by a terrible fire.

Dan-Tor luxuriated in the irony. Silently creeping into my domain again, Hawklan, he thought. Seeking to destroy my eyes and the food for my weapons with your treacherous cunning, and now destroyed in your turn by your own men.

A rumbling laugh began to form. So His enemies stumble and fall. Their every seeming success had been but a failure in disguise. Soon the rest would come clamouring across the plains of Narsindal to be destroyed in their turn; Cadwanol, Fyordyn, Orthlundyn and Riddinvolk; the old enemies, to be crushed this time at the very outset.

But through his malevolent delight shimmered a cold, sharp, sliver of uncertainty.

Hawklan had eluded destruction and capture so often; had appeared where he should not have been; had struck mysteriously beyond where he should be able to reach.

'Commander Aelang,' he said.

Aelang appeared from an adjacent room and saluted.

'You heard the message, commander?' Dan-Tor said.

'About the mines? Yes, Ffyrst,' Aelang replied.

Dan-Tor stood up. 'Take a company from the deep penetration patrol, go to the mines and destroy any of the attacking force who may have escaped to the north,' he said.

# *Chapter 29*

'You're a better rider than I imagined, Hylland,' Sylvriss said, as they trotted steadily along the valley towards Narsindalvak.

Hylland bowed his head. 'I merely follow your example, Majesty,' he said.

Sylvriss looked at him sideways. 'Your saddleside manner is more courtly than your bedside one,' she said, smiling.

Hylland nodded sagely. 'Ah, Majesty,' he said. 'Here I bask in the presence of my beautiful and honoured Queen. Elsewhere I often have to deal with wilfully obstreperous and difficult patients.'

Sylvriss laughed, and the sound mingled with that of the clattering hooves to echo along the towering rock face they were passing.

The valley was a harsh place, full of lowering crags, made all the darker by the grey, sullen, sky, but Sylvriss found herself immune to such influences. She reached forward and patted Serian's head. It was a strange experience to ride such an animal, both exhilarating and quietening. He responded unhesitatingly to her will, yet was quite beyond and above it. She knew that sooner or later, at a time of his own choosing, he would go on his own way in search of Hawklan but that now he was hers as utterly as he would be his.

On one occasion she became aware that she was riding with a stillness and awareness that she had neven known before. It came to her suddenly that Serian was teaching her how to ride, teaching her lessons that only someone who was a consummate rider could have the humility to understand and accept.

The experience brought tears flooding to her eyes.

Hylland saw the tears but sensed also their cause, albeit dimly, and kept his peace. Later he offered her a kerchief which she accepted, and for a good way they rode on, sharing a deep companionable silence.

As they neared the tower, a group of horsemen rode out to meet them. At their head was Lord Oremson; an old and trusted friend of Eldric's who had earned the odium of Dan-Tor for his passive obstructiveness following the suspension of the Geadrol and who had been imprisoned for a while after

Eldric's ill-fated attempt to demand an accounting of the Ffyrst.

'Majesty,' he said. 'I couldn't believe the messages we were receiving. You shouldn't be riding out here, it's far too dangerous. And with your baby too.'

Sylvriss smiled at the Lord's fatherly manner. 'Come now, Lord. The danger lies beyond Narsindalvak not before it,' she said. 'And how can I be in any danger with your look-outs and signallers watching my every step?' She smiled again and waved her hand along the high ridges above.

Oremson made to speak again, but she stopped him gently.

'Hylland and I will stay at the tower tonight, then we must leave to catch up with the army at daybreak,' she said.

Oremson's mouth dropped open. 'Majesty, I can't allow –'

'Lord,' she said, before he could continue. 'This is my intention, not a proposition to debate. Have no fear. I shall choose a suitable escort, and I'm not without some resource myself.' Her smile had faded and her whole manner was unequivocal.

Oremson's gaze went from his Queen's resolute face, to the baby slung about her shoulders and thence to the sword and staff hanging by her side. With an effort and a reproachful look at Hylland, who shrugged a wordless disclaimer, he managed a fretful acknowledgement of his Commander's will.

'And I want no ceremony, Lord,' Sylvriss added as they rode forward again. 'I'm here as your Commander and I wish to know the state of the war.'

When she arrived at the tower, however, Sylvriss found that a formal welcoming escort and a large cheering crowd were already waiting for her. The sight made her relent a little and she allowed herself a happy entry to the grim fortress.

The evening, was spent as she had promised, and the would-be revellers found themselves closeted with their Commander and poring over the various messages and reports that had been sent back by the advancing army.

The following morning, Oremson had almost given up all attempts at dissuading his Queen from her journey. Apart from her own determination, she would have an escort that would be more than adequate: a company of mounted High Guards routinely going to reinforce the forts, and a squadron of Muster riders who had followed late in the wake of their Ffyrst. He fought to the end, however.

'Majesty, you've studied all the reports and messages,' he

pleaded. 'There have been regular harrying attacks on the army. And serious assaults on at least two forts. I beg of you, reconsider, if only for your baby son.'

Sylvriss looked down at her baby and then at Oremson's anxious face. 'Lord,' she said. 'I'm travelling on an errand that's simply not of my choosing. When it's completed I'll return, and gladly. But in the meantime I'm bound by duties as you are; duty to my crown and duty to my son.'

Oremson yielded reluctantly. 'We shall be watching you for as long as we can, Majesty,' he said. 'And I'll have men stand by to come to your aid immediately if need arises.'

Sylvriss smiled and saluted then, mounting Serian, she gave the order to advance.

She did not look back as she rode down the valley away from the tower.


'Sit down, Lord, you look tired,' Loman and Eldric entered the tent.

Eldric accepted the offer and flopped into a nearby chair noisily. 'After we escaped from the Westerclave, I swore I'd never again complain about creature discomforts,' he said. 'But this place is just as bad as I remember it. It's as if even the air is tainted in some way.' He gazed up at the roof of the tent. 'I'm haunted by the thought of my favourite chair, and the carvings around my room, peaceful and homely in the light of the radiant stones . . .'

He fell silent and continued staring at the floor for some time then, with a sigh of self-reproach, he sat upright again.

'Sorry,' he said brusquely.

Loman smiled. 'I should think so, Lord. Any more of that and you'd have been on a charge for spreading despondency amongst the ranks.'

'No, no,' Eldric said. 'There's insufficient evidence for a charge. I'm only spreading my despondency to you. I'm quite hearty out there.'

Any further debate was ended by the arrival of Arinndier, Hreldar and Darek.

'A good day's progress,' Arinndier said.

Loman nodded off-handedly. 'Have you checked the perimeter fence?' he asked.

'Twice,' Arinndier replied. 'And there's no shortage of volunteers for guard duty these nights.'

Loman frowned. Would that it were otherwise, but Mandroc

raids during the night were becoming almost routine and while they had little effect, they could not be ignored. On the first few occasions they had caused great alarm, the Mandrocs showing a reckless wildness which, for the Orthlundyn, was quite different from the ferocity of the Morlider and, for the veteran Fyordyn, quite different from such few encounters as they might have had when riding the Watch.

Morale had wavered initially, but the perimeter fortifications which had been built each night with much grumbling had demonstrated their worth admirably, and Loman and the Lords had been able to change these strangely desperate forays by the enemy into valuable training exercises.

As a result, the Mandrocs suffered heavy casualties with little to show for their pains. Yet, despite the losses, the attacks continued and, in fact, they were becoming progressively more severe as the army moved further northwards. Such determination and such an indifference to life on the part of the enemy was a grim portent, and one which was burdening Loman profoundly. Looking at his companions, he raised this concern with them for the first time.

There was an odd silence when he had finished, and Loman had the feeling that these four foreigners were communing with one another in some silent fashion.

'Urthryn doesn't like his people manning the fences. He's bursting to go after the Mandrocs during the day on reprisal raids. And the Helyadin want to find their camps and attack them pre-emptively,' Hreldar said eventually. 'Give them their head.'

There was a note in Hreldar's voice which Loman could not identify at first. Then, quite suddenly, his foreboding was gone; despite themselves, and perhaps even unknowingly, these four old friends were anxious about this outlander commanding their army.

'No,' he said unequivocally. 'If we send people out into this country we'll be giving the enemy an advantage. They might find the odd camp and do some damage, but at what cost?' He looked around at the four Lords. 'We've agreed that it's highly probable we've been drawn into this conflict so that Sumeral could fight a defensive war and destroy His most powerful enemies with one single campaign. We march, knowing that. If now he chooses to attack and allow *us* the advantage of defence, then that's fine – we'll make the most of that advantage.'

458

He grimaced as the next words formed in his mind, but increasingly now, he knew that he must deliberately detach himself from the personal agonies of the individual soldiers and the price they must pay for this horror both now and in their future lives. He must concern himself with the broader cruel realities that those same soldiers demanded of him to ensure that they would *have* a future. Further, he must separate himself a little from these four stalwart leaders if he was to obtain their total support.

He went on, speaking as he knew Hawklan would. 'The simple fact is that every Mandroc that dies here can't fight us again. And, to be blunt, it's important that our troops get plenty of practice at killing and winning; the Muster not least. *That*'s why I've got them manning the perimeter. After what happened in Riddin they've been wearing their sense of failure like a wet cloak and it's been destroying their morale.'

The atmosphere in the tent eased perceptibly.

Loman moved in to finish his task. 'I don't mind your doubts about me, Lords,' he said, his voice unexpectedly stern. 'I take them as a sign of trust and affection. And, despite the opinion of your Queen and Hawklan, leaders of men such as yourselves would be rare fools not to be concerned about a bumpkin horse shoer from sleepy Orthlund suddenly given charge of this vast army. But in future, do as I do, speak your doubts to me as they occur. I knew I could speak freely to you here of the vague darkness looming in my mind, and that I would be heard and helped. In such manner we will win this war.'

Eldric lowered his gaze and there was an uncomfortable silence in the tent for some time.

'I'm sorry – we're sorry,' he said when he looked up. 'You shame us.'

Loman waved a dismissive hand. 'No, Lords,' he said. 'Sometimes doubts come because you are seeing the uncertainties more clearly, and there's no shame to be had in seeing the truth, and accepting it.'

He leaned forward before any of them could reply. 'Know this truth, Lords,' he said, quietly, but with chilling force. 'As we near this creature's lair and as we pile up his soldiers dead by the wayside, I am set on our original intention more strongly than ever. We march straight forward, to His very throne, and through His corrupt heart. If anything chooses to stand in our way we will crush it; as completely as we can and at as little cost to ourselves as our combined wits and ingenuity can allow. This is no more than His intention for us, and nothing less on our part will suffice.'

Flat on his stomach at the top of a small rise, Hawklan looked at the distant clutter of buildings, colourless and drab in the grey dawn. 'I didn't think your people lived in villages,' he said to Byroc.

Byroc shook his head. 'That is one of His slave places,' he said. 'Where weapons and other things are made. We must pass by carefully. There will be many black ones there and probably stinking Dowynai Vraen priests.' Hawklan shot him a sidelong glance. The Mandroc was trembling with rage and it seemed that at any moment he might leap up and charge into the camp to wreak what slaughter he could before he perished. It was a response he would have to watch for carefully.

'Control your anger, Byroc,' he said, his voice like ice. 'Or go your own way, now.'

Byroc's eyes narrowed viciously. 'You do not understand,' he growled after a moment.

'*I* above all, understand, the loss of a people,' Hawklan replied. 'Save your anger for the true creator of your ills.'

Dacu interrupted. 'Do you want me to find a way round?' he asked.

Hawklan nodded, but Byroc grunted. 'I know the way,' he said. 'Follow me.' And, without waiting for any debate, he wriggled backwards down the slope until he could stand without being seen from the slave camp. Hawklan and the others followed.

For some time they followed a wide circular route around the camp which took them through increasingly wet ground. After they had jumped over several rancid-smelling ditches, Byroc stopped, wrinkling his nose in disgust. 'This place has changed,' he said. 'And it stinks of His work. We must turn back.'

Hawklan looked down at the unpleasant mud clinging to his boots. It was black, with streaks of white running through it, and it was unlike anything he had ever seen before.

'Let's go a little further,' he said. 'It may be drier up ahead.'

Reluctantly Byroc agreed, and the party moved off again. They were soon brought to a halt, however, as they suddenly found themselves at the edge of a vast swamp-like area, flooded to a large extent by a black liquid. Several areas of tufted vegetation stood above the liquid but they were blackened as if they had been scorched, and the few trees that could be seen were not only leafless and stunted, but also a ghastly white.

'They're like the hands of drowned men,' someone said into the sudden silence.

Hawklan bent down a little and looked out over the silent black surface. It was alive with shimmering iridescence.

Cautiously he moved forward, but he had gone scarcely four paces, when his foot sank into the ground and suddenly he stumbled.

Several hands seized him immediately and dragged him back before he could fall. The ground released his foot with a noisy lingering slither, and a foul smell rose into the air.

Coughing and choking, the group retreated in disorder. When they stopped, Hawklan's flesh was crawling. 'What *is* that?' he said, turning to Andawyr wide-eyed.

The Cadwanwr shook his head but nodded towards Byroc. '*His* work,' he said, echoing the Mandroc's remark. 'Keep away from it.'

It was an unnecessary warning. Everyone was pale-faced and shocked. 'It's an obscenity,' Athyr said, holding his stomach uncertainly. 'Who could do such a thing, even to a benighted countryside like this?'

Byroc answered. 'This is the Groundshakers' work,' he said. 'It comes from what they do at the slave-place. In other parts it is very bad.'

'Worse than *that*?' Athyr said, aghast.

'Outside His bigger slave-places, yes,' Byroc replied. 'The air burns and the waters glow in the night. Even the wind from such will tear the throat and blind the eyes – sometimes forever.' His upper lip curled savagely to reveal his massive teeth. 'It bends and destroys even the unborn.' Hawklan turned away from the Mandroc's pain.

'Let's get well away, then,' he said, setting off again. 'We'll have to find a way round the other side of this slave-place, however difficult it is.'

'That might mean waiting until night-time,' Dacu said, looking up the small slope that was hiding them from the camp.

Hawklan scowled. 'We can't spend the whole day sitting about waiting. Time's against us here,' he said. 'And in any case I've no great desire to go wandering about in the dark with surprises like that waiting to be fallen into. We'll get around today if we have to crawl around on our bellies.'

They moved back along the route they had been following, cautiously helping one another over the ditches they had earlier jumped quite casually. Eventually the ground became drier and the air fresher, though to Hawklan it still carried some strange taint, and all of them found it difficult to rid themselves of the stench that had risen from the poisonous quagmire.

They crawled slowly to the top of the slope until they could see the camp again.

'It looks deserted,' Isloman said after a while.

Hawklan looked at Byroc. 'How many people would there be in a place that size?' he asked.

Byroc slapped his muscular hands together rapidly in a scissoring action. 'A few tens of tens,' he said. 'And much noise, smoke, and stink.'

'I can see no one,' Isloman said.

'Trust Gavor to wander off when he's needed,' Tirke said.

'He'll *be* here when he's *needed*,' Hawklan said sharply. 'I think we can reconnoitre a place like this on our own. Isloman, crawl forward. Dacu, go with him.'

Without comment, the two men set off.

Despite his bulk, it was the big carver, with his Goraidin training and his subtle shadow lore, who disappeared from view first. There was a soft whistle of appreciation from one of the watchers.

Then there was a long nervous pause as the group waited for a signal from the now invisible scouts, or a desperate alarm from the camp.

'They're there,' Yrain said abruptly, pointing. Peering between the long rough grass, Hawklan followed her hand to see the two men edging into the camp, shadows against the grey buildings.

What are they doing? he thought, in some alarm, but he said nothing out loud. Then they were gone, out of sight amid the buildings somewhere, and there was another long period of tense, silent waiting for the watchers.

Eventually they both reappeared, beckoning the others forward.

Despite the reassuring signals, however, Hawklan and the others ran low and crouching across the intervening open ground until they reached the camp.

'It's completely deserted,' Isloman said, before Hawklan

462

could ask. 'I don't think anyone's been here for several days.'

Hawklan turned to Byroc questioningly, but the Mandroc looked bewildered and nervous. 'This is a bad place,' he said. 'All His places are. We mustn't linger.'

'These buildings are like those monstrosities that Dan-Tor built outside Vakloss,' Yatsu said.

Hawklan looked around at the drab grey buildings. They were obviously not old, but they had a worn, neglected look which was peculiarly depressing. Further, he found that his inability to see into the distance all around was disconcerting.

'Let's move out,' he said. 'My instincts are with Byroc's, and we've wasted enough time here already.'

They moved through the eerily silent camp quickly and quietly, splitting into two groups and trotting down either side of the long street that ran through it. At its centre was a building with what appeared to be a watch-tower on top of it. As they passed it, Byroc paused and growled. 'Stinking priest hole,' but offered no further amplification of the remark when Hawklan looked at him.

They passed through the remainder of the camp without incident but as they reached the last buildings, Gavor came swooping along the street behind them. 'Look out –' he began, but his message was ended by the sudden appearance of a rider out of the scrubland that bounded the road where it left the camp.

He was a Mathidrin, and at his heels was a troop of some twenty of more Mandrocs.

'Whoops,' Gavor said as he landed on Hawklan's shoulder briefly and then took off again.

'Slave gatherers from the mines,' Byroc said. 'They will be looking for those who escaped.'

'Yatsu, Lorac, Tel-Odrel, move to the sides and look as if you're in charge,' Hawklan said urgently. 'The rest of you look beaten. Those at the back, string your bows discreetly. We'll have to go through this lot whether we like it or not, and we have to bring down as many as we can before they close with us.'

'They'll hardly take you for slaves, carrying swords and bows,' Yatsu said as he and the others moved to the side of the group and assumed the typical arrogant pose of a Mathidrin officers.

'Your Mathidrin uniforms and Byroc here will confuse them for long enough,' Hawklan replied. 'Are you ready at the back?'

There was grunted confirmation.

'On my command, come forward and start firing. Don't worry about the man, he'll be no problem. Take the Mandrocs, they're an unknown quantity. The rest of you string up as quickly as you can once the action starts.' He glanced at Andawyr. 'When they close with us, stay together. Andawyr is to be protected at all costs.'

He caught a glimpse of Dacu's hand signal: 'And Hawklan, too.'

'Yes, and me too,' he confirmed reluctantly.

Andawyr touched his arm. 'Don't use the Sword or the Bow, Hawklan,' he said. 'I doubt I can keep that from Him.'

Hawklan frowned. 'I understand,' he said.

Suddenly Byroc froze, and his mouth curled up into a horrifying gape. 'Dowynai Vraen!' he snarled savagely.

Hawklan felt the intention of the Mandroc and reached out to dissuade him, but Byroc evaded his grip and with an angry cry, broke ranks; not to run forward at the approaching patrol, but to disappear into a narrow alleyway between two buildings.

A flicker of surprise passed through Hawklan's mind at this apparent cowardice, but there was no time to dwell on it. The sudden movement galvanised the hesitant patrol and the Mathidrin barked out an order. At the same, so also did Hawklan.

As the Mandroc began running forward, Tirke, Jaldaric, Jenna and Yrain strode past their companions and released their four arrows. Three of them struck home, and even as the Mandrocs were falling, the four archers were firing again and the remainder of the group were preparing to fire.

For an instant the advancing Mandrocs faltered, then with a great cry of 'Amrahl! Amrahl!' they renewed their charge, seemingly oblivious to the hail of arrows being laid down by the archers.

The mindless ferocity of the attack took the defenders completely by surprise and they had barely chance to discard their bows and draw their swords before the Mandrocs struck. Several of the chanting creatures were already mortally wounded but the force of the charge scattered the group before it could form a defensive line.

Hawklan dragged Andawyr aside roughly and, pushing him against the wall of a building, stood in front of him.

A Mandroc charged at him, sword extended. Hawklan stepped forward and sideways outside the line of the attack.

His right hand gripped the extended wrist and deflected the blade across his opponent causing him to turn. At the same time his left hand reached up to rest almost gently on back of the Mandroc's neck. Then, effortlessly, he lowered the hand and the Mandroc crashed heavily to the gorund.

Hawklan followed him down and killed him instantly with a single crushing blow, at the same time seizing his sword.

It felt crude and ungainly in his hand, but its lack of finesse did not prevent him impaling a second Mandroc with a powerful upward blow as he rose to his feet.

He wrenched the sword free and thrust the dying creature into a third one who, catching the dreadful light in Hawklan's green eyes, suddenly stopped his chanting and turned to flee. The impact of Hawklan's hurled sword in his back sent him sprawling face downwards on to the hard stone ground.

Quickly Hawklan took in the condition of the others. He noted with a mixture of exhilaration and profound sadness that the beautiful and terrible fighting skills of the Helyadin and Goraidin were being practised with a ferocity that equalled the Mandroc's own. Weaving and turning, his companions were cutting and stabbing their way through their wild, chanting enemy, while threading through the scene moved the black shape of Gavor, bloodstained Mandrocs falling in his wake.

The dull grey street rang with the battle fury of the men and women who had chosen to join him in opposing Sumeral and who knew that to do so they must freely follow His way and accept the consequences that flowed from it.

As Hawklan paused, a blow in the back pushed him forward. Turning, he saw Andawyr delivering a powerful kick to the groin of a huge Mandroc who, less noisy and more experienced than the rest, had moved silently and swiftly along the side of the building. The creature looked more surprised than hurt at the blow, but as Hawklan made to attack him, Dar-volci emerged from behind Andawyr and clambered rapidly up to the hesitating Mandroc.

Hawklan half turned as the felci's rock-crushing teeth closed on the Mandroc's throat.

Then another sound rose above the din. It was a high-pitched, almost demented screaming. Alarmed at the prospect of perhaps some new and terrible foe, Hawklan instinctively reached for his Sword. Andawyr's hand gripped his wrist as the cause of the noise soon became apparent. It was Byroc. He came charging out from between two of the buildings wielding a large metal bar. The object of his attack, however, was not the body of the fray, but two Mandrocs who were standing aloof from it. They wore robes and strange head-dresses as opposed to the rough leather tunics of the others.

Both of them held up their hands and made authoritative and haughty gestures at the approaching apparition but this, if anything, roused the demented Byroc even more and with a series of swift and terrifying blows, he dispatched both of them bloodily. He paused briefly and let out a great howl then, discarding the bar, he took out his sword and fell upon the remaining fighters.

Almost abruptly, the battle was over. The last two Mandrocs slithered to the ground and the victors stood motionless amid the gaping wounds and hacked limbs of their enemy.

Only the raucous sound of heavy breathing could be heard.

The silence was only momentary, however.

'The rider. The Mathidrin. Where is he?' Hawklan's voice was strained as he ran forward into the middle of the street. 'Gavor, find him '

But even as Gavor rose up into the air, Dacu had snatched up his bow and was running to the end of the street. Hawklan and the others ran after him.

As they reached him, he was drawing the bow back to fire. Galloping rapidly into the distance was the Mathidrin officer.

'You'll never '–' someone began.

Hawklan's hands shot out, fingers extended, imposing an absolute silence and stillness on the spectators.

Dacu, bloodstained and still panting, became suddenly very still. Then to Hawklan it seemed that the entire world was filled with the sound of the release of the arrow.

No sooner had the arrow left the bow, however, than a light of knowledge came into Dacu's eyes; the shot was imperfect. Without a flicker of self-reproach or the least pause in his flowing movement, Dacu took a second arrow, nocked it on to the bow string, drew it and, slowly closing his eyes, released it.

The whole incident had been so rapid that the two arrows could be clearly seen arcing after the retreating Mathidrin like a pair of hunting hounds.

Not one of the watchers breathed.

The first arrow struck the horse, but before it stumbled, the second struck the rider. As both horse and rider crashed to the ground, Gavor dropped out of the sky on to them.

There was a brief flapping and thrashing, then he rose back into the air and headed towards the watchers.

Gently, Hawklan laid a hand on Dacu's shoulder.

'Thank you,' he said softly. Dacu was standing very still. He did not reply.

Turning to the others, Hawklan asked. 'Is anybody hurt?'

So close still to the fighting, and with most of the company covered in blood, there was some doubt about this at first, but a little careful testing showed that no serious injuries had been suffered.

'Good,' Hawklan said. 'You did well. Let's hide these bodies somewhere and then get out of here. Someone will come looking for them eventually and it's better they're thought lost than slaughtered by an enemy.'

A little later, the joyless task completed, they were moving out of sight of the camp and following Byroc across the harsh countryside.

'Were those two His priests?' Hawklan asked the Mandroc.

Byroc snarled and made a gesture mimicking that made by the two Mandrocs he had smashed down. 'Priests!' he said viciously. 'Dowynai Vraen. Too foul to blunt my blade on. We should have destroyed them generations ago.'

Hawklan frowned uncertainly, but Andawyr caught his eye and shook his head slightly. This was some deep tribal matter that would probably be beyond his true understanding. Suffice it that the Mandroc had fought with them, and fiercely at that.

He glanced at the others. They were in various degrees of shock, the younger ones, with the exception of Jaldaric being the most subdued.

He could give no subtle counsel. 'That was unfortunate,' he said. 'But you fought well and we survived with nothing more than some cuts and bruises. I won't tell you to forget it, but remember that you had no choice, and that your full attention belongs here, now, if we're to survive further. Remember also that the creatures charge on, fighting, even as they're dying.'

'Don't fret,' Isloman said to him later. 'Gulda and Loman have trained them properly. They have clear sight.'

Hawklan nodded. 'Perhaps I was speaking for my sake, not theirs,' he said. 'But I am a little concerned about Jaldaric. He seems almost elated.'

'He is,' Isloman replied simply. 'His burdens are being eased.'

Hawklan frowned.

Softly, Isloman enumerated Jaldaric's problems. 'He broke his High Guard's Oath when he kidnapped Tirilen. Then he was captured in his own tent by only three of us; faced with a Mandroc patrol.' He looked significantly at Hawklan. 'Remember what a shock that was for *us* let alone him. Then he was downed by that Mathidrin –' he searched for the name – 'Aelang. Thrown in jail without trial, and threatened with execution. And when all that was over and he was working to find himself again, he had to stand by and watch while Aelang and the militia massacred the villagers at Ledvrin.'

Hawklan put his hand to his head briefly and let out a long breath. 'I think I'll take up carving when we get back to Orthlund,' he said. '*You* can do the healing.'

Isloman smiled. 'Don't worry,' he said. 'Even I can't see a rock that's in front of me sometimes. Besides, you've helped him more than you know, as have Anderras Darion and Gulda and the Helyadin training.'

'I'll watch him more carefully in future,' the healer said, while the warrior inside him coldly assessed the value of the young man's torment as a goad to his fighting skill. The ambivalence no longer distressed him, however; both healer and warrior knew their roles and their worth.

He dropped back a little, thoughtfully, and found himself walking by Andawyr. The sight of the Cadwanwr with Darvolci scuttling along beside him made him smile despite himself. The little man was scruffier than ever after their long journey, and it was almost impossible to imagine him as their sole defence against the searching awareness of the terrible foe they were marching to meet.

Andawyr caught the scrutiny and eyed him narrowly. Hawklan's smile widened and Andawyr's scowled deepened in proportion.

'I'm sorry,' Hawklan said. 'I was just remembering you kicking that Mandroc. I'd no idea you were so . . . physical.'

Andawyr's frown turned into the teacher's look of exasperated despair such as Hawklan had seen so often on Gulda's face. He quailed a little in anticipation of the coming rebuke.

Andawyr snorted and lifted his hand to his broken nose. 'Some sight you have, healer,' he said. 'How did you think I got this?'

Aelang looked down at the fidgetting Mandroc and counselled himself to be patient. It was difficult. Of all the Mandrocs he loathed, these slobbering dim-witted trackers and their keepers were the worst.

The sight made him look up. The mountains lowered above the patrol, dark and grim, and the funeral pyre of the mines still belched forth a dense black smoke. At night it became a mass of leaping flames. It had been like a beacon for the latter part of the journey and now it streamed overhead like a great finger pointing to the north.

Arriving at the mines, Aelang had found them completely destroyed. Judging from what information he could obtain from the few surviving members of the garrison, the attacking force had been very large, but his own conclusion was that it had merely been well organised and ruthless. Judging too from the smoke and the flames pouring unabated from every known shaft and adit, and no small number of hitherto unknown ones, he presumed that that obscenity of a creature and its birds down in the depths had also been destroyed.

No great loss there, he thought again as he turned from the mountains to look again at the Mandroc tracker. What that creature did to people was only entertaining to a point, even for him, and there was always the lingering doubt that he too could go the same way if Dan-Tor judged it worthwhile. He suppressed a shudder and returned to the matter of the moment.

Having discovered that the attackers had fled south towards Fyorlund, Aelang had abandoned any thought of pursuing them. What was the point? Their whole army was moving into Narsindal anyway. Why go looking for trouble, pursuing what were presumably élite troops through dangerous mountain terrain?

He had intended to return to Dan-Tor with the news and then go to join the army waiting for the Fyordyn and their allies, but now this snivelling tracker had caught wind of something and was creating a stir. He had a powerful urge to kick the half-witted creature, but he restrained it, knowing that such a deed against one of their 'sighted ones' could well override the Mandrocs' otherwise dominant fear of Amrahl's black-clad servants.

'What does it want?' he snapped at the tracker's keeper. 'We haven't time to waste chasing slaves.'

'He says some went this way,' the keeper replied. 'Very little spoor. Not slaves. Soft movers.'

Aelang frowned. Soft movers. It was an unusual expression;

one the Mandrocs used about either particularly elusive game or their most skilled hunters.

'How many?' Aelang asked.

The keeper spoke to the tracker who grunted some unintelligible reply.

'One cum two tens,' the keeper said scissoring his hands together. '*All* soft movers.'

About fifteen 'skilled hunters'! Aelang's attention sprang to life. That was no small force. The departure of a force over the mountains must have been a feint. Perhaps the whole raid had been a feint. It was such a silent, behind-the-lines, attack that had cost them Vakloss, and with it all of Fyorlund.

He smiled, his pronounced canines predatory. Dan-Tor had told him to destroy any of the attacking force that had escaped to the north, but that had been in anticipation of their being random stragglers. Whoever these people were, they were certainly not that. But they would not have the speed of this patrol, nor be able to offer any effective resistance against such numbers. It occurred to him that the Ffyrst would appreciate having such a group captured alive for his later amusement, and that with the war about to be won and a distribution of the wealth of Fyorlund, Orthlund and Riddin imminent, the favour of Dan-Tor was well worth maintaining.

'Bring the other trackers up,' he ordered his Sirshiant. 'Tell them we're going after these "soft movers". They're to be captured for the Groundshaker.'

# *Chapter 30*

Loman started at the sound of the alarm. The Mandroc night raids had continued steadily, becoming, if anything, worse and certainly not abating despite the fearful casualties the Mandrocs were suffering. It was as if Sumeral were saying, 'I have such resources here that you may slay until you fall with fatigue and it will avail you nothing.' But surely they would not attack so early in the evening, when there was still sufficient light left for the Muster to pursue them with ease and make their casualties total?

He went to the entrance of his tent and looked out, but even as he did so the tone of the alarm changed. 'Friends approaching,' it said.

One of the sentries nearby signalled to him.

'Muster riders.'

Loman's concerned expression changed to a smile. Thanks to Sylvriss's endeavours many more squadrons had ridden to join Urthryn than he had started with after the retreat of the Morlider, but part of him was still concerned about the turmoil amongst his own people that he had left behind unresolved. He made no great stir about it, but if more of his countrymen were now arriving then it would undoubtedly hearten him. Loman set off enthusiastically towards the south gate to receive the new arrivals.

As he walked through the busy camp the noise ahead of him changed; people were cheering.

Puzzled, he ran the last part of the way and arrived just as the gate was being opened to admit the riders.

The cause of the cheering became immediately apparent. At the head of the riders was Sylvriss, her baby son hung about her neck in its simple sling and supported by one hand while with the other Sylvriss acknowledged the cheers of Fyordyn and Riddinvolk alike.

Loman strode forward as she dismounted, his face betraying a mixture of several emotions. Wherever Sylvriss was, affection dominated, but still . . .

'Lady . . . what . . . what are you doing here?' he burst out. 'And with your baby?'

'It's a pleasure to see you too, Commander,' Sylvriss replied raising her eyebrows as if surprised by this unexpected greeting.

Loman stuttered as he searched for a new beginning, but Sylvriss released him. 'Just a spot harness check, Commander,' she said, smiling. 'Nothing sinister.'

'We didn't even know you were coming,' Loman said, recovering slightly.

Sylvriss nodded, more serious now. 'I told Lord Oremson to send no word,' she said. 'I didn't want any messenger jeopardised on an unessential errand, and also I didn't want to risk the enemy finding out about my journey.'

Loman nodded appreciatively but reverted immediately to his original question. 'Lady, why have you come. It's . . .'

The question faded on his lips as his gaze drifted casually over her mount.

His eyes widened and his voice fell to an almost terrified whisper. 'That's Serian,' he said, stepping close and taking her arm urgently. 'Hawklan's horse. What –'

'Later, Loman,' Sylvriss said firmly. 'All things in their time. Let me tend him' – she wrinkled her nose and looked down at her offspring – 'and his most royal and pungent majesty, then we'll talk.'

The tending of both horse and heir did not take long, but when Sylvriss entered the Command Tent, it was to face the grim, concerned expression of her Commander and her four senior Lords.

She smiled disarmingly. 'Gentlemen,' she said. 'Why so fretful?' I've only been changing the baby, not giving birth to it.'

The sally, however, produced more exasperation than mirth but it disorganised her opponents' united protest long enough for her to sit down.

'Majesty, what are you doing here? And with Hawklan's horse?' Loman managed eventually.

'I don't know,' Sylvriss replied, suddenly almost solemn. 'The horse turned up at the Palace dirty and hungry, and needing my help. It carried me here. Now I've released it and told the guards to let it pass if it wishes.'

Loman shook his head, as if he were expecting to wake up. A swirling mass of questions fought for priority, but before any could be spoken, Eldric laid a hand on his arm.

'Forgive me, Loman,' he said gently. 'But set your questions

472

aside. You're not truly familiar with our ways. What you've just heard is all that her Majesty knows.' He looked at the Queen, who bowed in acknowledgement. 'If you ponder a little you'll see.'

Loman gazed at him intently, the Queen's few words echoing through his mind. He knew that the four Lords must be as bewildered as he about such a strange tale, but he knew too that they would be asking their own endless probing questions if they thought the Queen would be able to answer them. They were as fine craftsmen in such matters as he was with iron, or Isloman with stone. He must accept their judgement; it would be sound.

As he reached that decision, small fragments tumbled into position. By now, whatever route Hawklan had taken, he would be in Narsindal. And now the Queen seemingly at the horse's behest, had released Serian too into Narsindal.

It was a portentous event and more than sufficient to remind him that forces were at work in this conflict which were beyond even his discovering, let alone his understanding. It reminded him too that he must commit himself totally to what lay within his ability to affect.

'Thank you, Lord,' he replied. 'I won't pretend it's easy, but I *do* understand and accept what you say. This is some happening which is beyond us and we'll waste our time pursuing it. All we can do now is be happy that the Queen and her son have arrived safely, and concern ourselves with how we can have them escorted back to Narsindalvak.'

'We'll make a Gatherer of you yet, Loman,' Darek said with a chuckle.

'There'll be no need to consider my return, gentlemen,' Sylvriss said, cutting across this slight levity. 'I fear the way back will be too dangerous. I read your reports at Narsindalvak and have to tell you that matters to the rear were deteriorating even as we rode. The forts are hard pressed each night and twice we were attacked by Mandrocs on the road and saw bands of them in the mist, keeping station with us.' The men exchanged concerned glances. 'We suffered no serious casualties,' she added reassuringly. 'But we were a large force. I'd send no lightly escorted messengers back to the forts now. Nor look for any aid from that quarter. They seem confident that they can hold, but I suspect that any force plying between them will be assailed. The way is only forward now, for all of us.' Sylvriss looked down at the crib by her side. 'It isn't what

I'd intended or hoped for, but I'd no alternative than to do what I did. The horse demanded it. And now we're both trapped here.'

The Queen's news and her conclusion were chilling. A sudden commotion outside, however, forestalled any discussion, and suddenly the entrance to the tent was thrown open to reveal Urthryn; bobbing in his wake came Oslang.

The Ffyrst made no ceremony, but ploughed across the tent until he reached the crib. There, with an almost incongruous delicacy, he peered into it and, with a gentle finger, eased back a sheet to examine the face of his sleeping grandson. He smiled and nodded, then transferred his wide-eyed gaze to his daughter. 'Well, well,' he said slowly. 'Who's a clever girl then?'

Sylvriss stood up, and father and daughter embraced each other warmly. Urthryn shook his head reflectively as they parted. 'I can't tell you how happy I am,' he said. 'Your mother would've been . . .' The remark faded, and after a brief silence, Urthryn became businesslike.

'But what in the world possessed you to come here, child?' he said. 'We'll have to get you both back out of danger as soon as possible.' He looked round at the others for confirmation of this intention.

'Sit down, father,' Sylvriss said, laying a hand on his arm and indicating a nearby chair.

Though gentle, something in her manner brooked no argument and Urthryn did as he was bidden without comment.

Sylvriss told her tale again. Urthryn listened in silence. He took the news about Serian with scarcely a flicker of surprise, nodding understandingly, but he turned to Loman in disbelief when he heard about the daylight Mandroc attacks on the escort.

'Let me send a few squadrons back,' he said clenching his fist. 'We'll teach them to show their dog faces in daylight. My people are raring to go. They're weary of fighting these creatures from behind a fence.'

'No!' Loman said brusquely. 'The Mandrocs don't care whether they live or die, and whoever's organising them cares even less. You could lose any number of squadrons against such an enemy to gain nothing but two piles of dead.'

Urthryn opened his mouth to rebut this claim but Loman's hand came up to stop him. 'You know it's true, Ffyrst,' he went on. 'They're possessed by some unholy force. You've seen them fight. As have your people. That's one of the reasons I've given them such a liberal share of the night duties. There's no defence against an enemy so reckless and uncaring for their own lives, except to kill them before they get too close –'

'Or to kill whoever's leading them,' Oslang interrupted.

Loman nodded in acknowledgement. 'We'll do both,' Loman said. 'And I intend to lose no one in the process.'

'You may well fall short of that intention,' Eldric said, anxious at this extravagant ambition.

'I know,' Loman said quietly. 'But nonetheless, that's what we'll all aspire to. To aspire to save fewer, is to lose more, and I refuse to be cavalier with the lives of our people just for the want of our strong willpower.'

Loman's presence seemed to fill the tent and no one spoke as he looked round at his listeners.

'We have bows, pikes, and above all discipline,' he went on. 'We'll use all three to their maximum effect to try and avoid the need to use our swords and sinews against these creatures in close combat.'

'I don't dispute any of that, Loman,' Urthryn said. 'We *have* discussed it before at some length. But we can't afford to let the enemy cut off our supply lines and take possession of the rear.'

Loman leaned forward. 'So goes the tradition,' he said. 'But my feeling – my growing feeling – is that we'll best husband our resources by staying together and pressing on to strike at the heart of all this, than by draining ourselves trying to defend an ever-lengthening supply line. I think the more forces we commit to such a strategy, the more He'll harry us until we're spread out like a shaft with no spearhead. Very soon, I suspect, He'll look to meet us in the field, and we must be at our full strength then. When we defeat Him, I suspect the oppositon to our withdrawal will be minimal.'

'It's not what we intended at the outset,' Eldric said. 'But I agree, we hadn't envisaged such continuing and reckless assaults. It goes against the grain not to defend a supply line, but I fear you're right.'

'There will be another advantage,' Loman said.

'Everyone will know that there's no chance of retreat except through total victory.' Hreldar's voice was cold.

Loman nodded. 'If we allow Sumeral to cut us off then we limit all our options and He'll find out only too clearly just how well we've learned His lessons.'

The tent fell silent at this grim remark.

The baby stirred, then it opened its eyes and began to cry. Sylvriss picked it up. The child's innocent helplessness contrasted vividly with the stern faces of the gathered adults. Sylvriss smiled. 'You're very young to be mixing with such bad company,' she said cradling it comfortingly in her arms. After a while it fell silent.

Urthryn looked from his grandchild back to Loman, his face anxious but controlled. 'I suppose you're right,' he said, unconsciously resting his hand on his sword hilt. 'But being cut off is one thing, having a force come up behind us is another.'

Loman nodded. 'The Queen and her baby will have a special bodyguard,' he said, answering Urthryn's unspoken concern. 'And the Goraidin and Helyadin will watch for any major gathering of forces behind us. Depending on what they report we'll arrange our battle order accordingly when He finally takes to the field. A rear attack is only dangerous when you don't expect it.'

A trumpet call interrupted their discussion. Sylvriss started slightly. 'Just the night guards being set, Lady,' Loman said reassuringly. Then to the others: 'Duty calls, gentlemen. To your rounds.'

When Urthryn and the Lords had left, Loman turned to Oslang. 'What do *you* feel in the air, Cadwanwr?' he said.

'Him,' Oslang replied. 'His presence pervades everything increasingly. Those dank forests we passed through, the rivers we crossed, this damp, wretched wilderness we've reached.'

'But He doesn't assail us,' Loman said.

Oslang shook his head. 'Nor do the Uhriel,' he said. 'But they're merely waiting. We think as you do. He'll look to crush us all with one blow.'

Unexpectedly, Loman smiled. 'That, at least, is not a matter of His choosing,' he said. 'That much, *we* determine, by not responding to his harrying of our lines and by moving inexorably towards His lair. If He chooses not to stand there, then we'll take it down stone by stone.'

Oslang waved an anxious hand. 'That rhetoric's fine for the troops, Loman,' he said. 'But don't begin to believe it yourself. I agree with what you're doing. If we dawdle and fumble about here, of all places, He'll destroy us piecemeal just with His army, but if we threaten Derras Ustramel, be under no illusions, He'll set forth His power and if Ethriss isn't there to shield us, then we'll die – or worse.'

Loman dropped into a chair. 'Yes, I know,' he said. 'But it's as I said about the casualties. What we aspire to we tend to fall short of. I must have this image in my heart of Him under my sword, and His castle being tumbled into that lake. That way we'll go further than if I see us just fighting His army, and waiting for Hawklan to . . .' He faltered. He had almost blurted out the truth about Hawklan's mission. ' . . . to waken Ethriss and save us all.'

Oslang caught the stumble. 'I haven't asked before,' he said. 'But just where have Hawklan and Andawyr gone on this search for Ethriss?'

'You know as much as I do,' Loman lied. 'They told no one of their intentions so that no one would inadvertently betray them.'

Oslang seemd doubtful. 'If we knew, it's possible that we could help them in some way.'

Loman looked at him squarely. 'Your task is to protect the army against the Uhriel,' he said. 'Concentrate on that and that alone. I suspect it will take our every resource in due time. You lost one man facing Creost, as I recall. Let me attend to the fighting, and Hawklan and Andawyr to their tasks, wherever they are. I know nothing of the Power you wield, but I suspect you'll do more harm than good if you go using it indiscriminately in His land.'

Oslang bowed. 'I accept the rebuke,' he said. 'I'm sorry. It's just that I . . . we . . . seem to be doing so little. And His presence is so strong. I'm . . .' He paused.

'You're afraid,' Loman said, not unkindly.

Oslang blinked owlishly. 'Yes,' he said thoughtfully. 'Yes. I *am* afraid.'

Loman smiled and reached up to pat the Cadwanwr's arm. 'Let me tell you what you already know, Oslang,' he said. 'Say it out loud to yourself every now and then. It won't make you less afraid, but it'll make you less afraid of your fear.'

Oslang's brow furrowed. 'I'm suppose to be the wise one around here, soldier,' he said.

'Sorry,' Loman said unapologetically. 'Go and talk with your friends. They're probably all feeling the same way. This place is depressing enough for us so I shudder to think what it feels like to you. Tell them to sharpen whatever it is you people use for swords; it won't be long now.'

'I see I chose a good Commander,' Sylvriss said to Loman after Oslang had left.

Loman looked at her. 'Just tell me if you find I'm enjoying the work,' he said.

Sylvriss returned his gaze. 'Let me tell you what *you* already know then, wise one,' she said, her tone half serious, half mocking. 'You *do*, and *should*, enjoy the work, grim though it is and worse though it's going to be. You have the opportunity to use your considerable skills to protect the less fortunate and the weak and defenceless from a foe who would not only destroy them, but every precious thing that exists in our three countries, and beyond. Take it and relish it, man.'

Loman just managed to stop his mouth dropping open. 'Yes, Lady,' he said awkwardly.

'Good,' Sylvriss said. 'Now, where's Gulda?'

A messenger entered. His eyes flickered from Loman to the Queen and back again. Loman nodded.

'The horse has wandered off from the stables, Majesty,' the man said.

Unexpectedly, Sylvriss turned away quickly and began putting her baby into its carrying sling. Loman watched her. It came to him suddenly that she did not want her face to be seen.

'See that my orders are clearly understood,' she said, her hands toying busily but ineffectually with the straps to the sling. 'The horse is to be allowed to wander as it wishes, unhindered. If it seeks to leave then the gates are to be opened. Is that clear?'

'Yes, Majesty,' the messenge said, and, with a bow, he left.

Sylvriss turned round, her eyes shining wet in the torch-light. Loman looked at her helplessly, taken aback by this unexpected display of distress.

She reached into her pocket and pulled out a small stone disc. 'Your brother carved this for me when we were in Eldric's stronghold,' she said. Loman looked at it. It was Hawklan riding Serian and it was unmistakably Isloman's handiwork. Sylvriss's hand was trembling. 'Crude, he called it. But tell me, Loman,' she said. 'How does an Orthlundyn carver know more about the true nature of a horse than the Riddinvolk do?'

She wanted no answer, however, and waited for none. She took back the small carving. 'Where's Gulda?' she asked again, before Loman could speak. 'Why isn't she here, keeping you all in order?'

Loman floundered slightly then cleared his throat. 'She'll be in her tent,' he said. 'She become . . . strange . . . lately.

Withdrawn. As if she wasn't needed anymore. I've been so busy, I haven't had time –'

'I'll go and see her,' Sylvriss said, carefully positioning the baby's sling around her neck. 'Just show me the way, I need no escort.'

Following Loman's directions, Sylvriss made her way through the hectic, darkening camp. Despite the lights about her and the familiar Fyordyn and Riddin accents that she could hear, it was an oddly unpleasant place. There was an unhealthy dampness in the air which made her hold her baby tightly to her, and even the ground she walked on seemed to cling lingeringly to her feet.

After a few minutes she came to a small tent, standing slightly apart from the others. As she approached it, the entrance opened and the characteristic silhouette of Gulda stood back against the torchlight.

'Come in, my dear,' she said.

It seemed to Sylvriss that as she entered the tent, the aura of Narsindal fell away, and was replaced by an aura which she realised after a moment was like that she had felt around the sleeping Hawklan.

She took in the neat, simple quarters, with a single glance and sat down on the offered chair. Gulda sat opposite her and immediately reached out to take the baby. Sylvriss smiled and carefully handed the infant to her.

Gulda's arms enfolded it protectively and Sylvriss felt a strange, reassuring peace as she looked at the tiny form swaddled in its white sheets against the deep blackness of Gulda's robe.

Its eyes opened and it looked up at Gulda curiously. Then its mouth wrinkled into a smile and it released a delicate belch. Sylvriss smiled and Gulda laughed softly. She lifted her hand to chuck the child's chin gently.

Sylvriss looked at Gulda's hands. They were quite large, but very feminine – more like the hands of a young woman than an old one, Sylvriss thought. And yet despite their gentleness they seemed also to be muscular and powerful.

'So the line of the Lords of the Iron Ring runs still,' Gulda said, significantly.

Sylvriss raised a wry eyebrow. 'This is Rgoric's son, without a doubt,' she said. 'But before him, who can say *who* got in amongst the mares.'

The two women chuckled conspiratorially.

'Why are you here, and not helping guide this army, Memsa?' Sylvriss asked.

Gulda did not look up from the child. 'My help isn't needed for that any more,' she said. 'The Lords and your father are more than capable of doing what's necessary with Loman's Orthlundyn sight to guide them. I just potter about the hospital tent helping Tirilen and lusting after the young men.'

Sylvriss burst out laughing and for a moment could not reply. 'You've obviously got too little to do,' she said, wiping her eyes with the back of her hand. 'But you don't deceive me, Memsa Gulda, you're hiding from me and I can see you, whoever you are.'

The tears were suddenly a mixture of laughter and bewildered sadness.

'Why are you here, Queen?' Gulda asked blandly, ignoring the comment. 'In this awful land, and with Fyorlund's heir?'

'I don't know,' Sylvriss answered. 'Hawklan's horse needed to be here. Why I brought –'

Gulda looked up. 'Serian brought you?' she said without waiting for Sylvriss to finish.

Sylvriss nodded and briefly volunteered the story of the horse's mysterious appearance at the Palace and their subsequent journey into Narsindal.

'Well, well,' Gulda said incuriously when she had finished. 'How odd.'

She handed the baby back to Sylvriss with a smile. 'He's a fine child,' she said. 'I'm truly happy for you.' Then, abruptly, she began ushering Sylvriss gently towards the entrance of the tent. 'I'll have to ask you to excuse me now, my dear, I'm afraid all this marching has made me rather tired, and I'll need to catch some sleep. We'll be breaking camp early tomorrow as usual.'

As she held open the entrance, she looked intently at Sylvriss. 'You did well to trust the horse, girl!' she said. 'But have the armourer fit mail around this.' She fingered the sling. 'And sleep in your boots and riding clothes, and with your sword by your side, until this is over. We're nearly there, but we've all got harsh times ahead.'

Closing the entrance behind the Queen, Gulda turned round pensively. Then she moved towards a long chest by her bed and producing a key from her gown, unlocked it.

\* \* \*

As Sylvriss walked away from the tent, four large men emerged discreetly from the shadows. 'Majesty, Loman has asked us to protect you,' one of them said. For an instant Sylvriss considered protesting, but apart from the fact that she had the child to protect she knew that if she had no bodyguard then a far greater number of her subjects and countrymen than four would be distracted from their duties by fulfilling the role secretly.

She smiled. 'Thank you, Captain,' she said. 'That would be most reassuring.'

The Mandroc attack that night was worse than usual, and Sylvriss was glad of the four silent figures about her tent as the air began to fill with the relentless chanting of the Mandrocs and the shouted commands of the defenders. Eventually, though the baby seemed undisturbed by the noise, she took it from its crib and lay with it in her arms, staring up at the roof of the tent lit by the soft torchlight, and listening to furore outside until it merged into her dreams like the sound of a distant, pounding, ocean. Somewhere in them floated the faint memory of an awed remark she had once heard: 'The Memsa never sleeps.'


Aelang dismounted and looked around at the deserted slave camp. He needed no trackers to tell him there had been a battle here. The area had been cleared, but the dark skeins criss-crossing the stone streets were unmistakably bloodstains. Besides, it stank of it in some way.

'Find the bodies,' he said. 'Let's see how good these people really are.'

Within minutes the bodies of the ill-fated Mandroc patrol had been discovered in a windowless room in one of the buildings. Aelang showed a little surprise at the number but then examined them dispassionately. 'Slave gatherers from the mines,' he said. 'Out-shot and out-fought by the look of it. Skilled hunters indeed, our quarry – we must be careful of ambush.'

As he turned to leave, the Mandroc standing next to him let out a piercing yell. Mindful of his last remark, Aelang spun round, drawing his sword as he did, and braced himself for an attack.

But there was no attack. The Mandroc was pointing at the pile of bodies. Aelang frowned; what was it howling about?

They'd all seen and done worse than this to their own kind themselves.

Then he saw the bodies of the two priests killed by Byroc, their heads crushed in. He swore to himself. That was a heretic Mandroc killing and it could drive even his élite troops here into an uncontrollable frenzy if he didn't act quickly.

The Mandroc was beginning to roll its eyes and stamp its feet. Without hesitation, Aelang killed it with a single thrust of his sword. As he withdrew the blade he pushed the body so that it fell on top of the dead priests, then he turned round furiously on the other Mandrocs.

'Get out and form up!' he thundered offering them the smoking blade menacingly.

There was no debate. Aelang's savage and arbitrary discipline was as legendary amongst the Mandrocs as it was amongst the Mathidrin. No explanation would be given for his conduct; the Mandroc had offended in some way and been duly punished. To question the Commander's action would be to incur the same punishment.

Aelang slammed the doors behind him and set off towards the edge of the camp. He signalled to the trackers to move ahead.

Within a few minutes, however, they returned to him. 'They continue north, towards His Citadel, Great is His name, His will be done.'

Aelang finished wiping his sword. He cast away the small bruised sheaf of harsh grass then looked north and smiled, his canine teeth sharp in the grey daylight. 'Good,' he said. 'Then we need only go to the west.'

Sylvriss surveyed the destruction the next day as the camp was being broken. Outside the rudimentary palisade lay scores of dead Mandrocs, and fatigue details were hauling them away and recovering arrows and spears. Occasionally a knife was drawn to dispatch some badly wounded individual. Sylvriss started forward the first time she saw this, but Loman laid a hand on her arm.

'We can't tend them,' he said sadly. 'We tried at first, but once they gain the least strength, they'll try to kill anything that comes near.'

Sylvriss grimaced but made no comment. It was an unpleasant enough task for those involved without her displeasure adding to it.

She mounted her hitherto favourite horse. The animal had galloped faithfully behind with the remounts while she had ridden from Vakloss on Serian and now it reacted with pleasure as she settled into the saddle. Sylvriss felt like a faithless lover as she stroked its neck affectionately, for though the affection was genuine, her mind was full of the mystery of riding Hawklan's now vanished black horse.

Initially, with well-disguised reluctance, she took her place with the baggage train, Hylland and her four bodyguards riding escort. After a while, however, she was trotting up and down the huge column, talking, laughing, encouraging.

Loman turned and smiled as she approached. 'Lady,' he said. 'You're the only the thing so far that's managed to bring some lightness into this weary land. Just look at it.'

Sylvriss looked around. As ever, the mist obscured the horizons, but it held none of the mellowing haziness that might be expected. Sometimes it would be sparse, grey, and chill, fading coldly into the dull sky; at others it would be dense and white or, worse, yellow and clinging to the ground as if trying to suffocate it or obscure some aproaching menace. And it seemed to shift and change to some eerie law of its own, tendrils seeping forward and then retreating, or reaching up into the sky like eyeless spies.

The terrain itself was harsh and uneven, littered with rocks and boulders, stagnant lakes and sluggish rivers, and here and there pocked by ragged areas of discolouration as if something had lain there that had slain the ground for ever.

Trees and shrubs grew in watchful malevolent clusters as if fearful of attack, and even the grass seemed to cower.

'It's an ill land these creatures possess,' Sylvriss said. 'Perhaps if we'd looked to them more . . .'

She left the sentence unfinished. Oslang looked at her. 'Our whole journey here is littered with "ifs", lady,' he said. 'Perhaps in the future we might pay more heed to them.'

'Concern yourself with the present, Cadwanwr,' Loman said gently. 'Or there'll *be* no future for us.'

It started to rain. Cold, vertical, rain. Loman wiped his hand across his mouth. Even the rain seemed to be oily and tainted. He pulled up his hood.

Ahead, the large scattered groups of infantry who were acting as scouts started to disappear from view as the rain formed its own mist. Loman turned and looked back down the main column. That too was disappearing.

'Go back to the baggage train, Lady,' he said to Sylvriss. 'This is ambush weather.'

Sylvriss nodded and turned about.

When she had gone, Loman motioned to Oslang, and the two of them rode over to Eldric.

'Will we reach the central plain before nightfall?' Loman asked.

Eldric nodded tentatively. 'I think so,' he said. 'It must be generations since anyone rode the Watch this far north, but our old maps have been quite reasonable so far . . .'

Loman allowed himself a wry smile. 'Except for a few rivers and forests,' he said.

'I was about to say, with regard to the *major* features,' Eldric added defensively. 'If that remains the case then we should reach the edges of the plain well before dark. After that, I must admit, the maps become too vague to be of real value.'

Before Loman could reply, a rider drew up beside him. It was Fyndal, one of the Helyadin who had been sent out to assess the threat to the supply route following Sylvriss's observations. Despite the cold rain, both he and his horse were sweating.

'There are large groups of Mandrocs to our rear,' he said to Loman immediately. 'It'll take a substantial force to get through them. We're cut off from Narsindalvak unless we want to head back and make a fight of it.'

'I understand,' Loman said, then he cocked his head on one side as a faint whistling reached him. It was a relayed message from up ahead.

'It's the Goraidin coming back,' he said, urging his horse forward. 'Let's see what lies ahead of us now that we know what lies behind.'

Yengar, Olvric and Tel-Mindor looked substantially worse than Fyndal. They were tired and dishevelled, and their horses too were steaming in the steady rain. They had been riding hard for some time and it needed no subtle eye to see they brought ill news.

'Speak then rest, Goraidin,' Loman said simply, by way of greeting.

'There's an army camped on the plain two days' march away,' Yengar said.

'Mandrocs led by Mathidrin?' Loman asked.

Yengar nodded.

'How big is it?' Loman went on.

Yengar glanced briefly at his companions. 'Bigger than we are by far,' he said. Then, hesitantly, 'Three, perhaps four times our number.'

# Chapter 31

Hawklan looked down at the piece of meat on Dacu's knife. He pulled it off and began chewing it, trying to look appreciative.

'You're not hungry enough yet,' Dacu said, chuckling a little.

Gavor was less discreet. 'Eat it up, or you'll get it for your breakfast,' he said, mimicking Gulda, and laughing raucously.

Hawklan glowered at him. 'Thank you, Dacu,' he said graciously. 'And you Byroc, for your hunting.' Gavor continued to laugh.

'Indeed, Byroc,' Dacu seconded Hawklan's remark. 'I've never seen such wary game. We'd have been waiting a lot longer for food if you hadn't helped.'

Byroc grunted. 'No,' he said. 'You are a good hunter. Very quiet. You will soon learn.'

'Aren't there any herbs and roots we can eat round here?' Hawklan asked almost plaintively.

'If you wish to die, yes,' Byroc said. 'This is a bad place.' He waved a half-chewed bone at Hawklan. 'Full of His poisons. Nothing wholesome grows. Even this. We eat this now because we must, but we must not eat too often.'

Hawklan looked at the remnant he was holding, then began chewing it again. He was no great meat eater, but he knew that the Mandroc was speaking no more than the truth. He had examined some of the vegetation that surrounded them and it had a distinctly unpleasant aura. He looked at Byroc. The Mandroc had been an invaluable ally, and his knowledge of the country had enabled them to make far more progress than they would have been able to make alone.

'How much further to Lake Kedrieth?' Hawklan asked.

Byroc looked at him. 'We cannot go further this way,' he said. 'We must move to the road now.'

He became the focus of attention for everyone in the shelter. 'North are marshes,' he said. 'They move. There is no way through them.'

The road, however, seemed a bleak defenceless proposition.

'Can't we make raft of some kind?' Tirke offered.

Byroc crunched a bone noisily. 'Everything sinks in the mud,' he said. 'Everything. Byroc knows. Black ones, stinking

Dowynai Vraen.' He made an ominous slurping sound. 'They all sink. And the water flames, and the air burns and chokes. If you want to enter His place, you must use His road.'

There was a long silence. On their journey they had passed several deserted slave camps and on the occasions that they had seen the road it had apparently been deserted. It was as if the whole of Narsindal had been emptied of everyone save themselves. But still, they had encountered one patrol, and there must surely be others. The road was too exposed. The risk of discovery while using it was far too high.

But now Byroc left them no choice.

Hawklan looked around at the group. They were none of them in the best condition. Andawyr, being the oldest and least fit, was suffering the most, not least because he seemed to be bearing some kind of increasing burden as they moved nearer to Derras Ustramel. The others were suffering mainly from fatigue brought on by a combination of reduced, and dubious, rations, their long journeying, and the grim, depressing terrain. Time was against them.

'We must move soon, too,' Andawyr said unexpectedly. His words echoing Hawklan's thoughts. 'Something is happening.'

'What do you mean?' Hawklan asked, concerned at some note in the Cadwanwr's tone.

Andawyr screwed up his eyes and craned forward as if he were trying to hear some solitary voice amid a babble. 'Forces are gathering,' he said.

'What do you mean?' Hawklan repeated.

Andawyr shook his head. 'I don't know,' he said. 'His Will is . . . moving now . . . I think perhaps the army is drawing near.' He looked at Hawklan intently. 'We must destroy Him soon, *very soon*. Or He will destroy everyone. We must leave *now*.'

Hawklan felt Andawyr's bright eyes burning deep into him and it seemed that the path before him was becoming narrower and narrower.

'Very well,' he said slowly. 'This is no more than you're all trained for. We must truly be Helyadin and Goraidin. We must move through the midst of our enemies without them seeing us, and slay Him in His own lair.'

Byroc drew the Mathidrin sword he had taken during the fighting at the mines, and squinted along its edge. 'Amrahl is mine,' he said. 'If He would be chief of all the tribes, then He must face me.'

One or two were about to reply, but Hawklan shook his head at them. 'Whoever reaches Him must slay Him,' he said. 'Who can say what part we'll all play at the end? But use my Sword to do it. Use your own weapons for our lesser enemies.' He held out a beckoning hand towards Byroc's sword. The Mandroc looked at him for a moment, and then handed it to him. Hawklan passed it to Isloman, indicating its turned and chipped edge.

Isloaman nodded, and drew out a sharpening stone. Within minutes, the edge glinted and shone in the low torchlight, and so did Byroc's eyes as he received it back. As he hefted it menacingly, he bared his teeth in a predatory grimace.

'Almost as good as Loman could do with such poor metal,' Isloman said. 'Even though I shouldn't say it. Anyone else?'

When the party broke camp, there was not an edged weapon amongst them that did not bear the touch that had sharpened the chisels of Orthlund's master carver.

They abandoned the shelter and everything else that was unnecessary and, still following Byroc's lead, set off silently into the damp, grey, mist.

It was cold, grey morning that dawned on the allies' camp two days after the Goraidin had brought the news about the army waiting for them. They had reached the central plain that same day and marched across it through the next. Except for occasional flurries of spiky, thorn-laden vegetation, it was featureless and drab terrain, and despite its openness it offered no relief from the dank atmosphere that had pervaded their journey so far.

'Another reason for speed,' Loman mused to Eldric. 'A long campaign in this place would sap the morale of even the finest soldiers.'

Eldric agreed. 'It took no great subversion by Dan-Tor to engineer the abandonment of the Watch,' he said ruefully.

There were no Mandroc attacks during the two nights they camped on the plain though in the latter part of the second a long line of twinkling lights appeared on the northern horizon.

Eldric drew in a long hissing breath as he watched them. Yengar's words kept returning to him. 'Three, perhaps four times our number.' One purpose of the Mandroc raids became clear to him. Hitherto, they had been creatures of terror in legend. Now they had been shown to be just such, in real flesh and blood. Oslang had pronounced that their reckless disregard for their own lives was probably due to their being possessed by some unholy religious fervour but that did nothing to allay the terrifying prospect of facing them in open combat. And so many of them!

Worse, lurking in the mists of Eldric's thoughts, was the question: How many more of the enemy might be lurking in the mists of this benighted land?

Wilfully he repeated to himself Loman's words to Urthryn. 'We have bows, pikes and, above all, discipline.' For a while before the dawn, his mood oscillated between fearful depression and exhilaration until, seemingly by accident, his hand touched the small carving that Isloman had given him as he and Sylvriss had prepared to leave his mountain stronghold.

He sat down and looked at it quietly in the subdued torchlight of his tent. It had such depth, and as he moved it slightly, so the image of Hawklan riding Serian seemed to move, or rather, to become alive. And yet it was only a few scratches on a piece of stone. In his mind he saw again Isloman astride Serian, supporting the unconscious Hawklan. ' . . . and I only had my knife point . . .' the carver had said.

A few scratches, yet . . . so much; the wisdom and skill of generations.

He slipped the disc back into his pocket and found his mind full of the battle for Vakloss; how the army had force marched across Fyorlund to travel to the heart of its enemy like an arrow, and how, like the point of that arrow, he and his cavalry had crashed through the broken militia straight towards the distant figure of Dan-Tor.

His wavering concerns vanished and, though still fearful, he became calm. Stepping outside his tent he went to join Loman on a small watch-tower. Together they stood staring out at the lights filling the distant horizon.

Then Loman turned to him. 'Are you ready?' he asked simply.

Eldric nodded and took out the carving. 'Yes,' he said. 'I've just won the hardest part of *my* battle. Now we go straight for their heart.'

Loman took the disc and looked at it for a long moment.

'One day, I think my brother may look at this, and the one he gave the Queen, and say that for all their simplicity, they're his finest works,' he said. Then he smiled. 'But then, I'm no great judge of carving,' he said mocking himself gently.

'Suffice it that he tells us now that he's here with us, and Hawklan, and Serian.'

Then the camp was alive with activity.

The Goraidin and Helyadin came and went with their information about the enemy behind and the enemy ahead.

The cavalry – Muster, High Guard and Orthlundyn – checked their weapons and their horses and became one – more or less.

Tirilen walked among the healers in the hospital tent and, from somehere, found a quietness to help them face the bloody ordeal that must come. Gavor's feather, wilted and worn now, still adorned her green gown.

Quartermasters looked harassed.

Engineers checked the palisade and earthworks around the camp.

Bows were strung and tested, spare strings stowed safely, supplies of arrows confirmed with the runners. Slingers loosened their wrists and pocketed ' . . . just a few extra shot, Sirshiant.' Cautiously, countless cold thumbs tested countless sharp edges; swords, knifes, axes. Long pikes were hefted and grips bound and rebound. Shield straps were adjusted, armours were wriggled into some degree of comfort.

Some ate, some did not. Some sat silent, some swore, some wept – briefly. Some laughed – too much. Some checked their equipment – yet again.

All were afraid, but all would go forward.

Loman stood for a long time with Eldric on the watch-tower, watching the commotion. Relentlessly he willed his spirit into the vast gathering. And indeed, through all the ranks ran many of his words: 'Remember your drills . . . your orders . . . watch, listen . . . keep your wits about you, and use them . . . discipline and trust in your neighbour will win us the day . . . discipline and trust in your neighbour will sustain you even if your courage falters for the moment . . . don't be afraid to be afraid, it'll keep you alive . . .'

He wondered as he watched. The Riddinvolk and the Fyordyn had their military traditions, yet somehow it was the Orthlundyn and their unforeseen new aptitude that formed the heart of the army.

An army whose members could fight as one, or in groups, or as individuals. An army, whose every member knew why he or she was there.

This is a fine tool you've made, smith, he thought, both

sincerely and with bitter irony. Now use it as you must; as it deserves to be used.

Eventually he moved to the Command Tent and the final tactics of the day were agreed in the light of the information brought by the Goraidin and the Helyadin. They needed little debate; tactics had been discussed and rehearsed endlessly and were understood at every level throughout the army. There could be no other way; communication across the battlefield however well considered in advance, would almost certainly be disrupted once battle proper was joined; leaders and officers might be killed, or companies separated. 'Use your judgement as need arises. Have no fear, it'll be the same as mine,' Eldric had said before the battle for Vakloss. Now Loman echoed it.

As the various officers left, Loman turned his attention to the gathered Cadwanwr.

'Are you prepared, my friends?' he asked.

'Yes,' Oslang replied quietly.

Loman shrugged his shoulders helplessly. 'I'm at a loss to know what to say to you,' he said. 'We'll protect you from the fray, as far as we can protect ourselves . . .' He shrugged again.

'Thank you,' Oslang replied. 'That *is* all you can do for us and it *is* important to us.' He smiled and put his hand on Loman's shoulder with unexpected purposefulness. 'Have no fear for us,' he said. 'Like the Orthlundyn, we're not what we were but months ago. We're soldiers now, also. And we've every intention of both defeating our foe and coming away alive.'

Loman smiled in return, and echoed their earlier conversation. 'I'm supposed to be the warrior here, wise man,' he said.

'Sorry,' Oslang replied unapologetically, and the two men burst out laughing.

Finally, Loman, with Sylvriss and her father, and the Lords, rode along the length of the army. It took them some time, and when they returned to the centre, the damp, unpleasant air of Narsindal; rang to the sounds of cheering that it had not heard in countless generations.

As the Queen and her son returned to the camp with her escort, Loman pulled on a grim helm, and began to ride slowly forward.

Commands echoed along the line and the great army began to move after him.

491

It began to rain again.

Serian craned forward and examined the armoured figure in front of him intently, then he pranced a little, uncertain.

'Will you carry me?' the figure asked.

Serian pranced again, then bowed his head. 'Yes,' he said, knowing that the figure would hear him truly.

From the shelter of a cluster of gnarled and dying trees, Isloman gazed from side to side along the road. Then he moved from his hiding place and walked on to the road and looked again.

Satisfied, he signalled and, stealthily, the others ran forward to join him.

'At least the mist is on our side now,' he said as they set off.

Hawklan and Andawyr exchanged glances. From now, their whole venture would be balanced more finely than a sword standing on its point. They had moved along by the side of the road for as long as they could, but the ground had become increasingly marshy, and now they had no alternative but to use the road itself. Yatsu, Tel-Odrel and Lorac had salvaged what they could of their Mathidrin uniforms and Hawklan had donned that of the Captain they had killed.

'You are slave gatherers from the mines,' Byroc told them, tapping an insignia on Hawklan's uniform.

'Which means you're not highly thought of, as far as we can tell, but at least you're a Captain,' Yatsu added.

Hawklan nodded. 'I understand,' he said, adding needlessly, 'Stay aware, all of you.'

As they walked, the road widened considerably, and twice it gave them the opportunity to hide rather than test their crude disguises. On both occasions a group of mounted Mathidrin trotted out of the mist, to be followed by a large column of armed Mandrocs. Hawklan and the others, having heard the approach, lay flat at the foot of the wide shallow embankments that led down from the road.

The exercise demonstrated the correctness of Byroc's advice as they found themselves lying immediately adjacent to what appeared to be a field of lush, tufted vegetation which extended away from them into the mist. A single step however disabused them of any thoughts of travelling along this seemingly solid turf, as it yielded immediately with clinging relish, and emitted an appalling stench.

The smell of decay indeed pervaded everything, and occasionally the mist thinned out to show beyond the vegetation a dark glistening surface which seemed to be both still and uneasily mobile. In the distance, faint flickering lights could sometimes be seem, and from time to time, strange noises came softly out of the emcompassing greyness; splashing, slithering, bubbling.

Indeed, Hawklan frequently felt live things reaching out, but there was a quality about them so unnatural that he could do no other than turn away.

'What's the matter?' Isloman asked him at one point, but Hawklan just shook his head. 'Corruption,' he answered. 'Beyond any help I can offer.'

Then a dense mist, barely waist-high spilled over on to the road so that for a while they seemed to be wading through a shallow lake.

'Walk slowly. Do not disturb it,' Byroc said, without amplification.

After a while, it seemed to Hawklan that although the road was flat, he was straining up some great slope.

'How much further?' Hawklan asked Byroc.

'Not far,' came the reply, but it was from Andawyr not the Mandroc. Hawklan turned round to look at him. The Cadwanwr's face was grey with strain.

Hawklan signalled the group to stop and put his arm around Andawyr to support him. Andawyr however, waved a dismissive hand. 'I'm all right,' he said. 'It's just that His presence is more appalling than I could have imagined.' His face lightened momentarily. 'But His Will is elsewhere. We must hurry. We must take Him while His attention is towards the army.'

'Allow us to escort you to His presence.'

The voice was harsh and cold, and came out of the mist ahead.

# Chapter 32

Loman and the four Lords surveyed the enemy line as the army drew nearer. It was truly enormous. Loman thought of a debate that they had held at Anderras Darion concerning the social disruption involved in fielding a large army. They had concluded that Narsindal had become a warrior state and that to delay attacking it would benefit Sumeral and drain themselves. It had been one of the many small milestones they had passed on the journey to this point.

And the conclusion had been largely correct, Loman thought. Except that they had not foreseen the awful flux that Sumeral would have used to join together the many disparate and quarrelsome Mandroc tribes. Oklar had almost destroyed the Fyordyn by slow and subtle corruption of their ancient, civilised, ways from within. Creost had unified the semi-civilised Morlider by a combination of traditional tribal brute force, and self-interest against a common foe. Sumeral, however, so Oslang surmised from his observations of the night-raiding Mandrocs, had united the Mandrocs by becoming a god to them as He had during the First Coming.

Thus, obedience to His word would transcend all independent thought, all reason, all past traditions, everything. It was as savage and cruel an invention as war itself and its effectiveness was a shuddering affirmation of the power of ignorance. Who knew now what empty promises filled the minds of these demented creatures as they hurled themselves so frenziedly on to their enemies swords?

A rider came into view. It was Yengar, bringing final details of the enemy's disposition.

Loman raised his hand.

Commands echoed along the line and there was sound like the retreat of a wave down a pebbled beach as the advancing army halted. The forest of raised pikes wavered momentarily, like a field of tall grasses shaken by a sudden wind, then the air was full of the sound of thousands of waiting people, and the steadily falling rain.

Yengar saluted Loman and the Lords. 'Nothing's changed,' he said. 'One huge line of infantry, mainly Mandrocs, fronted by a pike line, and flanked by Mathidrin cavalry – of sorts – perhaps only a fifth of our cavalry strength. And a few archers.'

Loman nodded. 'What about the discipline of their infantry?' he asked.

'Minimal, as far as we can tell,' Yengar replied. 'There seem to be one or two orderly pike phalanxes. Ex-militia and High Guard probably, but I think the intention is to overwhelm us by sheer numbers.'

Loman looked at Yengar closely. 'That much we envisaged, but you seem more uneasy than that,' he said.

Yengar pulled a wry face. 'Something's not what it seems,' he replied. 'But I can't put my finger on it.'

'Be explicit, Goraidin,' Eldric said, frowning a little, but Loman raised a cautionary hand.

'Let it go for the moment, Yengar,' he said casually as he turned round to look at the Cadwanwr. Armed and armoured at Loman's express command, and to their own initial amusement, they were situated amongst the rearguard infantry and were quite indistinguishable from the rest of the troops.

Loman made a small hand signal and Oslang replied.

No attack had been launched by the Uhriel.

Loman turned back to Yengar thoughtfully.

'Did you see the Uhriel?' he asked.

Uncharacteristically for a Goraidin making a formal report, Yengar's reply betrayed his own feelings. 'Yes,' he said, almost snarling. He pointed, but even for Loman it was difficult to make out individuals. 'All three are standing in the centre as we are here, but riding . . .' His lip curled; Loman waited. ' . . . things . . . things that might have been horses, once.'

'You recognised them for certain?' Darek said, craning forward and staring through the rain.

'Oklar without a doubt, Lord, though he was out of his brown robe, and fully and foully armoured.' Yengar replied. 'The other two were also armoured but I knew them from the descriptions we got in Riddin.'

'What about *Him*?' Hreldar asked.

Yengar shook his head. 'Even to my eyes, those three stood stark and unnatural against all the others,' he said. 'There was no fourth figure.' He paused and then spat. 'But His flag was there. The One True Light – a silver star on a golden field.'

The Lords seemed discomfited by this display of emotion from their Goraidin, but Loman nodded and looking round again, smiled. 'Your people carry *your* ancient flag too, Goraidin. The Iron Ring on a red field. And the Muster have the flags of their houses.' He winked. 'And the flags of their cousins, and cousins' cousins,' he whispered.

Yengar's sourness faded before Loman's light touch and he laughed a little. 'But no flag from Orthlund,' he said.

Loman smiled and shrugged. 'We never got round to it,' he said. 'We're not soldiers really. We'll ride to His flag, and kill anyone who stands in the way.'

Yengar laughed out loud, then paused abruptly. He narrowed his eyes as if he were looking at something intently. 'The ground,' he said. 'The ground a few hundred paces in front of their line. It's been disturbed and they've tried to cover it up I'm sure. There's something wrong there.'

'Pits, trenches, to stop the cavalry?' Loman offered.

Yengar shook his head. 'It could be, but I don't think so,' he said. 'The rock's very near the surface here. We found it difficult to cut good observation trenches, that's why we couldn't get too near.' He gathered up his reins. 'I'll see if we can get closer. Don't send anyone in until you hear from us.'

Loman nodded and, and, and Yengar galloped off.

'Good advice, I think, Lords,' Loman said to his companions. 'Shall we continue slowly?'

The great line clattered into motion again.

'No changes of heart about our tactics, Lords?' Loman asked as they rode forward.

All four shook their heads. 'More than ever, we're right,' Hreldar said. 'From what we've seen of the Mandrocs I can't see them yielding until they've been utterly crushed. And against that number we'll have to crush them quickly if they're not going to curl round and envelop us.'

Loman nodded, and looked up into the rain. The sky overhead was grey and lowering.

Is there enough water there to wash away the blood that must be spilt today? he thought. Hawklan, Andawyr, in the name of pity, stop this if you can. I want to get back to my forge and my true life.

It was the only time that day, that Loman allowed his thoughts such a longing departure from the field.

'What's Yengar doing?' Arinndier asked, peering into the distance.

Loman wiped the rain off his face and followed the Lord's pointing hand. He had presumed that Yengar would fade quietly into the landscape to rejoin his colleagues in some secret obseravation post, but the Goraidin was trotting straight towards the enemy's centre.

Loman turned and signalled urgently to Oslang. The Cadwanwr broke ranks and galloped forward.

'Protect him,' Loman said pointing towards the distant figure of Yengar.

Oslang opened his mouth to speak.

'He'll take his chance against arrows and swords,' Loman said urgently. 'But protect him from the Uhriel. It's important.'

As he spoke, Yengar halted some way in front of the great horde. The allies' army continued to move relentlessly forward.

Yengar drew his sword, made a sweeping ceremonial salute, and began to parade up and down in front of the enemy. The rumble of distant voices began to make itself heard over the footsteps and rattling tackle of the advancing army.

'I don't believe it,' Arinndier exclaimed. 'He's doing a formal sword drill.'

As they watched, Yengar continued brandishing his sword and moving his horse to and fro; cut to the left, to the right, change hands, repeat, protect the head, protect the flank, change hands again, swing low out of the saddle to take a fallen weapon, to the right, to the left, on and on, the manoeuvres becoming progressively more complex and faster. The horse too twisted and turned, as it galloped round round in increasingly wider patterns. Then, with the horse rearing, he hurled the sword into the air several times, each higher than the last, finally sending it up in a great spinning arc, and galloping beneath to catch it as it tumbled back down.

It was an impressive display and an involuntary cheer went up from those in the army who could see what was happening.

Yengar completed his performance with another ceremonial bow to the enemy, backing his horse away as courtesy dictated.

There was no response from the Mandroc army other than what appeared to be abuse, but as Yengar finally turned to leave. Oklar raised a hand towards him. Loman became aware of Oslang beside him breathing deeply.

Yengar's horse suddenly tumbled, throwing him. The Goraidin rolled over several times and lay still. The sound of a distant triumphant roar reached the advancing army and there was a brief but perceptible surge in the enemy ranks. Oslang winced as if he had been struck, then he swore and, closing his eyes, extended both arms with the hand palm upwards. It was a gentle, open gesture, but Loman sensed the power being released next to him and found himself holding his breath.

Then he saw Oklar clearly. The Uhriel's horse reared, and Oklar himself raised a hand suddenly as if to protect himself from an unexpected blow. Yengar's horse struggled to its feet and began running away from the enemy. As it passed the motionless form of the Goraidin, Yengar surged up and began to run alongside it. For a moment, he seemed to be struggling for a grip, then he bounced twice off the sodden ground and swung up into the saddle.

As Yengar galloped a zig-zag course away from him at full speed, Oklar regained control of his mount, but he did not seem inclined to resume his assault on the fleeing Goraidin.

Loman looked at Oslang.

'He may have been bound at Vakloss, but he's bound no more,' Oslang said, squeezing his palms together. 'And he's angry now. He didn't expect to be so accurately thwarted in his petty spleen.' The Cadwanwr scowled. 'I presume that was done for a good reason, Loman, but send no more out on such antics,' he concluded. 'The cost of protecting them is too high, and *they'll* learn too much about us. I must return to the others now. The assault will begin in earnest soon I fear.'

'It *was* for a good reason, Oslang,' Loman said quietly. 'Thank you for what you did.'

Yengar did not return directly but seemingly fell exhausted from his horse near an advanced group of skirmishers who ran to tend to him. Eldric started forward, but Loman stopped him. 'He's all right,' he said. 'He's found something and he doesn't want to be seen bringing it directly to us.'

The army moved on, and the rumble of the Mandrocs grew louder and louder. Gradually, the familiar, 'Amrahl, Amrahl', began to punctuate the noise at regular intervals.

After a while, Yengar, on a different mount, emerged casually from the ranks alongside a messenger and rode up to Loman.

He was still trembling slightly.

'That was bravely done,' Loman said. 'But you owe your life to Oslang as well as to your horse and your wits. Thank him when you see him.'

'I will,' Yengar replied. 'It's Oklar's touch that's still making me shake. It was appalling. I've never been so frightened.' He shuddered. 'Then someone . . . something . . . lifted it from me like a spring breeze. I'm sorry if it's caused problems but I couldn't think of anything else to do. We couldn't get closer and I needed to see that ground. To be honest, I didn't think he'd bother to attack one foolish posturing soldier.'

'Never mind,' Loman said. 'What did you find?'

A few minutes later, after some coming and going of riders, the four Lords, their red cloaks resplendent even in the grey rain, were galloping to their respective units.

The chanting, with its periodic responses of, 'Amrahl, Amrahl', grew louder and louder, and a rhythmic accompaniment of stamping feet and swords banged against shields began to complement it. It was a prodigious, intimidating noise.

Loman grimaced then leaned over to one of his messengers and asked him a question. When the man answered, Loman motioned him towards the swaying mass of pikes following behind. The messenger galloped over to the nearest company leader.

Very soon the sound of the Fyordyn's Emin Rithid rose up to oppose the Mandroc's rumbling paean. It spread rapidly through the ranks and the pace drummers began to beat a determined tattoo about its imposing rhythm. As it reached the flanking and rearguard cavalry, the sound of the Muster's horns joined it in a sonorous counterpoint.

The length of the line meant that those near the flanks were singing well behind those at the centre, but the sound was massive and stirring and as it washed to and fro along the line like a great wave, Loman smiled.

'Gavor, my old tormentor, wherever you are,' he said to himself. 'You would appreciate this piece of theatre. And the one that's about to follow, if we can do it right.'

For, just as Oklar had sought to destroy the Fyordyn High Guards by fire, so he intended to destroy the allies.

He had failed in Fyorlund because of the discipline of his enemy. Now, one brave man out of the thousands on that plain had perhaps seen his scheme.

Steadily, the army drew nearer to Sumeral's waiting horde, and Oklar's fearful trap. Loman watched the skirmishers slowly falling back as he had ordered.

Then, the time was right.

Loman sent a signal down the line, and with a great shout, a section of the Lords' cavalry began to gallop forward raggedly.

The chanting from the Mandrocs rose in anticipation as the

noisy charge gathered momentum, but as the two leading riders reached the area where Yengar had performed his spectacular reconnaissance, they turned away suddenly and each threw something in the general direction of the enemy.

As the two objects landed, they burst into flames. But the two riders saw nothing; they, along with their companions were galloping back to the lines desperately.

Loman saw Oklar raise his hand, but he was too late. Almost immediately the whole area was engulfed by a roaring white sheet of flame.

Involuntarily the entire allied army halted and took several paces backwards, with a precision that no drill sirshiant could ever have inculcated.

Somehow, Loman managed to control his startled horse, though he found himself gaping as he stared up at the huge fiery wall that was tearing through the ground between the two armies. He looked from side to side and saw the flames were spreading along the entire length of the two armies.

Had they continued to advance, the whole army would have been utterly and horribly destroyed in the conflagration.

A vision of his forge back in Pedhavin came to him vividly; of times when in thoughtless absorption he had set his hand to metal just cooled below red heat. Even at this distance from the flames, the heat beat on his face appallingly. He had heard of the blazing destruction of the warehouse at Vakloss, but had taken tales of the escapade with some scepticism. Now however . . .

Something dark stirred deep within him.

Turning quietly to the wide-eyed signaller at his side, he sent a single message to every company. 'See the true nature of our enemy. His device has failed through our knowledge of the ways of His servants. Now He has only wild numbers, bathed in ignorance, to fight for His corruption, while we have discipline, skill and knowledge, to fight for our simple right to be. Look to one another today and light be with you all.'

Then, the army, hidden from the enemy by Oklar's own massive wall of fire, turned and began marching quickly to the left, while the High Guards' cavalry and some of the Muster trotted to the right.

Loman smiled broadly as the two riders who had ignited the trap fell in beside him. 'You're becoming rarely gifted incendiaries,' he said, shouting a little to make himself heard over the din of the roaring flames.

'I doubt there'll be much call for such skills when this is over,' Fel-Astian replied.

'Nor for many of the skills we've re-learned of late,' Loman agreed. 'But it doesn't alter their value. Still, this is no place for debate. How long is this going to last?'

Idrace glanced up at the flames, his eyes screwed tight against their brightness. 'They're dropping already,' he said. 'I'd say start preparing to move when they're about pike height.' He raised a cautionary finger. 'This is no ordinary fire, Loman,' he went on. 'At the end the flames will flicker out *very* quickly. You must be ready. Don't be too concerned about the temperature underfoot, this stuff burns to nothing. It leaves no ash or residue, and the ground won't be as hot as you'd imagine.'

As the flames gradually fell, Loman eyed them carefully and then turned the army forward to advance straight across them, though not without some trepidation. Idrace's comments about the flames however, proved accurate and, almost incongruously, the terrible blazing barrier suddenly disappeared. The flames did not gutter into leisurely extinction like a spent bonfire, but parted from the ground and rose into the air as they finally died, so that for a moment a low, blazing cloud hovered between the two armies.

The hissing of the rain falling on to the warm rock rose up to fill the strange silence that followed the roaring of the flames, and a low dense mist formed over the blighted area.

Slowly the sounds of the moving army began to dominate once more; the resolute tapping of the pace drummers, the clatter of thousands of silently marching people. Then, from the left came the horn calls that Loman had been anticipating, and several squadrons of the Muster slowly began to advance towards the enemy's right flank cavalry.

The phalanx infantry lowered their pikes into attack position and increased their speed to a fast walk.

Very rapidly, the Muster gathered speed and their battle cries began.

Loman glanced to the right to confirm that the Muster and the Lords' cavalry were also advancing. As he watched they began to move into close column formation.

Loman rode along the ranks to join his own squadron of Helyadin and Goraidin.

His decree had been that the enemy was to be crushed as quickly and totally as possible, and the Mathidrin cavalry guarding the right flank found themselves facing superior numbers, superior skills and pitiless intent as the unbroken wall of Urthryn's squadrons came towards them at full gallop with lances levelled and in almost parade ground order. Ahead of them, the air filled with the roaring of the men and the terrifying ululating cries of the women.

Such a sight was it, that the rout of the Mathidrin began even before contact was made; the few that had the courage to remain being eventually carried away by their wiser horses.

Those who survived the first, terrible, impact were cut down in the ensuing mêlée or fled blindly through and over the ranks of infantry they were supposed to be protecting. The Muster began its retribution for the drowning of its kin with awesome, vengeful, and bloody relish.

At the same time, the serried rows of glittering and unyielding pikes struck into the mass of Mandrocs and men that formed the enemy's right wing, sweeping aside the disordered pike lines that faced them and driving the surviving front ranks backwards in panic.

'Oklar put too much faith in his fire wall,' Yengar said, leaning across to Loman. 'Their fervour fades a little against such opposition.'

Loman nodded, but even as we watched this initial success, he felt the ground shake ominously. Then a feverish warmth passed through him and he began to gasp desperately as the air in his lungs seemed to be torn out of him.

From the attack in Riddin, he recognised the hand of the Uhriel in the attack and knew that he could do nothing about it. For a moment he felt himself slipping into unconsciousness, and he began to scream in terror and impotent rage, though no sound reached his lips. Around him he could see the others suffering similarly.

Then there was an uneasy stillness, and he could feel his body being fought over by other wills. Slowly, and fitfully the fearful sensation passed away and, as he recovered, his gaze was drawn to Oslang and the Cadwanwr. They were standing motionless. He galloped across to them.

'Can you hold them?' he shouted to Oslang above the din of the fighting.

Oslang turned to him, his eyes distant. He nodded slightly. Loman wanted to say more, but felt again his impotence in this battle within a battle. 'Fight the army, Loman,' Oslang said as if reading his mind. His voice was faint, but not weak.

As Loman turned to leave, Oslang spoke again. Loman had to lean forward to catch the words. '*They* are here,' the Cadwanwr said. 'The Guardians. Such consciousness as they have, is with us. Go now.' There was great strain in his voice, but also an unusual strength – triumph almost.

Loman seized a nearby messenger. 'Send to all the companies that the Uhriel are held and that the Guardians are among us.'

He returned to his companions and looked at the damage that had been wrought by the Uhriel's attack. It was considerable. The phalanx had lost some of its cohesion and had been broken at two points. He could see frantic hand-to-hand combat occurring as the infantry sought to beat back the incursion. The Muster too had been disarrayed by the attack and though they had not broken off contact, their advance had slowed considerably and they were beginning to suffer casualties in the mud-spattered mêlée where their mobility and power were less effective.

Break off, Urthryn, he thought. Pull back and use your archers against their infantry. We can't match them blow for blow.

The thought turned him to his right where the cavalry should have been assailing the enemy's left wing with arrow storms to prevent them moving round and surroundiung the attacking infantry. But they too had been thrown into confusion by the Uhriel's brief attack and though they were recovering quickly, they themselves were being threatened by the huge mass of the now advancing left wing.

As he watched, the fear that had haunted Loman ever since the first Mandroc attacks on their night camps, returned to him in full vigour.

It was only by turning the momentum of a large army against itself that a smaller one could hope to prevail. And yet while the discipline of the Mandrocs was less even than that of the Morlider, and the slaughter that they were suffering would have broken a normal army and sent them crashing over one another in rout, this was not happening. Certainly, sections of them were panicking and turning to flee through their own, but the majority were standing their ground. They would have to be cut down one at a time – and they took some killing.

Loman felt the strange stirring deep within him again.

Then it erupted to fill him like a living thing. A terrible dark knowledge, hung about with raging, soul-shaking anger at the

503

horror he was having to create. The Mandrocs would be put to flight only by the face of a will, an intention, more terrible, more inexorable, than that of their god and His servants.

He turned to the élite squadron around him. The two Goraidin, Yengar and Olvric were either side of him. Helmed and grim, he knew they saw what he saw, and assessed it as he did.

Olvric drew his sword as if anticipating Loman's order.

Yengar closed his eyes briefly and tightened his mouth, then he too drew his sword.

Loman looked at the others, his eyes cold and frightening. 'My friends,' he said. 'We are His creatures now. If we are to be ourselves again we can be nothing less. Will you ride with me to cut out the heart of this monster He has sent against us?'

He waited for no reply, but turned and urged his horse forward. There was a great roar from behind him and he felt his companions closing behind him in a tight wedge formation as his horse began to gather speed.

He was aware of the horse beneath him, and the wind, and the cold, tainted rain on his face. He was aware of the whole battle as if he were flying high above it, like Gavor, and yet he was present at every frightening, fearful, part of it; he was the hardened High Guard trooper counting his arrows and picking a target as he controlled his horse with his knees; he was the bewildered carving apprentice with rain in his eyes, gripping his pike and keeping station with his friends, though his feet were slipping in the mud; he was the unhorsed Muster rider repeatedly hacking a screaming Mandroc until it was still and then treading on its face to pull his sword free as he called desperately to his horse. He was their will and he was aware of them all.

But above all he was aware of His presence, watchful, malign, and patient.

You in your turn, you demon, came the thought through his unbridled rage.

Suddenly there were other riders ahead of and around him: Muster riders. Seeing his charge, some of the rearguard squadrons had been drawn inexorably after him – 'Use your judgement . . . it will be the same as mine.' Now they were shepherding and guiding him.

'We'll carry you through, commander,' came a voice from somewhere, and for a moment Loman was at one with the heart of the Muster; understood the bond between these wild-eyed riders and their wild-eyed horses; revelled in the straining sinews, the flying manes, the earth-shaking thunder of their hooves.

Then he was Loman the smith again, wielding the terrible tool he had forged to fill this terrible need.

And finally he was Loman the man again, as the Muster carried him into and over the Mandrocs who had rushed forward to protect the Uhriel from this onslaught.

Loman saw them flailing under the hooves of the horses, then abruptly the charge was over and he was part of a floundering, tumultuous mass of rearing horses and slashing blades. His horse lost its footing and fell heavily. Loman's own fall was softened by the bodies that he landed on, but his sword bounced from his hand.

He curled up and rolled over to avoid the stamping hooves, and the momentum of his roll carried him to his feet in long-practised manner. His two open hands followed the movement, driving upwards under the chin of a Mandroc in front of him. As the creature fell, Loman seized the axe it was holding and, spinning round, swung it into another approaching from his right.

The axe embedded itself in the Mandroc's side and Loman made no effort to relinquish it as the howling creature staggered back. A horse jostled him and he was aware of a high-pitched female shriek as a sword blade scythed past him to beat down a spear point driving towards him.

The Mandroc holding the spear towered over Loman, but the woman's blow had unbalanced it and, seizing the descending shaft, Loman caught the creature's momentum and sent it hurtling through the air to bring down several others as it landed.

He saw riders attempting to close about him but they were drawn away by their own needs. Two Mandrocs charged him. He swung the spear round and one fell with its throat cut by a short, flicking, lunge, while the other crashed to the sodden ground as it moved back to avoid another lunge only to have the spear swing over its head and sweep down to take its legs from under it. Loman finished it with a single blow.

A backward thrust sent a third reeling and a dreadful thrust sent the spear clear through a wildly charging fourth. As the dying creature fell forward, it slithered down the shaft, and the bloody spearhead rose to the vertical like an obscene plant before falling slowly to the ground.

Loman glanced round as he bent down to seize a longsword lying nearby. Several of his companions were fighting on foot; the Goraidin and the Helyadin with their terrible and strangely beautiful precison; the Muster riders, as savage, but less assured, in small self-protecting groups until they could remount or ride double. The majority, however, were still mounted and were forcing back the Mandrocs with terrible slaughter; swords and axes rose and fell against the grey sky and skeins of blood and gore flew up to join the incessant tumbling rain spattering down onto the mounds of dead and wounded.

A screaming horse crashed down beside him and as he snatched its rider upright, the momentum of Loman's purpose reasserted itself. He wrapped both hands about the grip of the sword, and charged towards the most densely packed section of the line in front of him with a great roar. He felt others, mounted and on foot, falling in behind him.

For an unknowable, timeless, age, the world became only a swirling, hacking, red-stained blaze of light, as the smith's forging will and his terrible strength cut through all that stood before him.

Slowly, somewhere in the turmoil, the fluttering, inspiring mote that was Loman felt the currents about him change; heard the all-pervasive rumbling ground bass rise into a whining, fleeing scream.

But then a sudden silence fell; and Loman stood shoulder to shoulder with Yengar and Olvric, staring down an aisle of white-eyed Mandroc faces into the grim-helmed visages of Oklar, Creost and Dar-Hastuin.

# *Chapter 33*

Andawyr laid a hand on Hawklan's arm as he reached for his Sword, but all the others drew theirs.

'I should prefer not to kill you all,' said the voice ahead of them. 'But the choice is yours.'

A solitary figure emerged from the mist, sword in hand.

It was Aelang.

As he walked forward, swaying shadows in the mist behind him darkened and slowly took form to reveal his Mandroc patrol.

Yatsu and the others slowly closed in front of Hawklan and Andawyr, but Jaldaric pushed past his companions and strode forward to stand in front of the Mathidrin, his sword levelled.

Aelang made no move other than to incline his head quizzically. 'Ah,' he said, after a moment, his tone contemptuous. 'I remember you. The solitary twig from Eldric's creaking tree. Stand aside, child, I'm in no mood for trifling with you as I did in Orthlund. Indeed I'm in no mood for trifling with any of you. We've been waiting for you for some time, and we're missing the slaughter of your friends.'

Jaldaric continued to stare at his erstwhile captor. 'Nor will I trifle with you, Aelang,' he said in a tone that, though calm, made his companions look at one another uneasily. Tirke made to step forward but Hawklan put a hand on his shoulder.

'In due course, you'll be charged with other crimes,' Jaldaric went on. 'But now I'm arresting you in the Queen's name for the crime that I witnessed; for the murders you committed at the village of Ledvrin. You'll be taken to Vakloss where'll you'll be given the opportunity for a full Accounting. I must ask you to surrender your sword.'

His manner was so authoritative that for a moment a flicker of doubt passed over Aelang's face and he glanced uncertainly at the swords behind his accuser. Then his face became livid. 'I see that blow to the head I gave you has addled what few wits you had,' he snarled. 'However, this one will end your confusion permanently.'

Without warning, he swung his sword round to beat Jaldaric's blade down. It was a swift and sudden blow, but

Jaldaric avoided it almost casually, and in turn beat Aelang's blade down.

'That was one more chance than was allowed to anyone at Ledvrin,' Jaldaric said, a hint of his inner rage creeping into his voice. 'You will have no other if you don't surrender.'

For an instant disbelief, then fear, filled Aelang's eyes as he stared into Jaldaric's emotionless face. He stepped back a pace, uncertain again.

Hawklan's hand tightened about Tirke's shoulder in anxious anticipation.

Then Aelang spun round, the sword following him with a scything power that would surely cleave the young Helyadin in two, from neck to hip.

Aelang had risen through the Mathidrin ranks not only by cunning and ruthlessness but also by displaying a fearful prowess in all manner of fighting techniques. He would have been a match even for the experienced Goraidin and as a swordsman he was far superior to Jaldaric.

But as Aelang had emerged out of the gloomy Narsindal mist, Jaldaric had recognised a terrible opportunity and knew that he must be prepared to accept death *now* if he was to be free of the doubts and guilt which lined the path of his life like mocking ghosts.

Thus it was with a deep inner stillness that Jaldaric entered the swirling maelstrom of Aelang's attack. As the Mathidrin's sword swept down, Jaldaric moved with the blow and stepping aside, drove his sword straight through his attacker.

'Go stand for your Accounting before your victims, then, Commander, if that's your wish,' Jaldaric said as disbelief returned to Aelang's eyes.

Jaldaric tugged at his sword, but the blade was wedged. Aelang made a strange noise and danced a brief, obscene dance. Gritting his teeth savagely, Jaldaric wrenched the sword free.

Aelang took a single step forward and stood for a moment like a stricken marionette. Then he dropped to his knees and slowly tumbled face forward on to the road.

His sword clattered noisily from his hand.

There was an eerie silence.

'Close ranks and follow at the double!' Yatsu's command was soft, whispered almost, but its power galvanised the stunned watchers.

Then they were all running, Tirke seizing Jaldaric and

dragging him forward, the others forming up around Hawklan and Andawyr.

Yatsu led them down and along the embankment past the Mandrocs, still bewildered by this sudden, unexpected happening.

Apart from his initial command, Yatsu made no sound as he ran, nor did any of the others, knowing that the silence would give them precious seconds where a roaring battle cry would soon bring their enemies to their senses.

Thus they were running back up on to the road before the Mandrocs began to respond.

'Hawklan, Andawyr, go,' Yatsu shouted. 'We'll hold them off.'

Hawklan hesitated briefly, but Andawyr grabbed his arm and dragged him forward along the road.

As the two men ran into the mist, the sound of desperate fighting began to follow them. Hawklan clenched his teeth as part of him rebelled against this flight from his friends in need. But the other part of him drove him forward beside the Cadwanwr. His friends might die without his help, but they might die with it, and their deaths then would be one of utter futility. They were here, in this awful land, solely that he could flee now, to find and face his true enemy.

Gradually, the sounds of battle faded, to be replaced by the sound of their footsteps and gasping breaths.

Suddenly, Andawyr tripped and fell awkwardly, crying out in pain. Hawklan bent to pick him, but as he did so, figures came running out of the mist ahead.

They were Mandrocs, Aelang's rearguard, Hawklan realised. Left here against the possibility of anyone escaping his trap.

One of them came charging forward, spear levelled. Another followed close behind. Hawklan reached for his Sword, but a glimpse of Andawyr's imploring face stopped him drawing it.

Instead, he twisted sideways and laid his hand on the shaft of the first spear as it passed by him. He pressed it downwards as it ran under his hand, and the sudden change in direction drove the point into the ground. The charging Mandroc ran into the butt end of the shaft with a grunt and then pivoted incongruously over it to fall heavily some distance away.

Even as the Mandroc was falling, Hawklan had swung the spear up and pushed it between the outstretched arms of the second attacker. Stepping forward, he twisted the spear to entangle its arms and then turned to send the creature hurtling through the air to join its fellow.

A straight thrust drove the butt of the spear into the gaping mouth of another and as it fell to the ground choking, Hawklan impaled a fourth.

The destruction of all four had taken scarcely as many heartbeats and the remainder pulled back a little way, uncertainly. Hawklan yanked Andawyr to his feet, but the Cadwanwr cried out in anguish, and Hawklan winced as the healer in him felt the jagged pain of a damaged ankle.

The cry seemed to give the watching Mandrocs the heart they needed and they charged forward as one. Hawklan dropped Andawyr and stood astride him.

'No!' Andawyr shouted in despair, seeing his intention. But no other path now lay before Hawklan. He drew Ethriss's Black Sword and in one seamless flowing movement cut down the attackers as if they had been no more than the dank Narsindal mist itself.

The blade rang out, joyous and clear in the gloom, as if every glittering star in its hilt was singing a hymn of triumph.


In their ghastly armour and mounted on their dreadful steeds the Uhriel struck a chilling fear into even Loman's burning anger, and he felt his body become rigid.

Oklar raised a mailed hand towards him, and his eyes blazed blood red as if from some terrible inner fire. His mount pawed the ground with its clawed foot, its head swaying from side to side and staring at the smith.

Then the hand clenched itself in frustration, and Loman felt hope bubbling up through the icy stillness that had descended on him.

He drove the longsword into the ground, snatched up a fallen spear, and with a great roar hurled it at the apparition threatening him. Impelled by the smith's great strength, the spear hissed as it cut through the rain-soaked air on its journey towards Oklar's heart.

The Uhriel, however, brushed it aside almost casually with a sweep of his arm. The force of the impact shattered the stout shaft.

Oklar urged his steed forward. The creature did not move at first, but its eyes shone with a deep malevolence, and its mouth opened to emit a rasping snarl. Oklar drove great spurs into its scarred sides and with another snarl it began loping slowly forward, its movements angular and peculiarly unnatural.

With its heightened awareness, Loman saw, albeit dimly, the true nature of the Uhriel, rending its way into the reality of this time and this place.

'Your old men protect you from our true wrath, for the moment, Orthlundyn, though they wilt and fade even as we speak.' Oklar's voice seemed to shake Loman's soul. 'But we are warrior kings whose empires spanned the world, even before we saw and knew the One True Light. *Nothing* can save you or your army from our swords when we deem it fit to draw them.'

As he spoke his actions imitated his words, and he drew a great sword. His steed let out a raucous cry of delight at the sound. Out of the corner of his eye Loman saw the watching Mandrocs moving back; some falling to their knees. He felt the two Goraidin involuntarily retreating from him.

But he could not move. His eyes were drawn to the Uhriel's blade. It seemed to be alive, flickering red and yellow as though it were the mobile, changing heart of his own forge. The sight fascinated him as much as it terrified him and, for all he knew that it was to be his death, he wanted to touch and handle it in its glory; or use its power to make those great creations that lay beyond the outer fringes of his great skill.

Yet even as these thoughts occurred, the image of Hawklan's Black Sword formed, with its transcendent chorus of wonder beyond all words.

From somewhere inside him he found the courage to denounce Oklar's work. 'Is there no end to your corruption, creature?' he said sadly.

Oklar's steed craned its neck forward and bellowed at him, its foetid breath making him grimace.

He wrenched the longsword out of the ground and levelled it at his approaching doom.

Oklar loomed tall and hideous in front of him, his sword suddenly blood red.

Loman felt his terror melt into raging anger and he gathered his mind and his body together for a strike that would cut down both horse and rider even as he died.

Suddenly, he felt a ringing song pass through him and the ominous form in front of him seemed to start in alarm. Its fearful eyes dimmed a little and then blazed out anew, more terrible than ever. The foul steed too was affected; it twisted its

511

serpentine neck to and fro, and let out a high-pitched snarl as though it were being strangled.

Then Oklar turned to his two companions and with a great screeching cry dragged his steed about and charged from the field, trampling underfoot any too slow to avoid his awful charge.

Loman stood aghast as he listened to the terrible cry of rage that rose over the tumult of the battle even as it faded into the distance. Relief surged over him.

'Strange fortunes look over you this day, smith.'

The voice brought Loman back to the heart of his terror again with its dark icy stillness. Oklar was gone, called by some strange event beyond this battle, but Creost and Dar Hastuin remained and it was Creost who had spoken.

So soon sentenced again after his reprieve, Loman was almost unmanned as he turned to face Sumeral's two other terrible aides. Creost with his flaccid, mouldering, skin, and his black, empty, eyes; and Dar Hastuin, gaunt and blasted, whose empty white-eyed gaze exuded a malevolence quite equal to that from Creost's dark pits and whose white hair writhed and twisted from under his helm like a mass of blind, venomous, snakes.

Creost's mount, like Oklar's, was a grotesque, predatory, caricature of a horse, but it was covered with scales, and it glistened with a clinging dampness that was not that from the teeming rain. Dar Hastuin rode Usgreckan.

Both carried longswords whose wrongness bit into Loman's soul as deeply as had Oklar's, but they offered him no temptation now and he tried to watch the approaching figures as he might any other two opponents.

As they neared, he noticed that both the Uhriel had newly healed and livid scars about their faces.

Gavor, he thought, finding strange solace in the sight. His trembling grip tightened on his sword.

He felt Yengar and Olvric come to his side again, swords raised, though neither affected anything other than terror in the face of the slowly advancing Uhriel.

'If they're men, they'll die as men,' Loman managed to say as he raised his sword to meet them.

'Indeed they will,' said the voice behind him.

Loman stared violently and looked quickly back over his shoulder.

A rider was there. For a moment he thought it was one of the Lords as he took in the red cloak and the white surcoat, emblazoned with the symbol of the Iron Ring, and covering a fine chain mail armour.

But the rider's face was covered with a visor and he saw that though blood had oozed through great scars in the armour, and the cloak and surcoat were torn and bloodstained, the blood was old and long dried. He blinked to clear his vision, and as he did so, he heard the song of the metal that formed the mail coat and the simple undecorated sword that the figure carried. It was a lesser song than that of the Black Sword of Ethriss, but it was beyond any that he had ever made or taken from the Armoury at Anderras Darion.

And the horse was Serian.

'Hawklan?' Loman asked, knowing the answer.

'These are my enemies before they are yours, smith,' said the figure, its voice muffled by the visor. 'Go to your true battle: it hangs in the balance, and will, no matter what the outcome here. It needs your heart, your will, your skill.'

Loman reached up and the figure took his hand briefly.

'Light be with you, Loman,' said the voice softly, then the figure saluted and eased Serian forward past the silent smith.

Loman stepped aside as the figure turned to face the Uhriel. 'Lord Vanas ak Tyrion, son of Alvan, and king and betrayer of the long dead Menidai. Duke Irgoneth, patricide and usurper of the throne of drowned Akiron. I greet you.'

The two Uhriel stopped their advance as if they had been struck, and Loman felt their terrible presence waver.

'In Ethriss's name I offer you redemption and release from your torment, if you forsake His way now,' the figure went on.

There was a long silence, then Dar Hastuin spoke, his voice hissing and shrieking like the winds he rode. 'What creature are you to know such ancient names, and to speak of the Great Heretic thus in *our* presence?'

'No creature, Lords,' the figure replied. Then slowly it reached up and raised the visor. Loman could not see the rider's face.

'I offer you redemption, or death, my Lords,' the voice said.

For a moment, Loman saw the two Uhriel become once again men; powerful men, ever seizing, ever fearing, but faced now with that which they had been ever fleeing.

Then the vision was gone.

Neither Uhriel spoke, but both suddenly raised their swords and charged towards the lone figure.

'We were great warrior kings . . . before . . .'

513

Oklar's words returned to Loman vividly as he felt the ferocity and power of their charge. No man could stand against such force. He and his two companions would have been brushed aside like chaff for all his strength and their skills.

Usgreckan rose from the ground, shrieking, its huge wings throwing up clouds of spray. Creost's steed crouched low like a great serpent.

Unexpectedly, Serian leapt forward to meet them. It was a seemingly reckless response to such an attack, but as the protagonists closed, Serian suddenly twisted to one side and the unknown rider struck Usgreckan a blow on the neck that half severed it.

With a terrible cry, the creature crashed into the ground sending its loathsome cargo tumbling among the heaps of dead and dying.

The fall, however, had little or no effect on the Uhriel, and as Serian turned, it was to the sight of Dar Hastuin clambering atop the bodies and shrieking as if the dying Usgreckan had entered his soul. His clawed hand reached out towards the rider who immediately dismounted and strode towards him.

Dar Hastuin screamed again at the approaching figure in some strange language, then he fell silent and the two were face to face sword to sword; both quite motionless save for the whirling mass of Dar Hastuin's clawing hair, and the rain running from the rider's armour.

There was a long silent stillness, filigreed about by the sounds of the battle around them. Loman watched, wide-eyed and intent. Then he started suddenly, as did Yengar and Olvric, though both were subtle and experienced swordsmen. There had been no apparent movement by either combatant but now, in the flicker of an eye, Dar Hastuin was impaled on the rider's sword.

His awful scream began, but petered out almost immediately, and the rider lowered him gently to the ground amid the other dead.

As he struggled to recall the beginning and end of this almost unbelievable slaying, Loman saw that Creost was charging again; silently and towards the rider's back.

He opened his mouth to shout a warning, but his responses felt slow and leaden, and even as he heard himself cry out, the rider was turning to face the onslaught.

To Loman's horror, however, the rider did not move back from the path of the charging creature, but stepped in front of it.

Loman's warning shout was still leaving him as the rider's sword cut the creature's throat and then swung round to deliver an upward lunge on Creost's unguarded side. The bloody swordpoint emerged from Creost's shoulder and he was torn from the saddle, such was the force of the blow.

With four strokes the rider had slain the two Uhriel and their steeds.

Then the rider struck two more terrible blows, mounted, and turned Serian towards the direction in which Oklar had fled.

Hawklan ran on and on, supporting the hobbling Andawyr.

It seemed to him that since he had used the Sword, everything was slipping from him and great forces were converging on him. He ran along Sumeral's road through the bleak mists of Narsindal, but he did not know where he was running, or scarcely why.

Some voice within him propelled him forward faster and faster.

And despite his pain, Andawyr propelled him also.

Skittering footsteps caught up with them. It was Dar-volci.

The sight of the felci apparently unaffected by the mounting horrors of their journey made Hawklan feel calmer.

'Where's Gavor?' he gasped.

'No idea,' Dar-volci replied. 'I saw him deal with a few Mandrocs then I got a little involved myself and I didn't see him before I left.'

Hawklan grimaced with self-reproach. In his own turmoil he had forgotten the others fighting to protect him.

'What about the rest,' he asked.

'Still fighting when I left,' Dar-volci replied. 'I thought I'd be more use here than there.'

They ran on in silence, until Andawyr slithered to the ground.

'I must rest,' he said desperately.

Hawklan stared to and fro into the mist. There were no sounds of pursuit, but still he felt a driving urgency.

He bent down and took Andawyr's ankle, but the Cadwanwr snatched it away.

'No,' he said. 'The pain focuses my mind so that I can remain where I am and still hide us from His will. Go on with Dar-volci, quickly before I'm overwhelmed.'

He reached out to stroke the anxious felci.

'I won't leave you,' Hawklan said. 'What's happening? Why's everything suddenly so . . . fraught, so . . . desperate?'

'I don't know,' Andawyr said. 'You used the Sword. I can feel terrible things happening somewhere. I can feel my brothers. I can feel the Uhriel. And other things too – the Guardians, perhaps. But no pattern, no shape. Just a chaos and disorder with you at its centre. Only He seems to be steadfast; watching, waiting. Go!'

Hawklan gazed up and down the mist-shrouded road. Its silence and stillness were bizarrely at odds with his own whirling inner confusion, and Andawyr's almost frenzied declamation.

Then, unceremoniously, he swept Andawyr up on to his shoulder and set off again. There was a brief protest from the Cadwanwr, but it foundered against Hawklan's patent resolution.

As Hawklan ran, he felt again as he had felt earlier; that he was climbing some interminably long and increasingly steep slope. Eventually he came to an exhausted halt.

'No more,' he said slumping. 'No more.'

Andawyr slithered down and stood in front of the despondent healer. He tried to smile encouragingly, but desperation leaked through and swept the smile aside.

'Lean on me,' he said eventually. 'I'm fresher now.'

'Hush, both of you,' Dar-volci said suddenly.

Hawklan bent his head forward. There were no sounds of pursuit. 'What –?' he began.

'Hush!'

Then into the silence came the soft lapping of waves.

Andawyr seized Hawklan's arm and, limping heavily, dragged him to the side of the road and down the embankment.

A line of dark, dripping waves came into view. Andawyr stopped, and hopped unsteadily on one leg as he looked at the grim turbulent surface that disappeared into the mist.

'We're here,' he said, his voice alive with a mixture of fear, disbelief and excitement. 'We're here. The causeway across Lake Kedrieth. We've reached His lair undiscovered, and His every resource is still turned towards the battle.'

Hawklan felt his confusion fall away. They *had* succeeded. Now, whatever the outcome, his journeying was truly near its end. Soon he would come face to face with the monstrous author of all the foulness that he had come upon since that fateful spring day when a twitching sharp-eyed tinker had pranced his spider's dance on the green at Pedhavin.

He helped Andawyr back to the road.

'Across this causeway to our enemy, Cadwanwr,' he said softly, loosening the Black Sword in its scabbard.

Andawyr nodded and ran the palms of his hands down his soiled robe as if preparing for some heavy task.

As they moved forward they began to pass abandoned carts and wagons; anonymous hulking shadows in the mist.

Then, abruptly, one of the dark shapes rose up in front of them. Hawklan cried out and drew his Sword. Dar-volci chattered his teeth and snarled.

'Welcome, Hawklan,' said Oklar. 'I see that, as ever, you come to strike at the heart of your foe; like an assassin, silent and treacherous. You would have been wiser to keep Ethriss's ringing Sword sheathed. I heard it amid the heart of the destruction of your army and drove my steed to its death so that *I* could lay it and your carcass before my Master.'

Hawklan released a long breath. 'I have no words for you, Uhriel. It is your Master from whom I seek an accounting. Stand aside or die. My sight is truer than it was.'

Oklar bowed. 'Then see this, healer,' he said, extending his hands.

Hawklan felt the dreadful presence of the Uhriel in all his power, tearing through the fabric of the reality around him. It afforded him an awesome measure of his own inadequacy.

And this is but a servant, a voice said somewhere inside him.

But then Andawyr stood in front of him, and the presence of the Uhriel receded.

'You above all will be punished when this day's work is finished,' Oklar said.

'No, Uhriel,' Andawyr said quietly. 'This day will be ours. Your time passed millennia ago when Ethriss struck you down. This is but a dream in the great sleep he sent you to.'

Oklar's eyes blazed red through the mist. 'The dream is yours, Cadwanwr,' he said, his voice taut with fury. 'Your brothers fall before us, your army falls before us. Where are your Guardians? And where is the great Heretic himself?'

'The Guardians are all around us, Uhriel,' Andawyr replied. 'Did you not wonder why your once great power is so weak?'

Oklar's anger was replaced by contemptuous amusement. 'A detail, learned one,' he said. 'One that time will overcome for

517

us as you, above all, know. And time we shall have when these irksome peoples about our southern borders have been crushed.'

'Enough,' Hawklan said, moving forward to stand by Andawyr. 'Each moment this puppet and his Master live, people are dying in bloody horror.'

Andawyr interposed himself again, but Oklar stepped forward and struck him a blow that sent him sprawling. With a roar, Dar-volci leapt forward, his great mouth agape.

Oklar swung round and caught him squarely with his foot. The felci arced into the air and fell with a thud near to the fallen Cadwanwr.

Oklar's eyes blazed again. 'Learn Cadwanwr, as your fellows did, that while your vaunted skills can stunt our powers for the moment, we were warriors great in a world of greatness before we bowed to His will. And as a warrior I shall slay you here.'

Hawklan stepped back involuntarily as Oklar drew his sword. It glowed a menacing, shifting red in the mist.

Hawklan took the Black Sword in both hands and let go such ties of fear as bound him.

For a timeless moment, the two assailants faced each other, then two objects landed with a dull thud on the ground between them.

As they rolled to a standstill, Hawklan stepped back in horror. The objects were the heads of Creost and Dar Hastuin, gaping and awful.

'Have you no word for the Lord Vanas and the Duke Irgoneth, mighty Lord?' said a muffled voice above his head. 'Your erstwhile comrades-in-arms, and bloody perpetrators of His will.'

A horse pushed gently past Hawklan. It was Serian and he was foam-covered and steaming. Riding him was a visored figure.

Oklar bent down to examine the two heads, then stared up at the newcomer.

His face was alive with emotion.

'It cannot be,' he said. 'No ordinary blade could hurt them, Cadwanwr or no. Who –?'

'Look at me, Uhriel,' the rider said.

Oklar stared up at the figure and his eyes opened in terror. 'It cannot be,' he began again. 'You wear the armour of the Lords of the Iron Ring; the true armour forged by the Heretic's smiths.'

'Why should I not, Lord?' said the rider. 'Did you not see me that day? Or did the ravens mocking you from above dim your true vision?' Oklar's hand clawed at the ground as he stared transfixed at the figure. 'Did you not see me stare into *His* eyes and show Him His own soul, so that even He faltered at the horror of it and fell before Ethriss's pity, and the Fyordyn's arrows?'

'It cannot be,' Oklar said again, like a soothing response in a dreadful litany. 'Who –?'

The rider moved forward and reached up to remove the visor.

'Do you not know me yet . . . father?'

Oklar staggered back; for the moment, Uhriel no more, but a man. 'Gwelayne?' he said softly. 'My . . .' His voice faded and Hawklan turned away from the torment in his face. Then Oklar let out a demented cry. 'No, no, no. Gwelayne is gone. Gone even before I became . . . Gone into . . .'

'Gone where, father?' the rider said. 'Gone into legend? Into some misty cloud at the edge of your conscience?' She leaned forward and her voice hissed with hatred. 'Know this, father. That I have the gift you sought. The gift you so lusted for that you betrayed and sold me in the hope it would be given to you. *Sold* me! Innocent and trusting; who could not have loved you more. Now it is I who have His greatest gift. It was His scornful, dismissive, blessing at our parting. "*Be* forever," he said, and I have walked the world ever since.'

Oklar shook his head, transfixed by the image in front of him.

The rider spoke again. 'Now He has struggled to rise again, I shall cast Him *down* again, as I have these creatures. And so utterly that there will be no further awakening. I will deny Him the gift he granted me.'

Oklar's head shook more and more, as if the action would dash all the words from his ears. 'You could be His again,' he gasped. 'Rule as you did. Powerful, haughty –'

He flinched back at some expression in the rider's face that Hawklan could not see. Man and Uhriel fought for possession of him, then suddenly, he let out a great scream and, plunging forward, seized the heads of his slain comrades. Hawklan started towards him, ready to strike, for he was Uhriel again, whole and terrible – more terrible even than before.

'Cadwanwr,' he said, rising to his feet holding a head in each hand. 'I see your hand in this foul charade, and you will live long to regret it.' Andawyr raised a hand towards him, then stepped as if held by some great force. 'I own I misjudged your power,' Oklar continued. 'But so did you mine. For in slaying these you gave me their power, and I am His equal now. His Will shall be mine. All things shall be mine.'

'No, father. Please –' The voice was pleading.

Oklar's eyes blazed and with a raging cry he swung his sword back to strike down this fearful spectre from his long-buried humanity.

The rider did not move, and briefly Oklar faltered in his terrible intent. As he did so Hawklan drove the Black Sword of Ethriss towards the Uhriel's heart with all the skill and power he possessed.

With effortless ease, Oklar knocked it from his grasp. It clattered to the ground, and he stood astride it.

'Now *no* weapon can injure me,' he said.

Strangely calm, his hand came round to point at Andawyr. '*Your* suffering shall begin now.'

But as he spoke, a sinuous brown body slithered from between the Cadwanwr's legs and ran towards him.

Oklar hesitated, and Dar-volci scrambled nimbly up his lank form until he was on his shoulder. A mailed hand moved to dislodge him, but Dar-volci reached out a powerful claw and slashed a great gash in it.

Then he whispered in Oklar's ear. 'We are creatures of the deep rock, corrupter,' he said. 'Here before your time and brought unwilling to this new world . . .'

Oklar stared at the welling blood, and terror suddenly filled his face. Desperately he reached back to seize the felci, but Dar-volci's claws were already about his throat and his formidable teeth were closing around the back of his neck.

'Noooo!' Oklar's scream rose above the sound of the crushing bones. It reached a terrible climax then faded suddenly, and his long frame fell to the ground almost silently.

Dar-volci jumped clear of the tumbling destruction, then, scratching his stomach, spat something out distastefully. The rider pulled the visor back over her face and dismounted. She bent down and with great tenderness lifted the dead Uhriel's head into her lap.

Hawklan knelt down beside her.

She turned to look at him. Hawklan could see no part of her face, but he could see tears shining in her eyes.

He touched her gently and she bowed her head gratefully.

520

Then she reached out and, picking up Ethriss's sword, handed it to him. 'Your people are dying, prince,' she said. 'All hangs at the point of balance, and all His power is returned to Him. You must destroy Him.'

Hawklan took hold of the Sword and, for the first time, felt its true power. He turned and looked at Andawyr. The little man nodded slightly, his eyes wide and desperate, and then Hawklan was running along the broad causeway, the only sound his soft footsteps and the icy lapping of Lake Kedrieth.

He felt the warrior in him listening, peering into the subtle shadows within the dense mist, and preparing every part of him for combat against any foe. He felt the healer too, silent but acquiescent, waiting for the terrible healing work that was to be done.

But above all, he felt alone.

Then a great coldness spoke inside him, like that which had touched him as he had fallen before Oklar's fury at the palace gate. But it was worse by far. And as beautiful as it was fearful.

'*Welcome, Hawklan, Prince of Orthlund, and greatest of My Uhriel.*'

# *Chapter 34*

Sylvriss's eyes opened in alarm and dismay as she looked at the group of men trudging wearily back into the camp. She wrapped her arm about her child protectively.

Since news had reached the camp that the battle had been joined, she had been pacing to and fro fretfully. Her responsibility to her child, and her deep need to be with her people, both Rgoric's Fyordyn and the Muster, shifted and changed relentlessly, and like ill-matched horses yoked together they twisted and turned her as they rampaged through the day.

Tirilen, bloodstained and strangely vital, had dismissed her from the groaning butchery of the Hospital Tent.

'You can do nothing here,' she had said without pausing in her work. 'We were prepared and you are not. You'll burden us.' There was no reproach or bitterness in the remark, just a gentle certainty. Sylvriss's baby cried out suddenly, the thin sound incongruous amid the inarticulate pain and the urgent tending that clamoured about them. Tirilen moved towards a young man standing nearby. His eyes were brave and afraid, and a portion of his upper arm had been hacked away to reveal torn muscles and white, splintered bone. Tirilen gave Sylvriss the healer's portion that her wounds merited. 'Look to your child and your army,' she said. 'The one needs you now, and as I read men's eyes here, the other may need you before the day's through.'

The remark had struck through to Sylvriss's heart in some way and she left silently.

She had found no solace with Gulda either. The comforting form of the old woman was nowhere to be seen, and her tent stood strangely still and silent under the noisy, pelting, rain, as if it were a faded picture in an ancient book of tales.

Now, Sylvriss ran forward to the leader of the group entering the camp. His face was grey with strain.

'Oslang, what's happened?' she cried out.

Oslang looked at her distantly and then, with difficulty, focused on her.

'What's happened?' she repeated almost desperately. 'Why are all your people here?'

'They're gone,' Oslang replied uncertainly after a moment.

'Gone? Who's gone?' Sylvriss exclaimed.

Oslang leaned against the wooden palisade and slowly sank down on to the wet ground. Ryath answered for him. 'The Uhriel, lady. They've gone.' His voice too, was weak.

Sylvriss put her fingers to her temples in an effort to understand what she was hearing.

'They're defeated?' she said. 'The Uhriel are defeated?'

'They're gone, lady.' Ryath repeated Oslang's words indifferently as he sat down on the damp earth beside him and, closing his eyes, turned his face up into the rain. 'Whether fled or dead we don't know, but their horror menaces us no more.'

Sylvriss's bewildered expression slowly changed to one of triumph, then it darkened. 'If they're gone, why are *you* here?' her voice was strident with reproach. 'Why aren't you on the field? Using your power on the enemy as Oklar did on Vakloss?'

Oslang started, as if out of a trance. He looked up at her, his face grim and angry. 'We cannot,' he said coldly.

'Cannot?' Sylvriss echoed. 'Cannot, or *will not* do you mean?' Her hand clutched at her child and her mouth curled into a vicious snarl. 'Would you protect His army with your misguided compassion, Cadwanwr?'

Oslang's own face became a mirror to the Queen's in its savagery. 'We *cannot*, lady,' he said, his eyes blazing. 'Do you think we'd stay our hand from anything that might bring an end to that horror out there?'

He struggled to his feet. The Queen's anger abated a little as the very effort of the deed showed in his face.

'We *cannot* lady,' he said again, more softly. 'We have the skill and the knowledge to redirect what is sent against us; even great Power. We know that now; these last hours have made us wiser by generations. But we are ordinary men. To use the Old Power as the Uhriel can use it would destroy our feeble frames before we brought down a fraction of that host.'

Sylvriss shook her head. 'But *they* are mortal men,' she said uncertainly.

Oslang took her arm. 'They're mortal, surely,' he said gently. 'As even is Sumeral. And, unlike Him, they *were* men. But they're His limbs now. They exist is many planes, and their mortality is no longer that of ordinary men. We've done all we can.'

Sylvriss bowed her head before Oslang's pain.

'How goes the battle?' she said without looking up.

'The balance swings against us, I fear,' Oslang said. 'The enemy dead are legion, but they have such numbers.'

'Be specific,' the Queen said, looking up calmly.

Oslang met her gaze. 'The lines hold,' he said. 'Infantry and cavalry. But they're nearly surrounded, and the circle tightens despite the carnage.'

Sylvriss closed her eyes briefly as if to picture the scene.

'If need arises can you use such skill as you have with your Power to defend the injured in this camp?' she said.

Oslang nodded. 'Yes,' he said, frowning. 'For a while we could use the Power thus.'

Slowly Sylvriss lifted the straps of the baby's sling from her shoulders and handed it to the Cadwanwr. Then, gently, she set aside its protective hood a little, and, removing her sodden glove, ran her finger over the warm, sleeping, face of her child.

'I shall withdraw the squadrons guarding our southern flank, and those guarding the camp, and lead them into the battle,' she said.

Oslang stared at her almost fearfully.

'This day will not be won unless we commit our every resource,' Sylvriss said simply, in answer to his unspoken question. She drew on her glove and straightened up. 'Guard this camp as . . . Hawklan would,' she said, smiling a little. 'And my . . .' Her voice broke a little. ' . . . my baby . . . as I would. Forgive my reproach to you and your brothers. It was intemperate.'

Oslang folded his arms around the child and bowed.

'Light be with you, Lady,' he said hoarsely.

Denial screamed through every fibre of Hawklan's body, but the cold words inside him allowed no escape.

'*Greatest of My Uhriel.*'

Hawklan's mind tumbled wildly in their icy wind. Only his hand tight about the hilt of his Sword seemed still.

'No,' he cried out silently. 'I am Ethriss's chosen. His hand snatched me from my very death to face you on this day.'

'*That hand was Mine, Hawklan. Ethriss spared none of his creations. I saw your true worth and I took you to be mine when I should rise again. Now you have brought Me my enemies and destroyed those who betrayed Me by their weakness and folly. You are worthy indeed. Their mantle becomes*'

524

*yours. See your inheritance, and deny it if you can.'*

Hawklan struggled to cry out again, but around him suddenly were worlds of beauty and perfection where such a cry could not be muttered.

Hawklan gazed in wonder for a timeless age, at the silent, glittering, revelation. His heart sang out.

*'Thus shall Ethriss's folly be remade.'*

Silence.

'It is without flaw,' Hawklan whispered.

*'And it shall be yours.'*

Silence.

*'Let slip Ethriss's cruel goad, and come forward to the power and glory of your rightful place.'*

Hawklan's hand opened, and the Black Sword of Ethriss fell from his grasp. He felt it falling, falling, falling, through the darkness of Ethriss's flawed and swirling world until it landed with a ringing, sonorous, chime.

The perfection closed about Hawklan and drew him forward.

But the ringing of the Sword rose and echoed, and its beating, beating, rhythm shook the perfection until it was the sound of flapping wings and His realm was but a faint shadow in a light that shone and danced with the great joy of being. At its heart stood the black, familiar form of Gavor.

Sylvriss looked at the tableau in front of her. It was as Oslang had described. The appalling toll of the day, though scarcely distinguishable from the mud, now carpeted the entire field. Isolated groups were strewn about the field, some in savage hand-to-hand combat, some larger, stabbing and thrusting from behind beleaguered shield walls.

But the greater part of the army, though intact, was struggling to prevent the encircling enemy closing about them.

Steadily they were losing ground, and against such numbers, exhaustion and sickness of heart must surely defeat them eventually.

Sylvriss checked her sword, then threw back her hood and let the rain fall cold about her head. She looked from side to side at her force. Fyordyn, Orthlundyn and Riddinvolk; cooks and clerks, ostlers and armourers; the too old and the too young who had been guarding the southern flanks of the force against the unknown strength that had cut their lines of supply; and such of the wounded as could hoist themselves into the saddle.

It was no Muster squadron, but it was all they had left, and she had spread the Riddinvolk through the ranks to help maintain its cohesion. Courage and will would win this battle, not horsemanship, she had announced.

She lifted her lance high above her head.

At the signal a great fanfare of horn calls sounded above the din of the battle.

The pace drumming began and the line started to walk forward.

Tackle clinked and jangled.

Slowly, the drums increased the pace.

Trotting, then cantering, the hooves splashed through the sodden Narsindal earth. The fanfare sounded again, purposeful and menacing.

Sylvriss tightened her grip on her lance as her Riddinvolk soul responded to the urgency of the horse beneath her.

Then, the blasting horns and rattling drums gave way to the shouting and screaming of battle cries, and the line came to the gallop; thundering through the teeming rain, over the dead, and those living foolish enough not to flee.

Hawklan became a mote; a spectator.

He trembled as he felt the gathering of great and terrible power.

*'I had thought my last cast slew you, brother.'*

The power was gathering still; drawn from all His many selves on many planes; frantically almost; its momentum seemingly uncontrollable.

'My prince of ravens with his true sight, caught my spirit as it fled the Iron Ring. Now *his* spirit has untimely wakened your own captive so that you may be destroyed.'

*'Only you can destroy me, brother, and you shall not this time, for now my power is undivided; unhindered by the tenancy of your flawed creations. Its totality is within and about me now and it is gathered for your doom.'*

There was a long silence, then:

'I have nothing with which to oppose your might.'

There was another time rending silence.

'YOU LIE!'

And the fullness of Sumeral's power was unleashed.

'GAVOR!'

Hawklan's voice filled his own universe in his despair for the fate of his friend.

But the tiny figure was gone even as the Ancient Power of the Great Searing, jagged with the barbs of humanity's every dark emotion, surged forth into the void where he had been. Only words lingered there.

'I forgive you your wickedness; forgive you me mine, I beseech you.'

Then they too were gone. Gone in the scream that rose into the grey misted sky of Narsindal and echoed into the world beyond and those other places that knew Him. The scream that came as His long-hoarded power flowed through His mortal frame and, being unopposed, slipped from its grasp and destroyed it utterly; the scream that came as He measured His folly in this deed, and, most terrible of all, the scream that came as Ethriss's forgiveness rent His tormented spirit into a myriad gibbering shards.

As it reached and rolled over the awful battlefield, Sylvriss's riders crashed into and over the crowded ranks of Mandrocs.

Hawklan swayed.

Faintly a voice spoke to him. 'Sumeral and I were but aberrations in the Great Searing. Now He is spent utterly, and I am among you all, as I should be, and as I *have* been for many eons. Forgive me my folly, Hawklan. Live well, and light be with you.'

Hawklan reached out to ease the poignant pain in the voice.

Then, dwindling finally, very human. 'Ah, prince, your touch is true. And it was good to soar awhile in the stout heart of your friend . . . It was . . . good . . .'

'Hawklan, Hawklan.' A loud voice, brought Hawklan back to the tumult of a solid, familiar, world. Someone was pulling at him desperately.

It was Andawyr. Hawklan succumbed to the little man's limping urgency.

The ground was shaking violently and a screaming wind was tearing at them as they staggered forward. Then the waters of the lake were boiling and foaming, and great waves began to spill across the causeway, threatening to wash them away.

Suddenly, out of the turmoil came figures running towards them. It was Yatsu and Isloman. Without preamble, Yatsu seized the hobbling Andawyr, hurled him over his shoulder indecorously and sped off, splashing through the waves and leaping over yawning cracks. Isloman did the same for the still bewildered Hawklan despite a feeble protestation.

As they reached the end of the disintegrating causeway, Hawklan looked up suddenly as if his name had been called. Briefly he saw three shadowy figures in the howling storm. Their hands were raised, in salute. Then they were gone, and a sound greater even that that of the destruction of the Viladrien over Riddin filled the air. Hawklan and the others fell to the ground, their hands over their ears in a vain attempt to shut out the appalling noise. In its wake the shaking of the ground became so violent that the ground was rippling beneath them as if it were the surface of the lake.

The noise rose to a climax and then faded suddenly. The shaking faded with it, and then all was still and quiet.

The four figures lay motionless, for a long time.

'It's over,' Andawyr whispered. 'He's gone. I can feel it. He's gone.'

'And the Guardians have cracked the foundations of Derras Ustramel,' Hawklan said. 'I saw them . . . again.'

The thought triggered a memory. 'Where's –?' he began.

He was interrupted by an oath from Andawyr who had scrabbled to his feet and put his weight on his injured ankle.

'The others are nearby,' Yatsu said, wrongly anticipating Hawklan's question, as he reached out to support the hopping Cadwanwr. 'Not in the best of shape, but alive. Those Mandrocs were rough. I was glad Dar-volci and Gavor were there.'

Hawklan raised his hands in self-reproach as a cascade of questions poured into his mind. Then came a surge of awful grief for his slaughtered friend. With an effort he set it aside. Time enough perhaps, to weep later, he thought.

'Where's . . . the woman? And Oklar's body?' he asked. 'And Serian.'

Yatsu looked at him blankly. 'They were here when I came to fetch you,' Andawyr said. 'She was still cradling his head and crying.'

'Come and look at the others,' Yatsu said as Hawklan and Andawyr looked around vaguely. 'Whoever you're talking about wasn't here when we arrived, and Jenna and Tirke need you *now*.'

As Hawklan tended to the casualties, the mist began to clear a little, though a dense cloud still hid the centre of the Lake. Other roads leading up to the broken causeway appeared; solid lines across the marshland.

'To the great plain,' Byroc said, indicating one.

Yatsu looked along it. 'No food, no shelter, debatable water and a long way to go through hostile territory,' he said. 'I'm open to suggestions.'

'How about one foot in front of the other?' Athyr said.

Yatsu nodded, then looked at his battered troops.

'Where's your Sword, Hawklan?' he asked.

Hawklan nodded towards the lake.

'Take Tirke's for now,' Yatsu said, putting his arm out to support Andawyr. 'It's better balanced for you than Jenna's, and we mightn't have finished fighting yet.'

They set off wearily, two being carried, several limping, all too exhausted to talk.

A low, blood-red sun was sinking into the mist shrouded west when a Muster squadron came upon them.

The following morning, Hawklan woke, aching and deeply weary. He was aware that the tale of the battle had been recounted to him on the journey back to the camp, but he had little recollection save that the Mandrocs had finally broken and fled under the onslaught of Sylvriss's great charge, and now none were to be found anywhere.

He walked to the entrance of his tent and stepped out. The eastern sky was lightening, and the camp was very quiet. The guards on the palisades were motionless silhouettes.

A noise made him turn. It was Serian. He reached up and patted the horse.

'We have some tales to tell,' he said.

The horse nuzzled him affectionately. 'Where's Gavor?' he asked.

Hawklan looked down, unable to speak at first. 'Later,' he said unsteadily. 'All our telling later, Serian. Take me to the battlefield.'

Hawklan did not speak as the great horse took him to the edge of the dreadful killing ground, and as they came there, he dismounted.

A yellow sun was beginning to rise, throwing long anxious shadows across the scene. Small lakes of water stood here and there, golden among the muddy, tousled ground, and slowly the shapes of slaughtered Mandrocs and men began to be distinguished. Numerous small hillocks became horses, and tall sparse grasses became spears and swords. Hawklan walked among them silently, Serian following behind him delicately.

Birds circled and squabbled overhead; animals scurried away briefly as they approached, then returned to their feasting when they had passed. Old revellers at an ancient banquet.

'Would that this horror could pass down through legend as the tales of courage and splendour will,' Hawklan said.

'It could not have been avoided,' Serian said. 'This does not compare to what would have been had He prevailed.'

Hawklan remembered the vision Sumeral had shown him. Beyond words in its endless, beautiful, perfection. It had seemed to become empty and futile in the light of Ethriss's will, yet . . .?

He walked on. Serian was right, he knew, though amid such carnage, the knowledge made his spirit no less heavy. A dreadful price had been paid, but a great evil was gone and the energy that had gone into its destruction could gradually be harnessed to the work of healing. Yet such a bargain was wrong. Such a savage accounting should never have come about when simple vigilance would have prevented it. Ethriss's greatest and most flawed creations must strive ever to know the measure of their imperfection or seal such bargains thus for ever. How the future, near and far, would learn from this event would depend on its telling now, but the greatest protection for all could only lie in the truth no matter how awful.

And, Hawklan thought, awful it would be – must be.

He looked around. Among these bodies would be people he knew. Eventually he would learn their names and carry the burden of his own grief and remorse and that of his friends and families. Yet he could grieve now only for the one whose death he did know of. That of Gavor, his companion since he had awakened in the snow-filled mountains, indeed, it seemed, his awakener.

Gavor, irreverent and hedonistic, yet faithful and true. Gavor, tormenting Loman, practising his bird impressions, gliding high in the sunlit mountain air, tumbling and laughing just out of joy at being. The true spirit of Ethriss and a fitting steed for him at the last.

He looked up in the hope that among the birds swooping and squabbling there, perhaps one of the black silhouettes might be his old companion. But he knew that nothing could have survived the onslaught that had destroyed even its own creator.

Suddenly, one of the birds swept low to land nearby. Hawklan stepped forward, heart lifting, but it was only some raucous

Narsindal crow and it flapped away noisily as he came near.

Sadly, he mounted Serian and turned back for the camp.

He had travelled only a little way when frantic cries reached him.

'Whoa, whoa, dobbin.'

The voice was unmistakable. Hawklan spun round and looked up again into the crowded air.

'Down here,' came the irritated response.

Hawklan looked down. A short distance away, the familiar form of Gavor appeared, stumping awkwardly through the corpses.

Hawklan dismounted and ran towards him. The raven was dirty and bedraggled and not at his most endearing. 'That's the last time I give a lift to any of *your* friends, I can assure you, dear boy,' he declaimed indignantly. 'I've never had to fly so fast in all my life when I had to get out of that place.'

Hawklan picked him up gently.

'Ow, ow, ow,' Gavor protested. 'Be careful.'

'What's the matter?' Hawklan asked anxiously.

Gavor was still indignant. 'I'll tell you what's the matter,' he said. 'I think I've bust my chuffing pectoral again. I've had to walk all the sodding way and my feet are killing me.'

Hawklan looked at him. '*Bust your pectoral*,' he echoed scornfully. 'Don't get technical with me, bird. I'll do the diagnosing, you just stick to the flying.'

Gavor snorted. 'Where are you going to drag us off to next?' he asked crossly.

Hawklan looked out across the grim, seething, battlefield.

'Home, I think, Gavor,' he replied. 'Home. Back to the light. Back to Anderras Darion.'

# And So . . .

Many events occurred after the Last Battle of the Second Coming which cannot be told here.

Sylvriss returned with her triumphant raggle-taggle squadron and relieved a harassed Oslang of his noisy burden.

The heads of Creost and Dar Hastuin were retrieved from the shattered causeway at Lake Kedreith and then burned together with their bodies and those of their awful steeds, so that all could see their destruction and know of it. Their ashes were scattered to the winds so that none could so easily worship them again.

The body of Oklar was not found, and Hawklan, looking into Serian's eyes sought no answer.

Gulda was not seen again, though the Alphraan sang of her journeying south, past Anderras Darion, giving her a name that no human could truly hear.

Tirilen and Hawklan tended the injured and sustained also the healers in their great pain.

Gavor developed hypochondria again for a while.

Under Loman's leadership, and through its deep discipline, the army of the allies had lost but a few hundred dead while their reckless enemy had lost countless thousands. Each of the dead was remembered then, and through the years, but all who had been there remembered that day every day of their lives thereafter.

'There is no healing for this, any more than there is truly for any hurt,' Hawklan said. 'Time will blur and cloud the memory of the pain, but your lives cannot be as they were. Make of it a learning and you will become whole, and worthy teachers for your children. Cherish it as a grievance and you will twist and turn through your lives seeing only your own needs, and burdening all around you.'

To Urthryn and the Lords, he said. 'Sumeral's teachings are deep within us. Only in the light of knowledge and truth can we truly see and understand them. You must begin the Watch again, but to study and learn about Byroc's people and their tortured land. Let Orthlundyn, Riddinvolk and Cadwanwr ride with you and let Narsindalvak become both a fortress and a repository of learning. Let its great seeing eyes see all things.'

Gavor glided along the unseen paths that came and went among the sunlit towers and spires of Anderras Darion. His black shadow leapt nimbly from wall to roof to keep pace with him. Far below, the villagers were preparing for the spring Festival and in one of the castle's many halls, Hawklan sat idly watching a splash of sun-carried colour move across the table, and pondering the worlds Sumeral had shown him.

Gavor dipped agilely and disappeared under a broad over-hanging roof.

He landed with consummate elegance on a ledge and stood for a moment presenting his best side in silhouette against the blue sky. Then he turned and peered through the drowsy, hovering, motes.

'Dear girl,' he said. 'I'm so sorry I've been such a time. Recuperating from my war wound. A damaged pectoral, you know.

'Now where were we . . . ?'

# ROGER TAYLOR

# THE CALL OF THE SWORD

## The Chronicles of Hawklan

Behind its Great Gate the castle of Anderras Darion has stood abandoned and majestic for as long as anyone can remember. Then from out of the mountains comes the healer, Hawklan – a man with no memory of anything that has gone before – to take possession of the keep with his sole companion, the raven Gavor.

Across the country, the great fortress of Narsindalvak, commanding the inky wastes of Lake Kedrieth, is a constant reminder of the peace won by the hero Ethriss and the Guardians in alliance with the three realms of Orthlund, Riddin and Fyorlund against the Dark Lord, Sumeral. But Rgoric, the ailing king of Fyorlund and protector of the peace, has fallen under the malign influence of the Lord Dan-Tor and from the bleakness of Narsindal come ugly rumours. It is whispered that Mandrocs are abroad again, that the terrible mines of the northern mountains have been re-opened, and that the Dark Lord himself is stirring.

And in the remote fastness of Anderras Darion, Hawklan feels deep within himself the echoes of an ancient power and the unknown, yet strangely familiar, call to arms . . .

**FICTION/FANTASY    0 7472 3117 6**

*More Fantasy Fiction from Headline:*

# ROGER TAYLOR

# THE FALL OF FYORLUND

## The Chronicles of Hawklan

The darkness of ancient times is spreading over the land of Fyorlund and tainting even the Great Harmony of Orthlund. The ailing King Rgoric has imprisoned the much-loved and respected Lords Eldric, Arinndier, Darek and Hreldar; he has suspended the ancient ruling council of the Geadrol; he has formed his own High Guard, filling its ranks with violent unruly men; and Mandrocs have been seen even in Orthlund. At the centre of this corruption is the King's advisor, the evil Lord Dan-Tor, who is determined to destroy the peace won by Ethriss and the Guardians eons ago, and surrender the land to his Dark Lord, Sumeral.

The people look to Hawklan to make a stand against Dan-Tor. But he is a healer and not a soldier – though, deep within himself, Hawklan has felt an ancient power, and when threatened has been seen to fight like a warrior out of legend. Hawklan knows he must confront Dan-Tor before the land falls forever to the encroaching, eternal night . . .

Also by Roger Taylor from Headline
THE CALL OF THE SWORD
The Chronicles of Hawklan

FICTION/FANTASY    0 7472 3118 4

# A selection of bestsellers from Headline

**FICTION**

| | | |
|---|---|---|
| THE EIGHT | Katherine Neville | £4.50 ☐ |
| THE POTTER'S FIELD | Ellis Peters | £5.99 ☐ |
| MIDNIGHT | Dean R Koontz | £4.50 ☐ |
| LAMPLIGHT ON THE THAMES | Pamela Evans | £3.99 ☐ |
| THE HOUSE OF SECRETS | Unity Hall | £4.50 ☐ |

**NON-FICTION**

| | | |
|---|---|---|
| TOSCANINI'S FUMBLE | Harold L Klawans | £3.50 ☐ |
| GOOD HOUSEKEEPING EATING FOR A HEALTHY SKIN | Alix Kirsta | £4.99 ☐ |

**SCIENCE FICTION AND FANTASY**

| | | |
|---|---|---|
| THE RAINBOW SWORD | Adrienne Martine-Barnes | £2.99 ☐ |
| THE DRACULA CAPER Time Wars VIII | Simon Hawke | £2.99 ☐ |
| MORNING OF CREATION The Destiny Makers 2 | Mike Shupp | £3.99 ☐ |
| SWORD AND SORCERESS 5 | Marion Zimmer Bradley | £3.99 ☐ |

*All Headline books are available at your local bookshop or newsagent, or can be ordered direct from the publisher. Just tick the titles you want and fill in the form below. Prices and availability subject to change without notice.*

Headline Book Publishing PLC, Cash Sales Department, PO Box 11, Falmouth, Cornwall, TR10 9EN, England.

Please enclose a cheque or postal order to the value of the cover price and allow the following for postage and packing:
UK: 60p for the first book, 25p for the second book and 15p for each additional book ordered up to a maximum charge of £1.90
BFPO: 60p for the first book, 25p for the second book and 15p per copy for the next seven books, thereafter 9p per book
OVERSEAS & EIRE: £1.25 for the first book, 75p for the second book and 28p for each subsequent book.

Name .................................................................................................

Address .............................................................................................

.............................................................................................................

.............................................................................................................